THE PENGUIN BOOK OF FRENCH VERSE

THE PENGUIN BOOK OF

FRENCH VERSE

*

Twelfth to Fifteenth Centuries

INTRODUCED AND EDITED BY
BRIAN WOLEDGE

Sixteenth to Eighteenth Centuries

INTRODUCED AND EDITED BY
GEOFFREY BRERETON

Nineteenth and Twentieth Centuries

INTRODUCED AND EDITED BY
ANTHONY HARTLEY

*

WITH PLAIN PROSE TRANSLATIONS
OF EACH POEM

PENGUIN BOOKS

Penguin Books Ltd, Harmondsworth, Middlesex, England
Penguin Books Inc., 7110 Ambassador Road, Baltimore, Maryland 21207, U.S.A.
Penguin Books Australia Ltd, Ringwood, Victoria, Australia
Penguin Books Canada Ltd, 41 Steelcase Road West, Markham, Ontario, Canada
Penguin Books (N.Z.) Ltd,
182-190 Wairau Road, Auckland 10, New Zealand

—

First published as *The Penguin Book of French Verse*, vols. 1 2, 3 and 4
Volume 1 first published 1961
Reprinted 1966, 1968
Volume 2 first published 1958
Reprinted 1964, 1967
Volume 3 first published 1957
Reprinted (with revisions) 1958, 1963, 1965, 1967, 1968
Volume 4 first published 1959
Reprinted 1963
Reprinted (with additional poems) 1966
Reprinted 1967, 1969
This revised edition incorporating the 4 volumes first published 1975

—

Copyright © Brian Woledge 1961, 1966, 1974
Geoffrey Brereton, 1958, 1974
Anthony Hartley, 1957, 1974; 1959, 1966, 1974

—

Made and printed in Great Britain by
Richard Clay (The Chaucer Press) Ltd, Bungay, Suffolk
Set in Monotype Fournier

CONTENTS

PART ONE

TWELFTH TO FIFTEENTH CENTURIES

Introduced and edited by Brian Woledge

v

RUTEBEUF (fl. *c.* 1250–*c.* 1285), a professional poet of whom we have more than fifty works, including a play, satirical poems, political poems, and lyrics with a direct and personal tone like the *Complainte Rutebeuf* represented here.

JEAN DE MEUNG (Jean Chopinel or Clopinel of Meung-sur-Loire, d. 1305?) probably about 1280 completed the *Roman de la Rose*, which had been left unfinished by Guillaume de Lorris. He added eighteen thousand lines not inspired by the courtly ideals of Guillaume de Lorris but serving as a vehicle for his strong and original mind and expressing ideas on almost every subject.

ANONYMOUS MOTETS. Motets were musical compositions for two, three, or four voices, each voice singing different words. A large number have come down to us, mostly anonymous and dating from the thirteenth century.

ANONYMOUS RONDEAUX (probably thirteenth-century). We have several Ms. collections of these early rondeaux, showing the form in its first stage before it had been strictly defined.

ANONYMOUS (probably thirteenth-century).

GUILLAUME DE MACHAUT (*c.* 1300–77), travelled widely in the service of Jean de Luxembourg, King of Bohemia. An outstanding figure in the history of music, and the acknowledged leader of the poets of his time. He is a master of the polished courtly style and was largely responsible for regularizing the ballade and rondeau, giving them a popularity that lasted until the end of the Middle Ages.

EUSTACHE DESCHAMPS (1346–1407). The principal disciple of Machaut and perhaps his nephew. He was employed in various capacities by the French King Charles VI, travelling widely and seeing service in the Hundred Years War. A prolific and uneven writer who left well over a thousand ballades, many of them reflecting incidents in his personal life or containing satirical comments on his times. He dealt with a wide range of subjects, but wrote very little love poetry, a thing which distinguishes him from most other poets of his time.

CHRISTINE DE PISAN (1365–1431?). Her father was an Italian doctor in the service of the French king, and she was brought up at Court. Left a widow with three children at the age of twenty-five, she became to some extent a professional writer. Her works in prose and verse are extremely varied and reveal an unusually vigorous and intelligent personality. She was a delicate lyric poet, sometimes capable of expressing deep personal feelings.

CHARLES D'ORLÉANS (1394–1465), a member of the French royal family who was captured at Agincourt (1415) and kept a prisoner in England till 1440. His last years were spent peacefully at Blois, where he gathered round him a circle of poets. His works consist mostly of *ballades* and *rondeaux*, which he wrote with unrivalled mastery.

FRANÇOIS VILLON (1431–63 or later). Took the degree of Master of Arts in Paris; concerned in various crimes; he was condemned to be hanged in 1463, but the sentence was changed to one of ten years' banishment from Paris. His most important work is his *Testament*, a half-serious, half-comic will, which includes most of his famous short poems. Though much of the *Testament* is of only ephemeral interest, it contains some great poetry.

PART TWO

SIXTEENTH TO EIGHTEENTH CENTURIES

Introduced and edited by Geoffrey Brereton

MELLIN DE SAINT-GELAIS (1491–1558) was a court poet of Marot's school whose work sometimes shows Italian Renaissance influences. He wrote some of the first French sonnets.

CLÉMENT MAROT (1496–1544), the dominant poet of the early sixteenth century. He wrote largely in the medieval tradition, but with new playfulness and humour. His songs, *ballades*, and *rondeaux* established a familiar vein to which later poets constantly returned.

MAURICE SCÈVE (1501?–c. 1563), the greatest of the Lyons group of poets. Condensed, learned, and passionate, he is the most nearly 'metaphysical' of French poets. The influences of late medieval rhetoric, of Petrarch, and of Neo-Platonism meet in his principal work, *Délie, objet de plus haute vertu* (1544), a collection of 450 *dizains* which was his amorous and spiritual diary.

PERNETTE DU GUILLET (c. 1520–45), the literary disciple of Scève and the human inspiration of his *Délie*. Her *Rimes* (1545) were published posthumously.

PONTUS DE TYARD (1521–1605), a youthful disciple of Scève who was later included in Ronsard's group. His *Erreurs amoureuses* (1549 etc.) is a typical product of French Neo-Platonism.

CONTENTS

JOACHIM DU BELLAY (1522–60) was Ronsard's companion in the early days of the Pléiade, whose manifesto he wrote in *La Défense et Illustration de la langue française*. His early verse, partly of Platonic inspiration, is in *L'Olive* and the *Treize Sonnets de l'honnête amour*. He then spent five years in Rome as steward to his relative, Cardinal Jean Du Bellay, dying shortly after his return to France. In Rome he wrote *Les Antiquités de Rome* and *Les Regrets*, in which his mastery of the sonnet reaches its peak.

LOUISE LABÉ (*c.* 1524–66) belonged to the Lyons group of poets. She wrote a score of sonnets and three elegies, all on the theme of unsatisfied physical passion (*Œuvres*, 1555).

PIERRE DE RONSARD (1524–85) was the leader of the Pléiade group and undoubtedly the greatest poet of the French Renaissance. He helped to renew French poetry by assimilating Greek, Latin, and Italian models, but most of his work reads as entirely native. His immense virtuosity appears

most effectively in his love-poems, from the early *Amours* to
the *Sonnets pour Hélène* of his late middle age, but his range
also includes philosophical verse, political verse, pastoral, light
poems, odd poems, and the sombre sonnets of his last years.

RÉMY BELLEAU (1528–77) was a member of the Pléiade group
who excelled in whimsical descriptions – of insects, fruit, and
other natural objects in the *Petites Inventions* (1556) and of
precious gems, with their physical and occult properties, in the
Amours et nouveaux échanges des pierres précieuses (1576).

ÉTIENNE JODELLE (1532–73). Another Pléiade poet, who
wrote the first experimental French tragedy. His posthumous
Amours are sonnets of intricate construction which exploit the
symbolism of the Moon-Goddess.

JEAN-ANTOINE DE BAÏF (1532–89) was also a member of
the Pléiade. He is best remembered for his experiments in
classical and other metres.

CONTENTS

JEAN PASSERAT (1534–1602) was a humanist scholar, a pamphleteer, and a satirist. His poetry was occasional. His *Villanelle* is the classic example of the form in French.

NICOLAS RAPIN (c. 1539–1608) was a legal official who experimented with rhythmic and quantitative verse. He fought at Ivry as a captain.

ROBERT GARNIER (c. 1544–90) was the most considerable French dramatist of the sixteenth century. He also wrote a number of occasional poems.

GUILLAUME DE SALLUSTE DU BARTAS (1544–90) was a Gascon Protestant who set out in *La Semaine* (1578) to describe the whole process and product of the Creation. His second *Semaine* (unfinished) continued the story of mankind from Eden. These long cosmic poems, packed with quaint and often fantastic information, are one of the noble curiosities of literature. They survive through Du Bartas's extraordinary powers of invention, verbal and otherwise.

PHILIPPE DESPORTES (1546–1606), a favourite court poet whom his contemporaries saw as the successor to Ronsard. In his love poems he drew freely on the Italians, from Petrarch to Ariosto, to produce verse of great sentimental sophistication, foreshadowing *préciosité*.

CONTENTS

JEAN-BAPTISTE CHASSIGNET (*c.* 1570–*c.* 1635) another 'baroque' religious poet, like Sponde and La Ceppède. The 434 sonnets of his *Mépris de la vie et consolation contre la mort* (1594) are meditations on the single theme of mortality, worked out through a rich variety of comparisons and metaphors.

THÉOPHILE DE VIAU (1590–1626) was the first of the 'libertine' poets, free-and-easy in manner and choice of subject. He invests his country scenes with a certain courtly artificiality.

ANTOINE-GIRARD DE SAINT-AMANT (1594–1661) was a courtier and soldier and a friend of Théophile de Viau. He has qualities of a Cavalier poet, added to a feeling for nature, a strain of melancholy, a pinch of *préciosité* and an overriding vein of exuberant humour. With such varied gifts, he could not be troubled to specialize.

VINCENT VOITURE (1598–1648), an outstanding writer of society verse, but not confined to the *précieuse* mentality. He is one of the wittiest of French poets. He revived the *rondeau* and the *ballade*, dead since Marot.

CHARLES VION DE DALIBRAY (1600?–1653?), a disciple of Saint-Amant who wrote both 'burlesque' and serious poetry.

TRISTAN L'HERMITE (c. 1601–55) wrote a number of plays and an autobiographical novel, *Le Page disgracié*. His verse, influenced by *préciosité*, shows an unusual blend of affectation and personal feeling. The passage given here is from his long poem, *Les Plaintes d'Acante* (1633).

PIERRE LE MOYNE (1602–72), a Jesuit theologian, author of an epic poem, *Saint Louis*, from which the lines on the pyramids are taken. He also wrote a series of descriptive sonnets on biblical and other heroines, *La Galerie des femmes fortes* (1647), in which morbidity and *préciosité* are strangely combined.

DU BOIS HUS (?). Nothing is known of him except that his poem *La Nuit des nuits et le Jour des jours, ou la Naissance des deux Dauphins du Ciel et de la Terre* appeared in 1640. The extract given appears reminiscent of Milton's *On the Morning of Christ's Nativity* (1629).

MARTIAL DE BRIVES (? – before 1655). This splendidly 'baroque' poet was a Capuchin friar, of whom little else is known. His *Œuvres poétiques et saintes* appeared in 1655.

JEAN DE LA FONTAINE (1621–95), the purest French 'classical' poet, apart from Racine. The fame of his *Fables* has sometimes overshadowed the qualities of his earlier mythological poetry. His varied talent could also move from humour in Marot's vein to the religious solemnity of the *Dies Iræ*.

NICOLAS BOILEAU (1636–1711), a satirist and critic with a shrewdly realistic outlook who represents the rational strain in classicism. His chief works were *L'Art poétique*, the *Satires* and the *Épîtres*.

JEAN-FRANÇOIS DE SAINT-LAMBERT (1716–1803), the author of *Les Saisons* (1769), inspired by James Thomson's *Seasons*. Using the noble diction of his time, he described nature with perception and feeling.

ANTOINE-LÉONARD THOMAS (1732–85), a man of letters and general essayist, remembered only for the poem given here.

ÉVARISTE DE PARNY (1753–1814) was born in Réunion of a minor aristocratic family. His love poems, light but tinged with sadness, appeared as the *Poésies érotiques* (1778). Some of them point forward to Romanticism.

ANDRÉ CHÉNIER (1762–94), born in Constantinople of a French father and a mother with a Greek background. He began a diplomatic career, wrote journalistic and other occasional prose, and was guillotined in the Revolution. His verse was hardly known in his lifetime and remained unpublished until 1819. It consists mainly of poems of Greek and Latin inspiration, fragments of ambitious descriptive poetry like *L'Amérique*, and the *Odes* and *Iambes*, which are largely concerned with political events. Whatever the subject, Chénier's passionate enthusiasms made him the most openly personal of

the eighteenth-century poets and commended him to the
Romantics.

PART THREE

THE NINETEENTH CENTURY

Introduced and edited by Anthony Hartley

JEAN-PIERRE DE BÉRANGER (1780–1857) wrote many
political songs and poems of social significance. Imprisoned
under the Restoration, his works helped to spread the Napo-
leon cult that brought about the advent of the Second Empire.

ALPHONSE DE LAMARTINE (1790–1869) had a career
spent in diplomacy and politics, first in the service of the re-
stored Bourbon monarchy and later on the Liberal side. His
best volume of poetry, *Méditations* (1820), owed something
of its inspiration to the death of Mme Charles, the Elvira
of *Le Lac*. In his later poetry the religious theme became
dominant, and the epic fragments *Jocelyn* and *La Chute d'un
ange* can hardly be called a success.

ALFRED DE VIGNY (1797–1863) was from the start of his
literary career one of the pillars of Romanticism, writing a
novel in the manner of Scott (*Cinq Mars*, 1826) and trans-
lating Shakespeare. The best of his poetry is to be found in
Les Destinées (published 1864), and his *Journal d'un poète*
contains a series of *pensées* on life and literature, which are
among the best of their kind.

CONTENTS

VICTOR HUGO (1802–85) in the course of a long life pro-
duced an immense quantity of work, including novels, plays,
and poetry. At first he placed himself at the head of the
Romantic movement, but his later verse goes far beyond this,
and his achievement is to be seen at its greatest in such works
as *La Légende des siècles*, *La Fin de Satan*, and *Dieu*, as well as
in the two late collections of verse, *Toute la lyre* and *Les
Quatre Vents de l'esprit*. *Les Contemplations* strikes a more
elegiac note than these, largely inspired, as it was, by the deaths
of his daughter and son-in-law, who were drowned near
Villequier in Normandy. In *Les Châtiments* he produced a col-
lection of political verse directed against the government of
Napoleon the Third, whose arrival in power had been the
cause of his exile in the Channel Islands. He returned to France
after the overthrow of the Second Empire in 1870.

GÉRARD DE NERVAL (1808–55) (his real name was Labrunie)
wrote a number of excellent short tales, of which *Sylvie* is
perhaps the best known. He also translated Goethe's *Faust*,
and produced a good deal of journalism. The main events in
his life were journeys to Italy, Germany, Austria, the Low
Countries and the Levant. Unfortunately, he suffered from
outbreaks of madness, which eventually culminated in his
suicide.

ALFRED DE MUSSET (1810–57) had a life only distinguished
by a catastrophic affair with George Sand. In addition to his
verse, he wrote many plays, the most famous of which is
probably *Lorenzaccio*. *Les Confessions d'un enfant du siècle*

is a romanticized autobiography in the most typical vein of the time and, like most of his best work, was written in the 1830s.

THÉOPHILE GAUTIER (1811–72) abandoned quickly enough the famous red waistcoat he had flaunted on the opening night of *Hernani* and led a peaceful life with his cats and sisters. The best of his volumes of verse is *Émaux et Camées* (1852). In the preface to *Mlle de Maupin*, a novel he published in 1836, he put forward the formula of Art for Art's sake. He was also a perceptive critic of literature and art.

LECONTE DE LISLE (1818–94) was born in the West Indies and came to France to study law, a pursuit he soon abandoned for journalism and poetry, becoming the acknowledged leader of the Parnassian school of poets. His best volumes are *Poèmes antiques* and *Poèmes barbares* (1852 and 1862).

CHARLES BAUDELAIRE (1821–67) made a voyage to Mauritius in 1841, which may have supplied some of the imagery of his poetry, but this was the first and last great event in a life harassed by debt, editors, illness, and his stepfather. In 1857 he published *Les Fleurs du mal*, which was the subject of a prosecution by the Imperial Government, taken with one of its periodical fits of morality, and this may be considered as the major work of his life, though the prose poems of *Le Spleen de Paris* (published in 1869 after his death) are noteworthy and his criticism, literary and artistic, is among the most revealing of the period (see *L'Art romantique* and *Curiosités Esthétiques*).

CONTENTS

JOSÉ-MARIA DE HÉRÉDIA (1842–1905) was born in
Cuba and educated in France. He studied at the *École des
Chartes*, and the archaeological training he received there
affected his poetry profoundly, as may be seen from the sonnet
sequence *Les Trophées* (1893), which is his main work. He
was also much under the influence of Leconte de Lisle and can
be said to be the best of the Parnassians.

STÉPHANE MALLARMÉ (1842–98) worked throughout
his life as a teacher of English in a *lycée*, and his struggle to
write poetry in conditions of discomfort and poverty provides
an illustrious example of devotion and sacrifice for art. Teach-
ing first at Tournon, then at Avignon, he was eventually ap-
pointed to a post in Paris, where his Tuesday *salon* in the Rue
de Rome became a rendezvous for young writers during the
last fifteen years of his life. His main works were *L'Après-
midi d'un faune* (1876), *Les Poésies* (1887), and *Divagations*
(1897).

PAUL VERLAINE (1844–96) varied Bohemian debauchery
with religious nostalgia throughout a life marked by a tragic
decline. His famous affair with Rimbaud culminated in
his wounding him with a revolver shot in Brussels and,

consequently, being sent to prison. After repenting and back-
sliding for some twenty years more, he died in a public in-
firmary. His best volumes of verse are *Fêtes galantes* (1869)
and *Romances sans paroles* (1874).

TRISTAN CORBIÈRE (1845–75) found many of the in-
gredients of his poetry in his native Brittany, its sea-coast and
sailors. He died young, but not before he published his
Amours jaunes (1873), a book of verse which was to set the
tone for a type of irony increasingly to be found in modern
French and English poetry.

ARTHUR RIMBAUD (1854–91) gave up writing at the age of
nineteen or twenty, after producing *Les Illuminations* and
Une Saison en Enfer (1872–3). His short, fiercely productive
literary life was marked by his liaison with Verlaine, and the
rest of his life was spent in Africa and the East, where he carried
on a series of trading operations.

ÉMILE VERHAEREN (1855–1916) brought to his poetry the
vision and the realism of his native Flanders. His Christian
Socialism led him to paint sombre pictures of the growth of

the modern city and the breakdown of traditional ways. His best volumes are *Les Villes tentaculaires* (1895) and *Les Forces tumultueuses* (1902).

JULES LAFORGUE (1860–87) died young, but not before having published a number of volumes of poetry. Originator of the apparently inconsequent poem written in *vers libres*, and guided by a free association of ideas and images, he was to enjoy considerable popularity abroad, where his irony was imitated by English and American poets. His main volumes of verse were *Complaintes* (1885), *Imitation de Notre-Dame la Lune* (1886), and the posthumous *Derniers vers* (1890).

PART FOUR

THE TWENTIETH CENTURY

Introduced and edited by Anthony Hartley

PAUL-JEAN TOULET (1867–1920) was born and lived in the south-west of France. With some of the nineteenth-century tastes of the *poète maudit* for dandyism, drink and drugs, he combined a poetic talent which had its roots in earlier times. *Les Contrerimes* (1921) recalls the seventeenth or eighteenth centuries in its epigrammatic eroticism. Into this one volume Toulet concentrated enough real poetry to ensure that there will always be readers to appreciate the *gauloiserie* of his verse.

FRANCIS JAMMES (1868–1938) during a long career did his best to reintroduce the poetry of sentiment into France. His best book of verse is *De l'angélus de l'aube à l'angélus du soir*

(1888–97), and many of his sentimental novels and stories had great success. The chief event in an otherwise calm life was his conversion to Catholicism – partly the result of Claudel's influence on him. In his verse sentiment easily falls into sentimentality, but sometimes his evocation of past moods is genuinely touching.

PAUL CLAUDEL (1868–1955) is better known for his plays than for his poetry. He combined literature with diplomacy, serving first in the Far East and ending as ambassador in Tokyo, Washington, and Brussels. The main spiritual event of his life was his return to Catholicism, which followed a mystical crisis experienced by him in the cathedral of Notre-Dame, and which he attributed to the influence of Rimbaud. His main works are *Tête d'or* (1890), *La Ville* (1892), *Partage de midi* (1907), *Art poétique* (1907), *Cinq Grandes Odes* (1910), *L'Ôtage* (1911), *L'Annonce faite à Marie* (1912), *Le Soulier de satin* (1930). Towards the end of his life he produced a number of impassioned commentaries on books of the Bible. His poetic style has been compared with that of Isaiah, Shakespeare, and Aeschylus, and its dramatic immediacy and tactile strength set it apart from anything that had gone before in French poetry. Despite his political opinions, most readers will be inclined to echo Auden and pardon him for writing well.

PAUL VALÉRY (1871–1945) united the tastes of a philosopher and scientist to the talents of a poet. He was born at Sète in the south of France, but came to Paris, where he frequented Mallarmé's *salon* in the Rue de Rome, meeting Pierre Louÿs and André Gide. He published his *Album de vers anciens* (1890–1900) early, but then printed no more poetry until *La Jeune Parque* (1917) and *Charmes* (1922). However, he also wrote much criticism as well as essays on different subjects distinguished by their prose and by the writer's lucid attempts to plumb the depths of his own complex mind. The most important of these are *Introduction à la methode de Léonard de*

Vinci (1895), *La Soirée avec M. Teste* (1896), and *L'Âme et la danse* (1923). His poetry is the result of a tension between being and becoming, which can give it great intensity, though the extreme self-consciousness of the poet sometimes leads to preciosity, when the dynamic behind it fails. However, this is a small flaw in the work of a great poet.

CHARLES PÉGUY (1873–1914) was born at Orléans of peasant stock, a fact that was to determine much of his thought and writing. After going to the École Normale, he founded the famous *Cahiers de la quinzaine* in 1900 and played a considerable part in the political battles of the time, at first on the side of Dreyfus, but later against the unworthy exploitation by the Dreyfusards of their victory. His prose works include *Victor Marie, Comte Hugo* (1911) and *L'Argent* (1912), as well as many other polemical and occasional writings. Among his large poetic production *Le Porche du mystère de la deuxième vertu* appeared in 1912, *Le Mystère des Saints Innocents* in 1912, and *Ève* in 1913. Perhaps his best-known works, however, are the two in which he took Joan of Arc as a subject: *Jeanne d'Arc* (1897) and *Le Mystère de la charité de Jeanne d'Arc* (1909). In all these works Péguy mingles nationalism and Catholicism in a style which is always powerful, though his immense capacity for repetition often spoils the effect of the whole work or even of the individual passage. He was killed at the battle of the Marne in September 1914.

MAX JACOB (1876–1944) expressed in a highly idiosyncratic manner much of the sentiment contained in 'popular' French poetry. His chosen themes are the simple joys and sorrows of peasant life, the poetry of the city, and the consolations of the Christian religion. With Apollinaire and André Salmon he formed part of a group of writers centred around the *Lapin agile* in Montmartre. His best volumes of verse were *Le Cornet à dés* (1918), *Le Laboratoire central* (1921), and *Derniers Poèmes* (1945). He died in a German concentration camp at Drancy.

OSCAR VENCESLAS DE LUBICZ MILOSZ (1877–1939) was a Lithuanian diplomat who represented his country in France and elsewhere between the wars. More than that of Jammes, his poetry succeeds in evoking the pathos of everyday life, though it sometimes lacks form, and his interest in occultism can be tiresome. His poems were first published in 1915, and he wrote two plays: *Miguel Manara* (1912) and *Mephiboseth* (1913).

LÉON-PAUL FARGUE (1876–1947) was best known as the poet of Paris, its sights, sounds, and smells. His most important books, which range from poems, through prose poems to poetic prose, are *Tancrède* (1911), *Poèmes* (1918), and *Sous la lampe* (1929). His mixture of realism and imaginative nostalgia is very typical of a certain climate of modern French sensibility – the feeling which helped to create the French realist film.

GUILLAUME APOLLINAIRE (1880–1918) was born in Rome of mixed Polish and Italian descent. His real name was Kostrowitzky. Having gone to school in France, he established himself in Paris, where he became a journalist and critic, earning money by writing, among other things, erotica. He helped to found various reviews and moved in a circle which included Max Jacob, André Salmon, Pablo Picasso, Alfred Jarry, and many other writers and artists. In 1911 he was accused of being involved in the theft of the Mona Lisa from the Louvre and spent a week in the Santé. In 1914 he joined the French Army and began his famous liaison with Louise de Coligny-Chatillon (Lou). Wounded in 1916, he was to die two years later of Spanish influenza. His poetry is largely contained in *Alcools* (1913), *Calligrammes* (1918), and *Poèmes à Lou* (first published 1955). His play *Les Mamelles de Tirésias* (1918) was the first work to be described as 'surrealist'. His peculiar combination of modernity and older French traditions, of plaintive melancholy and nostalgic passion, make the tone of his poetry unmistakable, though it has been much imitated.

VALÉRY LARBAUD (1881–1957) wrote a poetry largely based on his recollections of journeys and his nostalgia for far countries. His poems are contained in *Les Poésies de A. O. Barnabooth* (1913), and he also translated Coleridge and Whitman.

CATHERINE POZZI (1882–1934) managed to achieve an economy of sensual passion rare in women poets. She is not as well known as she deserves, since her poems – published in 1935 – are difficult to find.

JULES SUPERVIELLE (1884–1960) was born in Montevideo, and much of his poetry deals with South American scenes. He has written many volumes of verse as well as novels, short stories, and plays. His main volumes of poetry are *Débarcadères* (1922), *Gravitations* (1925), *Le Forçat innocent* (1930), *Les Amis inconnus* (1934), and *Poèmes de la France malheureuse* (1943). His poetry is the result of applying an innocent eye to the world around him combined with a sense of metaphysical disquiet which gives a deeper note to his writing. His tone is entirely individual, and his command of language and metre impressive.

SAINT-JOHN PERSE (1887–   ) is the pseudonym of Alexis Saint-Léger Léger, who was born in Guadeloupe and spent his life in the French diplomatic service, ending as Secretary-General of the Quai d'Orsay, a post from which he was dismissed by the Vichy Government. After 1940 he went into exile in the U.S.A., where he still lives. In 1960 he received the Nobel prize for literature. His poetry has been published spasmodically: *Éloges* in 1911, *Anabase* in 1924, *Exil* in 1942, *Vents* in 1946, and *Amers* in 1957. It is distinguished by an

epic tone, a wide and exotic vocabulary, and a highly idio-
syncratic use of syntax. The themes are drawn from the vast
matter suggested by man's discovery of the universe and of
himself. Since 1957 he has published three major poems:
Chronique (1960), *Oiseaux* (1963) and *Pour Dante* (1965).

Éloges:

Anabase:

PIERRE REVERDY (1889–1960) wrote poetry of a tortured
and disquieting lyricism, anticipating the Surrealists, many of
whose techniques and preoccupations he shared. Of the
younger poets prominent immediately after the First World
War, his was the greatest lyrical gift. The review to which he
contributed during the War, *Nord-Sud*, published many of
the poets who were later to be Dadaists or Surrealists. Collec-
tions in which most of his poems are to be found are *Plupart
du temps* (1945) and *Main d'œuvre* (1949). *Le Gant de crin*
(1924) contains some of his rather gnomic critical opinions.

PAUL ÉLUARD (1895–1952) was the pseudonym of Eugène
Grindel. After being a prominent member of the Surrealist
movement, he joined the Communist Party though he was
never as politically active as some who went the same way,
and his political poetry often sounds forced. His best verses
have an unfailing lyrical grace as well as something of the
intangible clarity of classical French poetry. His best-known

collections are *Capitale de la douleur* (1926), *Les Yeux fertiles* (1936), and *Le Livre ouvert* (1940–41). His *Œuvres complètes* now exist in the Bibliothèque de la Pléiade.

LOUIS ARAGON (1897–   ) began as a Surrealist, and, like Éluard, ended as a Communist. He is best known for his war poetry published in two volumes: *Le Crève-cœur* (1940) and *Les Yeux d'Elsa* (1942), but has also written novels partaking both of Surrealism and Social Realism, of which the best are: *Le Paysan de Paris* (1926), *Les Cloches de Bâle* (1934), and *Les Beaux Quartiers* (1936). Later in life he was to write a well-known historical novel *La Semaine sainte*. After Surrealism he returned to a more direct type of poetry and also to some of the forms of medieval French verse. The poems he wrote in 1940 are still effective, though much of his later output is ruined by its naïvely propagandist tone.

FRANCIS PONGE (1899–   ) has written poetry of a highly original kind, mostly contained in the two volumes *Le Parti pris des choses* (1942) and *Proèmes* (1948). These largely prose poems have for subject matter an impassioned meditation on the essence of objects, while Ponge's aphorisms have the authentic note of Pascal in them. In 1961 he published three volumes of *Le Grand Recueil*, a collection that contains new poems as well as an extensive discussion of his own poetic method. In 1967 *Nouveau Recueil* brought together a further instalment of his work.

HENRI MICHAUX (1899–   ) was influenced by journeys to South America and Asia, of which *Ecuador* (1929) and *Un Barbare en Asie* (1932) were the result. His best poetry is contained in the prose poems of *Épreuves, Exorcismes* (1945), which expresses better than the work of any other poet the Kafka-esque side of the German occupation. In *Un Certain Plume* (1930) he used his reading of Swift and Voltaire to advantage, creating his own Gulliver or Candide figure. His most recent major book is *Façons d' endormi; façons d'éveillé* (1969).

JACQUES PRÉVERT (1900–   ) has had the distinction of having his poems sung in most Parisian night-clubs. His two main volumes – *Paroles* (1946) and *Spectacles* (1951) – combine sentimentality with technical skill in a way more serious poets might envy. More recently his main collections are *La Pluie et le beau temps* (1955), *Histoires et d'autres histoires* (1963) and *Choses et autres* (1972).

ROBERT DESNOS (1900–1945) collected the majority of his poems in two volumes: *Corps et biens* (1930) and *Fortunes* (1942). At first he belonged to the Surrealist movement, but later broke with Breton to the accompaniment of some bitter polemics. His *Complainte de Fantomas* was written for the wireless (1933), and many of his poems were intended to be sung. His best poetry is to be found in the lyrical simplicity of his love poems, among which *Le Dernier Poème* was written to his wife, Youki, from a German concentration camp. Desnos died of typhus soon after being released by Allied Forces in the summer of 1945.

RENÉ CHAR (1907–   ) was a Surrealist before the War, and during it had a fine record in the Resistance. His main volumes of poetry are *Fureur et mystère* (1948) and *Les Matinaux* (1950). In both of them he draws his inspiration from the Midi, its countryside and the ways of its peasants. He has had much influence on recent French poetry – partly because of his affirmation of positive values at a time when they were hard to find elsewhere. His selected poems were published in 1964 under the title of *Commune Présence*. Since then he has produced *Dans la pluie giboyeuse* (1968) and *Recherche de la base et du sommet* (1971).

CONTENTS

ANDRÉ FRÉNAUD (1907–   ) has sometimes been called the poetic equivalent of Sartre or Camus, and certainly his volume *Les Rois-Mages* (1943) represents the same current of despair and nausea caused by the events of the occupation. More than the poetry of Aragon, it is an accurate expression of the mood of those days, both in its nihilism and in its rough vigour. Lately his most impressive poem has been *Les Paysans* (1949), which is, however, too long to be included here. It is now in print again in the important collected volume *Il n'y a pas de paradis* (1962), which gives an impressive selection of poems written between 1942 and 1960. The collection *Depuis toujours déjà* (1970) contains poems written between 1953 and 1968.

PATRICE DE LA TOUR DU PIN (1911–   ) has collected all his poems into one large volume, *Une Somme de poésie* (1947), joining them together with passages of prose description and dialogue. In this work he has created a mythology of his own, in which ghostly characters move on a background of landscapes from the Sologne, the poet's native province. Taken as a whole, this vast scheme is too hermetic and personal to be altogether successful, but individual poems are of great beauty. The second and third volumes of *Une Somme de poésie* appeared in 1959 and 1963.

YVES BONNEFOY (1923–   ) began by publishing two volumes of verse, *Du Mouvement et de l'immobilité de Douve* (1954) and *Hier régnant désert* (1958). His style may properly be called hermetic, and his poetry is often difficult, but this cryptic work, which seems to show that its writer has read both Valéry and Scève, contains the best poems to come out of France since the War. In 1965 he published his third major volume of poetry, *Pierre écrite*. He has also translated a number of plays of Shakespeare, and two collections of his critical essays, *L'Improbable* and *Un Rêve Fait à Mantore*, appeared in 1959 and 1967.

CONTENTS

PHILIPPE JACCOTTET (1925–   ) was born at Moudon in French-speaking Switzerland, but came to Paris in 1946, where he worked for a publishing house and was also for some years poetry critic of the *Nouvelle Revue Française*. His collections of poetry are *L'Effraie* (1953), *L'Ignorant* (1958) and *Airs* (1967). Like Yves Bonnefoy, he has chosen a traditional form for his poetry, but its content, whether an impassioned meditation on death or a lyrical celebration of the world of life and love, is conveyed with a passionate intensity that makes him one of the most exciting poets writing in French today.

JACQUES DUPIN (1927–   ) is a publisher in Paris who has written much art criticism as well as studies of Mirò (1961) and Giacometti (1962). His poetry has been collected in *Gravir* (1963) and *L'Embrasure* (1969). It is distinguished by a classical sense of form and a kaleidoscopic use of imagery. His poems are sometimes harsh and abrupt, but the harshness is mitigated by the careful finish of the style. He is a poet who makes demands on his readers, but who repays the trouble taken to understand his work and can also strike a note of pure and direct lyricism.

PART ONE

TWELFTH TO FIFTEENTH CENTURIES

Introduced and edited by
Brian Woledge

INTRODUCTION

THANKS to François Villon, English readers have long been familiar with the idea that great poetry was written in medieval France; yet many people are slow to venture beyond Villon, and some do not realize that Villon had behind him a tradition of French poetry stretching back for centuries. Others, who recognize that this vast literature exists, imagine that its artistic value is slight or that it is the preserve of the philologist. The truth is that Old French poetry, besides being of capital interest to the historian of civilization because of the influence it exerted in medieval Europe, is worth reading today for the simple reason that it offers us an immense amount of pleasure. This fact would be more widely recognized if the reader with an appetite for medieval poetry were better catered for; but anthologists tend to neglect the first six hundred years of French literature, and editors of single works generally write for the specialist and often pay more attention to literary history than to aesthetics. In the present volume French medieval poetry takes its natural place beside the later and better-known poetry of France. What is offered to the reader in this first part is a selection from the vast store of poetry written before 1500, chosen simply on the grounds of artistic merit.

*

From the ninth, tenth, and eleventh centuries only a handful of works in French verse have survived; doubtless other works existed, but we do not know how much literary activity there was in France at this stage. It is during the twelfth century that French poetry emerges as an immensely rich and varied literature, admired and imitated all over Western Europe. France was then, in many ways, the cultural and intellectual centre of Europe, the source not only of literary movements like the one that launched the romances of King Arthur and the Round Table but also of such new ideas and attitudes as those conveyed by the Old French words *courtesy* and *chivalry*.

3

Thanks to the Norman Conquest, England was closely associated with this great period of French literature. French was the language of the English Court and most of the nobility; many French works were written in England, and many copies of continental French works were made for English readers. In fact, Old French poetry of the twelfth century is a part of the literature of England.

By the fourteenth century the cultural leadership of Europe was passing to Italy, but literary output in French continued undiminished; there was perhaps less exciting experiment than in the twelfth and thirteenth centuries, and a larger output of inferior works, but there was also a continuous tradition of genuine poetry, at least until the disappearance of Villon in 1463.

The earliest surviving French poetry deals with Christian subjects, and the continuing importance of religion and the Church over the whole 600 years of medieval French literature may come as a surprise to the modern reader. It is not only that there is a steady stream of saints' lives, prayers and sermons in verse, and that canons, monks and bishops write some of the best poetry: for nearly 200 years the emotions aroused by the Crusades appear again and again in songs and epics, and indeed, throughout the Middle Ages, deep religious feeling may well up in almost any work, however much we label it 'secular'.

If the oldest poems can be seen as the natural product of a society so largely dominated by the Church, feudalism, the other face of medieval society, appears as the background against which we see the earliest secular literature. The oldest works of secular literature that have come down to us are the epic or heroic poems known as the *chansons de geste*. Nearly a hundred of these have survived, dating from about 1100 onwards. Though some of the authors seem to be concerned almost entirely with military prowess, the best of them are more interested in the moral questions of the knight's loyalty to his lord, to his companions, to his family, to God. The subjects are mostly taken from French history, but the historical element is small: thus in the *Chanson de Roland*, the earliest epic we possess, and the most famous as well as the greatest, the nucleus of the story is an event that happened in 778, but it has been completely transformed and re-created in the imagination of a man living 300 years later and taking his own feudal society and its values as a matter of course. The best of these epic authors handle their characters with superb understanding; they have considerable narrative skill, and achieve great dramatic intensity. Not all the poems are as tragic as the *Chanson de Roland*; some of them show an attractive blend of humour and seriousness, as in the *Moniage Guillaume*, where the author sees both the incongruity and the pathos of the warrior who turns monk in his old age.

It was probably towards the middle of the twelfth century that, side by side with these epics, the first romances appeared. The contrast between the two genres is striking. In the romances the love element comes to the fore, and the heroine takes her place beside the hero. This raises a host of new questions about the nature of love, its symptoms, its course, its place in life, questions which seem to have had an inexhaustible fascination for the French upper classes of the second half of the twelfth century. It is in these romances that the knight errant first enters literature, bringing with him new ideals of conduct and almost a new way of looking at life. He is a Christian, of course, but he is undeniably more secular than the epic warrior. He has felt the touch of Virgil and Ovid, though he does not know their names and their influence has reached him at second hand.

For this new matter a new style was evolved. The authors of the early epics used assonanced* groups of ten-syllable lines, with a slight pause at the end of each line, a style with a certain stiffness, though capable of great nobility. In the romances, verse becomes elegant and supple, the new metre being the rhymed octosyllabic couplet, which writers soon learned to break up and twist into any shape that suited their fancy.

It is impossible to discuss this new literature without some reference to Provençal (the language not only of Provence but

* The final words of the lines do not rhyme, but the final *vowel* is similar for all the lines of each group or *laisse*.

of all the southern half of France). It produced a sudden flowering of lyrical poetry in the first half of the twelfth century, and it was probably here that the new ideas were first expressed. The Provençal lyricists – the Troubadours – had well-established literary conventions; their matter was love, their manner closely prescribed: a new stanza form for each poem, five to seven stanzas metrically identical, and a tune composed by the poet.

Provençal differs so much from Old French that none of these poems has been included in this book, but the Provençal conventions had spread to Northern France by the last third of the twelfth century, if not sooner, and can be seen in the songs of the Châtelain de Coucy and Conon de Béthune, who achieved triumphs of metrical skill, and devoted their songs almost exclusively to the theme of love and the glorification of woman.

It is not surprising that such great changes in literature should have been described as a revolution – the 'courtly revolution'. It was not merely a literary movement, it was part of a profound and complex change in the outlook of the upper classes in Europe, a change shown by a more elegant and cultured life at the courts of the nobility, a higher standard of living, more leisure, more travel. The new and important place given to women in courtly literature no doubt reflects the change in their position in twelfth-century society, where they had become an important element in the poet's public.

The courtly revolution gave rise to the preoccupation with romantic love which was to be for so long the dominant idea of Western European literature, and many of the great and recurrent themes that have haunted that literature here first take literary shape. Benoît de Sainte-Maure, in his *Romance of Troy*, though drawing much of his material from the Ancients, greatly expanded episodes which gave him a chance of applying the new-found skill in the analysis of love, and completely invented others, for instance the story of Troilus and Cressida. It was French romance writers, drawing on Celtic legends, who gave to the world the story of Tristram and Iseult; others exploited the vast new field of Arthurian legend (we need not ask ourselves here how far their sources were Celtic, though this has long been a matter of dispute). It was Chrétien de Troyes who gave to Western Europe the stories of Lancelot and of the Grail: they doubtless existed in some form or other before he took them up, but they owed their success to his narrative skill and to his artistry in combining a realistic treatment of character with a setting full of magic and mystery. No doubt some of his public appreciated the realism more than the mystery, and they were soon catered for by other authors. Jean Renart is perhaps the best of a number of poets who gave their romances a realistic setting. His tales are full of lively wit and amused observation of his contemporaries. Altogether about sixty or seventy verse romances survive and most of them contain passages well worth quoting, but in a book of this kind it is obviously quite impossible to do them justice.

It must not be thought that all the literature of the time shared the courtly tone of the romances. A flourishing satirical vein was being developed at the same time in the *Roman de Renart* and the *fabliaux* and beginning to colour lyrical poetry. Meanwhile such social changes as the growth of town life were a potential threat to courtly ideas, though these were still powerful throughout the thirteenth century and persisted long after. In Arras, which in the thirteenth century was one of the most flourishing towns in France, there was great literary activity, and the most important poet of Arras, Adam de la Halle, still wrote the old courtly type of song and excelled at it. But in Paris, Rutebeuf, even when writing for aristocratic patrons, speaks of his own poverty in a direct, realistic, and personal style that is new to French literature, while Colin Muset in Lorraine is celebrating the pleasures of good food and an easy life.

The biggest change in the thirteenth-century outlook, however, came with the *Roman de la Rose*, the most famous of all Old French poems. Guillaume de Lorris, who started the work about 1240, set out to analyse the course of a love-affair. He cast his story in the form of a dream, narrated by the lover; the heroine never appears as a woman; she is symbolized by a rosebud, which the lover finds in the enchanted garden of the God of Love. His efforts to reach and pluck the rose represent the course of his love. He is helped and hindered by a crowd of allegorical characters, some standing for the characteristics and moods of his lady (Chastity, Shame, Fear, Pity, Fair Welcome), some for his own state of mind (Hope, Sweet Thought, and so on) and some for the society that surrounds the lovers (Slander, Riches, Reason, and many more). This was a subject very much to the taste of the courtly public, and the allegorical treatment was to set a fashion all over Europe; besides this, Guillaume de Lorris wrote brilliantly, so that the poem had all the ingredients of success; but it was left unfinished, presumably because of Guillaume's death.

About forty years later the story was taken up again by Jean de Meung, equally brilliant as a writer, but a man of a completely different turn of mind. Before he allowed the lover to pluck the rose, he added no less than eighteen thousand lines to the poem, pouring into it his ideas on every subject that interested him: social relations and morals, religion, philosophy, and science. In dealing with the love theme, he completely rejected the courtly tradition and dealt with love as Nature's device for the propagation of the species, while he made women the target for some of his most biting satire: the advice given to the lover about the treatment of women is full of the implications of the sex war. But in spite of their cynicism, his references to women are packed with instances of humorous observation and some-times of sympathetic understanding; they were to prove a rich quarry for subsequent writers: here Chaucer found very much of the *Wife of Bath* and Villon almost all of *La Belle Hëaumiere*. The complete poem enjoyed a tremendous and lasting success, probably owing more to the challenging ideas of Jean de Meung than to the charming fancies of Guillaume de Lorris. It must certainly have been by far the most widely read of all medieval French poems: the number of surviving manuscripts runs into hundreds.

When we reach the fourteenth and fifteenth centuries, poetry gradually assumes a look that is more familiar to the modern reader. Prose fiction gains new territory, so that there is less narrative poetry, and lyrical work forms a larger and larger proportion of the total output. There is less anonymous work and a keener sense of literary property; the greatest writers are less shadowy figures; we know about their lives and possess something like their complete works in something very near the form they intended them to have. The outline of literary history tends to become a procession of great names in lyrical poetry: Guillaume de Machaut, Eustache Deschamps, Christine de Pisan, Charles d'Orléans, Villon. There are plenty of lesser figures, certainly, and in the background a swarm of minor writers who turn out *ballades* and *rondeaux* because it is the fashionable amusement.

In fact, it had never before been so easy to write French poetry of a sort, and perhaps it has never been so easy since. The recipe was simple: take one or more allegorical figures, preferably from the *Roman de la Rose*, mix with the leftovers of courtly love (dying for love, inaccessible lady, etc.), and pour into the ready-made mould of *rondeau* or *ballade*. If done neatly, the result can be quite palatable, but the modern reader at least looks for some added ingredient. This can be found in Machaut's polished urbanity and technical perfection (it was he who created the moulds, perhaps a doubtful gain for French poetry) or in Deschamps's realism and his wide choice of unexpected subjects. Christine de Pisan, trying to turn the tide of anti-feminism and revive the courtly spirit, shows in her best work great delicacy and sincerity in portraying the woman in love. It is Charles d'Orléans who most successfully exploits the allegorical inheritance of the *Roman de la Rose*. Every mood, every sentiment, every season is personified, and he creates a whole world of his own with its own atmosphere of enchantment, a world in which we can feel immediately at home even today.

The latest poet represented in Part One is François Villon, who has long been by far the best-known of French medieval poets, at least in England. If he has perhaps sometimes been regarded too much as an innovator, he still stands out above all his contemporaries for intensity of feeling and force and directness of expression: he can convey to us the full poignancy of the situation of the Outsider, the failure in society.

*

The fact that so many of the best Old French poems are long narrative works creates a difficulty for the anthologist, which I have solved by including a good many extracts (wherever the complete poem is not given, omissions are shown by . . .). But in a book of this size it is not possible to give more than a taste of Old French narrative poetry, which is far too vast to be properly represented; moreover, some of the best works, too long to be given in full, defy quotation, and it has seemed best to exclude them altogether: the reader will find nothing here from *Aucassin et Nicolette* or the *Châtelaine de Vergy*, nor has it been possible to find room for examples of the drama, the *fabliaux*, or the *Roman de Renart*.

In Part One, as in the rest of the book, the English translations are intended merely as a help in understanding the original; it is hoped that the reader will submit them to no severer test.

LANGUAGE AND VERSIFICATION

For anyone who can read Modern French, it is not difficult to get used to reading Old French, but a few hints about the language may be useful.

An *s* at the end of a noun is nowadays almost always a sign of the plural; it is often not so in Old French, and for a number of poems in this book it is helpful to know the old system of declension, which can be summarized thus:

> 'The king' as subject of sentence: *li rois*
> 'The king' otherwise: *le roi*
> 'The kings' as subject of sentence: *li roi*
> 'The kings' otherwise: *les rois*

This system was at one time in use for most masculine nouns and adjectives, but our poems cover the period when it was gradually dying out, so that while some of them show declension used consistently, others show it spasmodically, and the later poets, such as Charles d'Orléans and Villon, do not use it at all. With so much variety, it is sometimes the verb that is the best guide to whether the subject is singular or plural: 'cling to the verb' is useful advice to anyone in difficulties with an Old French sentence.

Words such as *je*, *tu*, *il* are often not present in Old French sentences, so that, for example, *voit* by itself means 'he sees' (this and many other peculiarities will give no trouble to the reader who can think of Old French as a stage on the way from Latin to Modern French).

In some ways the English reader has an advantage over the French reader who tackles the medieval language: the constructions tend to be free and easy, more like those of English than the very formalized grammar of French as it has been since the classical period. English, too, which was so mixed up with French after 1066, has preserved some medieval words and meanings that have been given up on the Continent: *fail, remain, despise* all occur in the poems below, used much as we still use them.

Old French contains many more contractions than the modern language: *si les* becomes *ses*, *en le* becomes *el*, later *ou*, and so on. Fortunately, these forms gradually become rarer as we reach modern times (the only survivors today are *du*, *des*, *au*, and *aux*).

One of the commonest Old French words is *si*; its meaning is not 'if', but something more like 'and'; the Old French for 'if' is *se*. Other common words that are liable to be misunderstood are:

a, 'there is, there are'
aïe, 'help'
ainc . . . ne, 'never'

ainz, 'before'; 'but' (not to be confused with *ainsi*)

baillier, 'to give' and also 'to touch'

ça, 'here'

car is used to strengthen the imperative, as well as having its modern use

cheoir, 'to fall'

choisir, 'to notice'

ci, 'here'

ço, 'that'

corage, 'feeling, desire'

crient, 'he fears'

cuens, 'count, lord'

cui, 'whom, to whom'

cuider, 'to think'

dont, 'hence, so that' (also modern use)

el, (i) 'en le', (ii) 'otherwise', (iii) 'she'

ert, 'he was', 'he will be'

estuet, 'it is necessary'

ferir, 'to strike'

garir, 'to be saved', 'to recover' (modern *guérir*)

gesir, 'to lie'

hui, 'today'

i- can be prefixed to any demonstrative with no effect on the meaning, thus *ice* = *ce*. Also added to *donc, tant* and *tel*

illuec, 'there'

issir, 'to go out'

ja, 'soon'; its meaning is often a rather vague 'indeed'

jus, 'down'

lé, 'wide'

lès, 'beside'

li, (i) definite article, (ii) pronoun corresponding to certain modern uses of *lui* and *elle*

lié, 'glad'

mais has its modern meaning, but also others, of which the most important is 'henceforth'

mar, 'unfortunately'

ne, 'not'; 'and, or' (with a negative idea in the background); also has its modern uses

nen, 'not'

o, 'with'

onc, 'ever'

or, 'now'

ot, (i) 'he had', (ii) 'there was', (iii) 'he hears'

paor, 'fear'

pieça, 'some time ago'

que has most of its modern uses, and also corresponds to modern '*car*' and '*pourquoi*'

querre, 'to seek'

rien, 'thing'; *ne . . . rien*, 'not a thing, nothing'

talent, 'desire, wish, feelings'

tolir, 'to take away'

traire, 'to pull, draw, shoot'

trop, (i) 'very', (ii) 'too much'

truis, 'I find'

tuit, 'all' (masculine plural subject)

uis, 'door'

veuil, (i) 'I wish', (ii) 'wish' (noun)

vis, 'face'; *estre vis*, 'to seem'

voir, 'true, truly' ('to see' is *veoir*)

vois, 'I go' ('I see' is *voi*)

French spelling in the Middle Ages was not a matter of rules, and each scribe spelt as he liked, swayed by such influences as the sound of the word as he heard it, the look of the word as he was used to seeing it, and mere force of habit. The immense variety and inconsistency of Old French spelling has been considerably lessened in this book, though the spelling has been kept medieval. The main principle has been to spell in the most modern way that is consistent with medieval habits. Thus the line which appears in the Ms. of Charles d'Orléans' poem as

Alez vous ant allez ales

I have printed as

Allez vous en, allez, allez

(taking the most modern of the three spellings of *allez* used by the scribe, and rejecting *ant*, which was rare even in the fifteenth century, in favour of *en*, which was already almost universal). I have not attempted complete uniformity of spelling: it would have been impossible to achieve without giving an entirely false picture, since the language was changing rapidly and the spelling suitable for twelfth-century poems would have been quite unsuitable for Villon.

As for accents, medieval scribes hardly used any; modern scholars usually add a few when printing Old French, and I have added rather more than is usual.

Old French versification is fundamentally like that of Modern French, the main elements being rhyme (superseding the old system of assonance during the twelfth century) and the number of syllables in the line. To make the lines scan, it is necessary to pronounce a great many *e*'s which have since become silent, and to be prepared for adjacent vowels to form sometimes a single syllable, sometimes two. It is impossible to give all the rules here, but the following lines will show the system:

> *Se je i fuss(e) à tens venue*
>
> *Vie vous eüsse rendue,*
>
> *Et parlé doucement à vous*
>
> *De l'amour qui fu entre nous.*
>
> *Plaint(e) eüsse nostr(e) aventure,*
>
> *Nostre joie, nostr(e) envoisure.*

(Note that weak *e* at the end of a line is not counted, and that at the end of a word weak *e* disappears if the next word begins with a vowel.) The most common lines are of seven syllables (frequent in lyric verse), eight (normal in romances) and ten (normal in epics). It is useful to remember the so-called epic caesura, which allows an extra weak *e* at the pause in lines of ten or twelve syllables.

Apart from the rule about weak *e*, it is difficult to give much advice about pronunciation because of the immense changes that took place during the four centuries covered here. At the beginning of the period there were very few silent letters and spelling was largely phonetic (for example, the *s*'s in words like *escoles* could be heard as well as seen and in groups like *oi*, *au*, *eau* each vowel kept its own value). Changes came quickly, and by Villon's time French sounded much as it does today, although spelling was by then often archaic (we still show twelfth-century pronunciation when we write *rois*, which once rhymed with *voice*, and *faute*, which rhymed with *about*, and so on).

A few modern rules that will be familiar to the reader are valid for the Middle Ages. *U* already had its typical French sound; *c* and *g* were hard before *a*, *o*, *u* and soft before *i* and *e*; *ch* and soft *g* (both found in words like *charge*) took their modern sounds about the thirteenth century (in earlier poems the reader who wants accuracy should pronounce the consonants as in English 'charge'); the letter *j* has the same values as soft *g*.

*

Part One of this book, covering French poetry down to 1600, is an abridged version of *The Penguin Book of French Verse 1: To the Fifteenth Century*, edited and introduced by Brian Woledge, 1961; reprinted 1966 and 1968. Readers who want a more copious selection of Old French poetry can be recommended A. Pauphilet's anthology, *Poètes et romanciers du moyen âge*, Bibliothèque de la Pléiade, 1952.

...us les palefreis

...iens morz, si chevalchent estreis.

...ers fut li jors e.ls fut li soleilz,

Clargement ne fot ne reflambeit;

...por ce que plus bel seit;

...si s'oirent Franceis.

Dist Oliver: ...pains, ce crei,

De Sarrazins porrons bataille...

Respont Rollant: «Et Dieus la nos otreit!

Bien devons ci estre por nostre rei:

Por son seignor deit hom sofrir destreis

from THE SONG OF ROLAND

. . . THE Paynims arm themselves with Saracen hauberks, almost all of them with triple thickness of chain mail, they lace their excellent Saragossan helmets, and gird on their swords of Viana steel; they have noble shields and lances from Valence, and pennons white and blue and red; they have left the mules and palfreys and are mounted on chargers and ride in serried ranks. Clear was the day and bright was the sun; not a piece of armour that did not sparkle; they sound a thousand bugles so that [their array] may be more splendid. The noise is great; the French heard it. Said Oliver: 'Sir comrade, I believe we may come to battle with the Saracens.' Roland replied: 'May God grant that to us! We must hold out here for our king: for his lord, a man must suffer distress and endure

Paien ont tort et nos Olt...
Malvaise essample ja d'...
Oliver est desur... halçor,
Garde sur destre cele... un val ...
Si veit venir cele gpaienonbios;
Sin apela Rollant scomp...
«Devers Espaigne v...
Tanz blancs osber... ror.
Icil feront nos F..., li traitor,
Guenes le sa devant l'empereor.»
Qu... nos ...
«Tais, Oliver, li cuens Rollant respont,
Mis parrastre est, ne voeil que mot en sons.»

Oliver est desur un pui monté;
Or veit il bien d'Espaigne le regné

both great heat and great cold, and for his sake a man should be prepared to lose both skin and hair. Now let every man see that he deals mighty blows, so that a bad song may not be sung about us. The Pagans are in the wrong and the Christians in the right; my deeds shall never be told as a bad example.'AOI*

Oliver is on a lofty hill. He looks to the right through a grassy valley and sees the people of the Pagans coming; and he calls to Roland, to his companion: 'From Spain I see such a tumult coming, so many white hauberks, so many shining helmets. These will do great damage to our Frenchmen. Ganelon knew it, the coward, the traitor, when he proposed us before the emperor [for the rear-guard].' 'Be silent, Oliver,' Count Roland replies, 'he is my step-father, I do not want you to say a word against him.'

Oliver has climbed a height; now he can see the kingdom of Spain, and the Saracens who are assembled in such numbers, the

*These letters are repeated at intervals throughout the *Chanson de Roland*; their meaning is unknown.

from LA CHANSON DE ROLAND

... PAIEN s'adobent des osbercs sarazineis,
Tuit li plusor en sont doblés en treis;
Lacent lor helmes molt bons sarragozeis,
Ceignent espees de l'acier vianeis;
Escus ont genz, espiez valentineis
Et gonfanons blancs et blois et vermeils;
Laissent les muls et tos les palefreis,
Es destriers montent, si chevalchent estreis.
Clers fut li jors et bels fut li soleilz,
N'ont garnement que tot ne reflambeit;
Sonent mil grailes por ce que plus bel seit;
Grans est la noise, si l'oïrent Franceis.
Dist Oliver: «Sire compains, ce crei,
De Sarrazins porrons bataille aveir.»
Respont Rollant: «Et Dieus la nos otreit!
Bien devons ci estre por nostre rei:
Por son seignor deit hom sofrir destreis

from THE SONG OF ROLAND

... THE Paynims arm themselves with Saracen hauberks, almost
all of them with triple thickness of chain mail, they lace their excel-
lent Saragossan helmets, and gird on their swords of Viana steel;
they have noble shields and lances from Valence, and pennons
white and blue and red; they have left the mules and palfreys and
are mounted on chargers and ride in serried ranks. Clear was the
day and bright was the sun; not a piece of armour that did not
sparkle; they sound a thousand bugles so that [their array] may be
more splendid. The noise is great; the French heard it. Said Oliver:
'Sir comrade, I believe we may come to battle with the Saracens.'
Roland replied: 'May God grant that to us! We must hold out here
for our king: for his lord, a man must suffer distress and endure

Et endurer et granz chalz et granz freiz,
Sin deit hom perdre et del cuir et del peil.
Or gart chascuns que granz colps i empleit,
Que malvaise chançon de nos chanté ne seit!
Paien ont tort et chrestiens ont dreit;
Malvaise essample n'en sera ja de mei.» A O I

Oliver est desur un pui halçor,
Garde sur destre parmi un val herbos,
Si veit venir cele gent paienor,
Sin apela Rollant son compaignon:
«Devers Espaigne vei venir tel brunor,
Tanz blancs osbercs, tanz helmes flambios;
Icil feront nos Franceis grant iror.
Guenes le sout, li fel, li traïtor,
Qui nos jugea devant l'empereor.»
«Tais, Oliver, li cuens Rollant respont,
Mis parrastre est, ne voeil que mot en sons.»

Oliver est desur un pui monté;
Or veit il bien d'Espaigne le regné

both great heat and great cold, and for his sake a man should be prepared to lose both skin and hair. Now let every man see that he deals mighty blows, so that a bad song may not be sung about us. The Pagans are in the wrong and the Christians in the right; my deeds shall never be told as a bad example.'A O I*

Oliver is on a lofty hill. He looks to the right through a grassy valley and sees the people of the Pagans coming; and he calls to Roland, to his companion: 'From Spain I see such a tumult coming, so many white hauberks, so many shining helmets. These will do great damage to our Frenchmen. Ganelon knew it, the coward, the traitor, when he proposed us before the emperor [for the rear-guard].' 'Be silent, Oliver,' Count Roland replies, 'he is my step-father, I do not want you to say a word against him.'

Oliver has climbed a height; now he can see the kingdom of Spain, and the Saracens who are assembled in such numbers, the

---

*These letters are repeated at intervals throughout the *Chanson de Roland*; their meaning is unknown.

Et Sarrazins qui tant sont assemblé.
Luisent cil helme qui à or sont gemmé
Et cil escu et cil osbercs safré,
Et cil espié, cil gonfanon fermé;
Sol les escheles ne poet il aconter:
Tant en i a que mesure n'en set.
En lui meïsme en est moult esgaré;
Com il ainz pout, del pui est avalé,
Vint as Franceis, tot lor a aconté.

Dist Oliver: «Jo ai paiens veüs
Onc mais nuls hom en terre n'en vit plus.
Cil devant sont cent mile à escus,
Helmes laciés et blancs osbercs vestus,
Dreites ces hanstes, luisent cil espié brun.
Bataille avrez, onques mais tel ne fut.
Seignors Franceis, de Dieu aiez vertu;
El champ estez, que ne seions vencus.»
Dient Franceis: «Dehet ait qui s'en fuit.
Ja por morir ne vos en faldra uns.» AOI

helmets shining with gems set in gold, and the shields and the
yellow-burnished hauberks, and the lances with pennons fixed. He
cannot even count the battalions; there are so many that he does
not know the sum of them. Within his heart he is greatly distressed.
As fast as he could, he came down from the height, came to the
French and told them all.

Said Oliver: 'I have seen the Pagans; never before did any man
on earth see more of them. There before us are a hundred thousand
bearing their shields, helmets laced, wearing white hauberks, their
lances shining brown with shafts upraised. You will have a battle
such as never before was seen. French lords! may God give you
His strength. Hold your ground that we may not be defeated.' The
French say: 'Curse the man who flees. Not one will fail you, even
in the face of death.' AOI

Dist Oliver: «Paien ont grant esforz;
De nos Franceis m'i semble aveir moult poi.
Compaign Rollant, car sonez vostre corn,
Si l'orra Charles, si retornera l'ost.»
Respont Rollant: «Je fereie que fols;
En dolce France en perdreie mon los.
Sempres ferrai de Durendal grans colps,
Sanglant en ert li branz entresqu'à l'or.
Felon paien mar i vindrent as porz.
Je vos plevis, tos sont jugés à mort.» AOI

«Compaign Rollant, l'olifan car sonez!
Si l'orra Charles, fera l'ost retorner.
Soccorra nos li reis o son barné.»
Respont Rollant: «Ne place Damnedeu
Que mi parent por mei seient blasmé,
Ne France dolce ja chee en vilté.
Ainz i ferrai de Durendal assez,
Ma bone espee que ai ceint al costé:
Tot en verrez le brant ensanglanté.

Said Oliver: 'The Pagans are in great strength, and of our French it seems to me there are but few. Roland, my comrade, now sound your horn, and Charles will hear it and the army will come back.' Roland replies: 'I should behave like a madman [if I did]; I should lose my renown in sweet France. I shall straightway strike great blows with Durendal, his blade shall be bloody to the gold of the hilt. In an ill hour for them the Pagans have come to the pass: I swear to you they are all doomed to death.' AOI

'Comrade Roland, now sound the horn, and Charles will hear it and will make the host turn back. The king with his barons will come to our help.' Roland replies: 'May it never please God that my kin should be reproached for my sake, nor that sweet France should fall into contempt! Rather will I strike hard with Durendal, my good sword which I have girded at my side; you shall see the blade all stained with blood. In an ill hour for them the wicked

Felon paien mar i sont assemblés.
Je vos plevis, tos sont à mort livrés.» A O I

«Compaign Rollant, sonez vostre olifan,
Si l'orra Charles, qui est as porz passant.
Je vos plevis, ja retorneront Franc.»
«Ne place Dieu, ce li respont Rollant,
Que ce seit dit de nul home vivant
Ne por paien que je seie cornant!
Ja n'en avront reproece mi parent.
Quant je serai en la bataille grant
Et je ferrai et mil colps et set cenz,
De Durendal verrez l'acer sanglent.
Franceis sont bon, si ferront vassalment;
Ja cil d'Espaigne n'avront de mort garant.»

Dist Oliver: «D'iço ne sai je blasme;
Je ai veü les Sarrazins d'Espaigne:
Covert en sont li val et les montaignes
Et li lariz et trestotes les plaignes.
Grans sont les os de cele gent estrange,
Nos i avons moult petite compaigne.»
Respont Rollant: «Mis talenz en engraigne!

Pagans have assembled. I swear to you they are all delivered to death.' A O I

'Comrade Roland, sound your horn, and Charles will hear it as he goes through the pass; I swear to you the French will come back at once.' 'May it not please God,' Roland replies, 'that it should be said by any living man that I had sounded my horn for the Pagans. My kindred shall never be reproached for that. When I am in the great fight and I strike a thousand blows and seven hundred, you will see Durendal's blade all bloody. The French are brave and will strike boldly; the men of Spain will never escape death.'

Said Oliver: 'In this I know no blame. I have seen the Saracens of Spain; the valleys and the mountains are covered with them, and the hillsides and all the plains. Great are the hosts of these foreign people, and we have but a small company.' Roland replies: 'My

Ne place Damnedeu ne ses angles
Que ja por mei perde sa valor France!
Mielz voeil morir que hontage me vegne;
Por bien ferir l'emperere plus nos aime.» ...

... Li cuens Rollant des soens i veit grant perte.
Son compaignon Oliver en apele:
«Bel sire, chers compainz, por Dieu, que vos en haite?
Tanz bons vassals veez gesir par terre!
Plaindre poons France douce, la bele:
De tels barons com or remaint deserte!
E! reis, amis, que vos ici nen estes!
Oliver, frere, com le porrons nos faire?
Comfaitement li manderons noveles?»
Dist Oliver: «Jo nel sai coment querre.
Mielz voeil morir que honte nos seit retraite.» AOI

Ço dist Rollant: «Cornerai l'olifant,
Si l'orra Charles, qui est as porz passant.
Je vos plevis, ja retorneront Franc.»
Dist Oliver: «Vergoigne sereit grant
Et reprover à trestoz vos parenz;

eagerness is the greater because of that. May it never please God or
his angels that through me France should lose her good name. I
would rather die than that shame should come to me. For our hard
blows the emperor loves us better.' ...

... Count Roland sees the great losses of his men. He calls his
companion Oliver: 'Fair sir, dear companion, for God's sake, what
seems right to you? So many brave knights you see lying on the
ground! Well may we pity fair sweet France: how deeply she will
feel the loss of these noble men! Ah! king, friend, if only you were
here! Oliver, my brother, how can we do it? how can we send news
to him?' Said Oliver: 'I do not know how to send for him; I would
rather die than that a shameful tale should be told of us.' AOI

Said Roland: 'I will sound my horn, and Charles will hear it as
he goes through the pass; I swear to you, the French will come
back.' Said Oliver: 'It would be a great shame and reproach to all
your kin, and this disgrace would last to the end of their lives.

Iceste honte dureit al lor vivant.
Quant jel vos dis, n'en feïstes nient;
Mais nel ferez par le mien loement.
Se vos cornez, n'ert mie hardement:
Ja avez vos ambsdous les braz sanglanz.»
Respont li cuens: «Colps i ai fait molt genz.» AOI

Ço dit Rollant: «Forz est nostre bataille:
Je cornerai, si l'orra li reis Charles.»
Dist Oliver: «Ne sereit vasselage.
Quant jel vos dis, compainz, vos ne deignastes.
S'i fust li reis, n'i eüssons damage.
Cil qui là sont n'en deivent aveir blasme.»
Dist Oliver: «Par ceste meie barbe,
Se puis veeir ma gente soror Alde,
Ne gerreiez jamais entre sa brace.» AOI

Ço dist Rollant: «Por quei me portez ire?»
Et il respont: «Compainz, vos le feïstes,
Car vasselage par sens nen est folie;
Mielz valt mesure que ne fait estoltie.
Franceis sont mort par vostre legerie.

When I asked you to do it, you would not; you shall not do it now
by my counsel. If you blow your horn [now], it will look like
cowardice; by now your arms are both covered with blood.' The
count replies: 'I have been striking mighty blows.' AOI

Says Roland: 'Our battle is hard: I shall blow my horn, and
Charles the king will hear it.' Said Oliver: 'It would not be a
knightly deed. When I asked you, companion, you did not deign
to do it. If the king had been here, we should not have suffered
these losses. Those who lie dead here must not have shame brought
upon them.' Said Oliver: 'By this beard of mine, if ever I see my
sweet sister Alde again, you shall never lie in her arms.' AOI

Then spoke Roland: 'Why are you angry with me?' and he re-
plied: 'Companion, the fault is yours, for valour tempered with
prudence is a different thing from folly, and discretion is better
than recklessness. The French lie dead for your foolhardiness.

Jamais Charlon de nos n'avra servise.
Sem creïssez, venuz i fust mi sire;
Ceste bataille eüssons faite ou prise,
Ou pris ou mort i fust li reis Marsille.
Vostre proece, Rollant, mar la veïmes!
Charles li Magnes de nos n'avra aïe.
N'ert mais tel home dès qu'à Dieu juïse.
Vos i morrez et France en ert honie.
Hui nos defalt la leial compaigne:
Ainz le vespre molt ert grief la departie.» A O I

Li arcevesque les ot contrarier;
Le cheval broche des esperons d'or mier,
Vint tresqu'à els, sis prist à chastier:
«Sire Rollant, et vos, sire Oliver,
Por Dieu vos pri, ne vos contrariez.
Ja li corners ne nos avreit mestier,
Mais neporquant si est il assez mielz:
Vegne li reis, si nos porra venger.
Ja cil d'Espagne ne s'en deivent torner liez.
Nostre Franceis i descendront à pied,
Troveront nos et morz et detrenchés,

Never again will Charles have service from us. If you had taken
my advice, my lord would have come, we should have [won] this
battle, and King Marsille would have been killed or captured.
Little good has your bravery done us, Roland. Charlemagne will
never again have our help – there will never again be such a man
as he until the Day of Judgement. You will die here and France
will be shamed for it. Today is the end of our loyal companionship:
before evening will come our heavy parting.' A O I

The Archbishop heard them disputing. He pricked his horse
with his spurs of pure gold, came up to them, and began to reprove
them: 'Sir Roland, and you, Sir Oliver, for God's sake, I beseech
you, do not quarrel. It would not help us now to blow the horn,
but nevertheless it is better to do so: let the king come, and he will
be able to avenge us. These Spaniards must not go home rejoicing.
Our French knights will dismount here, they will find us dead, cut

Leveront nos en bieres sur somers,
Si nos plorront de duel et de pitié;
Enfueront nos en aitres de mostiers,
N'en mengeront ne lu ne porc ne chien.»
Respont Rollant: «Sire, molt dites bien.» . . .

from LE MONIAGE GUILLAUME

. . . Tant va li cuens et arriere et avant,
Qu'en un val entre moult soutil et moult grant.
Dessous un arbre foillu et verdoiant
Une riviere i ot bele et corant;
Sour la riviere troeve un habitement:
Uns sains hermites i prist herbergement,
Iluec sert Dieu moult enterinement.
De set grans lieues n'ot ne vile ne gent
De quoi il ait nesun confortement,
S'hermites non, ainsi com je l'entent,
Qui ens el bois ont lor estorement.
Et lor bestailles avoient voirement,
Lor cortisiaus, lor edefiement;

to pieces. They will raise us on biers, on packhorses, and will
mourn for us in grief and sorrow. They will bury us in the holy
ground of churches; we shall not be eaten by wolves or pigs or
dogs.' Roland replies: 'Sir, you have spoken well.' . . .

from HOW WILLIAM BECAME A MONK

. . . The count wanders here and there until he comes into a deep
and lonely valley. Beneath a green and leafy tree there was a fair,
swift-flowing river; on the bank of the river he finds a dwelling: a
holy hermit had settled in it and there served God with his whole
heart. For seven good leagues around there was neither town nor
people from whom he could have any help, except for hermits, as I
understand, who find all they need in the wood; they have their
cattle there, indeed, their little kitchen-gardens, their buildings;

Là se garissent et vivent saintement.
Mais li larron (se l'estoire ne ment)
Lor font maint mal et menu et souvent:
Prendent lor bestes et vendent à argent,
Lor maisons brisent, sachiés certainement,
Lor dras lor tolent et meinent malement,
Ses enkembelent et loient moult forment.
Douze en i ot de tel afaitement;
Mais je cuit bien que grans deus lor atent,
Car dans Guillaumes, qui moult a fier talent,
Ainz demain vespres les fera tous dolens:
Trestous li mieudres, sachiés certainement,
N'i voudroit estre pour plein un val d'argent.

Va s'en Guillaumes, si com Dieus li aprent;
De ses pechiés a grant repentement.
A l'ermitage s'en vient delivrement,
Le maillot troeve qui droit au postis pent;
Li cuens i fiert trois cous menuement.
La maisoncele est bien close en tous sens
De bone soif espinee forment,
Et un fossé i ot fait voirement;

there they provide for themselves and live a holy life. But the robbers, if the story does not lie, are always doing them some injury, over and over again. They take their cattle and sell them for money, break down their houses, you may be sure, steal their clothes, and ill-treat them, and tie them up and bind them very tightly. There are twelve of these robbers who did these things, but I think that there is great trouble in store for them, for Lord William, who is very stout-hearted, before tomorrow evening will make them all sorry. The very best of them, you may be sure, would not wish to be there for a valley full of silver.

William goes his way as God leads him; he deeply repents of his sins. He soon comes to the hermitage and finds the knocker which hangs on the gate. The count gives three rapid knocks. The little house is well fenced in on every side, with a good hedge bristling with thorns – and in fact there was a ditch dug too. The holy

Li sains hermites qui prie Dieu souvent
S'estoit hourdés ensifaitierement.
Le maillot ot, cele part vient errant,
Le postis oevre tost et isnelement:
«Qui'st la? fait il, por Dieu omnipotent.»
Li cuens respont moult debonairement:
«Pechieres sui, ainc hom ne vit plus grant.
Herbergiez moi, pour Dieu le vous demant!
Parmi ce bois ai alé traversant,
Plus de set jours, sachiés certainement;
Ainc n'i trovai maison n'habitement,
Au champ ai jut, à la pluie et au vent;
Or me herberge, se toi vient à talent.»
Li sains hermites l'esgarda durement;
Quant il le vit vestu si povrement,
Si malaisieu, si grant et si parant,
Au saint hermite si grant paor en prent,
N'i vousist estre pour plein un val d'argent.
La porte clot, si s'en fuit durement;
Pour cent mars d'or n'i fust plus longuement.
«Dieus, dist l'hermites, par ton commandement,
De cel maufé, se toi plaist, me defent,

hermit, who often prays to God, had fortified his dwelling in
this way. He hears the knocker and comes that way at once, and
immediately he quickly opens the gate. 'Who's there?' he says,
'in the name of Almighty God.' The count replies very meekly, 'I
am a sinner, never man saw a greater. Give me shelter, for God's
sake I ask it of you. I have been wandering through the midst of
this wood for more than seven days, I assure you, and never found
a house or a dwelling. I have slept in the open, in the wind, and
the rain; now give me lodging if it pleases you.' The holy hermit
looked hard at him. When he saw him so poorly dressed and so
evil-looking, so tall and so imposing, such great dread seized the
holy hermit that he would not willingly have been there for a valley
full of silver. He shuts the door and makes off as fast as he can; he
would not have stayed longer for a hundred gold marks. 'God,'
said the hermit, 'by Thy commandment, defend me, if it please

Car je sui mors se il as poins me prent;
Tout mon hostel et tout mon mandement
Ferroit il jus à un pié seulement:
Sainte Marie, dont vient si grande gent?»
Li cuens Guillaumes à la porte l'atent,
Iluec s'asiet, si pleure tendrement
Pour ses pechiés, dont se repent forment.
Lors en apele l'hermite doucement.

Li cuens Guillaumes a apelé l'hermite,
Mout doucement et par amour li prie:
«Oevre la porte, frere, Dieus le te mire,
Herberge moi, pour Dieu le fil Marie;
De moi n'as garde, se Dieus me beneïe:
Penëans sui, si ne le mescroi mie,
Tant ai fait mal, n'est hom qui le puist dire.»
L'hermite l'ot, li cuers li atendrie,
Vient à la porte, le postis à lui tire,
Le conte apele à la chiere hardie:
«Venez avant, de par Jesu, beaus sire,
De ce que j'ai vous ferai departie.»
Et dist Guillaumes: «Frere, Dieus le vous mire.»

Thee, from this devil, for I am as good as dead if he gets his hands
on me. All my house and all my dwelling he could knock down
with one foot only. St Mary! where do such tall people come from?'
Count William waits at the door; he sits down there and weeps
bitterly for his sins, which he deeply repents; then he calls gently
to the hermit.

Count William has called the hermit; very gently he begs him,
and for charity's sake, 'Open the door, brother, God reward you.
Give me lodging for the sake of God the son of Mary; you have
nothing to fear from me, as God may bless me; I am a penitent, do
not disbelieve me. I have done so much evil that no man could tell
it all.' The hermit hears him and his heart is softened. He comes to
the gateway and pulls the gate towards him. He calls to the count
with the bold face: 'Come in, for Jesu's sake, fair sir; what I have
I will share with you.' And William said: 'Brother, may God re-
ward you.'

Li cuens entra en la herbergerie,
Et li hermites la porte a veroillie
Pour les larrons, que Jesus maleïe.
Guillaumes a la chapele choisie;
Li cuens i va qui ne s'atarge mie,
Mais à l'entrer li dut estre petite,
Car li marchis se hurta à la liste.
«Abaissiez vous, sire» dist li hermite.
Et dist Guillaumes: «J'en ai ja une prise;
Trop par fesistes petite manandie.»
«Ele m'est grans, sire, dist li hermite,
El ne fu pas à vostre point taillie.»
Lors comencierent li doi preudome à rire.
Li cuens Guillaumes a ses orisons dites,
Puis si s'en vont andoi à la cuisine.
Li sains hermites, cui Dieus soit en aïe,
Dona Guillaume de ce qu'il ot à vivre
A grant plenté, ainc n'i fist avarice:
Eaue boulie à un poi de farine,
Et pain de soile; et si burent du cidre,
Et puis mengierent de pomes, de faïnes,
Les melles bletes n'i oublierent mie.

    The count entered into the dwelling, and the hermit bolted the
door because of the robbers, Jesu's curse upon them! William saw
the chapel; the count went straight there without lingering, but as
he went in, it must have been too low for him, for the marquis
knocked his head on the beam. 'Keep your head down, sir,' said
the hermit. And William said, 'I've got a bump already. You built
your house far too small.' 'It is big enough for me, sir,' said the
hermit, 'it was not cut to your measure.' Then the two good men
began to laugh. Count William has said his prayers, then they both
go to the kitchen. The holy hermit, may God be his help, gave
William a generous share of what he had to live on (he did not
treat him meanly!): water boiled with a little flour, and rye bread,
and they drank some cider, and then they ate apples and beech nuts
and did not forget the ripe medlars. When they had eaten, they

Quant mangié ont, Damedieu en mercient.
«Dieus, dist Guillaumes, com ci a bone vie!
Mieus aim ce mès que je ne fais un cisne,
Paon ne grue ne capon ne geline,
Ne cerf de lande, ours ne chevreul ne biche.»
L'hermites l'ot, s'a la teste baissie,
Un petit pense, si dist à soi meïsme:
«Je cuit cist hom a forment esté riches
Qui ci parole de si fiere devise.»
Li cuens l'apele, si li a pris à dire:
«Dites moi, frere, pour Dieu, où vous naquistes,
Com avez nom, ne le me celez mie.»
L'hermites l'ot, tous li sans li formie,
Pleure des ieus, la face en a mouillie.
Voit le li cuens, li cuers l'en atendrie:
«Frere, fait il, vous faites vilenie;
Dites vo nom, que il n'i ait detrie.»
E cil respont: «Volentiers, beaus dous sire.»

Or fu Guillaumes laiens en l'hermitage,
Dist à l'hermite: «Dites moi vo parage,
Dites vo nom, se Dieus grant bien vous face.»

gave thanks to the Lord. 'God,' said William, 'what a good life this is! I would rather have this food than a swan, peacock, or crane, or capon or fowl, stag from the moor or bear or roebuck or doe.' The hermit hears him and has bent his head. He thinks a moment, then says to himself: 'I think this man has been extremely rich, to talk here in this grand manner.' The count addresses him and has begun to say to him: 'Tell me, brother, for God's sake, where you were born and what your name is: do not hide it from me.' The hermit hears him and all his blood trembles. Tears fall from his eyes, his face is wet with them. The count sees it and his heart aches for him. 'Brother,' he says, 'you do wrong [to hesitate]. Tell your name, let there be no holding back.' And he replies, 'Willingly, fair sweet sir.'

Now was William inside the hermitage. He said to the hermit: 'Tell me your lineage, tell your name, as God may be good to

Dist li hermites: «Volentiers, par saint Jaque!
Nés sui de France, del païs honorable,
Gaidons ai nom, niés sui dame Anestasse,
Feme Garin d'Anseüne le large.
Fils fui d'un duc qui fu de grant parage,
Gerars ot nom et si tint quite Blaives.
Ma mere fu estraite d'un lignage
Qui ainc ne vout nule traïson faire:
Cuens Aimeris de Narbone le large
Fu ses cousins, ce me disoit mes maistre.
Je le servi moult grant piece pour armes,
Et si li fis mainte ruiste bataille.
Il m'adouba à Narbone en la sale;
Là fu Guillaumes, li marchis Fierebrace,
Hernaus li rous, Aïmers et li autre,
De Commarchis dus Bueves à la barbe:
Avec iceus fui norris en la sale.
Ne sai qu'en mente ne pour quoi le celasse:
Je ai tant fait de pechiés mortuables,
Tant home mort et tante cité arse,
Terres destruites et chasteaus fait abatre,

you.' Said the hermit: 'Willingly, by St James. I was born in France, that famous land. My name is Gaidon, I am the nephew of the lady Anastasia, wife of Garin of Anseüne the generous. I was the son of a duke who was of noble birth: Gerard was his name and he held Blaie freely. My mother came from a line that was never capable of treachery; the generous count Aimeri of Narbonne was her cousin, so my tutor used to tell me. I served him long to earn my arms, and fought many a fierce battle for him. He dubbed me knight at Narbonne in the hall. William the marquis Fierebrace was there, Hernaut the Red, Aimer and the others, Duke Bevis of Commarchis with the beard; with these men was I brought up in the hall. I know not why I should lie, or why I should conceal it. I have committed so many mortal sins, I have killed so many men and burnt so many cities, laid waste lands and destroyed castles, until

Que li pechié moult durement m'esmaient
Que je ne voise en enfer parmanable.
Vint et quatre ans avra à ceste Paque
Que je laissai mes viles et mes marches
Et que m'en ving çaiens en ce boscage;
En ceste terre qui tant par est sauvage
Deving hermites et pris cest herbergage.
Ainc puis du siecle, certes, ne me fu gaires.
Moult a d'hermites en icestui boscage,
Qui par ce bois lor viande porchacent,
Lor besteletes i nourrissent et paissent,
De quoi l'hiver et la saison trespassent.
Moult a bon tens, par Dieu l'esperitable,
Qui Damedieu sert de tres fin courage:
En Dieu servir a moult tres bon usage.
Or vous ai, sire, tout conté mon afaire.
Mais li larron me font souvent contraire,
Ma maison brisent, si me font grant damage.
Mais par cel Dieu qui me fist à s'image,
Se vous voulez, ja lairai l'hermitage,
O vous irai, sire, mais qu'il vous place.
Bien vous connois as poins et au visage,

my sins make me very much dread lest I should go to everlasting Hell. It will be twenty-four years this Easter since I left my towns and my lands and came away here into this wood. In this land which is so wild I became a hermit and took this dwelling, and since then, indeed, the world has meant little to me. There are many hermits in this forest who find their living in the woodland. They feed and nourish their few cattle here in order to get through the winter and the sowing season. He who serves God with a whole heart has a good life, by the Heavenly Lord. The service of God is a very good way of life. Now I have told you, sir, all my story; but the robbers often do me injury and destroy my house and do me great wrong. But by that God who made me in his image, if you wish it, I will leave the hermitage and go with you, sir, if only it is pleasing to you. I know you well by your hands and your face, your proud

Au fier courage et as lees espaules:
Mes cousins estes, s'avez à nom Guillaume,
D'Orange fustes sires et connestables,
Et si presistes à moullier dame Orable.»
A icest mot li cousin s'entrebaisent;
Chascuns d'eux deus a pleins les ieus de larmes . . .

Trestout li conte li marchis au vis fier:
Comment il fu moines saint Gratien,
Tout son affaire li dist de chief en chief,
Et des larrons qu'il ot mors el ramier,
Le prieus mort, les moines laidengiés;
«Mais or me doi envers Dieu amaisnier,
Hermites ere, se Dieus m'en veut aidier.»
Dist Gaidons: «Sire, Dieus en soit graciés!
O moi manrez, s'il à plaisir vous vient.»
«Naie, cousins, dist Guillaumes li fiers,
En autre lieu voudrai estre ostagiés.» . . .

bearing and your broad shoulders: you are my cousin, and your
name is William; you were lord and constable of Orange and you
took to wife the Lady Orable.' At these words, the cousins kissed
each other, and each of the two had his eyes full of tears . . .

The marquis with the proud face tells him all: how he was a
monk of St Gratien, and all his story he told him, and about the
robbers he had killed in the forest, the prior he killed and the monks
he wounded. 'But now I must make my peace with God: I shall be
a hermit, if God will help me to do so.' Said Gaidon: 'God be
thanked for that. You shall stay with me, if that will please you.'
'No, cousin,' says the proud William, 'in some other place I wish
to make my dwelling.' . . .

WACE

Le Roman de Rou

(Prologue)

POUR remembrer des ancessours
Les faiz et les diz et les mours,
Doit l'on les livres et les gestes
Et les estoires lire as festes,
Les felonies des felons
Et les barnages des barons.
Pour ce firent bien et savoir
Et grant pris durent cil avoir
Qui escristrent premierement,
Et li autour plenierement
Qui firent livres et escriz
Des nobles faiz et des bons diz
Que li baron et li seignour
Firent de tens ancianour.
Tourné fussent en oubliance,
Se ne fust tant de remembrance
Que li escriture nous fait
Qui les estoires nous retrait.

The History of Rollo

To keep in mind the deeds and words and ways of our ancestors, records and chronicles and histories ought to be read out at festivals: the crimes of the wicked and the good deeds of the noble. Therefore those men worked well and wisely, and should be greatly honoured, who first invented writing, and those authors should be fully esteemed who made books and writings about the noble feats and the good words of lords and barons in ancient days. These would have all sunk into oblivion were it not for the measure of remembrance brought to us by the written word which tells their stories.

Mainte cité a ja esté,
Et mainte riche poesté,
Dont nous or rien ne seüssons
Se les escriz n'en eüssons.
De Thebes est grant reparlance,
Et Babiloine ot grant puissance,
Et Troie fu de grant podnee,
Et Ninive fu grant et lee:
Qui or ireit querant les places,
A peine trouvereit les traces.
Rois fu Nabugodonosor,
Une image fist faire d'or,
Soissante coutes de hautour
Et sis coutes ot de laour;
Qui or voudreit son cors veoir,
Ne trouvereit, al mien espoir,
Qui moustrer ne dire seüst
Ou os de lui ne poudre eüst.
Mais par les bons clers qui l'escristrent,
Qui les gestes es livres mistrent,
Savons nous du vieil tens parler
Et des oevres plusours conter.

There has been many a city in the past, and many a wealthy empire, of which we should now know nothing if its chronicles had not come down to us. Thebes is famous in story, and great was the might of Babylon and great the power of Troy, and Nineveh was great and wide; but now, if you were to seek the places where they stood, you would hardly find a trace of them. Nebuchadnezzar was a king; he caused a golden image to be made sixty cubits high and six cubits wide; but now, if you were to try to find his body, I do not believe you would find anybody able to show or tell you where bone or ash of him is laid. But because of the worthy clerks who wrote and set down the chronicles in their books we can still speak of ancient times and tell of many of their works.

Alixandre fu rois puissanz,
Douze regnes prist en douze anz,
Moult ot terres, moult ot avoir,
Et rois fu de moult grant pooir;
Mais cil conquez poi li valut:
Envenimez fu, si mourut.

Cesar, qui tant fist et tant pot,
Qui tout le mont conquist et ot,
Onques nuls hom, puis ne avant,
Mien escient ne conquist tant,
Puis fu ocis en traïson
El Capitoile, ce savom.

Cil dui vassal qui tant conquistrent,
Tant orent terres et tant pristrent,
Après la mort, de lor honour
N'ot chascun fors que sa longour.
Quel bien lor fait, que mieuz lor est
De lor pris et de lor conquest,
Ne mais tant que l'on va disant,
Si com l'on le treuve lisant,

Alexander was a mighty king; twelve kingdoms he conquered in twelve years, many lands he had and great possessions, and was ruler of a vast empire; but all these conquests availed him little: he was poisoned and he died.

Caesar, who did so much and wielded such power, conquered and held the whole world; never any man before or after him, as I believe, was such a conqueror. Then, as we know, he was treacherously killed in the Capitol.

These two great men, who conquered so much, who had so many lands and seized so much territory, after their death, of all the lands they held, neither had more than his own length of earth. What good to them is all their honour and their conquest, and what better are they for it, except in so far as men still say of them — what they have learnt by reading — that they were Alexander and

Qu'Alixandre et Cesar furent?
Tant i a d'eus que lor nons durent,
Et si refussent oublié
S'il escrit n'eüssent esté.

Toute rien se tourne en declin,
Tout chiet, tout meurt, tout vait à fin;
Hom meurt, fer use, fust pourrist,
Tour font, mur chiet, rose flaistrist,
Cheval trebuche, drap vieillist,
Toute oevre faite o mains perist.
Bien entent et conois et sai
Que tuit mourront, et clerc et lai,
Et moult avra lor renomee
Apres lor mort courte duree,
Se par clerc nen est mise en livre:
Ne puet par el durer ne vivre. . .

Caesar? So much is left of them that their names endure, and
even these would have been forgotten if they had not been put
into writing.

Everything tends towards decay; all falls, all dies, all draws to-
wards its end; man dies, iron wears away, wood rots, towers come
to ruin, walls fall down, the rose withers, the horse stumbles, cloth
grows threadbare, and every work of man's hand perishes. Well do
I understand and realize and know that all men will die, both clerks
and laymen, and short-lived indeed will be their fame after their
death if no clerk sets it down in writing, for by no other means can
it endure or live. . .

BENOÎT DE SAINTE-MAURE

Le Roman de Troie

[Briseida's Monologue]

... DÉS or est toute en lui s'entente,
Dès or l'aime, dès or le tient,
Mais de lui perdre moult se crient.
Moult fu perilleuse la plaie;
Li oz des Greus moult s'en esmaie,
Et ele en plore o ses deus ieuz.
Ne remaint pour Calcas le vieuz,
Ne pour chasti ne pour manace,
Ne pour devié que il l'en face,
Que en l'aille sovent veoir.
Dès or peut on apercevoir
Que vers lui a tout atorné
S'amour, son cuer et son pensé.
Si set el bien certainement
Qu'el se mesfait trop laidement.
A grant tort et à grant boisdie
S'est si de Troïlus partie,

[*Briseida's Monologue*]

... Henceforth her mind is wholly set on him [Diomedes], henceforth she loves him, henceforth she clings to him; but she is very much afraid of losing him, for his wound is very dangerous; the Grecian army is in great dismay about it, and it brings tears to her two eyes. She will not desist because of old Calchas – neither for his admonishments nor for his threats, nor however much he forbids her to do so – from going often to see Diomedes. From now on it can clearly be seen that she has quite turned to him her love, her heart, and all her thoughts. And yet she knows very well how badly she is behaving. It is a great wrong and great treachery to have abandoned Troilus so; she has done very ill, it seems to her, and

Mesfait a moult, ce li est vis,
Et trop a vers celui mespris
Qui tant est beaus, riches et prouz
Et qui as armes les vaint touz.

A soi meïsmes pense et dit:
«De moi n'ert ja fait bon escrit
Ne chantee bonne chançon.
Tel aventure ne tel don
Ne vousisse ja jour avoir.
Mauvais sen oi et fol, espoir,
Quant je trichai à mon ami
Qui onc vers moi nel deservi.
Ne l'ai pas fait si com je dui:
Mes cuers deüst bien estre en lui
Si atachiés et si fermés
Qu'autre n'en fust ja escoutés;
Fausse fui, et legiere et fole
Là où j'en entendi parole.
Qui loiaument se veut garder
N'en doit ja parole escouter:
Par parole sont engeignié
Li sage et li plus veziié.

treated him very badly who is so handsome, noble, and full of valour, and who outshines them all in arms.

She thinks to herself and says: 'Of me nothing good will ever be written, and no good song be sung. Such a trick of fortune, such a gift of fate I never would have wished myself. It was wickedness in me – madness, perhaps – to be false to my lover who never deserved to be treated so; I have not behaved as I ought to have done: my heart should have been so fixed and so bound up in him that it would never listen to another. Faithless I was, wanton and foolish when I listened to another's words. She who would keep herself in loyal faith must never hear such words, for by words are deceived the wisest and the most cunning. Henceforth they will have plenty

Dès or avront pro que retraire
De moi cil qui ne m'aiment gaire;
Lor paroles de moi tendront
Les dames qui à Troie sont.
Honte i ai fait as damoiseles
Trop lait, et as riches puceles;
Ma tricherie et mes mesfais
Lor sera mais tous jours retrais.
Peser m'en doit, et si fait el.
Trop est mes cuers muable et fel,
Qu'ami avoie le meillour
Cui mais pucele doint s'amour;
Ceus qu'il amast deüsse amer
Et ceus haïr et eschiver
Qui pourchaçassent son damage.
Ici pert il com je sui sage,
Quant à celui qu'il plus haoit,
Contre raison et contre droit
Ai ma fine amor otroiee;
Trop en serai mais desproisiee.
Et que me vaut, se m'en repent?
En ço n'a mais recovrement.
Serai donc à cestui loiaus
Qui moult est prous et bons vassaus.

to say about me, those who do not like me. The ladies in Troy will be talking about me; I have brought great shame upon the maidens and the noble girls there; my treachery and my misdeeds will be a reproach to them for evermore. It should be a grief to me, and indeed it is. My heart is very wicked and fickle; for I had the best lover to whom a maiden ever gave her love. I should have loved those he loved and hated and avoided all who sought to do him evil. Here can be seen the measure of my worth, when on the man he hated most I have bestowed my love, against all reason and all right. But what good is it to repent of it? There is no going back now. So I will be true to this one, who is a noble and a valiant knight. I can no longer turn back, nor withdraw myself from him:

Je ne puis mais là revertir,
Ne de cestui moi resortir;
Trop ai ja en lui mon cuer mis,
Por c'en ai fait ce que j'en fis.
Et n'eüst pas ainsi esté,
Se fusse encore en la cité:
Ja jor mes cuers ne se pensast
Qu'il tressaillist ne qu'il changeast.
Mais ci estoie sans conseil
Et sans ami et sans feeil;
Si m'ot mestier tel atendance
Que m'ostast d'ire et de pesance.
Trop peüsse ore consirer
Et plaindre et moi desconforter
Et endurer jusqu'à la mort:
N'eüsse ja de là confort.
Morte fusse, pieça, ce croi,
Se n'eüsse merci de moi.
Sans ce que je ai fait folor,
Des jeus partis ai le meillor:
Tel ore avrai joie et leece
Que mes cuers fust en grant tristece;
Tels en porra en mal parler
Que me venist tart conforter.

I am already too much in love with him, that is why I have be-
haved as I have done. None of this would have happened if I had
still been in the city: the thought would never have come into my
heart of faltering or changing. But I was here without advice, with-
out a friend or anyone to trust in, and in great need of such a conso-
lation to save me sorrow and sad thoughts. Very sad indeed they
might have been, and bitterly I might be complaining and lamenting
now, and suffering until my death, but I should never have had any
comfort from there. I should have died long since, I think, if I had
not had pity on myself. Leaving aside the folly of my conduct, I
have chosen the best way out of my dilemma. I shall have joy and
gladness when my heart would have been in great sorrow; many a
one perhaps will blame me for it who would not have hastened to

Ne doit on mie por la gent
Estre en dolor et en torment.
Se touz li mondes est haitiés
Et mes cuers soit triste et iriés,
Iço ne m'est nule gaaigne;
Mais moult me deut li cuers et saigne
De ce que je sui en error;
Car nule rien qui a amor
Là où ses cuers soit point tiranz,
Troubles, doutos ne repentanz,
Ne peut estre ses jeus verais.
Sovent m'apai, sovent m'irais;
Sovent m'est bel et bien le vueil;
Sovent resont ploros mi ueil:
Ainsi est or, je n'en sai plus.
Dieus donge bien à Troïlus!
Quant nel puis avoir, ne il moi,
A cestui me doing et otroi.
Moult voudroie avoir cel talent
Que n'eüsse remembrement
Des euvres faites d'en arriere;
Ce me fait mal à grant maniere.
Ma conscience me reprent,

my help. One is not bound to suffer grief and torment for the sake of other people's opinion. If everyone else is well pleased but my own heart is sad and sorrowful, that is no gain for me; but all the same, my heart bleeds and grieves because I have done wrong. For no one who is in love, if his heart is divided, disturbed, uncertain, or troubled by remorse, can give free play to his affections. Often I feel at peace, but often full of care; often my love seems right and I accept it wholeheartedly, but then again my eyes are wet with tears; so it is now, I cannot help it. God send good fortune to Troilus; since I cannot have him nor he me, to the other I give and bind myself. How gladly would I have a mind that could banish all memory of things done in the past. This causes me great suffering; my conscience reproaches me and brings suffering to my heart. But

Qui à mon cuer fait grant torment.
Mais or m'estuet à ce torner
Tout mon corage et mon penser,
Veuille ou ne veuille, dès or mais,
Comfaitement Diomedès
Soit d'amor à moi atendanz,
Si qu'il en soit liez et joianz,
Et je de lui, puis qu'ainsi est.
Or truis mon cuer hardi et prest
De faire ce que lui plaira;
Ja plus orgueil n'i trovera.
Par parole l'ai tant mené
Qu'or li ferai sa volenté
Et son plaisir et son voloir.
Dieus m'en doint joie et bien avoir.» ...

CHRÉTIEN DE TROYES

Le Conte du Graal (Le Roman de Perceval)

... CE fu au tens qu'arbre foillissent,
Que glai et bois et pré verdissent,

now I must concentrate all my heart and all my thought, whatever I may wish, on making Diomedes confident of my love, so that he may be happy and glad because of me, and I because of him, as things have come about. Now I feel my heart bold and ready to do what will please him; no longer will he find any resistance in it. So far I have put him off with words, now I shall do all his will and his pleasure and desire. God grant that I may have joy and good from him.' ...

The Story of the Grail (The Romance of Perceval)

... IT was in the season when trees break into leaf, when iris plants and woods and meadows become green, when the birds in their

Et cil oisel en lor latin
Chantent doucement au matin
Et toute rien de joie aflamme,
Que li fils à la veve femme
De la gaste forest soutaine
Se leva; et ne li fu paine
Que il sa sele ne meïst
Sor son chaceor, et preïst
Trois javelos; et tout ainsi
Fors du manoir sa mere issi.
Il pensa que veoir iroit
Herceors que sa mere avoit,
Qui ses avaines li herçoient;
Bués douze et sis herces avoient.
Ainsi en la forest s'en entre,
Et maintenant li cuers du ventre
Pour le dous tens li resjoï,
Et pour le chant que il oï
Des oiseaus qui joie faisoient;
Toutes ces choses li plaisoient.
Pour la douçor du tens serain,
Osta au chaceor le frain,
Si le laissa aler paissant
Par l'herbe fresche verdoiant.

own language sing sweetly in the morning, when everything is
aflame with joy, that the son of the widow of the wild and lonely
forest arose; it was no trouble to him to saddle his horse and take
three darts; and thus he went out from his mother's dwelling. He
thought he would go and see his mother's labourers, who were
harrowing her oats; they had twelve oxen and six harrows. And so
he went out into the forest; and immediately his heart was glad
within him for the lovely weather and the song he heard from the
rejoicing birds; all these things pleased him. The weather was so
soft and mild that he took off the horse's bridle and let it loose to
graze on the fresh green grass.

Et cil qui bien lancier savoit
Des javelos que il avoit,
Aloit environ lui lançant,
Une heure arriere, l'autre avant,
Une heure bas et autre haut,
Tant qu'il oï parmi le gaut
Venir cinc chevaliers armés,
De toutes armes adoubés.
Et moult grant noise demenoient
Les armes de ceus qui venoient,
Que souvent hurtelent as armes
Li raim des chaisnes et des charmes.
Les lances as escus hurtoient
Et tout li hauberc fresteloient;
Sonent li fust, sone li fers;
Et des escus et des haubers.
Li vallés ot et ne voit pas
Ceus qui vers lui vienent le pas;
Moult se merveille et dist: «Par m'ame,
Voir se dist ma mere, ma dame,
Qui me dist que diable sont
Les plus laides choses du mont;
Et si dist por moi enseignier

And he, who was skilled at throwing with the darts that he had, went along hurling them now here, now there, now high, now low, until he heard coming through the wood five armed knights, equipped with all their arms; and the arms of the approaching knights made a very great noise, for often the branches of the oaks and the hornbeams clashed against their armour, and the lances struck against the shields, and all the hauberks jingled; both wood and iron resounded, from the shields and from the hauberks. The boy heard, but could not see, the men coming towards him at a walking pace. He marvelled greatly and said, 'On my soul, she told me the truth, my mother, my lady, when she said that devils are the most hideous things in the world. And she said too, to instruct me, that we should cross ourselves on meeting them. But I will scorn

Que pour eus se doit on seignier,
Mais cest ensaing desdaignerai,
Que ja voir ne m'en seignerai,
Ainz ferrai si tout le plus fort
D'un des javelos que je port
Que ja n'aprochera vers moi
Nuls des autres, si com je croi.»
Ainsi à soi meïsmes dist
Li vallés, ainz qu'il les veïst;
Et quant il les vit en apert,
Que du bois furent descovert,
Et vit les haubers fremians
Et les helmes clers et luisans,
Et vit le blanc et le vermeil
Reluire contre le soleil,
Et l'or et l'azur et l'argent,
Si li fu moult bel et moult gent,
Et dist «Ha! sire Dieus, merci!
Ce sont angle que je voi ci.
Et voir or ai je moult pechié,
Or ai je moult mal esploitié,
Qui dis que c'estoient diable.
Ne me dist pas ma mere fable,

this counsel, for indeed I will not cross myself, but will strike the very strongest of them with one of the darts that I am carrying so hard that none of the others will come near me, as I think.' So said the boy to himself before he saw them. And when he saw them clearly as they came out of the trees, and saw the glittering hauberks, and the bright shining helmets, and saw the white and the scarlet flashing in the sun, and the gold and the blue and the silver, it seemed to him most beautiful and noble, and he said, 'Ah Lord God, mercy! these are angels that I see here, and truly now have I sinned greatly; I did very wrong just now, when I said that they were devils. My mother was not deceiving me when she said that

Qui me dist que li angle estoient
Les plus beles choses qui soient,
Fors Dieus qui est plus beaus que tuit.
Ci voi je Damedieu, ce cuit,
Car un si bel en i esgart
Que li autre, se Dieus me gart,
N'ont mie de beauté la disme.
Ce me dist ma mere meïsme
Qu'on doit Dieu sor tous aorer
Et supplier et honorer;
Et je aorerai cestui
Et tous les angles après lui.»
Maintenant vers terre se lance
Et dist trestoute sa creance
Et oroisons que il savoit,
Que sa mere apris li avoit.
Et li maistres des chevaliers
Le voit, et dist «Estez arriers!
A terre est de paor cheüs
Uns vallés qui nous a veüs.
Se nous alions tuit ensemble
Vers lui, il avroit, ce me semble,
Si grant paor que il morroit,
Ne respondre ne me porroit
A rien que je li demandasse.»

angels were the most beautiful things in existence except God, who is more beautiful than all. And here I see the Lord God, I think, for one so handsome I see among them that the others (so help me God!) have not a tenth of his beauty. My mother herself told me that we must worship God above all others, and pray to him and honour him, and I shall worship this being and all the angels after him.' Straightway he threw himself on the ground and said all his creed and the prayers that he knew, that his mother had taught him. And the leader of the knights saw him and said, 'Stay behind! A boy who has seen us has fallen to the ground in fear; if we all went towards him together, I think he would be so terrified that he would

Cil s'arestent et il s'en passe
Vers le vallet grant aleüre,
Si le salue et asseüre
Et dist «Vallet, n'aiez paor.»
– «Non ai je, par le Salveor,
Fait li vallés, en qui je croi.
N'estes vous Dieus?» – «Naie, par foi.»
«Qui estes donc?» – «Chevaliers sui.»
– «Ainc mais chevalier ne conui,
Fait li vallés, ne nul n'en vi
N'onques mais parler n'en oï,
Mais vous estes plus beaus que Dieus.
Car fuisse je or autretieus,
Aussi luisanz et aussi fais.»
Maintenant pres de lui s'est trais,
Et li chevaliers li demande:
«Veïs tu hui par ceste lande
Cinc chevaliers et trois puceles?»
Li vallés à autres nouveles
Enquerre et demander entent;
A sa lance sa main li tent,
Sel prent et dist «Beaus sire chiers,
Vous qui avez nom chevaliers,
Que est or ce que vous tenez?»

die and would not be able to reply to anything I asked him.' They stopped, and he went on quickly towards the boy and greeted and reassured him, and said, 'Do not be afraid, boy.' 'I am not afraid,' said the boy, 'by the Saviour in whom I believe. Are you not God?' 'Not I, by my faith.' 'Who are you, then?' 'I am a knight.' 'I never knew a knight before,' said the boy, 'nor saw one, or ever before heard tell of one. But you are more beautiful than God. How I wish I were such another, just as shining and just like you.' At this he drew near to him and the knight asked him, 'Have you seen today on this moor five knights and three maidens?' The boy was intent on asking and inquiring about other matters; he stretched out his hand to the lance, grasped it, and said, 'Fair dear lord, you who are called "knight", now what is this that you are holding?' 'Now

– «Or sui je moult bien assenez,
Fait li chevaliers, ce m'est vis.
Je cuidoie, beaus dous amis,
Nouveles aprendre de toi,
Et tu les veus oïr de moi;
Sel te dirai: ce est ma lance.»
– «Dites vous, fait il, qu'on la lance
Si com je fais mes javelos?»
– «Naie, vallet, tu es tous sos!
Ainz en fiert on tout demanois.»
– «Donc vaut mieus li uns de ces trois
Javelos que vous veez ci;
Que quanques je vueil en oci,
Oiseaus et bestes au besoing
Et si les oci de si loing
Come on porroit d'un bojon traire.»
– «Vallet, de ce n'ai je que faire,
Mais des chevaliers me respont.
Di moi se tu sez où il sont,
Et les puceles veïs tu?»
Li vallés au pié de l'escu
Le prent et dist tout en apert
«Ce que est et de quoi vous sert?»

I am being very well directed,' said the knight, 'it seems to me. I thought, fair sweet friend, to learn news from you, and you want to hear news from me. And I will tell you: that is my lance.' 'Do you mean,' said he, 'that you throw it as I do my darts?' 'No, boy. How foolish you are! On the contrary, you strike with it directly.' 'Then one of these three darts you see here is more use, for I kill whatever I want with it, birds and beasts according to my need; and I kill from as far away as you can shoot an arrow.' 'Boy, that does not concern me. But give me an answer about the knights. Tell me if you know where they are, and if you saw the maidens.' The boy seized him by the bottom of his shield and said boldly, 'What is this, and what is it for?' 'Boy,' he said, 'this is a trick;

— «Vallet, fait il, ce est abés:
En autre nouvele me mes
Que je ne te quier ne demant.
Je cuidoie, se Dieus m'avant,
Que tu nouveles me deïsses
Ainz que de moi les apreïsses,
Et tu veus que je tes apreigne.
Je te dirai, coment qu'il preigne,
Car à toi volentiers m'acort:
Escu a nom ce que je port.»
— «Escu a nom?» — «Voire, fait cil,
Ne le doi mie tenir vil,
Car il m'est tant de bone foi
Que se nuls lance ou trait à moi,
Encontre tous les coups se met.
C'est li services qu'il me fet.»
    Atant cil qui furent arriere
S'en vindrent toute la charriere
Vers leur seigneur plus que le pas,
Si li dient isnellepas:
«Sire, que vous dist cist Galois?»
— «Il ne set pas toutes les lois,
Fait li sire, se Dieus m'ament,
Qu'a rien nule que li demant
Ne me respont il ainc à droit,

you are changing the subject from what I ask and seek of you. I thought, so God amend me, that you would give news to me rather than learn news from me, and you want me to tell news to you. I will tell you, come what may, for I have taken a liking to you: what I am carrying is called a shield.' 'It is called a shield?' 'Yes, indeed,' he replied, 'I must by no means scorn it, for it is so faithful to me that if anyone attacks me with lance or arrow it intercepts every blow. That is the service that it does me.' At this point, those that were behind came briskly up along the track towards their lord, and said to him without delay, 'Sire, what is this Welsh boy saying to you?' 'He is not quite right in his mind,' said the leader, 'so God amend me, for to nothing I ask him will he give a straight

Ainz demande de quanqu'il voit
Coment a nom et qu'on en fait,»
– «Sire, sachiez tout entresait
Que Galois sont tout par nature
Plus fol que bestes en pasture;
Cist est aussi come une beste.
Fols est qui dalez lui s'areste,
S'à la muse ne veut muser
Et le tens en folie user.»
– «Ne sai, fait il, mais se Dieu voie,
Ainz que soie mis à la voie,
Quanqu'il voudra tout li dirai;
Ja autrement n'en partirai.»
Lors li demande de rechief:
«Vallet, fait il, ne te soit grief,
Mais des cinc chevaliers me di
Et des puceles autresi
S'hui les encontras ne veïs.»
Et li vallés le tenoit pris
Par le hauberc, et si le tire.
«Or me dites, fait il, beaus sire,
Que c'est que vous avez vestu?»
– «Vallet, fait il, donc nel sez tu?»

answer, but asks about everything he sees, what it is called and
what it is used for.' 'Sire, you may know for certain that Welshmen
are all by nature more stupid than the cattle in the fields. This boy
is just like a beast. It is useless to stay with him, unless we want to
play the fool and waste our time on nonsense.' 'I don't know about
that,' said he, 'but, as I hope to see God, before I set off again I will
tell him everything he wants to know. Otherwise I will not leave
him.' Then he asked him again, 'Boy,' he said, 'I do not want to
bother you, but tell me about the five knights and also about the
maidens, if you met them or saw them today.' And the boy was
holding him by the hauberk, and pulled at it. 'Now tell me,' said
he, 'fair sir, what is this thing that you are wearing?' 'Boy,' said
he, 'do you not know then?' 'Not I.' 'Boy, it is my hauberk, and

— «Je non.» — «Vallet, c'est mes haubers,
S'est aussi pesans come fers,
Qu'il est de fer, ce vois tu bien.»
— «De ce, fait il, ne sai je rien,
Mais moult est beaus, se Dieus me saut.
Qu'en faites vous, et que vous vaut?»
— «Vallet, c'est à dire legier.
Se voloies à moi lancier
Javelot ou saiete traire,
Ne me porroies nul mal faire.»
— «Dans chevaliers, de tels haubers
Gart Dieus les biches et les cers,
Que nule ocirre n'en porroie
Ne jamais après ne courroie.»
Et li chevaliers li redit:
«Vallet, se Damedieus t'aït,
Se tu me sez dire nouveles
Des chevaliers et des puceles?»
Et cil qui petit fu senés
Li dist: «Fustes vous ainsi nés?»
— «Naie, vallet, ce ne peut estre
Qu'ainsi peüst ja nuls hom nestre.»
— «Qui vous atorna donc ainsi?»
— «Vallet, je te dirai bien qui.»
— «Dites le donc.» — «Moult volentiers:

it is as heavy as iron, for it is made of iron, as you see.' 'I don't
know anything about that,' he said, 'but it is very beautiful, so
God save me. What do you do with it, and what use is it to you?'
'Boy, that is easy to say. If you wanted to throw a dart or shoot
an arrow at me, you could not do me any harm.' 'Sir knight, may
God keep hinds and stags from such hauberks, for I should never
be able to kill any of them and I should no longer hunt them.' And
the knight said to him once more, 'Boy, so may God help you, can
you tell me news of the knights and the maidens?' And he, who
had but little sense, said, 'Were you born like this?' 'No, boy, that
could not be, for no man can be born like this.' 'Who equipped you
then like this?' 'Boy, I will tell you who.' 'Tell it then.' 'Willingly.

N'a pas encor cinc ans entiers
Que tout cest harnois me dona
Li rois Artus qui m'adouba.

Mais or me redi que devindrent
Li chevalier qui par ci vindrent,
Qui les trois puceles conduient.
Vont il le pas, ou il s'en fuient?»
Et cil dist: «Sire, or esgardez
Le plus haut bois que vous veez,
Qui cele montaigne avironne.
Là sont li destroit de Valbone.»
– «Et que de ce, fait il, beaus frere?»
– «Là sont li herceor ma mere,
Qui ses terres sement et erent,
Et se ces gens i trespasserent,
S'il les virent, sel vous diront.» . . .

THOMAS

Le Roman de Tristran

. . . LA nef desirent à la rive;
Encore ne la virent pas.

It is not yet five whole years since all this harness was given to me by King Arthur, who dubbed me knight. But now you tell me: what has become of the knights who passed this way, those who were leading the three maidens? Are they going slowly or are they in flight?' And he said, 'Sire, now look at the highest wood that you see surrounding that hill. That is the Pass of Valbone.' 'And what of that,' said he, 'fair brother?' 'There are my mother's harrowers, who sow and plough her land; and if those people passed that way and they saw them, they will tell you.'

The Romance of Tristram

. . . ON shore they are longing for the ship to come; as yet they have not seen it. Tristram is full of grief and weariness; often he

Tristrans en est dolenz et las,
Souvent se plaint, souvent sospire
Pour Iseut que il tant desire;
Plore des ieus, son cors deteurt,
A poi que du desir ne meurt.
En cele angoisse, en cel ennui
Vient sa femme Iseut devant lui.
Pourpensee de grant engin,
Dit: «Amis, or vient Kaherdin.
Sa nef ai veüe en la mer,
A grant peine l'ai veu sigler;
Nequedent je l'ai si veüe
Que pour la soe l'ai conue.
Dieus doint que tel novele aport
Dont vous au cuer aiez confort.»

Tristrans tresaut de la novele,
Dit à Iseut: «Amie bele,
Savez pour voir que c'est sa nef?
Or me dites quel est le tref.»
Ce dit Iseut: «Jel sai pour voir.
Sachez que le sigle est tout noir.
Trait l'ont amont et levé haut
Pour ice que li venz lor faut.»

moans, often he sighs for Iseult, whom he so longs to see. His tears fall down, he tosses about, he almost dies from his longing. In this anguish, in this trouble, his wife Iseult comes before him; her mind full of great treachery, she says: 'My love, now Kaherdin is coming: I have seen his ship on the sea; I could only just see it, but still I saw it well enough to know that it was his. God grant it brings us some news that will give comfort to your heart.'

Tristram starts up at this; he says to Iseult: 'Fair love, are you sure that it is his ship? Tell me, what kind of sail has it?' Iseult says: 'I am sure of it, and I can tell you that the sail is all black; they have hoisted it and raised it high because they have not wind

Donc a Tristrans si grant dolour
Onques n'ot ne n'avra maour,
Et torne soi vers la paroi;
Donc dit: «Dieus saut Iseut et moi!
Quant à moi ne voulez venir,
Pour vostre amour m'estuet mourir.
Je ne puis plus tenir ma vie;
Pour vous muer, Iseut, bele amie.
N'avez pitié de ma langour,
Mais de ma mort avrez dolour.
Ce m'est, amie, grant confort
Que pitié avrez de ma mort.»
«Amie Iseut» trois fois a dit,
A la quarte rent l'espirit.

Idonc plorent par la maison
Li chevalier, li compaignon.
Li criz est haut, la plainte grant.
Saillent chevalier et sergent
Et portent le cors de son lit,
Puis le couchent sur un samit,
Couvrent le d'un paile roié.

enough.' Then Tristram feels so sharp a pang as he had never felt
before, nor ever will again, and he turns his face to the wall and
says: 'God help Iseult and me! Since you will not come to me, I
must die for your love. I can cling to life no longer. I am dying for
you, Iseult, my fair love; you will not take pity on my suffering,
but my death will be a grief to you. My love, it is a great consola-
tion to me that you will mourn my death.' 'Iseult, my love,' he says
three times, and at the fourth gives up his spirit.

Then the knights his companions weep throughout the house;
the cry is loud, the lamentation great. Knights and servants leap
forward to carry the body from his bed and lay it down on a samite
cloth and cover it with one of striped silk.

Li venz est en la mer levé
Et fiert soi en milieu du tref;
A terre fait venir la nef.
Iseut est de la nef issue,
Ot les grans plaintes en la rue,
Les seins as mostiers, as chapeles;
Demande as homes quels noveles,
Pourquoi il font tel soneïs,
Et de quoi soit li ploreïs.
Uns anciens donques li dit:
«Bele dame, si Dieu m'aït,
Nous avons issi grant dolour
Que onques genz n'orent maour.
Tristran li prouz, li francs, est mort.
A tous ceus du regne ert confort.
Larges estoit as bosognous
Et grant aïe as dolorous.
D'une plaie qu'en son cors ut
En son lit orendroit morut.
Onques si grant chaitiveson
N'avint à ceste region.»

Tres que Iseut la novele ot,
De dolour ne peut soner mot.

The wind has risen over the sea and hurled itself upon the midst
of the sail, and it brings the ship to shore. Iseult has come out of
the ship, she hears the great lamentations in the street and the bells
in churches and chapels, and she asks the people what the news is
for which they make such ringing and what the cause of the
lamentations. An old man then says to her: 'Fair lady, as God may
help me, we have such a sorrow that no people ever had a greater.
Tristram the brave, the good, is dead. He was the comfort of all in
the kingdom. Generous he was to the needy, and full of help to those
in trouble. He died just now in his bed from a wound he had in his
body. Never so great a calamity befell this country.'
When Iseult hears the news, she cannot speak a word for sorrow.

De sa mort est si adolee
La rue va desafublee
Devant les autres el palais.
Breton ne virent onques mais
Femme de la soe beauté:
Merveillent soi par la cité
Dont ele vient, qui ele soit.
Iseut va là où le cors voit,
Si se tourne vers orient,
Pour lui prie pitousement:
«Amis Tristran, quant mort vous voi,
Par raison vivre puis ne doi.
Mort estes pour la moie amour,
Et je muer, amis, de tendrour,
Quant je à tens ne poi venir
Pour vous et vostre mal garir.
Amis, amis, pour vostre mort
N'avrai jamais de rien confort,
Joie, ne hait, ne nul deduit.
Icil orages soit destruit
Qui tant me fist, amis, en mer,
Que n'i poi venir, demourer!
Se je i fusse à tens venue,
Vie vous eüsse rendue,

She is so grief-stricken at his death that she goes without a cloak along the street to the palace before the others. The Bretons had never before seen a woman of her beauty; throughout the city they are wondering whence she comes and who she may be. Iseult goes to the place where she sees the body, and she turns towards the East and prays for him tenderly. 'Tristram, my love, when I see you dead, it is not reasonable that I should live any longer. You have died for my love and I am dying for sorrow that I could not come in time to cure you and heal your sickness. My love! my love! because of your death nothing can ever give me consolation nor joy nor gladness nor any pleasure. A curse upon the storm that kept me so long on the sea that I could not come. If I had been in time,

Et parlé doucement à vous
De l'amour qui fu entre nous;
Plainte eüsse nostre aventure,
Nostre joie, nostre envoisure,
Et la peine et la grant dolour
Qui a esté en nostre amour,
Et eüsse ice recordé
Et vous baisié et acolé.
Se je n'ai peü vous garir,
Qu'ensemble puissons donc mourir.
Quant je à tens venir n'i poi
Et je l'aventure ne soi,
Et venue sui à la mort,
De meisme boivre avrai confort.
Pour moi avez perdu la vie,
Et je frai com veraie amie:
Pour vous veuil mourir ensement.»
Embrace le et si s'estent,
Baise li la bouche et la face
Et moult estroit à li l'embrace,
Cors à cors, bouche à bouche estent,
Son espirit à itant rent,
Et meurt dejoste lui ainsi
Pour la dolour de son ami.

I would have brought you back to life and talked softly with you of the love that was between us. I should have spoken tenderly of all that has come to us, our joy and our delight, and all the sorrow and the great grief that there has been in our love. I should have recalled all this and kissed you and embraced you. Since I have not been able to heal you, let us then die both together; since I could not get here in time and did not know that this was happening, and have come at your death, I too will drink from the same cup. You have lost your life for me, and I shall do as a true lover should: I too shall die for you.' She embraces him and lies down beside him, kisses his mouth and his face and draws him very closely to her, body to body, mouth to mouth. Then she gives up her spirit, and so dies beside him, for grief for her lover. Tristram died of his

Tristrans morut pour son desir,
Iseut, qu'à tens n'i pot venir.
Tristrans morut pour soe amour
Et la bele Iseut pour tendrour . . .

LE CHÂTELAIN DE COUCY

Chanson d'Amour

LA douce voiz du rossignol sauvage,
Qu'oi nuit et jour cointoier et tentir,
Me radoucist mon cuer et rassouage:
Lors ai talent que chant pour esbaudir.
Bien doi chanter, puis qu'il vient à plaisir
Celi cui j'ai de cuer fait lige homage;
Si doi avoir grant joie en mon corage
S'ele me veut à son oés retenir.

Onques vers li n'oi faus cuer ne volage,
Si m'en devroit pour ço mieus avenir;
Ainz l'aim et serf et aour par usage,
Si ne li os mon penser descovrir,

longing, Iseult because she could not come in time; Tristram died
for love of her, and the fair Iseult for sorrow. . .

Love Song

THE sweet voice of the woodland nightingale that I hear night and
day trilling and calling softens and soothes my heart, and then I
have a mind to sing for joy. Well should I sing, since it is her
pleasure to whom I have done homage with my heart, and my soul
should be filled with joy if she is willing to accept me into her
service.

I never had a false or fickle thought towards her – and this should
make my case more hopeful – but I love and serve and adore her
with constancy; and yet I dare not disclose my thoughts to her, for

Car sa beauté me fait si esbahir
Que je ne sai devant li nul langage,
Ne regarder n'os son simple visage,
Tant en redout mes yeus à repartir.

Tant ai vers li ferm assis mon corage
Qu'ailleurs ne pens, et Dieus m'en laist joïr;
Qu'onques Tristrans, cil qui but le bevrage,
Si coraument n'ama sans repentir;
Car j'i met tout, cuer et cors et desir,
Sens et savoir, ne sai se faz folage;
Encor me dout qu'en trestout mon eage
Ne puisse assez li et s'amour servir.

Je ne di pas que je face folage,
Nis se por li me devoie mourir;
Qu'el mont ne truis si belle ne si sage,
Ne nule rien n'est tant à mon plaisir.
Moult aim mes yeus qui m'i firent choisir;
Lués que la vi, li laissai en ostage
Mon cuer, qui puis i a fait lonc estage,
Ne jamais jour ne l'en quier departir.

her beauty so dazzles me that I can find no words in her presence.
And I dare not even look at her sweet face, so much I dread to take
my eyes away.

I have so firmly set my heart on her that I can think of no one
else, and God grant that I may win her; for never Tristram, he who
drank the potion, loved so deeply or with such constancy; for I
give up all to loving, heart and body and every wish, all sense, all
reason; I do not know whether I am behaving like a madman – and
even so I fear that in all my life I shall not be able to serve her and
her love enough.

I do not say I am behaving like a fool, even if I were to die for
her, for in all the world I cannot find another so beautiful or so wise,
nor anyone to cause me such delight. I love my eyes for having
made me see her. As soon as I saw her, I left my heart a hostage in
her keeping, and there it has already made a long stay, and I never
wish to remove it from her.

Chançon, va t'en pour faire mon message
Là où je n'os trestorner ne guenchir;
Que tant redout la male gent ombrage
Qui devinent, ainz que puist avenir,
Les biens d'amour. Dieus les puist maleïr,
Qu'à maint amant ont fait ire et outrage,
Mais de ç'ai je touz jours mal avantage,
Qu'il les m'estuet sor mon gré obeïr.

CONON DE BÉTHUNE

Chanson d'Amour

Si voirement com cele dont je chant
Vaut mieuz que toutes les bonnes qui sont,
Et je l'aim plus que rien qui soit el mont,
Si me doint Dieus s'amour sans decevoir;
Que tel desir en ai et tel vouloir,
Ou tant ou plus, Dieus en set la verté,
Si com malades desirre santé,
Desir je li et s'amour à avoir.

Go, Song, and bear my message to that place where I myself dare neither go nor turn my steps, for I so greatly fear the wicked jealous people who guess the sweets of love before they can be savoured; God's curse upon such people: they have brought sorrow and injury to many a lover, but I am always unfortunate in this, that I have to obey them against my will.

Love Song

As truly as she of whom I sing surpasses all other women in goodness, and as I love her more than anything in the world, so may God grant me her love without fail; for I desire and wish for it so much that I long to have her and her love as much — or more — God knows the truth of it, as a sick man longs for health.

Or sai je bien que rien ne peut valoir
Tant com celi de qui j'ai tant chanté,
Qu'or ai veü et li et sa beauté,
Et si sai bien que tant a de valor
Que je doi faire et outrage et folor
D'amer plus haut que ne m'avroit mestier;
Et, nonporquant, maint povre chevalier
Fait riches cuers venir à haute honor.

Ainz que fusse sospris de ceste amor,
Savoie je autre gent conseillier,
Et or sai bien d'altrui jeu enseignier
Et si ne sai mie le mien juër;
Si sui com cil qui as eschés voit cler
Et qui tres bien ensengne as autres gens,
Et, quant il jue, si pert si son sens
Qu'il ne se set escore de mater.

Hé! las, dolanz, je ne sai tant chanter
Que ma dame parçoive mes tormenz,
N'encor n'est pas si granz mes hardemenz
Que je li os dire les maus que trai,
Ne devant li n'en os parler ne sai;

Now I know well that none can be the equal of her whose praises
I have sung so long, for now I have seen her and her beauty, and I
know too that she is of such worth that I must be guilty of pre-
sumption and folly in loving higher than I ought to do. And never-
theless a noble heart brings many a lowly knight to high honour.

Before this love had taken possession of me, I could give counsel
to other people, and now I can teach another his game but cannot
play my own, and I am like a man who sees clearly at chess and
teaches others very well, but when he plays, then he so loses his
head that he cannot escape being checkmated.

Alas, poor wretch, I know not how to sing so that my lady shall
perceive my torments, nor yet is my boldness so great that I dare
tell her of the sufferings I endure, and in her presence I dare not
and cannot speak of them. And when I am elsewhere before an-

Et quant je sui aillors devant autrui,
Lors i parol, mais si peu m'i dedui
Qu'un anui vaut li deduiz que j'en ai.

Encor devis comment je li dirai
La grant dolor que j'en trais senz anui;
Que tant l'ador et desir quant j'i sui,
Que ne li os descouvrir ma raison;
Si va de moi com fait du champion
Qui de lonc tens aprent à escremir,
Et quant il vient ou champ as cous ferir,
Si ne set rien d'escu ne de baston.

GUIOT DE DIJON

Chanson de Croisade

CHANTERAI por mon corage
Que je vueil reconforter,
Car avec mon grant damage
Ne quier mourir n'afoler,
Quant de la terre sauvage
Ne voi nului retorner

other, then I can speak, but it gives me so little pleasure that any joy I find there is no better than sorrow.

And still I plan how I shall tell her, without giving her offence, of the great pain I suffer for her; for I adore her and long for her so when I am with her, that I dare not tell her what is in my mind, and it is with me as it is with the champion who has long studied sword-play, but when he comes into the field and to the striking of blows, then he knows not a thing of either shield or weapon.

Song of the Crusade

FOR my heart's consolation I will sing, since I do not want to die or go out of my mind in my great suffering: for I see none returning from that wild country where he is who soothes my heart when

Où cil est qui m'assoage
Le cuer, quant j'en oi parler.
Dieus, quant crieront «Outree»,
Sire, aidiez au pelerin
Pour qui sui espoentee,
Car felon sont Sarrazin.

Soufrerai en tel estage
Tant quel voie rapasser.
Il est en pelerinage,
Dont Dieus le lait retorner.
Et maugré tout mon lignage
Ne quier ochoison trouver
D'autre face mariage;
Fols est qui j'en oi parler.
Dieus, quant crieront «Outree»,
Sire, aidiez au pelerin
Pour qui sui espoentee,
Car felon sont Sarrazin.

De ce sui au cuer dolente
Que cil n'est en Beauvoisis
Qui si souvent me tormente:
Or n'en ai ne jeu ne ris.
S'il est beaus, et je sui gente.

I hear him spoken of. God, when they cry '*Outree*', help, oh Lord,
that crusader for whose sake I go in fear, for cruel are the Saracens.

I will patiently keep my present state until I see him come back.
He is on pilgrimage: God grant he may return. And in spite of all
my kindred I do not wish to seek occasion to marry any other; he
is a fool whom I hear speaking of it. God, when they cry '*Outree*',
help, oh Lord, that crusader for whose sake I go in fear, for cruel
are the Saracens.

What grieves my heart is that he is not here in Beauvaisis, he
for whom I long so often. Now I have neither joy nor laughter. If
he is handsome, I too am comely. Lord God, why did you do it?

Sire Dieus, pour quel feïs?
Quant l'uns à l'autre atalente,
Pour quoi nous as departis?
Dieus, quant crieront «Outree»,
Sire, aidiez au pelerin
Pour qui sui espoentee,
Car felon sont Sarrazin.

De ce sui en bone atente
Que je son homage pris,
Et quant la douce ore vente
Qui vient de cel dous païs
Où cil est qui m'atalente,
Volentiers i tor mon vis;
Adonc, m'est vis que jel sente
Par desous mon mantel gris.
Dieus, quant crieront «Outree»,
Sire, aidiez au pelerin
Pour qui sui espoentee,
Car felon sont Sarrazin.

De ce sui moult deceue
Que ne fui au convoier.
Sa chemise qu'ot vestue
M'envoia pour embracier;

When one desires the other, why have you parted us? God, when they cry '*Outree*', help, oh Lord, that crusader for whose sake I go in fear, for cruel are the Saracens.

What gives me hope is that I have received his homage; and when the gentle breeze blows from that sweet country where my love is, I gladly turn my face towards it; and then, it seems to me, I feel his touch beneath my grey mantle. God, when they cry '*Outree*', help, oh Lord, that crusader for whose sake I go in fear, for cruel are the Saracens.

What I regret is that I was not there to escort him at his starting out. The pilgrim's gown he wore, he sent for me to hold in my

La nuit, quant s'amor m'argue,
La met delès moi couchier
Moult estroit à ma char nue
Pour mes maus assoagier.
Dieus, quant crieront «Outree»,
Sire, aidiez au pelerin
Pour qui sui espoentee,
Car felon sont Sarrazin.

JEAN RENART

L'Escoufle

... Que qu'il en vont parlant, tout droit
Vers la cité, grant aleüre,
Il a oï par aventure
Lès le chemin, en un jonchois,
Un ruisselet qui n'ert pas cois,
Ainz murmure sor la gravele.
Il a oï la fontenele
Dont l'eaue est plus clere qu'argens.
Fait il: «Or est ce li plus gens
Lieus d'eaue douce et de flors;

arms. At night, when love of him assails me, I put it beside me in my bed, close to my naked flesh, to allay my grief. God, when they cry '*Outree*', help, oh Lord, that crusader for whose sake I go in fear, for cruel are the Saracens.

The Kite

... As they rode on talking, straight towards the city, at a good speed, he heard by chance, beside the way, in a bed of rushes, a little stream that was not silent but murmured over the gravel. He heard the spring with water brighter than silver. Said he: 'This is the loveliest place of sweet water and flowers. Never before have I

Ainc mais ne vi de tans colors
En si peu de terre autretant.»
Il esgardent tout en estant
Le lieu delitable en esté.
La rosee ot si grans esté
Qu'encore en sont tout plein li oeil
Des flors, et li rais del soleil
Feroit si en chascune flor
Que l'eaue en reçoit la color
De chascune tèl comme el l'a.
«Beaus dous amis, fait ele, là
Vueil je descendre pour mangier.»
De tant la veut cil losengier
Qu'il li otroie volentiers.
Atant uns mout soutius sentiers
Ambedeus les conduit et maine
Du chemin jusqu'à la fontaine.

Il saut jus, si l'a descendue;
La pucele s'est estendue
As flouretes et au deduit.
Pour le chaut qui li grieve et nuit
Tolt sa chape et sa jupe fors:
Ele remest en pur le cors,
Tout desliee et desceinte.

seen such a quantity of flowers of so many different colours in such
a small space.' They stopped and looked at this place, so delightful
in the summer weather. The dew had been so heavy that the eyes
of the flowers were still full of it, and the sunlight shone into every
flower so that the water took on the colour of each one. 'Fair sweet
friend,' said she, 'this is where I should like to dismount to eat.'
He wished to please her so much that he willingly agreed. Then a
very winding path took them both from the road to the spring.

He leaped down and helped her to dismount. The girl gladly
stretched herself out among the flowers. Because of the oppressive
heat that was troubling her, she took off her cloak and her riding-
skirt and sat in indoor clothes, her robe loosened and ungirt, her

Sa cote li fait grant aceinte
Tout entour li, sor l'erbe drue.
(Moult est garis qui a tel drue;
Ne doit avoir nule destrece!)
Pour ce que sa bende destrece,
Li cort kavelet et li blont
Par moult grant maistrie li vont
Par devant le tour des oreilles
Desci jusqu'as faces vermeilles;
Sor son blanc col en rot floceaux ...

Galeran de Bretagne

... Tout sagement et deduisant
Entre Galeran en la ville
Où il ot de destriers dix mille
Parmi ces rues cler hennir,
Chevaliers aller et venir
Sur chevaux reposés et fres.
Cil autre y jouent aux eschés,
Et cil aux tables se deportent;
Cil varlet ces presens y portent
Par les hostels à ces pucelles
Et aux dames vaillans et belles.

gown making a great circle round her on the thick grass. (He is a fortunate man who has such a lover; he should never have any sorrows!) As she had unbraided her hair, the short, fair tresses fell charmingly round her ears and on to her rosy cheeks; and some curled on her white neck ...

Galeran of Brittany

... In good array and full of high spirits, Galeran enters the town, where he can hear the whinnying of ten thousand steeds ring out along the streets, as knights ride up and down on fresh well-rested horses. Others can be seen playing chess and still others back-gammon; servants are going from house to house carrying presents to maidens and to noble lovely ladies. There are young noblemen

Plenté y a de damoiseaux
Qui font gorges à leurs oiseaux.
Si sont fichees ces banieres
Et cil escu teint de manieres
Sus fenestres de tours perrines;
De covertoirs vairs et d'ermines,
Et d'autres chiers draps trais de malles
Ont pourtendues ces grans salles;
Autres ront mise leur entente
De jonchier ces rues de mente
Et de vers joncs et de jagleux.
Ci sont à vendre cist chevreux
Et cerfs et autres venoisons,
Et de là est la grant foisons
D'oues, de jantes et de grues,
Qu'on va portant parmi ces rues,
Et d'autres volailles assez;
Trop repourroie estre lassez
De nommer et de mettre en nombre
Les poissons que l'on vent en l'ombre;
Si pouez veoir el chemin
Plenté de poivre et de coumin,
D'autres espices et de cire.
Ci sont les changeürs en tire
Qui devant eux ont leur monnoie:

in plenty feeding their hawks. Banners with shields painted to match them are fixed outside the windows of stone turrets. Great halls have been draped with miniver and ermine rugs, and other precious hangings brought out of chests. Other people have made it their business to strew the streets with mint, and green rushes and wild iris. Here roebucks are for sale, and stags and other venison, and over there great stocks of geese, wild geese, and cranes are being hawked through the streets, and other fowl in plenty. It would be too wearisome a task to name and detail all the kinds of fish that are being sold in the shade; and you can see on your way plenty of pepper, and cummin and other spices, and beeswax. Here there are rows of money-changers, each with his coins before him:

Cil change, cil conte, cil noie,
Cil dit «C'est voir,» cil «C'est mençonge.»
Onques ivres, tant fust en songe,
Ne vit en dormant la merveille
Que cil peut ci veoir qui veille.

Cil n'i resert mie d'oiseuses
Qui y vent pierres precieuses,
Et images d'argent et d'or.
Autre ont devant eux grant tresor
De leur riche vesselement.
Là en a vint, là en a cent
Qui braire font lions et ours;
En mi la ville, es quarrefours,
Viele cil, et cist y chante,
Cil y tumbe, cist y enchante.
Ci orrïez cors et buisines,
Et les couteaux par ces cuisines
Dont cil queu les viandes coupent
(Qui des meilleurs morseaux s'en coupent.)
Ci a grant noise de mortiers,
Et des cloches de ces moustiers
Qu'on sonne par la ville ensemble.

this one is changing money, this one is counting up, the next disputes the sum: one cries, 'It's true,' another, 'It's a lie.' Never a man in drunken dream saw half the wonders in his sleep that you could see here while still wide awake. And the merchant is not wasting his time who deals in precious stones, and gold and silver images. Still others have before them a wealth of costly vessels. Here twenty people, there a hundred in a crowd set bears and lions roaring. In the middle of the town, at the cross-roads, one man is playing on the viol, another singing; here is an acrobat and there a conjurer; the noise of horns and trumpets mingles with that of sharpening knives in kitchens where cooks are carving up the joints (and cutting for themselves bits from the choicest parts). And there is a great noise of gongs and church bells which are all being rung at once throughout the town. Such festival is being kept, it

Telle feste court, ce me semble,
Mais or est morte en nostre eage:
Pas ne regnent li seigneurage ...

GUILLAUME DE LORRIS

Le Roman de la Rose (First Part)

... JOLIS, gais et pleins de leece,
Vers une riviere m'adrece
Que j'oï pres d'ilueques bruire;
Car ne me soi aller deduire
Plus bel que sus celle riviere.
D'un tertre qui pres d'iluec iere
Descendoit l'eaue grant et roide.
Clere estoit l'eaue et aussi froide
Comme puiz ou comme fontaine;
Si estoit peu mendre de Seine,
Mais qu'elle estoit plus espandue.
Onques mais n'avoie veüe
Cele eaue qui si bien seoit;
Si m'abelissoit et seoit
A regarder le lieu plaisant.

seems to me, as is no longer known in our times, for lordly living
is a thing of the past ...

The Romance of the Rose *(First Part)*

... BLITHE and gay and full of gladness, I made my way towards a
river that I heard flowing near by, for I could not have a better
place to take my pleasure than by that river. From a hillock close at
hand, the water flowed down wide and swift. The river was clear,
and as cold as if it came from a well or a spring, and it was a little
smaller than the Seine, although it was wider spread. Never before
had I seen this river in its lovely setting, and it rejoiced and glad-
dened me to gaze at this beautiful place. With the clear and shining

De l'eaue clere et reluisant
Mon vis rafreschi et lavai;
Si vi tout covert et pavé
Le fonz de l'eaue de gravele.
La praerie grant et bele
Tres au pié de l'eaue batoit.
Clere et serie et bele estoit
La matinee, et atempree;
Lors m'en alai par mi la pree,
Contreval l'eaue esbanoiant,
Tout le rivage costoiant.

Quant j'oi un peu avant alé,
Si vi un vergier grant et lé,
Tout clos de haut mur bataillié,
Portrait dehors et entaillié
A maintes riches escritures.
Les images et les peintures
Du mur volentiers remirai,
Si vous conterai et dirai
De ces images la semblance,
Si com moi vient en remembrance . . .

Après fu Vieillece portraite,
Qui estoit bien un pié retraite

water I refreshed and washed my face, and I saw the bottom of the
river all covered and paved with gravel. A beautiful wide meadow
came right to the water's edge. Clear and calm and lovely was the
morning, and temperate. Then I went on through the meadow,
happily wandering downstream, all along the river bank.

When I had gone a little way, I saw an orchard great and wide,
all enclosed with a high battlemented wall, painted and carved on
its outer side with many richly adorned inscriptions. I looked with
great pleasure at the images and paintings on the wall, and I will
describe to you the appearance of these pictures as I remember
them . . .

Next, Old Age was portrayed, shrunk a full foot from what she

De tel comme ele soloit estre;
A peine qu'el se pooit paistre,
Tant estoit vieille et redotee.
Mout estoit sa beauté gastee,
Mout estoit laide devenue.
Toute sa teste estoit chenue
Et blanche com s'el fust florie.
Ce ne fust mie grant morie
S'ele morist, ne granz pechiés,
Car touz ses cors estoit sechiés
De vieillece, et aneientiz.
Mout estoit ja ses vis flestiz,
Qui fu jadis soués et plains;
Or estoit tous de fronces pleins.
Les oreilles avoit moussues,
Et toutes les denz si perdues
Qu'ele n'en avoit mais nesune.
Tant par estoit de grant vieillune
Qu'el n'alast mie la montance
De quatre toises sanz potence.
Li Tens qui s'en va nuit et jour
Sanz repos prendre et sanz sejour,
Et qui de nous se part et emble
Si celeement qu'il nous semble
Qu'il s'arrest adès en un point,

used to be; hardly could she feed herself, she was so old and dod-
dering. Her beauty was all wasted away, and very ugly had she
become. Her head was all hoary and white, as if it was in blossom.
It would not be much of a death if she died, nor much of a pity, for
all her body was dried up with age and shrunk to nothing. Her face
was now all withered, which once was soft and smooth, but now
was full of wrinkles. Her ears were hairy, and she had lost all her
teeth until she had not a single one left. She was so far gone in age
that she could not walk the length of four ells without a stick. Time,
who speeds on both night and day, never resting, never staying,
and flees from us, and steals away so secretly that it seems to us
that he is always standing still, and yet he never stops but endlessly

Et il ne s'i arreste point,
Ainz ne fine de trespasser,
Que l'on ne puet neïs penser
Quels tens ce est qui est presenz,
Sel demandez as clers lisanz,
Car ainz que l'on l'eüst pensé
Seroient ja troi tens passé;
Li Tens qui ne peut sejourner,
Ainz va tousjours sans retourner,
Com l'eaue qui s'avale toute,
N'il n'en retourne arriere goute;
Li Tens vers qui neienz ne dure,
Ne fer ne chose tant soit dure,
Car Tens gaste tout et manjue;
Li Tens qui toute chose mue,
Qui tout fait croistre et tout norrist
Et qui tout use et tout porrist;
Li Tens qui envieilli nos peres,
Qui vieillist rois et empereres
Et qui tous nous envieillira,
Ou Mort nous desavancira;
Li Tens, qui tout a en baillie
Des genz vieillir, l'avoit vieillie
Si durement qu'au mien cuidier
El ne se pouoit mais aidier,

flies past, so that you cannot even seize the thought of present time if you inquire of learned men, for before you have thought it three separate presents will have passed away; Time, who cannot stay, but travels ever onwards without returning, as water flows forever down and never a drip turns back; Time, against whom nothing endures, not iron or anything however hard, for Time spoils all, eats everything away; Time, who changes all things, makes all things grow, nourishes all, then wears all out and turns all to decay; Time, who has aged our fathers, who ages kings and emperors, and who will age us all, unless death halts us first; Time, who is all-powerful to make all men old, had made her so very old that it seemed to me she could no longer help herself, but was already

Ainz retournoit ja en enfance;
Car certes el n'avoit puissance,
Ce cuit je, ne force ne sen,
Ne plus que uns enfes d'un an.
Neporquant, au mien escientre,
Ele avoit esté sage et entre,
Quant ele ert en son droit eage;
Mais je cuit qu'el n'ere mais sage,
Ainz estoit toute rassotee ...

RUTEBEUF

La Complainte Rutebeuf

... DIEUS m'a fait compagnon à Job,
Qu'il m'a tolu à un seul cop
Quanques j'avoie.
De l'ueil destre, dont mieus veoie,
Ne voi je pas aler la voie
Ne moi conduire:
A ci dolour dolente et dure,
Qu'à miedi m'est nuiz obscure
De celui ueil.

turning back to childhood. For certainly she had not power, I think, nor strength nor sense, more than a year-old child. None the less, she surely had been wise and judicious when she was in her prime, but I think she was no longer in her right mind, but was quite in her dotage ...

Rutebeuf's Complaint

... GOD has made me a fit companion for Job, for he has taken from me at one blow all that I had. With my right eye, which used to be my best, I can no longer see enough to find my way about. This is a dreadful grief to me, for it is dark night at midday for that

Or n'ai je pas quanques je vueil,
Ainz sui dolenz et si me dueil
      Parfondement;
Qu'or sui en grant afondement
Se par ceus n'ai relevement
      Qui jusque ci
M'ont secouru, la lor merci.
Le cuer en ai triste et noirci
      De cest mehain,
Car je n'i voi pas mon gaain.
Or n'ai je pas quanques je ain,
      C'est mes domages.
Ne sai se ç'a fait mes outrages;
Or devendrai sobres et sages
      Après le fait,
Et me garderai de forfait.
Mais ce que vaut? Ce est ja fait;
      Tart sui meüs,
A tart me sui aperceüs
Quant je sui en mes las cheüs.
      Cest premier an
Me gart cil Dieus en mon droit san
Qui pour nous ot paine et ahan,
      Et me gart l'ame.
Or a d'enfant geü ma fame;

eye. Now I cannot have anything I want and I am sunk in grief, for here I must stay in the depths of despair, unless I am raised up by those who have been so good as to help me in the past. My heart is heavy and cast down because of this infirmity, for I do not see how I can earn my living, and now I have nothing of what gives me pleasure, that is my sad case. I do not know whether this is the result of my own excesses; I shall become sober and wise now, after the event, and keep myself from doing wrong. But what is the good? The harm is done, I have changed too late. Too late I see the danger, when I have fallen into the trap. In this coming year, may God, who suffered and sorrowed for us all, keep me in my right mind and save my soul. Now my wife has given birth to a child, my

Mes chevaus a brisié la jame
    A une lice;
Or veut de l'argent ma norrice
Qui me destraint et me pelice
    Pour l'enfant paistre,
Ou il revendra braire en l'estre.
Cil Damedieus qui le fist naistre
    Li doint chevance,
Et li envoit sa sostenance,
Et me doint encore alejance
    Qu'aidier li puisse,
Et que mieus son vivre li truisse
Et que mieus mon ostel conduise
    Que je ne fais.
Se je m'esmai je n'en puis mais,
Car je n'ai dozaine ne fais
    En ma maison
De busche por ceste saison.
Si esbahi ne fu mais hom
    Com je sui, voir,
Qu'onques ne fui à meins d'avoir.
Mes ostes veut l'argent avoir
    De son osté,
Et j'en ai presque tout osté;

horse has broken his leg on a fence, and the nurse is asking for money, and pestering me and fleecing me for the child's keep, or else he'll be brought back to yell here in the house. May the Lord God, that caused him to be born, send him enough to live on and give him sustenance, and lighten my lot, too, so that I can help him and earn a better living for him, and manage my affairs better than I do now. I can't help feeling dismayed to think that I have not even a dozen logs, not a single bundle of firewood in the house for the winter. Never was a man so much at his wits' end as I am, truly, for I was never before so short of money. My landlord is demanding the rent for his house and I have taken almost everything out of it, and I have hardly a rag to my back to keep out the cold.

Et si me sont nu li costé
    Contre l'hiver.
Cist mal me sont dur et divers,
Dont moult me sont changié li vers
    Envers antan . . .

Li mal ne sevent seul venir;
Tout ce m'estoit à avenir,
    S'est avenu.
Que sont mi ami devenu
Que j'avoie si pres tenu
    Et tant amé?
Je cuit qu'il sont trop cler semé:
Il ne furent pas bien femé,
    Si sont failli.
Itel ami m'ont mal bailli,
Qu'onques tant com Dieus m'assailli
    En maint costé
N'en vi un seul en mon osté.
Je cuit li venz les m'a osté.
    L'amors est morte:
Ce sont ami que venz emporte,
Et il ventoit devant ma porte,
    Ses emporta,

These troubles are hard and cruel to bear, so that my verses are very different from what they used to be . . .

    Misfortunes never come singly; all this had to come upon me and it has come. What has become of my friends that I used to keep so near me and love so well? I think they were sown too far apart; they were not well manured, and they have wilted. Friends like these have not done me much good, for never, since God rained these blows on me from every side, have I seen one of them in my house. I think the wind has carried them away from me. Friendship is dead: these are the sort of friends that go with the wind, and when the wind blew before my door it bore them off, for never one of

Qu'onques nuls ne m'en conforta
Ne du sien rien ne m'aporta.
    Ice m'aprent:
Qui auques a, privé le prent;
Et cil trop à tart se repent
    Qui trop a mis
De son avoir pour faire amis,
Qu'il nes treuve entiers ne demis
    A lui secourre ...

JEAN DE MEUNG

Le Roman de la Rose (Second Part)

... ET s'il est tel qu'il ne veut mie
Loiauté porter à s'amie,
Si ne la voudrait il pas perdre,
Mais à autre se veut aerdre,
S'il veut à s'amie nouvele
Donner couvrechief ou toele,
Chapel, anel, fermail, ceinture,
Ou joyau de quelque faiture,
Gart que l'autre ne les connoisse;

them gave me either sympathy or help. This teaches me that those who have money keep it for themselves, and he repents too late who has wasted his money on making friends; for he doesn't find them true (or even half-true!) when he needs their help ...

The Romance of the Rose (Second Part)

... AND if he is the sort who does not want to be true to his mistress, and yet does not wish to lose her, but wants to attach himself to another, should he wish to give his new friend a kerchief or shawl, a hat, a ring, a clasp, a belt, or a jewel of any kind, let him take care that the first one does not know them, for she would be

Car trop avroit au cuer angoisse
Quant el les li verrait porter:
Rien ne l'en pourrait conforter.
Et gart que venir ne la face
En icele meïsme place
Où venait à lui la premiere,
Qui de venir est coutumiere;
Car s'ele y vient, pour qu'el la truisse,
N'est rien qui conseil metre y puisse.
Car nul vieuz sanglers hericiés,
Quant des chiens est bien aticiés,
N'est si crueus, ni lionesse
Si triste ne si felonesse,
Quant li venerres qui l'assaut
Li renforce en ce point l'assaut
Quant ele alaite ses chaiaus,
Ne nuls serpens si desloiaus
Quant on li marche sur la queue,
Qui du marchier pas ne se jeue,
Comme est feme quant ele treuve
O son ami s'amie neuve:
El jette partout feu et flame,
Preste de perdre cors et ame.

grieved to the heart to see her wearing them: nothing would console her for it. And let him take care never to get the new one to meet him in the same place where the other used to come to him and where she is in the habit of coming; for if she should come and find her rival there, nothing in the whole world would set that to rights! For no old bristly boar is so fierce, when the dogs are worrying him, nor is the lioness so cruel, so desperate, or so deadly when the hunter attacks her at the moment when she is feeding her cubs, nor is a snake so much to be feared when you tread on its tail and it doesn't consider it a joke, as is a woman when she finds a new mistress with her lover. She throws out fire and flame in all directions, ready to put both life and soul in peril.

Et s'el n'a pas prise prouvee
D'eus deus ensemble la couvee,
Mais bien en chiet en jalousie,
Qu'el set ou cuide estre acoupie,
Coment qu'il aut, ou sache ou croie,
Gart soi cil que ja ne recroie
De li nier tout pleinement
Ce qu'ele set certainement,
Et ne soit pas lent de jurer.
Tantost li reface endurer
En la place le jeu d'amours:
Lors ert quites de ses clamours.

Et si tant l'assaut et angoisse
Qu'il convient qu'il li reconnoisse,
Qu'il ne s'en set espeir defendre,
A ce doit lores, s'il peut, tendre
Qu'il li face à force entendant
Qu'il le fist sur soi defendant;
Car cele si court le tenait
Et si malement le menait
Qu'onques eschaper ne li pot
Jusqu'il orent fait ce tripot,
N'onc ne li avint fois fors cette.

And if she hasn't actually any real proof of what is going on between them, but still becomes suspicious of it, because she knows or thinks herself forsaken, however it may be, whether she really knows anything, or just suspects, let him never budge from a position of complete denial even of what she knows to be true, and let him not hesitate to swear it. Let him hasten to make love to her on the spot, then he will put a stop to her reproaches.

And if she worries and attacks him until he has to admit it, perhaps because it can't be denied, he must then, if he can, try to compel her to believe that he did it against his will, because the other woman had got him in her clutches and was persecuting him so that he simply could not get away from her without going to bed with her, and that it had never happened except this once.

Lors jure et fiance et promette
Que jamais ne li avendra:
Si loiaument se contendra
Que s'ele en ot jamais parole,
Bien veut qu'el le tut ou afole;
Car mieus voudrait qu'el fust noiee,
La desloiaus, la renoiee,
Qu'il jamais en place venist
Où cele en tel point le tenist;
Car s'il avient qu'ele le mant
N'ira mais à son mandement,
N'il ne souferra qu'ele viegne,
S'il peut, en lieu où el le tiegne.
Lors doit cele estroit embracier,
Baisier, blandir, et soulacier,
Et crier merci du mesfait,
Puis qu'il ne sera ja mais fait;
Qu'il est en vraie repentance
Pres de faire en tel penitance
Com cele enjoindre li savra
Puis que pardonné li avra.
Lors face d'Amour la besoigne,
S'il veut que ele li pardoigne . . .

Then let him take his oath, and swear and promise that it will
never happen again; he will be so true to her that if she ever hears a
word of such a thing he gives her full leave to kill or injure him, for
he would see that other woman drowned, the shameless baggage,
before he would go anywhere where she could put him in such a
position again; if she should send for him, he will never go to her,
nor will he allow her to come, as far as he can help it, to any place
where she can get hold of him. Then let him take the other tightly
in his arms and kiss, flatter, and caress her, and beg her to forgive
him for this injury, since it will never be repeated, for he is truly
sorry, ready to perform any penance she can lay upon him, once
she has forgiven him. Then let him set about love's work if he wants
her forgiveness . . .

Et s'ele chiet en maladie,
Droit est, s'il peut, qu'il s'estudie
En estre li moult serviables
Pour estre après plus agreables.
Gart que nuls ennuis ne le tiegne
De la maladie lointiegne;
Lès li le voie demourant,
Et la doit baisier en plourant,
Et se doit vouer, s'il est sages,
En mains lointains pelerinages,
Mais que cele les veus entende.
Viande pas ne li defende,
Chose amere ne li doit tendre
Ne riens qui ne soit douz et tendre.
Si li doit feindre nouveaus songes,
Tous farsis de plaisans mensonges;
Que quant vient au soir qu'il se couche
Tout seul en sa chambre en sa couche,
Avis li est, quant il sommeille, —
Car peu i dort et moult i veille, —
Qu'il l'ait entre ses bras tenue
Trestoute nuit trestoute nue,
Par soulas et par druerie,
Toute saine et toute guerie,

And if his mistress falls ill, he should, if possible, do everything he can to be of help to her, so as to be more pleasing to her afterwards. Let him take care not to be kept away from her sick-bed because he finds it tiresome. Let her see him always at her side; he should kiss her with tears in his eyes, and if he is wise he will vow himself to many a distant pilgrimage — but let him make sure she hears his vows! He must never withhold her food from her, or give her any bitter thing she has to take, or anything that is not tasty and tender. And he should make up new dreams for her benefit, all full of flattering lies: that when night comes and he lies down in his bedroom on his lonely bed, he imagines, when he does drop off (for he sleeps very little and lies awake a lot), that he holds her in his arms, all naked, all night long, in pleasure and in love, quite well

Et par jour en lieus delitables.
Tels fables li cont, ou semblables ...

Femes n'ont cure de chasti,
Ainz ont si leur engin basti
Qu'il leur est vis qu'els n'ont mestier
D'estre aprises de leur mestier;
Ne nul, s'il ne leur veut desplaire,
Ne deslot rien qu'els veuillent faire.
Si com li chas set par nature
La science de surgeüre,
Ne n'en peut estre destournés,
Qu'il est o tel sen tousjours nés
N'onques n'en fu mis à escole,
Ainsi set feme, tant est fole,
Par son naturel jugement,
De quanqu'el fait outreement,
Soit bien, soit maus, soit tors ou droiz,
Ou de tout quanque vous voudroiz,
Qu'el ne fait chose qu'el ne doie;
Si het quiconques la chastoie;
N'el ne tient pas ce sens de maistre,
Ainz l'a dès lors qu'ele pot naistre
Si n'en peut estre destournee;

and strong again – and by day as well in many a lovely spot. Let
him tell her these stories or others like them ...

Women do not like to be corrected, but their minds are so
formed that they think they know their own business without being
taught, and let no one who doesn't want to annoy them take excep-
tion to anything they do. Just as the cat knows by nature all about
catching mice, and can't be stopped from doing it, for it is born
with that instinct, and never had to learn; in the same way, a
woman, however stupid, has an inner conviction that whatever she
may do, good or bad, wrong or right, absolutely anything you like,
she is never doing anything but what she ought to do, so she hates
anyone who finds fault with her; and she hasn't learnt this convic-
tion, but she has it from the moment of her birth and can't be turned

Qu'ele est o tel sens tousjours nee
Que qui chastier la voudrait
Jamais de s'amour ne jourrait . . .

TROP ere lors de grant renon.
Partout courait la renomee
De ma grant beauté renomee;
Tele ale avait en ma maison
Qu'onques tele ne vit mais on;
Moult ert mes uis la nuit hurtés;
Trop leur faisaie de durtés
Quant leur faillaie de couvent,
Et ce m'avenait trop souvent,
Car j'avaie autre compagnie.
Faite en estait mainte folie,
Dont j'avaie courrous assez.
Souvent en ert mes uis cassés
Et faites maintes tels mellees
Qu'anceis qu'els fussent desmellees
Membres i perdaient et vies
Par haïnes et par envies. . .

from it; for a woman is born so sure of herself that if anyone tries
to put her right he will never have her love . . .

. . . I WAS very well known in those days; the fame of my renowned
beauty ran everywhere; there was such coming and going in my
house as no one ever saw: much knocking on my door at night;
I played them many a cruel trick when I failed to keep appoint-
ments – which happened very often, because I had other company.
Many a folly came of it and got me into trouble enough; my door
was often broken down, and there was many a fight where limbs
and even lives were lost in hatred and in envy before the scores
were settled . . .

Lors ert mes cors fors et delivres;
J'eüsse or plus vaillant mil livres
De blans esterlins que je n'ai,
Mais trop nicement me menai.
Bele ere et jeune et nice et fole,
N'onc ne fui d'Amours à escole
Où l'on leüst la theorique,
Mais je sai tout par la pratique:
Esperiment m'en ont fait sage,
Que j'ai hantés tout mon eage . . .

Et puis que j'oi sen et usage,
(Que je n'oi pas sans grant domage),
Maint vaillant homme ai deceü
Quant en mes las le tin cheü;
Mais ainz fui par mains deceüe
Que je me fusse aperceüe.
Ce fu trop tart, lasse dolente!
J'ere ja hors de ma jouvente;
Mes uis, qui ja souvent ouvrait,
– Car par nuit et par jour ouvrait –
Se tint adès près du lintier:
«Nuls n'i vint ui, nuls n'i vint hier,
Pensaie je, lasse chaitive!

In those days I was strong and supple; I should have had a
thousand pounds' worth more in silver sterling now than I have, if
I had not behaved so stupidly. Beautiful and young I was, and
simple and foolish, and I had never been schooled in the theory of
love, but I learnt all about it by practice: a lifetime of experience
has brought me wisdom . . .

And since I achieved wisdom and experience, which I didn't get
without great losses, I have tricked many a rich man when I have
had him in my toils, but I was tricked myself by many before my
eyes were opened. That came too late for me, alas! I was already past
my youth; my door, which formerly opened so often – for it was at
work both night and day – stayed henceforth close to the lintel.
'No one came today and no one yesterday,' I used to think, 'poor

En tristeur estuet que je vive.»
De deul me dut li cuers partir.
Lors me vos du païs partir
Quant vi mon uis en tel repos,
Et je meïsmes me repos,
Car ne poi la honte endurer.
Coment poïsse je durer,
Quant cil joli vallet venaient
Qui ja si chiere me tenaient
Qu'il ne s'en poaient lasser,
Et jes voaie trespasser,
Qu'il me regardaient de coste,
Et jadis furent mi chier oste?
Lès moi s'en alaient saillant
Sans moi prisier un euf vaillant,
Nes cil qui plus jadis m'amaient;
«Vielle ridee» me clamaient;
Et pis disait chascuns assez
Ainz qu'il s'en fust outre passez . . .

wretched me! I must live my life in sadness.' My heart was fit to break for sorrow. Then I wanted to leave the district when I saw my door so much at peace; and I myself hid away, for I could not endure the shame of it. How could I bear it when those elegant young men came along who used to hold me so dear that they could not weary of me, and now I saw them going by without giving me more than a passing glance – those who had been my dearest guests? They went pushing past me without considering me worth an egg, even those who used to love me most; they called me a wrinkled old woman, and every one of them said things much worse than that before he had passed by . . .

ANONYMOUS MOTETS

> EN mai quant naist la rosee,
> Que gelee s'en reva,
> Garis est qui amie a,
> Car sa joie en est doublee.
> Hé Dieus! mes cuers que fera?
> Comment tenir se pourra?
> Tant est ma joie doublee
> Quant cele qui mon cuer a,
> Que lonc tens ai deservie,
> Cele m'a s'amour donee
> Qui mon cuer et mon cors a.

> BEAUS douz amis, or ne vous enuit mie
> Se d'estre ensemble faisons tel demouree,
> Car on dit: «Qui bien aime à tart oublie.»
> Pour ce n'ert ja nostre amour desevree,
> Ne n'ai aillors ne desir ne pensee
> Fors seulement qu'ensemble estre puissomes.
> Hé! beau cuers douz, je vous aim sur tous homes:
> Aiez pitié de vo loial amie,

IN May, when dew begins to fall and frost goes away, happy is the man who has a lover, for his joy is doubled. Ah God! What is my heart to do? How can it contain itself? Now my joy is doubled, since she who has my heart, whose love I have earned by my long devotion, she has given me her love, who has my heart and my body.

FAIR sweet love, now do not let it grieve you if we have to wait so long to be together; for they say, 'He who loves well is slow to forget.' Therefore our love will not soon be ended, and I have not a single wish or thought except only to be with you. Oh fair sweet heart, I love you above all men. Take pity on your true love

Et si pensez que par tens i soiomes,
Pour mener joie, com amans à celee.
          Dieus! car nous herberjomes.

AMIS, dont est engendree
En vo cuer tel volentez
Qu'estre cuidiez refusez,
Pour ce que vous ai monstree
Chiere autre que ne voulez?

    Mais se bien saviez
Comment on doit retenir
Amant qu'on crient departir,
    Entendre porriez
Que le fis par tel desir
        Qu'enaigrir
Vous feïsse en moi amer.
Fins cuers, ne veuilliez cesser,
Car aillours que vous chierir
        Ne puis penser.

A LA clarté qui tout enlumina
    Nostre grant tenebrour,

and find some way for us soon to be alone as lovers for our delight.
In God's name, let us find some place to be together.

MY love, how has your heart conceived such an idea as to think
yourself rejected because I did not receive you exactly as you
wished?
    But if you knew how a woman has to hold a lover whom she
dreads to lose, you could understand that I did it in the hope that
I should sharpen your love for me.
    Sweet heart, do not cease to love me, for I cannot set my heart
on anything but loving you.

To the light which has illumined our great darkness, to the lad y

89

A la dame qui si grant mecine a
    Contre toute doulour,
Doivent venir trestuit li pecheour
Et devenir si serjant nuit et jour;
    N'autrui ne doit nul donner
    Son cuer, son cors ne s'amour
Fors à la douce mere au Creatour,
Vierge pucelle et de si sainte atour;
Rose est novelle et des dames la flour.

    BONE compaignie,
    Quant ele est bien privee,
   Maint jeu, mainte druerie
    Fait faire à celee.
Mais quant chascun tient s'amie
    Cointe et bien paree,
Lors a par droit bone vie
    Chascun d'eus trovee.

Li mangiers est atornez
    Et la table aprestee:
De bons vins i a assez
    Par quoi joie est menee.

who has such balm for every sorrow, all sinners should come, to be
her servants night and day. And to none other should any man give
his heart, his body, or his love, but only to the gentle Mother of
God, virgin, maid, clothed in such holiness. She is the rose newly
opened and the flower of all women.

GOOD company, among intimate friends, gives rise to many a
game and much jollity of a homely kind. But when every man has
his love at his side, elegant and beautifully dressed, then each of
them can truly say that life is good.

    The food is prepared and the table is laid; there are plenty of
good wines to make them merry. After dinner, they have the dice

Après mangier font les dez
  Venir en l'assemblee
   Sour la table lee.
Et si ai souvent trové
  Maint clerc, la chape ostee,
Qui n'ont cure que là soit logique desputee.
Li hostes est par delez,
     Qui dit: «Bevez!
Et quant vins faut, si criez:
Ci nous faut un tour de vin!
  Dieus, car le nous donez.»

  On parole de batre et de vanner
   Et de foïr et de hanner;
    Mais ces deduis trop me desplaisent,
Car il n'est si bone vie que d'estre à aise
    De bon cler vin et de chapons,
    Et d'estre avec bons compaignons,
       Liés et joians,
         Chantans,
          Truffans
Et amorous; et d'avoir quant qu'on a mestier
     Pour solacier,
    Beles dame à devis;
   Et tout ce treuve on à Paris.

set out for the company on the broad table. And I have often found
many a cleric there, his cowl cast off, happy to dispense with logical
disputation. The host is at their side saying, 'Drink up, and when
the wine runs out, call out, "We need a round of wine here, now for
God's sake let us have it!"'

Some talk of threshing and winnowing, digging and ploughing,
but I care nothing for these sports; for there is no life so good as
to be well supplied with good clear wine and capons, and to be
with good companions, happy and joyous, singing, joking, and
making love, and to have whatever you need for your pleasure, and
fair ladies to your liking. And all this can be found in Paris.

ANONYMOUS RONDEAUX

EST il paradis, amie,
Est il paradis qu'amer?
Nenil voir, ma douce amie.
Est il paradis, amie?
Cil qui dort es bras s'amie
A bien paradis trouvé.
Est il paradis, amie,
Est il paradis qu'amer?

TOUTE seule passerai le vert boscage,
        Puis que compagnie n'ai;
Se j'ai perdu mon ami par mon outrage,
Toute seule passerai le vert boscage.
Je li ferai à savoir par un message
        Que je li amenderai.
Toute seule passerai le vert boscage,
        Puis que compagnie n'ai.

Is there any Heaven, my darling, is there any Heaven but loving?
No, indeed, my sweet darling.
    Is there any Heaven, my darling?
    He who sleeps in his love's arms has found Heaven indeed.
    Is there any Heaven, my darling, is there any Heaven but loving?

I WILL walk through the greenwood alone, for I have no one to go with me. If I have lost my love through my own fault, I will walk through the greenwood alone. I will send a message to let him know that I will make him amends. I will walk through the greenwood alone, for I have no one to go with me.

ENCORE un chapelet ai
    Qui fut m'amie;
Donnés me fut de cuer gai.
Encore un chapelet ai;
Pour s'amour le garderai
    Toute ma vie;
Encore un chapelet ai
    Qui fut m'amie.

TROP me regardez, amie, souvent;
Vostre doux regart trahissent la gent.
Cuers qui veut amer jolietement
 – Trop me regardez, amie, souvent –
Ne se doit vanter pardevant la gent,
Ainz se doit garder pour les mesdisant.
Trop me regardez, amie, souvent;
Vostre douz regart trahissent la gent.

I STILL have a garland that belonged to my love. It was given to me
with a joyful heart. I still have a garland; for her sake I shall keep
it all my life. I still have a garland that belonged to my love.

YOU look at me too often, darling; others are intercepting your
sweet glances. A heart that would love happily – you look at me
too often, darling – should not boast its love in public, but should
keep on its guard because of the gossips. You look at me too often,
darling; others are intercepting your sweet glances.

ANONYMOUS

Une Branche d' Armes

QUI est li gentis bachelers?

Qui d'espee fu engendrés
Et parmi le heaume alaitiés,
Et dedans son escu berciés,
Et de char de lion nourris,
Et au grant tonnoire endormis,
Et au visage de dragon,
Ieus de liepart, cuer de lion,
Dens de sengler, isniaus com tigre,
Qui d'un estorbeillon s'enivre,
Et qui fait de son poing maçue
Qui cheval et chevalier rue
Jus à la terre comme foudre;
Qui voit plus cler parmi la poudre
Que faucons ne fait la riviere,
Qui torne ce devant derriere
Un tornoi, pour son cors deduire:
Ne cuide que rien li puist nuire;

Lines on Knighthood

WHO is the noble young knight?

He who was engendered of the sword, suckled in the helmet, and cradled in his shield; and fed on lion's flesh, and lulled to sleep by mighty thunder; he with the dragon's face, the leopard's eyes, the lion's heart, the wild boar's fangs; swift as a tiger, drunk with the whirlwind, making a club of his fist to strike down knight and horse like a thunderbolt; who sees more clearly through the dust of battle than the falcon sees the river below her; who reverses the whole fortunes of a tournament for his pleasure, and thinks that no man there can do him injury; who to accomplish adventure leaps

94

Qui tressaut la mer d'Engleterre
Pour une aventure conquerre,
Si fait il les mons de Mongeu:
Là sont ses festes et si jeu;
Et, s'il vient à une bataille,
Ainsi com li vens fait la paille,
Les fait fuir par devant lui,
Ne ne veut jouster à nului
Fors que du pié hors de l'estrier,
S'abat cheval et chevalier,
Et souvent le crieve par force.
Fer ne fust, platine n'escorce
Ne peut contre ses cops durer;
Et peut tant le heaume endurer
Qu'à dormir ne à sommeillier
Ne li covient autre oreillier;
Ne ne demande autres dragiees
Que pointes d'espees brisiees
Et fers de glaive à la moustarde
(C'est un mes qui forment li tarde)
Et haubers desmailliés au poivre;
Et veut la grant poudriere boivre
Avec l'alaine des chevaus;

across the English sea or over the Alps to Italy. Such are his feats
and such his sports, and if he comes to a battle, like straw before the
wind he makes them flee before him, and he never wishes to joust
with anyone except with his feet out of the stirrups, and he over-
turns both horse and knight and often kills by the force of the
blow. Iron nor wood nor metal plates nor hide can stand against his
blows, and he can endure his helmet for so long that for sleep and
for slumber he needs no other pillow; he seeks no better sweetmeat
than shattered swordpoints and lance-heads with mustard (that is a
dish he longs to eat) and hacked chainmail with pepper; and he
would drink battle-dust with the breath of horses; and over hills

Et chace par mons et par vaus
Ours et lions et cers de ruit
Tout à pié: ce sont si deduit;
Et donne tout sans retenir.

Cil doit moult bien terre tenir
Et maintenir chevalerie;
Que cil dont li hiraus s'escrie
Qui ne fu ne puns ne couvés
Mais el fiens des chevaus trouvés,
S'il savoient à quoi ce monte,
Sachiez qu'il li dient grant honte.

GUILLAUME DE MACHAUT

Ballade

Se vo grandeur vers moi ne s'humilie,
Tres douz ami, que j'aim sans decevoir,
Povre esperance avoir dois en ma vie;
Car j'ai douleur qui trop me fait douloir,
        Pour vous, où j'ai mon cuer mis,
Si que jamais n'en peut estre partis.

and valleys he hunts bears and lions and rutting stags, and all on
foot – such are his pleasures; and he gives away all that he has
without reserve.

Such a man well deserves to hold lands and uphold chivalry; for
this man whom the heralds announce as 'neither laid nor hatched
but found among the horse-dung', if they knew the whole truth,
believe me, they do him great injustice.

Ballade

If your great rank will not stoop down to me, my dearest friend,
whom I most truly love, then there is little hope in life for me, for
I endure most grievous pain for you, on whom I have so set my

Si ne dois pas toudis à vous penser
Sans vostre amour avoir ou esperer.

En deus amans qui s'aiment, signourie
Estre ne doit, ainçois doivent avoir
Un cuer, une ame et une maladie,
Une pensee, un desir, un vouloir;
       Donc se vo cuer n'est onnis
A mon desir, li miens sera honnis,
Car je ne puis pas longuement durer
Sans vostre amour avoir ou esperer.

Et se des biens de Fortune n'ai mie
Si largement comme autre peut avoir,
S'ai aussi bien vaillant un cuer d'amie,
Comme tele est roïne, à dire voir.
       Et bonne amour, ce m'est vis,
Ne demande que le cuer, si qu'amis
Le mien avez; si ne dois demourer
Sans vostre amour avoir ou esperer.

heart that it can never be removed. And I ought not to have you
always in my thoughts without your love or any hope of it.

Between two lovers who love each other, rank should not exist;
rather should they have one heart, one soul, one malady, one
thought, one longing, and one wish; so if your heart is not at one
with my heart's desire, mine will be shamed, for I cannot endure
much longer without your love or any hope of it.

And if I am not so well endowed with Fortune's goods as an-
other woman might be, yet have I, truth to tell, a loving heart as
good as any queen's, and True Love, so I think, asks only for the
heart, as you have mine, my dear. And so I ought not be left with-
out your love or any hope of it.

EUSTACHE DESCHAMPS

Ballade

MOULT se vantoit li cerfs d'estre legiers
Et de courir dix lieues d'une alaine,
Et li sengliers se vantoit d'estre fiers,
Et la brebis se louoit pour sa laine,
Et li chevreaux de sauter en la plaine
Se vantoit fort, li chevaux estre beaux,
Et de force se vantoit li toreaux,
L'ermine aussi d'avoir beau peliçon;
Adonc respont en sa coquille à ceaux:
«Aussi tost vient à Pasques limaçon.»

Les lions voy, ours et liepars premiers,
Loups et tigres, courir par la champaigne,
Estre chaciés de mastins et levriers
A cris de gens, et s'il est qu'on les preigne
Tant sont haïs que chascun les mehaigne,
Pour ce qu'ils font destruction de peaux;

Ballade

THE stag took great pride in his swiftness and in being able to run
ten leagues without stopping for breath, and the wild boar was
proud of his ferocity, and the sheep extolled her wool, and the roe-
buck was very proud of his ability to bound over the plain; the
horse took pride in his beauty and the bull in his strength, and the
ermine in the beauty of its fur; then to all these replied he from his
shell: 'The snail will get to Easter just as soon.'

I see first lions, bears, and leopards, then wolves and tigers run-
ning through the countryside, pursued by mastiffs and hounds, and
by the shouts of men; and if they are caught, they are so much de-
tested that everyone maims them because of the harm they cause
among the fleeces. They are wicked and treacherous thieves, and

Ravissables sont, fels et desloyaulx
Sans espargner, et pour ce les het on.
Courent ils bien? Sont ils fors et isneaux?
Aussi tost vient à Pasques limaçon.

Celui voient pluseurs par les sentiers;
Enclos se tient en la cruise qu'il maine,
Sans faire mal le laisse on volontiers,
Tousjours s'en va de semaine en semaine;
Si font pluseurs en leur povre domaine
Qui vivent bien sous leurs povres drapeaux,
Et, s'ils ne font au monde leurs aveaux,
Si courent ils par gracieus renom.
Quant desliés sont aux champs beufs et veaux,
Aussi tost vient à Pasques limaçon.

Prince, les gens fors, grans, riches, entr'eaulx
Ne tiennent pas toudis une leçon;
Pour eux haster n'approche temps nouveaux:
Aussi tost vient à Pasques limaçon.

merciless, and so they are hated. Do they run well? Are they both
strong and swift? The snail will get to Easter just as soon.

Many people see him on the path, housed in the shell he carries
with him; they do not harm him, but gladly let him be, and on he
goes from week to week; thus many men go on in their own poor
sphere, who live their lives well under their poor attire; and if they
do not get all they want from the world, yet they go on their way
with men's good will. When oxen and calves run free in the field,
the snail will get to Easter just as soon.

Prince, among the strong, the great, the rich, there is one thing
that is not always kept in mind; not all their haste can bring spring
any nearer. The snail will get to Easter just as soon.

Rondeau

Poux, puces, puor et pourceaux
Est de Behaigne la nature,
Pain, poisson salé et froidure,

Poivre noir, choux pourris, poreaux,
Char enfumee, noire et dure;
Poux, puces, puor et pourceaux.

Vint gens mangier en deux plateaux,
Boire cervoise amere et sure,
Mal couchier, noir, paille et ordure,
Poux, puces, puor et pourceaux
Est de Behaigne la nature,
Pain, poisson salé et froidure.

Ballade

Je deviens courbes et bossus,
J'oi tres dur, ma vie decline,
Je pers mes cheveux par dessus,

Rondeau

Lice and fleas and stink and pigs, that's the essence of Bohemia,
bread and salt fish and bitter cold,
   Black pepper, rotten cabbages and leeks, smoked meat, both
black and hard; lice and fleas and stink and pigs.
   Twenty people eating from two dishes, sour and bitter beer to
drink, hard sleeping in dark rooms on straw and filth, lice and fleas
and stink and pigs, that's the essence of Bohemia, bread and salt
fish and bitter cold.

Ballade

I am growing bent and hunchbacked, hard of hearing and short of
vigour; my hair is getting thin on top; and both my nostrils run;

Je flue en chascune narine,
J'ai grant douleur en la poitrine,
Mes membres sens ja tous trembler,
Je suis tres hastif à parler,
Impatient; Desdain me mort;
Sans conduit ne sai mais aler:
Ce sont les signes de la mort.

Couvoiteus suis, blans et chanus,
Eschars, courrouceux; j'adevine
Ce qui n'est pas, et loe plus
Le temps passé que la doctrine
Du temps present; mon corps se mine;
Je voi envis rire et jouer,
J'ai grant plaisir à grumeler,
Car le temps passé me remort;
Tousjours veuil jeunesse blamer:
Ce sont les signes de la mort.

Mes dens sont longs, foibles, agus,
Jaunes, flairans comme sentine;
Tous mes corps est frois devenus,
Maigres et secs; par medecine

I have a bad pain in my chest; I find my limbs beginning to tremble;
I am hasty in speech and lacking in patience; I feel the tooth of
Scorn; I can no longer walk without assistance: these are the signs
of Death.

I am greedy, and my hair is white and hoary; I am miserly and
irritable, suspicious without cause, more full of praise for old times
than for present-day opinions; my body is wasting away. I hate to
see other people laughing and enjoying themselves; I take great
pleasure in grumbling, for I look back with envy on the past; I am
always finding fault with youth: these are the signs of Death.

My teeth are long and weak and sharp, yellow and smelling like
bilge-water; all my body has become cold and thin and dried up;

Vivre me faut; char ne cuisine
Ne puis qu'à grant peine avaler;
Des jeusnes me faut baler,
Mes corps toudis sommeille ou dort,
Et ne veuil que boire et humer:
Ce sont les signes de la mort.

Prince, encor veuil ci ajouster
Soixante ans, pour mieux confermer
Ma vieillesse qui me nuit fort,
Quant ceux qui me doivent amer
Me souhaitent ja outre mer:
Ce sont les signes de la mort.

CHRISTINE DE PISAN

Rondeau

Source de plour, riviere de tristesse,
Flun de doulour, mer d'amertume pleine
M'avironnent, et noyent en grant peine
Mon povre cuer qui trop sent de destresse.

I have to live on a diet; it is only with great difficulty that I can
swallow meat or roast; I have to make my feasts of fasting; I am
always dozing or asleep and can only manage drinks and slops; all
these are signs of Death.

Prince, to all this I yet would wish to add sixty years more, to
put the seal upon this old age which bears hard on me, when those
who ought to love me already wish me over the sea: these are the
signs of Death.

Rondeau

A spring of tears, a river of sorrow, a stream of grief, a sea full of
bitterness surround me and drown in deep sadness my poor heart
overburdened with distress.

Si m'affondent et plongent en aspresse;
Car parmi moi courent plus fort que Seine
Source de plour, riviere de tristesse.

Et leurs grans flos cheent à grant largesse,
Si com le vent de Fortune les meine,
Tous dessus moi, dont si bas suis qu'à peine
Releverai, tant durement m'oppresse
Source de plour, riviere de tristesse.

Ballade

Ha! le plus doulz qui jamais soit formé!
Le plus plaisant qu'onques nulle acointast!
Le plus parfait pour estre bon clamé!
Le mieuz amé qu'onques mais femme amast!
De mon vrai cuer le savoreux repast!
Tout quanque j'aim, mon savoreux desir!
Mon seul amé, mon paradis en terre
Et de mes yeuz le tres parfait plaisir!
Vostre douceur me meine dure guerre.

And I am sunk and plunged in trouble, for over me there flows, stronger than the Seine, a spring of tears, a river of sorrow.

And their great waves break over me again and again, as the wind of Fortune blows them, bringing me so low that I shall hardly rise again, so heavily they press upon me, a spring of tears, a river of sorrow.

Ballade

GENTLEST of all men ever made, most charming lover any woman ever knew, most perfect ever to be acclaimed for his worth, best beloved ever loved by woman, sweet food of my true heart, sum of all I love, my dearest desire, my only love, my Heaven on earth, the very perfect delight of my eyes, the thought of your sweetness works havoc in me.

Vostre douceur voirement entamé
A le mien cuer, qui jamais ne pensast
Estre en ce point, mais si l'a enflammé
Ardent desir qu'en vie ne durast
Se Doulz Penser ne le reconfortast;
Mais Souvenir vient avec lui gesir,
Lors en pensant vous embrace et vous serre,
Mais quant ne puis le doulz baisier saisir
Vostre douceur me meine dure guerre.

Mon doulz ami de tout mon cuer amé,
Il n'est penser qui de mon cuer jetast
Le doulz regard que vos yeuz enfermé
Ont dedans lui; rien n'est qui l'en ostast, –
Ne le parler et le gracieux tast
Des douces mains qui, sans lait desplaisir,
Veulent partout encerchier et enquerre;
Mais quant ne puis de mes yeuz vous choisir
Vostre douceur me meine dure guerre.

Tres bel et bon, qui mon cuer vient saisir,
Ne m'oubliez, ce vous vueil je requerre;

In very truth, your sweetness has broken into my heart, which never thought to be in this state; but burning desire has so inflamed it that it could never keep alive if Musing did not bring it consolation. But then comes Memory to lie down with my heart, then in my thoughts I hold you and embrace you; but when I cannot savour your sweet kiss, the thought of your sweetness works havoc in me.

My dear love, beloved of my whole heart, that thought does not exist which could drive from my heart that sweet look which your eyes have enclosed within it. Nothing could drive it out or make me forget your voice or the gentle touch of those dear hands, never resented, ever eager to search and to explore. But when I cannot see you with my eyes, the thought of your sweetness works havoc in me.

Fairest and best, oh! captor of my heart, do not forget me, this I

Car quant veoir ne vous puis à loisir
Vostre douceur me meine dure guerre.

Ballade

Tu soies le tres bien venu,
M'amour! Or m'embrace et me baise.
Et comment t'es tu maintenu
Puis ton depart? Sain et bien aise
As tu esté toujours? Ça vien,
Coste moi te sié et me conte
Comment t'a esté, mal ou bien;
Car de ce vueil savoir le compte.

– Ma dame, à qui je suis tenu
Plus qu'autre, (à nul n'en desplaise!)
Sachez que desir m'a tenu
Si court qu'onques n'oz tel mesaise,
Ne plaisir ne prenoie en rien
Loin de vous: Amour, qui cuers dompte,
Me disoit: «Loyauté me tien,
Car de ce vueil savoir le compte.»

will beg of you, for when I cannot see you as often as I wish, the
thought of your sweetness works havoc in me.

Ballade

'WELCOME back, my darling! Now put your arms round me and
kiss me. How have you been since you went away? Have you been
well and happy all the time? Come here, sit down beside me, and
tell me how things have been with you, both ill and well, for I must
know the full account of that.'

'My Lady, whom I love more than any other (be it said without
offence) know that my longing kept me so tight-reined that I was
never so unhappy before, and I could not take pleasure in anything,
parted from you. Love, who tames all hearts, said to me: "Keep
faith with me, for I must know the full account of that."

– Dont m'as tu ton serment tenu;
Bon gré t'en sai, par saint Nicaise.
Et puis que sain es revenu,
Joie avrons assez; or t'apaise
Et me dis se ses de combien
Le mal qu'en as eu à plus monte
Que cil qu'a souffert le cuer mien;
Car de ce vueil savoir le compte.

– Plus mal que vous, si com retien,
Ai eu; mais dites sans mescompte
Quans baisiers en avrai je bien?
Car de ce vueil savoir le compte.

CHARLES D'ORLÉANS

Ballade

BIEN moustrez, printemps gracieux,
De quel mestier savez servir,
Car hiver fait cuers ennuieux
Et vous les faites resjouir;

'Then you have kept your word to me; I thank you for it, by St Nicasius; and since you have come back safely, we shall have joy enough; now be at peace, and tell me if you know by how much your pain has surpassed what my heart has suffered; for I must know the full account of that.'

'More pain than you, as I maintain, I have had; but now tell me exactly how many kisses I shall have for it; for I must know the full account of that.'

Ballade

GRACIOUS Springtime, well you show what trade you can ply, for Winter makes hearts heavy and you make them rejoice. As soon

Si tost comme il vous voit venir,
Lui et sa meschant retenue
Sont contrains et prestz de fuir
A vostre joyeuse venue.

Hiver fait champs et arbres vieux,
Leurs barbes de neige blanchir,
Et est si froit, ort et pluieux
Qu'emprés le feu couvient croupir.
On ne peut hors des huis issir,
Comme un oiseau qui est en mue;
Mais vous faites tout rajeunir
A vostre joyeuse venue.

Hiver fait le soleil, es cieux,
Du manteau des nues couvrir;
Or maintenant, loué soit Dieux,
Vous estes venue esclercir
Toutes choses et embellir;
Hiver a sa peine perdue,
Car l'an nouveau l'a fait bannir
A vostre joyeuse venue.

as he sees you on your way, he and his evil retinue are forced to flee in haste at your joyous coming.

Winter makes fields and trees grow old, their beards grow white with snow. He is so cold, so muddy and rainy that we must crouch over the fire. A man cannot go out of doors; he is like a bird in the moult. But you make all things young again at your joyous coming.

Winter hides the sun in the heavens behind the mantle of the clouds; but now, praised be God, you are come to shine on everything and make it beautiful. Winter's work is all in vain, for the new year has banished him at your joyous coming.

Ballade

LE premier jour du mois de mai
S'aquitte vers moi grandement;
Car, ainsi qu'à present je n'ai
En mon cuer que dueil et tourment,
Il est aussi pareillement
Troublé, plein de vent et de pluie;
Estre souloit tout autrement
Ou temps qu'ai conneu en ma vie.

Je croi qu'il se met en essai
De m'accompaignier loyaument;
Content m'en tiens, pour dire vrai,
Car meschans, en leur pensement,
Reçoivent grant allegement
Quant en leurs maux ont compaignie;
Essayé l'ai certainement
Ou temps qu'ai conneu en ma vie.

Las! j'ai veu mai joyeux et gai
Et si plaisant à toute gent
Que raconter au long ne sai
Le plaisir et esbatement
Qu'avoit en son commandement;

Ballade

MAY Day is treating me with great generosity; for just as I have now nothing in my heart but grief and torment, he too is stormy, full of wind and rain. How different he used to be in days that I have known!

I think that he is doing all he can to keep me loyal company, and I am glad of it, to tell the truth; for the unfortunate find that their thoughts are greatly lightened when they have a companion in their ills; I have made certain proof of this in days that I have known.

Alas! I have seen May joyful and gay, and so delightful to everyone that I could not tell all the sport and pleasure that he had at his

Car Amour en son abbaye
Le tenoit chief de son couvent,
Ou temps qu'ai conneu en ma vie.

Le temps va je ne sai comment,
Dieu l'amende prochainement!
Car Plaisance s'est endormie,
Qui souloit vivre liement,
Ou temps qu'ai conneu en ma vie.

Ballade

EN tirant d'Orléans à Blois,
L'autre jour par eaue venoie.
Si rencontrai, par plusieurs fois,
Vaisseaux, ainsi que je passoie,
Qui cingloient leur droite voie
Et alloient legierement,
Pour ce qu'eurent, comme veoie,
A plaisir et à gré le vent.

Mon cuer, Penser et moi, nous trois,
Les regardames à grant joie;

bidding; for in the Abbey of Love he was appointed head in days
that I have known.

The world has come to such a pass, may God amend it soon!
For Pleasure is fast asleep, who used to lead a merry life in days
that I have known.

Ballade

GOING from Orleans to Blois the other day, I was travelling by
river, and I met, time after time, vessels, as I passed, sailing straight
before the wind and scudding lightly along, because they had, as I
saw, a favourable wind at will.

My heart, my thought, and I, we three, watched them with great

Et dit mon cuer à basse vois:
«Volentiers en ce point feroie:
De Confort la voile tendroie,
Se je cuidoie seurement
Avoir, ainsi que je voudroie,
A plaisir et à gré le vent.

«Mais je treuve, le plus des mois,
L'eaue de Fortune si quoie
Quant ou bateau du monde vois
Que, s'avirons d'Espoir n'avoie,
Souvent ou chemin demouroie
En trop grant ennui longuement;
Pour neant en vain attendroie
A plaisir et à gré le vent.»

Les nefs dont ci devant parloie
Montoient, et je descendoie
Contre les vagues de Tourment;
Quant il lui plaira, Dieu m'envoie
A plaisir et à gré le vent.

joy, and my heart murmured: 'I should like to do like that: I would spread the sail of comfort if I could only be sure of having at my command a favourable wind at will.

'But I find, most months of the year, Fortune's waters so motionless as I voyage in the ship of the world that, if I had not Hope for oars, often I should be quite becalmed, lingering in the midst of troubles; and all for nothing I should await in vain a favourable wind at will.'

The ships I spoke of just now were going upstream, and I was coming down against the waves of Trouble. When it shall please Him, may God send me a favourable wind at will.

Rondeau

EN regardant ces belles fleurs
Que le temps nouveau d'amours prie,
Chascune d'elles s'ajolie
Et farde de plaisans couleurs.

Tant embasmees sont d'odeurs
Qu'il n'est cuer qui ne rajeunie
En regardant ces belles fleurs.

Les oiseaus deviennent danseurs
Dessus mainte branche flourie,
Et font joyeuse chanterie
De contres, deschans et teneurs,
En regardant ces belles fleurs.

Rondeau

ALLEZ vous en, allez, allez,
Soussy, Soing et Merencolie!

Rondeau

WHILE looking at these lovely flowers to whom the Spring pays
court, [we see] each one adorn herself and paint herself with splen-
did colours.

They are so fragrant with perfume that every heart grows
younger while looking at these lovely flowers.

The birds turn dancers on many a flowery branch and make a
joyful carolling – altos, descants, and tenors – while looking at
these lovely flowers.

Rondeau

AWAY with you, begone, begone, Grief, Care, and Melancholy!

Me cuidez vous, toute ma vie,
Gouverner, comme fait avez?

Je vous promets que non ferez:
Raison aura sur vous maistrie.
Allez vous en, allez, allez,
Soussy, Soing et Merencolie!

Se jamais plus vous retournez
Avecques vostre compaignie,
Je pri à Dieu qu'il vous maudie,
Et ce par qui vous revendrez:
Allez vous en, allez, allez,
Soussy, Soing et Merencolie!

Rondeau

QUANT j'ai ouy le tabourin
Sonner pour s'en aller au mai,
En mon lit fait n'en ai effrai
Ne levé mon chef du coissin,

Do you think to rule me all your life, as you have done?

I promise you, you shall not do it: Reason shall have the upper hand of you. Away with you, begone, begone, Grief, Care, and Melancholy!

If ever you come back again, you and your wretched crew, I pray to God that he will curse both you and whatever brings you back. Away with you, begone, begone, Grief, Care, and Melancholy!

Rondeau

WHEN I heard the drum sounding a call to go and fetch the may, I did not start up out of bed nor lift my head up from the pillow,

En disant: il est trop matin,
Un peu je me rendormirai,
Quant j'ai ouy le tabourin.

Jeunes gens partent leur butin:
De Nonchaloir m'acointerai,
A lui je m'abutinerai;
Trouvé l'ai plus prochain voisin
Quant j'ai ouy le tabourin.

Rondeau

NE hurtez plus à l'uis de ma Pensee,
Soing et Souci, sans tant vous traveiller,
Car elle dort et ne veut s'esveiller;
Toute la nuit en peine a despensee.

En dangier est, s'elle n'est bien pensee:
Cessez, cessez, laissez la sommeiller.
Ne hurtez plus à l'uis de ma Pensee,
Soing et Souci, sans tant vous traveiller.

Saying: it is still too early, I shall sleep a little longer – when I heard the drum.

Let the young folk share their spoils: I shall make friends with Indifference; he is the one who shall share mine; for him I found my nearest neighbour when I heard the drum.

Rondeau

KNOCK no more at the door of my thought, Care and Trouble, cease your turmoil. For he is asleep and does not wish to wake; he has spent all the night in pain.

He is in danger if he is not well tended. Stop! stop! and let him sleep. Knock no more at the door of my thought, Care and Trouble, cease your turmoil.

Pour la guerir Bon Espoir a pensee
Medecine qu'a fait appareiller;
Lever ne peut son chief de l'oreiller,
Tant qu'en repos se soit recompensee.
Ne hurtez plus à l'uis de ma Pensee.

Rondeau

LES en voulez vous garder,
Ces rivieres, de courir,
Et grues prendre et tenir
Quant haut les veez voler?

A telles choses muser
Voit on fols souvent servir:
Les en voulez vous garder,
Ces rivieres, de courir?

Laissez le temps tel passer
Que Fortune veut souffrir,
Et les choses avenir
Que l'on ne set destourber.
Les en voulez vous garder?

To cure him, Good Hope has thought of a medicine which she has had prepared. He cannot lift his head up from his pillow until he has refreshed himself with sleep. Knock no more at the door of my thought.

Rondeau

WOULD you stop them, these running rivers, or catch and hold cranes when you see them flying high in the air?

To dream of such things is a pastime for fools; would you stop them, these running rivers?

Let time pass by just as Fortune wills it, and let things happen that you cannot prevent. Would you stop them?

FRANÇOIS VILLON

LE TESTAMENT

... JE plains le temps de ma jeunesse,
Ouquel j'ai plus qu'autre gallé
Jusqu'à l'entree de vieillesse,
Qui son partement m'a celé.
Il ne s'en est à pié allé
N'a cheval: helas! comment don?
Soudainement s'en est volé
Et ne m'a laissié quelque don.

Allé s'en est, et je demeure,
Povre de sens et de savoir,
Triste, failli, plus noir que meure,
Qui n'ai ne cens, rente, n'avoir;
Des miens le mendre, je dis voir,
De me desavouer s'avance,
Oubliant naturel devoir
Par faute d'un peu de chevance.

Si ne crains avoir despendu
Par friander ne par leschier;

LAST WILL AND TESTAMENT

... I REGRET the days of my youth, when I enjoyed myself more than another man, right up to the threshold of old age, while youth was slipping away. He did not leave on foot, nor yet on horseback; alas! how then? He suddenly flew away, and left no gift for me behind him.

He is gone, and I am left, poor in wisdom and in knowledge, sad, worn out, blacker than a mulberry, with neither property, income, nor money. The least of my relations, I can truly say, hastens to disown me, forgetting his natural obligations because I lack a few worldly goods.

And I need have no regrets for having spent money on feasting

Par trop amer n'ai rien vendu
Qu'amis me puissent reprochier,
Au moins qui leur couste moult chier.
Je le dis et ne croi mesdire;
De ce me puis je revenchier:
Qui n'a mesfait ne le doit dire.

Bien est verté que j'ai amé
Et ameroie volentiers;
Mais triste cuer, ventre affamé
Qui n'est rassasié au tiers
M'oste des amoureux sentiers.
Au fort, quelqu'un s'en recompense
Qui est rempli sur les chantiers!
Car la dance vient de la pance.

Hé! Dieu, se j'eusse estudié
Ou temps de ma jeunesse folle
Et à bonnes meurs dedié,
J'eusse maison et couche molle.
Mais quoi? Je fuyoie l'escole
Comme fait le mauvais enfant.
En escrivant ceste parole,
A peu que le cuer ne me fent.

and dissipation; and too much loving has not made me sell anything that my friends could reproach me with, nothing at least that cost them very dear. I think I can say that without lying; from that accusation I can defend myself; he who has done no wrong need not confess.

It is very true that I have loved, and would willingly love again, but a sad heart and a famished stomach, not a third part filled, keep me from the paths of love. Ah! well, let someone with a well-filled belly profit from my absence, for a man can't dance on an empty stomach.

Oh! God, if only I had studied in the days of my foolish youth, and taken up good habits, I should now have a home and a soft bed. But alas! I ran away from school like a naughty child. As I write these words my heart is fit to break.

Le dit du Sage trop lui fis
Favorable (bien en puis mais!)
Qui dit: «Esjouis toi, mon fils,
En ton adolescence»; mais
Ailleurs sert bien d'un autre mes,
Car «Jeunesse et adolescence»
C'est son parler, ne moins ne mais,
«Ne sont qu'abus et ignorance.»

Mes jours s'en sont allés errant
Comme, dit Job, d'une touaille
Font les filets, quant tisserant
En son poing tient ardente paille:
Lors, s'il y a nul bout qui saille,
Soudainement il le ravit.
Si ne crains plus que rien m'assaille,
Car à la mort tout s'assouvit.

Où sont les gracieux gallans
Que je suivoie ou temps jadis,
Si bien chantans, si bien parlans,
Si plaisans en fais et en dis?
Les aucuns sont morts et roidis,
D'eux n'est il plus rien maintenant:

I gave the Sage too much credit (much good did it do me!) when
he says, 'Rejoice, oh! young man in thy youth'; but elsewhere he
serves up a very different dish, for 'Childhood and youth are
vanity', these are his words, neither more nor less.

My days have flown by, as Job says, like the threads of the
weaver's cloth, when he holds in his hand a burning straw: then if
any end of thread projects he has it off in a moment. And I have no
fear now of anything that may assail me, for Death pays all scores.

Where are those handsome gallants whose company I used to
keep in the old days, singing so true, speaking so fair, pleasant in
all they did and said? Some of them are dead and stiff, nothing now

Repos aient en Paradis,
Et Dieu sauve le remenant!

Et les autres sont devenus,
Dieu merci! grans seigneurs et maistres;
Les autres mendient tous nus
Et pain ne voient qu'aux fenestres;
Les autres sont entrés en cloistres
De Celestins et de Chartreux,
Botés, housés, com pescheurs d'oistres.
Voyez l'estat divers d'entre eux.

Aux grans maistres Dieu doint bien faire,
Vivans en paix et en requoi;
En eux il n'y a que refaire,
Si s'en fait bon taire tout quoy.
Mais aux povres qui n'ont de quoi,
Comme moi, Dieu donne patience!
Aux autres ne faut qui ne quoi,
Car assez ont pain et pitance.

Bons vins ont, souvent embrochiés,
Sauces, brouets, et gros poissons,

is left of them; may they have rest in Paradise, and God save those that are left!

And others have become, thanks be to God, great lords and masters; others go naked, begging, and never see bread except in shop windows; others have gone into monasteries of Celestines or of Carthusians, booted and gaitered like oyster-fishers: see to what varying estates they have come!

As for those in high estate, may God grant them to do good, living in peace and quiet; in them there is nothing to amend, and it is best to say no more about them. But to the poor who have nothing to live on, like me, may God give patience; as for the rest, they want for nothing, they have bread and they have their monk's ration.

Good wines they have, often freshly broached, sauces, broth and

Tartes, flans, oefs frits et pochiés,
Perdus et en toutes façons.
Pas ne ressemblent les maçons,
Que servir faut à si grant peine:
Ils ne veulent nuls eschançons,
De soi verser chascun se peine.

En cest incident me suis mis
Qui de rien ne sert à mon fait;
Je ne suis juge, ne commis
Pour punir n'absoudre mesfait:
De tous suis le plus imparfait,
Loué soit le doux Jhesu Crist!
Que par moi leur soit satisfait!
Ce que j'ai escrit est escrit.

Laissons le moustier où il est;
Parlons de chose plus plaisante:
Ceste matiere à tous ne plaist,
Ennuyeuse est et desplaisante.
Povreté, chagrine, dolente,
Tousjours, despiteuse et rebelle,
Dit quelque parolle cuisante;
S'elle n'ose, si la pense elle.

fine fish, tarts, flans, eggs fried, poached, scrambled, and cooked in every kind of way. They are not like the masons, who have to be served with so much trouble; they do not need any butlers, each one takes the trouble to pour out for himself.

I have embarked on this digression, which in no way serves my purpose; for I am neither judge nor appointed to punish or absolve crime. I am the most imperfect of all men, praise be to the sweet Jesus Christ. Let them be satisfied as far as I am concerned: what I have written is written.

So much for that! Now let us speak of something more attractive; for that subject does not please everyone, it is tiresome and unpleasant. Vexed and grieving Poverty, spiteful and rebellious, is ever apt to speak the wounding word – and if she does not speak it, still she thinks it.

Povre je suis de ma jeunesse,
De povre et de petite extrace;
Mon pere n'eut onc grant richesse,
Ne son aieul nommé Horace;
Povreté tous nous suit et trace.
Sur les tombeaux de mes ancestres,
Les ames desquels Dieu embrasse!
On n'y voit couronnes ne sceptres.

De povreté me guementant,
Souventesfois me dit le cuer:
«Homme, ne te doulouse tant
Et ne demaine tel douleur:
Se tu n'as tant qu'eut Jacques Cuer,
Mieux vaut vivre sous gros bureau
Povre, qu'avoir esté seigneur
Et pourrir sous riche tombeau.»

Qu'avoir esté seigneur! . . . Que dis?
Seigneur, las! et ne l'est il mais?
Selon les davitiques dis
Son lieu ne connoistras jamais.
Quant du surplus, je m'en desmets:

I have been poor from my childhood, of poor and humble origins; my father never had great riches, nor his father, who was called Horace. Poverty follows us all, and tracks us down: on the tombs of my ancestors, whose souls may God take to himself, you will see no crowns or sceptres.

When I lament my poverty, my heart often tells me: 'Do not grieve like that, man, and bewail yourself so much: if you are not so well provided as Jacques Cœur, it is better to be a poor man alive under the coarsest woollen garment than to have been a lord and lie rotting in a rich tomb.'

Than to have been a lord? What am I saying? A lord – alas! is he that no longer? According to the words of David, 'Thou shalt not find his place.' Further than that I will not venture; it would ill

Il n'appartient à moi, pecheur;
Aux theologiens le remets,
Car c'est office de prescheur.

Si ne suis, bien le considere,
Fils d'ange portant diademe
D'estoile ne d'autre sidere.
Mon pere est mort, Dieu en ait l'ame!
Quant est du corps, il gist sous lame.
J'entens que la mere mourra,
El le set bien, la povre femme,
Et le fils pas ne demourra.

Je connois que povres et riches,
Sages et fols, prestres et lais,
Nobles, vilains, larges et chiches,
Petiz et grans, et beaux et lais,
Dames à rebrassés collets,
De quelconque condicion,
Portans atours et bourrelets,
Mort saisit sans excepcion.

become me, a sinner. I leave it to the theologians, for it is the province of a preacher.

And I am well aware that I am not the son of an angel crowned with a star or any other heavenly body. My father is dead, God save his soul. As for his body, it lies beneath the tombstone. I realize that my mother is going to die, and she, poor woman, knows it well; and her son will not stay long behind.

I know that poor and rich, wise and foolish, priests and laymen, nobles, peasants, the open-handed and the miserly, the small, the great, the handsome, and the ugly, ladies in their upturned collars, whatever their rank, whether they wear *atours** or *bourrelets*,† death takes them all without exception.

---

*Head-dress of noble women.
†Head-dress of citizens' wives.

Et meure Paris ou Helaine,
Quiconques meurt, meurt à douleur
Telle qu'il pert vent et alaine;
Son fiel se creve sur son cuer,
Puis sue, Dieu set quelle sueur!
Et n'est qui de ses maux l'alege:
Car enfant n'a, frere ne seur,
Qui lors voulsist estre son plege.

La mort le fait fremir, pallir,
Le nez courber, les veines tendre,
Le col enfler, la chair mollir,
Jointes et nerfs croistre et estendre.
Corps femenin, qui tant es tendre,
Poli, souef, si precieux,
Te faudra il ces maux attendre?
Oui, ou tout vif aller es cieux.

Ballade des Dames du Temps jadis

DITES moi, où, n'en quel pays
Est Flora la belle Romaine,

And even if it be Paris or Helen who is dying, whoever dies,
dies in such pain that he loses air and breath; his gall bursts over his
heart, and then he sweats, God knows with what a sweat, and none
can relieve him of his ills, for he has neither child nor brother nor
sister who would take his place.

Death makes him shiver and turn pale, curves his nose and draws
tight his veins, swells out his neck and makes his flesh go limp,
stretches and extends his joints and muscles. Body of woman, so
tender, polished, smooth, so precious, must you, too, expect these
ills? Yes, or go straight to Heaven alive.

Ballade of the Ladies of Days Gone by

TELL me where, or in what country, is Flora the fair Roman girl,

Archipiades, ne Thaïs,
Qui fut sa cousine germaine,
Echo, parlant quant bruit on maine
Dessus riviere ou sus estan,
Qui beauté eut trop plus qu'humaine.
Mais où sont les neiges d'antan?

Où est la tres sage Heloïs
Pour qui chastré fut et puis moine
Pierre Esbaillart à Saint Denis?
Pour son amour eut ceste essoine.
Semblablement, où est la roine
Qui commanda que Buridan
Fust jeté en un sac en Seine?
Mais où sont les neiges d'antan?

La roine Blanche comme lis
Qui chantoit à vois de seraine,
Berte au grant pié, Bietris, Alis,
Haremburgis qui tint le Maine,
Et Jehanne la bonne Lorraine
Qu'Anglois brulerent à Rouan;
Où sont ils, où, Vierge souvraine?
Mais où sont les neiges d'antan?

or Archipiades, or Thaïs, who was her counterpart, or Echo, reply-
ing whenever sound is made over river or pool, who had more than
human beauty. But where are last year's snows?

Where is that wisest lady Heloise, for whose sake Pierre Abelard
was first castrated, then became a monk at Saint-Denis? It was
through love that he suffered this misfortune. And where, too, is
the queen who ordered Buridan to be thrown into the Seine in a
sack? But where are last year's snows?

Queen Blanche, white as a lily, who sang with a siren's voice,
Berte of the big foot, Beatrice, Alice, Haremburgis, who ruled over
Maine, and Joan the good maid of Lorraine, who was burnt by the
English at Rouen, where are they, where, oh! sovereign Virgin?
But where are last year's snows?

Prince, n'enquerez de semaine
Où elles sont, ne de cest an,
Qu'à ce refrain ne vous remaine:
«Mais où sont les neiges d'antan?» ...

La Vieille en Regrettant le Temps de sa Jeunesse

(*Les Regrets de la Belle Hëaumiere*)

Avis m'est que j'oi regreter
La belle qui fut hëaumiere,
Soi jeune fille souhaiter
Et parler en telle maniere:
«Ha! vieillesse felonne et fiere,
Pourquoi m'as si tost abatue?
Qui me tient, qui, que ne me fiere,
Et qu'à ce coup je ne me tue?

«Tollu m'as la haute franchise
Que beauté m'avoit ordonné
Sur clercs, marchans et gens d'Eglise:

Prince, do not ask within the week where they are, nor within this year, or I shall quote you this refrain: 'But where are last year's snows?' ...

The Old Woman's Lament for the Days of her Youth
(*The Lament of the Fair Armouress*)

I seem to hear the lamentations of the once-lovely Armouress, wishing herself a girl again, and speaking thus: 'Ah! wicked and cruel Old Age, why have you struck me down so soon? What is it, what indeed, that holds me back from striking myself and killing myself with the blow?

'You have bereft me of the high command that Beauty had ordained for me over clerks, merchants, and churchmen, for in

Car lors il n'estoit homme né
Qui tout le sien ne m'eust donné,
Quoi qu'il en fust des repentailles,
Mais que lui eusse abandonné
Ce que refusent truandailles.

«A maint homme l'ai refusé,
Qui n'estoit à moi grant sagesse,
Pour l'amour d'un garçon rusé,
Auquel j'en fis grande largesse.
A qui que je feisse finesse,
Par m'ame je l'amoie bien!
Or ne me faisoit que rudesse,
Et ne m'amoit que pour le mien.

«Si ne me sut tant detrainer,
Fouler aux piez, que ne l'aimasse;
Et m'eust il fait les reins trainer,
S'il m'eust dit que je le baisasse,
Que tous mes maux je n'oubliasse.
Le glouton, de mal entechié,
M'embrassoit . . . J'en suis bien plus grasse!
Que m'en reste il? Honte et pechié.

those days there was not a man born who would not have given me
all that he possessed, however much he might have repented later,
if only I would have yielded to him what now the very beggars
refuse.

'To many a man I have refused it – and this was not great wis-
dom on my part – for the sake of one crafty lad to whom I gave it
with the greatest freedom. Whoever else I may have cheated, upon
my soul I loved him dearly, while he did nothing but ill-treat me
and only loved me for my money.

'Yet however much he bullied me and trampled me underfoot,
I loved him still; and if he had dragged me about on the ground, if
only he asked me to kiss him, I would forget all my ills. The
black-hearted scoundrel would take me in his arms – and little good
it did me! What now remains for me? Only shame and sin.

«Or est il mort, passé trente ans,
Et je remains, vieille, chenue.
Quant je pense, lasse! au bon temps,
Quelle fus, quelle devenue!
Quant me regarde toute nue,
Et je me voi si tres changiee,
Povre, seche, megre, menue,
Je suis presque toute enragiee.

«Qu'est devenu ce front poli,
Cheveux blons, ces sourcils voutiz,
Grant entr'oeil, ce regart joli
Dont prenoie les plus soubtilz;
Ce beau nez droit grant ne petiz,
Ces petites jointes oreilles,
Menton fourchu, cler vis traitiz,
Et ces belles levres vermeilles?

«Ces gentes espaulles menues,
Ces bras longs et ces mains traitisses,
Petis tetins, hanches charnues,
Elevees, propres, faitisses
A tenir amoureuses lisses;

'Now he is dead – more than thirty years ago – and I am left old and grey. Alas, when I think of the good time that was, what I was then, and what I have become! When I look at myself all naked, and see myself so very changed, wretched, dried up, thin, and withered, I almost go out of my mind.

'What has become of that smooth forehead, that fair hair, those arched eyebrows, those well-spaced eyes, that merry glance with which I would entrap even the most wary, that fine straight nose, neither large nor small, those dainty little ears, that dimpled chin, the curve of those bright cheeks, and those beautiful red lips?

'Those lovely slender shoulders, those long arms, and those shapely hands, small breasts, high and rounded hips, perfectly

Ces larges reins, ce sadinet
Assis sur grosses fermes cuisses,
Dedans son petit jardinet?

«Le front ridé, les cheveux gris,
Les sourcils cheus, les yeux estains
Qui faisoient regars et ris
Dont mains marchans furent attains;
Nez courbe de beauté lointains,
Oreilles pendantes, moussues,
Le vis pali, mort et destains,
Menton froncé, levres peaussues:

«C'est d'humaine beauté l'issue!
Les bras cours et les mains contraites,
Les espaulles toutes bossues;
Mamelles, quoi? toutes retraites;
Telles les hanches que les tetes;
Du sadinet, fi! Quant des cuisses
Cuises ne sont plus, mais cuissetes
Grivelees comme saucisses.

shaped for holding jousts of love, those wide loins, that mount of Venus set over full, firm thighs within its little garden?

'Lined brow, grey hair, eyebrows all fallen out; those eyes grown dull that used to cast glances and smiles that were the undoing of many a merchant, nose hooked and far from beauty, ears pendulous and hairy, cheeks pale, lifeless, and dull, wrinkled chin, and skinny lips:

'This is the end that human beauty comes to! Short arms, gnarled hands, shoulders all humped. What of the breasts? all shrunk away, and the hips no better than the dugs. The mount of Venus? ugh! As for the thighs, they are no longer worth the name, poor shrivelled things speckled like sausages.

«Ainsi le bon temps regretons
Entre nous, povre vieilles sotes,
Assises bas, à crouppetons,
Tout en un tas comme pelotes,
A petit feu de chenevotes
Tost allumees, tost estaintes;
Et jadis fumes si mignotes!
– Ainsi en prent à mains et maintes.»

... Premier, je donne ma povre ame
A la benoite Trinité,
Et la commande à Nostre Dame,
Chambre de la Divinité,
Priant toute la charité
Des dignes neuf Ordres des cieux
Que par eux soit ce don porté
Devant le trosne precieux.

Item, mon corps j'ordonne et laisse
A nostre grant mere la terre;
Les vers n'y trouveront grant gresse,
Trop lui a fait faim dure guerre.
Or lui soit delivré grant erre:

'So we lament the good old days among ourselves, poor, silly old women, squatting on our haunches, each one hunched up like a ball, around a wretched fire of hemp-twigs, soon lit, soon dying down; and in our time we were so lovely. . . But that's the way it goes with many men and women.'

. . . First, I give my soul to the Blessed Trinity, and commend it to Our Lady, the dwelling-place of God, beseeching all the charity of the worthy nine Orders of Heaven, that this gift may be carried by them before the precious throne.

Item, I give and bequeath my body to our great mother the earth; the worms won't find much fat on it, hunger has waged too fierce a war against it. And let it be delivered speedily: from earth

De terre vint, en terre tourne;
Toute chose, se par trop n'erre,
Volentiers en son lieu retourne.

Item, et à mon plus que pere,
Maistre Guillaume de Villon,
Qui esté m'a plus doux que mere
A enfant levé de maillon:
Degeté m'a de maint bouillon,
Et de cestui pas ne s'esjoie,
Si lui requier à genouillon
Qu'il m'en laisse toute la joie;

Je lui donne ma librairie,
Et le Rommant du Pet au Diable,
Lequel maistre Guy Tabarie
Grossa, qui est hom veritable.
Par cahiers est sous une table;
Combien qu'il soit rudement fait,
La matiere est si tres notable
Qu'elle amende tout le mesfait.

it came, to earth let it return; everything, unless I am much mistaken, goes back gladly to its own place.

Item, to my more than father, Master Guillaume de Villon, who has been more tender to me than a mother to a child just out of swaddling-clothes; he has got me out of many a tight corner, and is not happy about the one I am in now, and I beg him on my knees that he will leave all the joy of it to me.

I give him my library, and the Romance of the Devil's Fart,* which was copied by Master Guy Tabarie, who is a trustworthy man. It is in quires under a table. Although it is roughly written, the matter is so notable that it makes up for all defects.

---

*This refers to a students' rag in which a huge stone was removed from the Hotel du Pet au Diable.

Item, donne à ma povre mere
Pour saluer nostre Maistresse,
(Qui pour moi eut douleur amere,
Dieu le set, et mainte tristesse),
Autre chastel n'ai, ne fortresse,
Où me retraie corps et ame,
Quant sur moi court male destresse,
Ne ma mere, la povre femme!

Ballade pour prier Nostre Dame

DAME du ciel, regente terrienne,
Emperiere des infernaux palus,
Recevez moi, vostre humble chrestienne,
Que comprise soie entre vos esleus,
Ce non obstant qu'onques rien ne valus.
Les biens de vous, ma Dame et ma Maistresse,
Sont trop plus grans que ne suis pecheresse,
Sans lesquels biens ame ne peut merir
N'avoir les cieux. Je n'en suis jangleresse:
En ceste foi je vueil vivre et mourir.

Item, I give to my poor mother, who suffered for my sake bitter grief, God knows, and many a sorrow, [this ballad] to offer in praise of Our Lady; I have no other stronghold nor fortress where I can take refuge, body and soul, when evil fortune falls upon me, nor has my mother, poor woman.

Ballade of Prayer to Our Lady

LADY of Heaven, Sovereign over earth, empress of the infernal swamps, receive me, your humble Christian woman, let me be counted among your elect, for all my unworthiness. For your goodness, my Lady and my Mistress, is far greater than all my sinfulness, that goodness without whose help no soul can merit Heaven nor win it. This is no idle chatter: in this faith I desire to live and die.

A vostre Fils dites que je suis sienne;
De lui soient mes pechiés abolus;
Pardonne moi comme à l'Egipcienne,
Ou comme il fist au clerc Theophilus,
Lequel par vous fut quitte et absolus,
Combien qu'il eust au diable fait promesse.
Preservez moi de faire jamais ce,
Vierge portant, sans rompure encourir,
Le sacrement qu'on celebre à la messe:
En ceste foi je vueil vivre et mourir.

Femme je suis povrette et ancienne,
Qui rien de sai; onques lettre ne lus.
Au moustier voi dont suis paroissienne
Paradis peint, où sont harpes et lus,
Et un enfer où damnez sont boullus;
L'un me fait peur, l'autre joie et liesse.
La joie avoir me fai, haute Deesse,
A qui pecheurs doivent tous recourir,
Comblés de foi, sans feinte ne paresse:
En ceste foi je vueil vivre et mourir.

Say to your Son that I am His; by Him may my sins be swept away; may He forgive me as He did the Egyptian woman or as He did the clerk Theophilus, who through you was acquitted and absolved, although he had made a compact with the Devil. Preserve me from ever doing that, oh! Virgin who bore without defilement the Sacrament we celebrate at Mass. In this faith I desire to live and die.

I am only a poor old woman, quite unlearned and unlettered. On the walls of my parish church I see a picture of Heaven with harps and lutes, and one of Hell where the damned are boiled. One fills me with terror, the other with joy and gladness. Make that joy be mine, oh! high Goddess, to whom all sinners must resort, brimming with faith in all sincerity and zeal. In this faith I desire to live and die.

Vous portastes, digne Vierge, princesse,
Iesus regnant qui n'a ne fin ne cesse.
Le Tout puissant, prenant nostre foiblesse,
Laissa les cieux et nous vint secourir,
Offrit à mort sa tres chiere jeunesse;
Nostre Seigneur tel est, tel le confesse:
En ceste foi je vueil vivre et mourir. . .

L'Épitaphe Villon (*La Ballade des Pendus*)

FRERES humains qui après nous vivez,
N'ayez les cuers contre nous endurcis,
Car, se pitié de nous povres avez,
Dieu en aura plus tost de vous mercis.
Vous nous voyez ci attachés cinq, six;
Quant de la chair, que trop avons nourrie,
Elle est pieça devoree et pourrie,
Et nous, les os, devenons cendre et poudre.
De nostre mal personne ne s'en rie,
Mais priez Dieu que tous nous veuille absoudre.

You bore, oh! worthy Virgin Princess, Jesus, who reigns for ever without end. The Almighty, taking on our frailty, left the Heavens and came to succour us, gave up to death His dear young life; such is Our Lord and such I acknowledge Him. In this faith I desire to live and die. . .

Villon's Epitaph (*The Ballade of the Hanged*)

BROTHERS, fellow-men, you who live on after we are dead, do not harden your hearts against us. For if you feel pity for us poor wretches God will the sooner have mercy on you. You see us hanging here, five or six of us. As to the flesh we fed so well, it has long ago been devoured or rotted away, and we, the bones, are turning to dust and ashes. Let no one laugh at our sufferings, but pray God to forgive us all.

Se freres vous clamons, pas n'en devez
Avoir desdain, quoi que fusmes occis
Par justice. Toutesfois, vous savez
Que tous hommes n'ont pas bon sens rassis;
Excusez nous, puis que sommes transis,
Envers le fils de la Vierge Marie,
Que sa grace ne soit pour nous tarie,
Nous preservant de l'infernale foudre.
Nous sommes morts, ame ne nous harie;
Mais priez Dieu que tous nous veuille absoudre.

La pluie nous a debués et lavés,
Et le soleil dessechiés et noircis;
Pies, corbeaux, nous ont les yeux cavés,
Et arrachié la barbe et les sourcis.
Jamais nul temps nous ne sommes assis;
Puis ça, puis là, comme le vent varie,
A son plaisir sans cesser nous charie,
Plus becquetés d'oiseaux que dés à coudre.
Ne soiez donc de nostre confrerie;
Mais priez Dieu que tous nous veuille absoudre.

If we call you brothers, you must not be offended, although we died at the hands of the hangman; after all, you know that all men are not endowed with good judgement. Now that we are gone, intercede for us with the Son of the Virgin Mary, that for us the spring of His grace may not run dry but may preserve us from the thunderbolt of Hell. We are dead, let no one molest us, but pray God to forgive us all.

The rain has washed and scoured us; the sun has dried and blackened us. Magpies and crows have pecked out our eyes and plucked our beards and eyebrows. We are never left at peace for a moment, driven endlessly this way and that at the whim of every changing wind. The birds have pecked at us until we are more pitted than a thimble. Take care, then, that you never join our company, but pray God to forgive us all.

Prince Jesus, qui sur tous a maistrie,
Garde qu'Enfer n'ait de nous seigneurie;
A lui n'ayons que faire ne que soudre.
Hommes, ici n'a point de moquerie;
Mais priez Dieu que tous nous veuille absoudre.

May Prince Jesus, who rules over all men, save us from the power of Hell; may we have no dealings there and no account to pay there. Men, here is no subject for your mirth; but pray God to forgive us all.

PART TWO

SIXTEENTH TO EIGHTEENTH CENTURIES

Introduced and edited by
Geoffrey Brereton

INTRODUCTION

I

THE French poetry of nearly three hundred years is represented in this section, which runs from poets still influenced by medieval tradition to the precursors of Romanticism. Between those two limits, the great poetic movement of the Renaissance grew up and declined, to be succeeded by types of verse which were neglected for too long and whose rediscovery entailed a new assessment of the resources of French poetry. The face of this, it is now recognized, differs appreciably from the older presentation. Although, on a long view, it does not need to be redrawn completely, the changes of emphasis are considerable and for the modern reader the results seem pure gain. The chief beneficiaries are the poets writing between about 1580 and 1650. They have an interest scarcely suspected by critics who regarded most of that period as a long and somewhat uninspired prelude to classicism. Classicism itself, however – with the outstanding exceptions of La Fontaine and the great dramatists – still appears as inimical to poetry as before. Its final triumph as an academic doctrine marked a decline of the lyrical faculty which became fully apparent in the eighteenth century. The Age of Reason, so rich in prose-writers, confronts the verse-anthologist with a relatively barren field, only partially redeemed by Chénier towards its end.

Since the literature of France forms an inseparable part of Western culture as a whole, one might expect her poetry to have gone through the same phases as the poetry of neighbouring countries. On broadly general lines, it is possible to say that it did. But a reader who approaches this anthology with an ordered picture of the development of the English poetry of the same period in his mind is just as likely to be struck by differences as by resemblances. The two outlines have roughly the same shape but at no point do they truly coincide. It would, in fact, be surprising if they did. Quite apart from such fundamentals as language and national character, the temporary circumstances which influence poets to write as they do can hardly combine in the same proportions in two literatures simultaneously. They include the social moment, the religious and philosophical climate, the impact of foreign literatures, and a number of other factors. In the period represented here, the Renaissance reached the two countries with somewhat different emphasis, the Counter-Reformation set up different reactions (especially since it failed in England while succeeding in France), and the standing and tone of the various courts, universities and urban societies had diverse effects on the poets who lived and worked in them.

Yet in spite of this the English reader of this section will sometimes find himself on more familiar ground than he would in the nineteenth and twentieth centuries. Ronsard, Du Bellay, and Desportes are likely to remind him of the Elizabethan sonneteers, some of whom imitated the French poets directly. He will quite often be reminded of Milton, although there was no Milton in France. Again, one cannot point with confidence to any French 'metaphysical' poets, but one recognizes features of metaphysical poetry across the Channel. So long as one does not try to match two patterns and is prepared for things to occur at different times and in different orders, it is remarkable how frequently they prove to be the same things. A common background of literary culture – the Bible, or Greek, Latin, and Italian poetry – explains many of them. Yet sometimes the resemblance is harder to define: it may be a mere tone of voice, a similar way of looking at physical objects, an unconscious mannerism which has only become noticeable through the passage of time. To recognize these without always scrutinizing them very closely is one of the minor yet real pleasures to be had from the French poetry of this period. But even without it the principal pleasure remains. Most of the original qualities of good poetry should be able to reach the reader directly over any interval of space and time. If they completely failed to do that, the poem would hardly be worth reprinting.

The historical outline which follows may help to place those qualities in better perspective.

In the sixteenth century French poetry was dominated by the Pléiade, the group of poets whose work marked the coming of the full Renaissance. Their achievement was so considerable that it has tended to obscure their immediate predecessors, some of whom deserve a better fate. It is true that at the beginning of the century French poetry was at a low ebb. The old medieval forms and themes were still in use, but the spirit had died out of them. The wind was beginning to blow from Italy, but so far its force had hardly been felt. In those circumstances Clément Marot wrote his verse. He had something of the new humanist learning; he wrote some of the earliest French sonnets – as did his disciple and contemporary, Mellin de Saint-Gelais – but he still belonged essentially to the medieval tradition, the tradition of Villon. His main achievement was to have developed this at a time when other poets were either continuing it mechanically or preparing to reject it. He combined the blunt humour and naïveté of an earlier age with a lightness of touch which was novel and still natively French. Particularly by his skill in the traditional *rondeau* and *ballade*, he succeeded in handing on some of the medieval vein, even if only in a playful form. Much later poets, from Voiture and La Fontaine to Voltaire, looked on him as a model for familiarly satirical verse. Even today his short song-poems can awaken a more immediate response than the more sophisticated work of the Pléiade.

Like his contemporary Rabelais, Marot was entirely untouched by Neo-Platonism, the new idealism which was spreading from Italy and which represented the most serious attempt of the Renaissance mind to bridge the medieval distinction between the physical and the spiritual. For the Neo-Platonists, intent on finding some kind of wholeness in man and in the universe, the activities of the senses were reflections of those of the soul – lower in degree but not essentially different in nature. Such a philosophy transformed love, which for Marot had been little more than an agreeable pastime, into something approaching a religious cult, in which earthly beauty was revered as an image of divine beauty. Neo-Platonism in France is often inseparable from the influence of Petrarch and other Italian poets who imitated him. For these, the poet's mistress becomes assimilated – in pagan terms – to a goddess, or, in Christian terms, takes on some of the prestige enjoyed by the Virgin in medieval literature. Combined or separately, Neo-Platonism and Petrarchism colour a great deal of sixteenth-century poetry, though they often take on distorted forms. They were first given memorable expression by a group of poets who flourished at Lyons, a city whose geographical position made it particularly open to Italian influences. Maurice Scève, the leader of the group, followed the Petrarchan pattern in his best work, *Délie*, in which he traces his love for an idealized mistress in terms which make a complete human experience of it. The work is at once sensual and abstract, but its chief originality lies in the intellectual element which controls its beautifully regulated symbolism. In form it is a long succession of short separate poems known as *dizains*, and has analogies with the sonnet sequence. The brevity of the *dizain* is intimately connected with Scève's condensed thought and carefully chosen language. Its discipline and compression occasionally suggest Mallarmé, but Scève is a much clearer – if also a more limited – poet.

Two poetesses also belonged to the Lyons group. The more varied was Pernette du Guillet, a young woman who was Scève's literary disciple and in part, at least, the model for his *Délie*. She replies to his verse in hers which, unlike his, is fluid and caressing, full of a half-playful love casuistry which is still largely medieval. Some of her songs are not so far from Marot's manner. Her delightfully intelligent verse has none of the intensity of Louise Labé's better-known elegies and sonnets, which harp very movingly on the single theme of frustrated passion. In contrast to this, the Platonic abstractions of Pontus de Tyard – a follower of Scève who later entered Ronsard's orbit – may seem mathematical and bloodless. But such a poem as *Disgrâce* shows how the cosmogony of the Platonists could be used to suggest an always valid picture of a universe which seems to have turned black and hostile in sympathy with some personal depression. The theme is basically that of Marot's light little song:

> *D'amours me va tout au rebours,*
>
> In love it goes all the wrong way for me,

but de Tyard has built it up by intellectual elaboration into a total disorganization of life.

All this verse belongs to the dawn of the Renaissance. The decisive innovations were made by Ronsard's group in the middle of the century. The Pléiade poets began by consciously turning their backs on medieval tradition and seeking their models in Greek and Latin literature. They continued also to absorb Italian influences and enthusiastically adopted the sonnet, so that it became very easily the dominant short verse-form of the age and the vehicle of much of its best poetry. They gave France what was virtually a new metre – the *alexandrin* – and in other ways, also, greatly increased the scope and suppleness of French verse. Of their two major poets, Du Bellay can be seen at his best in the sonnet. He used it for his early verse, which is largely Platonic in inspiration, as well as for the *Antiquités* and the *Regrets* of his maturity. These last books were the fruit of his exile in Rome, where he spent five unhappy years in the suite of his uncle, Cardinal Jean du Bellay. They show the wide variation of tone of which he was capable. In the same narrow form he can lament the fall of ancient Rome with all the appropriate pomp, can achieve a fastidious elegance in such a sonnet as *Cependant que Magny suit son grand Avanson*, or evoke a chatty session with his barber or a carnival outing with his girl-friend. Another manner appears in the *Jeux rustiques*, whose main originality consists in their metrical lightness, since they were adaptations of Latin pieces by the Italian poet Andrea Navagero. Such borrowings, sometimes hardly distinguishable from free translations, were too common in the sixteenth and seventeenth centuries to need constantly pointing out. They were not considered as plagiarisms and can be judged now, as they were then, on their poetic merits in their new language.

Du Bellay died comparatively young, and in any case his more volatile talent was never likely to challenge Ronsard's title to supremacy. Ronsard was a court poet with a scholarly formation and a wide culture. Within the inescapable limits of his age he comes nearer to being a universal poet than any other in France, with the possible exception of Hugo. He is a virtuoso in several domains. His love-sonnets – often courtly but never Platonic – are as varied in their way as Du Bellay's, but the diversity is as much an effect of art as of changing mood. The passionate rhythms of certain sonnets are quite unlike the formal precision of others. The grave pathos of the sonnets on the death of Marie, or of *Quand vous serez bien vieille, au soir, à la chandelle*, has little in common with the swirl and sway of the lines describing the dance in *Le soir qu'Amour vous fit dans la salle descendre*. The rhetorical opening of the *Sonnet pour Sinope* differs again from the generally colloquial tone of many of the *Sonnets pour Hélène*, a work of his mature years and undoubtedly his masterpiece. The virtue of this poetry is more in its execution than in any particular intensity of feeling, beyond the direct human appeal. When Ronsard writes on less personal themes, he does so in poems which are usually too long to be anthologized, though an occasional passage can be extracted. As an unofficial poet laureate he commanded a firm and noble style fully adequate to the political occasion. He brooded on destiny with a pomp of language which Malherbe would hardly surpass. He speculated on the natural and the supernatural with a picturesque curiosity which may now seem quaint, but which was in step with the current knowledge of his time. He could write delightful pastoral and did not disdain the humour of the *folâtrie* and the drinking-song.

While Ronsard and Du Bellay between them represent the highest achievements of the Pléiade, its range is extended in various directions by several lesser poets. The 'scientific' impulse to catalogue knowledge of the natural world and to give it some kind of philosophical explanation underlies Rémy Belleau's charming descriptive verse, light and playful though it is in the main. (This is the same tendency that appeared in Du Bartas's much vaster work, undertaken in a completely serious spirit.) Among the numerous sonneteers who followed Du Bellay, Pontus de Tyard and Ronsard in writing their sequences of *Amours*, Jodelle strikes a distinctive note which is sometimes reminiscent of Scève. In form, he cultivated a curious 'ternary' technique, used to good effect in the sonnet printed in this book. Other poets were to use it after him, including Sponde in the sonnet beginning:

> *Tout s'enfle contre moi, tout m'assaut, tout me tente.*
>
> Everything swells up against me, everything assails me, everything tempts me.

More radical experiments with metre were made by Jean-Antoine de Baïf, as well as by poets who were not of the Pléiade, such as Passerat and Rapin. Though their attempts to write in Greek and Latin metres came to nothing, some of their pieces are much better than curiosities. They deserve remembering as some of the earliest poets who questioned the purely syllabic basis of French verse and who did not invariably consider rhyme to be sacrosanct.

III

Most French critics have refused to see the Pléiade movement as an early phase of classicism. They prefer to reserve that term for the seventeenth century. Nevertheless, it is plain that Ronsard and his group were 'classical' in intention, even if their performance was incomplete. They believed in a fixed hierarchy of literary standards, at the summit of which they placed the Greeks and Latins. They set out to create new forms and styles which would be permanently suitable for French poetry, not merely for the individual poet and the moment. Here, they had a large measure of success. They established the rule for their own century, while few of the prosodic innovations of the seventeenth century are not to be found already in Ronsard, if only in embryo. The Pléiade were also classical in another sense of the word in supposing an ordered universe which could be known and described by the poet, and within that conception of a settled order some of them achieved a noteworthy serenity of outlook and style. One may point to some of Du Bellay's more turbulent poems or to an occasional fantastic piece by Ronsard, but these were not typical of their work as a whole. Their mature work at least is distinguished by its simplicity and sobriety and by that balance between imagination and reason which is a dominant feature of classicism in any age.

If one sees the Pléiade as a classicist movement which for various reasons failed to establish itself conclusively, the succeeding developments follow the theoretically normal order. (The norm is based on the development of Italian art and, to a certain degree, on that of the ancient Greek and Latin literatures.) According to theory, a classical period is followed by a decadent phase, in which its forms are aped and elaborated by writers who have lost touch with its spirit. In France the poetry of Desportes, who, in his more mannered way, attempted to continue the Pléiade tradition, answers to such a description. The next important phase is the baroque, which in the plastic arts means a rejection of the classical harmony and purity of line in favour of fluid and swirling forms; these are often accompanied by an excessive love of decoration for its own sake. The underlying state of mind is taken to be one of anguish and uncertainty. The balanced order of classicism has broken down and in its place is a whirlpool which the human eye cannot reduce to any rational design. It can only perceive constant movement and a series of disquieting impressions.

To call poetry 'baroque' on the analogy of painting and architecture is to risk some confusion. The term is not really well enough defined, and different critics have applied it to different kinds of poetry. However, it can be pressed into service as the best guide so far available to some newly-discovered territory. The baroque doubt may be said to have affected all the great religious poets of the late sixteenth century with the single exception of Du Bartas. In setting out to describe the divine ordering of the universe, Du Bartas seems to have felt no inner misgivings at all. Where he appears baroque is in his exuberant use of language and in his ostensibly fantastic vision of the natural world. Plants can move and animals have roots; the stars dance and the earth is constituted anthropomorphically. Such things, however, belonged for the most part to contemporary theories of the physical universe and cannot be credited to the poet's individual imagination. Yet there still remains something basically anti-rational and anti-classical in his attitude towards them. The greater the excess, the more enthusiastically he elaborates upon it.

In d'Aubigné the baroque strain goes deeper. The strength and strangeness of his language derive principally from the Bible, and he lacks the loquacious exuberance of Du Bartas. But the underlying anguish is intense. It was already apparent in the morbid violence of his early love-poems. When he came to write his epic poem, *Les Tragiques*, he had canalized it by an effort of will and, by making the Protestant cause his own, had identified his psychological conflict with the struggle between the two religious parties. The scenes of suffering and destruction which recur throughout this long poem remain as evidence of his obsessions. His contemporary, Sponde, and a younger poet, Chassignet, are also at war with themselves. They are afflicted by a spiritual disquiet which makes them profoundly aware of the impermanence of human life and of worldly values. This had been one of Ronsard's favourite themes, expressed in terms of the flower which fades – a universally accepted metaphor which he presents with a calm and almost static melancholy. But Sponde treats the matter as one of spiritual survival and fights out the issues before the reader with a display of highly mannered antitheses which give his verse an extraordinary flavour of decadence without detracting from its urgency. Chassignet, who published his sonnets at the age of about twenty-four and then ceased to write original verse, conveys the effect of mutability by an almost inexhaustible range of similes, from the constantly changing waters of a river to the evanescent smell of fruit. Here again the contrast with Ronsard is apparent and even more pointed. Such a sonnet as *A beaucoup de danger est sujette la fleur* opens with the exact idea of the doomed rose, but Chassignet immediately expands and varies this in compliance with his own shifting vision. There is none of the unity which gives a sense of slow inevitability and finally of acceptance to Ronsard's classically lovely *Comme on voit sur la branche, au mois de mai, la rose*. Instead, there is a fluidity of metre and of thought, which is one of the characteristics of the literary baroque.

In La Ceppède, another remarkable sonneteer, the variety of the imagery and of the allusions has a different purpose. His sonnets, called 'theorems' by their author, were intended to suggest the various mystic implications of the Passion and Resurrection of Christ and to encourage meditation by the use of a symbolism which is sometimes deliberately abstruse. La Ceppède weaves together the biblical and the classical, draws similes from astrology, alchemy, hunting and other sources, and succeeds in erecting one of the strangest monuments to piety which France or any other Catholic country has produced.

All these poets have a basic violence or restlessness which belongs to the dark period of the Wars of Religion, although neither La Ceppède nor d'Aubigné was published until the next century. From then on, the baroque entered a lighter phase, which for some critics, who see it as essentially a seventeenth-century mode of art, is its only true form.

IV

In the baroque poetry of the seventeenth century the interest is transferred to external qualities. The poet may still harbour a sense of instability, but he quickly projects it on to the outward scene, leaving the impression that he is not moved by deep feeling. The most that he reveals is the quiet melancholy of the 'fantastical' mind. One of the reasons for this widespread melancholia was evidently the removal of religion as a poetic catalyst.

The victory of the Counter-Reformation – which in France looked more like a return to civic sanity than the triumphant conclusion of a crusade – had put an end to a conflict with which the poet could openly identify his emotions. He was now limited to the ordinary sentiments of piety, which found abundant expression in numerous volumes of conventional verse. The most vital element left for religious poetry was praise – praise of the Deity, of his goodness and his works. This is the theme of almost every religious poem which rises above the average, from some of Malherbe's paraphrases of the Psalms to Martial de Brives's rich and ecstatic *Paraphrase du Cantique des Trois Enfants*. A poet can appropriately express his delight in nature or a mood of personal exultation in such verse, but it offers him no means of expressing the mood of frustration or of discontent. Denied this outlet, sharpness of feeling became diffused in a more vague and passive melancholy, which often reached the surface in eccentric forms.

An English poet of the early seventeenth century throws out a definition which fits much of the French poetry of the time:

> From witty men and mad
> All poetry conception had.
>
> ... Only these two poetic heat admits:
> A witty man, or one that's out of's wits.

This notion of 'wit' was common to all the West European literatures. Combined in various degrees with the 'fantastic' element, it complicates and enriches the conception of the baroque. It appears in a relatively pure state in French *précieux* verse, where it takes the form of an ingenious ringing of the changes on a limited number of sentiments and metaphors. This cultivated strain owed much to the literary *salons* and was connected with a social movement towards greater refinement in language and manners. It also reflected the influence of a new generation of Italian poets headed by Marino, in whose work the same qualities of ingenuity were developed to the full. A sonnet such as *La Belle Matineuse*, of which a version by Voiture of an Italian original is printed in this book, is typical of this kind of poetry. Vincent Voiture was the most accomplished of the various writers of *salon* verse and his reputation has suffered since because of it. He deserves rehabilitating as one of the best of French light poets, by no means limited to the *précieux* conventions. He parodies these as often as he obeys them and he is quite capable of ignoring them altogether and writing with a humour as open as that of Marot, whom he consciously imitated.

A type of wit which is often deliberately anti-*précieux* and always anti-idealistic flourished at the same time. It appears in numerous epigrammatists, in 'burlesque' poets like Scarron, in minor humorists like Vion de Dalibray and in such poems as Saint-Amant's *Le Melon* and *L'Enamouré*. Some of the same poets who affect this bluff Philistine manner can write on other occasions in the most delicate *précieux* vein.

Préciosité cannot be confined to society verse. It mingles with the baroque to introduce the conceit and the ornamental classical allusion both into religious poetry and into what is now thought of as nature-poetry. The descriptive verse of seventeenth-century poets admits a degree of artificiality quite at variance with post-Wordsworthian ideas of the way 'nature' should be approached. Yet to conclude that these poets were looking only with an urban eye, or were technically ill-equipped for their subjects, would be to ignore the true qualities of their work.

There is much direct observation of the countryside in poems such as Saint-Amant's *La Solitude*, or Théophile de Viau's *Lettre à son frère* (both are too long to be given in their entirety). The first is coloured with melancholy, the second with nostalgia, and conventional classical allusions appear in both, yet the predominant vision in each is realistic. Elsewhere, the same poets write with greater artificiality. The reason is certainly not incompetence, but because they are seeking a different effect. In Théophile's poem *Le Matin* the mythological and the natural alternate to present a kaleidoscopic succession of small, clearly-defined pictures appropriately capped by the conceit in the final verse:

> Il est jour, levons-nous, Philis:
> Allons à notre jardinage
> Voir s'il est, comme ton visage,
> Semé de roses et de lis.

It is day, let us get up, Phyllis: let us go to our garden and see if, like your face, it is sprinkled with roses and lilies.

The conceits in such a poem as Saint-Amant's *L'Hiver des Alpes* help to convey the impression of whiteness and glitter more strongly than merely naturalistic description would do:

> Ces atomes de feu qui sur la neige brillent,
> Ces étincelles d'or, d'azur et de cristal
> Dont l'hiver, au soleil, d'un lustre oriental
> Pare ses cheveux blancs que les vents éparpillent.

These fiery atoms glittering on the snow, these sparks of gold, of azure and of crystal, with which Winter, in sunshine, with oriental splendour, adorns its white hair tossed by the winds.

Other poets in their various landscapes and skyscapes – among them Tristan l'Hermite and Du Bois Hus – show us a world of changing lights and colours, of little mechanical figures moving to the sound of running water, of flowers, birds and fishes constantly transformed by the imagination into something else: in short a world of movement and metamorphosis in which nothing retains the same shape for very long. Conventionalized, these transformations can become tedious – Phyllis outshines the sun and appears herself to be the daystar – but in fresher contexts they represent a particular way of looking at phenomena which goes deeper than mere literary fashion. They tend to show that the sense of mutability, which for the earlier religious poets had gone to the foundations of the individual and of the universe, still ran through the more polished poetry of the seventeenth century. To suggest it on this more superficial level was a delicate art, very open to abuse by exaggeration and to the ridicule of common sense. Once lost, it disappeared almost entirely from French poetry, to reappear only in quite recent times.

V

After 1650 the whole trend of French literature was towards a definitive classicism and against the kind of poetry just described. The positive virtues of classicism are those associated with the clean, clear line and with a sense of proportion in fitting the means to the end. Such a conception of art precludes 'madness' and requires 'wit' to be kept under close control – an almost crippling condition for the poetic imagination as this is usually conceived. It happens that the greatest of the classical poets, Racine, was a dramatist. His best verse is all in his plays and so is outside the scope of this anthology. His non-dramatic verse, which is predominantly religious, cannot be taken to represent him worthily. Similar considerations exclude Corneille, who belonged, however, to an earlier generation and whose verse is less purely classical. There remains La Fontaine – justly remembered as the best of all writers of verse fables (so familiar that I have included only a single example here), but also a poet of much wider accomplishment whose early work, such as *Adonis* and *Le Songe de Vaux*, illustrates the classical qualities at their most attractive. There is also Boileau, the theorist of late seventeenth-century classicism and the satirist of the *précieux* and the baroque (though even Boileau's work shows traces of a mild 'fantasy', just as Racine's still shows traces of 'wit'). Although not one of the great creative writers, Boileau represented the doctrine of the golden mean and set an example of sound sense and sound craftsmanship in the making of verse. In this last field he and his contemporaries were generally supposed to have continued and completed the reform begun by Malherbe earlier in the century. This was one of those half-truths which can now be seen to require some adjustment.

Malherbe had laid down certain principles of verse-technique which were aimed at achieving greater regularity and dignity. He had also set up models for 'official' poetry in some of his odes. But his influence had been neither conclusive nor continuous. The verse of his immediate disciples, Maynard and Racan, appears elegantly empty today and, although these poets were esteemed in their own time, their prestige was considerably lower than that of Théophile de Viau, who stood for ease and naturalness of style. As a reformer of language and prosody, Malherbe represented at first little more than an interlude between the two phases of the baroque, and even this would be untrue of the earlier part of his career. He himself was unequivocally a baroque poet when he began writing. He indulged without restraint in the hyperbolic flourish and the far-fetched simile. A poem such as his *Ode pour Marie de Médicis*, written in 1600, shows this flamboyant manner only partially tamed: it may well appeal more strongly to the modern reader than the more cramped though still rhetorical manner of his later verse. It was, in fact, the *panache* of his poetry, combined with its firm metrical basis, which seems to have impressed later poets; they included the youthful Racine, who admired and quoted the ode just mentioned in his correspondence. But this was only one kind of poetry, and for some thirty years after Malherbe's death it was not the chief kind. When the true classical movement emerged, it contained much more than had ever been in Malherbe. In spite of Boileau's rather tendentious praise, it is only very partially true to say of Malherbe that 'everything recognized his laws'. His influence had not predominated up to the sixteen-sixties, nor, although strongly felt, was it to do so afterwards. One of his most lasting legacies to French poetry was the ten-line stanza which he handled with such assurance. It will be found in several of the longer poems in this book and it continued in favour long after the eighteenth century.

VI

The eighteenth century inherited an exhausted tradition from Racine, La Fontaine, and Boileau. When those three had ceased to write there remained little more than the empty shell of classicism for their successors. Grandiloquent verse, derived ultimately from Malherbe, but modified by Boileau and others, had wide currency and occasional successes. 'Wit' was still alive, but it was divorced from the fantasy which had once made it a poetic force. It could be pointed and amusing, but it was the wit of the clubman and no longer of the eccentric. The subtler wit of the Vicomte de Parny, a minor poet who was one of Lamartine's models, should no doubt be excepted. Parny combines it with a pervading tone of nostalgia which, if it went rather deeper, might be called Romantic.

'Madness' has disappeared, but in its place an entirely new kind of personal feeling begins to manifest itself dimly. In the descriptive and didactic poetry of the time, flat and excessively long though much of it is, there is sometimes an attempt to discern a spirit in the scene described and even to associate it with the mood of the poet. Such emotions may be only faintly present in Saint-Lambert, whose religious-conditioned contemplation of the universe renewed Du Bartas in an eighteenth-century spirit. But there is something of the true Romantic ecstasy in Thomas's remarkable *Ode sur le Temps*, and much more in such a poem as Chénier's *Invocation*.

Chénier, who perished in the Revolution while he was still young, was easily the greatest poet of the century. With his emotional enthusiasms, his impassioned rhetoric, he is as much an eighteenth-century figure as Edmund Burke. His satirical manner reaches its height in the savage oratory of the *Ode à Charlotte Corday*. It appears as well in the *Iambes*, which he composed during the last months of his life in prison. Rather than give one of the more smoothly polished of these well-known poems, I have preferred a short, unfinished fragment which catches more realistically the peculiar absurdity and horror of a situation still actual in too many countries today. As for Chénier's earlier poems on classical themes, they may appear excessively sentimental in places, yet they have a suppleness and flow hardly matched elsewhere in French poetry, and certainly not in their own century. Chénier fittingly closes an epoch. He stands at the limit of the classical tradition: a step or two further and it would relax and cease to be classical altogether.

VII

The ideal anthology would no doubt consist only of complete poems, but within any practical limits of space that would mean omitting the best work of too many poets. I have therefore compromised with principle in a number of cases by including extracts from longer poems, but have aimed at choosing passages which are reasonably complete in themselves and do not smack of the specimen. I must ask the reader's indulgence where I have failed, and point in compensation to the greater variety of work which cutting has made it possible to include. Cuts are indicated by three dots, usually at the beginning of the line which immediately follows an omitted passage. Spelling has been modernized throughout, except where requirements of rhyme or metre (and, exceptionally, other considerations) demand the retention of an old form.* The punctuation of early editions has also been modified where it was misleadingly archaic. When the title of a poem is in square brackets, it has been supplied editorially.

*During most of the period covered in this section the endings *-ois* and *-oit* were pronounced *oué. Je vois* rhymed with the modern *j'appelais.* The old spelling has been used wherever the rhyme depends on it.

MELLIN DE SAINT-GELAIS

Sonnet

Il n'est point tant de barques à Venise,
D'huîtres à Bourg, de lièvres en Champagne,
D'ours en Savoie et de veaux en Bretagne,
De cygnes blancs le long de la Tamise;

Ni tant d'amours se traitant en l'église,
Ni différends aux peuples d'Allemagne,
Ni tant de gloire à un seigneur d'Espagne,
Ni tant se trouve à la cour de feintise;

Ni tant y a de monstres en Afrique,
D'opinions en une république,
Ni de pardons à Rome aux jours de fête;

Ni d'avarice aux hommes de pratique,
Ni d'arguments en une Sorbonnique,
Que m'amie a de lunes en la tête.

Sonnet

There are not so many boats in Venice, oysters at Bourg, hares in Champagne, bears in Savoy, and calves in Brittany, white swans along the Thames;

Nor so many love-affairs negotiated in church, nor disputes among the peoples of Germany, nor haughtiness in a Spanish grandee, nor is so much deceit found at court;

Nor are there so many monsters in Africa, opinions in a republic, nor pardons at Rome on feast days;

Nor avarice among lawyers, nor arguments in a disputation at the Sorbonne, as my darling has whims in her head.

CLÉMENT MAROT

De sa grande amie

Rondeau

DEDANS Paris, ville jolie,
Un jour passant mélancolie,
Je pris alliance nouvelle
A la plus gaie demoiselle
Qui soit d'ici en Italie.

D'honnêteté elle est saisie,
Et crois – selon ma fantaisie –
Qu'il n'en est guère de plus belle
   Dedans Paris.

Je ne la vous nommerai mie,
Sinon que c'est ma grand'amie,
Car l'alliance se fit telle
Par un doux baiser que j'eus d'elle,
Sans penser aucune infamie
   Dedans Paris.

On His Darling

Rondeau

IN Paris, that pretty town, throwing off melancholy one day, I began a new friendship with the gayest young lady that there is from here to Italy.

   She's as virtuous as she could be and I think – according to my ideas – that there is hardly a prettier girl in Paris.

   I shall certainly not tell you her name, except [to say] that she's my darling, for our friendship was sealed by a sweet kiss I had from her, with no thought of any harm, in Paris.

Du baiser de s'amie

Rondeau

EN la baisant m'a dit: Ami, sans blâme
Ce seul baiser, qui deux bouches embâme,
Les arrhes sont du bien tant espéré.
Ce mot elle a doucement proféré,
Pensant du tout apaiser ma grand'flamme.

Mais le mien cœur adonc plus elle enflamme,
Car son haleine, odorant plus que bâme,
Soufflait le feu qu'Amour m'a préparé
　　En la baisant.

Bref, mon esprit sans connaissance d'âme
Vivait alors sur la bouche à ma Dame,
Dont se mourait le corps enamouré:
Et si la lèvre eût guère demouré
Contre la mienne, elle m'eût sucé l'âme
　　En la baisant.

On His Darling's Kiss

Rondeau

WHEN I kissed her, she said: 'Darling, in all good faith, this single
kiss which makes two mouths fragrant is on account for the bliss
so much desired.' She uttered these words softly, meaning entirely
to calm my hot flame.

　　But by this she inflamed my heart all the more, for her breath,
more fragrant than balsam, fanned the fire which Love prepared
for me when I kissed her.

　　Yes, though not a soul knew it, my spirit lived at that moment
on the mouth of my lady, whose amorous body seemed to die. And
if her lips had stayed much longer against mine, she would have
sucked out my soul, when I kissed her.

De trois couleurs

Rondeau

GRIS, Tanné, Noir porte la fleur des fleurs
Pour sa livrée, avec regrets et pleurs;
Pleurs et regrets en son cœur elle enferme,
Mais les couleurs dont ses vêtements ferme,
Sans dire mot exposent ses douleurs.

Car le Noir dit la fermeté des cœurs;
Gris le travail; et Tanné les langueurs:
Par ainsi c'est *langueur en travail ferme,*
    Gris, Tanné, Noir.

J'ai ce fort mal par elle et ses valeurs,
Et en souffrant ne crains aucuns malheurs,
Car sa bonté de mieux avoir m'afferme:
Ce nonobstant, en attendant le terme,
Me faut porter ces trois tristes couleurs:
    Gris, Tanné, Noir.

On Three Colours

Rondeau

GREY, tan, black the flower of flowers wears for her livery, with
sorrow and tears; tears and sorrow in her heart she hides, but the
colours with which she decks her clothes show out her grief with-
out a word said.

For black spells constancy of heart; grey, distress; and tan,
sighs: so it is *sighing in constant distress,* grey, tan, black.

I have this affliction through her and her emblems, and in suffer-
ing I fear no misfortune, for her kindness assures me of better
things: this notwithstanding, until the time is up I have to wear
these three sad colours: grey, tan, black.

Ballade de Frère Lubin

Pour courir en poste à la ville
Vingt fois, cent fois, ne sais combien,
Pour faire quelque chose vile,
Frère Lubin le fera bien.
Mais d'avoir honnête entretien,
Ou mener vie salutaire,
C'est à faire à un bon chrétien,
Frère Lubin ne le peut faire.

Pour mettre, comme un homme habile,
Le bien d'autrui avec le sien
Et vous laisser sans croix ni pile,
Frère Lubin le fera bien:
On a beau dire: Je le tiens,
Et le presser de satisfaire,
Jamais il ne vous rendra rien;
Frère Lubin ne le peut faire.

Pour débaucher par un doux style
Quelque fille de bon maintien,

Ballade of Brother Lubin*

To hurry post-haste to the town, twenty times, a hundred times, I don't know how often, to do some dirty thing, Brother Lubin will do it gladly. But to have honest dealings with you, or lead a wholesome life, that's a matter for a good Christian, Brother Lubin cannot do it.

To place, like a smart fellow, other people's property with his, and leave you without a dime, Brother Lubin will do it gladly. It is no good saying: 'I have got him', and pressing him to settle, he will never give you back a thing: Brother Lubin cannot do it.

To seduce with smooth words some attractive-looking girl, no

---

* 'Brother Lubin' was a stock name given to mendicant friars.

Point ne faut de vieille subtile,
Frère Lubin le fera bien.
Il prêche en théologien,
Mais pour boire de belle eau claire,
Faites-la boire à votre chien,
Frère Lubin ne le peut faire.

Envoi

Pour faire plus tôt mal que bien,
Frère Lubin le fera bien:
Mais si c'est quelque bonne affaire,
Frère Lubin ne le peut faire.

Chanson

D'AMOURS me va tout au rebours,
Jà ne faut que de cela mente.
J'ai refus en lieu de secours:
M'amie rit, et je lamente.
C'est la cause pourquoi je chante:
D'amours me va tout au rebours,
Tout au rebours me va d'amours!

crafty old woman is needed: Brother Lubin will do it gladly. He preaches like a true theologian, but as for drinking clean clear water – give it to your dog to drink: Brother Lubin cannot do it.

Envoi

To do harm rather than good, Brother Lubin will do it gladly: but if it is some good matter, Brother Lubin cannot do it.

Song

In love it goes all wrong for me; I really must not lie about that. I get refusal instead of encouragement; my darling laughs and I lament. That's the reason why I sing: In love it goes all wrong for me, all wrong for me it goes in love!

MAURICE SCÈVE

Délie
Objet de Plus Haute Vertu

Dizains

LIBRE vivais en l'avril de mon âge,
De cure exempt, sous cette adolescence
Où l'œil, encor non expert de dommage,
Se vit surpris de la douce présence
Qui par sa haute et divine excellence
M'étonna l'âme et le sens tellement
Que de ses yeux l'archer, tout bellement,
Ma liberté lui a tout asservie:
Et dès ce jour continuellement
En sa beauté gît ma mort, et ma vie.

COMME Hécaté tu me feras errer,
Et vif et mort, cent ans parmi les ombres;
Comme Diane au ciel me reserrer,

Delia, object of highest virtue
Dizains

I LIVED free in the April of my life, untouched by care, in that youthful time when my eye, not yet accustomed to danger, saw itself surprised by that sweet presence which, by its high and divine excellence, so stunned my soul and my sense that the archer of her eyes, without more ado, wholly enslaved my freedom to her. And since that day continually, in her beauty lies my death and my life.

LIKE Hecate you will make me wander alive and dead a hundred years among the shades; like Diana, will shut me up in heaven,

D'où descendis en ces mortels encombres;
Comme régnante aux infernales ombres,
Amoindriras ou accroîtras mes peines.
    Mais comme Lune infuse dans mes veines,
Celle tu fus, es, et seras DÉLIE,
Qu'Amour a jointe à mes pensées vaines
Si fort que Mort jamais ne l'en délie.

LE voir, l'ouïr, le parler, le toucher
Finaient le but de mon contentement,
Tant que le bien, qu'amants ont sur tout cher,
N'eut onques lieu en notre accointement.
    Que m'a valu d'aimer honnêtement
En sainte amour chastement éperdu?
Puisque m'en est le mal pour bien rendu,
Et qu'on me peut pour vice reprocher
Qu'en bien aimant j'ai promptement perdu
La voir, l'ouïr, lui parler, la toucher.

whence you came down among these mortal pitfalls; as queen of
the infernal shades, will lessen or increase my torments.

But as Moon infused in my veins, this you were, are, and will be
Delia – whom love has joined to my fruitless thoughts so closely
that death can never separate her from them.

SEEING, hearing, speaking, touching, marked the limit of my
satisfaction, so that that supreme happiness, which lovers hold dear
above all else, never had place in our intercourse.

What has it profited me to love virtuously, chastely beguiled
in a sacred love? Since evil is given me in exchange for good, and
it can be imputed to me as a fault that by loving rightly I have sud-
denly lost [the right] to see her, to hear her, to speak to her, to
touch her.

En devisant un soir me dit ma Dame:
Prends cette pomme en sa tendresse dure,
Qui éteindra ton amoureuse flamme,
Vu que tel fruit est de froide nature:
Adonc aura congrue nourriture
L'ardeur qui tant d'humeur te fait pleuvoir.
   Mais toi, lui dis-je, ainsi que je puis voir,
Tu es si froide, et tellement en somme
Que, si tu veux de mon mal cure avoir,
Tu éteindras mon feu mieux que la pomme.

Délia ceinte, haut sa cotte attournée,
La trousse au col, et arc et flèche aux mains,
Exercitant chastement la journée,
Chasse et prend cerfs, biches, et chevreuils maints.
   Mais toi, Délie, en actes plus humains
Mieux composée, et sans violents dards,
Tu vènes ceux par tes chastes regards
Qui tellement de ta chasse s'ennuient,
Qu'eux tous étant de toi saintement ards,
Te vont suivant, où les bêtes la fuient.

While we were chatting one evening, my lady said to me: 'Take this apple so firmly tender, and it will quench your amorous flame, since this fruit is cold by nature. So the ardour which makes you rain so much moisture will have appropriate food.'

   'But you,' I said to her, 'as I can well see, you are so cold, and in short such that, if you are willing to treat my disease, you will quench my fire better than the apple.'

Delia (Diana) belted, her tunic girded up, the quiver round her neck, the bow and arrow in her hands, chastely occupying the day, hunts and catches stags, does, and many a roe-deer.

   But you, my Delia, more pacific in less cruel acts and without brutal arrows, you hunt with your chaste looks those who are so harried by your pursuit that, all being burnt by your virtuous fire, they follow after you, while the beasts flee from her.

SEUL avec moi, elle avec sa partie,
Moi en ma peine, elle en sa molle couche:
Couvert d'ennui je me vautre en l'ortie,
Et elle nue entre ses bras se couche.

   Ah, lui indigne, il la tient, il la touche:
Elle le souffre et, comme moins robuste,
Viole amour par ce lien injuste
Que droit humain, et non divin, a fait.

   O sainte loi à tous, fors à moi, juste,
Tu me punis pour elle avoir méfait!

SANS lésion le Serpent Royal vit
Dedans le chaud de la flamme luisante:
Et en l'ardeur qui à toi me ravit
Tu te nourris sans offense cuisante;
Et, bien que soit sa qualité nuisante,
Tu t'y complais, comme en ta nourriture.

I ALONE with myself, she with her husband, I in my pain, she in her soft bed: covered with torments, I wallow in nettles, and she lies naked in his arms.

Ah, unworthy he, he holds her, he touches her: she suffers him and, though the weaker, violates love by that unjust bond, which human equity, not divine, has made.

O holy law, just to all except to me, you punish me for her mis-doing.

THE Royal Serpent* lives unscathed in the heat of the shining flame; and in the fire which bars me from you, you feed with no scorching hurt; and, though its properties are harmful, you delight in it, as though it were your native food.

---

*'Royal' because the salamander was the emblem of Francis I, with the motto: *Nutrisco et extinguo* (I feed on fire and extinguish it).

O fusses-tu par ta froide nature
La Salamandre en mon feu résidente!
Tu y aurais délectable pâture
Et éteindrais ma passion ardente.

Tu cours superbe, ô Rhône, florissant
En sablon d'or et argentines eaux.
Maint fleuve gros te rend plus ravissant,
Ceint de cités et bordé de châteaux,
Te pratiquant par sûrs et grands bateaux
Pour seul te rendre en notre Europe illustre.
  Mais la vertu de ma Dame t'illustre
Plus qu'autre bien qui te fasse estimer.
Enfle-toi donc au parfait de son lustre,
Car fleuve heureux plus que toi n'entre en mer.

Nouvelle amour, nouvelle affection,
Nouvelles fleurs parmi l'herbe nouvelle:
Et, jà passée, encor se renouvelle
Ma primevère en sa verte action.

O would that by your cold nature you were the salamander
dwelling in my fire; there you would find delectable nourishment
and would quench my ardent passion.

You proudly flow, O Rhône, prospering in golden sands and sil-
very waters. Many a swollen river makes you more delightful,
girded with cities and fringed with castles, navigating you with
stout and great ships, to send you on alone through our noble
Europe.
  But the virtue of my lady ennobles you more than any other
quality for which you are prized. Swell yourself, then, to the height
of her perfection, for no more fortunate river joins the sea.

New love, new feeling, new flowers in the new grass: and, though
now past, my spring renews itself yet again in its green effects.

Ce néanmoins, la rénovation
De mon vieux mal et ulcère ancienne
Me détient tout en cette saison sienne,
Où le meurtrier m'a meurtri, et noirci
Le cœur si fort que plaie égyptienne,
Et tout tourment me rend plus endurci.

LA blanche aurore à peine finissait
D'orner son chef d'or luisant et de roses,
Quand mon esprit, qui du tout périssait
Au fond confus de tant diverses choses,
Revint à moi sous les custodes closes
Pour plus me rendre envers Mort invincible.
    Mais toi qui as – toi seule – le possible
De donner heur à ma fatalité,
Tu me seras la Myrrhe incorruptible
Contre les vers de ma mortalité.

This notwithstanding, the recurrence of my old pain and former wound shackles me wholly in this its season, when the slayer slew me and darkened my heart with the virulence of a plague of Egypt, and every torment hardens me still more.

THE white dawn had scarcely finished bedecking her head with gleaming gold and roses, when my spirit, which was wholly perishing in the confused depths of so many various things, came back to me under the drawn curtains, to make me more invincible against death.

    But you who have – you only – the power to bring happiness to my destiny, you will be for me the incorruptible myrrh against the worms of my mortality.

PERNETTE DU GUILLET

Rimes

QUI dira ma robe fourrée
De la belle pluie dorée
Qui Daphnès enclose ébranla:
Je ne sais rien moins que cela.

    Qui dira qu'à plusieurs je tends
Pour en avoir mon passetemps,
Prenant mon plaisir çà et là:
Je ne sais rien moins que cela.

    Qui dira que t'ai révélé
Le feu longtemps en moi celé
Pour en toi voir si force il a:
Je ne sais rien moins que cela.

    Qui dira que, d'ardeur commune
Qui les jeunes gens importune,
De toi je veux … et puis holà!
Je ne sais rien moins que cela.

    Mais qui dira que la vertu,
Dont tu es richement vêtu,

Rhymes

IF they say that my dress is lined with the beautiful golden rain which stirred imprisoned Danaë, I know nothing at all of that.

If they say that I incline to several to have my amusement with them, taking my pleasure here and there, I know nothing at all of that.

If they say that I have revealed to you the fire long hidden within me to see what power it has on you, I know nothing at all of that.

If they say that [fired] with the common ardour by which young people are importuned I want from you … and then, hey there! I know nothing at all of that.

But if they say that the virtue with which you are richly clad

En ton amour m'étincela:
Je ne sais rien mieux que cela.
　　Mais qui dira que d'amour sainte
Chastement au cœur suis atteinte,
Qui mon honneur onc ne foula:
Je ne sais rien mieux que cela.

A QUI plus est un amant obligé:
Ou à Amour, ou vraiment à sa Dame?
Car son service est par eux rédigé
Au rang de ceux qui aiment los et fame.
　　A lui il doit le cœur, à elle l'âme,
Qui est autant comme à tous deux la vie.
L'un à l'honneur, l'autre à bien le convie.
Et toutefois voici un très grand point,
Lequel me rend ma pensée assouvie:
C'est que sans Dame, Amour ne serait point.

kindled a love for you in me, there's nothing I know better than
that.

　　If they say that I am chastely stricken in my heart with a vir-
tuous love which has never stained my honour, there's nothing I
know better than that.

To whom is a lover most beholden? Is it to Love, or in truth to his
Lady? For Love's service is by them (those who ask such ques-
tions) reduced to the level of those who love praise and fame.

　　To Love he owes his heart, to her his soul, which is the same as
owing both of them his life. One invites him to honour, the other
to joy. And yet here is a very important point, which sets my
doubts at rest: it is that without Lady there would not be Love.

PONTUS DE TYARD

Disgrâce

LA haute Idée à mon univers mère,
Si hautement de nul jamais comprise,
M'est à présent ténébreuse Chimère.

Le Tout, d'où fut toute ma forme prise,
Plus de mon tout, de mon tout exemplaire,
M'est simplement une vaine feintise.

Ce qui soulait mon imparfait parfaire
Par son parfait, sa force a retirée,
Pour mon parfait en imparfait refaire.

Le Ciel, qui fut mon haut Ciel Empyrée,
Fixe moteur de ma force première,
Pour m'affaiblir rend sa force empirée.

La grand' clarté, à luire coutumière
En mon obscur, me semble être éclipsée,
Pour me priver du jour de sa lumière.

Desolation

THE high Idea which is the mother of my universe, in its height never understood by any, is now a dark illusion to me.

The Whole, from which my whole form was taken – more than my whole, the pattern of my whole – is simply a vain pretence to me.

That which used to perfect my imperfection by its perfection has withdrawn its power, to throw back my perfection into imperfection.

Heaven, which was my high Empyrean, the fixed mover of my primal force, decreases its force to weaken me.

The great brightness which was accustomed to shine in my darkness appears eclipsed to me, in order to deprive me of the light of its day.

La Sphère en rond, de circuit lassée
Pour ma faveur, malgré sa symétrie
En nouveau cours contre moi s'est poussée.

La harmonie, en doux concens nourrie
Des sept accords, contre l'ordre sphérique
Horriblement entour mon ouïr crie.

Le clair Soleil par la ligne écliptique
De son devoir mes yeux plus n'illumine,
Mais (puisque pis ne peut) se fait oblique.

La déité, qui de moi détermine,
De ne prévoir que mon malheur m'asseure,
Et au passer du temps mon bien termine.

L'âme, qui fit longtemps en moi demeure,
Iniquement d'autre corps s'associe,
Et, s'éloignant de moi, veut que je meure,
Pour s'exercer en palingénésie.

The round sphere, weary of turning in my favour, denies its symmetry and launches out on a new course against me.

The harmony, fed by sweet attunings of the seven chords, against the order of the spheres screeches hideously around my ears.

The bright sun no longer lights my eyes by the ecliptic line of its true function, but – since it can do no worse – becomes oblique.

The divine power which disposes of me confirms me only in the promise of misfortune, and with the passing of time ends my happiness.

The soul, which long dwelt within me, joins iniquitously with another body and, deserting me, desires me to die in order to practise palingenesis.*

---

*Palingenesis: the revival of an apparently dead body by the introduction of another soul.

JOACHIM DU BELLAY

L'Olive

DÉJÀ la nuit en son parc amassait
Un grand troupeau d'étoiles vagabondes,
Et pour entrer aux cavernes profondes,
Fuyant le jour, ses noirs chevaux chassait.

Déjà le ciel aux Indes rougissait,
Et l'aube encor de ses tresses tant blondes
Faisant grêler mille perlettes rondes,
De ses trésors les prés enrichissait:

Quand d'occident, comme une étoile vive,
Je vis sortir dessus ta verte rive,
O fleuve mien! une nymphe en riant.

Alors, voyant cette nouvelle aurore,
Le jour honteux d'un double teint colore
Et l'Angevin et l'Indique orient.

SI notre vie est moins qu'une journée
En l'éternel, si l'an qui fait le tour

The Olric

NIGHT was already gathering into its fold a great flock of wandering stars, and to enter the deep caves, fleeing from day, was driving its black horses.

The sky was already reddening in the Indies and the dawn, still raining down a thousand round pearlets from its fair tresses, was enriching the meadows with its treasures:

When from the west, like a living star, I saw coming out upon your green bank, O river of mine, a smiling nymph.

Then, seeing this new dawn, the day, ashamed, colours with a double flush both the Angevin and the Indian east.

IF our life is less than a day in eternity, if the returning year carries

Chasse nos jours sans espoir de retour,
Si périssable est toute chose née,

Que songes-tu, mon âme emprisonnée?
Pourquoi te plaît l'obscur de notre jour,
Si pour voler en un plus clair séjour,
Tu as au dos l'aile bien empennée?

Là est le bien que tout esprit désire,
Là, le repos où tout le monde aspire,
Là est l'amour, là le plaisir encore.

Là, ô mon âme, au plus haut ciel guidée,
Tu y pourras reconnaître l'Idée
De la beauté qu'en ce monde j'adore.

Sonnets de l'honnête amour

Non autrement que la prêtresse folle,
En grommelant d'une effroyable horreur,
Secoue en vain l'indomptable fureur
Du Cynthien, qui brusquement l'affole:

off our days without hope of recall, if each thing born is perishable,

Why do you linger here, my imprisoned soul? Why does the darkness of our day please you, if, to fly to a brighter home, you have a well-fledged wing on your back?

There is the joy which all spirits desire, there the repose to which all men aspire, love is there, and pleasure still.

There, O my soul, guided to the highest heaven, you will be able to recognize the Idea [ideal pattern] of the beauty which I adore in this world.

Sonnets of Virtuous Love

Not otherwise than the demented priestess, muttering with a fearful abhorrence, tries in vain to shake off the irresistible frenzy of the Cynthian [Apollo] who suddenly maddens her:

Mon estomac, gros de ce dieu qui vole,
Épouvanté d'une aveugle terreur
Se fait rebelle à la divine erreur,
Qui brouille ainsi mon sens et ma parole.

Mais c'est en vain: car le dieu qui m'étreint
De plus en plus m'aiguillonne, et contraint
De le chanter, quoique mon cœur en gronde.

Chantez-le donc, chantez mieux que devant,
O vous mes vers! qui volez par le monde,
Comme feuillards éparpillés du vent.

Divers Jeux rustiques

D'un vanneur de blé aux vents

A vous, troupe légère,
Qui d'aile passagère
Par le monde volez,
Et d'un sifflant murmure
L'ombrageuse verdure
Doucement ébranlez,

My stomach, big with this flying god, stricken with a blind terror, revolts against the divine madness, which confuses thus my senses and my speech.

But it is in vain: for the god who clasps me spurs me on more and more and forces me to sing him, although my heart murmurs against it.

Sing him then, sing better than before, O my verses which flutter through the world, like dead leaves scattered by the wind.

(The reference in the first four lines is to the oracle at Delphi.)

Rustic Diversions

From a Winnower of Corn to the Winds

To you, airy troop, who on passing wing fly over the world, and with a whistling whisper softly shake the shady foliage,

J'offre ces violettes,
Ces lis et ces fleurettes,
Et ces roses ici,
Ces vermeillettes roses,
Tout fraîchement écloses,
Et ces œillets aussi.

De votre douce haleine
Éventez cette plaine,
Éventez ce séjour:
Cependant que j'ahane
A mon blé, que je vanne
A la chaleur du jour.

A Vénus

AYANT après long désir
Pris de ma douce ennemie
Quelques arrhes du plaisir
Que sa rigueur me dénie,
  Je t'offre ces beaux œillets,
Vénus, je t'offre ces roses,

I offer these violets, these lilies and these flowerets and these
roses here, these reddening roses all freshly blooming, and these
carnations too.

With your soft breath fan this plain, fan this farmstead; while I
toil away at my corn which I winnow in the heat of the day.

To Venus

HAVING, after long desire, taken from my sweet enemy some small
advance of the pleasure which her cruelty refuses me, I offer you
these fine carnations, Venus, I offer you these roses whose ruby buds

Dont les boutons vermeillets
Imitent les lèvres closes
    Que j'ai baisé par trois fois,
Marchant tout beau dessous l'ombre
De ce buisson, que tu vois:
Et n'ai su passer ce nombre,
    Pource que la mère était
Auprès de là, ce me semble,
Laquelle nous aguettait:
De peur encore j'en tremble.
    Or je te donne des fleurs:
Mais si tu fais ma rebelle
Autant piteuse à mes pleurs
Comme à mes yeux elle est belle,
    Un myrte je dédierai
Dessus les rives de Loire
Et sur l'écorce écrirai
Ces quatre vers à ta gloire:

Thénot sur ce bord ici,
A Vénus sacre et ordonne
Ce myrte, et lui donne aussi
Ces troupeaux, et sa personne.

imitate the pouting lips which I kissed three times, walking softly in the shade of that bush which you see. And I was not able to exceed that number because the mother was near at hand – it seemed to me – and she was spying on us: I still tremble with fear at the thought.

Now I give you flowers; but if you make my rebel as compassionate to my tears as she is lovely in my eyes, I will dedicate a myrtle to you on the banks of the Loire, and on the bark I will write these four lines in your honour:

Thenot here on this bank to Venus consecrates and dedicates this myrtle, and gives her also these flocks and his own person.

Les Antiquités de Rome

TELLE que dans son char la Bérécynthienne,
Couronnée de tours et joyeuse d'avoir
Enfanté tant de dieux, telle se faisait voir
En ses jours plus heureux cette ville ancienne:

Cette ville, qui fut plus que la Phrygienne
Foisonnante en enfants, et de qui le pouvoir
Fut le pouvoir du monde, et ne se peut revoir
Pareille à sa grandeur, grandeur sinon la sienne.

Rome seule pouvait à Rome ressembler,
Rome seule pouvait Rome faire trembler:
Aussi n'avait permis l'ordonnance fatale

Qu'autre pouvoir humain, tant fût audacieux,
Se vantât d'égaler celle qui fit égale
Sa puissance à la terre, et son courage aux cieux.

The Antiquities of Rome

As in her chariot the Berecynthian, crowned with towers and joyful at having given birth to so many gods, so in its happier days appeared this ancient city:

This city, which was more than the Phrygian abounding in children, and whose power was world-wide, and the like of whose greatness cannot be seen again, since no greatness approaches hers.

Rome alone could resemble Rome, Rome alone could make Rome tremble. Therefore the decree of fate had not allowed

Any other human power, however daring, to boast that it could equal her who made her sway equal to the earth and her courage to the heavens.

(The Berecynthian was Cybele, mother of the gods. By the Phrygian city, Du Bellay probably meant Troy.)

PÂLES esprits et vous, ombres poudreuses,
Qui, jouissant de la clarté du jour,
Fîtes sortir cet orgueilleux séjour
Dont nous voyons les reliques cendreuses:

Dites, esprits – ainsi les ténébreuses
Rives de Styx non passable au retour,
Vous enlaçant d'un trois fois triple tour,
N'enferment point vos images ombreuses –

Dites-moi donc – car quelqu'une de vous
Possible encor se cache ici dessous –
Ne sentez-vous augmenter votre peine,

Quand quelquefois de ces coteaux romains
Vous contemplez l'ouvrage de vos mains
N'être plus rien qu'une poudreuse plaine?

Les Regrets

FRANCE, mère des arts, des armes et des lois,
Tu m'as nourri longtemps du lait de ta mamelle:
Ores, comme un agneau qui sa nourrice appele,
Je remplis de ton nom les antres et les bois.

PALE spirits and you, dusty ghosts, who, when you enjoyed the light of day, raised up this proud city whose crumbling remains we see:

Say, spirits – unless the dark banks of un-recrossable Styx, entwining you in a ninefold circle, imprison your shadowy phantoms –

Tell me, then – for one of you is perhaps still hidden underneath here – do you not feel your sorrow increase

When sometimes from these Roman slopes you contemplate the work of your hands and see that it is no more than a dusty plain?

Regrets

FRANCE, mother of the arts, of arms, and of laws, you have long fed me with the milk from your breast; now, like a lamb calling for its mother, I fill the caves and the woods with your name.

Si tu m'as pour enfant avoué quelquefois,
Que ne me réponds-tu maintenant, ô cruelle?
France, France, réponds à ma triste querelle:
Mais nul, sinon Écho, ne répond à ma voix.

Entre les loups cruels j'erre parmi la plaine;
Je sens venir l'hiver, de qui la froide haleine
D'une tremblante horreur fait hérisser ma peau.

Las, tes autres agneaux n'ont faute de pâture,
Ils ne craignent le loup, le vent, ni la froidure:
Si ne suis-je pourtant le pire de troupeau.

CEPENDANT que Magny suit son grand Avanson,
Panjas son Cardinal, et moi le mien encore,
Et que l'espoir flatteur, qui nos beaux ans dévore,
Appâte nos désirs d'un friand hameçon,

Tu courtises les rois, et d'un plus heureux son
Chantant l'heur de Henri, qui son siècle décore,

If at one time you owned me as your child, why do you not
answer me now, O cruel one? France, France, answer my plaintive
cry: but none, except Echo, replies to my voice.

Among the cruel wolves I stray over the plain; I feel the winter
coming and its cold breath makes my hair rise in trembling horror.

Alas, your other lambs have food in plenty, they do not fear the
wolf, the wind, or the cold: and yet I am not the worst of the
flock.

WHILE Magny follows his great Avanson,* Panjas his Cardinal,*
and I mine, too, and deceitful hope, consuming our best years, lures
on our desires with a tempting bait,

You [Ronsard] pay court to kings, and with more fortunate
strains singing the fortune of Henry,† who adorns his age, you

---

*Patrons of Du Bellay's friends in Rome, the poets Olivier de
Magny and Jean de Panjas.

†Henri II, King of France.

Tu t'honores toi-même et celui qui honore
L'honneur que tu lui fais par ta docte chanson.

Las, et nous cependant nous consumons notre âge
Sur le bord inconnu d'un étrange rivage,
Où le malheur nous fait ces tristes vers chanter,

Comme on voit quelquefois, quand la mort les appelle,
Arrangés flanc à flanc parmi l'herbe nouvelle,
Bien loin sur un étang trois cygnes lamenter.

HEUREUX qui, comme Ulysse, a fait un beau voyage,
Ou comme cestui-là qui conquit la toison,
Et puis est retourné, plein d'usage et raison,
Vivre entre ses parents le reste de son âge!

Quand reverrai-je, hélas, de mon petit village
Fumer la cheminée, et en quelle saison
Reverrai-je le clos de ma pauvre maison,
Qui m'est une province, et beaucoup d'avantage?

bring honour to yourself and to him who honours the honour
which you bring him by your learned song.

Meanwhile we, alas, consume our days on the unknown brink
of a foreign shore, where sorrow makes us sing these sad verses,

As one sees sometimes, when death is summoning them, drawn
up side by side on the young grass, far across a pond three swans
lamenting.

HAPPY the man who, like Ulysses, has had a good journey, or like
that man who won the fleece [Jason – the golden fleece], and then
came home full of experience and wisdom to live the rest of his days
among his family.

Ah, when shall I see the chimneys of my little village smoking,
and in what season shall I see the garden of my humble house,
which is a province, and much more, to me?

Plus me plaît le séjour qu'ont bâti mes aïeux
Que des palais romains le front audacieux;
Plus que le marbre dur me plaît l'ardoise fine,

Plus mon Loire gaulois que le Tibre latin,
Plus mon petit Liré que le Mont Palatin,
Et plus que l'air marin la douceur angevine.

Tu ne me vois jamais, Pierre, que tu ne die
Que j'étudie trop, que je fasse l'amour,
Et que d'avoir toujours ces livres à l'entour
Rend les yeux éblouis, et la tête alourdie.

Mais tu ne l'entends pas, car cette maladie
Ne me vient du trop lire ou du trop long séjour,
Ains de voir le bureau qui se tient chacun jour:
C'est, Pierre mon ami, le livre où j'étudie.

Ne m'en parle donc plus, autant que tu as cher
De me donner plaisir et de ne me fâcher:
Mais bien en cependant que d'une main habile

The home which my ancestors built pleases me more than the
lofty front of the Roman palaces: delicate slate pleases me more
than hard marble, my Gallic Loire more than the Latin Tiber, my
little Liré more than the Palatine Hill, and more than the sea air
the mildness of Anjou.

You never see me, Peter,* without telling me that I study too
much, that I should do some love-making, and that having these
books always around makes the eyes dull and the head heavy.

But you don't understand, for this sickness comes, not from
reading too much or staying indoors too long, but from seeing how
people behave in the daily round. That, Peter my friend, is the book
in which I study.

So stop talking about it, if you really want to give me pleasure
and not annoy me. Instead, while with skilful hand you are washing

---

*His Roman barber.

Tu me laves la barbe et me tonds les cheveux,
Pour me désennuyer, conte-moi si tu veux,
Des nouvelles du Pape, et du bruit de la ville.

Voici le Carnaval, menons chacun la sienne,
Allons baller en masque, allons nous pourmener,
Allons voir Marc-Antoine, ou Zany bouffonner
Avec son Magnifique à la Vénitienne:

Voyons courir le pal à la mode ancienne,
Et voyons par le nez le sot buffle mener:
Voyons le fier taureau d'armes environner,
Et voyons au combat l'adresse italienne:

Voyons d'œufs parfumés un orage grêler,
Et la fusée ardent' siffler menu par l'air.
Sus donc, dépêchons-nous, voici la pardonnance.

Il nous faudra demain visiter les saints lieux;
Là nous ferons l'amour, mais ce sera des yeux,
Car passer plus avant c'est contre l'ordonnance.

my beard and trimming my hair, tell me if you will, to cheer me up,
the news of the Pope and the gossip of the town.

THE Carnival is here, let's each take his girl, let us dance in masks,
let us walk about the town, let us go and see Mark Antony, or
Zanny* clowning, with his Venetian magnifico character.
   Let us go and see them racing for the *palio* [banner] in the old
style, and see the stupid buffalo led around by the nose; let us see
the fierce bull hemmed in with weapons, and see the Italian skill in
fighting.
   Let us see a shower of scented eggs raining down and the fiery
rockets hissing thick and fast through the air. Come on, let's hurry,
the pardoning has started.
   Tomorrow we must visit the holy places; there we will make
love, but it will be with our eyes, for to go any further is against the
regulation.

_____

*Names of actors or characters in the *Commedia dell'arte*.

LOUISE LABÉ

CLAIRE VÉNUS, qui erres par les cieux,
Entends ma voix qui en plaints chantera,
Tant que ta face au haut du ciel luira,
Son long travail et souci ennuyeux.

Mon œil veillant s'attendrira bien mieux,
Et plus de pleurs te voyant jettera.
Mieux mon lit mol de larmes baignera,
De ses travaux voyant témoins tes yeux.

Donc des humains sont les lassés esprits
De doux repos et de sommeil épris.
J'endure mal tant que le soleil luit:

Et quand je suis quasi toute cassée,
Et que me suis mise en mon lit lassée,
Crier me faut mon mal toute la nuit.

OH, si j'étais en ce beau sein ravie
De celui-là pour lequel vais mourant,

BRIGHT Venus, roving through the skies, hear my voice which, as long as your face shines in the height of heaven, will sing in plaintive tones of its long torment and heavy care.

My wakeful eye will be more easily grieved and will shed more tears for seeing you. It will bathe my soft bed more freely with tears when it sees that your eyes witness its sufferings.

Now the wearied spirits of men are overcome by sweet rest and sleep. I endure pain as long as the sun shines.

And when I am almost wholly broken and have lain down wearily on my bed, I must cry my pain the whole night through.

OH, if I were ravished in that sweet breast of him for whom I lan-

Si avec lui vivre le demeurant
De mes courts jours ne m'empêchait envie.

Si m'accolant me disait: «Chère amie,
Contentons-nous l'un l'autre,» s'assurant
Que jà tempête, Euripe, ni courant
Ne nous pourra disjoindre en notre vie:

Si, de mes bras le tenant accolé,
Comme du lierre est l'arbre encercelé,
La mort venait, de mon aise envieuse,

Lorsque, souef, plus il me baiserait
Et mon esprit sur ses lèvres fuirait,
Bien je mourrais, plus que vivante, heureuse.

BAISE-M'ENCOR, rebaise-moi et baise:
Donne-m'en un de tes plus savoureux,
Donne-m'en un de tes plus amoureux:
Je t'en rendrai quatre plus chauds que braise.

---

guish, if the spiteful world did not prevent me from living the remainder of my short days with him,

If, clasping me, he said: 'Dear love, let us content one another,' swearing that now neither tempest, Euripus* nor current would be able to separate us in our lives:

If, while I held him clasped in my arms as the tree is entwined by the ivy, death came, envious of my pleasure,

While softly he kissed me the more and my spirit fled upon his lips, I could well die, better than alive – happy.

KISS me again, re-kiss me and kiss: give me one of your most delicious, give me one of your most amorous: I will give you back four hotter than coals.

*A narrow strait in Greece.

Las, te plains-tu? ça, que ce mal j'apaise
En t'en donnant dix autres doucereux.
Ainsi, mêlant nos baisers tant heureux,
Jouissons-nous l'un de l'autre à notre aise.

Lors double vie à chacun ensuivra.
Chacun en soi et son ami vivra.
Permets-m'Amour penser quelque folie:

Toujours suis mal, vivant discrètement,
Et ne me puis donner contentement,
Si hors de moi ne fais quelque saillie.

PIERRE DE RONSARD

MIGNONNE, allons voir si la rose
Qui ce matin avait déclose
Sa robe de pourpre au soleil,
A point perdu cette vêprée
Les plis de sa robe pourprée,
Et son teint au vôtre pareil.

Las! voyez comme en peu d'espace,
Mignonne, elle a dessus la place
Las! las! ses beautés laissé choir!

There, is it hurting? Come, let me soothe that pain by giving you ten more soft ones. So, mingling our happy kisses, let us enjoy each other at our ease.

Then a double life will follow for both. Each will live in himself and in his dear. Allow me, Love, to think a little wildly:

I am always unhappy, living discreetly, and I can find no contentment if I do not sometimes sally out of myself.

MY sweet, let us go and see if the rose, which this morning opened its crimson robe to the sun, has not lost this evening the folds of its crimson dress and its colour like yours.

Ah! see how in so short a time, my sweet, it has, ah me, shed its

O vraiment marâtre Nature,
Puisqu'une telle fleur ne dure
Que du matin jusques au soir!

Donc, si vous me croyez, mignonne,
Tandis que votre âge fleuronne
En sa plus verte nouveauté,
Cueillez, cueillez votre jeunesse:
Comme à cette fleur, la vieillesse
Fera ternir votre beauté.

Ode

PLUSIEURS de leurs corps dénués
Se sont vus en diverse terre
Miraculeusement mués,
L'un en serpent et l'autre en pierre;

L'un en fleur, l'autre en arbrisseau,
L'un en loup, l'autre en colombelle:
L'un se vit changer en ruisseau,
Et l'autre devint arondelle.

beauties upon the ground! O truly stony-hearted Nature, since such a flower lasts only from the morning till the evening.

So, if you will heed me, sweet, while your young years bloom in their freshest newness, gather, gather your youth: as with this flower, age will wither your beauty.

MANY, divested of their bodies, have seen themselves in various lands miraculously transformed, one into a serpent and another into a stone;

One into a flower, another into a shrub, another into a wolf, another into a dove: one saw himself changed into a stream and another became a swallow.

Mais je voudrais être miroir
Afin que toujours tu me visses:
Chemise je voudrais me voir,
Afin que souvent tu me prisses.

Volontiers eau je deviendrais,
Afin que ton corps je lavasse:
Être du parfum je voudrais,
Afin que je te parfumasse.

Je voudrais être le ruban
Qui serre ta belle poitrine:
Je voudrais être le carcan
Qui orne ta gorge ivoirine.

Je voudrais être tout autour
Le corail qui tes lèvres touche,
Afin de baiser nuit et jour
Tes belles lèvres et ta bouche.

OR que Jupin, époint de sa semence,
Hume à longs traits les feux accoutumés,
Et que du chaud de ses reins allumés
L'humide sein de Junon ensemence;

But I would like to be a mirror, so that you should always see me: I would like to be a shift, so that you should often take me up.
Gladly would I become water, so that I should wash your body: I would like to be perfume, so that I should perfume you.
I would like to be the ribbon which clasps your lovely breast: I would like to be the necklace which adorns your ivory throat.
I would like to be the coral which colours your lips all around, so as to kiss night and day your lovely lips and your mouth.

Now that Jove, spurred on by his seed, snuffs in long draughts the familiar fires, and with the heat of his kindled loins makes fertile the moist bosom of Juno;

Or que la mer, or que la véhémence
Des vents fait place aux grands vaisseaux armés,
Et que l'oiseau parmi les bois ramés
Du Thracien les tensons recommence:

Or que les prés et or que les fleurs
De mille et mille et de mille couleurs
Peignent le sein de la terre si gaie,

Seul et pensif, aux rochers plus secrets
D'un cœur muet je conte mes regrets,
Et par les bois je vais celant ma plaie.

MARIE, levez-vous, vous êtes paresseuse:
Jà la gaie alouette au ciel a fredonné,
Et jà le rossignol doucement jargonné,
Dessus l'épine assis, sa complainte amoureuse.

Sus debout! allons voir l'herbelette perleuse,
Et votre beau rosier de boutons couronné,
Et vos œillets mignons auxquels aviez donné
Hier au soir de l'eau d'une main si soigneuse.

Now that the sea, now that the violence of the winds makes way
for the great rigged vessels, and the bird among the branchy woods
pipes the Thracian's [Orpheus'] madrigals anew:
Now that the fields and now that the flowers, with thousand,
thousand, and thousand colours paint the breast of the earth so gay,
Alone and pensive, to the most hidden rocks I tell my sorrows
with a silent heart and wander through the woods hiding my
wound.

GET UP, Marie, you lazy girl: the gay lark has already trilled in the
sky and the nightingale, sitting on the hawthorn, has already
sweetly warbled its amorous lay.
Get up! Get up! Let us go and see the pearly lawn and your
pretty rose-bush crowned with buds, and your pretty pinks to
which last night you gave water with so loving a hand.

Harsoir en vous couchant vous jurâtes vos yeux
D'être plus tôt que moi ce matin éveillée:
Mais le dormir de l'aube aux filles gracieux

Vous tient d'un doux sommeil encor les yeux sillée.
Ça! ça! que je les baise, et votre beau tétin
Cent fois pour vous apprendre à vous lever matin.

COMME on voit sur la branche, au mois de mai, la rose
En sa belle jeunesse, en sa première fleur,
Rendre le ciel jaloux de sa vive couleur,
Quand l'aube de ses pleurs au point du jour l'arrose:

La grâce dans sa feuille et l'amour se repose,
Embaumant les jardins et les arbres d'odeur:
Mais, battue ou de pluie ou d'excessive ardeur,
Languissante elle meurt feuille à feuille déclose.

Ainsi en ta première et jeune nouveauté,
Quand la terre et le ciel honoraient ta beauté,
La Parque t'a tuée, et cendre tu reposes.

Last night when you went to bed you swore by your eyes that
you would be awake earlier than me this morning; but the slumber
of dawn, so gracious to girls,
Keeps your eyes still sealed with a gentle sleep. There, there, let
me kiss them, and your pretty breast, a hundred times to teach you
to get up early.

As the rose appears on the branch, in May, in its lovely youth, in
its newest bloom, making the sky jealous of its brilliant hue, when
the dawn waters it with its tears at daybreak:
Grace in its petals and love lie hidden, filling the garden and
the trees with scent: but, beaten down by the rain or by excessive
heat, it languishes and dies, laid open petal by petal.
So in your early and youthful freshness, when earth and heaven
acclaimed your beauty, Fate slew you and you lie as dust.

Pour obsèques reçois mes larmes et mes pleurs,
Ce vase plein de lait, ce panier plein de fleurs,
Afin que vif et mort ton corps ne soit que roses.

l'Hymne des Démons

... Tout ainsi les Démons, qui ont le corps habile,
Aisé, souple et dispos, à se muer facile,
Changent bientôt de forme, et leur corps agile est
Transformé tout soudain en tout ce qu'il leur plaît:
Ores, en un tonneau grossement s'élargissent,
Ores, en peloton rondement s'étrécissent,
Ores, en un chevron les verriez allonger,
Ores mouvoir les pieds, et ores ne bouger.
Bien souvent on les voit se transformer en bête
Tronque par la moitié: l'une n'a que la tête,
L'autre n'a que les yeux, l'autre n'a que les bras,
Et l'autre que les pieds tout velus par là-bas.
... Les autres sont nommés par divers noms, Incubes,
Larves, Lares, Lémurs, Pénates et Succubes,

For your funeral receive my sobs and my tears, this vase full of
milk, this basket full of flowers, so that in life and in death your
body may be only roses.

The Hymn of the Demons

... In the same way demons, which have nimble bodies, lithe,
supple and alert, easily able to transform themselves, quickly change
their shape, and their agile bodies are rapidly turned into whatever
they please: now into a barrel they swell out fatly, now into a
ball they contract roundly, now into a rafter you would see them
lengthening, now moving their feet, and now not stirring. Often
they are seen turning into a beast with only part of a body: one has
only a head, another only eyes, another only arms, another only
feet all hairy underneath.
... The others are called by various names, Incubi, Larvae, Lares,
Lemures, Penates and Succubi, Night-Walkers, Lamians, which do

Empouses, Lamiens, qui ne vaguent pas tant
Que font les aérins; sans plus vont habitant
Autour de nos maisons, et de travers se couchent
Dessus notre estomac, et nous tâtent et touchent;
Ils remuent de nuit bancs, tables et tréteaux,
Clefs, huis, portes, buffets, lits, chaires, escabeaux,
Ou comptent nos trésors, ou jettent contre terre
Maintenant une épée, et maintenant un verre;
Toutefois au matin on ne voit rien cassé,
Ni meuble qui ne soit en sa place agencé.

On dit qu'en Norovègue ils se louent à gages
Et font comme valets des maisons les ménages,
Ils pansent les chevaux, ils vont tirer le vin,
Ils font cuire le rôt, ils serencent le lin,
Ils filent la fusée, et les robes nettoient
Au lever de leurs maîtres, et les places baloient.
Or' qui voudrait narrer les contes qu'on fait d'eux,
De tristes, de gaillards, d'horribles, de piteux,
On n'aurait jamais fait, car homme ne se treuve
Qui toujours n'en raconte une merveille neuve.

Les autres moins terrains sont à part habitants
Torrents, fleuves, ruisseaux, les lacs et les étangs,

not roam so much as the aerial spirits do; they are content to live round our homes and lie across our chests and prod and touch us; at night they move benches, tables and trestles, keys, doors, presses, beds, chairs, stools, or count our treasures, or sometimes fling down a sword, sometimes a glass. Yet in the morning nothing is found broken, nor any furniture disturbed from its place.

They say that in Norway they hire themselves out and do the work of the house like servants, they groom the horses, they draw the wine, they cook the roast, they rinse the washing, they spin the wool and brush the clothes when their masters rise, and sweep the rooms. If one tried to relate all the stories that are told of them, sad, comic, horrifying, or pitiful, one would never have finished, for every man you meet will always tell some wonderful new tale about them.

The other, less earthy kind are dwellers apart in torrents, rivers,

Les marais endormis et les fontaines vives,
Or' paraissant sur l'eau et ores sur les rives.
   Tant que les aérins ils n'ont d'affections,
Aussi leur corps ne prend tant de mutations:
Ils n'aiment qu'une forme, et volontiers icelle
Est du nombril en haut d'une jeune pucelle
Qui a les cheveux longs, et les yeux verts et beaux,
Contre-imitant l'azur de leurs propres ruisseaux.
Pour ce ils se font nommer Naïades, Néréides,
Les filles de Téthys, les cinquante Phorcydes,
Qui errent par la mer sur le dos des dauphins,
Bridant les esturbots, les fouches et les thins,
Aucunefois vaguant tout au sommet des ondes,
Aucunefois au bas des abîmes profondes . . .

Épitaphe de François Rabelais

  . . . JAMAIS le soleil ne l'a vu,
Tant fût-il matin, qu'il n'eût bu,
Et jamais au soir la nuit noire,
Tant fût tard, ne l'a vu sans boire,

streams, lakes and ponds, stagnant marshes and gushing springs, appearing now on the water and now on the banks.

They have not such varied feelings as the aerial ones, and so their bodies do not take on so many different shapes. They like a single form, and usually that is from the navel up the form of a young maiden with long hair and fair green eyes, resembling the azure of their own streams. Therefore they are called naiads, nereids, daughters of Tethys, the fifty daughters of Phorcys [sirens], who roam the seas on the backs of dolphins, bridling the turbots, the seals, and the tunnies, sometimes moving on the crest of the waves, sometimes at the bottom of the deep gulfs . . .

Epitaph on François Rabelais

. . . NEVER did the sun see him, however early it was, before he had drunk, and never in the evening did dark night, however late it

Car altéré sans nul séjour
Le galant buvait nuit et jour.
... Il chantait la grande massue
Et la jument de Gargantue,
Le grand Panurge, et le pays
Des Papimanes ébahis,
Leurs lois, leurs façons et demeures,
Et frère Jean des Antoumeures,
Et d'Epistème les combats;
Mais la Mort qui ne buvait pas
Tira le buveur de ce monde,
Et ores le fait boire en l'onde
Qui fuit trouble dans le giron
Du large fleuve d'Achéron.

    Or toi quiconque sois qui passes,
Sur sa fosse répands des tasses,
Répands du bril et des flacons,
Des cervelas et des jambons,
Car si encor dessous la lame
Quelque sentiment a son âme,
Il les aime mieux que des lis
Tant soient-ils fraîchement cueillis.

was, see him *not* drinking, for – thirsty without respite – the fellow drank night and day.
... He hymned the great club and the mare of Gargantua, great Panurge, and the country of the gaping Papimanes, their laws, their customs, and their dwellings, and Friar Jean des Entommeures and the battles of Epistemon; but Death, who did not drink, dragged the drinker from this world and now makes him drink in the water which flows muddily in the bosom of the wide River Acheron.

    Now, passer-by, whoever you be, spread cups upon his grave, spread foliage and flagons, saveloys and hams, for if his soul beneath the sod still has any feeling, he loves them better than lilies, however freshly gathered.

PIERRE DE RONSARD

Sonnet pour Sinope

Si j'étais Jupiter, maîtresse, vous seriez
Mon épouse Junon; si j'étais roi des ondes,
Vous seriez ma Téthys, reine des eaux profondes,
Et pour votre palais le monde vous auriez;

Si le monde était mien, avec moi vous tiendriez
L'empire de la terre aux mamelles fécondes,
Et dessus un beau coche, en longues tresses blondes,
Par le peuple en honneur déesse vous iriez.

Mais je ne suis pas dieu, et si ne le puis être;
Le ciel pour vous servir seulement m'a fait naître.
De vous seule je prends mon sort aventureux.

Vous êtes tout mon bien, mon mal, et ma fortune;
S'il vous plaît de m'aimer, je deviendrai Neptune,
Tout Jupiter, tout roi, tout riche et tout heureux.

Sonnet for Sinope

If I were Jupiter, mistress, you would be my spouse Juno; if I
were king of the waves, you would be my Tethys, queen of the
deep waters, and for your palace you would have the world.

If the world were mine, you would hold sway with me over the
earth with its fertile breasts, and in a splendid coach, with your
long fair tresses, you would ride among the people honoured as a
goddess.

But I am not a god, and I cannot be one; heaven gave me life
only to serve you. My hazardous fate depends on you alone.

You are my whole pleasure, my pain, and my fortune. If it
pleases you to love me, I shall become Neptune, wholly Jupiter,
wholly king, wholly rich, and wholly happy.

Sonnets pour Hélène

JE liai d'un filet de soie cramoisie
Votre bras l'autre jour, parlant avecques vous;
Mais le bras seulement fut captif de mes nouds,
Sans vous pouvoir lier ni cœur ni fantaisie.

Beauté que pour maîtresse unique j'ai choisie,
Le sort est inégal: vous triomphez de nous;
Vous me tenez esclave, esprit, bras et genoux,
Et Amour ne vous tient ni prise ni saisie.

Je veux parler, maîtresse, à quelque vieil sorcier,
Afin qu'il puisse au mien votre vouloir lier,
Et qu'une même plaie à nos cœurs soit semblable.

Je faux: l'amour qu'on charme est de peu de séjour.
Être beau, jeune, riche, éloquent, agréable,
Non les vers enchantés, sont les sorciers d'amour.

Sonnets for Helen

I BOUND a ribbon of crimson silk to your arm the other day while I was talking to you; but only the arm was captured by my knots, I could not bind your heart or your fancy.

Beauty whom I have chosen as my sole mistress, the chances are not even, you triumph over us; you hold me enslaved – mind, arms, and knees – and Love has neither hold nor grip upon you.

I mean to speak, mistress, to some old sorcerer, in order that he should bind your will to mine, and that the same shaft should pierce our two hearts.

I deceive myself: conjured love does not last long. To be handsome, young, rich, eloquent, agreeable, not enchanted verses, are the sorcerers of love.

Vous me dîtes, maîtresse, étant à la fenêtre,
Regardant vers Montmartre et les champs d'alentour:
«La solitaire vie et le désert séjour
Valent mieux que la Cour; je voudrais bien y être.

«A l'heure mon esprit de mes sens serait maître,
En jeûne et oraison je passerais le jour,
Je défierais les traits et les flammes d'Amour;
Ce cruel de mon sang ne pourrait se repaître.»

Quand je vous répondis: «Vous trompez de penser
Qu'un feu ne soit pas feu pour se couvrir de cendre;
Sur les cloîtres sacrés la flamme on voit passer;

«Amour dans les déserts comme aux villes s'engendre;
Contre un dieu si puissant, qui les dieux peut forcer,
Jeûnes ni oraisons ne se peuvent défendre.»

Le soir qu'Amour vous fit en la salle descendre
Pour danser d'artifice un beau ballet d'amour,

You said to me, mistress, as you stood at the window, looking
towards Montmartre and the fields around: 'A cloistered life and a
solitary existence are better than the Court; I wish I were there.

'Even now my mind would be master of my senses, I should
spend the day in fasting and prayer, I should defy the arrows and
the flames of Love; that cruel god would not be able to batten on
my blood.'

Then I answered you: 'You are mistaken to think that a fire is
not fire when it is covered with ashes; one sees the flame pass over
the holy cloisters.

'Love breeds in desert places as it breeds in towns; against so
powerful a god, who can command the gods, neither fasts nor
prayers are of any avail.'

That evening when Love brought you down into the hall to
dance so skilfully a fine ballet of love, your eyes, though it was

Vos yeux, bien qu'il fût nuit, ramenèrent le jour,
Tant ils surent d'éclairs par la place répandre.

Le ballet fut divin, qui se soulait reprendre,
Se rompre, se refaire, et tour dessus retour
Se mêler, s'écarter, se tourner à l'entour,
Contre-imitant le cours du fleuve de Méandre.

Ores il était rond, ores long, or étroit,
Or en pointe, en triangle en la façon qu'on voit
L'escadron de la grue évitant la froidure.

Je faux, tu ne dansais, mais ton pied voletait
Sur le haut de la terre; aussi ton corps s'était
Transformé pour ce soir en divine nature.

Te regardant assise auprès de ta cousine
Belle comme une aurore, et toi comme un soleil,
Je pensai voir deux fleurs d'un même teint pareil,
Croissantes en beauté sur la rive voisine.

night, brought back the day, so much light did they shed upon that scene.

The ballet was divine, as it went on linking up, breaking back, coming together again and, turning this way and that, mingling, drawing away, wheeling around, imitating the course of the river Meander.

Now it was round, now long, now narrow, now pointed, triangular in the shape of a flight of cranes fleeing south from the cold.

I am wrong, sweet, you did not dance, but your foot fluttered over the ground; and so your body took on for that evening a divine quality.

As I watched you sitting beside your cousin, she lovely as the dawn and you as the sun, I seemed to see two flowers of the same hue, growing in beauty on the bank near by.

La chaste, sainte, belle et unique Angevine,
Vite comme un éclair sur moi jeta son œil;
Toi, comme paresseuse et pleine de sommeil,
D'un seul petit regard tu ne m'estimas digne.

Tu t'entretenais seule au visage abaissé,
Pensive toute à toi, n'aimant rien que toi-même,
Dédaignant un chacun d'un sourcil ramassé,

Comme une qui ne veut qu'on la cherche ou qu'on l'aime.
J'eus peur de ton silence et m'en allai tout blême,
Craignant que mon salut n'eût ton œil offensé.

QUAND vous serez bien vieille, au soir, à la chandelle,
Assise auprès du feu, dévidant et filant,
Direz, chantant mes vers, en vous émerveillant:
«Ronsard me célébrait du temps que j'étais belle.»

Lors vous n'aurez servante oyant telle nouvelle,
Déjà sous le labeur à demi sommeillant,
Qui au bruit de mon nom ne s'aille réveillant,
Bénissant votre nom de louange immortelle.

The chaste, virtuous, lovely, and peerless Angevine girl turned her eyes towards me as swift as a flash: you, as though indolent and full of sleep, did not count me worthy of a single little glance.

You communed with yourself with your head bent low, wholly self-absorbed, loving nothing but yourself, disdaining each and all with knitted brow,

Like one who does not want to be sought out or loved. I was frightened by your silence and went away very pale, fearing that my greeting had offended your eye.

WHEN you are very old, at evening, by candlelight, sitting near the fire spooling and spinning the wool, you will say, in wonder, as you sing my verses: 'Ronsard praised me in the days when I was beautiful.'

Then not one of your servants who hears that news, though already half asleep over her work, but will start awake at the sound of my name, and bless your name of immortal renown.

Je serai sous la terre et, fantôme sans os,
Par les ombres myrteux je prendrai mon repos;
Vous serez au foyer une vieille accroupie,

Regrettant mon amour et votre fier dédain.
Vivez, si m'en croyez, n'attendez à demain:
Cueillez dès aujourd'hui les roses de la vie.

Derniers Vers

Il faut laisser maisons et vergers et jardins,
Vaisselles et vaisseaux que l'artisan burine,
Et chanter son obsèque en la façon du cygne
Qui chante son trépas sur les bords Méandrins.

C'est fait, j'ai dévidé le cours de mes destins,
J'ai vécu, j'ai rendu mon nom assez insigne:
Ma plume vole au ciel pour être quelque signe,
Loin des appâts mondains qui trompent les plus fins.

I shall be under the ground, a boneless ghost, taking my rest in the myrtles' shade; you will be an old woman crouching by the hearth, regretting my love and your own proud scorn. Heed me and live now, do not wait till tomorrow. Gather today the roses of life.

Last Verses

It is time to leave houses and orchards and gardens, vessels and plate which the craftsman engraves, and to sing one's passing as does the swan, when it sings its death on the banks of the Meander.

It is over, I have unravelled the course of my destiny, I have lived, I have made my name famous enough; my quill flies to heaven to become some sign there, far from the worldly lures which deceive the most subtle.

Heureux qui ne fut onc, plus heureux qui retourne
En rien comme il était, plus heureux qui séjourne,
D'homme fait nouvel ange, auprès de Jésus-Christ,

Laissant pourrir çà-bas sa dépouille de boue,
Dont le sort, la fortune et le destin se joue,
Franc des liens du corps pour n'être qu'un esprit.

RÉMY BELLEAU

Le Béril

LE Béril que je chante est une pierre fine,
Imitant le vert gai des eaux de la marine,
Quand les fiers Aquilons mollement accoisés
Ont fait place aux Zéphyrs sur les flots reposés.
Quelquefois le Béril a la face dorée
Comme liqueur de miel fraîchement épurée,
Dont le lustre est faiblet s'il n'est fait à biseau,
Car le rebat de l'angle hausse son lustre beau:
Autrement languissant, morne et de couleur paille,
Sans les rayons doublés que lui donne la taille.

Happy is he who never was, happier he who returns to the nothingness which he was, happier [still] he who dwells, transformed from man into a new angel, at the side of Jesus Christ,

Leaving to rot down here his body of clay, with which fate and fortune and destiny sport, free from the bonds of flesh to be nothing but a spirit.

The Beryl

THE Beryl of which I sing is a precious stone, resembling the gay green of the waters of the sea when the stormy blasts, gently appeased, have given place to the zephyrs on the calmed waves. Sometimes the Beryl has a golden surface like newly-strained liquid honey, but its lustre is feeble if it is not bevelled, for the blow of the tool's edge heightens its fine lustre which is otherwise sickly, dull, and straw-coloured, lacking the double gleams which cutting gives to it.

Le meilleur est celui dont le visage peint
De l'Émeraude fine imite le beau teint:
Seul le rivage Indois le Béril nous envoie,
Soit ou vert ou doré: pour les durtés du foie
Et pour le mal des yeux il est fort souverain,
Les soupirs trop hâtés il appaise soudain,
Le hoquet et les rots: entretient le ménage
De l'homme et de la femme ès lois de mariage:
Il chasse la paresse, et d'un pouvoir ami
Il rabaisse l'orgueil d'un cruel ennemi.

Béril, je te suppli', si telle est ta puissance,
Chasse notre ennemi hors les bornes de France;
Trop de peuple français a senti les efforts
De son bras enivré du sang de tant de morts.

Prière

TES mains m'ont fait et repétri de chair,
Comme un potier qui de grâce gentille
Tourne en vaisseau une masse d'argille:
Puis tout soudain tu me fais trébucher.

The best is the sort whose tinted surface resembles the lovely hue of fine emeralds. Only the Indian shore sends us the Beryl, either green or golden. For hardenings of the liver and for eye diseases it is a sovereign remedy, it immediately calms panting, hiccups, and belching. It maintains the union of man and woman within the laws of marriage. It drives away sloth and with its friendly influence humbles the pride of a cruel enemy.

Beryl, I beg you, if such is your power, drive our enemy beyond the frontiers of France; too many Frenchmen have felt the weight of his arm made drunk by the blood of so many dead.

Prayer

YOUR hands have made me and modelled me from flesh, like a potter who with delicate skill turns a lump of clay into a vessel: then suddenly You make me stumble.

Souvienne-toi avant que me damner
Que de limon et de bourbe fangeuse
Tu m'as formé, et qu'en terre poudreuse
Après ma mort me feras retourner.

Tu m'as coulé comme le lait nouveau,
Qui s'épaissit et se caille en présure,
De nerfs et d'os assemblé ma figure,
Puis, revêtu et de chair et de peau,

Tu m'as donné et la vie et les ans,
Me conduisant au sentier de ta grâce,
Et aux rayons de ta divine face
Guidé mes pas, mon esprit et mes sens.

ÉTIENNE JODELLE

DES astres, des forêts, et d'Achéron l'honneur,
Diane au monde haut, moyen et bas préside,
Et ses chevaux, ses chiens, ses Euménides guide,
Pour éclairer, chasser, donner mort et horreur.

Remember before You damn me that You formed me from mire
and slimy mud, and that after my death You will make me return to
dusty earth.

You poured me like fresh milk, which thickens and curdles in
rennet, You put together my body from nerves and bones, then,
clothed with flesh and skin,

You gave me life and years, leading me in the way of your grace,
and by the light of your divine face have guided my steps, my
spirit, and my senses.

THE pride of the heavens, of the forests, and of Acheron, Diana
presides over the upper, middle, and lower worlds, and guides her
horses, her hounds, and her Furies to illumine, hunt, sow death and
horror.

Tel est le lustre grand, la chasse et la frayeur
Qu'on sent sous ta beauté claire, prompte, homicide,
Que le haut Jupiter, Phébus, et Pluton cuide
Son foudre moins pouvoir, son arc, et sa terreur.

Ta beauté par ses rais, par son rets, par la crainte,
Rend l'âme éprise, prise, et au martyre étreinte:
Luis-moi, prends-moi, tiens-moi, mais hélas, ne me perds

Des flambeaux forts et griefs, feux, filets et encombres,
Lune, Diane, Hécate, aux cieux, terre et enfers
Ornant, quétant, gênant nos dieux, nous, et nos ombres.

JEAN-ANTOINE DE BAÏF

L'Hippocrène

Vers baïfins

MUSE, reine d'Hélicon, fille de mémoire, ô déesse,
O des poètes l'appui, favorise ma hardiesse.

Such is the bright lustre, the hunt, and the fear which springs
from your clear, swift, murderous beauty, that mighty Jupiter,
Phoebus Apollo, and Pluto think they can do less with thunder,
with bow, and with terror.

Your beauty by its beams, by its snares, by fear, leaves the heart
captivated, captured, and martyred. Shine on me, seize me, hold
me, but ah, do not destroy me

With your bright and hurtful torches, fires, nets, and pitfalls –
Moon, Diana, Hecate, in heaven, earth, and hell gracing, harrying,
tormenting our gods, us, and our ghosts.

The Horse's Fountain

(In Baïfin verse – a name coined by de Baïf for the fifteen-foot
line of his own invention.)

MUSE, Queen of Helicon, Daughter of Memory, O Goddess, O
protectress of poets, prosper my adventurous undertaking; I wish

Je veux donner aux Français un vers de plus libre
accordance,
Pour le joindre au luth sonné d'une moins contrainte
cadence.
Fais qu'il oigne doucement des oyants les pleines oreilles,
Dedans dégouttant flatteur un miel doucereux à mer-
veilles.
Je veux d'un nouveau sentier m'ouvrir l'honorable
passage
Pour aller sur votre mont m'ombroyer sous votre bocage,
Et ma soif désaltérer en votre fontaine divine
Qui sourdit du mont cavé dessous la corne Pégasine,
Lorsque le cheval ailé bondit en l'air hors de l'ondée
Du sang qui coulait du col de la Méduse outrecuidée.
... Et nulle bête depuis n'a touché cette onde argentine,
Qu'en mémoire du cheval ils surnommèrent chevaline,
Fors les chantres oisillons qui par le laurierin bocage
Fredonnetant leurs chansons dégoisent un mignot
ramage.
Mais les corbeaux croassants ni les corneilles jaseresses
Ni les criards chats-huants ni les agaces jangleresses
Ne touchent à la belle eau, qui, coulant de la nette source,

to give the French a line of freer harmony, to be linked to the lute
played with a less constrained cadence. Make it anoint sweetly the
open ears of its hearers, caressingly dropping in a marvellously
suave honey. I want to blaze for myself a glorious new path, by
which to go up to your mountain and sit in the shade of your grove
and quench my thirst at your divine spring which gushed from the
hollow mount beneath the hoof of Pegasus, when the winged horse
bounded skywards out of the torrent of blood which flowed from
the neck of the overweening Medusa.
... And no creature since has touched that silvery water, which
in memory of the horse they dubbed the Horse's Fountain, except
the fledgling songsters which, warbling their songs through the
laurelled grove, pour out a pretty twittering. But neither the cawing
crows nor the chattering rooks nor the screeching owls nor the
noisy magpies touch the fine water which, flowing from the clear

Sur un sablon argentin crêpe sa tournoyante course
Alentour de cent préaux et cent verdoyantes îlettes,
Là où la fraîche moiteur abreuve dix mille fleurettes. . .

Épitaphe

[*des protestants tués le jour de la Saint-Barthélemy*]

PAUVRES corps où logeaient ces esprits turbulents,
Naguère la terreur des princes de la terre,
Même contre le ciel osant faire la guerre,
Déloyaux, obstinés, pervers et violents:

Aujourd'hui le repas des animaux volants
Et rampants charogniers, et de ces vers qu'enserre
La puante voirie, et du peuple qui erre
Sous les fleuves profonds en la mer se coulant:

Pauvres corps, reposez; si vos malheureux os,
Nerfs et veines et chair, sont dignes de repos,
Qui ne purent souffrir le repos de la France.

spring, winds its twisting course over silvery sand around a hundred meadows and a hundred green islets, upon which the cool moisture waters ten thousand flowers...

Epitaph

[*On the Protestants killed on St Bartholomew's Day*]

POOR bodies in which those turbulent spirits lodged, once the terror of the princes of the earth, presuming to make war even against heaven, disloyal, stubborn, perverse, and violent:
Today the pasture of the flying creatures and the creeping carrion-beasts, and of those worms which the stinking sewers contain, and of the nation which roams under the deep rivers flowing down to the sea:
Poor bodies, rest in peace; if your unhappy bones, nerves, veins, and flesh are worthy of peace which could not allow France to be at peace.

Esprits dans les carfours toutes les nuits criez:
O mortels avertis, et voyez et croyez
Que le forfait retarde et ne fuit la vengeance.

JEAN PASSERAT

Villanelle

J'AI perdu ma tourterelle:
Est-ce point celle que j'ois?
Je veux aller après elle.

Tu regrettes ta femelle.
Hélas! aussi fais-je, moi.
J'ai perdu ma tourterelle.

Si ton amour est fidèle,
Aussi est ferme ma foi;
Je veux aller après elle.

Ta plainte se renouvelle,
Toujours plaindre je me dois;
J'ai perdu ma tourterelle.

Spirits every night cry at the crossroads: O mortals now warned, see and believe that crime delays vengeance, but does not escape it.

Villanelle

I HAVE lost my turtle-dove: Is that not she whom I hear? I want to go after her.

You pine for your mate. So, alas, do I. I have lost my turtle-dove.

If your love is faithful, so is my faith constant; I want to go after her.

Your grieving is renewed, I must grieve always; I have lost my turtle-dove.

En ne voyant plus la belle,
Plus rien de beau je ne vois;
Je veux aller après elle.

Mort, que tant de fois j'appelle,
Prends ce qui se donne à toi!
J'ai perdu ma tourterelle;
Je veux aller après elle.

Ode

(*Vers mesurés rimés*)

CE petit dieu, colère archer, léger oiseau,
    A la parfin ne me lairra que le tombeau,
Si du grand feu que je nourris ne s'amortit la vive ardeur.
    Une été froid, un hiver chaud, me gèle et fond,
        Mine mes nerfs, glace mon sang, ride mon front:
Je me meurs vif, ne mourant point: je sèche au temps de
    ma verdeur.
        Sotte, trop tard à repentir tu te viendras:
        De m'avoir fait ce mal à tort tu te plaindras.

No longer seeing my fair one, nothing fair can I see; I want to
go after her.

Death, on whom I call so often, take what is offered you. I have
lost my turtle-dove; I want to go after her.

Ode

(*Rhymed rhythmic verse*)

THIS little god, angry archer, light-winged bird, in the end will
leave me only the tomb, if the sharp heat of the great fire which I
feed is not cooled. A cold summer, a hot winter, freezes and melts
me, saps my nerves, ices my blood, furrows my brow: I am dying
alive, not dying: I wither in the time of my greenness. Fool, too
late will you come to repent: you will complain wrongly that you

Tu t'attends donc à me chercher remède au jour que je
    mourrai?
    D'un amour tel méritait moins la loyauté
   Que de goûter du premier fruit de ta beauté?
Je le veux bien, tu ne veux pas, tu le voudras, je ne
    pourrai.

NICOLAS RAPIN

Sur la bataille d'Ivry

(*Vers anapestiques rimés*)

CHEVALIERS généreux, qui avez le courage françois,
Accourez, accourez secourir l'héritier de vos rois,
Secourez votre roi naturel, si vaillant, si guerrier,
A la peine, à la charge, à l'assaut le premier, le dernier:
    Un roi ne s'est jamais vu
    De tant de grâce pourvu.

have done this harm to me. Are you waiting until the day of my
death to find me a remedy? Did the constancy of such a love de-
serve less than to taste the first-fruits of your beauty? I am willing,
you are not willing, you will be willing, I shall not be able.

The Battle of Ivry

(*Anapaestic verse with rhymes*)

NOBLE knights, brave French hearts, ride up, ride up and rally to
the heir of your Kings, rally to your natural King, so brave, so
soldierly, in the thick of the battle, in the charge, in the assault the
first and the last [to remain]; no king has ever been seen endowed
with so much grace.

A cheval, à cheval, casaniers, tout affaire laissé;
Le loyal coutelas à la main et le casque baissé,
Débattez courageux votre honneur, votre vie et vos
      biens;
Ne souffrez ce tyran, qui s'accroît de la perte des siens,
    Ravir le sceptre et les lois
    Du grand royaume françois.

Ne craignez de donner la bataille et le choc commencer,
Attaquez et donnez à ce gros qui se veut avancer;
Ce ne sont que mutins, maladroits à la guerre et aux
      coups,
Qui jamais ne sauront soutenir ni tenir devant vous:
    Au traître, lâche et trompeur,
    L'écharpe blanche fait peur.

De clairons, de tambours et de voix animez le combat,
Côtoyez votre roi, qui premier à la presse combat,
Désireux de trouver ce voleur que l'Érynne poursuit;
Il a honte, il a peur, je le vois, le renard, qui s'enfuit:
    Io péan! s'en est fait,
    Io! triomphe parfait.

    To horse, to horse, home-keepers, leaving all [other] business; with your faithful swords in hand and your helms lowered, fight bravely for your honour, your lives and possessions; do not allow that tyrant who grows fat on the woes of his countrymen to usurp the sceptre and the rule of the great kingdom of France.

    Do not fear to give battle and to begin the clash, attack and charge on that main body which offers to advance; they are only rebels, unskilled in war and at blows, who will never be able to stand or hold fast before you: into the traitor, cowardly and deceitful, the white scarf strikes fear.

    Stir up the fight with bugles, drums and cries, advance beside your King, fighting in the forefront of the fray, bent on finding that brigand whom the vengeful Fury pursues; he is ashamed, he is afraid, I see him, the fox, slipping away:

    Io pœan! the day is won. *Io!* victory is complete.

ROBERT GARNIER

Élégie sur la mort de Ronsard

... A<small>DIEU</small>, mon cher Ronsard; l'abeille en votre tombe
    Fasse toujours son miel;
Que le baume arabic à tout jamais y tombe,
    Et la manne du ciel,
Le laurier y verdisse avecque le lierre
    Et le myrte amoureux;
Riche en mille boutons, de toutes parts l'enserre
    Le rosier odoreux,
Le thym, le basilic, la franche marguerite,
    Et notre lis françois,
Et cette rouge fleur où la plainte est écrite
    Du malcontent Grégeois.
Les nymphes de Gâtine et les naïades saintes
    Qui habitent le Loir,
Le venant arroser de larmettes épreintes,
    Ne cessent de douloir.
Las! Cloton a tranché le fil de votre vie
    D'une piteuse main,

Elegy on the Death of Ronsard

... F<small>AREWELL</small>, my dear Ronsard, may the bee always make its honey in your tomb; may gum Arabic drip for ever in there and the heavenly manna, may the laurel grow green there with the ivy and the amorous myrtle; rich with a thousand buds, may the fragrant rosebush enclose it on every side, with thyme, basil, the simple daisy, and our French lily, and that red flower on which the complaint of the discontented Greek is written.* May the nymphs of Gâtine and the sacred naiads who dwell in the Loire, coming to water it with flowing tears, not cease to mourn. Alas, Clotho has snipped the thread of your life with a merciful hand, seeing it pur-

---

*A kind of hyacinth which sprang from the blood of Ajax.

La voyant de vieillesse et de goutte suivie,
　　　Torturage inhumain;
Voyant la pauvre France, en son corps outragée
　　　Par le sanglant effort
De ses enfants qui l'ont tant de fois ravagée,
　　　Soupirer à la mort;
Le Suisse aguerri, qui aux combats se loue,
　　　L'Anglais fermé de flots,
Ceux qui boivent le Pô, le Tage et la Danoue
　　　Fondre dessus son dos,
Ainsi que le vautour, qui de griffes bourrelles
　　　Va sans fin tirassant
De Prométhé' le foie, en pâtures nouvelles
　　　Coup sur coup renaissant.
Les meurtres inhumains se font entre les frères,
　　　Spectacle plein d'horreur,
Et déjà les enfants courent contre leurs pères
　　　D'une aveugle fureur;
Le cœur des citoyens se remplit de furies;
　　　Les paysans écartés
Meurent contre une haie; on ne voit que tûries
　　　Par les champs désertés.

sued by old age and gout, an inhuman torture; seeing poor France, outraged in her body by the murderous assault of her children who have ravaged her so often, sighing for death; [seeing] the warlike Switzer, who hires himself for fighting, the Englishman fenced with waves, those who drink of the Po, the Tagus, and the Danube swooping down upon her like the vulture, which with racking claws endlessly tears out the liver of Prometheus, time after time reborn as new food for it. Inhuman killings take place between brothers – a sight full of horror – and already children leap upon their fathers in blind fury; the citizens' hearts are filled with rage; the isolated peasants die against a hedge; only slaughters are seen in the deserted fields. And then go and sing the glory of our France in

Et puis allez chanter l'honneur de notre France
    En siècles si maudits!
Attendez-vous qu'aucun vos labeurs récompense
    Comme on faisait jadis?
La triste pauvreté nos chansons accompaigne;
    La Muse, les yeux bas,
Se retire de nous, voyant que l'on dédaigne
    Ses antiques ébats.
Vous êtes donc heureux, et votre mort heureuse,
    O Cygne des François;
Ne lamentez que nous, dont la vie ennuyeuse
    Meurt le jour mille fois.
Vous errez maintenant aux campaignes d'Élise,
    A l'ombre des vergers,
Où chargent en tout temps, assurés de la bise,
    Les jaunes orangers,
Où les prés sont toujours tapissés de verdure,
    Les vignes de raisins,
Et les petits oiseaux gazouillant au murmure
    Des ruisseaux cristallins . . .

such accursed times! Do you think that any will reward your labours as they used to do? Sad poverty accompanies our songs; the Muse, with eyes downcast, withdraws from us, seeing that her ancient revels are despised. So you are happy, and your death is happy, O Swan of the French; mourn only for us, whose dismal lives die a hundred deaths a day. You wander now in the fields of Elyseum in the shade of the orchards, where in all seasons, secure from the storm, the yellow orange-trees are laden with fruit, where the meadows are always covered with green, the vines with grapes, and the little birds twittering to the murmur of the crystalline streams . . .

GUILLAUME DE SALLUSTE DU BARTAS

Les Semaines

[Louanges de la terre]

JE te salue, ô Terre, ô Terre porte-grains,
Porte-or, porte-santé, porte-habits, porte-humains,
Porte-fruits, porte-tours, alme, belle, immobile,
Patiente, diverse, odorante, fertile,
Vêtue d'un manteau tout damassé de fleurs,
Passementé de flots, bigarré de couleurs.
Je te salue, ô cœur, racine, base ronde,
Pied du grand animal qu'on appelle le Monde,
Chaste épouse du Ciel, assuré fondement
Des étages divers d'un si grand bâtiment.
Je te salue, ô sœur, mère, nourrice, hôtesse
Du Roi des Animaux. Tout, ô grande princesse,
Vit en faveur de toi. Tant de cieux tournoyants
Portent pour t'éclairer leurs astres flamboyants.
Le feu, pour t'échauffer, sur les flottantes nues
Tient ses pures ardeurs en arcade étendues.

The Weeks

[In Praise of the Earth]

HAIL to you, O Earth, grain-bearer, gold-bearer, health-bearer, clothes-bearer, man-bearer, fruit-bearer, tower-bearer, kindly, beautiful, immovable, patient, various, sweet-smelling, fertile, clad with a mantle all damasked with flowers, braided with waters, motley with colours. Hail to you, O heart, root, round base, foot of the great creature which is called the Universe, chaste spouse of heaven, sure foundation of the different storeys of so great an edifice. Hail to you, O sister, mother, nurse, hostess of the King of the Animals. Everything, O great princess, exists for your benefit. So many wheeling heavens bear their flaming stars to give light to you. To warm you, the fire stretches its pure ardours arch-like

L'air, pour te raffraîchir, se plaît d'être secous
Or d'un âpre Borée, or d'un Zéphyre doux.
L'eau, pour te détremper, de mers, fleuves, fontaines,
Entrelace ton corps tout ainsi que de veines.
Hé! que je suis marri que les plus beaux esprits
T'ayent pour la plupart, ô Terre, en tel mépris;
Et que les cœurs plus grands abandonnent superbes
Le rustique labeur et le souci des herbes
Aux hommes plus brutaux, aux hommes de nul prix,
Dont les corps sont de fer et de plomb les esprits . . .

[La Création des oiseaux]

LE céleste Phénix commença son ouvrage
Par le Phénix terrestre, ornant d'un tel plumage
Ses membres revivants que l'annuel flambeau
De Cairan jusqu'en Fez ne voit rien de plus beau.
   Il fit briller ses yeux, il lui planta pour crête
Un astre flamboyant au sommet de sa tête:
Il couvrit son col d'or, d'écarlate son dos
Et sa queue d'azur, puis voulut qu'Atropos

above the floating clouds. To refresh you, the air is content to be shaken, now by a biting north wind, now by a gentle zephyr. To bathe you, the water interlaces your body with seas, rivers, springs, as though with veins. Ah, it grieves me to think that the finest minds hold you, in general, O Earth, in such disdain; and that the noblest hearts contemptuously leave rustic toil and the care of the plants to the most sottish men, men of no account, whose bodies are of iron and whose minds are of lead . . .

[The Creation of the Birds]

THE heavenly Phoenix began his work with the earthly Phoenix, adorning his constantly resurrected members with such plumage that the yearly torch [of the sun] from Cairo to Fez sees nothing more beautiful.

   He made his eyes shine, he planted a flaming star as a crest for him on the top of his head: he covered his neck with gold, his back with scarlet and his tail with azure, then ordained that Death should

Lui servît de Vénus, et qu'une mort féconde
Rendît son âge égal au long âge du monde.
... L'unique oiseau ramant par des sentes nouvelles
Se voit bientôt suivi d'une infinité d'ailes,
Diverses en grandeur, couleur et mouvement,
Ailes que l'Éternel engendre en un moment.
La flairante Arondelle à toutes mains bricole,
Tournoie, virevolte, et plus raide s'envole
Que la flèche d'un Turc, qui voulant décocher,
Fait la corde au tétin et l'arc au fer toucher.
Jà volant elle chante, et chantant, elle pense
D'employer en lieu sûr plus d'art que de dépense
A bâtir un palais, qui, rond par le devant,
Servira de modèle au maçon plus savant.
Elle charge déjà son bec de pailles frêles,
Et ses ongles de terre et d'eau ses noires ailes;
Elle en fait un mortier, et jette proprement
D'un logis demi-rond l'assuré fondement.

do him the service of Love, and that a fertile death should make his life equal to the long life of the world.*

... The sole bird of its kind, soaring on new paths, soon sees itself followed by an infinite number of wings, various in size, colour, and motion, wings which the Almighty engenders in a moment. The scenting swallow casts to and fro, wheels, swoops back, and darts off more swiftly than the arrow of a Turk who, about to let fly, makes the bowstring touch his breast and the barb touch the bow. Now flying, she sings, and as she sings she plans to exercise in some safe place more skill than expenditure by building a house which, rounded in front, will serve as a model to the most cunning mason. Already she loads her beak with slender straws, her claws with earth and her dark wings with water; she makes mortar from this and neatly throws up the firm foundation of a half-round dwelling.

---

*The Phoenix of the legend was the sole bird of its species and so could not mate. On ageing, it plunged into fire and was reborn periodically from its own ashes. The 'heavenly Phoenix' of the first line is God, who became the resurrected Christ.

La gentille Alouette avec son tire-lire
Tire l'ire à l'iré, et tire-lirant tire
Vers la voûte du ciel: puis son vol vers ce lieu
Vire, et désire dire: adieu Dieu, adieu Dieu.
Le peint Chardonneret, le Pinson, la Linotte
Jà donnent aux frais vents leur plus mignarde note.
... Le Colchide Faisan, le fécond Étourneau,
La chaste Tourterelle et le lascif Moineau,
Le Tourt becque-raisin, la Pie babillarde,
La friande Perdrix, la Palombe grisarde,
Le petit Benarric, mets digne des grands rois,
Et le vert Papegai, singe de notre voix,
Font la cour au Phénix, son divin chant admirent,
Et dans l'or et l'azur de ses plumes se mirent ...

[*La Tour de Babel*]

Ici pour dur ciment nuit et jour on amasse
Des étangs bitumeux l'eau gluantement grasse.

The pretty lark with its *tirra-lirra* draws the wrath from the wrathful and, carolling, draws towards the vault of heaven, then turns its flight towards this place (the earth) and tries to say: Goodbye God, goodbye God. The bright-painted goldfinch, the chaffinch, the linnet, now give to the fresh winds their prettiest notes. ... The pheasant of Colchis, the fast-breeding starling, the chaste turtle-dove and the wanton sparrow, the grape-pecking blackbird, the talkative magpie, the dainty partridge, the greyish wood-pigeon, the little blackcap – a dish fit for great kings – and the green parakeet, the aper of our voice, pay court to the Phoenix, admire his divine song, and see themselves reflected in the gold and azure of his feathers...

[*The Tower of Babel*]

Here for hard cement they collect night and day the glutinously greasy water of the bituminous lakes. Here the tiler bakes the dust

Le tuilier cuit ici dans ses fourneaux fumants
En brique la poussière. Ici les fondements
Jusqu'aux enfers on creuse, et les impures âmes
Revoyent contre espoir du beau soleil les flammes.

Tout le ciel retentit au dur son des marteaux,
Et les poissons du Tigre en tremblent sous les eaux.
De tour et de longueur les murs rougeâtres croissent;
Leur ombre s'étend loin, jà de loin ils paroissent;
Tout bouillonne d'ouvriers, et les faibles humains
Pensent au premier jour toucher le ciel des mains.

Quoi voyant, l'Éternel renfrogne son visage,
Et d'un son qui, grondant, roule comme un orage
Par les champs nuageux, déracine les monts,
Et fait crouler du ciel les immobiles gonds:

«Voyez (dit-il) ces nains, voyez cette racaille,
Ces fils de la poussière. Oh, la belle muraille!
Oh, l'imprenable tour! Oh, que ce fort est seur
Contre tant de canons braqués par ma fureur!

into bricks in his smoking kilns. Here they dig the foundations
down to hell and, against all hope, the impure souls see the flames
of the sweet sun again.

The whole sky rings with the hard sound of the hammers, and
the fishes of the Tigris tremble to hear it beneath the waters. In cir-
cuit and length the reddish walls grow; their shadow stretches far,
now from afar they can be seen; the whole place seethes with work-
men, and those weak human beings expect daily to touch the sky
with their hands.

Seeing this, the Almighty puckers his brow and, with a noise
which, rumbling, rolls like a storm over the cloudy fields [of the
sky], uproots the mountains and bursts open the fixed hinges of
heaven:

'Look,' he says, 'at these dwarfs, look at this rabble, these sons
of the dust. Oh, the marvellous wall! Oh, the impregnable tower!
Oh, how secure is this fortress against so many cannons trained
[against it] by my wrath! I swore to them that the fertile earth

Je leur avais juré que la terre féconde
Ne craindrait désormais la colère de l'onde;
Ils s'en font un rempart. Je voulais qu'épandus
Ils peuplassent le monde; et les voici rendus
Prisonniers en un parc. Je désirais seul être
Leur loi, leur protecteur, leur pasteur, et leur maître;
Ils choisissent pour prince un voleur inhumain,
Un tyran qui veut faire à leurs dépens sa main,
Qui dépite mon bras; et qui, plein de bravade,
A ma sainte maison présente l'escalade.
Sus, rompons leur dessein; et puisqu'unis de voix
Aussi bien que de sang, de vouloir et de lois,
Ils s'obstinent au mal et d'un hardi langage
S'animent, forcenés, nuit et jour à l'ouvrage,
Mettons un enrayoir à leur courant effort;
Frappons-les vivement d'un esprit de discord;
Confondons leur parole, et faisons que le père
Soit barbare à son fils, et sourd le frère au frère.»

should not fear the fury of the waters again; they take that (my promise) as a rampart. I wished them to disperse and people the earth, and here they are imprisoned in a pen. I desired to be their sole law, protector, shepherd, and master; they choose for their prince an inhuman bandit, a tyran who means to profit at their expense, who defies my arm and who, full of bravado, sets scaling-ladders against my holy house. Up, let us confound their plan; and since, united in tongue, as well as in blood, intention, and laws, they persist in evil and with rash words urge each other wildly on day and night to the task, let us put a curb on their galloping onslaught; let us strike them swiftly with a spirit of discord; let us confuse their speech and cause the father to be foreign to his son and the brother deaf to his brother.'

PHILIPPE DESPORTES

Si la foi plus certaine en une âme non feinte,
Un honnête désir, un doux languissement,
Une erreur variable et sentir vivement,
Avec peur d'en guérir, une profonde atteinte:

Si voir une pensée au front toute dépeinte,
Une voix empêchée, un morne étonnement,
De honte ou de frayeur naissant soudainement,
Une pâle couleur de lis et d'amour teinte:

Bref, si se mépriser pour une autre adorer,
Si verser mille pleurs, si toujours soupirer,
Faisant de sa douleur nourriture et breuvage,

Si de loin se voir flamme, et de près tout transi,
Sont cause que je meurs par défaut de merci,
L'offense en est sur vous, et sur moi le dommage.

If the most constant faithfulness in an unfeigning heart, virtuous desire, a gentle languishing, a bemused uncertainty, and the keen sensing – with fear of healing – of a deep wound,

If to see a mind openly depicted in a face, a stammering tongue, a dull bewilderment, suddenly arising from timidity or misgiving, a pale complexion tinted with lilies and love:

In short, if to despise oneself in order to adore another, if to shed a thousand tears, if to sigh continually, making food and drink of one's distress,

If to find oneself flame afar off and be benumbed when near, are the causes of my dying deprived of pity, the blame falls upon you and the hurt on me.

(This is a fairly close translation of Petrarch's sonnet beginning:
S'una fede amorosa, un cor non finto . . .

Cf. Wyatt's English version of the same original:
If amorous faith, or if an heart unfeigned . . .)

ICARE est chu ici, le jeune audacieux,
Qui pour voler au ciel eut assez de courage:
Ici tomba son corps dégarni de plumage,
Laissant tous braves cœurs de sa chute envieux.

O bienheureux travail d'un esprit glorieux,
Qui tire un si grand gain d'un si petit dommage!
O bienheureux malheur plein de tant d'avantage
Qu'il rende le vaincu des ans victorieux!

Un chemin si nouveau n'étonna sa jeunesse,
Le pouvoir lui faillit mais non la hardiesse,
Il eut pour le brûler des astres le plus beau.

Il mourut poursuivant une haute aventure,
Le ciel fut son désir, la mer sa sépulture:
Est-il plus beau dessein, ou plus riche tombeau?

AUTOUR des corps, qu'une mort avancée
Par violence a privés du beau jour,
Les ombres vont, et font maint et maint tour,
Aimant encor leur dépouille laissée.

ICARUS fell here, the daring youth, who had the courage to fly up to heaven; here fell his body shorn of its plumage, leaving all gallant hearts envious of his fall.

O blessed anguish of a proud spirit, which extracts such gain from so small a hurt! O fortunate misfortune so full of benefits that it makes the vanquished a victor over the years!

So new a road did not daunt his youth, his power failed him but not his daring, he had the loveliest of the stars to burn him.

He died pursuing a noble quest, heaven was his desire, the sea his sepulchre. Is there a finer purpose or a richer tomb?

AROUND bodies which a premature death has violently robbed of the light of day, the ghosts go and turn and twist, loving still their abandoned remains.

Au lieu cruel où j'eus l'âme blessée
Et fus meurtri par les flèches d'Amour,
J'erre, je tourne et retourne à l'entour,
Ombre maudite, errante et déchassée.

Légers esprits plus que moi fortunés,
Comme il vous plaît vous allez et venez
Au lieu qui clôt votre dépouille aimée.

Vous la voyez, vous la pouvez toucher,
Où las! je crains seulement d'approcher
L'endroit qui tient ma richesse enfermée.

JEAN DE LA CEPPÈDE

Théorèmes Spirituels

Aux monarques vainqueurs la rouge cotte d'armes
Appartient justement. Ce Roi victorieux
Est justement vêtu par ces moqueurs gens d'armes
D'un manteau qui le marque et prince et glorieux.

In that cruel spot in which my heart was stricken and I was slain by the arrows of Love, I roam, I turn and turn around it, a ghost accursed, wandering and expelled.

Airy spirits more happy than I, as you please you come and go in the place which encloses your beloved remains.

You see them, you can touch them, while I, alas, fear even to approach the place in which my treasure is contained.

Spiritual Theorems

To conquering monarchs the red surcoat belongs of right. This victorious King is rightly clad by these mocking men-at-arms in a cloak which stamps Him both a prince and glorious.

Ô pourpre, emplis mon têt de ton jus précieux
Et lui fais distiller mille pourprines larmes,
A tant que, méditant ton sens mystérieux,
Du sang trait de mes yeux j'ensanglante ces carmes.

Ta sanglante couleur figure nos péchés
Au dos de cet Agneau par le Père attachés:
Et ce Christ t'endossant se charge de nos crimes.

Ô Christ, ô saint Agneau, daigne-toi de cacher
Tous mes rouges péchés, brindelles des abîmes,
Dans les sanglants replis du manteau de ta chair.

L'AMOUR l'a de l'Olympe ici-bas fait descendre:
L'amour l'a fait de l'homme endosser le péché:
L'amour lui a déjà tout son sang fait épandre:
L'amour l'a fait souffrir qu'on ait sur lui craché:

L'amour a ces halliers à son chef attaché:
L'amour fait que sa Mère à ce bois le voit pendre:

O [royal] purple, fill my head with your precious liquid and make it distil a myriad crimson tears, until at last, contemplating your mysterious meaning, I stain these songs with the blood milked from my eyes.

Your blood-red colour symbolizes our sins, bound by the Father on the back of this Lamb; and this Christ, putting you on, takes our offences upon Himself.

O Christ, holy Lamb, deign to hide all my red sins, kindling-twigs of hell, in the bleeding folds of the cloak of your flesh.

LOVE has brought Him down here from Olympus: love has made Him take the sin of man upon Himself; love has already made Him pour out all his blood: love has made Him suffer them to spit upon Him:

Love has bound these thorns on his head: love causes his Mother

L'amour a dans ces mains ces rudes clous fiché:
L'amour le va tantôt dans le sépulcre étendre.

Son amour est si grand, son amour est si fort
Qu'il attaque l'Enfer, qu'il terrasse la mort,
Qu'il arrache à Pluton sa fidèle Eurydice.

Belle pour qui ce beau meurt en vous bien-aimant,
Voyez s'il fut jamais un si cruel supplice,
Voyez s'il fut jamais un si parfait amant.

L'autel des vieux parfums dans Solyme encensé
Fait or' d'une voirie un temple vénérable,
Où du Verbe incarné l'Hypostase adorable
S'offre très-odorante à son Père offensé.

Le vieux pal, sur lequel jadis fut agencé
En Édom le serpent aux mordus secourable,
Élève ores celui qui piteux a pansé
Du vieux serpent d'Éden la morsure incurable.

to see Him hanging on this tree: love has driven these hard nails
into these hands: love will presently lay Him in the sepulchre.

His love is so great, his love is so strong, that He attacks Hell,
that He lays death low, that He snatches his faithful Eurydice from
Pluto.

Fair one for whom this fair groom dies adoring you, consider if
there was ever so cruel a death, consider if there was ever so perfect
a lover.*

The altar censed with the old perfumes in Solyma now makes of a
place of slaughter a temple to be venerated, in which the adorable
hypostasis of the Word Incarnate (the person of Christ) is offered
sweet-smelling to his offended Father.

The old stake, on which the serpent helpful to the bitten was
once set in Edom, now raises up Him who has compassionately
tended the incurable bite of the old serpent of Eden.

---

*In a note on this sonnet, La Ceppède explains 'the fair one'
('la belle') as a metaphor for the faithful soul, or the Church.

Le pressoir de la vigne en Calvaire est dressé,
Où ce fameux raisin ce pressoir a pressé
Pour noyer dans son vin nos léthales vipères.

L'échelle Israëlite est posée en ce lieu,
Sur laquelle aujourd'hui s'appuyant l'homme-Dieu,
Nous fait jouir des biens qu'il promit à nos pères.

Ce grand Soleil, de qui l'autre n'est qu'une flamme,
Par quatre des maisons du grand Cercle a passé:
Par celle de la Vierge, où neuf mois sa belle âme
A de son corps égal l'organe compassé:

Par celle du Verseau, quand son œil a tracé
Sa douleur par son pleur, en maint acte sans blâme:
Par celle du Taureau, quand son corps terrassé
S'est pour victime offert sur le gibet infâme.

The press of the vine is set up on Calvary, where that press has pressed that famous grape to drown our deadly vipers in its wine.

Jacob's ladder is put up in this place, and the Man-God supported on it today makes us enjoy the blessings He promised to our fathers.*

That great Sun [Christ], of which the other is only a flame, has passed through four of the houses of the great Circle [of the Zodiac]: through that of the Virgin, in which during nine months his fair soul formed the organism of his matching body;

Through that of the Waterbearer, when his eye portrayed his sorrow with its tears in many a blameless act; through that of the Bull, when his body was pulled down and offered itself as a victim on the shameful gallows.

---

*The key to the first two lines is in Numbers 16, in which a rebellious faction of the Israelites offer incense to the altar and are 'swallowed up by the earth' as a sign of Jehovah's refusal. The second quatrain refers first to the brazen serpent set up by Moses as a cure for snake-bite (Numbers 21, ix) and then to the serpent of the Garden of Eden.

Or à ce jour il entre en celle du Lion.
Perruqué de lumière, il darde un million
De rayons flamboyants sur les deux hémisphères,

Et sa voix rugissante et son frémissement
Au sortir de la tombe épouvantent les fères
Et les rangent au joug de leur amendement.

L'OISEAU dont l'Arabie a fait si grande fête
Est de ce grand Héros le symbole assuré.
Le Phénix est tout seul. Le Christ est figuré
Seul libre entre les morts par son royal prophète.

Le Phénix courageux se porte à sa défaite
Sur du bois parfumé: l'amour démesuré
Fait que Christ a la mort sur ce bois enduré,
Qui parfume le ciel d'une odeur très-parfaite.

De sa moüelle après le Phénix renaissant
Enlève tout son bois et l'emporte puissant
Sur un autel voisin des arènes brûlées.

Now on this day He enters the house of the Lion. Bemaned with light, He darts a million fiery beams on the two hemispheres,
And his bellowing voice and his roar as he comes out from the grave strike terror into the beasts and bring them to the yoke of their reclaiming.

THE bird which Arabia cherished so highly is the certain symbol of this great Hero. The Phoenix is alone of its kind. Christ is represented by his royal prophet [David] as alone unenslaved among the dead.
The Phoenix bravely goes to its destruction on scented wood: measureless love led Christ to suffer death on the wood of that tree which sweetens heaven with its most excellent perfume.
Reborn afterwards from its ashes [marrow], the Phoenix takes up all its wood and carries it powerfully to an altar near to the burnt sands.

Par sa divinité le Christ ressuscitant,
Sur l'azuré lambris des voûtes étoilées
Élèvera son bois de rayons éclatant.

AGRIPPA D'AUBIGNÉ

[*Sonnet pour Diane*]

Un clairvoyant faucon en volant par rivière
Planait dedans le ciel, à se fondre apprêté
Sur son gibier blotti. Mais voyant à côté
Une corneille, il quitte une pointe première.

Ainsi de ses attraits une maîtresse fière
S'élevant jusqu'au ciel m'abat sous sa beauté,
Mais son vouloir volage est soudain transporté
En l'amour d'un corbeau pour me laisser arrière.

Ha! beaux yeux obscurcis qui avez pris le pire,
Plus propres à blesser que discrets à élire,
Je vous crains abattu, ainsi que fait l'oiseau

Qui n'attend que la mort de la serre ennemie:
Fors que le changement lui redonne la vie,
Et c'est le changement qui me traîne au tombeau.

Christ, resurrected by his divine essence, against the azure ceiling of the starry vaults will raise up his tree resplendent with light.

Sonnet for Diana

A KEEN-EYED falcon flying over riverland was hovering in the sky, ready to swoop on its crouching prey. But seeing a crow at one side, it abandons its first aim.

So a cruel mistress, raised to heaven by her charms, strikes me down beneath her beauty, but her fickle fancy is suddenly transferred to the love of a crow, leaving me behind.

Ah, sweet clouded eyes which have picked the worse, more fitted to wound than skilled to choose, I fear you cowering here, as does the bird which expects only death from the hostile talons: except that the change gives it back its life, and the change is what draws me towards the grave.

Stances

[Misères de l'amour]

... Sɪ quelquefois poussé d'une âme impatiente
Je vais précipitant mes fureurs dans les bois,
M'échauffant sur la mort d'une bête innocente,
Ou effrayant les eaux et les monts de ma voix,

Milles oiseaux de nuit, mille chansons mortelles
M'environnent, volant par ordre sur mon front:
Que l'air en contrepoids fâché de mes querelles
Soit noirci de hiboux et de corbeaux en rond.

Les herbes sècheront sous mes pas, à la vue
Des misérables yeux dont les tristes regards
Feront tomber les fleurs et cacher dans la nue
La lune et le soleil et les astres épars.

Ma présence fera dessécher les fontaines
Et les oiseaux passants tomber morts à mes pieds,
Étouffés de l'odeur et du vent de mes peines:
Ma peine, étouffe-moi, comme ils sont étouffés!

Stanzas

[Miseries of Love]

... Iғ sometimes, driven by my impatient heart, I go and vent my
frenzy in the woods, waxing hot over the death of some innocent
beast, or startling the waters and the hills with my voice,

A thousand night birds, a thousand baleful songs [bird-cries] sur-
round me, flying in order across my face: let the sky, grieved in
sympathy by my lamentations, be darkened all around with owls
and crows.

The grass will wither under my footsteps, at the sight of these
miserable eyes whose sad looks will cause the flowers to droop and
the moon and the sun and the scattered stars to hide in the clouds.

My presence will make the springs run dry and the passing birds
fall dead at my feet, choked with the stench and the wind of my
sorrows; my sorrow, choke me, as they are choked.

. . . Il reste qu'un démon connaissant ma misère
Me vienne un jour trouver aux plus sombres forêts,
M'essayant, me tentant pour que je désespère,
Que je suive ses arts, que je l'adore après.

Moi je résisterai, fuyant la solitude
Et des bois et des rocs, mais ce cruel, suivant
Mes pas, assiégera mon lit et mon étude,
Comme un air, comme un feu, et léger comme un vent.

Il m'offrira de l'or, je n'aime la richesse;
Des états, des faveurs, je méprise les cours;
Puis me promettera le corps de ma maîtresse:
A ce point Dieu viendra soudain à mon secours.

Le menteur, empruntant la même face belle,
L'idée de mon âme et de mon doux tourment,
Viendra entre mes bras apporter ma cruelle,
Mais je n'embrasserai pour elle que du vent.

Tantôt une fumée épaisse, noire ou bleue,
Passant devant mes yeux me fera tressaillir;
En bouc et en barbet, en fascinant ma veue,
Au lit de mon repos il viendra m'assaillir.

. . . It remains for a demon who knows my misery to seek me out
one day in the darkest forests, trying me, tempting me to make me
despair, to obey his arts and worship him afterwards.

I shall resist, fleeing from the solitude of woods and rocks, but
that cruel being, dogging my steps, will beset my bed and my study,
like a draught, like a fire, and light as a breeze.

He will offer me gold – I do not love wealth; estates, favours – I
despise courts; then he will promise me the body of my mistress:
at that point God will come quickly to my help.

The deceiver, putting on the same lovely face, the ideal of my
soul and of my sweet torments, will come and place my cruel one
in my arms, but instead of her I shall embrace only air.

Sometimes a thick smoke, black or blue, will make me start as it
drifts before my eyes; in the form of a he-goat or a spaniel, be-
witching my sight, he will come to assail me on my couch.

Neuf gouttes de pur sang naîtront sur ma serviette,
Ma coupe brisera sans coup entre mes mains,
J'oirai des coups en l'air, on verra des bluettes
De feu que pousseront les démons inhumains.

... Et lorsque mes rigueurs auront fini ma vie
Et que par le mourir finira mon souffrir,
Quand de me tourmenter la fortune assouvie
Voudra mes maux, ma vie et son ire finir,

Nymphes qui avez vu la rage qui m'affole,
Satyres que je fis contrister à ma voix,
Baptisez en pleurant quelque pauvre mausole
Aux fonds plus égarés et plus sombres des bois ...

Les Tragiques

[*Prière à Dieu pour venger les Protestants*]

... Tu vois, juste vengeur, les fleaux de ton Église,
Qui, par eux mise en cendre et en masure mise,
A contre tout espoir son espérance en toi,
Pour son retranchement le rempart de la foi.

Nine drops of pure blood will appear on my napkin, my glass will break untouched in my hands, I shall hear thuds in the air, flashes of fire given out by inhuman demons will be seen.
... And when my afflictions have brought my life to a close and death puts an end to my suffering, when fortune, sated with tormenting me, is willing to end my woes, my life, and its own wrath—
Nymphs who have seen the frenzy which maddens me, satyrs whom I have saddened by my cries, baptise with your tears some humble tomb in the most hidden and darkest depths of the woods ...

The Tragic One

[*Prayer to God to Avenge the Protestants*]

... You see, just avenger, the scourges of your Church, which, reduced to ashes and ruins by them, places against all hope its hope in you, and has for its bulwark the rampart of faith.

... Veux-tu longtemps laisser en cette terre ronde
Régner ton ennemi? N'es-tu Seigneur du monde,
Toi, Seigneur, qui abats, qui blesses, qui guéris,
Qui donnes vie et mort, qui tue' et qui nourris?

Les princes n'ont point d'yeux pour voir tes grand'-
   merveilles;
Quand tu voudras tonner, n'auront-ils point d'oreilles?
Leurs mains ne servent plus qu'à nous persécuter;
Ils ont tout pour Satan, et rien pour te porter.

Sion ne reçoit d'eux que refus et rudesses,
Mais Babel les rançonne et pille leurs richesses;
Tels sont les monts cornus qui, avaricieux,
Montrent l'or aux enfers et les neiges aux cieux.

Les temples du païen, du Turc, de l'idolâtre,
Haussent au ciel l'orgueil du marbre et de l'albâtre;
Et Dieu seul, au désert pauvrement hébergé,
A bâti tout le monde et n'y est pas logé!

... Will you allow your enemy to reign for long on this round
earth? Are you not Lord of the world – you, Lord, who casts down,
who smites, who heals, who gives life and death, who slays, and
who feeds?

The princes have no eyes to see your great marvels; when you
decide to thunder, will they have no ears? Their hands now serve
no purpose but to persecute us; they have everything for Satan, and
nothing to bring you.

Zion [the Reformed Church] receives only refusals and harsh-
ness from them, but Babylon [Rome] holds them to ransom and
plunders their wealth; they are like the horny mountains which, in
miser-fashion, show gold to the nether regions and snow to the
skies.

The temples of the heathen, of the Turk, of the idolater, raise to
heaven the pomp of marble and alabaster; and God alone, poorly
lodged in the wilderness, has built the whole world and has no
dwelling in it.

Les moineaux ont leurs nids, leurs nids les hirondelles;
On dresse quelque fuie aux simples colombelles;
Tout est mis à l'abri par le soin des mortels,
Et Dieu seul, immortel, n'a logis ni autels.

Tu as tout l'univers, où ta gloire on contemple,
Pour marchepied la terre et le ciel pour un temple:
Où te chassera l'homme, ô Dieu victorieux?
Tu possèdes le ciel et les cieux des hauts cieux!

Nous faisons des rochers les lieux où on te prêche,
Un temple de l'étable, un autel de la crèche;
Eux, du temple une étable aux ânes arrogants,
De la sainte maison la caverne aux brigands.

Les premiers des chrétiens priaient aux cimetières:
Nous avons fait ouïr aux tombeaux nos prières,
Fait sonner aux tombeaux le nom de Dieu le fort,
Et annoncé la vie aux logis de la mort.

Tu peux faire conter ta louange à la pierre,
Mais n'as-tu pas toujours ton marchepied en terre?

The sparrows have their nests, their nests the swallows; some cote is put up for the simple doves; everything is given shelter by the care of mortal men, and only God, immortal, has no dwelling nor altars.

You have the whole universe, in which we contemplate your glory, for your footstool the earth and the heavens for a temple: whither will man drive you, O victorious God? You possess heaven and the heaven of high heaven!

We make the rocks places where your name is preached, the stable a temple, the manger an altar; they make of the temple a stable for arrogant asses, of the holy house a robber's cave.

The earliest Christians prayed in the cemeteries; we have spoken our prayers in the tombs, made the name of mighty God ring in the tombs, and proclaimed the living way in the dwellings of death.

You can have your praises told to the stone, but have you not still your footstool upon earth? Do you no longer wish to have

Ne veux-tu plus avoir d'autres temples sacrés
Qu'un blanchissant amas d'os de morts massacrés?

Les morts te loueront-ils? Tes faits grands et terribles
Sortiront-ils du creux de ces bouches horribles?
N'aurons-nous entre nous que visages terreux
Murmurant ta louange aux secrets de nos creux?

En ces lieux caverneux tes chères assemblées,
Des ombres de la mort incessamment troublées,
Ne feront-elles plus résonner tes saints lieux,
Et ton renom voler des terres dans les cieux?

... Soient tes yeux adoucis à guérir nos misères,
Ton oreille propice ouverte à nos prières,
Ton sein déboutonné à loger nos soupirs
Et ta main libérale à nos justes désirs.

Que ceux qui ont fermé les yeux à nos misères,
Que ceux qui n'ont point eu d'oreille à nos prières,
De cœur pour secourir, mais bien pour tourmenter,
Point de mains pour donner, mais bien pour nous ôter,

other holy temples than a whitening heap of bones of the slaughtered dead?

Will the dead praise you? Will your great and terrible deeds issue from the hollows of those ghastly mouths? Shall we have among us only earthy faces murmuring your praise in the secret of our caves?

Your beloved congregations in these cavernous places, continually haunted by the shadow of death – shall they never again make your holy places ring, and your praise rise up from the earth to the heavens?

... Let your eyes grow kind to heal our afflictions, your merciful ear be opened to our prayers, your breast be unbuttoned to receive our sighs, and your hand be bountiful to our just desires.

Let those who have shut their eyes to our afflictions, let those who have had no ear for our prayers, no heart to succour but rather to torment, no hands to give but rather to take from us,

Trouvent tes yeux fermés à juger leurs misères;
Ton oreille soit sourde en oyant leurs prières;
Ton sein ferré soit clos aux pitiés, aux pardons;
Ta main sèche stérile aux bienfaits et aux dons.

Soient tes yeux clairvoyants à leurs péchés extrêmes,
Soit ton oreille ouverte à leurs cris de blasphèmes,
Ton sein déboutonné pour s'enfler de courroux,
Et ta main diligente à redoubler tes coups.

Ils ont pour un spectacle et pour jeu le martyre,
Le méchant rit plus haut que le bon n'y soupire;
Nos cris mortels n'y font qu'incommoder leurs ris,
Les ris de qui l'éclat ôte l'air à nos cris.

Ils crachent vers la lune et les voûtes célestes:
N'ont-elles plus de foudre et de feux et de pestes?
Ne partiront jamais du trône où tu te sieds
Et la Mort et l'Enfer qui dorment à tes pieds?

Find your eyes shut to judge their afflictions; let your ear be deaf to hear their prayers, let your mailed breast be closed to pity, to pardon, and your dry hand be barren of blessings and gifts.

Let your eyes be keen for their fearful sins, let your ear be open to their blasphemous cries, your breast be unbuttoned to swell with anger, your hand be active to multiply your blows.

They have martyrdom for a spectacle and a sport, the wicked laugh more loudly than the righteous man groans; our dying cries serve only to disturb their laughter – that laughter whose outbursts stifle our cries.

They spit towards the moon and the heavenly vaults: have these no more thunderbolts and fires and plagues? Will Death and Hell sleeping at your feet never come forth from the throne on which you sit?

Lève ton bras de fer, hâte tes pieds de laine;
Venge ta patience en l'aigreur de ta peine:
Frappe du ciel Babel: les cornes de son front
Défigurent la terre et lui ôtent son rond!

FRANÇOIS MALHERBE

Ode pour Marie de Médicis

PEUPLES, qu'on mette sur la tête
Tout ce que la terre a de fleurs;
Peuples, que cette belle fête
A jamais tarisse nos pleurs;
Qu'aux deux bouts du monde se voie
Luire le feu de notre joie,
Et soient dans les coupes noyés
Les soucis de tous ces orages
Que pour nos rebelles courages
Les dieux nous avaient envoyés.

Raise your iron arm, make swift your feet of wool [i.e. too slow]: avenge your long-suffering by the sharpness of the punishment: strike Babylon from heaven; the horns on its brow disfigure the earth and spoil its round symmetry.

Ode for Marie de Médicis*

LOYAL subjects, let us deck our heads with all the flowers of the earth; subjects, may this happy day for ever dry our tears; let our fireworks blaze out from end to end of the world, and in the goblets let there be drowned the anxieties of all those storms which the gods sent us to punish our rebel hearts.

---

*Ode presented to Marie de Médicis in 1600, on the occasion of her arrival in France to marry Henri IV.

A ce coup iront en fumée
Les vœux que faisaient nos mutins
En leur âme encor affamée
De massacres et de butins;
Nos doutes seront éclaircis
Et mentiront les prophéties
De tous ces visages pâlis,
Dont la vaine étude s'applique
A chercher l'an climatérique
De l'éternelle fleur de lis.

Aujourd'hui nous est amenée
Cette princesse, que la foi
D'amour ensemble et d'hyménée
Destine au lit de notre Roi.
La voici, la belle Marie,
Belle merveille d'Étrurie,
Qui fait confesser au soleil,
Quoi que l'âge passé raconte,
Que du ciel depuis qu'il y monte
Ne vint jamais rien de pareil.

Telle n'est point la Cythérée
Quand, d'un nouveau feu s'allumant,

On this day will vanish in smoke the prayers which our rebels
murmured in their hearts still athirst for massacres and plunder;
our doubts will be dispelled and there will prove to be only lies in
the prophecies of all those pallid faces, whose vain study it is to
discover the climacteric year [critical year in life] of the eternal
fleur de lis.

Today this princess is brought to us, she whom the pledge of
love and of marriage alike destine for the bed of our King. This is
she, the lovely Marie, lovely marvel of Etruria, who forces the sun
to confess that, whatever history relates, since he has been in the
heavens nothing came from them equal to her.

The Cytherean [Venus] cannot match her, when, kindling with a

Elle sort pompeuse et parée
Pour la conquête d'un amant;
Telle ne luit en sa carrière
Des mois l'inégale courrière,
Et telle dessus l'horizon
L'Aurore au matin ne s'étale,
Quand les yeux mêmes de Céphale
En feraient la comparaison.

Le sceptre que porte sa race,
Où l'heur aux mérites est joint,
Lui met le respect en la face,
Mais il ne l'enorgueillit point;
Nulle vanité ne la touche;
Les Grâces parlent par sa bouche,
Et son front, témoin assuré
Qu'au vice elle est inaccessible,
Ne peut que d'un cœur insensible
Être vu sans être adoré.

Quantesfois, lorsque sur les ondes
Ce nouveau miracle flottait,
Neptune en ses caves profondes
Plaignit-il le feu qu'il sentait?

new fire, she goes forth gloriously arrayed to the conquest of a lover; nor does the irregular harbinger of the months shine so upon its course, and the dawn above the horizon does not display itself so to the morning, even if the eyes of Cephalus* were to make the comparison.

The sceptre borne by her line, in which high fortune joins with worth, gives dignity to her face but does not make her proud; no vanity touches her; the graces speak through her mouth, and her brow, a certain witness that she is inaccessible to evil, can be seen only by a heart of stone without being adored.

How often, when this modern miracle was floating over the waves, did Neptune in his deep caves complain of the fire which he

---

*The lover of Aurora, the dawn.

Et quantesfois en sa pensée
De vives atteintes blessée,
Sans l'honneur de la royauté
Qui lui fit celer son martyre,
Eût-il voulu de son empire
Faire échange à cette beauté?

Dix jours ne pouvant se distraire
Du plaisir de la regarder,
Il a par un effort contraire
Essayé de la retarder;
Mais à la fin, soit que l'audace
Au meilleur avis ait fait place,
Soit qu'un autre démon plus fort
Aux vents ait imposé silence,
Elle est hors de sa violence
Et la voici dans notre port.

La voici, peuples, qui nous montre
Tout ce que la gloire a de prix:
Les fleurs naissent à sa rencontre
Dans les cœurs et dans les esprits;

---

felt. And how often in his secret thoughts, stricken with smarting wounds – but for his kingly honour which made him hide his torments – would he have been ready to exchange his empire for that beauty?

Unable for ten days to tear himself away from the pleasure of looking at her, he tried by an adverse effort to delay her; but at last, either because his boldness yielded to better counsels, or because another, stronger, daemon, reduced the winds to silence, she has escaped from his violence and here she is in our port.*

Here she is, Frenchmen, to show us the full value of her fame: flowers spring up to greet her in our hearts and minds; and the

---

*The arrival of the royal bride in France was delayed by a particularly stormy sea-crossing.

Et la présence des merveilles
 Qu'en oyaient dire nos oreilles
Accuse la témérité
De ceux qui nous l'avaient décrite
D'avoir figuré son mérite
Moindre que n'est la vérité.

O toute parfaite Princesse,
L'étonnement de l'univers,
Astre par qui vont avoir cesse
Nos ténèbres et nos hivers;
Exemple sans autres exemples,
Future image de nos temples:
Quoi que notre faible pouvoir
En votre accueil ose entreprendre,
 Peut-il espérer de vous rendre
Ce que nous vous allons devoir?

Ce sera vous qui de nos villes
Ferez la beauté refleurir,
Vous, qui de nos haines civiles
Ferez la racine mourir;
Et par vous la paix assurée
N'aura pas la courte durée
Qu'espèrent infidèlement,
Non lassés de notre souffrance,

presence of this marvel of which our ears had heard condemns the presumption of those who had described her to us for having represented her at less than her true worth.

O wholly perfect princess, amazement of the universe, star thanks to whom our darkness and our winters will cease; unexampled example, future image in our churches; whatever our feeble powers dare to attempt in your welcome, can we hope to repay you for what we are going to owe you?

It will be you who will make the beauty of our towns flower again, you who will kill the root of our civil discords; and peace, ensured by you, will not have the short duration which is treacherously hoped for by those Frenchmen — not yet wearied of our

Ces Français qui n'ont de la France
Que la langue et l'habillement.

Par vous un Dauphin nous va naître,
Que vous-même verrez un jour
De la terre entière le maître,
Ou par armes ou par amour;
Et ne tarderont ses conquêtes
Dans les oracles déjà prêtes
Qu'autant que le premier coton,
Qui de jeunesse est le message,
Tardera d'être en son visage
Et de faire ombre à son menton.

O combien lors aura de veuves
La gent qui porte le turban!
Que de sang rougira les fleuves
Qui lavent les pieds du Liban!
Que le Bosphore en ses deux rives
Aura de sultanes captives!
Et que de mères à Memphis
En pleurant diront la vaillance
De son courage et de sa lance
Aux funérailles de leurs fils! . . .

sullerings – who of France have only the language and the costume.

Through you a prince will be born to us, whom you yourself will one day see master of the whole earth, by force either of arms or of love; and his conquests, which the oracles are already preparing to announce, will be delayed only for as long as the first down, the sign of young manhood, delays to appear on his face and to darken his chin.

Oh, how many widows will the folk who wear the turban have then! How much blood will redden the rivers which wash the feet of the Lebanon! How many captive sultanesses will the Bosphorus have on its two shores! And how many mothers in Memphis will speak in tears of the stoutness of his heart and lance at the funerals of their sons! . . .

Imitation du Psaume Lauda anima mea Dominum

N'ESPÉRONS plus, mon âme, aux promesses du monde:
Sa lumière est un verre, et sa faveur une onde,
Que toujours quelque vent empêche de calmer;
Quittons ces vanités, lassons-nous de les suivre:
  C'est Dieu qui nous fait vivre,
  C'est Dieu qu'il faut aimer.

En vain, pour satisfaire à nos lâches envies,
Nous passons près des rois tout le temps de nos vies,
A souffrir des mépris et ployer les genoux;
Ce qu'ils peuvent n'est rien: ils sont comme nous sommes,
  Véritablement hommes,
  Et meurent comme nous.

Ont-ils rendu l'esprit, ce n'est plus que poussière
Que cette majesté si pompeuse et si fière
Dont l'éclat orgueilleux étonne l'univers;
Et dans ces grands tombeaux où leurs âmes hautaines
  Font encore les vaines,
  Ils sont mangés des vers.

Inspired by the Psalm 'Praise the Lord, O my soul'*

LET us trust no more, my soul, in the world's promises: its light is a glinting glass and its favour a shifting wave which some wind always prevents from calming. Let us renounce these vanities, let us turn from following them. It is God who gives us life, it is God whom we must love.

Vainly, to satisfy our base desires, we spend in courts of kings the whole span of our lives, enduring contempt and bending our knees. Their power is nothing, they are as we are, in very truth men, and die as we do.

When they give up the ghost, it is no more than dust – that majesty so stately and so proud whose pomp and splendour awes the world. And in those great tombs where their haughty souls still make a vain display, they are eaten by the worms.

---

*No. 146 in the English Psalter.

Là se perdent ces noms de maîtres de la terre,
D'arbitres de la paix, de foudres de la guerre:
Comme ils n'ont plus de sceptre ils n'ont plus de flatteurs,
Et tombent avec eux d'une chute commune
      Tous ceux que leur fortune
      Faisait leurs serviteurs.

JEAN DE SPONDE

Sonnet

Si j'avais comme vous, mignardes colombelles,
Des plumages si beaux sur mon corps attachés,
On aurait beau tenir mes esprits empêchés
De l'indomptable fer de cent chaînes nouvelles.

Sur les ailes du vent je guiderais mes ailes,
J'irais jusqu'au séjour où mes biens sont cachés:
Ainsi, voyant de moi ces ennuis arrachés,
Je ne sentirais plus ces absences cruelles.

There vanish those titles of lords of the earth, of arbiters of peace, of thunderbolts of war. As they have lost their sceptres, they have lost their flatterers. And with them go down in a common fall all those whom their fortune once made their servants.

Sonnet

PRETTY doves, if I had like you such fine plumage fastened to my body, in vain would they try to shackle my spirit with the unbreakable iron of a hundred fresh chains.

I would slant my wings on the wings of the wind, I would go to the abode where my treasure is hidden: so, seeing these sorrows plucked from me, I would no longer feel this cruel absence.

Colombelles, hélas! que j'ai bien souhaité
Que mon corps vous semblât autant d'agilité
Que mon âme d'amour à votre âme ressemble.

Mais quoi! je le souhaite, et me trompe d'autant.
Ferais-je bien voler un amour si constant
D'un monde tout rempli de vos ailes ensemble?

Stances de la mort

Mes yeux, ne lancez plus votre pointe éblouie
Sur les brillants rayons de la flammeuse vie;
Sillez-vous, couvrez-vous de ténèbres, mes yeux:
Non pas pour étouffer vos vigueurs coutumières,
Car je vous ferai voir de plus vives lumières,
Mais sortant de la nuit vous n'en verrez que mieux.

Je m'ennuie de vivre et mes tendres années,
Gémissant sous le faix de bien peu de journées,
Me trouvent au milieu de ma course cassé:

Little doves, alas, how much have I longed that my body should be as like you in its lightness as my soul resembles your soul in love.

Alas, I long for it and deceive myself no less. Could I ever make so constant a love take flight from a world filled full with all your wings together?

Stanzas on Death

My eyes, no longer dart your dazzled looks upon the bright beams of fiery life; close, cover yourselves with darkness, my eyes: not in order to dim your normal keenness, for I will cause you to see [yet] brighter lights, but because you will see all the better on coming out of the dark.

I am weary of living and my tender years, groaning beneath the load of few enough days, find me broken in the middle of my jour-

Si n'est-ce pas du tout par défaut de courage,
Mais je prends, comme un port à la fin de l'orage,
Dédain de l'avenir pour l'horreur du passé.

... La chair, des vanités de ce monde pipée,
Veut être dans sa vie encor enveloppée,
Et l'esprit pour mieux vivre en souhaite la mort.
Ces partis m'ont réduit en un péril extrême:
Mais, mon Dieu, prends parti de ces partis toi-même,
Et je me rangerai du parti le plus fort.

Sans ton aide, mon Dieu, cette chair orgueilleuse
Rendra de ce combat l'issue périlleuse,
Car elle est en son règne et l'autre est étranger:
La chair sent le doux fruit des voluptés présentes,
L'esprit ne semble avoir qu'un espoir des absentes,
Et le fruit pour l'espoir ne se doit point changer.

... C'est assez enduré que de cette vermine
La superbe insolence à ta grandeur domine.
Tu lui dois commander, cependant tu lui sers:

ney. Yet it is in no way for lack of courage; but I have attained, like
a port after the storm, contempt of the future through horror of the
past.
... The flesh, duped by the vanities of this world, desires still to be
clothed with life, and the spirit, in order to live better, desires the
death of the flesh. These factions have brought me into mortal
danger. But, Lord, side with [one of] these factions yourself, and
I will rally to the strongest side.
   Without your aid, Lord, this proud flesh will make the outcome
of this struggle uncertain, for the flesh is in its own kingdom and
the other is alien here: the flesh tastes the sweet fruit of present de-
lights, the spirit seems to have only a hope of absent ones – and the
fruit must [surely] not be exchanged for the hope.
... We have suffered the overbearing insolence of that vermin to
dominate your greatness long enough. You should command it, yet

Tu dois purger la chair, et cette chair te souille;
Voire, de te garder un désir te chatouille,
Mais cuidant te garder, mon esprit, tu te perds.

... Je sais bien, mon esprit, que cet air et cette onde,
Cette terre, ce feu, ce ciel qui ceint le monde,
Enfle, abîme, retient, brûle, éteint tes désirs:
Tu vois je ne sais quoi de plaisant et d'aimable,
Mais le dessus du ciel est bien plus estimable,
Et de plaisants amours et d'aimables plaisirs.

Ces amours, ces plaisirs dont les troupes des anges
Caressent du grand Dieu les merveilles étranges
Aux accords rapportés de leurs diverses voix,
Sont bien d'autres plaisirs, amours d'autre nature:
Ce que tu vois ici n'en est pas la peinture,
Ne fût-ce rien sinon pour ce que tu le vois.

Invisibles beautés, délices invisibles,
Ravissez-moi du creux de ces manoirs horribles,
Fondez-moi cette chair et rompez-moi ces os:

you serve it. You should purge the flesh, and the flesh defiles you.
Indeed, a desire to preserve yourself tempts you, but thinking to
preserve yourself, my spirit, you destroy yourself.
... I well know, my spirit, that this air and this ocean, this earth, this
fire, this sky which girdles the world, swells up, engulfs, holds back,
burns, extinguishes your desires: you see I know not what that is
pleasant and lovable; but the height of heaven is far more to be
prized, both for pleasant love and for lovable pleasure.

That love, that pleasure with which the bands of angels caress
the strange marvels of mighty God, to the concerted harmonies of
their various voices, is very different pleasure, love of another
nature. What you see here below is not the portrait of it, if only
because you do see it.

Invisible beauties, delights invisible, snatch me up from the
depths of these horrible dwellings, melt this flesh of mine and break

Il faut passer vers vous à travers mon martyre,
Mon martyre en mourant, car hélas! je désire
Commencer au travail et finir au repos.

Mais dispose, mon Dieu, ma tremblante impuissance
A ces pesants fardeaux de ton obéissance;
Si tu veux que je vive encore, je le veux.
Et quoi? m'envies-tu ton bien que je souhaite?
Car ce ne m'est que mal que la vie imparfaite
Qui languit sur la terre, et qui vivrait aux cieux.

Non, ce ne m'est que mal, mais mal plein d'espérance
Qu'après les durs ennuis de ma longue souffrance,
Tu m'étendras ta main, mon Dieu, pour me guérir.
Mais tandis que je couve une si belle envie,
Puisqu'un bien est le bout et le but de ma vie,
Apprends-moi de bien vivre, afin de bien mourir.

these my bones; I must go towards you through my own suffering, the suffering of my death, for ah, I desire to begin in travail and to end in rest.

But incline, my God, my trembling impotence to those heavy burdens of your obedience; if you wish me to live still, I too wish it. So then, do you grudge me your bliss, for which I long? For there is only pain for me in this imperfect life which languishes on earth, and would live in heaven.

Yes, it is only pain for me, but pain full of hope that after the harsh tortures of my long suffering, you will stretch out your hand, my God, to heal me. But while I cherish so sweet a longing, since good is the end and the aim of my life, teach me to live well in order to die well.

Sonnets de la mort

QUI sont, qui sont ceux-là dont le cœur idolâtre
Se jette aux pieds du monde et flatte ses honneurs,
Et qui sont ces valets, et qui sont ces seigneurs?
Et ces âmes d'ébène et ces faces d'albâtre?

Ces masques déguisés, dont la troupe folâtre
S'amuse à caresser je ne sais quels donneurs
De fumées de cour, et ces entrepreneurs
De vaincre encor le ciel qu'ils ne peuvent combattre?

Qui sont ces louvoyeurs qui s'éloignent du port,
Hommagers à la vie et félons à la mort,
Dont l'étoile est leur bien, le vent leur fantaisie?

Je vogue en même mer et craindrais de périr,
Si ce n'est que je sais que cette même vie
N'est rien que le fanal qui me guide au mourir.

Sonnets on Death

WHO are these, who are these, whose idolatrous hearts fawn at the feet of the world and ogle its honours, and who are these lackeys and who are these lords? These ebony souls and these alabaster faces?

These disguised maskers, whose giddy band wastes its time in flattering some vague dispensers of courtly vanities, and these who again undertake to conquer that heaven which they are powerless to fight?

Who are these tacking schemers sailing ever further from port, fawners on life and traitors to death, whose pole-star is their profit, whose wind is their caprice?

I sail on the same sea and should fear to perish, did I not know that this same life is only the beacon which shows me the way to die.

Tout s'enfle contre moi, tout m'assaut, tout me tente,
Et le monde, et la chair, et l'ange révolté,
Dont l'onde, dont l'effort, dont le charme inventé
Et m'abîme, Seigneur, et m'ébranle, et m'enchante.

Quelle nef, quel appui, quelle oreille dormante,
Sans péril, sans tomber, et sans être enchanté,
Me donras-tu? Ton temple où vit ta sainteté,
Ton invincible main, et ta voix si constante?

Et quoi? Mon Dieu, je sens combattre maintesfois
Encor avec ton temple et ta main et ta voix
Cet ange révolté, cette chair, et ce monde.

Mais ton temple pourtant, ta main, ta voix sera
La nef, l'appui, l'oreille, où ce charme perdra,
Où mourra cet effort, où se rompra cette onde.

EVERYTHING swells up against me, everything assails me, everything tempts me: the world, the flesh, and the rebel angel, whose wave, whose onslaught, whose deceitful spell engulfs me, Lord, and weakens and enchants me.

What ship, what stay, what sleeping ear, will you give me against danger, against falling, and against enchantment? Your temple in which your holiness dwells, your invincible arm, and your steadfast voice?

But what is this? My God, I feel many a time still warring against your temple and your arm and your voice, this rebel angel, this flesh and this world.

And yet your temple, your arm, and your voice will be the ship, the stay, the ear, on which that spell will lose its power, that onslaught will die, that wave will break.

JEAN-BAPTISTE CHASSIGNET

Le Mépris de la vie et consolation contre la mort

ASSIEDS-TOI sur le bord d'une ondante rivière:
Tu la verras fluer d'un perpétuel cours,
Et flots sur flots roulant en mille et mille tours
Décharger par les prés son humide carrière.

Mais tu ne verras rien de cette onde première
Qui naguère coulait; l'eau change tous les jours,
Tous les jours elle passe, et la nommons toujours
Même fleuve, et même eau, d'une même manière.

Ainsi l'homme varie, et ne sera demain
Telle comme aujourd'hui du pauvre corps humain
La force que le temps abrévie et consomme:

Le nom sans varier nous suit jusqu'au trépas,
Et combien qu'aujourd'hui celui ne sois-je pas
Qui vivais hier passé, toujours même on me nomme.

Contempt of Life and Reassurance upon Death

SIT down on the bank of a rippling river; you will see it flowing in a perpetual current, and, rolling wave after wave in a thousand twists and turns, outpouring its watery course through the meadows.

But you will see nothing of that first wave which once flowed by. The water changes every day, every day it passes and we still call it the same river, and the same water, in the same way.

So does man vary, and tomorrow the strength of the poor human body which time shortens and consumes will not be the same as today:

The name follows us until death without changing and, although today I am not the same man who was living yesterday, yet am I still called the same.

Donne l'enseigne au vent, étendant tes conquêtes
Du Midi jusqu'au Nord et, publiant tes lois
Au Ponant et Levant, fais trembler sous ta voix
Des potentats voisins les couronnes sujettes.

Tiens dans tes ports guerriers cent mille flottes prêtes
Pour écorner l'orgueil des arrogants Chinois,
Et, mettant sous le joug les félons Japonois,
Dépouille les trésors des terres plus secrètes.

Refrène le François, captive l'Allemand,
Supplante l'Espagnol, dompte le Musulman,
Et porte en Italie et la peste et la guerre:

Si mourras-tu, chétif, et ne posséderas
De tant de régions que tu délaisseras
Que le tour du tombeau: sept ou huit pieds de terre.

Cingle depuis la France au royaume Turquesque,
De là va visiter les murs de Sun-Tien
Et des fiers Japonais le royaume ancien,
Puis fais tourner la voile à la côte Moresque.

Unfurl your banner to the wind, extending your conquests from
the south to the north and, proclaiming your laws in the east and
the west, make the subject crowns of the neighbouring princes
tremble at the sound of your voice.

In your ports of war keep a hundred thousand ships ready to
whittle the pride of the arrogant Chinese and, fastening the yoke
on the false Japanese, ransack the treasures of the remotest lands.

Curb back the Frenchman, enchain the German, drive out the
Spaniard, subdue the Muslim, and carry to Italy plague and war:

Yet you will die, puny man, and of so many domains which you
will abandon you will possess only the length of the grave, seven or
eight feet of earth.

Sail away from France to the realm of the Turks, from there go
and visit the walls of Tsungsin and the ancient realm of the fierce
Japanese, then set your course back to the Moorish coast.

Passe encore au-delà de la mer Arabesque,
Et si tu n'es content du noir Égyptien,
Va remarquer les ports de l'empire Indien
Furetant les trésors de la gent barbaresque.

Si tu treuve' un seul homme affranchi de la mort
Partout où tu courras, dis qu'elle te fait tort
D'aigrir contre toi seul sa vengeante rancune:

Mais si tout homme est né pour choir au monument,
Apprends à tout le moins à mourir constamment;
Moindre se fait le mal par la perte commune.

Les poissons écaillés aiment les moites eaux,
Les fleuves et les lacs; les animaux sauvages
Aiment les bois touffus, les creux et les bocages,
Et l'air doux et serein est aimé des oiseaux;

Les grillons babillards aiment l'émail des preaux,
S'égayant au printemps parmi le vert herbage,
Les lézards et serpents envenimés de rage
Aiment des murs rompus les humides caveaux.

Pass again beyond the Arabian sea, and if the dark Egyptian does
not please you, go and see the ports of the empire of Ind, ran-
sacking the treasures of the Barbary folk.

If you find a single man not subject to death wherever you go,
say that death wrongs you in venting its spite on you alone.

But if every man was born to go down to the tomb, then learn at
least to die steadfastly. The evil becomes less when it is the common
lot.

The scaly fishes love the wet waters, the rivers, and the lakes; the
wild beasts love the thick woods, the caves, and the copses, and the
mild, clear sky is loved by the birds;

The chattering crickets love the bright hues of the meadows,
making merry in spring among the green grass, the lizards and ser-
pents envenomed with fury love the damp crannies in ruined walls.

Bref, naturellement chacun aime et désire
Le lieu originel d'où sa naissance il tire,
Auquel mêmes il doit résider longuement:

L'homme seul, dérivant comme plante divine
Du ciel spirituel sa féconde origine,
Préfère à sa patrie un long bannissement.

A BEAUCOUP de danger est sujette la fleur:
Ou l'on la foule au pied ou les vents la ternissent,
Les rayons du soleil la brûlent et rôtissent,
La bête la dévore, et s'effeuille en verdeur.

Nos jours, entremêlés de regret et de pleur,
A la fleur comparés comme la fleur fleurissent,
Tombent comme la fleur, comme la fleur périssent,
Autant comme du froid tourmentés de l'ardeur.

Non de fer ni de plomb, mais d'odorantes pommes
Le vaisseau va chargé, ainsi les jours des hommes
Sont légers, non pesants, variables et vains,

In short, each naturally loves and desires the place of origin from
which it draws its being, and which also it must inhabit for a long
time:
   Only man, like a divine plant deriving his fertile origin from the
spiritual sky, prefers a long exile to his true home.

To many a peril the flower is exposed: either it is trampled under-
foot or the winds wither it, the beams of the sun burn and scorch it,
the animal devours it, and its leaves fall while they are still green.
   Our days, intermingled with sorrow and tears, compared to the
flower like the flower blossom, fall like the flower, like the flower
perish, tormented by heat as much as by cold.
   Not with iron or with lead but with sweet-smelling apples does
the vessel go laden: so the days of man are light, unsubstantial,
variable, and vain,

Qui, laissant après eux d'un peu de renommée
L'odeur en moins de rien comme fruit consommée,
Passent légèrement hors du cœur des humains.

THÉOPHILE DE VIAU

Lettre à son frère

MON frère, mon dernier appui,
Toi seul dont le secours me dure,
Et qui seul trouves aujourd'hui
Mon adversité longue et dure;
Ami ferme, ardent, généreux,
Que mon sort le plus malheureux
Pique davantage à le suivre,
Achève de me secourir:
Il faudra qu'on me laisse vivre
Après m'avoir fait tant mourir.

And, leaving after them the scent of a little fame, in less than an instant consumed like fruit, pass lightly away out of human hearts.

Letter to His Brother

(Written to his brother Paul, a Huguenot captain from the prison in which he spent two years under suspicion of impiety. He died broken a year after his release. Boussères in the second stanza was their country home on the Garonne.)

MY brother, my last support, who alone continues to help me and who alone today thinks my misfortune long and hard; staunch, eager, generous friend, whom the extreme misery of my lot prompts to sympathize with it all the more, make a last effort to help me. They will have to let me live after having made me die for so long.

... Quelque lac qui me soit tendu
Par de si subtils adversaires,
Encore n'ai-je point perdu
L'espérance de voir Boussères.
Encore un coup, le dieu du jour
Tout devant moi fera sa cour
Aux rives de notre héritage,
Et je verrai ses cheveux blonds
Du même or qui luit sur le Tage
Dorer l'argent de nos sablons.

Je verrai ces bois verdissants
Où nos îles et l'herbe fraîche
Servent aux troupeaux mugissants
Et de promenoir et de crèche.
L'aurore y trouve à son retour
L'herbe qu'ils ont mangée le jour.
Je verrai l'eau qui les abreuve,
Et j'oirai plaindre les graviers
Et repartir l'écho du fleuve
Aux injures des mariniers.

... Whatever snare is laid for me by such subtle adversaries, I have still not lost hope of seeing Boussères. Once again the god of day will pay his court right before me on the banks of our estate, and I shall see his yellow locks gilding the silver of our sands with the same gold that gleams on the Tagus.

I shall see those green woods among which our islands and the fresh grass provide the lowing herds both with a place to walk in and a manger. The dawn finds at its return the same grass on which they grazed the day before. I shall see the water which slakes their thirst and I shall hear the gravel-banks murmuring and the river-echoes startled by the oaths of the boatmen.

... Je cueillerai ces abricots,
Ces fraises à couleur de flammes
Dont nos bergers font des écots
Qui seraient ici bons aux dames,
Et ces figues et ces melons
Dont la bouche des aquilons
N'a jamais su baiser l'écorce,
Et ces jaunes muscats si chers
Que jamais la grêle ne force
Dans l'asile de nos rochers.

Je verrai sur nos grenadiers
Leurs rouges pommes entr'ouvertes,
Où le ciel, comme à ses lauriers,
Garde toujours des feuilles vertes.
Je verrai ce touffu jasmin
Qui fait ombre à tout le chemin
D'une assez spacieuse allée,
Et la parfume d'une fleur
Qui conserve dans la gelée
Son odorat et sa couleur.

... I shall pick those apricots, those flame-coloured strawberries from which our shepherds make snack meals which here would be good enough for the ladies, and those figs and melons whose skin the mouth of the cold winds has never been able to kiss, and those precious yellow muscat grapes which the hail never violates in the shelter of our rocks.

I shall see the red, half-opened fruit on our pomegranate-trees, on which heaven, as with its own laurels, always keeps green leaves. I shall see that leafy jasmine which shades the whole length of quite a broad garden-walk and scents it with a flower which keeps its fragrance and its colour through the frosts.

Je reverrai fleurir nos prés
Je leur verrai couper les herbes;
Je verrai quelque temps après
Le paysan couché sur les gerbes;
Et, comme ce climat divin
Nous est très libéral de vin,
Après avoir rempli la grange
Je verrai du matin au soir
Comme les flots de la vendange
Écumeront dans le pressoir.

Là, d'un esprit laborieux,
L'infatigable Bellegarde
De la voix, des mains et des yeux
A tout le revenu prend garde.
Il connaît d'un exacte soin
Ce que les prés rendent de foin,
Ce que nos troupeaux ont de laine,
Et sait mieux que les vieux paysans
Ce que la montagne et la plaine
Nous peuvent donner tous les ans.

I shall see our meadows flower again; I shall see their grass being cut; some time later I shall see the peasant lying on the corn-sheaves; and as that divine climate gives us wine in abundance, after the barn has been filled I shall see the floods of the grape-harvest foaming from morning till evening in the wine-press.

There, industriously inclined, the tireless Bellegarde supervises the whole yield of the estate with voice, hands, and eyes. He knows exactly how much hay the meadows give, how much wool our flocks have, and can tell better than the old peasants what the mountain and the plain can give us each year.

... Si je passais dans ce loisir
Encore autant que j'ai de vie,
Le comble d'un si cher plaisir
Bornerait toute mon envie.
Il faut qu'un jour ma liberté
Se lâche en cette volupté.
Je n'ai plus de regret au Louvre,
Ayant vécu dans ces douceurs.
Que la même terre me couvre
Qui couvre mes prédécesseurs.

Ode

Un corbeau devant moi croasse,
Une ombre offusque mes regards;
Deux belettes et deux renards
Traversent l'endroit où je passe;
Les pieds faillent à mon cheval,
Mon laquais tombe du haut mal;
J'entends craqueter le tonnerre;
Un esprit se présente à moi;
J'ois Charon qui m'appelle à soi,
Je vois le centre de la terre.

... If I were to spend all the life that is left me in that calm spot, the satisfaction of so dear a pleasure would be the limit of my desire. One day I must surely be set free among those delights. Having lived that sweet life, I have no more regrets for the Louvre. Let the same earth cover me which covers my ancestors.

Ode

A RAVEN croaks in front of me, a shadow startles my eyes; two weasels and two foxes cross the path down which I pass; my horse's feet slip, my servant falls in a fit; I hear the thunder crackling; a spectre appears before me; I hear Charon calling me to him, I see the earth opening under me.

Ce ruisseau remonte à sa source;
Un bœuf gravit sur un clocher;
Le sang coule de ce rocher;
Un aspic s'accouple d'une ourse;
Sur le haut d'une vieille tour
Un serpent déchire un vautour;
Le feu brûle dedans la glace;
Le soleil est devenu noir;
Je vois la lune qui va choir;
Cet arbre est sorti de sa place.

Le Matin

L'AURORE sur le front du jour
Sème l'azur, l'or et l'ivoire,
Et le soleil, lassé de boire,
Commence son oblique tour.

Ses chevaux au sortir de l'onde,
De flamme et de clarté couverts,
La bouche et les naseaux ouverts,
Ronflent la lumière du monde.

That stream is flowing backwards; an ox climbs a belfry; blood flows from that rock; an asp couples with a she-bear; at the top of an old tower a snake is tearing up a vulture; fire burns in the ice; the sun has turned black; I see the moon about to fall; that tree has moved from its place.

Morning

OVER the face of the day the dawn sows azure, gold, and ivory, and the sun, weary of drinking [in the sea], begins its slanting course.

Its horses, coming out of the waves, covered with flame and brightness, with open mouths and nostrils snort out the light of the world.

La lune fuit devant nos yeux,
La nuit a retiré ses voiles,
Peu à peu le front des étoiles
S'unit à la couleur des cieux.

Déjà la diligente avette
Boit la marjolaine et le thym,
Et revient riche du butin
Qu'elle a pris sur le mont Hymette.

Je vois le généreux lion
Qui sort de sa demeure creuse,
Hérissant sa perruque affreuse
Qui fait fuir Endymion.

Sa dame, entrant dans les bocages,
Compte les sangliers qu'elle a pris,
Ou dévale chez les esprits
Errants aux sombres marécages.

The moon flees before our eyes, night has withdrawn her veils, slowly the face of the stars merges into the colour of the skies.

Already the industrious bee drinks of the marjoram and thyme and comes back rich with the loot which it has taken on Mount Hymettus.

I see the noble lion coming out of his hollow cave, bristling his frightful mane which makes Endymion flee.

His lady,* retreating into the woods, counts the wild boars she has taken, or goes down among the spirits which wander in the dark marshes.

---

*Endymion's lady, the Moon – that is, Diana, huntress and goddess of the underworld.

Je vois les agneaux bondissants
Sur les blés qui ne font que naître:
Cloris, chantant, les mène paître
Parmi ces coteaux verdissants.

Les oiseaux d'un joyeux ramage
En chantant semblent adorer
La lumière qui vient dorer
Leur cabinet et leur plumage.

La charrue écorche la plaine,
Le bouvier qui suit les sillons
Presse de voix et d'aiguillons
Le couple de bœufs qui l'entraîne.

Alix apprête son fuseau;
Sa mère, qui lui fait la tâche,
Presse le chanvre qu'elle attache
A sa quenouille de roseau.

Une confuse violence
Trouble le calme de la nuit,
Et la lumière avec le bruit
Dissipent l'ombre et le silence.

I see the lambs leaping over the young corn; Chloris, singing, leads them out to graze among those green slopes.

With joyous twitterings the birds seem, as they sing, to worship the light which gilds their little houses and their plumage.

The plough galls the plain; the ploughman, walking along the furrows, urges on with voice and goad the pair of oxen which draw it.

Alix gets her spindle ready; her mother, preparing her work for her, presses the hemp which she attaches to her distaff made of reed.

Confused activity disturbs the calm of the night, and light and noise drive away darkness and silence.

Alidor cherche à son réveil
L'ombre d'Iris qu'il a baisée,
Et pleure en son âme abusée
La fuite d'un si doux sommeil.

Les bêtes sont dans leur tanière
Qui tremblent de voir le soleil;
L'homme, remis par le sommeil,
Reprend son œuvre coutumière.

Le forgeron est au fourneau:
Ois comme le charbon s'allume!
Le fer rouge dessus l'enclume
Étincelle sous le marteau.

Cette chandelle semble morte:
Le jour la fait évanouir;
Le soleil vient nous éblouir:
Vois qu'il passe au travers la porte.

Il est jour, levons-nous, Philis:
Allons à notre jardinage
Voir s'il est, comme ton visage,
Semé de roses et de lis.

Alidor, awakening, looks for the ghost of Iris which he kissed, and weeps in his deluded heart to find that so sweet a dream has fled.

The beasts are in their lairs, trembling to see the sun; man, refreshed by sleep, takes up his usual tasks.

The blacksmith is at the forge; hear the coal roaring into flame! The red-hot iron on the anvil sparks beneath the hammer.

This candle seems dead: the daylight makes it fade; the sun comes to dazzle us: see him coming through the door!

It is day; let us get up, Phyllis: let us go to our garden and see if, like your face, it is sprinkled with roses and lilies.

ANTOINE-GIRARD DE SAINT-AMANT

La Solitude

O H, Q U E j'aime la solitude!
Que ces lieux sacrés à la nuit,
Éloignés du monde et du bruit,
Plaisent à mon inquiétude!
Mon Dieu! que mes yeux sont contents
De voir ces bois, qui se trouvèrent
A la nativité du temps,
Et que tous les siècles révèrent,
Être encore aussi beaux et verts,
Qu'aux premiers jours de l'univers!

... Que j'aime ce marais paisible!
Il est tout bordé d'alisiers,
D'aulnes, de saules et d'osiers,
A qui le fer n'est point nuisible.
Les nymphes, y cherchant le frais,
S'y viennent fournir de quenouilles,
De pipeaux, de joncs et de glais,
Où l'on voit sauter les grenouilles

Solitude

O H, how I love solitude! How much these places, sacred to night, far removed from men and noise, please my unquiet mind. God, how contented are my eyes to see these woods, which were there at the birth of time and which all the ages respect, still as lovely and as green as in the first days of creation.
... How I love this peaceful pond! It is fringed with rowan-trees, alders, willows, and osiers, which the axe never harms. The nymphs, seeking some cool place, come here to provide themselves with bulrushes, reed-pipes, reeds, and irises, among which you see

Qui de frayeur s'y vont cacher
Sitôt qu'on veut s'en approcher.

Là, cent mille oiseaux aquatiques
Vivent, sans craindre, en leur repos,
Le giboyeur fin et dispos,
Avec ses mortelles pratiques.
L'un, tout joyeux d'un si beau jour,
S'amuse à becqueter sa plume;
L'autre alentit le feu d'amour
Qui dans l'eau même se consume,
Et prennent tous innocemment
Leur plaisir en cet élément.

Jamais l'été ni la froidure
N'ont vu passer dessus cette eau
Nulle charrette ni bateau,
Depuis que l'un et l'autre dure;
Jamais voyageur altéré
N'y fit servir sa main de tasse;
Jamais chevreuil désespéré
N'y finit sa vie à la chasse;
Et jamais le traître hameçon
N'en fit sortir aucun poisson.

the frogs jumping and hiding themselves in panic as soon as you try to approach.

There, a myriad water-fowl live peacefully with no fear of the cunning, watchful fowler with his deadly practices. One, delighting in such a lovely day, passes the time preening its feathers. Another abates the fire of love, which is consumed in the water itself, and all of them innocently take their pleasure in that element.

Never have summer or winter's cold seen cart or boat pass over this water since either [winter or summer] endures. Never has thirsty traveller cupped his hand in it. Never has desperate roebuck ended his life there in the hunt; and never did the treacherous hook bring any fish from out of it.

Que j'aime à voir la décadence
De ces vieux châteaux ruinés,
Contre qui les ans mutinés
Ont déployé leur insolence!
Les sorciers y font leur sabat;
Les démons follets s'y retirent,
Qui d'un malicieux ébat
Trompent nos sens et nous martirent;
Là se nichent en mille trous
Les couleuvres et les hiboux.

L'orfraie, avec ses cris funèbres,
Mortels augures des destins,
Fait rire et danser les lutins
Dans ces lieux remplis de ténèbres.
Sous un chevron de bois maudit
Y branle le squelette horrible
D'un pauvre amant qui se pendit
Pour une bergère insensible,
Qui d'un seul regard de pitié
Ne daigna voir son amitié.

How I love to see the decay of these old ruined castles, against which the rebellious years have flaunted their insolence! The wizards hold their sabbath there, in there lurk the elfish goblins, who delude our senses and plague us with their mischievous sport; there in countless holes adders and owls nest.

The screech-owl, with its baleful cries, deadly harbingers of doom, makes the goblins laugh and dance in these haunts filled with darkness. Under a beam of wood accursed jigs the fearful skeleton of a poor lover who hanged himself for a stony-hearted shepherd-ess, who did not deign to favour his love with a single pitying glance.

Aussi le Ciel, juge équitable,
Qui maintient les lois en vigueur,
Prononça contre sa rigueur
Une sentence épouvantable:
Autour de ces vieux ossements
Son ombre, aux peines condamnée,
Lamente en longs gémissements
Sa malheureuse destinée,
Ayant, pour croître son effroi,
Toujours son crime devant soi.

Là se trouvent sur quelques marbres
Des devises du temps passé;
Ici l'âge a presque effacé
Des chiffres taillés sur les arbres;
Le plancher du lieu le plus haut
Est tombé jusque dans la cave
Que la limace et le crapaud
Souillent de venin et de bave;
Le lierre y croît au foyer,
A l'ombrage d'un grand noyer . . .

And so heaven, the impartial judge who enforces the laws, pronounced a dreadful sentence upon her cruelty: around these ancient bones, her ghost, condemned to torments, laments its unhappy fate with long-drawn moans – having, to increase its horror, its crime always present before it.

There are seen on marble slabs emblems of times gone by; here, the years have almost effaced initials carved on the trees; the floor of the topmost room has fallen right through to the cellar, which the slug and the toad foul with poison and with slime; there, the ivy grows on the hearth in the shade of a great walnut-tree. . . .

L'Hiver des Alpes

Ces atomes de feu qui sur la neige brillent,
Ces étincelles d'or, d'azur et de cristal
Dont l'hiver, au soleil, d'un lustre oriental
Pare ses cheveux blancs que les vents éparpillent;

Ce beau coton du ciel de quoi les monts s'habillent,
Ce pavé transparent fait du second métal,
Et cet air net et sain, propre à l'esprit vital,
Sont si doux à mes yeux que d'aise ils en pétillent.

Cette saison me plaît, j'en aime la froideur;
Sa robe d'innocence et de pure candeur
Couvre en quelque façon les crimes de la terre.

Aussi l'Olympien la voit d'un front humain;
Sa colère l'épargne, et jamais le tonnerre
Pour désoler ses jours ne partit de sa main.

Winter in the Alps

These fiery atoms glittering on the snow, these sparks of gold, of azure and of crystal with which Winter, in sunshine, with oriental splendour adorns its white hair tossed by the winds;

That fine skiey cotton with which the mountains clothe themselves, that transparent pavement made of the second metal [silver], and this clean, healthy air, favourable to the vital spirit, are so sweet to my eyes that they sparkle with delight.

This season pleases me, I like its cold. Its mantle of innocence and of candid purity in some sort covers the crimes of the earth.

And so Olympian Jove turns a kindly face upon it. His anger spares it and never was the thunder loosed from his hand to sadden its days.

Plainte sur la mort de Sylvie

RUISSEAU qui cours après toi-même
Et qui te fuis toi-même aussi,
Arrête un peu ton onde ici
Pour écouter mon deuil extrême.
Puis, quand tu l'auras su, va-t'en dire à la mer
Qu'elle n'a rien de plus amer.

Raconte-lui comme Sylvie,
Qui seule gouverne mon sort,
A reçu le coup de la mort
Au plus bel âge de la vie,
Et que cet accident triomphe en même jour
De toutes les forces d'Amour.

Las! je n'en puis dire autre chose,
Mes soupirs tranchent mon discours.
Adieu, ruisseau, reprends ton cours
Qui, non plus que moi, se repose;
Que si, par mes regrets, j'ai bien pu t'arrêter,
Voici des pleurs pour te hâter.

Dirge for the Death of Sylvia

STREAM who hasten after yourself, and flee from yourself also, halt your waters here for a moment and give ear to my heavy grief. Then, when you have heard it, go and tell the sea that it has nothing more bitter than this.

Tell it how Sylvia, sole mistress of my fate, has suffered death's blow in the flower of life, and that this disaster has discomfited in one day all the forces of love.

Alas, I can say no more. My sighs cut short my words. Farewell stream, flow on your course, which knows repose no more than I. And if my lamentations have been able to halt you, here are tears to hasten you on.

Le Melon

... C'en est fait, le voilà coupé,
Et mon espoir n'est point trompé.
O dieux! que l'éclat qu'il me lance
M'en confirme bien l'excellence!
Qui vit jamais un si beau teint!
D'un jaune sanguin il se peint;
Il est massif jusques au centre,
Il a peu de grains dans le ventre,
Et ce peu-là, je pense encor
Que ce soient autant de grains d'or;
Il est sec, son écorce est mince;
Bref, c'est un vrai manger de prince;
Mais, bien que je ne le sois pas,
J'en ferai pourtant un repas.

   Ha! soutenez-moi, je me pâme!
Ce morceau me chatouille l'âme.
Il rend une douce liqueur
Qui me va confire le cœur;
Mon appétit se rassasie
De pure et nouvelle ambroisie,
Et mes sens, par le goût séduits,
Au nombre d'un sont tous réduits.

The Melon

... Well, that's it. Now it is cut, and my hopes are not disappointed. O gods, the radiance that it casts leaves no doubt of its excellence! Who ever saw such a lovely hue! It is tinted a reddish yellow; it is firm right to the centre, it has few pips in its belly, and those few, I really believe, are so many grains of gold. It is not watery, its rind is thin: in short, a feast for a king. But, although I am not one, yet will I make a meal of it.

Ha! Hold me up, I swoon! This delicious morsel tickles my very soul. It oozes a sweet juice which will steep my heart in ecstasy. My appetite is sated with a new and pure ambrosia, and all my senses, captivated by taste, are concentrated into one.

Non, le coco, fruit délectable,
Qui lui tout seul fournit la table
De tous les mets que le désir
Puisse imaginer et choisir,
Ni les baisers d'une maîtresse,
Quand elle-même nous caresse,
Ni ce qu'on tire des roseaux
Que Crète nourrit dans ses eaux,
Ni le cher abricot, que j'aime,
Ni la fraise avecque la crème,
Ni la manne qui vient du ciel,
Ni le pur aliment du miel,
Ni la poire de Tours sacrée,
Ni la verte figue sucrée,
Ni la prune au jus délicat,
Ni même le raisin muscat
(Parole pour moi bien étrange),
Ne sont qu'amertume et que fange
Au prix de ce MELON divin,
Honneur du climat angevin.

. . . O manger précieux! délices de la bouche!
O doux reptile herbu, rampant sur une couche!

No, neither the coconut, that delectable fruit which by itself pro-
vides the table with all the dishes which desire can imagine and
choose, nor the kisses of a mistress when she herself caresses us, nor
what is drawn from the [sugar] canes which Crete grows in its
waters, nor the dear apricot which I love, nor the strawberry with
cream, nor the manna which falls from heaven, nor the pure food of
honey, nor the sacred pear of Tours, nor the green and sugared
fig, nor the plum with delicate juice, nor even the muscat grape
(strange indeed that *I* should say so), are more than gall and mud
compared to this divine MELON, the glory of the Angevin clime.

. . . O precious food, delight of the palate! O sweet grassy reptile,
crawling on your green couch! O better far than gold, O Sun God's

O beaucoup mieux que l'or, chef-d'œuvre d'Apollon!
O fleur de tous les fruits! O ravissant MELON!
Les hommes de la cour seront gens de parole,
Les bordels de Rouen seront francs de vérole,
Sans vermine et sans gale on verra les pédants,
Les preneurs de petun auront de belles dents,
Les femmes des badauds ne seront plus coquettes,
Les corps pleins de santé se plairont aux cliquettes,
Les amoureux transis ne seront plus jaloux,
Les paisibles bourgeois hanteront les filous,
Les meilleurs cabarets deviendront solitaires,
Les chantres du Pont-Neuf diront de hauts mystères,
Les pauvres Quinze-Vingts vaudront trois cents argus,
Les esprits doux du temps paraîtront fort aigus,
Maillet fera des vers aussi bien que Malherbe,
Je haïrai Faret, qui se rendra superbe,
Pour amasser des biens avare je serai,
Pour devenir plus grand mon cœur j'abaisserai,
Bref, O MELON sucrin, pour t'accabler de gloire,
Des faveurs de Margot je perdrai la mémoire
Avant que je t'oublie et que ton goût charmant
Soit biffé des cahiers du bon gros SAINT-AMANT.

masterpiece! O flower of all the fruits, ravishing MELON! The men of the Court will be men of their word, the brothels of Rouen will be free of the pox, de-loused and clear-skinned will pedants be seen, tobacco-users will have white teeth, fools will no longer have flighty wives, healthy bodies will delight in lepers' rattles, moonstruck lovers will cease to be jealous, peaceful citizens will consort with thieves, the best inns will become deserted, the ballad-singers of the Pont Neuf will speak high mysteries, the poor Fifteen-Score [an institution for the blind] will be as good as three hundred Arguses, the simple-minded of this age will seem very acute, Maillet will write verses as good as Malherbe's, I shall take to hating Faret, who will grow pompous, I shall be greedy to amass riches, to become greater I will demean my heart; in short, O sugary MELON, to heap you with glory, I will lose the memory of Margot's favours before I forget you and your delightful taste is crossed off the books of good fat SAINT-AMANT.

L'Enamouré

PARBLEU! j'en tiens, c'est tout de bon,
Ma libre humeur en a dans l'aile,
Puisque je préfère au jambon
Le visage d'une donzelle.
Je suis pris dans le doux lien
De l'archerot idaliën.
Ce dieutelet, fils de Cyprine,
Avecques son arc mi-courbé,
A féru ma rude poitrine
Et m'a fait venir à jubé.

Mon esprit a changé d'habit:
Il n'est plus vêtu de revêche;
Il se raffine et se fourbit
Aux yeux de ma belle chevêche.
Plus aigu, plus clair et plus net
Qu'une dague de cabinet,
Il estocade la tristesse,
Et, la chassant d'autour de soi,
Se vante que la politesse
Ne marche plus qu'avecques moi.

The Lovesick Swain

OD'S LIFE! I've caught it, properly. My roving fancy has been winged, since I prefer the face of a damsel to ham. I am caught in the sweet snare of the Idalian archer-boy. The godlet son of the Cyprian with his curving bow has pierced my rugged breast and made me come to heel.

My wit has changed its garb: it is no longer clad in homespun. It grows refined and polished before the eyes of my pretty owl. Sharper, brighter, and more sparkling than some toy dagger, it thrusts and cuts at melancholy and, driving it from all around, boasts that true refinement walks only now with me.

Je me fais friser tous les jours,
On me relève la moustache;
Je n'entrecoupe mes discours
Que de rots d'ambre et de pistache;
J'ai fait banqueroute au petun;
L'excès du vin m'est importun;
Dix pintes par jour me suffisent:
Encore, ô falotte beauté
Dont les regards me déconfisent,
Est-ce pour boire à ta santé!

VINCENT VOITURE

La Belle Matineuse

DES portes du matin l'amante de Céphale
Ses roses épandait dans le milieu des airs,
Et jetait sur les cieux nouvellement ouverts
Ces traits d'or et d'azur qu'en naissant elle étale,

I have my beard curled every day, the ends of my moustache are twirled up. I only punctuate my conversation with belches of pistachio and amber. I have driven the tobacconists bankrupt. Excess of wine is distasteful to me. Ten pints a day suffice me*; and then, O pallid beauty, whose looks undo me utterly, it is to drink to your health.

The Fair Nymph of Dawn

FROM the gates of the morning the mistress of Cephalus [the Dawn] was scattering her roses through the air, and was casting on the newly opened skies those shafts of gold and azure which she displays at her birth,

---

*More accurately, about sixteen pints. The *pinte* is a larger measure than the English pint.

Quand la nymphe divine, à mon repos fatale,
Apparut, et brilla de tant d'attraits divers
Qu'il semblait qu'elle seule éclairait l'univers
Et remplissait de feux la rive orientale.

Le Soleil, se hâtant pour la gloire des cieux,
Vint opposer sa flamme à l'éclat de ses yeux
Et prit tous les rayons dont l'Olympe se dore.

L'onde, la terre et l'air s'allumaient à l'entour;
Mais auprès de Philis on le prit pour l'aurore,
Et l'on crut que Philis était l'astre du jour.

Rondeau

Vous l'entendez mieux que je ne pensois.
Si quelque amant bien-disant et matois
Vous croit payer en vous nommant son âme,
C'est du latin qui passe votre gamme;
Vous n'entendez des termes si courtois.

When that heavenly nymph, fatal to my peace, appeared and
shone with so many varied charms that it seemed that she alone
gave light to the world and filled the eastern shore with fire.

The Sun, hastening on for the honour of the heavens, came to
parry the brightness of her eyes with his flame, and took all the
beams with which Olympus is gilded.

The sea, the earth, and the sky grew bright all around; but beside
Phyllis he was taken for the dawn, and they thought that Phyllis
was the star of day [the sun himself].

Rondeau

You understand better than I thought. If some smooth-tongued
and crafty lover thinks to pay you by speaking of his heart, that is
Greek and quite beyond you; you do not understand such courtly
terms.

Mais s'il en vient qui dise à haute voix
Qu'il veut prouver, fût-il Turc ou Anglois,
Par beaux effets la grandeur de sa flamme,
   Vous l'entendez.

Je donnerai telle somme par mois:
Outre cela, joyaux, perles de choix,
Satin, velours à souhait, à madame.
Cet entretien vous charme et vous enflamme;
C'est dire d'or et parler bon françois.
   Vous l'entendez.

Rondeau

SIX rois prièrent l'autre jour
Tyrcis de leur faire la cour;
Mais il soufflait un vent de bise
Qui perçait jusqu'à la chemise.
Cela le fit demeurer court.

But if one comes proclaiming loudly that he will prove, be he Turk or Englishman, the strength of his passion with goods and cash, you understand him.

I will give such-and-such a sum per month; in addition jewels, choice pearls, satin, velvet as required, to Madam. This declaration delights and inflames you. 'Tis golden speech and good plain French. You understand.

Rondeau*

SIX kings begged Tircis to pay court to them the other day; but an icy wind was blowing which cut right through to your shirt. That pulled him up short.

---

*Written for a certain François Coquet, renowned for his fatness, who once remarked: 'I would not go for six kings.'

Il a le ventre d'un tambour,
Ce qui le rend tant soit peu lourd
Et fait que parfois il méprise
     Six rois.

Il ne fait point cas de l'amour.
Quand on l'appelle il fait le sourd;
Mais pour prêter son entremise
En quelque fâcheuse entreprise,
Il ne le ferait jamais pour
     Six rois.

Étrenne d'une tortue

POUR vous venir baiser la main
Je partis, au mois de septembre,
Du bout du faubourg Saint-Germain;
Et nuit et jour faisant chemin,
J'arrivai hier céans à la fin de décembre.

He has a belly like a drum, which makes him just a little sluggish and causes him occasionally to despise six kings.

He doesn't think much of love. When you call him he pretends not to hear. But as for lending his services for any dubious enterprise, he would never do it for six kings.

On the New Year Gift of a Tortoise*

To come and kiss your hand, I set out in September from the end of the Faubourg Saint-Germain; and travelling night and day, I arrived in this house yesterday at the end of December. Sometimes

---

*Sent by a lady with three other animals to a certain Monsieur Esprit.

Quelquefois Salladin va plus diligemment,
Mais il n'est rien de tel que d'aller sûrement.
    Voulant doncque vous étrenner,
    Pour vous faire heureusement vivre
Je n'ai rien de meilleur que je puisse donner
    Si ce n'est mon exemple à suivre.
Vous autres beaux esprits battez trop de pays.
    Croyez-moi, suivez mon avis.
Soit que vous poursuiviez évêché, femme ou fille,
Faites tout comme moi, hâtez-vous lentement;
Ne formez qu'un dessein, suivez-le constamment.
Mais c'est trop discourir, je rentre en ma coquille.

CHARLES VION DE DALIBRAY

Sonnet bachique

JE ne vais point aux coups exposer ma bedaine,
Moi qui ne suis connu ni d'Armand ni du Roi;

Salladin* goes more speedily, but there is nothing like going surely.

So wishing to bring you a New Year gift, to help you to live happily I have nothing better to offer you than my own example. You brilliant minds race about too much. Believe me, follow my advice. Whether you are after a bishopric, a woman, or a girl, do everything as I do, make haste slowly. Form a single plan and follow it through steadily. But that's quite enough talk, I'm going back into my shell.

Drinking Sonnet

I AM not going to expose my paunch to blows, I who am unknown both to Armand [Richelieu] and the King; I want to find out how

*Richelieu's courier.

Je veux savoir combien un poltron comme moi
Peut vivre n'étant point soldat ni capitaine.

Je mourrais, s'il fallait qu'au milieu d'une plaine
Je fusse estropié de ce bras dont je bois;
Ne me conte donc plus qu'on meurt autant chez soi
A table, entre les pots, qu'où ta valeur te mène.

Ne me conte donc plus qu'en l'ardeur des combats
On se rend immortel par un noble trépas,
Cela ne fera point que j'aille à l'escarmouche.

Je veux mourir entier, et sans gloire et sans nom,
Et crois-moi, cher Clindor, si je meurs par la bouche,
Que ce ne sera pas par celle du canon.

Sur une horloge de sable

CETTE poussière que tu vois
Qui tes heures compasse
Et va recourant tant de fois
Par un petit espace:

long a coward like myself can live without being a soldier or
captain.

I should die, if in the middle of some plain I were to lose this
arm that I drink with; so stop telling me that one is as likely
to die in one's home, at table among the pots, as where your valour
leads you.

Stop telling me that in the heat of battle one becomes immortal
through a noble death; that won't get me to go out soldiering.

I want to die in one piece, unfamed and unsung, and believe me,
dear Clindor, if I die by the mouth, it will not be by the mouth of
the cannon.

On an Hourglass

THIS dust which you see, which measures your hours, and so often
goes running through a narrow space:

Jadis Damon je m'appelois,
Que la divine grâce
De Philis pour qui je brûlois
A mis en cette place.

Le feu secret qui me rongea
En cette poudre me changea
Qui jamais ne repose:

Apprends, amant, que par le sort
L'espérance t'est close
De reposer même en ta mort.

TRISTAN L'HERMITE

[Les Fleurs et la grotte]

... JE vous pourrais montrer si vous veniez un jour
En un parc qu'ici près depuis peu j'ai fait clore,
Mille amants transformés, qui des lois de l'Amour
    Sont passés sous celles de Flore;
Ils ont pour aliment les larmes de l'aurore.
    Dieux! que ne suis-je entre ces fleurs
Si vous devez un jour m'arroser de vos pleurs?

Damon I was once called, whom the divine grace of Phyllis for whom I burned put in this place.

The hidden fire which gnawed me changed me into this powder which is never at rest.

Learn, lover, that by fate you are sealed off from hope of resting even in death.

[The Flowers and the Grotto]

... IF you came one day to a garden which I have lately had enclosed near here, I could show you a thousand transformed lovers, who have passed from the rule of Love into the rule of Flora. They have the tears of the dawn for food. O gods! why am I not among those flowers, if you are to water me one day with your tears?

Vous y verriez Clytie, aux sentiments jaloux,
Qui n'a pu jusqu'ici guérir de la jaunisse;
Et la fleur de ce Grec dont le bouillant courroux
    Ne peut souffrir une injustice;
Vous y verriez encore Adonis et Narcisse,
    Dont l'un fut aimé de Cypris,
L'autre fut de son ombre aveuglément épris.

Je vous ferais savoir tout ce que l'on en dit,
Vous contant leurs vertus et leurs métamorphoses:
Quelle fleur vint du lait que Junon répandit,
    Et quel sang fit rougir les roses
Qui grossissent d'orgueil dès qu'elles sont écloses,
    Voyant leur portrait si bien peint
Dans la vive blancheur des lis de votre teint.

Piqué secrètement de leur éclat vermeil,
Un folâtre Zéphire à l'entour se promène,
Et, pour les garantir de l'ardeur du soleil,
    Les évente de son haleine;

There you would see Clytie, the jealous-natured thing, who so far has not been able to recover from jaundice; and the flower of that Greek* whose boiling rage cannot stomach an injustice; you would also see Adonis and Narcissus, of which the one was loved by Cypris and the other was blindly infatuated by his own reflection.

I would teach you all that is told of them, relating their virtues and their metamorphoses: which flower came from the milk which Juno shed, and which blood reddened the roses which swell with pride as soon as they bloom, seeing their portrait so well painted amid the gleaming whiteness of the lilies of your complexion.

Secretly spurred by their rosy beauty, a playful zephyr roams around, and, to protect them from the heat of the sun, fans them

---

*Ajax, who killed himself in fury when the arms of Achilles were awarded to Odysseus instead of to himself. A kind of hyacinth sprang from his blood. See Garnier's *Élégie sur la mort de Ronsard*.

Mais lorsqu'il les émeut, il irrite ma peine,
    Car aimant en un plus haut point,
Je vois que mes soupirs ne vous émeuvent point.

Là, mille arbres chargés des plus riches présents
Dont la terre à son gré les mortels favorise,
Et sur qui d'un poinçon je grave tous les ans
   ·   Votre chiffre et votre devise,
Font en mille bouquets éclater la cerise,
    La prune au jus raffraîchissant,
Et le jaune abricot au goût si ravissant.

Là, parmi des jasmins dressés confusément,
Et dont le doux esprit à toute heure s'exhale,
Cependant que partout le chaud est véhément,
    On se peut garantir du hâle,
Et se perdre aisément dans ce plaisant dédale,
    Comme entre mille aimables nœuds
Mon âme se perdit parmi vos beaux cheveux.

Une grotte superbe et des rochers de prix,
Que des pins orgueilleux couronnent de feuillage,
Y garde la fraîcheur sous ses riches lambris,
    Qui sont d'un rare coquillage.

with his breath; but when he stirs them he exasperates my pain, for, loving on a higher level, I see that my sighs stir you not at all.

There, a thousand trees loaded with the richest gifts with which the earth liberally favours mortal men, and on which I engrave your emblem and your motto with an etching-tool every year, burst into countless clusters of cherries, plums with refreshing juice, and the yellow apricot with its delicious taste.

There, among jasmines planted at hazard, whose sweet essence is breathed out night and day, while everywhere the heat is intense one can find protection from sunburn and easily lose oneself in that agreeable maze – as among countless pleasant curls my heart lost itself in your lovely hair.

A magnificent grotto and rocks of costly stone, which proud pines crown with foliage, preserves the cool inside its rich walls,

Mille secrets tuyaux cachés sur son passage
      Mouillent soudain les imprudents
Qui sans discrétion veulent entrer dedans.

D'un côté l'on y voit une petite mer
Que traverse en nageant un amoureux Léandre;
De rage autour de lui l'onde vient écumer,
      Et lui tâche de s'en défendre,
Apercevant Héro qui veille pour l'attendre
      Et d'impatience et d'amour
Brûle avec son flambeau sur le haut d'une tour.

Aux niches de rocher qui sont aux environs
On voit toujours mouvoir de petits personnages:
Ici des charpentiers et là des forgerons,
      Qui travaillent à leurs ouvrages;
Et force moulinets, faits à divers usages,
      Qui tournent bien diligemment
A la faveur de l'eau qui coule incessamment.

Une table de marbre, où je vais me mirer
Alors que je n'ai pas le visage si blême,

which are made of rare sea-shells. Numberless secret pipes hidden along the entrance suddenly drench incautious intruders who indiscreetly venture in there.

On one side is to be seen a little sea, which an amorous Leander is swimming across; the water foams in fury around him and he tries to breast it, catching sight of Hero who sits up waiting for him and, with impatience and love, burns with her torch at the top of a tower.

In recesses in the rock near by, one sees little figures continually moving; carpenters here and blacksmiths there, working at their tasks; and many little wheels, for various purposes, turning busily by means of the water which flows continuously.

A marble table, in which I go to look at my reflection when my

Pourrait bien de beau linge et de fleurs se parer
　　　Quand la chaleur serait extrême,
Si vous vouliez venir y manger de la crême
　　　Et des fraises, que chèrement
Je ne fais conserver que pour vous seulement.

Vous n'y trouveriez pas de superbes apprêts
Comme ceux que mérite une beauté divine,
Mais vous pourriez à l'ombre au moins y boire frais
　　　En des vases de cornaline,
Et vos yeux, en vingt plats de porcelaine fine
　　　Pourraient confronter à souhait
La blancheur de vos mains avec celle du lait . . .

PIERRE LE MOYNE

[*Au cœur des pyramides*]

. . . Sous le pied de ces monts taillés et suspendus
Il s'étend des pays ténébreux et perdus,

face is not so pallid as now, might well be embellished with fine linen and flowers on some day of excessive heat, if you cared to come and eat strawberries and cream which I keep lovingly for you alone.

You would not find any of the luxurious preparations which a divine beauty deserves, but you could at least have cool drinks in the shade from vases of cornelian, and your eyes, in twenty dishes of delicate porcelain, could compare as long as they pleased the whiteness of your hands with that of the milk . . .

[*In the Heart of the Pyramids*]

. . . Beneath the foot of these hewn and hanging mountains there stretch dark and lost regions, wide deserts, sombre solitudes,

De spacieux déserts, des solitudes sombres
Faites pour le séjour des morts et de leurs ombres.
Là sont les corps des Rois et les corps des Sultans,
Diversement rangés selon l'ordre du temps.
Les uns sont enchâssés dans les creuses images
A qui l'art a donné leur taille et leurs visages,
Et dans ces vains portraits, fastueux monuments,
Leur orgueil se conserve avec leurs ossements.
Les autres, embaumés, sont posés en des niches
Où leurs ombres, encore éclatantes et riches,
Semblent perpétuer, malgré les lois du sort,
La pompe de leur vie en celle de leur mort.
    De ce muet sénat, de cette cour terrible,
Le silence épouvante et l'aspect est horrible.
Là sont les devanciers joints à leurs descendants;
Tous les règnes y sont, on y voit tous les temps;
Et cette Antiquité, ces siècles dont l'histoire
N'a pu sauver qu'à peine une obscure mémoire,
Réunis par la mort en cette sombre nuit,
Y sont sans mouvement, sans lumière et sans bruit . . .

made to be inhabited by the dead and their ghosts. There are the bodies
of the kings and the sultans, variously ranked in the order of the ages.
Some are enshrined in hollow images, to which the artist has given
their shape and their faces, and in those vain likenesses, pompous
memorials, their pride is preserved together with their bones.
Other, embalmed, are laid in niches, where their shades, still
splendid and rich, seem to perpetuate – in defiance of the laws of
destiny – the pomp of their life in the pomp of their death.
    Of this mute senate, of this terrible court, the silence horrifies
and the sight is dreadful. There are the ancestors together with their
descendants. All the reigns are there, all the ages are seen. And that
Antiquity, those centuries of which history has been able to preserve
only a dim memory, assembled by death in that gloomy darkness,
are there without movement, without light and without sound . . .

Judith

HOLOPHERNE est couché, le flambeau qui sommeille
A mêlé sa lumière avec l'obscurité,
Et Judith fait de l'ombre un voile à sa beauté
De peur qu'à son éclat le Barbare s'éveille.

Le fer que tient en main cette chaste merveille
Ajoute à son visage une fière clarté,
Et pour la confirmer en cette extrêmité
Son bon ange lui fait ce discours à l'oreille:

«Assure-toi, Judith, tu vas tuer un mort;
Le sommeil et le vin par un commun effort
Ont déjà commencé son meurtre et ta conquête;

«Ton captif ne doit pas te donner de la peur,
Et ton bras sans danger pourra couper la tête
D'un homme à qui tes yeux ont arraché le cœur.»

Judith

HOLOPHERNES is lying down, the slumbering torch has merged
its light into the darkness, and Judith makes a veil for her beauty
with the shadow, for fear that the Barbarian should be awakened by
its splendour.

The blade which that chaste marvel holds in her hand adds a
savage gleam to her face, and to strengthen her in this supreme
moment, her good angel whispers these words in her ear:

'Fear nothing, Judith, you are about to kill a dead man; sleep
and wine by a mutual onslaught have already begun his slaying
and your triumph;

'Your captive ought not to inspire you with fear, and your arm
can safely cut off the head of a man whose heart your eyes have
torn out.'

La Madeleine

ICI, d'un repentir célèbre et glorieux,
Madeleine, à soi-même indulgente et cruelle,
Guérit de son péché la blessure mortelle
Et par ses larmes tire un nouveau feu des cieux.

Son luxe converti devient religieux.
L'esprit de ses parfums se fait dévot comme elle.
Ces rubis sont ardents de sa flamme nouvelle
Et ces perles en pleurs se changent à ses yeux.

Beaux yeux, sacrés canaux d'un précieux déluge,
Innocents corrupteurs de votre amoureux juge,
Ne serez-vous jamais sans flammes et sans dards?

Au moins pour le moment faites cesser vos charmes:
La terre fume encor du feu de vos regards,
Et déjà vous brûlez le ciel avec vos larmes.

The Magdalen

HERE [in this picture], by a famous and glorious repentance, the Magdalen, indulgent and cruel to herself, heals the mortal wound of her sin and draws a new fire from heaven with her tears.

Her luxury, converted, becomes religious. The essence of her perfumes becomes pious like her. Those rubies are glowing with her new fire, and those pearls change into tears in her eyes.

Sweet eyes, sacred channels of a precious flood, innocent corruptors of your loving judge, will you never be without flames and arrows?

At least for a time discontinue your charms: the earth still smokes with the fire of your glances, and already you are burning heaven with your tears.

DU BOIS HUS

La Nuit des nuits

LE jour, ce beau fils du soleil
Dont le visage nonpareil
Donne le teint aux belles choses,
Prêt d'entrer en la mer, enlumine son bord
De ses dernières roses,
Et ses premiers rayons vont lui marquer le port.

Ce doux créateur des beautés,
Roi des glorieuses clartés
Qui dessus nous sont répandues,
Nous donnant le bonsoir se cache dans les eaux,
Et les ombres tendues
Avertissent le ciel d'allumer ses flambeaux.

Les bois ne paraissent plus verts,
La nuit entrant dans l'univers
Couvre le sommet des montagnes,

*The Night of Nights**

THE day, that fair son of the sun whose peerless face gives colour
to all fair things, ready to plunge into the sea, flushes its shore with
its last roses, and its first beams [tomorrow] will show it its haven.

That gentle creator of beauties, king of the glorious lights which
are scattered above us, bidding us good-night, hides in the waters,
and the spreading shadows warn the sky to kindle its torches.

The woods no longer appear green; the night, coming into the
universe, covers the tops of the mountains; already the orphaned

---

*Christmas Eve.

284

Déjà l'air orphelin arrose de ses pleurs
    La face des campagnes,
Et les larmes du soir tombent dessus les fleurs.

    Le monde change de couleur:
    Une générale paleur
    Efface la beauté des plaines,
Et les oiseaux surpris sur le bord des marais,
    Courtisans des fontaines,
Se vont mettre à couvert dans le sein des forêts.

    Quelques brins d'écarlate et d'or
    Paraissent attachés encor
    A quelque pièce de nuage:
Des restes de rayon peignant tout à l'entour
    Le fond du paysage,
Font un troisième temps qui n'est ni nuit ni jour.

    Les rougeurs qu'on voit dans les airs
    Jeter ces languissants éclairs
    Qui meurent dans les plis de l'onde,

sky waters the face of the fields with its tears and the sobs of the evening fall upon the flowers.

The world changes colour: a general pallor effaces the beauty of the plains, and the birds, surprised on the edge of the water-meadows – courtiers of the pools – go to find shelter in the heart of the forests.

A few streaks of scarlet and gold can still be seen hanging to some fragment of cloud; lingering gleams of sun, painting the distant landscape all around, make a third time which is neither night nor day.

That red flush, which is to be seen in the sky giving out those languishing beams which die in the folds of the waves, is the blushes

Sont les hontes du jour fuyant le successeur
    Qui le chasse du monde,
L'astre des belles nuits que gouverne sa sœur.

    Le silence vêtu de noir,
    Retournant faire son devoir,
    Vole sur la mer et la terre,
Et l'océan, joyeux de sa tranquillité,
    Est un liquide verre
Où la face du ciel imprime sa beauté.

    Le visage du firmament
    Descendu dans cet élément
    Y fait voir sa figure peinte;
Les feux du ciel sans peur nagent dedans la mer
    Et les poissons sans crainte
Glissent parmi ces feux qui semblent les aimer.

    Dans le fond de ce grand miroir
    La Nature se plaît à voir
    L'onde et la flamme si voisines,
Et les astres tombés en ces pays nouveaux,

of the day fleeing from the successor who drives it from the world, the luminary of the fair nights which are ruled by its sister [the day's sister, the moon].

Black-clad silence, returning to its task, glides over earth and sea, and the ocean, rejoicing in its own quiet, is a liquid glass on which the face of the sky imprints its beauty.

The face of the firmament, come down into this [liquid] element, shows its features painted there; the lights of heaven swim unafraid in the sea, and the fish glide fearlessly among those lights which seem to love them.

In the depths of that great mirror Nature rejoices to see water and fire so close, and the stars, fallen into this new region – sala-

Salamandres marines,
Se baignent à plaisir dans le giron des eaux.

L'illustre déesse des mois,
Quittant son arc et son carquois,
Descend avec eux dedans l'onde;
Son croissant est sa barque, où, l'hameçon en main
Fait de sa tresse blonde,
Elle pêche à loisir les perles du Jourdain.

Le ciel en ce soir bienheureux,
S'habillant de ses plus beaux feux,
Éclate plus qu'à l'ordinaire,
Et la nuit infidèle à son obscurité
A sur notre hémisphère
Beaucoup moins de noirceur qu'elle n'a de clarté.

Soleil, quitte-lui ta maison;
Celle qui vient sur l'horizon
Est grosse du Dieu que j'adore;
Les torches qu'elle allume en la place du jour,
Plus belles que l'aurore,
Lui couronnent le front de lumières d'amour.

manders of the sea – bathe to their hearts' content in the bosom of the waters.

Thè honoured goddess of the months, putting aside her bow and her quiver, goes down with them into the water. Her crescent is her boat, from which, holding the hook made from her blond tresses, she fishes at her ease for the pearls of the Jordan.

The sky on this blessed evening, clothing itself with its loveliest lights, shines more brightly than usual, and the night, abandoning its gloom, has above our hemisphere much less darkness than it has light.

Sun, yield your house to her; she who comes over the horizon is big with the God I adore; the torches which she kindles in place of the day – lovelier than the dawn – crown her brow with beams of love.

. . . Riche et miraculeuse Nuit
Qui sans bouche et sans aucun bruit
Enfantes pourtant la PAROLE,
Sois toujours révérée en ce vaste univers,
Et que ta gloire vole
De l'un à l'autre bout sur l'aile de mes vers . . .

MARTIAL DE BRIVES

Paraphrase du Cantique des Trois Enfants

ÊTRES qui n'avez rien que l'être,
Êtres qui croissez seulement,
Êtres bornés au sentiment,   *Benedicite*
Êtres capables de connaître,   *omnia opera*
Venez par des transports sacrés   *Domini*
Franchir les différents degrés,   *Domino*
Soit du genre, soit de l'espèce,
Et prenez soin de vous unir
A bénir le Seigneur sans cesse,
Puisque sans cesse il prend le soin de vous bénir.

. . . Rich and miraculous Night, which without mouth and with no sound yet brings forth THE WORD, be for ever revered in this vast universe, and may your glory fly from end to end of it on the wing of my verse . . .

*Paraphrase of the Song of the Three Young Men**

All the works of the Lord, bless the Lord
BEINGS who have only being, beings who are only growing, beings limited to feeling, beings capable of knowledge, come by holy ecstasies to transcend the various degrees, either of genus or of species, and take heed to come together to bless the Lord without ceasing, since without ceasing He takes heed to bless you.

---

*The original Latin 'Song of the Three Young Men' (in the fiery furnace) is an apocryphal addition to the Book of Daniel.

Anges, substances immortelles,
Dépendantes divinités,
Du flambeau des éternités   *Benedicite*
Intelligentes étincelles,   *Angeli*
Esprits en qui sans mouvement   *Domini*
Pendant un éternel moment   *Domino*
Dieu prend plaisir de se répandre,
Bénissez les saintes beautés
Que vous ne pouvez pas comprendre,
Et portez vos ardeurs plus loin que vos clartés.

... Vertus qu'en faveur de l'espèce
Dieu loge dans l'individu,
Afin que, l'un étant perdu,   *Benedicite*
L'autre lui succède sans cesse,   *omnes*
Propriétés qui déclarez   *virtutes*
Dans les Êtres confédérés   *Domini*
Les titres de leurs alliances,   *Domino*
Traits d'un même être en divers corps,
Unions dans les différences,
Bénissez le Seigneur de ces rares accords.

Angels of the Lord, bless the Lord
  Angels, immortal substances, dependent divine beings, sparks
endowed with mind from the torch of the eternities, spirits in whom
God, unmoving, delights to diffuse Himself during an eternal
moment, bless the holy loveliness which you cannot understand,
and let [the fire of] your ardour outrun the light of your under-
standing.

All virtues of the Lord, bless the Lord
  ... Virtues which, in the interest of the species, God lodges in the
individual, so that, when one is lost, another succeeds it continually,
properties which proclaim their titles of alliance in the confederate
Essences, features of the same being in various bodies, unions in
differences, bless the Lord for these rare harmonies.

... Paillettes d'or, claires étoiles
Dont la nuit fait ses ornements,
Et que comme des diamants   *Benedicite*
Elle sème dessus ses voiles,   *stellae caeli*
Fleurs des parterres azurés,   *Domino*
Points de lumière, clous dorés
Que le ciel porte sur sa roue,
De vous soit à jamais béni
L'Esprit souverain qui se joue
A compter sans erreur votre nombre infini.

... Ondes subtilement tracées
D'un azur si sombre et si clair,
Qu'on prend dans les plaines de l'air   *Et nubes*
Pour des collines entassées,   *Domino*
Longs ordres de riches bouillons,
Plis de l'air, célestes sillons,
Belles rides, pompeux nuages,
Bénissez le Maître des Cieux,
Et que vos couleurs soient langages
Pour parler hautement de sa gloire à nos yeux.

Stars of heaven, bless the Lord
... Golden spangles, bright stars which the night wears as its orna-
ments and which it strews like diamonds upon its veils, flowers of
the azure borders, points of light, gilded studs which heaven bears
on its wheel, be praised by you for ever the Sovereign Spirit which
makes light of counting your infinite numbers unerringly.

And the clouds, bless the Lord
... Waves cunningly traced in so dark and so clear a blue, which
look like hills piled up in the plains of the sky, long chains of rich
foam, airy folds, skiey furrows, lovely ripples, splendid clouds,
bless the Master of the Heavens, and let your colours be languages
to speak loudly of his glory to our eyes.

Simples précieux et vulgaires,
Herbes de toutes les saisons,
D'où coulent les mortels poisons   *Benedicite*
Ou les remèdes salutaires,   *universa*
Lignes peintes, filets mouvants   *germinantia*
Qu'on voit flotter au gré des vents   *in terra*
Comme une verte chevelure,   *Domino*
Vif émail qui vivez si peu,
Froides languettes de verdure,
A bénir le Seigneur soyez langues de feu.

... Vaste océan, monde liquide,
Lice des carrosses ailés
Que les quatre vents attelés   *Benedicite*
Traînent où la fureur les guide,   *maria*
Monstre qu'on voit toujours caché
Et dans votre lit attaché
Comme un frénétique incurable,
Baisez d'un flot humilié
Vos augustes chaînes de sable
Et bénissez la main qui vous en a lié.

All things growing upon earth, bless the Lord
Rare and common medieval herbs, herbs of all the seasons, from which come mortal poisons or health-giving remedies, coloured lines, moving nets which we see swaying at the will of the winds like green hair, bright hues which live so short a time, cold little tongues of verdure, to bless the Lord be tongues of fire.

Bless Him, you seas
... Vast ocean, liquid world, arena of the winged coaches which the four harnessed winds drag wherever their wild course takes them, monster always seeming hidden and fastened to your bed like a raving madman, kiss with humbled waves your noble chains of sand, and bless the hand which bound you with them.

... Vous dont les nochers se retirent
S'ils veulent sauver leurs vaisseaux,
Baleines qu'on voit sur les eaux   *Benedicite*
Comme des îles qui respirent,   *cete et omnia*
Et vous, tous petits habitants   *quae*
De ces palais creux et flottants   *moventur*
Que forme le marbre de l'onde,   *in aquis*
Bénissez Dieu, muets poissons,   *Domino*
Puisque sa conduite profonde
A mis votre silence au rang de nos chansons.

Oiseaux qui par vos beaux plumages
Tenez l'œil de l'homme ravi,
Et qui ravissez à l'ennui   *Benedicite*
Son oreille par vos ramages,   *omnes*
Voix visibles, sons emplumés,   *volucres*
Orgues de chair, luths animés,   *caeli*
Chantres qui sur la tablature   *Domino*
Que vous lisez en votre cœur
Chantez avec art par nature,
Invitez la nature à bénir son Auteur.

Whales and all things which move in the waters, bless the Lord
... You from whom the sailors draw away if they wish to save their
vessels, whales appearing on the waters like breathing islands, and
you, tiny inhabitants of those hollow floating palaces formed by the
marble of the sea, praise God, mute fishes, since his mysterious
ways have made your silence equal to our songs.

All fowls of the air, bless the Lord
Birds which delight the eye of man with your fine plumage and
distract his ear from care with your songs, visible voices, feathered
sounds, organs of flesh, living lutes, singers who, from the score
which you read in your hearts, sing with art by nature's light, bid
nature to bless her Author.

Esprits de chair, âmes de boue,
Bêtes esclaves de vos sens,
Ouvrages bas et languissants   *Benedicite*
De la nature qui se joue,   *omnes bestiae*
Cerfs et lions, brebis et loups,   *et pecora*
Animaux farouches et doux,   *Domino*
Ne soyez plus incompatibles,
Adorez Dieu paisiblement,
Et puisqu'il vous a fait sensibles,
Bénissez son saint nom avecque sentiment.

Homme, en qui ces diverses choses
Dont ce vaste monde est rempli,
Comme en un monde recueilli   *Benedicite*
Sont délicatement encloses,   *filii*
Pierre et plante conjointement   *hominum*
Par l'être et par l'accroissement,   *Domino*
Bête en la chair, en l'esprit ange,
Puisque tous êtres sont en vous,
Honorez Dieu d'une louange
Qui seule ait la vertu de le bénir pour tous.

All beasts and cattle, bless the Lord
    Spirits of flesh, souls of clay, beasts enslaved by your senses, low and dull-brained works of frolicsome Nature, stags and lions, sheep and wolves, fierce and gentle animals, be no longer incompatible, worship God in peace and, since He has given you feeling, with feeling bless His holy name.

Sons of man, bless the Lord
    Man, in whom these various things with which this great world is filled are contained in miniature as though in a contracted world — stone and plant conjointly in essence and through growth, beast in the flesh, angel in the spirit — since all beings are in you, glorify God with praises which alone have the virtue to bless Him in the name of all.

JEAN DE LA FONTAINE

Invocation

Ô DOUCE Volupté, sans qui, dès notre enfance,
Le vivre et le mourir nous deviendraient égaux,
Aimant universel de tous les animaux,
Que tu sais attirer avecque violence!
    Par toi tout se meut ici-bas,
    C'est pour toi, c'est pour tes appas,
    Que nous courons après la peine:
    Il n'est soldat, ni capitaine,
Ni ministre d'État, ni prince, ni sujet,
    Qui ne t'ait pour unique objet.
Nous autres nourrissons, si, pour fruit de nos veilles,
Un bruit délicieux ne charmait nos oreilles,
Si nous ne nous sentions chatouillés de ce son,
    Ferions-nous un mot de chanson?
Ce qu'on appelle gloire en termes magnifiques,
Ce qui servait de prix dans les jeux olympiques,
N'est que toi proprement, divine Volupté,
Et le plaisir des sens n'est-il de rien compté?

Invocation

O SENSUOUS Delight, without whom, from our childhood, life
and death would seem the same to us; universal magnet of all living
things, how violently you are able to attract! Everything here be-
low takes its motion from you, it is for you, for your charms, that
we court hardship: there is no soldier, nor captain, nor minister of
state, nor prince, nor subject, who does not have you for his sole
object. We nurslings of the Muses – if, to reward our vigils, a de-
lightful sound did not charm our ears, if we did not feel pleasurably
moved by that sound, should we trouble to compose a word of
song? What is called 'glory' in lofty style, what constituted the
prize at the Olympic games, is really only you, divine Delight – and
is the pleasure of the senses counted as nothing? What is the pur-

Pour quoi sont faits les dons de Flore,
Le soleil couchant et l'aurore,
Pomone et ses mets délicats,
Bacchus, l'âme des bons repas,
Les forêts, les eaux, les prairies,
Mères des douces rêveries?
Pour quoi tant de beaux arts, qui tous sont tes enfants?
Mais pour quoi les Chloris aux appas triomphants
Que pour maintenir ton commerce?
J'entends innocemment: sur son propre désir
Quelque rigueur que l'on exerce,
Encor y prend-on du plaisir.

Volupté, Volupté, qui fus jadis maîtresse
Du plus bel esprit de la Grèce,
Ne me dédaigne pas, viens-t'en loger chez moi;
Tu n'y seras pas sans emploi:
J'aime le jeu, l'amour, les livres, la musique,
La ville et la campagne, enfin tout; il n'est rien
Qui ne me soit souverain bien,
Jusqu'au sombre plaisir d'un cœur mélancolique.
Viens donc; et de ce bien, ô douce Volupté,
Veux-tu savoir au vrai la mesure certaine?

pose of Flora's gifts, the setting sun and the dawn, Pomona and her delicate foods, Bacchus – the soul of good meals – the forests, the waters, the meadows, mothers of sweet musings? For what are so many fine arts, all of them your children? And for what the Chlorises with their conquering charms, if not to maintain our intercourse with you? I mean, innocently: for, whatever discipline one exercises over one's own desires, one still finds pleasure in them.

Delight, Delight who once was mistress of the finest mind in Greece, do not disdain me, come and dwell with me; you will not be idle here. I like gaming and cards, love, books, music, town and country, in short everything; there is nothing which is not supremely enjoyable to me, even to the sombre pleasure of a melancholy heart. Come, then; and of that enjoyment, O sweet Delight,

Il m'en faut tout au moins un siècle bien compté;
Car trente ans, ce n'est pas la peine.

Adonis

[*Vénus et Adonis*]

... TOUT ce qui naît de doux en l'amoureux empire,
Quand d'une égale ardeur l'un pour l'autre on soupire,
Et que, de la contrainte ayant banni les lois,
On se peut assurer au silence des bois:
Jours devenus moments, moments filés de soie,
Agréables soupirs, pleurs enfants de la joie,
Vœux, serments et regards, transports, ravissements,
Mélange dont se fait le bonheur des amants,
Tout par ce couple heureux fut lors mis en usage.
    Tantôt ils choisissaient l'épaisseur d'un ombrage.
Là, sous des chênes vieux où leurs chiffres gravés
Se sont avec les troncs accrus et conservés,
Mollement étendus ils consumaient les heures,
Sans avoir pour témoins, en ces sombres demeures,

would you know truly the exact extent? I need at the very least a
full century of it; for thirty years is not worth while.

[*Venus and Adonis*]

... ALL that springs sweet from the empire of love when with equal
ardour each sighs for the other, and when, having banished the laws
of constraint, one can entrust oneself to the silence of the woods:
days turned into moments, moments spun with silk, pleasant sighs,
tears born of joy, vows, pledges and glances, ecstasies, delight – a
blend which makes up the happiness of lovers – all this was then
practised by that fortunate pair.
    Sometimes they sought out a shady bower. There, under ancient
oaks on which their carved emblems have grown and endured with
the trunks, softly pillowed they whiled away the hours, observed in
those twilit haunts by none but the woodland songsters, counselled

Que les chantres des bois, pour confidents qu'Amour,
Qui seul guidait leurs pas en cet heureux séjour.
    Tantôt sur des tapis d'herbe tendre et sacrée
Adonis s'endormait auprès de Cythérée,
Dont les yeux, enivrés par des charmes puissants,
Attachaient au héros leurs regards languissants.
Bien souvent ils chantaient les douceurs de leurs peines;
Et quelquefois assis sur le bord des fontaines,
Tandis que cent cailloux, luttant à chaque bond,
Suivaient les longs replis du cristal vagabond,
«Voyez, disait Vénus, ces ruisseaux et leur course;
Ainsi jamais le temps ne remonte à sa source.
Vainement pour les dieux il fuit d'un pas léger;
Mais vous autres mortels le devez ménager,
Consacrant à l'Amour la saison la plus belle.»
        Souvent, pour divertir leur ardeur mutuelle,
Ils dansaient aux chansons, de nymphes entourés.
Combien de fois la lune a leurs pas éclairés,
Et, couvrant de ses rais l'émail d'une prairie,
Les a vus à l'envi fouler l'herbe fleurie!
Combien de fois le jour a vu les antres creux
Complices des larcins de ce couple amoureux . . .

by none but Love, who alone guided their steps in that happy place.
    Sometimes, on carpets of soft and sacred grass, Adonis fell asleep
at the side of Cytherea, whose eyes, bewitched by powerful spells,
fixed their languishing looks on the hero. Often they sang of the
sweetness of their sufferings; and sometimes as they sat on the edge
of a brook, while a myriad pebbles, rolled down by the bounding
water, followed the long coils of the wandering crystal: 'See,' said
Venus, 'these streams and their course. So Time never flows back
to its source. For the gods it passes light-footed and unheeded. But
you mortals should be sparing of it, dedicating your springtime
to love.'
    Often, to beguile their mutual fire, they danced to songs, by
nymphs surrounded. How often the moon lit their steps and,
flooding with its beams some bright-hued meadow, saw them tread
together the flowery grass. How often did daylight see the hollow
caves abetting the stolen pleasures of that amorous pair! . . .

Épitaphe de Molière

Sous ce tombeau gisent Plaute et Térence,
Et cependant le seul Molière y gît.
Il les faisait revivre en son esprit,
Par leur bel art réjouissant la France.
Ils sont partis! et j'ai peu d'espérance
De les revoir malgré tous nos efforts.
Pour un long temps, selon toute apparence,
Térence et Plaute et Molière sont morts.

Fables

L'Éducation

Laridon et César, frères dont l'origine
Venait de chiens fameux, beaux, bien faits et hardis,
A deux maîtres divers échus au temps jadis,
Hantaient, l'un les forêts, et l'autre la cuisine.
Ils avaient eu d'abord chacun un autre nom:

Epitaph on Molière

Under this tombstone lie Plautus and Terence, yet Molière alone lies there. He made them live again in his mind, delighting France with their excellent art. They have gone, and I have little hope of seeing them again for all that we may do. For a long time, to all appearances, Terence and Plautus and Molière are dead.

Education

Pincher and Caesar, brothers whose pedigree sprang from famous dogs, good-looking, well-shaped, and bold, falling to two different masters in times gone by, frequented, one the forests, the other the kitchen. At first each had had another name, but their

Mais la diverse nourriture
Fortifiant en l'un cette heureuse nature,
En l'autre l'altérant, un certain marmiton
Nomma celui-ci Laridon.
Son frère ayant couru mainte haute aventure,
Mis maint cerf aux abois, maint sanglier abattu,
Fut le premier César que la gent chienne ait eu.
On eut soin d'empêcher qu'une indigne maîtresse
Ne fît en ses enfants dégénérer son sang.
Laridon négligé témoignait sa tendresse
A l'objet le premier passant.
Il peupla tout de son engeance:
Tourne-broches par lui rendus communs en France
Y font un corps à part, gens fuyant les hasards,
Peuple antipode des Césars.

On ne suit pas toujours ses aïeux ni son père:
Le peu de soin, le temps, tout fait qu'on dégénère.
Faute de cultiver la nature et ses dons,
Oh! combien de Césars deviendront Laridons!

different upbringing having strengthened their natural qualities in one and debased them in the other, a certain kitchen-boy named the second Pincher.

His brother, having accomplished many a noble deed, bayed the death of many a stag, brought down many a boar, was the first Caesar that the doggy race has had. Care was taken to ensure that no unworthy mistress should allow his line to degenerate in his children. Pincher, neglected, gave proof of his affection to any fair object who passed by. He peopled the whole place with his progeny. Turnspits, having grown common in France thanks to him, form a body apart, danger-avoiding, a tribe antipodal to the Caesars.

We do not always follow our forbears or our father. Neglect, time, everything causes us to degenerate. For want of cultivating nature and her gifts, oh! how many Caesars will become Pinchers.

NICOLAS BOILEAU

A Mon Jardinier

... ANTOINE, de nous deux, tu crois donc, je le vois,
Que le plus occupé dans ce jardin c'est toi?
Oh! que tu changerais d'avis et de langage,
Si deux jours seulement, libre du jardinage,
Tout à coup devenu poète et bel esprit,
Tu t'allais engager à polir un écrit
Qui dît, sans s'avilir, les plus petites choses,
Fît des plus secs chardons des œillets et des roses,
Et sût même aux discours de la rusticité
Donner de l'élégance et de la dignité.
... Bientôt de ce travail revenu sec et pâle,
Et le teint plus jauni que de vingt ans de hâle,
Tu dirais, reprenant ta pelle et ton râteau:
«J'aime mieux mettre encor cent arpents au niveau,
Que d'aller follement, égaré dans les nues,
Me lasser à chercher des visions cornues,
Et, pour lier des mots si mal s'entr'accordants,
Prendre dans ce jardin la lune avec les dents.»

To My Gardener

... So, Antoine, you think, I am sure, that the busier of us two in
this garden is yourself. Oh, how differently you would think and
speak if only for two days, freed from gardening, having suddenly
become a poet and wit, you undertook to polish a piece of writing
which would express the most trivial things without demeaning it-
self, would turn the thorniest thistles into carnations and roses, and
would even succeed in giving elegance and dignity to rustic speech.
... Soon, emerging from this work fevered and pale, with your face
more yellowed than by twenty years of sunburn, you would say, as
you took up your spade and rake again: 'I would rather level a hun-
dred more acres than crazily, lost in the clouds, exhaust myself pur-
suing phantom shapes, and – in order to put together such re-
fractory words – stand in this garden reaching for the moon.'

Approche donc, et viens; qu'un paresseux t'apprenne,
Antoine, ce que c'est que fatigue et que peine.
L'homme ici-bas, toujours inquiet et gêné,
Est, dans le repos même, au travail condamné.
La fatigue l'y suit. C'est en vain qu'aux poètes
Les neuf trompeuses Sœurs dans leurs douces retraites
Promettent du repos sous leurs ombrages frais.
Dans ces tranquilles bois, pour eux plantés exprès,
La cadence aussitôt, la rime, la césure,
La riche expression, la nombreuse mesure,
Sorcières dont l'amour sait d'abord les charmer,
De fatigue sans fin viennent les consumer.
Sans cesse poursuivant ces fugitives fées,
On voit sous les lauriers haleter les Orphées.
Leur esprit toutefois se plaît dans son tourment,
Et se fait de sa peine un noble amusement.
Mais je ne trouve point de fatigue si rude
Que l'ennuyeux loisir d'un mortel sans étude,
Qui, jamais ne sortant de sa stupidité,
Soutient, dans les langueurs de son oisiveté,
D'une lâche indolence esclave volontaire,
Le pénible fardeau de n'avoir rien à faire.

Draw near, then, come. Let an idle man show you, Antoine,
what weariness and labour are. Man here below, always anxious
and tormented, is condemned to work even when at rest. Fatigue
pursues him. In vain do the nine deceitful Sisters [the Muses] in
their quiet retreats promise rest to poets under their cool shade. In
those peaceful woods planted specially for them, cadence, rhyme,
caesura, richness of expression, rhythmic harmony – sorceresses
whose love can at first enchant them – quickly come to consume
them with endless weariness. Ceaselessly pursuing those elusive
fairies, the Orpheuses are seen panting beneath their laurels. And
yet their minds find pleasure in their torment and make a noble
distraction of their suffering. But I find no weariness so great as the
dull leisure of a man with no studious interests, who, never emerg-
ing from his stupidity, bears in the tedium of his idleness (the
willing slave of a slothful indolence) the heavy burden of having
nothing to do.

... Je te vais sur cela prouver deux vérités:
L'une, que le travail, aux hommes nécessaire,
Fait leur félicité plutôt que leur misère;
Et l'autre, qu'il n'est point de coupable en repos.
C'est ce qu'il faut ici montrer en peu de mots.
Suis-moi donc ... Mais je vois, sur ce début de prône,
Que ta bouche déjà s'ouvre large d'une aune,
Et que, les yeux fermés, tu baisses le menton.
Ma foi, le plus sûr est de finir ce sermon.
Aussi bien j'aperçois ces melons qui t'attendent,
Et ces fleurs qui là-bas entre elles se demandent
S'il est fête au village, et pour quel saint nouveau
On les laisse aujourd'hui si longtemps manquer d'eau.

JEAN-FRANÇOIS DE
SAINT-LAMBERT

L'Été

O TOI dont l'Éternel a tracé la carrière,
Toi, qui fais végéter et sentir la matière,

... Whereupon I will prove two truths to you: The first, that work,
necessary to men, brings them happiness rather than misery. And
the other, that no guilty man enjoys peace. That is what I must now
demonstrate briefly. So try to follow me... But I see, as I begin
my homily, that your mouth is already opening a foot wide and
that, your eyes having shut, your chin drops. Well, well, the best
thing is to end this sermon. I also notice those melons waiting for
you, and those flowers over there which are asking each other if
it is a holiday in the village, and for what new saint they are left
so long without water today.

Summer

You* whose course the Eternal Spirit has marked out, you who
give growth and feeling to matter, who measure out time and mete

---

*The sun.

Qui mesures le temps et dispenses le jour,
Roi des mondes errants qui composent ta cour,
Du Dieu qui te conduit noble et brillante image:
Les saisons, leurs présents, nos biens, sont ton ouvrage.

　　Tu disposas la terre à la fécondité
Quand tu la revêtis de grâce et de beauté;
Tu t'élevas bientôt sur la céleste voûte,
Et des traits plus ardents répandus sur ta route
De l'équateur au pôle ont pénétré les airs,
Le centre de la terre et l'abîme des mers.

　　A des êtres sans nombre ils donnent la naissance,
Tout se meut, s'organise, et sent son existence.
Le sable et le limon se sont-ils animés?
Dans les bois, dans les eaux, sur les monts enflammés,
Les germes des oiseaux, des poissons, des reptiles
S'élancent à la fois de leurs prisons fragiles.
Ici, le faon léger se joue avec l'agneau;
Là, le jeune coursier bondit près du chevreau;
Sur les bords opposés de ces feuilles légères
Résident des tribus l'une à l'autre étrangères;
Les calices des fleurs, les fruits, sont habités;

out the day, king of the wandering worlds who compose your court, bright and noble image of the God who guides you: the seasons, their gifts, our riches, are your work.

You prepared the earth to be fertile when you clothed it with grace and beauty; soon you mounted to the height of the heavenly vault and hotter beams, shed about your path, penetrated the atmosphere, the depths of the earth and of the seas from the equator to the pole.

They give birth to innumerable beings, everything stirs, organizes itself, and is conscious of existence. Have the sand and the mud come to life? In the woods, in the waters, on the burning mountains, the germs of birds, fish, reptiles, burst out all at once from their fragile prisons. Here, the nimble fawn plays with the lamb; there, the young steed bounds near the kid; on the opposite edges of those light leaves, tribes dwell which are foreign to one another; the calyxes of the flowers, the fruits, are inhabited; in humble clods

Dans les humbles gazons s'élèvent des cités;
Et des eaux de la nue une goutte insensible
Renferme un peuple atome, une foule invisible.
    Comme un flot disparaît sous le flot qui le suit,
Un être est remplacé par l'être qu'il produit.
Ils naissent, Dieu puissant, lorsque ta voix féconde
Les appelle à leur tour sur la scène du monde.
Dévorés l'un par l'autre, ou détruits par le temps,
Ils ont à tes desseins servi quelques instants. . .

ANTOINE-LÉONARD THOMAS

Ode sur le Temps

LE compas d'Uranie a mesuré l'espace.
O Temps, être inconnu que l'âme seule embrasse,
Invisible torrent des siècles et des jours,
Tandis que ton pouvoir m'entraîne dans la tombe,
        J'ose, avant que j'y tombe,
M'arrêter un moment pour contempler ton cours.

of turf, cities spring up; and an inanimate drop of rain-water contains a people full of atoms, an invisible multitude.

As a wave disappears beneath the following wave, a being is replaced by the being it produces. They are born, O mighty God, when your life-giving voice calls them in their turn on to the stage of the world. Devoured by each other, or destroyed by time, they have served your purpose for a few moments. . .

Ode on Time

THE compasses of Urania* have measured out space. O Time, unknown being which the soul alone conceives, invisible torrent of the ages and the days, while your power carries me towards the grave, I dare, before I go down into it, to halt for a moment to contemplate your course.

------

*The Muse of astronomy.

Qui me dévoilera l'instant qui t'a vu naître?
Quel œil peut remonter aux sources de ton être?
Sans doute ton berceau touche à l'éternité.
Quand rien n'était encore, enseveli dans l'ombre
    De cet abîme sombre,
Ton germe y reposait, mais sans activité.

Du chaos tout à coup les portes s'ébranlèrent;
Des soleils allumés les feux étincelèrent;
Tu naquis; l'Éternel te prescrivit ta loi.
Il dit au mouvement: «Du Temps sois la mesure.»
    Il dit à la nature:
«Le Temps sera pour vous, l'Éternité pour moi.»

Dieu, telle est ton essence: oui, l'océan des âges
Roule au-dessous de toi sur tes frêles ouvrages,
Mais il n'approche pas de ton trône immortel.
Des millions de jours qui l'un l'autre s'effacent,
    Des siècles qui s'entassent,
Sont comme le néant aux yeux de l'Éternel.

Mais moi, sur cet amas de fange et de poussière,
En vain contre le Temps je cherche une barrière;
Son vol impétueux me presse et me poursuit.

Who will reveal to me the instant which saw your birth? What eye can look back to the sources of your being? Doubtless your cradle touches eternity. When nothing yet was, buried in the night of that dark abyss, your germ was there, waiting but inactive.

Suddenly the gates of chaos swung open; the lights of the kindled suns flashed out; you were born; the Everlasting gave you your law. He said to motion: 'Be the measure of Time.' He said to nature: 'Time will be for you, Eternity for me.'

Such, God, is your essence: yes, the ocean of the ages rolls beneath You over your frail works, but it does not approach your immortal throne. Millions of days effacing one another, ages accumulating, are as void and nothing in the sight of the Everlasting.

But I, on this heap of mire and dust, seek in vain some rampart against Time; its rushing wing drives me on and pursues me. I

Je n'occupe qu'un point de la vaste étendue,
    Et mon âme éperdue
Sous mes pas chancelants voit ce point qui s'enfuit.

De la destruction tout m'offre des images.
Mon œil épouvanté ne voit que des ravages:
Ici de vieux tombeaux que la mousse a couverts,
Là des murs abattus, des colonnes brisées,
    Des villes embrasées:
Partout les pas du Temps empreints sur l'univers.

Cieux, terres, éléments, tout est sous sa puissance.
Mais tandis que sa main, dans la nuit du silence,
Du fragile univers sape les fondements,
Sur des ailes de feu loin du monde élancée,
    Mon active pensée
Plane sur les débris entassés par le Temps.

Siècles qui n'êtes plus, et vous qui devez naître,
J'ose vous appeler: hâtez-vous de paraître.
Au moment où je suis venez vous réunir.
Je parcours tous les points de l'immense durée
    D'une marche assurée:
J'enchaîne le présent, je vis dans l'avenir.

occupy only a point in the vast expanse, and my bewildered soul sees that point slipping away from beneath my tottering feet.

Everything shows me images of destruction. My eyes, appalled, see only devastation: here, ancient tombs which the moss has covered; there, ruined walls, broken columns, burnt-out cities; everywhere Time's footsteps imprinted on the universe.

Heavens, worlds, elements, all are under its power. But while its hand, in the night of silence, undermines the foundations of the fragile universe, my active mind, borne far from the earth on wings of fire, soars above the ruins heaped up by Time.

Centuries which are no more, and you still to be born, I dare to summon you: make haste to appear. Come and assemble at the moment where I am. I visit every point of the immense duration with confident steps: I enchain the present, I live in the future.

Le soleil épuisé dans sa brûlante course
De ses feux par degrés verra tarir la source,
Et des mondes vieillis les ressorts s'useront.
Ainsi que des rochers qui du haut des montagnes
      Roulent sur les campagnes,
Les astres l'un sur l'autre un jour s'écrouleront.

Là, de l'Éternité commencera l'empire,
Et dans cet océan où tout va se détruire,
Le Temps s'engloutira comme un faible ruisseau.
Mais mon âme immortelle, aux siècles échappée,
      Ne sera point frappée,
Et des mondes brisés foulera le tombeau . . .

ÉVARISTE DE PARNY

Le Revenant

J'IGNORE ce qu'on fait là-bas.
Si du sein de la nuit profonde
On peut revenir en ce monde,
Je reviendrai, n'en doutez pas.

The sun, exhausted in its burning course, will see the source of its light gradually quenched, and the motive forces of the ageing worlds will wear out. Like rocks rolling down on the fields from the tops of the mountains, the stars will one day tumble one upon another.

Then will begin the reign of Eternity, and in that ocean in which everything will be destroyed, Time will be engulfed like a tiny stream. But my immortal soul, having escaped from the ages, will not be struck down, and will walk over the grave of the shattered worlds. . .

The Ghost

I DON'T know what they do down there. If from the heart of deepest night one can come back to this world, I shall come back, you

Mais je n'aurai jamais l'allure
De ces revenants indiscrets,
Qui, précédés d'un long murmure,
Se plaisent à pâlir leurs traits,
Et dont la funèbre parure,
Inspirant toujours la frayeur,
Ajoute encore à la laideur
Qu'on reçoit dans la sépulture.
De vous plaire je suis jaloux,
Et je veux rester invisible.
Souvent du zéphyr le plus doux
Je prendrai l'haleine insensible,
Tous mes soupirs seront pour vous:
Ils feront vaciller la plume
Sur vos cheveux noués sans art,
Et disperseront au hasard
La faible odeur qui les parfume.
Si la rose que vous aimez
Renaît sur son trône de verre,
Si de vos flambeaux rallumés
Sort une plus vive lumière,
Si l'éclat d'un nouveau carmin
Colore soudain votre joue,

may be sure. But I shall never appear like those indiscreet ghosts which, heralded by long-drawn moans, see fit to whiten their features, and whose funereal attire, always arousing fear, increases the ugliness one acquires in the tomb.

I am eager to please you and I would choose to remain invisible. Often I will borrow the scarcely perceptible breath of the lightest breeze. All my sighs will be for you. They will sway the feather on your carelessly knotted hair and will disperse at random the subtle scent which perfumes it. If the rose you love revives on its glass throne, if from your lighted candles a brighter flame shines out, if the glow of a fresh carmine suddenly colours your cheek, and

Et si souvent d'un joli sein
Le nœud trop serré se dénoue,
Si le sofa plus mollement
Cède au poids de votre paresse,
Donnez un souris seulement
A tous ces soins de ma tendresse.

　　Quand je reverrai les attraits
Qu'effleura ma main caressante,
Ma voix amoureuse et touchante
Pourra murmurer des regrets;
Et vous croirez alors entendre
Cette harpe qui, sous mes doigts,
Sut vous redire quelquefois
Ce que mon cœur savait m'apprendre.
Aux douceurs de votre sommeil
Je joindrai celles du mensonge;
Moi-même, sous les traits d'un songe,
Je causerai votre réveil.
Charmes nus, fraîcheur du bel âge,
Contours parfaits, grâce, embonpoint,
Je verrai tout: mais, quel dommage,
Les morts ne ressuscitent point.

if often on a pretty breast the knot, too tight, is loosened, if the sofa
yields more softly under your sleepy weight, spare just a smile for
all these marks of my love.

　　When I see again those charms which my hand brushed caress-
ingly, my voice, touching and tender, may well murmur my regrets.
And then you will think you hear that harp which sometimes,
under my fingers, managed to repeat to you what my heart man-
aged to teach me. To the sweetness of your sleep, I will add the
sweetness of illusion. In the guise of a dream, I myself will cause
your awakening. Naked charms, freshness of youth, perfect lines,
grace, agreeable plumpness, I shall see all. But, more's the pity, the
dead do not come back again.

ANDRÉ CHÉNIER

Bacchus

VIENS, ô divin Bacchus, ô jeune Thyonée,
Ô Dionyse, Évan, Iacchus et Lénée;
Viens, tel que tu parus aux déserts de Naxos,
Quand tu vins rassurer la fille de Minos.
Le superbe éléphant, en proie à ta victoire,
Avait de ses débris formé ton char d'ivoire.
De pampres, de raisins, mollement enchaînés,
Le tigre aux larges flancs de taches sillonnés,
Et le lynx étoilé, la panthère sauvage,
Promenaient avec toi ta cour sur ce rivage.
L'or reluisait partout aux axes de tes chars.
Les Ménades couraient en longs cheveux épars
Et chantaient Évoé, Bacchus et Thyonée,
Et Dionyse, Évan, Iacchus et Lénée,
Et tout ce que pour toi la Grèce eut de beaux noms.
Et la voix des rochers répétait leurs chansons,
Et le rauque tambour, les sonores cymbales,

Bacchus

COME, divine Bacchus, O young Thyoneus, O Dionysus, Euan,
Iacchus, and Lenaeus. Come, as you appeared on the deserted
shores of Naxos, when you came to console the daughter of Minos.
The proud elephant, a trophy of your victory, had formed your
ivory car with his spoils. Softly enchained with vines, with grapes,
the broad-flanked tiger streaked with stripes, and the star-marked
lynx and the savage panther drew you and your court along that
shore. Gold gleamed everywhere on the axles of your chariots.
The Maenads ran with their long hair flowing and sang Evoe,
Bacchus, Thyoneus, and Dionysus, Euan, Iacchus, and Lenaeus,
and all t he fair names that Greece had for you. And the voice of the
rocks repeated their songs, with the harsh drum, the ringing cym-

Les hautbois tortueux, et les doubles crotales
Qu'agitaient en dansant sur ton bruyant chemin
Le Faune, le Satyre et le jeune Sylvain,
Au hasard attroupés autour du vieux Silène,
Qui, sa coupe à la main, de la rive indienne
Toujours ivre, toujours débile, chancelant,
Pas à pas cheminait sur son âne indolent.

Néære

MAIS telle qu'à sa mort, pour la dernière fois,
Un beau cygne soupire, et de sa douce voix,
De sa voix qui bientôt lui doit être ravie,
Chante, avant de partir, ses adieux à la vie:
Ainsi, les yeux remplis de langueur et de mort,
Pâle, elle ouvrit sa bouche en un dernier effort:
«O vous, du Sébéthus Naïades vagabondes,
Coupez sur mon tombeau vos chevelures blondes.
Adieu, mon Clinias! moi, celle qui te plus,
Moi, celle qui t'aimai, que tu ne verras plus.

bals, the curving oboes and the twin castanets which were shaken
as they danced on your noisy way by the Faun, the Satyr, and the
young Sylvan, flocking in disorder round old Silenus, who, cup in
hand, and always drunk since the Indian shore, always feeble, reel-
ing, rode slowly along on his sleepy ass.

Neæra

BUT as at its death, for the last time, a beautiful swan laments, and
with its sweet voice, its voice which is soon to be taken from it,
sings before it goes its farewell to life: so, her eyes filled with lan-
guor and death, pale, she opened her mouth in a last song:
'O you, wandering Naiads of the Sebethus, cut your fair tresses
upon my tomb. Farewell, my Clinias! I, she who pleased you, I,
she who loved you, whom you will see no more. O skies, earth,

O cieux, ô terre, ô mer, prés, montagnes, rivages,
Fleurs, bois mélodieux, vallons, grottes sauvages,
Rappelez-lui souvent, rappelez-lui toujours
Néære tout son bien, Néære ses amours;
Cette Néære, hélas! qu'il nommait sa Néære,
Qui pour lui criminelle, abandonna sa mère;
Qui pour lui fugitive, errant de lieux en lieux,
Aux regards des humains n'osa lever les yeux.
Oh, soit que l'astre pur des deux frères d'Hélène
Calme sous ton vaisseau la vague ionienne,
Soit qu'aux bords de Pæstum, sous ta soigneuse main,
Les roses deux fois l'an couronnent ton jardin,
Au coucher du soleil, si ton âme attendrie
Tombe en une muette et molle rêverie,
Alors, mon Clinias, appelle, appelle-moi,
Je viendrai, Clinias, je volerai vers toi.
Mon âme vagabonde à travers le feuillage
Frémira; sur les vents ou sur quelque nuage
Tu la verras descendre, ou du sein de la mer
S'élevant comme un songe, étinceler dans l'air,
Et ma voix, toujours tendre et doucement plaintive,
Caresser, en fuyant, ton oreille attentive.»

sea, meadows, mountains, shores, flowers, melodious woods, valleys, wild caves, remind him often, remind him always, of Neæra his whole joy, Neæra his love; that Neæra, alas, whom he called his Neæra, who, sinning for his sake, deserted her mother; who an outcast for his sake, roaming from place to place, dared not raise her eyes to meet the eyes of men.

'Whether the pure star of the two brothers of Helen [Castor and Pollux] calms the Ionian wave beneath your ship, or on the shores of Paestum, under your diligent hand, the roses crown your garden twice every year, at sunset if your soul, moved, falls into soft and silent musings, then, my Clinias, call me, call me. I will come, Clinias, I will hasten to you. My wandering soul will tremble in the foliage; on the winds or on some cloud you will see it descend, or, rising from the heart of the sea like a dream, glitter in the air, and my voice, still tender and softly plaintive, will caress as it passes your listening ear.'

ANDRÉ CHÉNIER

L'Amérique

Invocation

SALUT, ô belle nuit, étincelante et sombre . . .
Qui n'entend que la voix de mes vers et les cris
De la rive aréneuse où se brise Thétis.
Muse, Muse nocturne, apporte-moi ma lyre.
Comme un fier météore, en ton brûlant délire,
Lance-toi dans l'espace et, pour franchir les airs,
Prends les ailes des vents, les ailes des éclairs,
Les bonds de la comète aux longs cheveux de flamme.

Mes vers impatients élancés de mon âme
Veulent parler aux dieux, et volent où reluit
L'enthousiasme errant, fils de la belle nuit.
Accours, grande Nature, ô mère du génie.
Accours, reine du monde, éternelle Uranie,
Soit que tes pas divins sur l'astre du Lion
Ou sur les triples feux du superbe Orion
Marchent, ou soit qu'au loin, fugitive emportée,
Tu suives les détours de la voie argentée,
Soleils amoncelés dans le céleste azur

Invocation

HAIL, lovely night, glittering and dark . . . you who hear only the voice of my verse and the cries of the sandy shore on which Tethys [Ocean] breaks. Muse, Muse of night, bring me my lyre. Like a proud meteor in your burning ecstasy, launch yourself into space and, to pass through the skies, take the wings of the winds, the wings of the lightning, the bounds of the comet with long hair of flame.

My eager verses, springing from my soul, would speak with the gods, and they fly where roving Enthusiasm, the son of the fair night, shines out. Come to me, great Nature, mother of genius. Come, queen of the universe, eternal Urania: whether your feet walk on the star of the Lion, or on the triple lights of proud Orion, or whether afar, an impetuous fugitive, you follow the windings of the silvery way, those suns heaped together in the azure of heaven,

Où le peuple a cru voir les traces d'un lait pur;
  Descends, non, porte-moi sur ta route brûlante,
Que je m'élève au ciel comme une flamme ardente.
Déjà ce corps pesant se détache de moi,
Adieu, tombeau de chair, je ne suis plus à toi.
Terre, fuis sous mes pas. L'éther où le ciel nage
M'aspire. Je parcours l'océan sans rivage.
Plus de nuit. Je n'ai plus d'un globe opaque et dur
Entre le jour et moi l'impénétrable mur.

  Plus de nuit, et mon œil et se perd et se mêle
Dans les torrents profonds de lumière éternelle.
Me voici sur les feux que le langage humain
Nomme Cassiopée et l'Ourse et le Dauphin,
Maintenant la Couronne autour de moi s'embrase,
Ici l'Aigle et le Cygne et la Lyre et Pégase,
Et voici que plus loin le Serpent tortueux
Noue autour de mes pas ses anneaux lumineux.
Féconde immensité, les esprits magnanimes
Aiment à se plonger dans tes vivants abîmes,
Abîmes de clartés où, libre de ses fers,

in which the common people thought they saw the traces of a pure milk.*

Come down – no, rather bear me up on your fiery path, let me rise to heaven like a burning flame. Already this solid body falls away from me, farewell, fleshly tomb, I am no longer yours. Earth, flee from under my feet. The ether in which the sky swims draws me up. I move through the shoreless ocean. There is no more night. I no longer have the impenetrable wall of a hard, opaque globe between the day and me.

No more night, and my sight is lost and mingles in the deep torrents of eternal light. Now I am upon those lights which in human speech are called Cassiopeia and the Bear and the Dolphin, now the Crown bursts into fire around me, here the Eagle and the Swan and the Lyre and Pegasus, and further now the twisting Serpent winds its luminous coils around my feet. Fertile vastness, noble spirits love to plunge into your living gulfs, gulfs of light where, free from his

---

*The Milky Way: according to legend, the milk of Juno.

L'homme siège au conseil qui créa l'univers,
Où l'âme remontant à sa grande origine
Sent qu'elle est une part de l'essence divine.

Ode à Marie-Anne-Charlotte Corday

QUOI! tandis que partout, ou sincères ou feintes,
Des lâches, des pervers, les larmes et les plaintes
Consacrent leur Marat parmi les immortels,
Et que, prêtre orgueilleux de cette idole vile,
Des fanges du Parnasse un impudent reptile
Vomit un hymne infâme au pied de ses autels,

La Vérité se tait! Dans sa bouche glacée,
Des liens de la peur sa langue embarrassée
Dérobe un juste hommage aux exploits glorieux!

chains, man sits in the council which created the universe, where the soul, reascending to its great origin, feels that it is a part of the divine essence.

Ode to Marie-Anne-Charlotte Corday*

AH, while on all sides the tears and moans, sincere or feigned, of cowardly, perverted minds consecrate their Marat among the immortals, while – arrogantly officiating before that vile idol – an impudent reptile from the slime of Parnassus† vomits a foul hymn at the foot of his altars,

Truth is silent! In her numbed mouth, her tongue, impeded by the trammels of fear, denies the homage justly due to [such] glorious deeds! Is it so sweet to live, then? Of what value is life when

---

*Executed on 18 July 1793 for having assassinated the extremist revolutionary leader Marat in his bath.

†Probably a certain Michel de Cubières-Palmézeaux, who had written a poem in Marat's honour.

Vivre est-il donc si doux? De quel prix est la vie,
Quand, sous un joug honteux la pensée asservie,
Tremblante, au fond du cœur se cache à tous les yeux?

Non, non, je ne veux point t'honorer en silence,
Toi qui crus par ta mort ressusciter la France
Et dévouas tes jours à punir des forfaits.
Le glaive arma ton bras, fille grande et sublime,
Pour faire honte aux dieux, pour réparer leur crime,
Quand d'un homme à ce monstre ils donnèrent les traits.

Le noir serpent, sorti de sa caverne impure,
A donc vu rompre enfin sous ta main ferme et sûre
Le venimeux tissu de ses jours abhorrés!
Aux entrailles du tigre, à ses dents homicides,
Tu vins redemander et les membres livides
Et le sang des humains qu'il avait dévorés!

... Longtemps, sous les dehors d'une allégresse aimable,
Dans ses détours profonds ton âme impénétrable
Avait tenu cachés les destins du pervers.

thought, enslaved beneath a shameful yoke, hides itself timorously
from every eye in the depths of the heart?

No, no, I will not honour you in silence, you who thought to
resurrect France by your death and gave up your life to punish
evil deeds. You took the sword in your hand, great and noble girl,
to shame the gods, to make good their crime, when they gave the
features of a man to that monster.

So that black serpent, coming out from his foul cave, had the
poisonous web of his hateful days broken at last by your true, un-
faltering hand. From the tiger's bowels, from his murderous teeth,
you came to claim back the livid members and the blood of the
human beings whom he had devoured!

... For long, under a cheerful and pleasing surface, your inscrut-
able heart had kept the fate of the monster hidden in its subtle

Ainsi, dans le secret amassant la tempête,
Rit un beau ciel d'azur, qui cependant s'apprête
A foudroyer le monts, à soulever les mers.

Belle, jeune, brillante, aux bourreaux amenée,
Tu semblais t'avancer sur le char d'hyménée;
Ton front resta paisible et ton regard serein.
Calme sur l'échafaud, tu méprisas la rage
D'un peuple abject, servile et fécond en outrage,
Et qui se croit alors et libre et souverain.

La Vertu seule est libre. Honneur de notre histoire,
Notre immortel opprobre y vit avec ta gloire.
Seule tu fus un homme, et vengeas les humains.
Et nous, eunuques vils, troupeau lâche et sans âme,
Nous savons répéter quelque plainte de femme,
Mais le fer pèserait à nos débiles mains.

Non, tu ne pensais pas qu'aux mânes de la France
Un seul traître immolé suffît à sa vengeance,
Ou tirât du chaos ses débris dispersés.

depths. So, while it gathers the storm in secret, the clear blue sky smiles, yet prepares to strike the mountains with thunder, to lash the seas.

Fair, young, resplendent, led to the executioners, you seemed to be riding in your bridal car; your brow was still untroubled and your look serene. Calm on the scaffold, you despised the rage of an abject populace, servile and rich in insults, and which yet believes that it is free and sovereign.

Only Virtue is free. Glory of our history, our eternal shame lives on there [in history] with your fame. You alone were a man and vindicated the human race. And we, vile eunuchs, a cowardly and soulless herd, we know how to repeat some womanly whimper, but the steel would weigh heavy in our feeble hands.

No, you did not intend that a single traitor sacrificed to the angry spirit of France should suffice to avenge her, or should recover her scattered remains from chaos. You meant, by firing timorous hearts,

Tu voulais, enflammant les courages timides,
Réveiller les poignards sur tous ces parricides,
De rapine, de sang, d'infamie engraissés.

Un scélérat de moins rampe dans cette fange.
La Vertu t'applaudit. De sa mâle louange
Entends, belle héroïne, entends l'auguste voix.
O Vertu, le poignard, seul espoir de la terre,
Est ton arme sacrée, alors que le tonnerre
Laisse régner le crime et te vend à ses lois.

Iambes *VIII*

On vit; on vit infâme. Eh bien? il fallut l'être;
　　L'infâme après tout mange et dort.
Ici même, en ses parcs, où la mort nous fait paître,
　　Où la hache nous tire au sort,
Beaux poulets sont écrits; maris, amants sont dupes;
　　Caquetage, intrigues de sots.
On y chante; on y joue; on y lève des jupes;
　　On y fait chansons et bons mots;

to awaken daggers over all these parricides – fattened on plunder, blood, and dishonour.

One scoundrel less crawls in this slime. Virtue applauds you. Hear the majestic sound of its virile praise, heroic maid. O Virtue, the dagger, the only hope of the world, is your holy weapon, as long as the thunder [God's vengeance] allows crime to prevail and sells you into its power.

Iambes *VIII*

We live, we live degraded. What of it? It had to be. Degraded, you still eat and sleep. Even here, in its pens, where death puts us to graze, where the axe draws lots for us, fine love-letters are written; husbands, lovers are duped; tittle-tattle, intrigues of fools. There is singing, gambling, skirts are lifted; songs and jokes are made up;

L'un pousse et fait bondir sur les toits, sur les vitres,
    Un ballon tout gonflé de vent,
Comme sont les discours des sept cents plats bélîtres,
    Dont Barère est le plus savant.
L'autre court; l'autre saute; et braillent, boivent, rient
    Politiques et raisonneurs;
Et sur les gonds de fer soudain les portes crient.
    Des juges tigres nos seigneurs
Le pourvoyeur paraît. Quelle sera la proie
    Que la hache appelle aujourd'hui?
Chacun frissonne, écoute; et chacun avec joie
    Voit que ce n'est pas encor lui . . .

someone sends up and bounces on the roofs, on the panes, a balloon swollen with wind, like the speeches of the seven hundred dreary imbeciles, of which the wisest is Barère.*

Another runs, another jumps; 'politicians' and discussers bray, drink, laugh ; and on their iron hinges the doors suddenly grate. The purveyor of our masters the tiger-judges appears. Who will be the prey which the axe calls for today? Each shudders, listens, and each with joy sees that it is not yethe. . .

---

* One of the seven hundred members of the *Convention Nationale* during the Terror. Writing this fragment in prison while in constant fear of execution, Chénier ciphered Barère's name and disguised his meaning in the previous line by writing:

    Comme sont les discours des heptsad (700) *plats bélit.*

PART THREE

THE NINETEENTH CENTURY

Introduced and edited by
Anthony Hartley

INTRODUCTION

AN English reader encountering French poetry for the first time is bound to feel an overwhelming impression of strangeness. Poetry is notoriously the most difficult part of any literature for a foreigner to appreciate, and when the two languages concerned are as different in their traditions as French and English, the difficulty becomes acute. Of course these traditions were not always far apart: a reader of Chaucer can appreciate Guillaume de Machaut or Eustace Deschamps (if he has a sufficient knowledge of medieval French) without feeling that any fresh approach is required from him. Ronsard is near enough to Sidney for an English-speaking reader to be at home with him, and the same is true of most of the French sixteenth-century poets. It was the process of purification and abstraction of language that went on in France in the seventeenth century that changed matters. This winnowing had no parallel in English, and one of its effects was to make French poetry more rigid and classical in its structure than that of any other European language. The divorce between it and common speech was completed by the time of Racine, and there took shape at this moment those general characteristics which are likely to cause trouble to the foreign reader.

I

The most mechanical of these is metre. As opposed to the English verse line, which is governed by stress, French verse has a syllabic basis. The Alexandrine, for instance, which is one of the most commonly used lines, has twelve syllables with a caesura (the main pause) after the sixth. But the variation in importance of the elements of the line is given by the pitch of the vowels, and, even in classical verse, there are other pauses to provide variety. In a line like this famous one from *Phèdre*:

> *Le jour n'est pas plus pur que le fond de mon cœur.*
>
> The day is not more pure than the depth of my heart.

jour, *plus*, and *pur* seem to benefit from what might be called an accent of pitch, and consequently have rather more prominence than the other words. The main pause comes after *pur* with a minor one after *jour*. But, in spite of variations, classical French verse had a comparatively rigid rhythmical structure, and throughout the nineteenth century attempts were to be made to break up the line. Victor Hugo moved the caesura in the Alexandrine and introduced *enjambement* (the carrying-on of a sentence from one line to another; the classical Alexandrine has a stop at the end of each), but little was done to revolutionize the rhythms of poetry until the end of the century and the introduction of *vers libres* (poems with lines of all lengths, much repetition and a free use of rhyme and assonance) and the prose poem. Rhyme, indeed, was disputed in the second half of the century:

> Ô qui dira les torts de la Rime?
> Quel enfant sourd ou quel nègre fou
> Nous a forgé ce bijou d'un sou
> Qui sonne creux et faux sous la lime?

O who will tell of the wrongs done by Rhyme? What deaf child or mad Negro made us this halfpenny jewel that sounds hollow and false under the file?

Significantly enough, Verlaine's sweeping judgement is, itself, not merely rhymed, but rhymed with the classical alternation of masculine and feminine endings (endings without and with *e mute*). Rhyme has persisted in French poetry, and its latest apologist is M. Louis Aragon, Surrealist and Communist. By and large, attempts to revolutionize the metrical structure of French poetry have failed – except, of course, in recent literary movements (like *Dada* or the *Lettristes*), where the single word has become the only poetic unit. For the English reader these rhythms of French poetry are less emphatic than those he is used to, and he may fail to catch the delicate variations within the line. It is necessary to develop an ear for French verse, and this can only be done by reading a good deal of it or, better still, by listening to French people reading it.

Another inheritance from classical French poetry is rhetoric. The greatest French poet, Racine, was not only a dramatist, but a dramatist writing a type of play which did not give much scope for anything other than the set speech. There are no songs, for instance, as in Shakespeare (the choruses from *Esther* are hardly comparable). Right up to and beyond Baudelaire poets tended to write as if they were addressing someone. Even a light piece like Musset's *Une Soirée perdue* is a sustained argument-cum-narration. Only in a song, like the same poet's *Chanson de Barberine*, was there what might be called gratuitous poetry, and this neglect of what the English reader usually regards as the purer poetic elements presents an obstacle which has often led foreign critics to deny French poetry the place in European culture that it deserves. Moreover, we have become unaccustomed to the theatrical side of rhetoric.

> *O drapeaux de Wagram! Ó pays de Voltaire!*
> O banners of Wagram! O country of Voltaire!

sounds uncomfortably like *O Sophonisba, Sophonisba O!* We can far more easily put up with ten low words creeping in one dull line than we can with this exclamatory inflation. However, the dangers of the declamatory style were quickly realized. When Baudelaire praised Hugo for expressing 'avec *l'obscurité indispensable*, ce qui est obscur et confusément révélé',* he was expressing his own revolt against rhetorical inflation and a falsely logical order of development. One of the aims of the innovations attempted by Baudelaire and the poets who followed him was to strip French poetry of its rhetorical coverings. They tried to write a type of poetry that could be received more directly by the reader. 'Prends l'éloquence et tords-lui son cou',† wrote Verlaine, and Mallarmé's attempt to destroy logic went as far as the destruction of syntax itself.

---

*With the indispensable obscurity, what is obscure and confusedly revealed.

†Take eloquence and wring its neck!

The poets of the latter half of the nineteenth century therefore largely escape the dangers of declamation and its accompanying bathos. However, they do present another difficulty for the foreigner – a difficulty that has to do with the way in which what is called poetic emotion is communicated through the medium of words. One of the results of the formation of classical French in the seventeenth century was an increased precision in use and abstraction in meaning of words. And, of course, precision in the application of words does necessarily carry with it a considerable degree of generalization. A *house* can only always be exactly a house, if it refers more to the idea of a house than to the individual building on the horizon. But, in referring to the idea, it will have lost some of its power of affective communication. It will be a *house*, but it will not strike anyone as particularly the house in which they live. This process is part of the normal development of civilized languages, but it has been carried further in France than elsewhere, since the opposition to new words and slang managed for a long time to prevent the normal renewal of affective language from those sources. A poet like Baudelaire, who wanted to write more directly affective poetry, was therefore faced with a problem. He could not restore its primitive solidity to his vocabulary, though he could, and did, add new words to it. Continuing to use a language far more intellectualized than that of an English poet, he achieves his effects by a sort of lucid intensity, which had always been the mark of French poetry, but which the Romantics had abandoned in favour of the declamatory side of the classical inheritance. Lines like those in *Les Bijoux*:

> *Quand il jette en dansant son bruit vif et moqueur,*
> *Ce monde rayonnant de métal et de pierre*
> *Me ravit en extase, et j'aime à la fureur*
> *Les choses où le son se mêle à la lumière.*

When dancing it throws off its bright, mocking noise, this shining world of metal and stone transports me into ecstasy, and I love to distraction things where sound is mingled with light.

are sensuous indeed, but their sensuality is of a kind that does not exist in English. One has the impression of looking through sheet after sheet of glass, until the idea presented dies away in the shimmering of multiple refracted images. The eye is not on the object, but on the idea of the object. The description is sensuous, but not tactile, and the English reader, accustomed as he is to a more concrete imagery, may find this difference of level of abstraction one of the greatest obstacles to his appreciation of French poetry.

Difference of consciousness, too. French poets almost invariably give the impression of being well aware of what they are doing. Their creations are constructed with a theory behind them (that the final result may be very different from what was originally intended does not matter; the important thing is the conscious effort to create according to certain formulas). Hence the predominance of the school and the manifesto, hence the highly Byzantine discussions on poetry which went on throughout the second half of the nineteenth century. Of course, many of the consequences of this consciousness of a literary position are repugnant, and among them are the showing off, brawling, and shady behaviour, which were the by-products of the Parisian literary underworld and have been widely adopted since as the correct bardic insignia. Yet, much of the more eccentric practice and theory of French poets of this period must be accepted as proceeding from ideas, which, however wrong in themselves, nonetheless provided myths on which poetry could conveniently and legitimately be based.

*

I have dealt rather fully with the difficulties that an English reader might find on a first encounter with French nineteenth-century poetry, because such a discussion has not always been present in the writings of either English or French critics of these works. There has been a tendency among foreign critics to lose themselves in an *O altitudo* (supposing that they were not hostile to French poetry in the first place), and this was all the more comprehensible in that French academic criticism until relatively recently was largely still at the stage of the demonstration of *beauties*. At its worst, this *Ô que c'est beau** can involve an assent to entirely mediocre poems. At its best it does not go much beyond saying that lines are good because they are good. French poetry (and literature in general) could do with a thorough academic revaluation and, over the last fifteen years, there have been many signs that this is on the way. But the central guide still remains Marcel Raymond's *De Baudelaire au Surréalisme* – an old work that gives a convincing account of the development of French poetry from Baudelaire onwards and which, for want of competition, is the starting-point for all discussion of the subject. Suggestive ideas about nineteenth-century literature in general will be found in Sartre's essay *Qu'est-ce que la littérature?* (*Situations* 2) and in *Le degré zéro de l'écriture* by Roland Barthes. There is much helpful criticism of French nineteenth-century poets in Georges Poulet's series of studies *Études sur le temps humain* (Vols. 1 and 2) and in two works by Jean-Pierre Richard: *Poésie et profondeur* and *Études sur le Romantisme*. Gaston Bachelard's studies of poetic imagery also illuminate the subject, though their purpose is not primarily that of literary criticism. It would seem, in fact, as though the foundations have now been laid for a more modern view of nineteenth-century French poetry – one that takes into account that twentieth-century sensibility which so many of these poets helped to form.

I do not propose to give here a detailed history of French poetry during the nineteenth century, but a few facts and dates would seem to be inevitable. Three dates in particular are important: 1830, 1857, and 1866. The first marks the apogee of the Romantic movement in France. The second is the date of the first (unbowdlerized) version of Baudelaire's *Fleurs du mal*. The last is the date of publication of the anthology *Le Parnasse contemporain*, in which Mallarmé and Verlaine appeared side by side and which marks conveniently the appearance of a generation of poets who had been influenced by Baudelaire. The history of

*O how beautiful it is!

French nineteenth-century poetry, then, is that of two revolutions – one effected by the Romantics and the other by Baudelaire and his successors. Before we look at these transformation scenes, however, we should glance at the situation in 1815, just after Waterloo.

II

To say that the greatest poet of the French eighteenth century was thought at the time to be Voltaire is to reveal at once its entire poverty from the point of view of the production of poetry. With the achievements of the previous century culminating in Racine it is perhaps not surprising that sterility should have overtaken this branch of literature. Racine is certainly an example of the tendency (common in France) to produce works incapable of further development and, in fact, it was not until the end of the century that André Chénier (significantly enough a poet of Greek origin) managed to write beautiful and original verse, the effect of which, however, was not fully felt until the publication of his works in 1819. Apart from him – nobody. For the beginnings of the Romantic movement we have to look to prosewriters or foreign models. A French poet writing in 1815 or the years following would have heard something of German literature from Mme de Stael (her book *De l'Allemagne* was published in a French edition in 1814); he would have encountered the troubadours and *trouvères* of his own country in Simone de Sismondi's *De la Littérature du midi de l'Europe* (1813); he would certainly know about Scott, Shakespeare, and Byron – not to mention Ossian and the horror comics of Mrs Radcliffe, 'Monk' Lewis and Maturin. The French emigration to England during the Terror, the past cultural contacts between the two countries, the *odi et amo* relationship in which they lived, combined to make the English influence by far the most powerful force affecting French literature at this time. While Stendhal was subscribing to the *Edinburgh Review* (an event which he regarded as marking an epoch in his intellectual life), Delacroix was applying to his painting principles he had learned from Constable, and the English actors, whose performances of Shakespeare in Paris in 1822 provided one of the more picturesque episodes of the Romantic struggle to arrive – they had to be given police protection, since the Liberals regarded their appearance on the French stage as an insult to the memory of Napoleon and the Revolution – could hardly complain of a lack of publicity.

But there were French Romantics already in the field. Rousseau had set the example of an individual aesthetic. The subjectivity of his works, the importance accorded in them to passion and above all his attitude towards nature and the tranced feeling of unity into which he entered on contemplating it – all these things were to influence the Romantics profoundly. Chateaubriand in his *Atala* and *René* (1801 and 1802) helped to diffuse Rousseau's attitudes, while adding one or two of his own (the Romantic concept of religion and history, for example). From Rousseau through Chateaubriand to Lamartine is not far. The *Méditations* were published in 1820, and a poem like *Le Lac* is simply rhymed Rousseau – beautifully rhymed Rousseau, I hasten to add. It is, indeed, difficult to overestimate the part played by Rousseau and Chateaubriand in the history of nineteenth-century poetry. In them our poet would have found all the main themes of French Romanticism (we have to wait till Baudelaire or the later Hugo for any really novel subject-matter to appear) expressed in a marvellously cadenced prose by the two most influential purveyors of ideas of their respective generations. Their works were the first demonstration of the power of the new forces which were to possess French poetry.

III

In the years between 1820 and 1830 the Romantic movement took shape. However, both Lamartine and Marceline Desbordes-Valmore, who are the first to appear on the scene, follow on from Chateaubriand. Both of them had sensitive, if not particularly strong talents, which were quite at home with the poetry of sensibility, the first type of Romantic poetry. For themes a rather arbitrary association of love, nature, and sometimes religion; for style a soft, mellifluous manner, conserving in large part the eighteenth-century vocabulary of the passions – by 1820 there was nothing very revolutionary about all this. The essential passivity of a poet like Lamartine, his willingness to abandon himself to the impact of a beautiful landscape or a beautiful woman, defines and limits his talent, though the manner was to be continued and transformed by Verlaine. His poems can hardly be called constructed, and his conception of poetry is almost that of a mere Aeolian harp. He was, of course, a considerable craftsman, but few are likely to want to read his works as a whole. He lacks the essential surprise of poetry. For a more decisive individuality we have to turn to other Romantics, whose intention of transforming their poetry was both stronger and more conscious.

In the preface to *Cromwell* (1827), which may be considered as the principal manifesto of French Romanticism, Hugo uttered the battle-cry, which is invariably produced whenever any question of literary reform arises: 'La nature et la vérité'.* 'Mettons le marteau dans les théories, les poétiques et les systèmes,' he wrote. 'Jetons bas ce vieux plâtrage qui masque la façade de l'art!'† The opposition to the old aesthetic of classicism (a classicism degraded into Laharpe's *Cours*) is total, but the constructive part of the preface is limited to the advocacy of a number of technical innovations both in poetry and drama. What is new is the urgency of the feeling, which informs Hugo's writing, that poetry and drama (for the preface to *Cromwell* is naturally more concerned with the latter) are important. The claims made for the poet's status throughout the nineteenth century begin here.

For one of the keys to an understanding of French nineteenth-century poetry is the poet's conception of the part to be played by his own work in relation to society and the universe. The idea of the poet's mission, always present in the minds of the Romantics, led them to think of him, in Shelley's words, as 'the

---

*Nature and truth.

†Let us take the hammer to theories, poetics, and systems. Let us throw down this old plaster-work masking art's façade.

unacknowledged legislator of mankind'. Poets are seers or law-
givers, prophets or mages, and though Baudelaire, Mallarmé
and Rimbaud were to produce more complex versions of this
myth, in substance it remained the same. Moreover, this idea of
a mission was to be directed as to its form by the increasing
alienation of the poets from a society in the process of being
transformed by the Industrial Revolution. What could a Vigny
find to say to the hard-faced industrialists, *haute bourgeoisie*, and
bankers of the French monarchy of the 1830s? Reacting to an
unsympathetic milieu, the poets were to become ever more
concerned to affirm their own necessarily aristocratic view of life,
and after the disillusion of the failed revolution of 1848
this alienation was to develop into an active revolt against society.
The rise of the concept of the *poète maudit* coincides with the
victory of a *bourgeoisie* that conquered society, not only (as in
England) by its power, but also by its manners.

The effect of this growing separation between society and the
poet is clearly to be seen in their idea of their own work.
Lamartine had been content to regard poetry simply as a vehicle
for the expression of his own personal feelings. The dissatis-
faction that the younger Romantics felt with the trends of their
time led them to write poetry intended to influence their con-
temporaries directly either from a political (and revolutionary)
standpoint or else morally. Indeed, the 1820s saw far more dis-
cussion of politics than of literature, and Hugo's later political
volumes (*Les Châtiments* and *L'Année terrible*, for example)
were in the true Romantic tradition. The Romantics' concern
with moral lessons is best expressed by Vigny:

> *Seul et dernier anneau de deux chaines brisées,*
> *Je reste. Et je soutiens encor dans les hauteurs,*
> *Parmi les maîtres purs de nos savants musées,*
> *L'IDÉAL du poète et des graves penseurs.*

Sole and last ring of two broken chains, I remain. And still I bear
up on the heights, amid the pure masters of our learned
museums, the poet's and the solemn thinkers' IDEAL.

Yet this concept of the poet's mission as being the propagation of the moral and political good was unsatisfactory. First, because morals and politics have a bad effect on poetry itself; Gautier's protest in this sense was made soon after 1830. Secondly, because, especially after 1848, it was no longer possible for the poet to think of society as being affected by his works. That being so, his only alternative was to exalt his art from some other point of view, proclaiming the primacy of the creation of the beautiful over all other forms of human activity (as did the devotees of Art for Art's sake), or else regarding his poetry as having some more mystic significance. From *law-giver* the poet would become *mage* (i.e. one aspiring to power through magical operations). If he could not change the world around him, he would create new worlds from language, worlds that should be no less real than the tangible one and that should, indeed, correspond to the most secret rhythms of the universe. And the production of this occult poetry would naturally widen the gap between the poet/adept and his reader/acolyte. In this way the poets of the latter half of the nineteenth century compensated themselves for the increasing lack of comprehension with which they were regarded by the society around them.

IV

Of all the Romantics, Hugo is without doubt the greatest, but his greatness has been hidden by the insufficient attention paid to the last part of his work. He is not the *garde-national épique**
which he appears to be in the school books, but a poet more akin to Blake, filling his works with monstrous cosmologies, where the terror of the abyss draws the poet's mind cascading from void to void in unending vertigo. Valéry wrote of his last poems: 'Dans la *Corde d'airain*, dans *Dieu*, dans la *Fin de Satan*, dans la pièce sur la mort de Gautier . . . le vieillard très illustre atteint le plus haut point de la puissance poétique et de la noble science

---

*The epic national guard.

du versificateur.'* Hugo's cosmic epic style can be seen in some of these poems. It is a style which achieves the feat of giving imprecision to the French language. Reading it is like looking into a fog, and this is not the obscurity of a Mallarmé or of Valéry himself, where the individual phrase is clearly outlined, but an obscurity which makes it hard to focus any but the most hazy visual image:

> Oh! quelle nuit! là, rien n'a de contour ni d'âge;
> Et le nuage est spectre, et le spectre est nuage.

Oh! What night! Nothing there has contour or age: and the cloud is a phantom and the phantom is a cloud.

These poems are rhetorical – they are highly dramatic even – but their rhetoric is broken and gasping. The rhythms pant and labour, changing with the changing of the emotions, and in this great flood of language Hugo brings to life a weird universe of absence, in which God only appears as a gulf, an imperative question. Wherever Hugo took his cosmology from (the Kabbala or Swedenborg? It does not much matter), he made it peculiarly his own, and embodied it in a series of poems which, for epic sweep and primitive strength, have hardly their equal. Ironically they remain largely unknown, while *Ruy Blas* and *Hernani* are still performed on the stage. Of course, to praise Hugo's later poems is not to say that the well-known pieces like *L'Expiation* and *A Villequier* are not fine poetry. They, too, should be read, but with an eye to the kind of poetry that makes Hugo unique.

The works of the other Romantics present no necessity for any such revaluation. Vigny, indeed, may be thought to have been given too high a place in the past. His long philosophical poems, inculcating, as they do, a stoicism before a hostile universe, sometimes fall into a rather embarrassing bathos, which makes denigration of his talent a little too easy. But poems such

---

*In the *Brazen Cord*, in *God*, in the *End of Satan*, in the piece on the death of Gautier ... the celebrated old man reaches the highest point of poetic power and of the verse-maker's noble art.

as *Le Cor* or *L'Esprit pur* deserve their fame, and his style can only be fairly represented by periods rather than by the individual line. It may be a platitude to say that in his faults and virtues he resembles Wordsworth, but the English reader will find the comparison helpful. They both lack a sense of humour.

Musset, on the other hand, brought to Romanticism some of the traditional wit and *esprit gaulois* of French poetry. A poem like *A Julie* comes at the end of a long line of seventeenth- and eighteenth-century erotica. Musset's poetry is always charming and accomplished and, if there are not many people who can put up with *Les Nuits* nowadays, the poems in which he puts off the *persona* of the melancholy Romantic hero and assumes that of the Byronic boulevardier will always be read with pleasure. The colloquialism and psychological accuracy of *Une Soirée perdue* make it very modern in feeling – the reverse side of the *Lettre à M. de Lamartine*, which, however, is saved by its *naïveté*. Musset stands as the representative in his own generation of a tradition that is permanent in French poetry, and which he did not need Byron to teach him: a tradition of sentiment conveyed in a light, but classically perfected form.

Among other poets in operation between 1830 and 1850, Aloysius Bertrand may fairly be attached to the Romantics. His strange, hauntingly beautiful prose poems seem to me infinitely superior to the much-vaunted farrago produced by Isidore Ducasse, Comte de Lautréamont. Jean-Pierre Béranger is really an older Romantic; his political songs had had an important influence on public opinion under the Restoration, and he also wrote some poems of merit, of which *Le Vieux Vagabond* is the most moving. 'Le pauvre a-t-il une patrie?' anticipates much that has happened since, and it is hard not to be touched by this sincere early statement of a truth that has since been disgraced. One other poet must be mentioned, who, though he was one of Gautier's *Jeune France* group, does not come comfortably under any heading. Gérard de Nerval, one of the greatest poets of the nineteenth century, owes his fame to a handful of works in verse and prose. In the twelve sonnets of *Les Chimères* there is as much

of the miraculous as most poets achieve in a lifetime. 'Jusqu'ici rien n'a pu guérir mon cœur qui souffre toujours du mal du pays.'* 'La Muse est entrée dans mon cœur comme une déesse aux paroles dorées; elle s'en est echappée comme une pythie en jetant des cris de douleur. Seulement, ses derniers accents se sont adoucis à mesure qu'elle s'éloignait. Elle s'est détournée un instant, et j'ai revu comme en un mirage les traits adorés d'autre-fois ...'† The poetry of Nerval is commonly referred to as 'hermetic', but nothing more than these words of his is neces-sary to seize its inspiration. One can decode the end of a sonnet like:

> La déesse avait fui sur sa conque dorée,
> La mer nous renvoyait son image adorée,
> Et les cieux rayonnaient sous l'écharpe d'Iris.

The goddess had fled on her golden shell, the sea sent us back her sweet image, and the skies shone beneath Iris's scarf.

Much scholarship has in fact been expended on *Quellenforschung*, but I do not think that it adds anything more to the poem. Homesickness for a land where the sea is blue and the women beautiful, a glimpse of a most fugitive beauty now lost for ever – these are the themes of this poetry, which may properly be called pure or gratuitous, since the means which it employs to effect its ends owe almost nothing to the non-poetic. The intensity is that of a style, where every word carries a dense weight of passion, and there is a total absence of rhetoric.

The urge towards a purer poetry, unconscious in Nerval, had already led Gautier to revolt against the moralizing of the Romantics. 'L'art pour nous n'est pas le moyen, mais le but; – tout artiste qui se propose autre chose que le beau n'est pas un

---

*Up to now nothing has been able to cure my heart, which still suffers from homesickness.

†The Muse entered into my heart like a goddess with golden words; she left it like a pythoness giving forth shrieks of pain. Only, her last words became softer as she went away, and I saw again as in a mirage the adored features of former days ...

artiste à nos yeux',* he was to write in a famous article. His own poetry is cultivated, but usually falls into an epigrammatic preciosity, which comes between it and the big attempt. It would seem that Art for Art's sake is not necessarily a battle-cry that brings inspiration with it, though Gautier found in it the means for giving a *raison d'être* to the poet's work. Leconte de Lisle, the founder of what only became the Parnassian school of poets some years after he had written his best poems, carried Gautier's ideas still further. For him art was not only superior to all other forms of human activity, but summed them up and made them incarnate. He is not a terribly good poet, but those of his poems which come off owe their success to the contrast between the stoical indifference with which he regarded nature and life (the starting-point of the famous Parnassian impassibility) and the exotic imagery he drew from mythology and landscape. Leconte de Lisle's only true successor was Hérédia, who was far more adroit at putting his ideals into practice, but his attempt to base poetry on a theory, which, for want of a better word, can be called philosophical, is highly significant. It was a step on the road towards the erection of poetry into a religious or magical operation.

v

With the publication of *Les Fleurs du mal* in 1857 this process is almost complete; at least all the elements of completion are present. The dissociation of the artist from society had progressed so far by 1848, the year of revolutions, and the disillusionment after the failure of the hopes that year had aroused had been so bitter that, from a strong dislike of the conquering *bourgeoisie*, the French intelligentsia passed to a stage of revolt against it: a revolt which might take the form of Socialism, but which, for the majority of writers and artists, expressed itself in a withdrawal from society into the certainty of the transcendence of art. Not that Baudelaire was an adherent of Art for Art's sake. 'Dans ce

*Art for us is not the means, but the end; – any artist who aims at something other than the beautiful is not an artist in our eyes.

livre atroce,' he wrote of *Les Fleurs du mal*, 'j'ai mis tout mon cœur, toute ma tendresse, toute ma religion (travestie), toute ma haine. Il est vrai que j'écrirai le contraire, que je jurerai mes grands dieux que c'est un livre d'art pur ...'* Certainly his achievement had a technical side to it; Valéry's judgement on his work is well known: 'L'œuvre romantique, *en général*, supporte assez mal une lecture ralentie et hérissée des résistances d'un lecteur difficile et raffiné ... Baudelaire était ce lecteur',† and nobody who has studied these poems would think to deny the part of the conscious artist in them (metrical innovations, fresh imagery, avoidance of obvious rhetoric, etc.). But the inspiration behind them is cosmological; Baudelaire had a system, which, it is true, can hardly be taken seriously as a philosophy, but whose existence is of the greatest importance as a directing myth of his poetry. At its base is the idea of *correspondances* set out in the poem of that name:

> *La Nature est un temple où de vivants piliers*
> *Laissent parfois sortir de confuses paroles;*
> *L'homme y passe à travers des forêts de symboles*
> *Qui l'observent avec des regards familiers.*

Nature is a temple where living pillars sometimes allow confused words to escape; man passes there through forests of symbols that watch him with familiar glances.

And, since everything is fixed in a hierarchy of relationships, it follows that when the poet uses a metaphor or even when he simply names an object, he is invoking something *real*. His use of language is *magical*, his poems are *spells*, since they have a reality which comes from their real correspondence with the objects described. The universe has a mystical unity; no part of it can be altered without affecting the rest. From this concept of mystical unity comes the idea (which was so popular with Baudelaire

*In this dreadful book I have put all my heart, all my tenderness, all my religion (disguised), all my hatred. It is true that I shall write the contrary, that I shall swear by the great gods that it is a work of pure art.

†The work of the Romantics, in general, stands up rather badly to a slow reading, bristling with the resistance of a critical and refined reader ... Baudelaire was that reader.

and other poets in the nineteenth century) of the unity of the arts and also of the sensations (*synaesthesia*). The equivalence of colours and sounds, of music and poetry, which was to play so large a part in the discussions which went on around the Symbolist movement, is the natural consequence of this view of the universe. The exaltation of the *dandy* too, which is, however, of more importance in Baudelaire's prose than in his poetry, comes, not only from the necessity of the poet/mage's creating for himself a personality apart from the common run of men, but also from the vague feeling that this personality should be of a kind that displayed some equivalence with his creation (to the artifice of the poem corresponds the artifice of the dandy).

This system provided Baudelaire with a controlling myth or a series of controlling myths, which were not merely arbitrary, but were deeply seated in his nature. In his attitude towards women, for example, he instinctively uses the same sense of correspondences as a mechanism for his sexual sensibility. 'La femme est sans doute une lumière, un regard, une invitation au bonheur, une parole quelquefois; mais elle est surtout une harmonie générale, non-seulement dans son allure et le mouvement de ses membres, mais aussi dans les mousselines, les gazes, les vastes et chatoyantes nuées d'étoffes dont elle s'enveloppe, et qui sont comme les attributs et le piédestal de sa divinité . . .'* Evidently, for Baudelaire, these sensuous trappings of woman held as much charm as she herself, and this fetishism is continually displayed in those of his poems with a sexual theme, where the sensual communication with his mistress is usually achieved via her hair, her perfume, or something she is wearing (cf. *Les Bijoux*, *La Chevelure*, etc.). What might be called mere woman is repugnant to him: 'La femme est *naturelle*, c'est-à-dire abominable'.† The artifice that Baudelaire demands in his creation of

*Woman is doubtless a light, a glance, an invitation to happiness, a word sometimes; but she is above all a general harmony, not only in her carriage and the movement of her limbs, but also in the muslins, the gauzes, the vast glistening clouds of cloth, in which she swathes herself and which are as the attributes and the pedestal of her divinity.

†Woman is *natural*, that is: abominable.

himself he also requires in his mistress, even in his way of making love to her, a way that often seems to be that of the *voyeur*.

Sartre has reproached Baudelaire with his inability to create his own values. Revolting against a *bourgeois* society, but accepting its values by his denial rather than transcendence of them, paying an inverted homage to Christianity by his Satanism, for Sartre Baudelaire seems engaged in a monstrous game, erecting around himself card-houses of false revolt and false suffering, of false belief and false emotion. Now it is undoubtedly true that much of the apparatus thas Baudelaire used to sustain his poetry is ridiculous as thought. The one completely puerile attitude in face of Christianity is that of the Satanist. To revolt against a system of belief, while appearing to accept its premises, is justifiable from only one point of view: that of the poet. The poet is concerned with the communication of experience and, for this communication, he must use what myths he has to hand. Moreover, these myths must be sufficiently well known to strike a resonant chord in his audience. I do not think Baudelaire was a Christian, even of an inverted kind, but he was a man of what is called religious feeling, and he wished to communicate certain things which could be expressed only in terms of Christian imagery. The question of belief does not enter into this poetic expression. Baudelaire would be quite justified in creating a mythical structure for his poems in which he himself did not believe, in the sense in which one believes in a religion. That most of his thought is valueless except in relation to his poetry I should not dispute, but it is equally true that it is not the least use considering it except in such a relationship. It is here that Sartre has gone wrong; to try to separate Baudelaire's philosophy of life from his poetry is to forget that he was primarily a poet, and, as such, has a right to a phoney philosophy. Perhaps Sartre is right in saying that 'ses poèmes sont comme des succédanés de la création du Bien, qu'il s'est interdite',* but anyone concerned with poetry must regard them as a good in themselves.

*His poems are like substitutes for the creation of the Good, which he has forbidden himself.

In fact there is one value ceaselessly affirmed in Baudelaire's poems, and from it comes most of the novelty of his poetic achievement. His definition of the Beautiful is well known: 'C'est quelque chose d'ardent et de triste, quelque chose d'un peu vague, laissant carrière à la conjecture ... Le mystère, le regret sont aussi des caractères du Beau.'* And this uncertain objective, this mixture of the emotions represents a carrying of the romantic ideal further than it had been carried before. Baudelaire's insistence on the entry of every emotion, every passion into art, together with his love of the grotesque 'grand sourire dans un beau visage de géant',† led him to create a value out of experience itself, an experience necessarily in flux, alternating between *Spleen* and *Idéal*, between God and Satan, including both the beautiful and the grotesque. This attribution of a value to the flow of life is the basic element in Romanticism, and Baudelaire pushed it to a greater extreme than it had been carried by the poets more properly called Romantics, by refusing any exclusions and by declining the idealization of the universe which is to be found in their works. The tide of experience must continue to run, whatever happens; the great enemy is boredom (*ennui*). Baudelaire described himself in *Le Voyage*:

> *Mais les vrais voyageurs sont ceux-là seuls qui partent*
> *Pour partir ...*

> But the true travellers are only those who depart for the
> sake of departing...

It was the value placed upon experience (necessarily egocentric) that gave Baudelaire's universe its real unity as opposed to the mythical unity he imposed on it by his system of correspondences. And this consuming thirst made him include new themes and new images in his poetry. He was the first poet to write that *poésie des villes*, which was to become one of the chief innovations of nineteenth-century French poetry. His psychological

* It is something passionate and sad, something a little vague, leaving room for conjecture ... Mystery and regret are also characteristics of the Beautiful.

† A wide smile on a handsome giant's face.

observation of his own and other people's comportment brought a new realism into his descriptions of human behaviour (particularly as regards sexual relations), and his consciousness of the homesickness that afflicts modern man enabled him to reach that strange tone (half-revolt, half-melancholy) which has marked so much French poetry and prose ever since. His own estrangement from society gave a new anguish to his realization of the essential loneliness of the poet, and in his poems this feeling of isolation, and the material presented by a new age and new emotions are seized upon by an aesthetic of impermanence, which in some ways is curiously near to that of the baroque. This poetry, incarnate in a style where the surprising epithet is never wanting, might be called the poetry of romantic realism, and a combination of time and quality make of Baudelaire the most revolutionary poet of the nineteenth century, the first to express the shifting sensibility of modern man.*

'Enfin Malherbe vint.'† The coming of Baudelaire has as much importance for the nineteenth century as a literary landmark. Whether or not the new generation of poets needed his example to write as they did, he was their precursor, and they all paid tribute to him. Their first appearance can conveniently be dated in 1866, when the anthology *Le Parnasse contemporain* came out with poems by Verlaine and Mallarmé, and by 1870 these two poets were beginning to be known; Rimbaud was

---

*Marcel Aymé's attack on Baudelaire in his book *Le Confort intellectuel* seems to be due to a recognition of the basically romantic character of much of his poetry. His hostile analysis of the sonnet *La Beauté*, exaggerated as it is, makes some legitimate points about Baudelaire's vocabulary which does sometimes stray into the inflation common to all the Romantics. On the other hand, the moral strictures put into the mouth of M. Lepage seem to me purely paradoxical. Moreover, M. Aymé's Johnsonian interlocutor admits in the course of his dialogue with his creator that he finds the sonnet beautiful in spite of the faults he points out in it. That is surely enough. As any critic knows, it is only too easy to destroy the total effect of a poem by questioning individual words. Which is not to say that M. Aymé has not touched on a weak spot in Baudelaire's poetry: its frequently absurd inheritance from the Romantics.

†At last Malherbe came.

to publish *Une Saison en Enfer* in 1873 and Corbière's *Amours jaunes* date from the same year. Of these poets it is Rimbaud and Mallarmé who continue Baudelaire's work most directly.

VI

Baudelaire's magical view of language had not led him to demand of it feats beyond its power. All he had wanted was a re-creation of experience, with no desire to put into practice the occult powers he attributed to poetry. In Rimbaud, however, the transfiguration of the poet into the demiurge is carried to its furthest limit. In him can be seen incarnate the revolt against society and the attempt to realize it in poetry. He is the poet/mage *par excellence*, and, like other mages, he envisages an asceticism: 'Je dis qu'il faut être *voyant*, se faire *voyant*. Le poète se fait *voyant* par un long, immense et raisonné dérèglement de tous les sens.'* The anarchic side of Rimbaud's nature is complemented by a desire to create and, since it is by language that he must achieve this creation, the word necessarily takes on its full power of invocation (the primitivism of this view of language is quite in accordance with his character). By language he would destroy a world and create a world. And the change from poet to demiurge is marked by the famous statement 'Je est un autre'.†

Rimbaud's poetry is that of a man struggling to find firm ground in a world whose values he rejected, and no system entirely solves the riddle of his poignant and tormented writings. It seems that he believed in his own myths to a dangerous point. To expect other than purely poetic results from an exaltation of poetry into sorcery could only lead to disappointment, and *Une Saison en Enfer* is probably an account of one such check, but why Rimbaud began to write and why he ceased writing at the age of nineteen or twenty remains conjectural. What is left is the marvellous incantatory power of his verse, the tender realism of

*I say that it is necessary to be a *seer*, to make oneself a *seer*. The poet makes himself a *seer* by a long, vast and reasoned disordering of all his senses.

†I is another.

a poem like *Les Premières Communions* or the nostalgia and the vision of *Matin*:

> *Le chant des cieux, la marche des peuples! Esclaves, ne maudissons pas la vie.*

> The song of the heavens, the advance of the peoples! Slaves, let us not blaspheme life.

But it would be too easy to think that Rimbaud ever succeeded in creating a certainty for himself. He was never able either to fall back on a traditional solution or to establish the foundations of his own values firmly enough to rest from his ceaseless effort towards creation. Like other poets of the time he avails himself of the myth of the city and of the myth of childhood (complementary aspects of the same nostalgia), but there is also another element in his poetry which is to be found nowhere else: an acute sense of historic movement. Over twenty years after the first Communist manifesto we can feel in Rimbaud's poetry a sense that the tribes are on the move with the old hierarchies and national states breaking down. A poem like *Qu'est-ce pour nous, mon cœur, que les nappes de sang* . . . is the sharpest expression of revolutionary nihilism, just as *Matin* is the most touching hymn to revolutionary aspiration. What makes Rimbaud so near to us today is that he saw the break-up of civilization around him at a time when hardly anyone else saw it. For him history was *le temps des assassins*,* and he was forced to do his best about it. It is this that gives his poetry its urgent, direct quality; it was the instrument of a personal salvation. That Rimbaud was not, could not be saved by it increases the gravity of the tragedy. He was the first poet in our historic plight.

VII

While Rimbaud represents the claims of poetry in their most active connection with man in history, Mallarmé is the type of the poet-contemplative, interested in the cultivation of an inner purity. Rimbaud had given himself to the creation of a world

*The time of the assassins.

through language; Mallarmé gave himself to the creation of a language. For him it was an end sufficient in itself as virtue is sufficient. At the age of twenty-five he had written in a letter to a friend: 'Il n'y a que la Beauté; – et elle n'a qu'une expression parfaite – la Poésie.'* And Valéry has spoken of his conviction of 'l'éminente dignité de la Poésie, hors de laquelle il n'apercevait que le hasard'.† Thus the work of art was established as an absolute, incarnating something approaching the Platonic Ideas. But the poem had to be constructed from language, and how to give to language, shopsoiled from its association with the particular, the burning generality that Mallarmé desired? For his poetry differs from that of other great poets in that it moves from the general to the particular. 'Je dis: une fleur! et, hors de l'oubli où ma voix relègue aucun contour, en tant que quelque chose d'autre que les calices sus, musicalement se lève, idée même et suave, l'absente de tous bouquets.'‡ An aesthetic of absence of the particular, in which the creative act itself appears an impurity, must necessarily carry with it some obscurity. 'Toute chose sacrée et qui veut demeurer sacrée s'enveloppe de mystère.'§ The poems of Mallarmé, however, are not as difficult as they seem. The dissolution of syntax, which was for him one means of renewing language, sometimes complicates matters and gives to the poem an ambiguity that cannot be resolved in favour of any one interpretation. The *Prose pour des Esseintes* is an extreme case of a poem which does not seem meant to be understood; there Mallarmé speaks directly of the Ideas, and his language is unavoidably a description of the unfathomable, but the sonnet for Verlaine, for instance, only seems obscure because of the great compression of language and imagery. Mallarmé

*There is only Beauty; – and it has only one perfect expression – Poetry.

†The eminent dignity of Poetry, outside of which he only saw chance.

‡I say: a flower! and, out of the forgetfulness where my voice banishes any contour, inasmuch as it is something other than known calyxes, musically arises, an idea itself and fragrant, the one absent from all bouquets.

§Every holy thing wishing to remain holy surrounds itself with mystery.

also owes his reputation for coldness to his fundamental conception of poetry. Concerned as he was with the non-presence of the object, much of his imagery is drawn from the vertigo he felt before Space or the Ideal (it comes to the same thing). But the warm sensuality of a poem like *L'Après-midi d'un faune* serves to refute the legend of a poet dedicated to lunar sterility.

Dedicated, however, he was. To make of a poem at once the summit and explanation of the universe required dedication, but, as M. Raymond has pointed out, this was not an attempt which could in any sense succeed. Mallarmé could not make of language an absolute. 'Donner un sens plus pur aux mots de la tribu'*– that he could do. What was impossible was to make them the equivalent of a transcendance. Yet all was not lost; the famous *salon* at the rue de Rome was thronged with young writers – Valéry, Gide, and Claudel among them – who learned from Mallarmé what toil and self-abnegation the poet's task demands. Like Rimbaud, like Baudelaire, he had a directing myth that enabled him to justify his sacrifices for poetry. Withdrawn from society rather than revolting against it (but this was certainly his form of revolt), he appealed from it to eternity, and the language broke under him. Nineteenth-century poetry was bought at the price of such failures.

VIII

Verlaine's poetry shows no sign of such perilous spiritual adventures. His work is largely lyrical and resists attempts at analysis. His talent (naïve as it was) links up with the sentimental lyricism of Lamartine or Mme Desbordes-Valmore. Like them, he is given to sensibility; like theirs his poems are not the products of strength, technically perfect though they are. But he owes to Baudelaire a certain self-mocking irony in the presentation of his poetic *persona*, which had not been present in earlier poets of this type, and he extended his range to cover modern city life as well as the beauties of nature. It is curious to compare his *Art poétique* with Gautier's *Art* and see what a long

*Give a purer meaning to the words of the tribe.

way ideas on aesthetics had travelled. The jewels and statues in which Gautier chose to typify art have changed to Verlaine's misty ideal:

> *C'est des beaux yeux derrière des voiles,*
> *C'est le grand jour tremblant de midi . . .*

It is lovely eyes behind veils, it is the full shimmering light of noon. . .

What had come between? Baudelaire: 'quelque chose d'ardent et triste, quelque chose d'un peu vague, laissant carrière à la conjecture . . .'*

It is Verlaine's wonderful skill with verse and word that most readers will choose to remember. When he tries to elaborate any other philosophy than that of the sentimentally cynical vagabond, he becomes over-pathetic. Sincere he no doubt was, but lines like:

> *Je ne veux plus aimer que ma mère Marie.*

> I want to love no one but my mother Mary.

are positively embarrassing. However, we can forget the *fadaises* of *Sagesse* in the exquisite formality of a poem like *Clair de Lune* or the equally exquisite impressionism of *Dans l'interminable* . . .

What other poets are there to talk of? Tristan Corbière wrote harsh ironic poems – some of them in the *argot* of the sea, others full of puns and *double-entendres*. His best poetry comes when he is speaking of his native Brittany, or when he is judging himself, as in *Paria*. His manner was to be taken up on a lighter note by Jules Laforgue, a poet who, like Corbière, died young. His poems, in turn sentimental, humorous, and tragic, were to have great influence on English and American poetry. The *persona*, which he created for himself, of the little man with a wry smile and lack of self-confidence anticipates Charlie Chaplin and Eliot (J. Alfred Prufrock attests his influence, not to mention such early poems of Eliot as *Conversation Galante*, which are pure Laforgue pastiche), and the mingling of images in a poem like *L'Hiver qui vient* was to be found later in the poetry of

*Something passionate and sad, something a little vague, leaving room for conjecture.

Surrealism and the humour of a Queneau or a Prévert. Laforgue and Corbière were, in fact, one possible line of development from Baudelaire and they both represent the self-critical irony which informs so much French writing. Émile Verhaeren, who was almost a very great poet, develops the poetry of the town to a point where his Flemish vision of a countryside eaten away by industrial tentacles becomes almost apocalyptic. His Socialism and intense pity for the miseries of peasant and worker give his poetry great force, even if it occasionally shows the formlessness which so displeased Rémy de Gourmont. Formless too are the vast prose poems of Lautréamont, which were to influence the Surrealists by their apparent unchaining of a purely visionary talent. These wild, often sadistic, reveries have been much overrated, but Lautréamont cannot be denied a gift of language and delirium. Towards the turn of the century a return to classicism brought about the appearance of the *École Romane*, of whom Raymond de la Tailhède is one of the more presentable members. Their inspiration was Mediterranean, and they looked back to the poets of the sixteenth century as their masters. The result was a rather Levantine *Latinità*. Nearer to Athens and Rome is Emmanuel Signoret, whose poems, sparkling with light and the southern sea, foreshadow Valéry. With this tentative reaction towards classicism the story of French nineteenth-century poetry closes.

IX

Finally, a word about this selection. I have tried to give only complete poems, and this has necessarily meant some exclusions – notably in the case of Hugo, most of whose best works were far too long to include. I have also tried to represent fully the great poets of the time, and this has meant leaving out some others. For instance, there is no Théodore de Banville and no Sully Prudhomme, as I was unable to find a poem of theirs I liked sufficiently to justify the omission of something else. A poem is not necessarily bad because it has figured in many anthologies, so the reader will find a number of very familiar poems in this selection. But I hope he will also find some he does not know, but will like on acquaintance, and that he will not hold the vagaries of my taste against me. A selection is bound to be personal, and there is nothing that can be done about it. As to the translations, it has been my aim to provide as literal a rendering as is compatible with reasonable English prose. Occasionally I have had to be more approximate: a poet like Mallarmé, for instance, is bound to impose on his translator an interpretation which is only one of several possible versions. In one or two cases, where it has been impossible to render some play on or opposition of words, I have given an explanatory note. But I have tried to keep these down to the minimum.

My thanks are due to Dr Joseph Chiari for checking my translations and putting his knowledge of his native language and literature at my disposal; to Mr Donat O'Donnell for his criticism of the introduction; and to Mr J. D. Scott for advising me on the translations and the introduction.

This new edition of the Penguin Book of French Verse, in which all four volumes are being published in one, has inevitably meant some excisions in the nineteenth- and twentieth-century sections. I have tried to preserve a balance between poets, to keep as many of them as possible while representing adequately the more important figures, and to preserve what I consider to be the best poems. However, I am aware that it has not always been possible to reconcile these conflicting criteria. I have left the two introductions largely unchanged since it seemed to me that, even if a poet (like Emmanuel Signoret or Saint-Pol-Roux) had to be cut out, there was an interest for the reader in learning about him and, possibly, being encouraged to seek out his works. An anthologist, indeed, would not be doing his job if he were to give the impression that all the good poetry and poets of a period were contained in his own selection. In relation to the copious meal provided by French nineteenth- and twentieth-century poetry what is presented here is an *hors d'œuvre* – I hope, a good one.

A.H.

JEAN-PIERRE DE BÉRANGER

Le Vieux Vagabond

Dans ce fossé cessons de vivre.
Je finis vieux, infirme et las.
Les passants vont dire: Il est ivre;
Tant mieux! ils ne me plaindront pas.
J'en vois qui détournent la tête;
D'autres me jettent quelques sous.
Courez vite; allez à la fête.
Vieux vagabond, je puis mourir sans vous.

Oui, je meurs ici de vieillesse,
Parce qu'on ne meurt pas de faim.
J'espérais voir de ma détresse
L'hôpital adoucir la fin,
Mais tout est plein dans chaque hospice,
Tant le peuple est infortuné!
La rue, hélas! fut ma nourrice:
Vieux vagabond, mourons où je suis né.

The Old Tramp

Let me end my life in this ditch. I finish old and sick and tired. The passers-by will say: he is drunk; so much the better! they will not pity me. I see some turning away their heads; others throw me a few coppers. Run quickly; go to your feasting. An old tramp can die without you.

Yes, I am dying here of old age, because people do not die of hunger. I hoped to see the hospital soften the end of my distress, but everything is full up in every poor-house, so unfortunate are the common people! The street, alas, was my nurse: let an old tramp die where he was born.

Aux artisans, dans mon jeune âge,
J'ai dit: Qu'on m'enseigne un métier.
Va, nous n'avons pas trop d'ouvrage,
Répondaient-ils, va mendier.
Riches, qui me disiez: Travaille,
J'eus bien des os de vos repas;
J'ai bien dormi sur votre paille.
Vieux vagabond, je ne vous maudis pas.

J'aurais pu voler, moi, pauvre homme;
Mais non: mieux vaut tendre la main.
Au plus, j'ai dérobé la pomme
Qui mûrit au bord du chemin.
Vingt fois pourtant on me verrouille
Dans les cachots de par le roi.
De mon seul bien on me dépouille.
Vieux vagabond, le soleil est à moi.

Le pauvre a-t-il une patrie?
Que me font vos vins et vos blés,
Votre gloire et votre industrie,
Et vos orateurs assemblés?
Dans vos murs ouverts à ses armes,
Lorsque l'étranger s'engraissait,

In my youth I said to the craftsmen: Teach me a trade. Go away,
we have not too much work, they replied; go away and beg. Rich
folk, who said to me: Work, I had many a bone from your meals;
I have slept well on your straw. An old tramp does not curse you.

I, poor man, could have thieved; but no: it is better to hold out
my hand. At most, I stole an apple ripening on the roadside. Yet
twenty times they locked me up in dungeons by order of the king.
They robbed me of my only possession. The sun belongs to an old
tramp.

Has the poor man a country? What do your wine and wheat,
your fame and industry, and your assemblies of orators mean to
me? When the foreigner grew fat within your walls thrown open

Comme un sot j'ai versé des larmes.
Vieux vagabond, sa main me nourrissait.

Comme un insecte fait pour nuire,
Hommes, que ne m'écrasiez-vous?
Ah! plutôt vous deviez m'instruire
A travailler au bien de tous.
Mis à l'abri du vent contraire,
Le ver fût devenu fourmi;
Je vous aurais chéris en frère.
Vieux vagabond, je meurs votre ennemi.

ALPHONSE DE LAMARTINE

Le Lac

Ainsi, toujours poussés vers de nouveaux rivages,
Dans la nuit éternelle emportés sans retour,
Ne pourrons-nous jamais sur l'océan des âges
Jeter l'ancre un seul jour?

to his arms, like a fool I shed tears. His hand used to feed an old tramp.

Men, why did you not crush me like an insect made to harm you? Ah! rather you should teach me to work for the good of all. Sheltered from the unkind wind, the maggot would have become an ant; I would have loved you as a brother. As an old tramp I die your enemy.

The Lake

So, always impelled towards new shores, carried for ever into eternal night, can we never cast anchor in time's ocean for a single day?

Ô lac! l'année à peine a fini sa carrière,
Et, près des flots chéris qu'elle devait revoir,
Regarde! je viens seul m'asseoir sur cette pierre
    Où tu la vis s'asseoir!

Tu mugissais ainsi sous ces roches profondes;
Ainsi tu te brisais sur leurs flancs déchirés;
Ainsi le vent jetait l'écume de tes ondes
    Sur ses pieds adorés.

Un soir, t'en souvient-il? nous voguions en silence;
On n'entendait au loin, sur l'onde et sous les cieux,
Que le bruit des rameurs qui frappaient en cadence
    Tes flots harmonieux.

Tout à coup des accents inconnus à la terre
Du rivage charmé frappèrent les échos;
Le flot fut attentif, et la voix qui m'est chère
    Laissa tomber ces mots:

«Ô temps, suspends ton vol! et vous, heures propices,
    Suspendez votre cours!
Laissez-nous savourer les rapides délices
    Des plus beaux de nos jours!

O lake! The year has hardly finished its course, and behold! I come alone to sit upon this stone where you saw her sit, near the beloved waves that she was to have seen once more!

Thus you murmured beneath these steep rocks; thus you broke upon their torn sides; thus the wind threw the foam from your waves on her adorable feet.

One evening, do you remember? we were sailing noiselessly; we only heard far off, on the water and beneath the skies, the sound of rowers rhythmically striking the melodious waves.

All at once strains unknown to earth struck the echoes of the spell-bound shore; the waves were attentive, and the voice dear to me let fall these words:

'O time, suspend your flight! And you, propitious hours, suspend your course! Let us taste the swift delights of the fairest of our days!

«Assez de malheureux ici-bas vous implorent:
      Coulez, coulez pour eux;
Prenez avec leurs jours les soins qui les dévorent;
      Oubliez les heureux.

«Mais je demande en vain quelques moments encore,
      Le temps m'échappe et fuit;
Je dis à cette nuit: «Sois plus lente»; et l'aurore
      Va dissiper la nuit.

«Aimons donc, aimons donc! de l'heure fugitive,
      Hâtons-nous, jouissons!
L'homme n'a point de port, le temps n'a point de rive:
      Il coule, et nous passons!»

Temps jaloux, se peut-il que ces moments d'ivresse,
Où l'amour à longs flots nous verse le bonheur,
S'envolent loin de nous de la même vitesse
      Que les jours de malheur?

Hé quoi! n'en pourrons-nous fixer au moins la trace?
Quoi! passés pour jamais? quoi! tout entiers perdus?
Ce temps qui les donna, ce temps qui les efface
      Ne nous les rendra plus?

'Enough unhappy beings pray to you down here on earth: flow on, flow on for them; together with their days take away the cares that consume them; forget those that are happy.

'But in vain I ask for a few more moments; time escapes me and flees away; I say to this night: "Go more slowly"; and dawn will scatter the night.

'Let us love then, let us love! Let us hasten to enjoy the fleeting hour! Man has no harbour, time has no shore: it flows on, and we pass by!'

Jealous time, can it be that these moments of intoxication, when love pours us happiness in long draughts, fly far away from us with the same speed as days of misfortune?

What! Can we not preserve their trace at least? What! Gone for ever? What! All quite lost? The time that gave them, the time that blots them out will give them back to us no more?

Éternité, néant, passé, sombres abîmes,
Que faites-vous des jours que vous engloutissez?
Parlez: nous rendrez-vous ces extases sublimes
   Que vous nous ravissez?

Ô lac! rochers muets! grottes! forêt obscure!
Vous que le temps épargne ou qu'il peut rajeunir,
Gardez de cette nuit, gardez, belle nature,
   Au moins le souvenir!

Qu'il soit dans ton repos, qu'il soit dans tes orages,
Beau lac, et dans l'aspect de tes riants coteaux,
Et dans ces noirs sapins, et dans ces rocs sauvages
   Qui pendent sur tes eaux!

Qu'il soit dans le zéphyr qui frémit et qui passe,
Dans les bruits de tes bords par tes bords répétés,
Dans l'astre au front d'argent qui blanchit ta surface
   De ses molles clartés!

Que le vent qui gémit, le roseau qui soupire,
Que les parfums légers de ton air embaumé,
Que tout ce qu'on entend, l'on voit ou l'on respire,
   Tout dise: «Ils ont aimé!»

Eternity, nothingness, past – dark abysses – what do you do with
the days you swallow up? Speak: will you give us back those sub-
lime raptures that you snatch from us?

O lake! Silent rocks! Caves! Dark forest! You whom time spares
or can make young again, keep at least the memory of that night;
keep it, fair landscape!

Let it be in your calms or in your storms, sweet lake, and in the
sight of your laughing hillsides, and in these black pines, and in
these wild rocks overhanging your waters!

Let it be in the breeze trembling and passing by, in the sounds of
your shores and their echoes, in the silver-browed star that whitens
your surface with its soft lights!

Let the moaning wind, the sighing reed, the light perfumes of
your scented air, let everything that is heard, seen, or breathed, let
everything say: 'They loved!'

Tristesse

RAMENEZ-MOI, disais-je, au fortuné rivage
Où Naples réfléchit dans une mer d'azur
Ses palais, ses coteaux, ses astres sans nuage,
Où l'oranger fleurit sous un ciel toujours pur.
Que tardez-vous? Partons! Je veux revoir encore
Le Vésuve enflammé sortant du sein des eaux;
Je veux de ses hauteurs voir se lever l'aurore;
Je veux, guidant les pas de celle que j'adore,
Redescendre en rêvant de ces riants coteaux.
Suis-moi dans les détours de ce golfe tranquille:
Retournons sur ces bords à nos pas si connus,
Aux jardins de Cynthie, au tombeau de Virgile,
Près des débris épars du temple de Vénus:
Là, sous les orangers, sous la vigne fleurie
Dont le pampre flexible au myrte se marie
Et tresse sur ta tête une voûte de fleurs,
Au doux bruit de la vague ou du vent qui murmure,
Seuls avec notre amour, seuls avec la nature,
La vie et la lumière auront plus de douceurs.

Sorrow

TAKE me back, I said, to the happy shore where Naples reflects its palaces, its hillsides, and its cloudless stars in a blue sea, where the orange-tree blooms beneath a sky that is always clear. Why do you delay? Let us depart! I want to see once again flaming Vesuvius rising from the bosom of the waves; from its heights I want to see the dawn rise; I want to come down those laughing slopes once again in a dream, guiding the steps of her whom I adore.

Follow me among the windings of this calm bay: let us return to those shores so well known to our footsteps, to Cynthia's gardens, to Virgil's tomb, near the scattered ruins of the temple of Venus: there, beneath the orange-trees, beneath the flowering vine whose lithe stem is united to the myrtle and weaves a vault of flowers above your head, there, to the gentle noise of the waves or of the murmuring wind, alone with our love, alone with nature, life and light will have more sweetness.

De mes jours pâlissants le flambeau se consume,
Il s'éteint par degrés au souffle du malheur,
Ou s'il jette parfois une faible lueur,
C'est quand ton souvenir dans mon sein le rallume.
Je ne sais si les dieux me permettront enfin
D'achever ici-bas ma pénible journée:
Mon horizon se borne, et mon œil incertain
Ose l'étendre à peine au delà d'une année.
      Mais s'il faut périr au matin,
S'il faut, sur une terre au bonheur destinée,
      Laisser échapper de ma main
      Cette coupe que le destin
Semblait avoir pour moi de roses couronnée,
Je ne demande aux dieux que de guider mes pas
Jusqu'aux bords qu'embellit ta mémoire chérie,
De saluer de loin ces fortunés climats,
Et de mourir aux lieux où j'ai goûté la vie!

The torch of my paling days burns itself out, it goes out gradually at the breath of misfortune, or, if sometimes it throws a faint light, it is when your memory rekindles it in my breast. I do not know if at last the gods will allow me to conclude my wearisome day down here on earth: my horizon is confined, and my uncertain eye hardly dares to stretch it beyond a year. But if I must die in the morning, if, in a land appointed for happiness, I must let fall from my hand this cup which fate seemed to have crowned with roses for me, I only ask the gods to guide my steps to shores made more beautiful by your beloved memory, to hail from afar those happy climes, and to die in the places where I tasted life.

ALFRED DE VIGNY

Le Cor

Poème

I

J'AIME le son du Cor, le soir, au fond des bois,
Soit qu'il chante les pleurs de la biche aux abois,
Ou l'adieu du chasseur que l'écho faible accueille
Et que le vent du nord porte de feuille en feuille.

Que de fois, seul dans l'ombre à minuit demeuré,
J'ai souri de l'entendre, et plus souvent pleuré!
Car je croyais ouïr de ces bruits prophétiques
Qui précédaient la mort des Paladins antiques.

Ô montagnes d'azur! ô pays adoré!
Rocs de la Frazona, cirque du Marboré,
Cascades qui tombez des neiges entraînées,
Sources, gaves, ruisseaux, torrents des Pyrénées;

The Horn

A poem

I

I LOVE the horn's sound in the evening in the depth of the woods, whether it sings the tears of the doe at bay, or the hunter's farewell greeted by the faint echo and carried from leaf to leaf by the north wind.

How many times, lingering alone in the shade at midnight, have I smiled to hear it and more often wept! For I thought to hear those prophetic sounds that preceded the death of the old Paladins.

O blue mountains! O beloved country! Rocks of the Frazona, valley of the Marboré, waterfalls coming down from the moving snows, springs, burns, streams, torrents of the Pyrenees;

Monts gelés et fleuris, trône des deux saisons,
Dont le front est de glace et le pied de gazons!
C'est là qu'il faut s'asseoir, c'est là qu'il faut entendre
Les airs lointains d'un Cor mélancolique et tendre.

Souvent un voyageur, lorsque l'air est sans bruit,
De cette voix d'airain fait retentir la nuit;
A ses chants cadencés autour de lui se mêle
L'harmonieux grelot du jeune agneau qui bêle.

Une biche attentive, au lieu de se cacher,
Se suspend immobile au sommet du rocher,
Et la cascade unit, dans une chute immense,
Son éternelle plainte au chant de la romance.

Âmes des Chevaliers, revenez-vous encor?
Est-ce vous qui parlez avec la voix du Cor?
Roncevaux! Roncevaux! dans ta sombre vallée
L'ombre du grand Roland n'est donc pas consolée!

Frozen and flowered mountains, throne of both seasons, whose
brow is made of ice and foot of grass! It is there one must sit, it is
there one must hear the far-off notes of a tender, melancholy Horn.

Often a traveller, when the air is still, makes night resound with
that brazen voice; around him is mingled with his rhythmic song
the melodious bell of the young bleating lamb.

An attentive doe stays motionless on top of a rock instead of hid-
ing, and the cascade in its huge fall joins its eternal complaint to the
song of the ballad.

Souls of the Knights, do you still linger here? Is it you who speak
with the voice of the Horn? Roncesvalles! Roncesvalles! In your
dark valley great Roland's shade has found no rest!

2

Tous les preux étaient morts, mais aucun n'avait fui.
Il reste seul debout, Olivier près de lui;
L'Afrique sur les monts l'entoure et tremble encore.
«Roland, tu vas mourir, rends-toi, criait le More,

«Tous tes Pairs sont couchés dans les eaux des torrents.»
Il rugit comme un tigre, et dit: «Si je me rends,
Africain, ce sera lorsque les Pyrénées
Sur l'onde avec leurs corps rouleront entraînées.»

«Rends-toi donc, répond-il, ou meurs, car les voilà.»
Et du plus haut des monts un grand rocher roula.
Il bondit, il roula jusqu'au fond de l'abîme,
Et de ses pins, dans l'onde, il vint briser la cime.

«Merci, cria Roland; tu m'as fait un chemin.»
Et jusqu'au pied des monts le roulant d'une main,
Sur le roc affermi comme un géant s'élance,
Et, prête à fuir, l'armée à ce seul pas balance.

2

All the valiant were dead, but none had fled. He alone remains
standing, Oliver near him; on the hills Africa surrounds him and
still trembles. 'Roland, you are going to die, yield,' cried the Moor,

'All your Peers are laid low in the waters of the streams.' He
roared like a tiger, and said: 'If I yield, African, it will be when the
Pyrenees tumble carried away on the water with their bodies.'

'– Yield then, he answers, or die, for there they are.' And from
the top of the mountains a great rock fell. It bounced, rolled to the
bottom of the abyss and broke the crest of its pines in the water.

'Thanks,' cried Roland; 'you have made me a path.' And rolling
it with one hand to the foot of the mountains, he springs like a giant
on the steady rock, and the army ready to flee sways at this single
step.

3

Tranquilles cependant, Charlemagne et ses preux
Descendaient la montagne et se parlaient entre eux.
A l'horizon déjà, par leurs eaux signalées,
De Luz et d'Argelès se montraient les vallées.

L'armée applaudissait. Le luth du troubadour
S'accordait pour chanter les saules de l'Adour;
Le vin français coulait dans la coupe étrangère;
Le soldat, en riant, parlait à la bergère.

Roland gardait les monts; tous passaient sans effroi.
Assis nonchalamment sur un noir palefroi
Qui marchait revêtu de housses violettes,
Turpin disait, tenant les saintes amulettes:

«Sire, on voit dans le ciel des nuages de feu;
Suspendez votre marche; il ne faut tenter Dieu.
Par monsieur saint Denis, certes ce sont des âmes
Qui passent dans les airs sur ces vapeurs de flammes.

3

Meanwhile Charlemagne and his knights were calmly descending the mountains and talking among themselves. The valleys of Luz and Argelès, marked out by their streams, were already visible on the horizon.

The army applauded. The troubadour's lute was tuned to sing the willows of the Adour; French wine flowed in foreign cups; laughing, the soldier spoke to the shepherdess.

Roland was guarding the mountains; they all passed over without fear. Carelessly seated on a black palfrey that walked clothed in violet trappings, Turpin said, holding the holy amulets:

'Sire, we see clouds of fire in the sky; halt your march; you must not tempt God. By Saint Denis, for sure these are souls passing by in the air of those flaming mists.

«Deux éclairs ont relui, puis deux autres encor.»
Ici l'on entendit le son lointain du Cor.
L'Empereur étonné, se jetant en arrière,
Suspend du destrier la marche aventurière.

«Entendez-vous? dit-il. – Oui, ce sont des pasteurs
Rappelant les troupeaux épars sur les hauteurs,
Répondit l'archevêque, ou la voix étouffée
Du nain vert Obéron qui parle avec sa Fée.»

Et l'Empereur poursuit; mais son front soucieux
Est plus sombre et plus noir que l'orage des cieux.
Il craint la trahison, et, tandis qu'il y songe,
Le Cor éclate et meurt, renaît et se prolonge.

«Malheur! c'est mon neveu! malheur! car si Roland
Appelle à son secours, ce doit être en mourant.
Arrière, chevaliers, repassons la montagne!
Tremble encor sous nos pieds, sol trompeur de
    l'Espagne!»

'Two flashes of lightning have shone, then two others again.'
Here they heard the distant sound of the Horn. The astonished Emperor, throwing himself back, halts the bold march of his charger.
    'Do you hear?' said he. '– Yes, those are herdsmen calling in the flocks scattered on the heights,' answered the archbishop, 'or the muffled voice of the green dwarf Oberon talking to his fairy queen.'
    And the Emperor goes on his way; but his careworn brow is darker and blacker than the storm of the skies. He fears treason, and, while he thinks of it, the Horn bursts forth and dies, is reborn and prolonged.
    'Ill luck! it is my nephew! ill luck! for if Roland calls for help, he must be dying. Back, knights, let us pass back over the mountains! Tremble once more beneath our feet, deceitful soil of Spain!'

4

Sur le plus haut des monts s'arrêtent les chevaux;
L'écume les blanchit; sous leurs pieds, Roncevaux
Des feux mourants du jour à peine se colore.
A l'horizon lointain fuit l'étendard du More.

«Turpin, n'as-tu rien vu dans le fond du torrent?
– J'y vois deux chevaliers: l'un mort, l'autre expirant.
Tous deux sont écrasés sous une roche noire;
Le plus fort, dans sa main, élève un Cor d'ivoire,
Son âme en s'exhalant nous appela deux fois.»

Dieu! que le son du Cor est triste au fond des bois!

L'Esprit pur

A Éva

I

Si l'orgueil prend ton cœur quand le peuple me nomme,
Que de mes livres seuls te vienne ta fierté.

4

On the very highest of the mountains the horses stop; they are white with foam; beneath their feet Roncesvalles is hardly tinted by the dying fires of day. On the far horizon flees the banner of the Moor.

'Turpin, do you see nothing in the depth of the stream? – I see two knights there: one dead, the other dying. Both are crushed beneath a black rock; the stronger raises an ivory Horn in his hand, his soul in going forth called us twice.'

God! how sad the Horn's sound is in the depth of the woods!

The Pure Spirit

To Eva

IF pride takes your heart when the people name me, let your arrogance come from my books alone. I have placed on the gentleman's

J'ai mis sur le cimier doré du gentilhomme
Une plume de fer qui n'est pas sans beauté.
J'ai fait illustre un nom qu'on m'a transmis sans gloire.
Qu'il soit ancien, qu'importe? Il n'aura de mémoire
Que du jour seulement où mon front l'a porté.

2

Dans le caveau des miens plongeant mes pas nocturnes,
J'ai compté mes aïeux, suivant leur vieille loi.
J'ouvris leurs parchemins, je fouillai dans leurs urnes
Empreintes sur le flanc des sceaux de chaque Roi.
A peine une étincelle a relui dans leur cendre.
C'est en vain que d'eux tous le sang m'a fait descendre;
Si j'écris leur histoire, ils descendront de moi.

3

Ils furent opulents, seigneurs de vastes terres,
Grands chasseurs devant Dieu, comme Nemrod, jaloux
Des beaux cerfs qu'ils lançaient des bois héréditaires
Jusqu'où voulait la mort les livrer à leurs coups;

gilded crest an iron plume that is not without beauty. I have made
illustrious a name that was left to me without fame. What does it
matter that it is old? It will only be remembered from the day my
brow bore it.

Plunging my nightly steps into my people's vault, I counted my
ancestors according to their ancient law. I opened their parchments,
I ransacked their caskets stamped on the side with the seals of every
King. Hardly a spark shone in their ashes. In vain my blood has
made me descend from all of them; if I write their history, they will
descend from me.

They were rich, the lords of vast lands, great hunters before God,
like Nimrod, jealous of the lovely stags they started from their
hereditary woods to where death would deliver them to their blows;

Suivant leur forte meute à travers deux provinces,
Coupant les chiens du Roi, déroutant ceux des Princes,
Forçant les sangliers et détruisant les loups;

4

Galants guerriers sur terre et sur mer, se montrèrent
Gens d'honneur en tout temps comme en tous lieux,
    cherchant
De la Chine au Pérou les Anglais, qu'ils brûlèrent
Sur l'eau qu'ils écumaient du Levant au Couchant;
Puis, sur leur talon rouge, en quittant les batailles,
Parfumés et blessés revenaient à Versailles
Jaser à l'Œil-de-bœuf avant de voir leur champ.

5

Mais les champs de la Beauce avaient leurs cœurs, leurs
    âmes,
Leurs soins. Ils les peuplaient d'innombrables garçons,
De filles qu'ils donnaient aux chevaliers pour femmes,
Dignes de suivre en tout l'exemple et les leçons;

following their strong cry of hounds across two provinces, cutting off the King's hounds, turning those of the Princes, forcing the boars and exterminating the wolves;

Gallant warriors on land and sea, they showed themselves men of honour in all times and places, from China to Peru searching out the English, burning them on the water they scoured from East to West; then on their red heels, leaving battles behind, they returned perfumed and wounded to Versailles to chat in the *Œil-de-bœuf* before going to see their fields.

But the fields of the Beauce had their hearts, their souls, their care. They populated them with innumerable boys, with daughters whom they gave to the knights for wives, worthy to follow their example and lessons in all things; simply satisfied if each one of their

366

Simples et satisfaits si chacun de leur race
Apposait saint Louis en croix sur sa cuirasse,
Comme leurs vieux portraits qu'aux murs noirs nous
    plaçons.

6

Mais aucun, au sortir d'une rude campagne,
Ne sut se recueillir, quitter le destrier,
Dételer pour un jour ses palefrois d'Espagne,
Ni des coursiers de chasse enlever l'étrier
Pour graver quelque page et dire en quelque livre
Comme son temps vivait et comment il sut vivre,
Dès qu'ils n'agissaient plus, se hâtant d'oublier.

7

Tous sont morts en laissant leur nom sans auréole,
Mais sur le Livre d'or voilà qu'il est écrit,
Disant: «Ici passaient deux races de la Gaule
Dont le dernier vivant monte au temple et s'inscrit,
Non sur l'obscur amas des vieux noms inutiles,
Des orgueilleux méchants et des riches futiles,
Mais sur le pur tableau des titres de l'ESPRIT.»

race placed St Louis in a cross on his breastplate, like their old por-
traits which we hang on blackened walls.

But none, coming from a hard campaign, knew how to lose him-
self in meditation, leave his charger, unsaddle his Spanish palfreys
for a day, or take the stirrups from his hunting horses to engrave
some page and say in some book how his time lived and how he
lived himself; as soon as they ceased to act, they hurried to forget.

They are all dead, leaving their name without fame, but in the
Golden Book here is what is written, saying: 'Here two races of
Gaul passed by, whose last descendant climbs to the temple and in-
scribes his name, not in the obscure heap of useless old names, of
proud evil-doers and the futile rich, but on the pure tablet of the
SPIRIT's title-deeds.'

8

Ton règne est arrivé, PUR ESPRIT, roi du monde!
Quand ton aile d'azur dans la nuit nous surprit,
Déesse de nos mœurs, la guerre vagabonde
Régnait sur nos aïeux. Aujourd'hui, c'est l'ÉCRIT,
L'ÉCRIT UNIVERSEL, parfois impérissable,
Que tu graves au marbre ou traces sur le sable,
Colombe au bec d'airain! VISIBLE SAINT-ESPRIT!

9

Seul et dernier anneau de deux chaînes brisées,
Je reste. Et je soutiens encor dans les hauteurs,
Parmi les maîtres purs de nos savants musées,
L'IDÉAL du poète et des graves penseurs.
J'éprouve sa durée en vingt ans de silence,
Et toujours, d'âge en âge, encor je vois la France
Contempler mes tableaux et leur jeter des fleurs.

10

Jeune postérité d'un vivant qui vous aime!
Mes traits dans vos regards ne sont pas effacés;

Your kingdom has come, PURE SPIRIT, king of the world!
When your blue wing surprised us in the night, goddess of our
ways, roving war reigned over our ancestors. Today it is the
WRITTEN WORD, the UNIVERSAL WRITTEN WORD, sometimes
imperishable, that you engrave in marble or trace on sand, dove
with the brazen beak! VISIBLE HOLY SPIRIT!

Sole and last ring of two broken chains, I remain. And still I bear
up on the heights, amid the pure masters of our learned museums,
the poet's and solemn thinkers' IDEAL. In twenty years of silence
I test its duration, and ever from age to age I see France gaze on my
pictures and throw flowers on them.

Young posterity of a man who loves you! In your gaze my fea-
tures are not blotted out; in this mirror, this ever-new judge of our

Je peux en ce miroir *me connaître moi-même*,
Juge toujours nouveau de nos travaux passés!
Flots d'amis renaissants! Puissent mes destinées
Vous amener à moi, de dix en dix années,
Attentifs à mon œuvre, et pour moi c'est assez!

VICTOR HUGO

Puisque j'ai mis ma lèvre . . .

PUISQUE j'ai mis ma lèvre à ta coupe encor pleine,
Puisque j'ai dans tes mains posé mon front pâli,
Puisque j'ai respiré parfois la douce haleine
De ton âme, parfum dans l'ombre enseveli,

Puisqu'il me fut donné de t'entendre me dire
Les mots où se répand le cœur mystérieux,
Puisque j'ai vu pleurer, puisque j'ai vu sourire
Ta bouche sur ma bouche et tes yeux sur mes yeux;

---

past works, I can *know myself*! Waves of friends reborn! May my fate lead you to me, from decade to decade, attentive to my work, and that is enough for me!

Since I have put my lip . . .

SINCE I have put my lip to your still brimming cup, since I have placed my pale brow in your hands, since I have sometimes breathed the sweet breath of your soul, a perfume buried in the shadow.

Since it was given to me to hear you say the words in which the mysterious heart pours itself forth, since I have seen weep, since I have seen smile your mouth on my mouth and your eyes on my eyes;

Puisque j'ai vu briller sur ma tête ravie
Un rayon de ton astre, hélas! voilé toujours,
Puisque j'ai vu tomber dans l'onde de ma vie
Une feuille de rose arrachée à tes jours,

Je puis maintenant dire aux rapides années:
— Passez! passez toujours! je n'ai plus à vieillir!
Allez-vous-en avec vos fleurs toutes fanées;
J'ai dans l'âme une fleur que nul ne peut cueillir!

Votre aile en le heurtant ne fera rien répandre
Du vase où je m'abreuve et que j'ai bien rempli.
Mon âme a plus de feu que vous n'avez de cendre!
Mon cœur a plus d'amour que vous n'avez d'oubli!

Nuits de Juin

L'ÉTÉ, lorsque le jour a fui, de fleurs couverte
La plaine verse au loin un parfum enivrant;
Les yeux fermés, l'oreille aux rumeurs entr'ouverte,
On ne dort qu'à demi d'un sommeil transparent.

Since over my enraptured head I have seen a beam of your star shine, alas! always veiled, since I have seen a rose leaf snatched from your days fall into my life's sea,

Now I can say to the swift years: — pass by! ever pass by! I have no longer to age! Away with you and your withered flowers; in my soul I have a flower that none may pluck!

Your wing brushing it will cause nothing to spill from the cup where I quench my thirst and that I have filled right up. My soul has more fire than you have ashes! My heart has more love than you have forgetfulness!

June Nights

IN summer, when day has fled, the plain covered with flowers pours out far away an intoxicating scent; eyes shut, ears half open to noises, we only half sleep in a transparent slumber.

Les astres sont plus purs, l'ombre paraît meilleure;
Un vague demi-jour teint le dôme éternel;
Et l'aube douce et pâle, en attendant son heure,
Semble toute la nuit errer au bas du ciel.

Demain, dès l'aube . . .

DEMAIN, dès l'aube, à l'heure où blanchit la campagne,
Je partirai. Vois-tu, je sais que tu m'attends.
J'irai par la forêt, j'irai par la montagne.
Je ne puis demeurer loin de toi plus longtemps.

Je marcherai les yeux fixés sur mes pensées,
Sans rien voir au dehors, sans entendre aucun bruit,
Seul, inconnu, le dos courbé, les mains croisées,
Triste, et le jour pour moi sera comme la nuit.

Je ne regarderai ni l'or du soir qui tombe,
Ni les voiles au loin descendant vers Harfleur,
Et quand j'arriverai, je mettrai sur ta tombe
Un bouquet de houx vert et de bruyère en fleur.

The stars are purer, the shade seems pleasanter; a hazy half-day
colours the eternal dome; and the sweet pale dawn awaiting her
hour seems to wander all night at the bottom of the sky.

Tomorrow at dawn . . .

TOMORROW at dawn, the hour when the countryside whitens, I
shall depart. You see, I know you are waiting for me. I shall go
through the forest, I shall go over the mountain. I cannot remain
away from you any longer.

I shall walk with eyes fixed on my thoughts, without seeing any-
thing outside, without hearing any noise, alone, unknown, back
bent, hands folded, sorrowful, and day for me shall be as night.

I shall gaze neither at the falling gold of evening nor at the far-
off sails dropping down towards Harfleur, and when I arrive, I shall
place on your grave a bunch of green holly and flowering heather.

Booz endormi

BOOZ s'était couché de fatigue accablé;
Il avait tout le jour travaillé dans son aire;
Puis avait fait son lit à sa place ordinaire;
Booz dormait auprès des boisseaux pleins de blé.

Ce vieillard possédait des champs de blés et d'orge;
Il était, quoique riche, à la justice enclin;
Il n'avait pas de fange en l'eau de son moulin,
Il n'avait pas d'enfer dans le feu de sa forge.

Sa barbe était d'argent comme un ruisseau d'avril.
Sa gerbe n'était point avare ni haineuse;
Quand il voyait passer quelque pauvre glaneuse:
— Laissez tomber exprès des épis, disait-il.

Cet homme marchait pur loin des sentiers obliques,
Vêtu de probité candide et de lin blanc;
Et, toujours du côté des pauvres ruisselant,
Ses sacs de grains semblaient des fontaines publiques.

Boaz Sleeping

BOAZ had lain down overwhelmed by fatigue; he had worked all day on his threshing-floor; then had made his bed in his usual place; Boaz slept beside bushels full of corn.

This old man owned fields of corn and barley; though rich, he was given to justice; he had no dirt in the water of his mill, he had no inferno in the fire of his forge.

His beard was silver like an April stream. His sheaves of corn were not mean or hateful; when he saw some poor woman pass gleaning: — 'Let some ears fall on purpose,' he said.

This man walked pure far from crooked paths, dressed in shining righteousness and white linen; and his sacks of grain seemed public fountains, ever pouring forth towards the poor.

Booz était bon maître et fidèle parent;
Il était généreux, quoiqu'il fût économe;
Les femmes regardaient Booz plus qu'un jeune homme,
Car le jeune homme est beau, mais le vieillard est grand.

Le vieillard, qui revient vers la source première,
Entre aux jours éternels et sort des jours changeants;
Et l'on voit de la flamme aux yeux des jeunes gens,
Mais dans l'œil du vieillard on voit de la lumière.

*

Donc, Booz dans la nuit dormait parmi les siens.
Près des meules, qu'on eût prises pour des décombres,
Les moissoneurs couchés faisaient des groups sombres;
Et ceci se passait dans des temps très anciens.

Les tribus d'Israël avaient pour chef un juge;
La terre, où l'homme errait sous la tente, inquiet
Des empreintes de pieds de géant qu'il voyait,
Était encor mouillée et molle du déluge.

*

Boaz was a good master and faithful kinsman; he was generous,
though he was sparing; women looked at Boaz more than at a
young man, for the young man is fair, but the old man is great.

The old man returning towards the first fountain-head enters on
eternal days and emerges from changing days; and flame is seen in
the eyes of young folk, but in the old man's eyes we see light.

*

So Boaz in the night slept among his people. Near the mill-stones
which you would have taken for ruins, the sleeping harvesters made
dark groups; and this took place in times long past.

The tribes of Israel had a judge for head; the earth, where men
wandered with tents, troubled by the giants' footprints which they
saw, was still damp and soft from the flood.

*

Comme dormait Jacob, comme dormait Judith,
Booz, les yeux fermés, gisait sous la feuillée;
Or, la porte du ciel s'étant entre-bâillée
Au-dessus de sa tête, un songe en descendit.

Et ce songe était tel, que Booz vit un chêne
Qui, sorti de son ventre, allait jusqu'au ciel bleu;
Une race y montait comme une longue chaîne;
Un roi chantait en bas, en haut mourait un dieu.

Et Booz murmurait avec la voix de l'âme:
«Comment se pourrait-il que de moi ceci vînt?
Le chiffre de mes ans a passé quatre-vingt,
Et je n'ai pas de fils, et je n'ai plus de femme.

«Voilà longtemps que celle avec qui j'ai dormi,
O Seigneur! a quitté ma couche pour la vôtre;
Et nous sommes encor tout mêlés l'un à l'autre,
Elle à demi vivante et moi mort à demi.

«Une race naîtrait de moi! Comment le croire?
Comment se pourrait-il que j'eusse des enfants?
Quand on est jeune, on a des matins triomphants;
Le jour sort de la nuit comme d'une victoire;

As Jacob slept, as Judith slept, Boaz, his eyes shut, lay beneath the bower; now, the gate of heaven having half-opened above his head, a dream came down from it.

And this dream was such that Boaz saw an oak, which, issuing from his stomach, went up to the blue sky; a people ascended it like a long chain; a king was singing at the bottom, a god dying at the top.

And Boaz murmured with the voice of the soul: 'How could it be that this came from me? The number of my years has passed eighty, and I have no son and I have no longer a wife.

'It is a long time ago that she with whom I slept, O Lord! left my bed for yours; and we are still mingled the one to the other, she half living and I half dead.

'A people to be born of me! How should I believe it? How could it be that I should have children? When we are young, we have triumphant mornings, day emerges from night as from a victory;

«Mais vieux, on tremble ainsi qu'à l'hiver le bouleau;
Je suis veuf, je suis seul, et sur moi le soir tombe,
Et je courbe, ô mon Dieu! mon âme vers la tombe,
Comme un bœuf ayant soif penche son front vers l'eau.»

Ainsi parlait Booz dans le rêve et l'extase,
Tournant vers Dieu ses yeux par le sommeil noyés;
Le cèdre ne sent pas une rose à sa base,
Et lui ne sentait pas une femme à ses pieds.

*

Pendant qu'il sommeillait, Ruth, une moabite,
S'était couchée aux pieds de Booz, le sein nu,
Espérant on ne sait quel rayon inconnu,
Quand viendrait du réveil la lumière subite.

Booz ne savait point qu'une femme était là,
Et Ruth ne savait point ce que Dieu voulait d'elle.
Un frais parfum sortait des touffes d'asphodèle;
Les souffles de la nuit flottaient sur Galgala.

'But, old, we tremble like the birch-tree in winter. I am a widower, I am alone, and evening falls upon me, and I bend, O my God! my soul towards the tomb, as a thirsty ox inclines his brow towards the water.'

So Boaz spoke in dream and ecstasy, turning his eyes, drowned by sleep, towards God; the cedar does not feel a rose at its base, and he did not feel a woman at his feet.

*

While he slept, Ruth, a Moabite, had lain down at the feet of Boaz, with naked breast, hoping we know not what unknown gleam, when the sudden light of awakening should come.

Boaz did not know that a woman was there, and Ruth did not know what God wanted of her; a cool perfume came from the tufts of asphodel; the breath of night floated over Galgala.

L'ombre était nuptiale, auguste et solennelle;
Les anges y volaient sans doute obscurément,
Car on voyait passer dans la nuit, par moment,
Quelque chose de bleu qui paraissait une aile.

La respiration de Booz qui dormait,
Se mêlait au bruit sourd des ruisseaux sur la mousse.
On était dans le mois où la nature est douce,
Les collines ayant des lys sur leur sommet.

Ruth songeait et Booz dormait; l'herbe était noire;
Les grelots des troupeaux palpitaient vaguement;
Une immense bonté tombait du firmament;
C'était l'heure tranquille où les lions vont boire.

Tout reposait dans Ur et dans Jérimadeth;
Les astres émaillaient le ciel profond et sombre;
Le croissant fin et clair parmi ces fleurs de l'ombre
Brillait à l'occident, et Ruth se demandait,

Immobile, ouvrant l'œil à moitié sous ses voiles,
Quel dieu, quel moissonneur de l'éternel été,
Avait, en s'en allant, négligemment jeté
Cette faucille d'or dans le champ des étoiles.

The shadow was nuptial, august, and solemn; doubtless angels flew darkly there, for from time to time there was seen to pass in the night something blue that seemed to be a wing.

The breathing of the sleeping Boaz mingled with the hollow sound of streams upon the moss. It was in the month when nature is gentle; the hills had lilies on their tops.

Ruth mused and Boaz slept; the grass was dark; the bells of the flocks vaguely quivered; a vast beneficence fell from the sky; it was the quiet hour when lions go to drink.

Everything slept in Ur and in Jerimadeth; the stars enamelled the deep, dark sky; the small bright crescent shone in the west among those flowers of the shade, and Ruth asked herself,

Lying motionless and half-opening her eye beneath her veils, what god, what harvester of the eternal summer, departing, had negligently thrown down this golden sickle in the field of stars.

A Théophile Gautier

AMI, poète, esprit, tu fuis notre nuit noire,
Tu sors de nos rumeurs pour entrer dans la gloire;
Et désormais ton nom rayonne aux purs sommets.
Moi qui t'ai connu jeune et beau, moi qui t'aimais,
Moi qui, plus d'une fois, dans nos altiers coups d'aile,
Éperdu, m'appuyais sur ton âme fidèle,
Moi, blanchi par les jours sur ma tête neigeant,
Je me souviens des temps écoulés, et songeant
A ce jeune passé qui vit nos deux aurores,
A la lutte, à l'orage, aux arènes sonores,
A l'art nouveau qui s'offre, au peuple criant: oui,
J'écoute ce grand vent sublime évanoui.

Fils de la Grèce antique et de la jeune France,
Ton fier respect des morts fut rempli d'espérance;
Jamais tu ne fermas les yeux à l'avenir.
Mage à Thèbes, druide au pied du noir menhir,

To Théophile Gautier

FRIEND, poet, spirit, you flee our dark night; you emerge from our clamours to enter into fame, and henceforward your name will shine on the pure hilltops. I who knew you when you were young and handsome, I who loved you; I who more than once, when dismayed in our proud flights, supported myself on your faithful soul; I, whitened by the days snowing upon my head; I recall times gone by, and, thinking of that recent past which saw the dawn of both of us, of the struggle, of the storm, of the resounding arenas, of the new art being offered, and the people crying: yes, I hear that vast sublime wind that has passed away.

Son of ancient Greece and modern France, your proud respect for the dead was filled with hope; you never shut your eyes to the future. A mage in Thebes, a druid at the foot of the dark menhir, a

Flamine aux bords du Tibre et brahme aux bords du
    Gange,
Mettant sur l'arc du dieu la flèche de l'archange,
D'Achille et de Roland hantant les deux chevets,
Forgeur mystérieux et puissant, tu savais
Tordre tous les rayons dans une seule flamme;
Le couchant rencontrait l'aurore dans ton âme;
Hier croisait demain dans ton fécond cerveau;
Tu sacrais le viel art aïeul de l'art nouveau;
Tu comprenais qu'il faut, lorsqu'une âme inconnue
Parle au peuple, envolée en éclairs dans la nue,
L'écouter, l'accepter, l'aimer, ouvrir les cœurs;
Calme, tu dédaignais l'effort vil des moqueurs
Écumant sur Eschyle et bavant sur Shakspeare;
Tu savais que ce siècle a son air qu'il respire,
Et que, l'art ne marchant qu'en se transfigurant,
C'est embellir le beau que d'y joindre le grand.
Et l'on t'a vu pousser d'illustres cris de joie
Quand le Drame a saisi Paris comme une proie.
Quand l'antique hiver fut chassé par Floréal,
Quand l'astre inattendu du moderne idéal

Priest on Tiber's banks, and a Brahmin on those of the Ganges,
placing the archangel's arrow in the god's bow, haunting the bed-
sides of both Achilles and Roland, like a smith of mysterious power
you knew how to twist all sunbeams into a single flame; in your
soul the sunset met the dawn; yesterday encountered tomorrow in
your fertile brain; you consecrated ancient art ancestor of the new;
you understood that, when an unknown soul speaks to the people,
flying away in lightnings to the clouds, we must hear it, accept it,
love it, open our hearts to it; you calmly scorned the base attempt
of the mockers drooling on Aeschylus and dribbling on Shake-
speare; you knew that this age has its own air which it breathes, and
that, since art only progresses by transforming itself, to join the
great to the beautiful makes it more beautiful still. And you were
seen to utter noble cries of joy, when the drama seized Paris like a
prey, when old winter was expelled by Spring, when the unexpected

Est venu tout à coup, dans le ciel qui s'embrase,
Luire, et quand l'Hippogriffe a relayé Pégase!

*

Je te salue au seuil sévère du tombeau.
Va chercher le vrai, toi qui sus trouver le beau.
Monte l'âpre escalier. Du haut des sombres marches,
Du noir pont de l'abîme on entrevoit les arches;
Va! meurs! la dernière heure est le dernier degré.
Pars, aigle, tu vas voir des gouffres à ton gré;
Tu vas voir l'absolu, le réel, le sublime.
Tu vas sentir le vent sinistre de la cime
Et l'éblouissement du prodige éternel.
Ton olympe, tu vas le voir du haut du ciel,
Tu vas du haut du vrai voir l'humaine chimère,
Même celle de Job, même celle d'Hòmère,
Âme, et du haut de Dieu tu vas voir Jéhovah.
Monte! esprit! Grandis, plane, ouvre tes ailes, va!

Lorsqu'un vivant nous quitte, ému, je le contemple,
Car entrer dans la mort, c'est entrer dans le temple

star of the modern ideal suddenly came to shine in the glowing sky,
and when the hippogriff took Pegasus' place.

*

On the severe threshold of the tomb I salute you. Go to seek truth,
you who knew how to find beauty. Climb the harsh staircase. From
the top of the dark steps the arches of the black bridge over the
abyss can just be seen; Go! Die! The last hour is the last step! De-
part, eagle, you will see gulfs to your taste; you will see the abso-
lute, the real, the sublime, feel the ominous wind of the summit and
the dizziness of perpetual wonder. You will see your Olympus from
the height of heaven; you will see human unreality from the height
of truth, even Job's, even Homer's unreality, soul, and you will see
Jehovah from the height of God. Soar! Spirit! Tower, hover, open
your wings, go!

When a living being leaves us, I gaze upon him with emotion,
for to enter into death is to enter into the temple; and when a man

Et quand un homme meurt, je vois distinctement
Dans son ascension mon propre avènement.
Ami, je sens du sort la sombre plénitude;
J'ai commencé la mort par de la solitude,
Je vois mon profond soir vaguement s'étoiler.
Voici l'heure où je vais, aussi moi, m'en aller.
Mon fil trop long frissonne et touche presque au glaive;
Le vent qui t'emporta doucement me soulève,
Et je vais suivre ceux qui m'aimaient, moi banni.
Leur œil fixe m'attire au fond de l'infini.
J'y cours. Ne fermez pas la porte funéraire.

Passons; car c'est la loi; nul ne peut s'y soustraire;
Tout penche; et ce grand siècle avec tous ses rayons
Entre en cette ombre immense où pâles nous fuyons.
Oh! quel farouche bruit font dans le crépuscule
Les chênes qu'on abat pour le bûcher d'Hercule!
Les chevaux de la Mort se mettent à hennir,
Et sont joyeux, car l'âge éclatant va finir;
Ce siècle altier, qui sut dompter le vent contraire,
Expire . . . Ô Gautier! toi, leur égal et leur frère,
Tu pars après Dumas, Lamartine et Musset.

dies, in his ascent I clearly see my own accession. Friend, I feel the
dark plenitude of fate; I have begun death by solitude; I see my
own deep evening vaguely covered with stars; here is the hour when
I too shall depart; my extenuated thread shudders and almost
touches the sword; the wind that carried you away lifts me gently,
and I shall follow those who loved me when I was banished. Their
fixed eye draws me to the depth of the infinite. I hasten. Do not shut
the funereal door.

Let us pass by, for it is the law; no one can escape it; everything
declines, and this great age with all its luminaries enters that vast
shadow, where palely we vanish. Oh! What a wild sound the oaks
being cut for Hercules' pyre make in the twilight! Death's horses
begin to neigh and are joyful, for the brilliant age is ending; this
proud century, which knew how to conquer the opposing wind, is
dying . . . O Gautier, you their equal and their brother, depart after
Dumas, Lamartine, and Musset. The ancient wave, where men grew

L'onde antique est tarie où l'on rajeunissait;
Comme il n'est plus de Styx, il n'est plus de Jouvence.
Le dur faucheur avec sa large lame avance
Pensif et pas à pas vers le reste du blé;
C'est mon tour; et la nuit emplit mon œil troublé
Qui, devinant, hélas, l'avenir des colombes,
Pleure sur des berceaux et sourit à des tombes.

GÉRARD DE NERVAL

El Desdichado

Je suis le ténébreux, – le veuf, – l'inconsocé,
Le prince d'Aquitaine à la tour abolie:
Ma seule *étoile* est morte, – et mon luth constellé
Porte le *soleil* noir de la *Mélancolie*.

Dans la nuit du tombeau, toi qui m'as consolé,
Rends-moi le Pausilippe et la mer d'Italie,
La *fleur* qui plaisait tant à mon cœur désolé,
Et la treille où le pampre à la rose s'allie.

young again, is dried up; since there is no more Styx, there is no
more fountain of youth, and the harsh reaper, thoughtfully, step by
step advances with his broad blade towards the remainder of the
corn; it is my turn; and night fills my anxious eye which, guessing,
alas! the future of doves, weeps over cradles and smiles at tombs.

El Desdichado

I AM the shadow, the widower, the unconsoled, the Aquitanian
prince with the ruined tower: my only *star* is dead, and my star-
strewn lute bears the black *sun* of *Melancholy*.

You who consoled me, in the night of the tomb, give me back
Posilipo and the Italian sea, the *flower* which pleased my grief-
stricken heart so much, and the arbour where the vine joins with the
rose.

Suis-je Amour ou Phébus? ... Lusignan ou Biron?
Mon front est rouge encor du baiser de la reine;
J'ai rêvé dans la grotte où nage la sirène ...

Et j'ai deux fois vainqueur traversé l'Achéron:
Modulant tour à tour sur la lyre d'Orphée
Les soupirs de la sainte et les cris de la fée.

Myrtho

JE pense à toi, Myrtho, divine enchanteresse,
Au Pausilippe altier, de mille feux brillant,
A ton front inondé des clartés d'Orient,
Aux raisins noirs mêlés avec l'or de ta tresse.

C'est dans ta coupe aussi que j'avais bu l'ivresse,
Et dans l'éclair furtif de ton œil souriant,
Quand aux pieds d'Iacchus on me voyait priant,
Car la Muse m'a fait l'un des fils de la Grèce.

Am I Love or Phoebus? ... Lusignan or Biron? My brow is still red from the queen's kiss; I have dreamed in the cave where the siren swims ...

And I have twice crossed Acheron victoriously: tuning in turn on Orpheus' lyre the sighs of the saint and the fairy's cries.

Myrtho

I THINK of you, Myrtho, divine sorceress, of proud Posilipo shining with a thousand fires, of your brow flooded with the lights of the East, of the black grapes mingled with the gold of your plait.

It was in your cup too that I had drunk intoxication and in the stealthy lightning of your smiling eye, when I was seen praying at the feet of Iacchus, for the Muse made me one of the sons of Greece.

Je sais pourquoi là-bas le volcan s'est rouvert . . .
C'est qu'hier tu l'avais touché d'un pied agile,
Et de cendres soudain l'horizon s'est couvert.

Depuis qu'un duc normand brisa tes dieux d'argile,
Toujours, sous les rameaux du laurier de Virgile,
Le pâle hortensia s'unit au myrte vert!

Horus

LE dieu Kneph en tremblant ébranlait l'univers:
Isis, la mère, alors se leva sur sa couche,
Fit un geste de haine à son époux farouche,
Et l'ardeur d'autrefois brilla dans ses yeux verts.

«Le voyez-vous, dit-elle, il meurt, ce vieux pervers,
Tous les frimas du monde ont passé par sa bouche,
Attachez son pied tors, éteignez son œil louche,
C'est le dieu des volcans et le roi des hivers!

I know why the volcano opened down there again . . . It was be-
cause yesterday you had touched it with a nimble foot, and sud-
denly the horizon was covered with ashes.

Since a Norman duke broke your clay gods, beneath the branches
of Virgil's laurel, the pale hydrangea is still joined to the green
myrtle!

Horus

TREMBLING the god Kneph shook the universe: then Isis, the
mother, raised herself on her couch, made a gesture of hatred to-
wards her savage husband, and the passion of former days shone in
her green eyes.

'Do you see him?' she said; 'he is dying, the old lecher; all the
hoar-frosts of the world have passed through his mouth; bind his
crooked foot, put out his squinting eye, he is the god of volcanoes
and the king of winters!

«L'aigle a déjà passé, l'esprit nouveau m'appelle,
J'ai revêtu pour lui la robe de Cybèle ...
C'est l'enfant bien-aimé d'Hermès et d'Osiris!»

La déesse avait fui sur sa conque dorée,
La mer nous renvoyait son image adorée,
Et les cieux rayonnaient sous l'écharpe d'Iris.

Antéros

Tu demandes pourquoi j'ai tant de rage au cœur
Et sur un col flexible une tête indomptée;
C'est que je suis issu de la race d'Antée,
Je retourne les dards contre le dieu vainqueur.

Oui, je suis de ceux-là qu'inspire le Vengeur,
Il m'a marqué le front de sa lèvre irritée,
Sous la pâleur d'Abel, hélas! ensanglantée,
J'ai parfois de Caïn l'implacable rougeur!

Jéhovah! le dernier, vaincu par ton génie,
Qui du fond des enfers, criait: «O tyrannie!»
C'est mon aïeul Bélus ou mon père Dagon ...

'Already the eagle has passed by, the new spirit calls me, for him I have put on the dress of Cybele ... He is the beloved child of Hermes and Osiris!'

The goddess had fled on her golden shell, the sea sent us back her sweet image, and the skies shone beneath Iris' scarf.

Anteros

You ask why I have so much anger in my heart and an undaunted head on a neck that inclines; it is because I am sprung from the race of Antaeus; I turn back the arrows against the conquering god.

Yes, I am of those whom the Avenger inspires; he marked me on the brow with his angry lip; sometimes I have the implacable crimson of Cain beneath Abel's pallor, covered in blood, alas!

Jehovah! the last to be conquered by your genius, who from the depth of hell cried: 'O tyranny!', was my grandfather Belus or my father Dagon ...

Ils m'ont plongé trois fois dans les eaux du Cocyte.
Et, protégeant tout seul ma mère Amalécyte,
Je ressème à ses pieds les dents du vieux dragon.

Delfica

La connais-tu, Dafné, cette ancienne romance,
Au pied du sycomore, ou sous les lauriers blancs,
Sous l'olivier, le myrte, ou les saules tremblants,
Cette chanson d'amour qui toujours recommence? ...

Reconnais-tu le TEMPLE au péristyle immense,
Et les citrons amers où s'imprimaient tes dents,
Et la grotte, fatale aux hôtes imprudents,
Où du dragon vaincu dort l'antique semence? ...

Ils reviendront, ces Dieux que tu pleures toujours!
Le temps va ramener l'ordre des anciens jours;
La terre a tressailli d'un souffle prophétique ...

They dipped me three times in the waters of Cocytus, and, while alone protecting my Amalekite mother, I sow the old dragon's teeth again at her feet.

Delfica

Daphne, do you know this old ballad, at the sycamore's foot or beneath the white laurels, beneath the olive tree, the myrtle or the trembling willows, this love song which always begins anew? ...

Do you recognize the TEMPLE with the vast peristyle, and the bitter lemons which were marked by your teeth, and the cave, fatal to rash guests, where sleeps the old seed of the defeated dragon? ...

They will return, those Gods for which you still weep! Time will lead back the order of ancient days; the earth has shuddered at a prophetic breath ...

Cependant la sibylle au visage latin
Est endormie encor sous l'arc de Constantin
– Et rien n'a dérangé le sévère portique.

Artémis

LA Treizième revient ... C'est encor la première;
Et c'est toujours la seule, – ou c'est le seul moment;
Car es-tu reine, ô toi! la première ou dernière?
Es-tu roi, toi le seul ou le dernier amant? ...

Aimez qui vous aima du berceau dans la bière;
Celle que j'aimai seul m'aime encore tendrement:
C'est la mort – ou la morte ... O délice! o tourment!
La rose qu'elle tient, c'est la *Rose trémière*.

Sainte napolitaine aux mains pleines de feux,
Rose au cœur violet, fleur de sainte Gudule:
As-tu trouvé ta croix dans le désert des cieux?

Yet the sibyl with the Latin face is still asleep beneath the arch
of Constantine – and nothing has disturbed the severe porch.

Artemis

THE thirteenth woman returns ... Still she is the first; and still the
only one – or it is the only moment; for are you queen, O you who
are the first or last woman? Are you king, you who are the sole or
last lover? ...

Love him who loved you from the cradlet o the grave; she whom
I loved alone still loves me tenderly; she is death – or the dead ...
O delight! O torment! The rose she holds is the *Hollyhock*.*

Neapolitan saint with your hands full of fires, rose with the
violet heart, Saint Gudula's flower: did you find your cross in the
desert of the skies?

---

*The contrast between *rose* and *rose tremière* is lost in the English
rose and *hollyhock*, but I thought it better to stick to the literal
translation.

Roses blanches, tombez! vous insultez nos dieux,
Tombez, fantômes blancs, de votre ciel qui brûle:
– La sainte de l'abîme est plus sainte à mes yeux!

ALFRED DE MUSSET

A Julie

ON me demande, par les rues,
Pourquoi je vais bayant aux grues,
Fumant mon cigare au soleil,
A quoi se passe ma jeunesse,
Et depuis trois ans de paresse
Ce qu'ont fait mes nuits sans sommeil.

Donne-moi tes lèvres, Julie;
Les folles nuits qui t'ont pâlie
Ont séché leur corail luisant.
Parfume-les de ton haleine;
Donne-les-moi, mon Africaine,
Tes belles lèvres de pur sang.

White roses, fall! you insult our gods, fall, white, white spec-
tres, from your burning heaven:- the saint from the abyss is more
holy in my eyes!

To Julia

IN the streets they ask me why I go gaping at the tarts, smoking
my cigar in the sun, how my youth is passed, and what my sleep-
less nights have produced during three years of idleness.

Give me your lips, Julia; the wild nights that made you pale have
dried their shining coral. Perfume them with your breath; give them
me, my Barbary, your lovely lips of pure blood-stock.

Mon imprimeur crie à tue-tête
Que sa machine est toujours prête,
Et que la mienne n'en peut mais.
D'honnêtes gens, qu'un club admire,
N'ont pas dédaigné de prédire
Que je n'en reviendrai jamais.

Julie, as-tu du vin d'Espagne?
Hier, nous battions la campagne;
Va donc voir s'il en reste encor.
Ta bouche est brûlante, Julie;
Inventons donc quelque folie
Qui nous perde l'âme et le corps.

On dit que ma gourme me rentre,
Que je n'ai plus rien dans le ventre,
Que je suis vide à faire peur;
Je crois, si j'en valais la peine,
Qu'on m'enverrait à Sainte-Hélène,
Avec un cancer dans le cœur.

Allons, Julie, il faut t'attendre
A me voir quelque jour en cendre,
Comme Hercule sur son rocher.

My printer cries with all his might that his machine is always ready and that mine can do nothing any more. Honest folk, whom clubs admire, have not disdained to say that I shall never recover from it.

Julia, have you Spanish wine? Yesterday we were roving; go then and see if there is any left. Your mouth is burning, Julia; let us find out some madness to destroy us body and soul.

They say I am reaping my wild oats, that I have nothing more in my belly, that I am frightfully hollow; I think, if I were worth it, they would send me to Saint Helena with a cancer in my heart.

Come, Julia, you must be prepared to see me in ashes some day

Puisque c'est par toi que j'expire,
Ouvre ta robe, Déjanire,
Que je monte sur mon bûcher.

Une Soirée perdue

J'ÉTAIS seul, l'autre soir, au Théâtre Français,
Ou presque seul; l'auteur n'avait pas grand succès.
Ce n'était que Molière, et nous savons de reste
Que ce grand maladroit, qui fit un jour *Alceste*,
Ignora le bel art de chatouiller l'esprit
Et de servir à point un dénoûement bien cuit.
Grâce à Dieu, nos auteurs ont changé de méthode,
Et nous aimons bien mieux quelque drame à la mode
Où l'intrigue, enlacée et roulée en feston,
Tourne comme un rébus autour d'un mirliton.

J'écoutais cependant cette simple harmonie,
Et comme le bon sens fait parler le génie.
J'admirais quel amour pour l'âpre vérité
Eut cet homme si fier en sa naïveté,

like Hercules on his rock. Since it is through you I die, open your
dress, Dejanira, let me climb upon my pyre.

A Wasted Evening

I WAS alone the other evening at the *Comédie Française*, or almost
alone; the author had not much success. It was only Molière, and,
moreover, we know that this great bungler, who created *Alceste* one
day, was not aware of the fine art of tickling the mind and of serving
medium done a well-cooked conclusion. Thank God, our authors
have changed their methods, and we far prefer some fashionable
drama where the intrigue, twined and rolled in festoons, is twisted
like a pun round a doggerel verse.

Yet I listened to this simple harmony, and how common sense
makes genius speak. I marvelled at the love this man, so proud in

Quel grand et vrai savoir des choses de ce monde,
Quelle mâle gaieté, si triste et si profonde
Que, lorsqu'on vient d'en rire, on devrait en pleurer!
Et je me demandais: Est-ce assez d'admirer?
Est-ce assez de venir, un soir, par aventure,
D'entendre au fond de l'âme un cri de la nature,
D'essuyer une larme, et de partir ainsi,
Quoi qu'on fasse d'ailleurs, sans en prendre souci?
Enfoncé que j'étais dans cette rêverie,
Çà et là, toutefois, lorgnant la galerie,
Je vis que, devant moi, se balançait gaiement
Sous une tresse noire un cou svelte et charmant;
Et, voyant cet ébène enchâssé dans l'ivoire,
Un vers d'André Chénier chanta dans ma mémoire,
Un vers presque inconnu, refrain inachevé,
Frais comme le hasard, moins écrit que rêvé.
J'osai m'en souvenir, même devant Molière;
Sa grande ombre, à coup sûr, ne s'en offensa pas;
Et, tout en écoutant, je murmurais tout bas,
Regardant cette enfant, qui ne s'en doutait guère:
«Sous votre aimable tête, un cou blanc, délicat,
Se plie, et de la neige effacerait l'éclat.»

his simplicity, had for the harsh truth, what great and true know-
ledge of the things of this world, what virile gaiety, so sad and so
deep that, when one has just been laughing at it, one should be
weeping! And I asked myself: Is it enough to marvel? Is it enough
to come one evening by chance to hear nature's cry in the depth of
the soul, to wipe away a tear and to depart so, without taking heed,
whatever one does besides? Immersed as I was in this meditation,
yet glancing here and there at the gallery, I saw gaily poised in
front of me a slim and charming neck beneath a black plait; and, see-
ing this ebony set in the ivory, a line from André Chénier sang in
my memory, an almost unknown line, an unfinished song, fresh as
chance, less written than dreamed. I dared to recall it even before
Molière; most certainly his great shade was not offended; and, while
still listening, I whispered softly, glancing at that child, who hardly
suspected it: 'Beneath your fair head, a white delicate neck inclines
and would outshine the brightness of snow.'

Puis je songeais encore (ainsi va la pensée)
Que l'antique franchise, à ce point délaissée,
Avec notre finesse et notre esprit moqueur,
Ferait croire, après tout, que nous manquons de cœur;
Que c'était une triste et honteuse misère
Que cette solitude à l'entour de Molière,
Et qu'il est *pourtant temps*, comme dit la chanson,
De sortir de ce siècle ou d'en avoir raison;
Car à quoi comparer cette scène embourbée,
Et l'effroyable honte où la muse est tombée?
La lâcheté nous bride, et les sots vont disant
Que, sous ce vieux soleil, tout est fait à présent;
Comme si les travers de la famille hùmaine
Ne rajeunissaient pas chaque an, chaque semaine.
Notre siècle a ses mœurs, partant, sa vérité;
Celui qui l'ose dire est toujours écouté.

Ah! j'oserais parler, si je croyais bien dire,
J'oserais ramasser le fouet de la satire,
Et l'habiller de noir, cet homme aux rubans verts,
Qui se fâchait jadis pour quelques mauvais vers.

Then I thought again (so thought goes) that the old frankness being abandoned thus far, together with our subtlety and mocking wit, would make one believe, after all, that we lack heart; that this solitude around Molière was a sad and shameful disgrace, and that it is *time indeed*, as the song says, to quit this age or get the better of it; for to what are we to compare this muddy stage and the frightful shame into which the muse has fallen? Cowardice reins us in, and fools say that everything has now been done beneath this aged sun; as if the human family's whims were not renewed every year, every week. Our age has its manners, consequently its truth; he who dares tell it is always listened to.

Ah! I would dare to speak if I thought I could speak well, I would dare to take up satire's whip and dress in black that man in green ribbons who once was angered by some bad lines of verse.

S'il rentrait aujourd'hui dans Paris, la grand'ville,
Il y trouverait mieux pour émouvoir sa bile
Qu'une méchante femme et qu'un méchant sonnet;
Nous avons autre chose à mettre au cabinet.
Ô notre maître à tous, si ta tombe est fermée,
Laisse-moi dans ta cendre, un instant ranimée,
Trouver une étincelle, et je vais t'imiter!
Apprends-moi de quel ton, dans ta bouche hardie,
Parlait la vérité, ta seule passion,
Et, pour me faire entendre, à défaut du génie,
J'en aurai le courage et l'indignation!

Ainsi je caressais une folle chimère.
Devant moi cependant, à côté de sa mère,
L'enfant restait toujours, et le cou svelte et blanc
Sous les longs cheveux noirs se berçait mollement.
Le spectacle fini, la charmante inconnue
Se leva. Le beau cou, l'épaule à demi nue,
Se voilèrent; la main glissa dans le manchon;
Et, lorsque je la vis au seuil de sa maison
S'enfuir, je m'aperçus que je l'avais suivie.
Hélas! mon cher ami, c'est là toute ma vie.

If he came back today to Paris, the great town, he would find
more to move him to anger than a bad woman and a bad sonnet;
we have other things to put down the drain. O master of us all, if
your tomb is closed, let me find a spark in your ashes, brought to
life again for a moment, and I shall follow your example! Teach me
in what strain your passion, truth, spoke in your bold mouth,
and, to make myself heard, for want of genius, I shall have its
courage and indignation!

So I indulged a foolish fancy. Meanwhile in front of me, beside
her mother, the child still remained, and her slim white neck swayed
gently beneath the long black hair. The play finished, the charming
stranger rose. The lovely neck, the half-naked shoulder were veiled;
the hand slipped into the muff; and, when I saw her disappear on
the threshold of her home, I realized that I had followed her. Alas!
my dear friend, there is my whole life. While my soul sought its

Pendant que mon esprit cherchait sa volonté,
Mon corps avait la sienne et suivait la beauté;
Et, quand je m'éveillai de cette rêverie,
Il ne m'en restait plus que l'image chérie:
«Sous votre aimable tête, un cou blanc, délicat,
Se plie, et de la neige effacerait l'éclat.»

Sur une morte

ELLE était belle, si la Nuit
Qui dort dans la sombre chapelle
Où Michel-Ange a fait son lit,
Immobile peut être belle.

Elle était bonne, s'il suffit
Qu'en passant la main s'ouvre et donne,
Sans que Dieu n'ait rien vu, rien dit,
Si l'or sans pitié fait l'aumône.

Elle pensait, si le vain bruit
D'une voix douce et cadencée,
Comme le ruisseau qui gémit
Peut faire croire à la pensée.

will, my body had its own, and followed beauty; and, when I awoke from this dream, there only remained to me the sweet image: 'Beneath your fair head, a white delicate neck inclines and would outshine the brightness of snow.'

On a Dead Lady

SHE was fair, if Night that sleeps motionless in the dark chapel, where Michelangelo made her bed, can be fair.

She was generous, if it is enough for the hand to open and give while passing by, without God seeing or saying anything, if gold without pity is charity.

She thought, if the empty noise of a sweetly modulated voice, like the murmuring stream, can make one believe in the existence of thought.

Elle priait, si deux beaux yeux,
Tantôt s'attachant à la terre,
Tantôt se levant vers les cieux,
Peuvent s'appeler la Prière.

Elle aurait souri, si la fleur
Qui ne s'est point épanouie
Pouvait s'ouvrir à la fraîcheur
Du vent qui passe et qui l'oublie.

Elle aurait pleuré si sa main,
Sur son cœur froidement posée,
Eût jamais, dans l'argile humain,
Senti la céleste rosée.

Elle aurait aimé, si l'orgueil
Pareil à la lampe inutile
Qu'on allume près d'un cercueil,
N'eût veillé sur son cœur stérile.

Elle est morte, et n'a point vécu.
Elle faisait semblant de vivre.
De ses mains est tombé le livre
Dans lequel elle n'a rien lu.

She prayed, if two fair eyes, sometimes fixed on earth, sometimes raised towards heaven, can be called Prayer.

She would have smiled, if the flower, which has not bloomed, could open to the coolness of the passing, forgetful wind.

She would have wept, if her hand coldly placed upon her heart had ever felt the heavenly dew in human clay.

She would have loved, if pride, like the useless lamp lighted beside a coffin, had not watched over her barren heart.

She is dead and has not lived. She made a pretence of living. From her hands the book has fallen in which she read nothing.

THÉOPHILE GAUTIER

La Mansarde

SUR les tuiles où se hasarde
Le chat guettant l'oiseau qui boit,
De mon balcon une mansarde
Entre deux tuyaux s'aperçoit.

Pour la parer d'un faux bien-être,
Si je mentais comme un auteur,
Je pourrais faire à sa fenêtre
Un cadre de pois de senteur,

Et vous y montrer Rigolette
Riant à son petit miroir,
Dont le tain rayé ne reflète
Que la moitié de son œil noir;

Ou, la robe encor sans agrafe,
Gorge et cheveux au vent, Margot
Arrosant avec sa carafe
Son jardin planté dans un pot;

The Garret

ON the tiles where the cat risks his life to watch the bird drinking, from my balcony I can see a garret between two drain-pipes.

To adorn it with a false comfort, if I were to lie like an author, I could put a box of sweet peas at its window.

And show you Rigolette laughing in her little mirror, whose streaky quicksilver only reflects half of her black eye;

Or Margot, her dress still not hooked up, bosom and hair in the wind, watering with her jug her garden planted in a pot;

Ou bien quelque jeune poète
Qui scande ses vers sibyllins,
En contemplant la silhouette
De Montmartre et de ses moulins.

Par malheur, ma mansarde est vraie;
Il n'y grimpe aucun liseron,
Et la vitre y fait voir sa taie
Sous l'ais verdi d'un vieux chevron.

Pour la grisette et pour l'artiste,
Pour le veuf et pour le garçon,
Une mansarde est toujours triste:
Le grenier n'est beau qu'en chanson.

Jadis, sous le comble dont l'angle
Penchait les fronts pour le baiser,
L'amour, content d'un lit de sangle,
Avec Suzon venait causer;

Mais pour ouater notre joie,
Il faut des murs capitonnés,
Des flots de dentelle et de soie,
Des lits par Monbro festonnés.

Or else some young poet scanning his sibylline lines, while gazing at the silhouette of Montmartre and its windmills.

Unfortunately my garret is real; no convolvulus climbs there, and the window shows its frosted glass beneath the green rotting timber of an old rafter.

For the girl of easy virtue and for the artist, for the widower and for the bachelor, a garret is always dismal: the attic is only pleasant in songs.

In former times, beneath the roof whose angle bent brows together for the kiss, love, contented with a camp bed, came to chat with Suzon.

But, to cosset our joy, there must be quilted walls, floods of lace and silk, beds festooned by Monbro.

Un soir, n'étant pas revenue,
Margot s'attarde au mont Bréda,
Et Rigolette entretenue
N'arrose plus son réséda.

Voilà longtemps que le poète,
Las de prendre la rime au vol,
S'est fait *reporter* de gazette,
Quittant le ciel pour l'entresol.

Et l'on ne voit contre la vitre
Qu'une vieille au maigre profil,
Devant Minet, qu'elle chapitre,
Tirant sans cesse un bout de fil.

L'Art

Oui, l'œuvre sort plus belle
D'une forme au travail
    Rebelle,
Vers, marbre, onyx, émail.

Not having returned one evening, Margot delays at the Mount Breda, and Rigolette waters her mignonette no more since she is a kept woman.

The poet a long time ago, tired of catching rhyme in its flight, has become a *reporter* on a paper, leaving the sky for the mezzanine.

And against the window one only sees an old woman with a lean profile, ceaselessly pulling a piece of thread in front of pussy, while she scolds him.

Art

Yes, the work of art emerges more beautiful from a form that resists working, verse, marble, onyx, enamel.

Point de contraintes fausses!
Mais que pour marcher droit
    Tu chausses,
Muse, un cothurne étroit.

Fi du rhythme commode,
Comme un soulier trop grand,
    Du mode
Que tout pied quitte et prend!

Statuaire, repousse
L'argile que pétrit
    Le pouce
Quand flotte ailleurs l'esprit;

Lutte avec le carrare,
Avec le paros dur
    Et rare,
Gardiens du contour pur;

Emprunte à Syracuse
Son bronze où fermement
    S'accuse
Le trait fier et charmant;

No false hindrances! But to march straight, put on, O Muse, a narrow buskin.

Shame on the easy rhythm, like a shoe that is too large, of the kind that every foot takes off and puts on!

Sculptor, reject clay moulded by the thumb when the mind hovers elsewhere;

Struggle with Carrara marble, with the hard, rare Parian, keepers of the pure outline;

Borrow from Syracuse its bronze where the proud enchanting stroke is firmly marked;

D'une main délicate
Poursuis dans un filon
    D'agate
Le profil d'Apollon.

Peintre, fuis l'aquarelle,
Et fixe la couleur
    Trop frêle
Au four de l'émailleur;

Fais les sirènes bleues,
Tordant de cent façons
    Leurs queues,
Les monstres des blasons;

Dans son nimbe trilobe
La Vierge et son Jésus,
    Le globe
Avec la croix dessus.

Tout passe. – L'art robuste
Seul a l'éternité:
    Le buste
Survit à la cité.

With a delicate hand hunt the profile of Apollo in a vein of agate.
    Painter, flee the water-colour, and fix too delicate a tint in the enameller's oven.
    Create blue sirens, writhing their tails in a hundred ways, create the monsters of heraldry,
    Create the Virgin and her Jesus in their three-lobed halo, create the globe with the cross above it.
    Everything passes. – Only strong art possesses eternity. The bust outlives the city.

Et la médaille austère
Que trouve un laboureur
　　Sous terre
Révèle un empereur.

Les dieux eux-mêmes meurent.
Mais les vers souverains
　　Demeurent
Plus forts que les airains.

Sculpte, lime, cisèle;
Que ton rêve flottant
　　Se scelle
Dans le bloc résistant!

LECONTE DE LISLE

Midi

Midi, roi des étés, épandu sur la plaine,
　Tombe en nappes d'argent des hauteurs du ciel bleu.
Tout se tait. L'air flamboie et brûle sans haleine;
　La terre est assoupie en sa robe de feu.

And the austere medal found by a ploughman beneath the earth reveals an emperor.

The gods themselves die. But sovereign lines of verse remain stronger than brass.

Carve, file, and chisel; let your hazy dream be sealed in the hard block!

Noon

Noon, king of summers, spread over the plain, falls in silver sheets from the heights of the blue sky. Everything is quiet. Breathlessly the air flames and burns; earth drowses in its fiery dress.

L'étendue est immense, et les champs n'ont point d'ombre,
Et la source est tarie où buvaient les troupeaux;
La lointaine forêt, dont la lisière est sombre,
Dort là-bas, immobile, en un pesant repos.

Seuls, les grands blés mûris, tels qu'une mer dorée,
Se déroulent au loin, dédaigneux du sommeil;
Pacifiques enfants de la terre sacrée,
Ils épuisent sans peur la coupe du soleil.

Parfois, comme un soupir de leur âme brûlante,
Du sein des épis lourds qui murmurent entre eux,
Une ondulation majestueuse et lente
S'éveille, et va mourir à l'horizon poudreux.

Non loin, quelques bœufs blancs, couchés parmi les
    herbes,
Bavent avec lenteur sur leurs fanons épais,
Et suivent de leurs yeux languissants et superbes
Le songe intérieur qu'ils n'achèvent jamais.

Homme, si, le cœur plein de joie ou d'amertume,
Tu passais vers midi dans les champs radieux,

The expanse is vast, the fields have no shade, and the spring
where the flocks used to drink is dried up; the distant forest, whose
edge is dark, motionlessly slumbers over there in a heavy sleep.

Only the great ripe cornfields, like a golden sea, roll far away dis-
daining sleep; as peaceful children of the sacred earth, fearlessly they
drain the sun's cup.

Sometimes, like a sigh from their burning soul, from the bosom
of the heavy ears, murmuring among themselves, a majestically
slow undulation awakens and goes to die on the dusty horizon.

Not far away some white oxen lying in the grass dribble slowly
on their heavy dewlaps and follow with their proud, languid eyes
the inner dream they never finish.

Man, if towards noon you passed into the blazing fields with

Fuis! la nature est vide et le soleil consume:
Rien n'est vivant ici, rien n'est triste ou joyeux.

Mais si, désabusé des larmes et du rire,
Altéré de l'oubli de ce monde agité,
Tu veux, ne sachant plus pardonner ou maudire,
Goûter une suprême et morne volupté,

Viens! Le soleil te parle en paroles sublimes;
Dans sa flamme implacable absorbe-toi sans fin;
Et retourne à pas lents vers les cités infimes,
Le cœur trempé sept fois dans le néant divin.

CHARLES BAUDELAIRE

Harmonie du soir

Voici venir les temps où vibrant sur sa tige
Chaque fleur s'évapore ainsi qu'un encensoir;
Les sons et les parfums tournent dans l'air du soir;
Valse mélancolique et langoureux vertige!

---

your heart full of joy or bitterness, flee! nature is empty and the sun devours: nothing is living here, nothing is sad or joyful.

But if, disillusioned with tears or laughter, parched for forgetfulness of this busy world, no longer knowing how to pardon or to curse, you wish to taste a last desolate pleasure,

Come! The sun speaks to you in sublime words; be endlessly absorbed in its relentless flame; and return with slow steps towards the abject cities, your heart seven times bathed in the divine void.

Evening Harmony

HERE comes the time when, vibrating on its stem, every flower fumes like a censer; noises and perfumes circle in the evening air; O melancholy waltz and languid vertigo!

Chaque fleur s'évapore ainsi qu'un encensoir;
Le violon frémit comme un cœur qu'on afflige;
Valse mélancolique et langoureux vertige!
Le ciel est triste et beau comme un grand reposoir.

Le violon frémit comme un cœur qu'on afflige,
Un cœur tendre, qui hait le néant vaste et noir!
Le ciel est triste et beau comme un grand reposoir;
Le soleil s'est noyé dans son sang qui se fige.

Un cœur tendre, qui hait le néant vaste et noir,
Du passé lumineux recueille tout vestige!
Le soleil s'est noyé dans son sang qui se fige ...
Ton souvenir en moi luit comme un ostensoir!

Je t'adore à l'égal de la voûte nocturne ...

JE t'adore à l'égal de la voûte nocturne,
Ô vase de tristesse, ô grande taciturne,
Et t'aime d'autant plus, belle, que tu me fuis,
Et que tu me parais, ornement de mes nuits,

Every flower fumes like a censer; the violin shudders like an afflicted heart; O melancholy waltz and languid vertigo! The sky is sad and beautiful like a vast station of the Cross.

The violin shudders like an afflicted heart, a tender heart that hates the great dark void! The sky is sad and beautiful like a vast station of the Cross; the sun is drowned in its own congealing blood.

A tender heart that hates the great dark void gathers up every remnant of the bright past! The sun is drowned in its own congealing blood ... Your memory shines within me like a monstrance!

I adore you as much as the vault of night ...

I ADORE you as much as the vault of night, O vessel of sorrow,
O tall, silent woman, and I love you the more, my beauty, the more

Plus ironiquement accumuler les lieues
Qui séparent mes bras des immensités bleues.

Je m'avance à l'attaque, et je grimpe aux assauts,
Comme après un cadavre un chœur de vermisseaux,
Et je chéris, ô bête implacable et cruelle!
Jusqu'à cette froideur par où tu m'es plus belle!

La Chevelure

Ô TOISON, moutonnant jusque sur l'encolure!
Ô boucles! Ô parfum chargé de nonchaloir!
Extase! Pour peupler ce soir l'alcôve obscure
Des souvenirs dormant dans cette chevelure,
Je la veux agiter dans l'air comme un mouchoir!

La langoureuse Asie et la brûlante Afrique,
Tout un monde lointain, absent, presque défunt,
Vit dans tes profondeurs, forêt aromatique!
Comme d'autres esprits voguent sur la musique,
Le mien, ô mon amour! nage sur ton parfum.

you flee me, and seem, O ornament of my nights, to pile up ironically the leagues that separate my arms from the blue spaces.

I advance to the attack and I climb to the assault like a band of worms on a corpse, and I hold dear, O mercilessly cruel beast!, even that coldness through which you appear more beautiful to me!

The Hair

O FLEECE curling right down on the neck! O ringlets! O perfume laden with indifference! Ecstasy! This evening to people the dark alcove with the memories sleeping in this hair, I want to wave it in the air like a handkerchief!

Languorous Asia and burning Africa, the whole of a distant world, far away, almost extinct, lives in your depths, aromatic forest! As other spirits drift upon music, mine, O my love! floats upon your perfume.

J'irai là-bas où l'arbre et l'homme, pleins de sève,
Se pâment longuement sous l'ardeur des climats;
Fortes tresses, soyez la houle qui m'enlève!
Tu contiens, mer d'ébène, un éblouissant rêve
De voiles, de rameurs, de flammes et de mâts:

Un port retentissant où mon âme peut boire
A grands flots le parfum, le son et la couleur;
Où les vaisseaux, glissant dans l'or et dans la moire,
Ouvrent leurs vastes bras pour embrasser la gloire
D'un ciel pur où frémit l'éternelle chaleur.

Je plongerai ma tête amoureuse d'ivresse
Dans ce noir océan où l'autre est enfermé;
Et mon esprit subtil que le roulis caresse
Saura vous retrouver, ô féconde paresse!
Infinis bercements du loisir embaumé!

Cheveux bleus, pavillon de ténèbres tendues,
Vous me rendez l'azur du ciel immense et rond;
Sur les bords duvetés de vos mèches tordues
Je m'enivre ardemment des senteurs confondues
De l'huile de coco, du musc et du goudron.

I shall go to the land where trees and men, full of sap, slowly swoon beneath the passionate heat of the climate; strong locks, be the swell that carries me away! O ebony sea, you hold a dazzling dream of sails, rowers, pennants, and masts:

An echoing harbour where my soul can drink scent, sound, and colour in great waves; where the ships, slipping through the gold and watered silk, open their huge arms to clasp the glory of a pure sky trembling with eternal heat.

I shall plunge my head, which loves intoxication, into this dark ocean where the other ocean is enclosed; and my keen spirit caressed by the swell will know how to seek you out, O fertile idleness! Infinite rocking of scented leisure!

Blue hair, tent of stretched shadows, you give me back the blue of the vast round sky; on the downy verges of your twisted locks passionately I drink the intoxication of the mingled scents of coconut oil, musk, and tar.

Longtemps! toujours! ma main dans ta crinière lourde
Sèmera le rubis, la perle et le saphir,
Afin qu'à mon désir tu ne sois jamais sourde!
N'es-tu pas l'oasis où je rêve, et la gourde
Où je hume à longs traits le vin du souvenir?

Correspondances

LA Nature est un temple où de vivants piliers
Laissent parfois sortir de confuses paroles;
L'homme y passe à travers des forêts de symboles
Qui l'observent avec des regards familiers.

Comme de longs échos qui de loin se confondent
Dans une ténébreuse et profonde unité,
Vaste comme la nuit et comme la clarté,
Les parfums, les couleurs et les sons se répondent.

Il est des parfums frais comme des chairs d'enfants,
Doux comme les hautbois, verts comme les prairies,
– Et d'autres, corrompus, riches et triomphants,

For many a day! For ever! My hand will sow the ruby, pearl, and sapphire in your heavy mane so that you may never be deaf to my desire! Are you not the oasis where I dream and the gourd where I drink memory's wine in long draughts?

Correspondences

NATURE is a temple where living pillars sometimes allow confused words to escape; man passes there through forests of symbols that watch him with familiar glances.

Like long-drawn-out echoes mingled far away into a deep and shadowy unity, vast as darkness and light, scents, colours, and sounds answer one another.

There are some scents cool as the flesh of children, sweet as oboes and green as meadows, – and others corrupt, rich, and triumphant,

Ayant l'expansion des choses infinies,
Comme l'ambre, le musc, le benjoin et l'encens,
Qui chantent les transports de l'esprit et des sens.

Moesta et errabunda

DIS-MOI, ton cœur, parfois, s'envole-t-il, Agathe,
Loin du noir océan de l'immonde cité,
Vers un autre océan où la splendeur éclate,
Bleu, clair, profond, ainsi que la virginité?
Dis-moi, ton cœur, parfois, s'envole-t-il, Agathe?

La mer, la vaste mer, console nos labeurs!
Quel démon a doté la mer, rauque chanteuse
Qu'accompagne l'immense orgue des vents grondeurs,
De cette fonction sublime de berceuse?
La mer, la vaste mer, console nos labeurs!

Emporte-moi, wagon! enlève, moi, frégate!
Loin! loin! ici la boue est faite de nos pleurs!

Having the expansion of things infinite, like amber, musk, benzoin, and incense, singing the raptures of the mind and senses.

Moesta et errabunda

TELL me, does your heart sometimes fly away, Agatha, far from the dark ocean of the filthy city, towards another ocean where splendour blazes, an ocean blue, clear, and deep as virginity? Tell me, does your heart sometimes fly away, Agatha?

The sea, the great sea, comforts our toil! What demon has given the sea, that hoarse singer accompanied by the vast organ of the complaining winds, this sublime office of lullaby? The sea, the great sea, comforts our toil!

Coach, carry me off! Frigate, take me away! Far away! far away! here the mud is made from our tears! — Is it true that sometimes

– Est-il vrai que parfois le triste cœur d'Agathe
Dise: Loin des remords, des crimes, des douleurs,
Emporte-moi, wagon, enlève-moi, frégate?

Comme vous êtes loin, paradis parfumé,
Où sous un clair azur tout n'est qu'amour et joie,
Où tout ce que l'on aime est digne d'être aimé!
Où dans la volupté pure le cœur se noie!
Comme vous êtes loin, paradis parfumé!

Mais le vert paradis des amours enfantines,
Les courses, les chansons, les baisers, les bouquets,
Les violons vibrant derrière les collines,
Avec les brocs de vin, le soir, dans les bosquets,
– Mais le vert paradis des amours enfantines,

L'innocent paradis, plein de plaisirs furtifs,
Est-il déjà plus loin que l'Inde et que la Chine?
Peut-on le rappeler avec des cris plaintifs,
Et l'animer encor d'une voix argentine,
L'innocent paradis plein de plaisirs furtifs?

Agatha's sad heart says: far from remorse, from crime, from grief,
coach, carry me off, frigate, take me away?

How distant you are, scented paradise, where beneath a clear blue
sky there is only love and joy, where everything we love is worthy
to be loved! Where the heart is drowned in pure pleasure! How dis-
tant you are, scented paradise!

But the green paradise of childish loves, the races, the songs, the
kisses, the bouquets, the violins throbbing behind the hills, with the
jugs of wine in the evening in the groves – but the green paradise of
childish loves,

The innocent paradise, full of secret pleasures; is it already
further away than India or China? Can we call it back with plaintive
cries, and give it life again with a silvery voice, the innocent paradise
full of secret pleasures?

Spleen

JE suis comme le roi d'un pays pluvieux,
Riche, mais impuissant, jeune et pourtant très-vieux,
Qui, de ses précepteurs méprisant les courbettes,
S'ennuie avec ses chiens comme avec d'autres bêtes.
Rien ne peut l'égayer, ni gibier, ni faucon,
Ni son peuple mourant en face du balcon.
Du bouffon favori la grotesque ballade
Ne distrait plus le front de ce cruel malade;
Son lit fleurdelisé se transforme en tombeau,
Et les dames d'atour, pour qui tout prince est beau,
Ne savent plus trouver d'impudique toilette
Pour tirer un souris de ce jeune squelette,
Le savant qui lui fait de l'or n'a jamais pu
De son être extirper l'élément corrompu,
Et dans ces bains de sang qui des Romains nous viennent
Et dont sur leurs vieux jours les puissants se souviennent,
Il n'a su réchauffer ce cadavre hébété
Où coule au lieu de sang l'eau verte du Léthé.

Spleen

I AM like the king of a rainy country, rich but impotent, young and yet aged, who, scorning his tutors' obeisances, passes his time in boredom with his dogs as with other beasts. Nothing can cheer him, neither game nor falcon nor his people dying opposite his balcony. The comical ballad of his favourite fool no longer distracts the brow of this cruel invalid; his bed with the fleur-de-lys is changed to a tomb, and the ladies of the bedchamber, for whom any prince is beautiful, can no longer find a shameless dress to draw a smile from the young skeleton. The scholar who makes gold for him has never been able to drive out the corrupt element from his being, and could not heat this dull corpse, where, instead of blood, flows the green water of Lethe, in those baths of blood which come to us from the Romans and which the powerful recall in the days of their old age.

Les Bijoux

La très-chère était nue, et, connaissant mon cœur,
Elle n'avait gardé que ses bijoux sonores,
Dont le riche attirail lui donnait l'air vainqueur
Qu'ont dans leurs jours heureux les esclaves des Mores.

Quand il jette en dansant son bruit vif et moqueur,
Ce monde rayonnant de métal et de pierre
Me ravit en extase, et j'aime à la fureur
Les choses où le son se mêle à la lumière.

Elle était donc couchée et se laissait aimer,
Et du haut du divan elle souriait d'aise
A mon amour profond et doux comme la mer,
Qui vers elle montait comme vers sa falaise.

Les yeux fixés sur moi, comme un tigre dompté,
D'un air vague et rêveur elle essayait des poses,
Et la candeur unie à la lubricité
Donnait un charme neuf à ses métamorphoses;

The Jewels

The darling was naked, and, knowing my heart, she had only kept on her sonorous jewels, whose rich accoutrement gave her the conquering air that Moorish slaves have in their happy days.

When dancing it throws off its bright, mocking noise, this shining world of metal and stone transports me into ecstasy, and I love to distraction things where sound is mingled with light.

She was lying down and let herself be loved, and from the divan's height she smiled for pleasure at my passion, deep and gentle as the sea, rising towards her as towards its cliff.

Her eyes fixed on me, like a tame tiger, with a vague dreamy air she tried various positions, and ingenuousness joined to lubricity gave a new charm to her metamorphoses;

Et son bras et sa jambe, et sa cuisse et ses reins,
Polis comme de l'huile, onduleux comme un cygne,
Passaient devant mes yeux clairvoyants et sereins;
Et son ventre et ses seins, ces grappes de ma vigne,

S'avançaient, plus câlins que les Anges du mal,
Pour troubler le repos où mon âme était mise,
Et pour la déranger du rocher de cristal
Où, calme et solitaire, elle s'était assise.

Je croyais voir unis par un nouveau dessin
Les hanches de l'Antiope au buste d'un imberbe,
Tant sa taille faisait ressortir son bassin.
Sur ce teint fauve et brun le fard était superbe!

— Et la lampe s'étant résignée à mourir,
Comme le foyer seul illuminait la chambre,
Chaque fois qu'il poussait un flamboyant soupir,
Il inondait de sang cette peau couleur d'ambre!

And her arm and her leg and her thigh and her loins, polished as oil, sinuous as a swan, passed before my calm, clear-sighted eyes; and her belly and breasts, those clusters of my vine,

Advanced more coaxing than evil Angels to disturb the quiet in which my soul was stationed, and to displace it from the crystal rock where, calm and solitary, it had taken up its seat.

Her waist set off her hips so well that I thought I saw the haunches of the Antiope joined to the bust of a young boy in a new drawing. On that dark tawny complexion the rouge was magnificent!

— And the lamp having decided to die, as the fire alone lighted the room, each time it uttered a sigh of flame, it flooded with blood that amber-coloured skin!

Le Voyage

A Maxime du Camp

I

POUR l'enfant, amoureux de cartes et d'estampes,
L'univers est égal à son vaste appétit.
Ah! que le monde est grand à la clarté des lampes!
Aux yeux du souvenir que le monde est petit!

Un matin nous partons, le cerveau plein de flamme,
Le cœur gros de rancune et de désirs amers,
Et nous allons, suivant le rhythme de la lame,
Berçant notre infini sur le fini des mers:

Les uns, joyeux de fuir une patrie infâme;
D'autres, l'horreur de leurs berceaux, et quelques-uns,
Astrologues noyés dans les yeux d'une femme,
La Circé tyrannique aux dangereux parfums.

The Voyage

To Maxime du Camp

I

FOR the child fond of maps and prints the universe equals his huge appetite. Ah, how large the world is by lamplight! How small in the eyes of memory!

One morning we depart, our brains full of flame, hearts swollen with rancour and bitter desires, and we travel following the rhythm of the waves and rocking our infinity on the finite sea:

Some, glad to leave an infamous country; others, the horror of their cradles, and some, astrologers drowned in a woman's eyes, the tyrant Circe with the dangerous perfume.

Pour n'être pas changés en bêtes, ils s'enivrent
D'espace et de lumière et de cieux embrasés;
La glace qui les mord, les soleils qui les cuivrent,
Effacent lentement la marque des baisers.

Mais les vrais voyageurs sont ceux-là seuls qui partent
Pour partir; cœurs légers, semblables aux ballons,
De leur fatalité jamais ils ne s'écartent,
Et, sans savoir pourquoi, disent toujours: Allons!

Ceux-là dont les désirs ont la forme des nues,
Et qui rêvent, ainsi qu'un conscrit le canon,
De vastes voluptés, changeantes, inconnues,
Et dont l'esprit humain n'a jamais su le nom!

2

Nous imitons, horreur! la toupie et la boule
Dans leur valse et leurs bonds; même dans nos sommeils
La Curiosité nous tourmente et nous roule,
Comme un Ange cruel qui fouette des soleils.

Not to be changed into beasts, they drink the intoxication of
space and light and glowing skies; the ice that gnaws them, the suns
that bronze them slowly blot out the mark of the kisses.

But the true travellers are only those who depart for the sake of
departing; with hearts light as balloons, they never avoid their
destiny and always say: Let us go! without knowing why.

Those whose desires have the shape of clouds, and who dream,
as a conscript dreams of cannon, of vast, secretly shifting pleasures,
whose name the human mind has never known!

2

O horror! We follow the top and the ball in their waltzing and
bouncing; even in our sleep curiosity torments and rolls us along
like a cruel angel whipping on the suns.

Singulière fortune où le but se déplace,
Et, n'étant nulle part, peut être n'importe où!
Où l'Homme, dont jamais l'espérance n'est lasse,
Pour trouver le repos court toujours comme un fou!

Notre âme est un trois-mâts cherchant son Icarie;
Une voix retentit sur le pont: «Ouvre l'œil!»
Une voix de la hune, ardente et folle, crie:
«Amour . . . gloire . . . bonheur!» Enfer! c'est un écueil!

Chaque îlot signalé par l'homme de vigie
Est un Eldorado promis par le Destin;
L'Imagination qui dresse son orgie
Ne trouve qu'un récif aux clartés du matin.

Ô le pauvre amoureux des pays chimériques!
Faut-il le mettre aux fers, le jeter à la mer,
Ce matelot ivrogne, inventeur d'Amériques
Dont le mirage rend le gouffre plus amer?

Tel le vieux vagabond, piétinant dans la boue,
Rêve, le nez en l'air, de brillants paradis;
Son œil ensorcelé découvre une Capoue
Partout où la chandelle illumine un taudis.

What a curious destiny where the goal is always moved and, being nowhere, can be anywhere! Where Man, whose capacity for hope is tireless, ever runs like a madman to find rest!

Our soul is a three-master seeking its Icaria; a voice resounds on the bridge: 'Alert!' A wild, passionate voice from the crow's nest cries: 'Love . . . fame . . . happiness!' Hell! It is a rock!

Every islet pointed out by the look-out is fate's promised Eldorado; Imagination preparing her orgy only finds a reef in the morning light.

O the poor lover of mythical countries! Should we put him in irons or throw him in the sea, this drunken sailor, the inventor of Americas, whose mirage makes the gulf more bitter?

As the old tramp paddling in the mud with his nose in the air dreams of shining Paradises; his bewitched eye discovers a Capua wherever a candle lights up a slum.

3

Étonnants voyageurs! quelles nobles histoires
Nous lisons dans vos yeux profonds comme les mers!
Montrez-nous les écrins de vos riches mémoires,
Ces bijoux merveilleux, faits d'astres et d'éthers.

Nous voulons voyager sans vapeur et sans voile!
Faites, pour égayer l'ennui de nos prisons,
Passer sur nos esprits, tendus comme une toile,
Vos souvenirs avec leurs cadres d'horizons.

Dites, qu'avez-vous vu?

4

«Nous avons vu des astres
Et des flots; nous avons vu des sables aussi;
Et, malgré bien des chocs et d'imprévus désastres,
Nous nous sommes souvent ennuyés, comme ici.

La gloire du soleil sur la mer violette,
La gloire des cités dans le soleil couchant,
Allumaient dans nos cœurs une ardeur inquiète
De plonger dans un ciel au reflet alléchant.

3

Surprising travellers! What noble tales we read in your eyes, deep
as the seas! Show us the coffers of your rich memories, those mar-
vellous jewels made out of stars and ether.

We wish to travel without steam or sail! To cheer the boredom
of our prison let your memories framed by the horizon pass over
our spirits set for them like a sail.

Say, what have you seen?

4

'We saw stars and waves; we saw sand dunes as well; and, in spite
of many shocks and unforeseen catastrophes, we were often bored
as we are here.

'The glory of the sun on the purple sea, the glory of cities in the
setting sun lighted in our hearts a restless longing to plunge into a
sky, whose reflection was so alluring.

Les plus riches cités, les plus grands paysages,
Jamais ne contenaient l'attrait mystérieux
De ceux que le hasard fait avec les nuages.
Et toujours le désir nous rendait soucieux!

– La jouissance ajoute au désir de la force.
Désir, vieil arbre à qui le plaisir sert d'engrais,
Cependant que grossit et durcit ton écorce,
Tes branches veulent voir le soleil de plus près!

Grandiras-tu toujours, grand arbre plus vivace
Que le cyprès? – Pourtant, nous avons, avec soin,
Cueilli quelques croquis pour votre album vorace,
Frères qui trouvez beau tout ce qui vient de loin!

Nous avons salué des idoles à trompe;
Des trônes constellés de joyaux lumineux;
Des palais ouvragés dont la féerique pompe
Serait pour vos banquiers un rêve ruineux;

Des costumes qui sont pour les yeux une ivresse;
Des femmes dont les dents et les ongles sont teints,
Et des jongleurs savants que le serpent caresse.»

'The richest cities, the widest landscapes never held the mysterious attraction of those that chance constructs with the clouds. And desire always made us anxious!

'– Enjoyment adds strength to desire. Desire, old tree that pleasure serves to fertilize, as your bark thickens and hardens, your branches wish to see the sun nearer to!

'Will you always grow, great tree, longer-lived than the cypress? – Yet with care we gathered some sketches for your greedy album, brothers who find everything beautiful that comes from afar!

'We have hailed idols with elephants' trunks; thrones studded with shining gems; carved palaces whose fairy pomp would be a ruinous dream for your bankers;

'Clothes that are an intoxication for the eyes; women, whose teeth and nails are dyed, and skilful jugglers fondled by snakes.'

5

Et puis, et puis encore?

6

«Ô cerveaux enfantins!

Pour ne pas oublier la chose capitale,
Nous avons vu partout, et sans l'avoir cherché,
Du haut jusques en bas de l'échelle fatale,
Le spectacle ennuyeux de l'immortel péché:

La femme, esclave vile, orgueilleuse et stupide,
Sans rire s'adorant et s'aimant sans dégoût;
L'homme, tyran goulu, paillard, dur et cupide,
Esclave de l'esclave et ruisseau dans l'égout;

Le bourreau qui jouit, le martyr qui sanglote;
La fête qu'assaisonne et parfume le sang;
Le poison du pouvoir énervant le despote,
Et le peuple amoureux du fouet abrutissant;

5

And then, and then again?

6

'O childish minds!

'Not to forget the main thing, without having searched we saw everywhere, from top to bottom of the fatal ladder, the tedious spectacle of immortal sin:

'Woman, a base slave, arrogant and stupid, worshipping herself without laughter and loving herself without disgust; man, a gluttonous, lecherous tyrant, hard and avaricious, slave of a slave and gutter pouring into a sewer;

'The happy torturer, the sobbing martyr; the feast flavoured and scented with blood; power's poison enfeebling the despot and the people loving the brutalizing whip;

Plusieurs religions semblables à la nôtre,
Toutes escaladant le ciel; la Sainteté,
Comme en un lit de plume un délicat se vautre,
Dans les clous et le crin cherchant la volupté;

L'Humanité bavarde, ivre de son génie,
Et, folle maintenant comme elle était jadis,
Criant à Dieu, dans sa furibonde agonie:
«Ô mon semblable, ô mon maître, je te maudis!»

Et les moins sots, hardis amants de la Démence,
Fuyant le grand troupeau parqué par le Destin,
Et se réfugiant dans l'opium immense!
– Tel est du globe entier l'éternel bulletin.»

7

Amer savoir, celui qu'on tire du voyage!
Le monde, monotone et petit, aujourd'hui,
Hier, demain, toujours, nous fait voir notre image:
Une oasis d'horreur dans un désert d'ennui!

'Several religions like ours, all storming heaven; Sanctity seeking
pleasure in nails and hair-shirts, like a sybarite wallowing in a
feather-bed;
'Loquacious humanity drunk with its own genius and, mad now
as it was before, crying to God in its wild agony: "O my fellow,
O my master, I curse you!"
'And the less foolish, bold lovers of Lunacy, shunning the great
herd corralled by fate and taking refuge in the immensity of opium!
– Such is the perpetual news of the whole globe.'

7

What bitter knowledge one gets from travelling! The monotonous-
ly small world today, yesterday, tomorrow, always, makes us see
our own likeness: an oasis of horror in a desert of boredom!

Faut-il partir? rester? Si tu peux rester, reste;
Pars, s'il le faut. L'un court, et l'autre se tapit
Pour tromper l'ennemi vigilant et funeste;
Le Temps! Il est, hélas! des coureurs sans répit,

Comme le Juif errant et comme les apôtres,
A qui rien ne suffit, ni wagon ni vaisseau,
Pour fuir ce rétiaire infâme; il en est d'autres
Qui savent le tuer sans quitter leur berceau.

Lorsque enfin il mettra le pied sur notre échine,
Nous pourrons espérer et crier: En avant!
De même qu'autrefois nous partions pour la Chine,
Les yeux fixés au large et les cheveux au vent,

Nous nous embarquerons sur la mer des Ténèbres
Avec le cœur joyeux d'un jeune passager.
Entendez-vous ces voix, charmantes et funèbres,
Qui chantent: «Par ici! vous qui voulez manger

Must we depart? Or stay? If you can stay, stay; depart if you must. One man runs and another crouches to trick the sinister watchful enemy: Time! Alas! there are some runners who can take no rest,

Like the Wandering Jew and like the apostles, for whom nothing, neither coach nor ship, suffices to flee this infamous retiary; there are others who can kill him without leaving their cradle.

When at last he places his foot upon our spine, we can take hope and cry: Forward! In the same way as before we left for China, our eyes on the horizon and our hair in the wind,

We shall embark upon the sea of shadows with the joyful heart of a young voyager. Do you hear those charming funereal voices singing: 'This way! You who would eat

Le Lotus parfumé: c'est ici qu'on vendange
Les fruits miraculeux dont votre cœur a faim;
Venez vous enivrer de la douceur étrange
De cette aprés-midi qui n'a jamais de fin!»

A l'accent familier nous devinons le spectre;
Nos Pylades là-bas tendent leurs bras vers nous.
«Pour rafraîchir ton cœur nage vers ton Électre!»
Dit celle dont jadis nous baisions les genoux.

8

Ô Mort, vieux capitaine, il est temps! levons l'ancre!
Ce pays nous ennuie, ô Mort! Appareillons!
Si le ciel et la mer sont noirs comme de l'encre,
Nos cœurs que tu connais sont remplis de rayons!

Verse-nous ton poison pour qu'il nous réconforte!
Nous voulons, tant ce feu nous brûle le cerveau,
Plonger au fond du gouffre, Enfer ou Ciel, qu'importe?
Au fond de l'Inconnu pour trouver du *nouveau*!

'The scented Lotus! Here is the harvest gathered of the wondrous fruits for which your heart hungers; come and get drunk on the strange sweetness of this unending afternoon!'

At the familiar voice we guess who the ghost is; there our Pylades stretch their arms towards us. 'To cool your heart swim towards your Electra!' says she whose knees we once kissed.

8

O Death, old captain, it is time! Raise anchor! This country bores us, Death! make ready! If the sky and sea are black as ink, our hearts, which you know, are filled with sunbeams!

Pour us your poison to comfort us! This fire burns our brains so, that we want to plunge to the bottom of the gulf, Hell or Heaven, what does it matter? To find something *new* in the depth of the Unknown!

JOSÉ-MARIA DE HÉRÉDIA

La Trebbia

L'aube d'un jour sinistre a blanchi les hauteurs.
Le camp s'éveille. En bas roule et gronde le fleuve
Où l'escadron léger des Numides s'abreuve.
Partout sonne l'appel clair des buccinateurs.

Car malgré Scipion, les augures menteurs,
La Trebbia débordée, et qu'il vente et qu'il pleuve,
Sempronius Consul, fier de sa gloire neuve,
A fait lever la hache et marcher les licteurs.

Rougissant le ciel noir de flamboîments lugubres,
A l'horizon, brûlaient les villages Insubres;
On entendait au loin barrir un éléphant.

Et là-bas, sous le pont, adossé contre une arche,
Hannibal écoutait, pensif et triomphant,
Le piétinement sourd des légions en marche.

The Trebbia

The dawn of an ominous day whitened the heights. The camp awakens. Below rolls and murmurs the river, where the light squadron of Numidians is watering its horses. Everywhere sounds the clear call of the trumpeters.

For in spite of Scipio, the lying augurs, the Trebbia in flood, and the wind and the rain, the Consul Sempronius, proud of his new glory, has raised the axe and made the lictors advance.

Reddening the dark sky with a melancholy blaze, the Insubri villages burned on the horizon; far off the trumpeting of an elephant was heard.

And down there beneath the bridge, with his back against an arch, triumphant and thoughtful, Hannibal listened to the dull tramp of the marching legions.

Antoine et Cléopâtre

Tous deux ils regardaient, de la haute terrasse,
L'Égypte s'endormir sous un ciel étouffant
Et le Fleuve, à travers le Delta noir qu'il fend,
Vers Bubaste ou Saïs rouler son onde grasse.

Et le Romain sentait sous la lourde cuirasse,
Soldat captif berçant le sommeil d'un enfant,
Ployer et défaillir sur son cœur triomphant
Le corps voluptueux que son étreinte embrasse.

Tournant sa tête pâle entre ses cheveux bruns
Vers celui qu'enivraient d'invincibles parfums,
Elle tendit sa bouche et ses prunelles claires;

Et sur elle courbé, l'ardent Imperator
Vit dans ses larges yeux étoilés de points d'or
Toute une mer immense où fuyaient des galères.

Antony and Cleopatra

From the high terrace they both watched Egypt sleeping beneath a stifling sky and the river rolling its oily waves towards Bubastis or Sais through the black delta that it divides.

And beneath his heavy armour, the Roman, a captive soldier cradling a child's slumber, felt the voluptuous body grasped in his embrace yielding and fainting on his triumphant heart.

Turning her head, pale amid her dark hair, towards him who was maddened by irresistible perfumes, she offered her mouth and her clear eyes;

And bent over her the passionate Imperator saw in her wide eyes starred with golden specks a whole vast sea where galleys were in flight.

La Mort de l'aigle

Quand l'aigle a dépassé les neiges éternelles,
A sa vaste envergure il veut chercher plus d'air
Et le soleil plus proche en un azur plus clair
Pour échauffer l'éclat de ses mornes prunelles.

Il s'enlève. Il aspire un torrent d'étincelles.
Toujours plus haut, enflant son vol tranquille et fier,
Il monte vers l'orage où l'attire l'éclair;
Mais la foudre d'un coup a rompu ses deux ailes.

Avec un cri sinistre, il tournoie, emporté
Par la trombe, et, crispé, buvant d'un trait sublime
La flamme éparse, il plonge au fulgurant abîme.

Heureux qui pour la Gloire ou pour la Liberté,
Dans l'orgueil de la force et l'ivresse du rêve,
Meurt ainsi d'une mort éblouissante et brève!

The Death of the Eagle

When the eagle has passed beyond the everlasting snows, he desires to seek more air for his vast spread of wing and a nearer sun in a clearer blue to rouse the brightness of his dull eyes.

He soars. He breathes a stream of sparks. Ever higher, raising his calm, proud flight, he climbs towards the storm allured by the lightning; but the thunder has broken both his wings with a single blow.

With a dismal cry, he whirls round and round, carried away by the whirlwind, and, shrivelled, drinking the scattered flame at one sublime draught, he dives into the abyss of lightnings.

Happy he who, for Fame or Freedom, in the pride of his strength and the intoxication of a dream, dies so dazzling and swift a death!

STÉPHANE MALLARMÉ

Le Pitre châtié

YEUX, lacs avec ma simple ivresse de renaître
Autre que l'histrion qui du geste évoquais
Comme plume la suie ignoble des quinquets,
J'ai troué dans le mur de toile une fenêtre.

De ma jambe et des bras limpide nageur traître,
A bonds multipliés, reniant le mauvais
Hamlet! c'est comme si dans l'onde j'innovais
Mille sépulcres pour y vierge disparaître.

Hilare or de cymbale à des poings irrité,
Tout à coup le soleil frappe la nudité
Qui pure s'exhala de ma fraîcheur de nacre,

Rance nuit de la peau quand sur moi vous passiez,
Ne sachant pas, ingrat! que c'était tout mon sacre,
Ce fard noyé dans l'eau perfide des glaciers.

The Clown Punished

EYES, lakes with my simple intoxication to be reborn other than
the actor, who, with his gestures as with a pen, evoked the disgust-
ing soot of the lamps, I have pierced a window in the wall of cloth.

Limpid, treacherous swimmer with my leg and arms in many a
bound renouncing the evil Hamlet! It is as if I began a thousand
tombs in the waves to disappear into them virgin.

Merry gold of the cymbal beaten with fists, all at once the sun
strikes the nakedness purely breathed from my cool mother-of-
pearl,

When you passed over me, rancid night of the skin, not knowing,
ingrate! that it was my whole anointing, this rouge drowned in the
deceitful water of glaciers.

Brise Marine

LA chair est triste, hélas! et j'ai lu tous les livres.
Fuir! là-bas fuir! Je sens que des oiseaux sont ivres
D'être parmi l'écume inconnue et les cieux!
Rien, ni les vieux jardins reflétés par les yeux
Ne retiendra ce cœur qui dans la mer se trempe
Ô nuits! ni la clarté déserte de ma lampe
Sur le vide papier que la blancheur défend,
Et ni la jeune femme allaitant son enfant.
Je partirai! Steamer balançant ta mâture,
Lève l'ancre pour une exotique nature!
Un Ennui, désolé par les cruels espoirs,
Croit encore à l'adieu suprême des mouchoirs!
Et, peut-être, les mâts, invitant les orages
Sont-ils de ceux qu'un vent penche sur les naufrages
Perdus, sans mâts, sans mâts, ni fertiles îlots . . .
Mais, ô mon cœur, entends le chant des matelots!

Sea Breeze

THE flesh is sad, alas! and I have read all the books. To escape! To
escape far away! I feel that birds are drunk to be among unknown
foam and the skies! Nothing – not old gardens reflected in the eyes –
will keep back this heart soaking itself in the sea, O nights! nor the
desolate light of my lamp on the empty paper, defended by its own
whiteness, nor the young wife feeding her child. I shall depart!
Steamer with swaying masts, raise anchor for exotic landscapes!

A tedium saddened by cruel hopes still believes in the last fare-
well of handkerchiefs! And perhaps the masts, inviting storms, are
among those that a gale bends above shipwrecks lost without masts,
without masts or fertile islands . . . But, O my heart, listen to the
sailors' song!

Don du poème

JE t'apporte l'enfant d'une nuit d'Idumée!
Noire, à l'aile saignante et pâle, déplumée,
Par le verre brûlé d'aromates et d'or,
Par les carreaux glacés, hélas! mornes encor,
L'aurore se jeta sur la lampe angélique.
Palmes! et quand elle a montré cette relique
A ce père essayant un sourire ennemi,
La solitude bleue et stérile a frémi.
Ô la berceuse, avec ta fille et l'innocence
De vos pieds froids, accueille une horrible naissance:
Et ta voix rappelant viole et clavecin,
Avec le doigt fané presseras-tu le sein
Par qui coule en blancheur sibylline la femme
Pour les lèvres que l'air du vierge azur affame?

Gift of the Poem

I BRING you the child of an Idumean night! Dark, with bleeding wing and pale, its feathers plucked, through the glass burned with spices and gold, through the icy panes, still dreary, alas! the dawn threw itself on the angelic lamp. O palms! and when it showed this relic to the father trying out a hostile smile, the blue, sterile solitude shuddered.

O nurse, with your daughter and the innocence of your and her cold feet, welcome a horrid birth: and, your voice recalling viol and harpsichord, with your withered finger will you press the breast whence woman flows in enigmatic whiteness for lips made hungry by the air of the blue, virginal sky?

STÉPHANE MALLARMÉ

L' Après-midi d'un faune

Églogue

Le Faune

CES nymphes, je veux les perpétuer.

                      Si clair,
Leur incarnat léger, qu'il voltige dans l'air
Assoupi de sommeils touffus.

                         Aimai-je un rêve?
Mon doute, amas de nuit ancienne, s'achève
En maint rameau subtil, qui, demeuré les vrais
Bois mêmes, prouve, hélas! que bien seul je m'offrais
Pour triomphe la faute idéale de roses.
Réfléchissons...

                 ou si les femmes dont tu gloses
Figurent un souhait de tes sens fabuleux!
Faune, l'illusion s'échappe des yeux bleus
Et froids, comme une source en pleurs, de la plus chaste:
Mais l'autre, tout soupirs, dis-tu qu'elle contraste

A Faun's Afternoon

Eclogue

The Faun

I DESIRE to perpetuate these nymphs.

So bright their light rosy flesh that it hovers in the air drowsy with tufted slumbers.

Did I love a dream? My doubt, heap of old night, ends in many a subtle branch, which, remaining the true woods themselves, proves, alas! that alone I offered myself the ideal error of roses for triumph. Let us reflect ...

Or if the women that you tell of represent a desire of your fabulous senses! Faun, illusion flows like a weeping spring from the cold blue eyes of the most chaste: but the other, all sighs, do you say that

Comme brise du jour chaude dans ta toison?
Que non! par l'immobile et lasse pâmoison
Suffoquant de chaleurs le matin frais s'il lutte,
Ne murmure point d'eau que ne verse ma flûte
Au bosquet arrosé d'accords; et le seul vent
Hors des deux tuyaux prompt à s'exhaler avant
Qu'il disperse le son dans une pluie aride,
C'est, à l'horizon pas remué d'une ride,
Le visible et serein souffle artificiel
De l'inspiration, qui regagne le ciel.

Ô bords siciliens d'un calme marécage
Qu'à l'envi de soleils ma vanité saccage,
Tacite sous les fleurs d'étincelles, CONTEZ
«Que je coupais ici les creux roseaux domptés
«Par le talent; quand, sur l'or glauque de lointaines
«Verdures dédiant leur vigne à des fontaines,
«Ondoie une blancheur animale au repos:
«Et qu'au prélude lent où naissent les pipeaux
«Ce vol de cygnes, non! de naïades se sauve
«Ou plonge. . .»

she contrasts like the day breeze warm on your fleece? No! Through
the motionless, lazy swoon suffocating with heat the cool morning
if it struggles, there murmurs no water not poured by my flute on
the thicket sprinkled with melody; and the only wind, quick to
breathe itself forth out of the two pipes, before it scatters the sound
in an arid rain, is, on the horizon unmoved by any wrinkle, the
visible, calm and artificial breath of inspiration returning to the
sky.

O Sicilian shores of a calm pool that my vanity plunders, vying
with the sun, silent beneath flowers of sparkling light, TELL '*That
here I was cutting the hollow reeds subdued by talent; when, on the
green gold of far-off verdures that offer their vine to fountains, an
animal whiteness ripples to rest: and that at the slow prelude in which
the pipes are born this flight of swans, no! of naiads runs away or
dives . . .*'

Inerte, tout brûle dans l'heure fauve
Sans marquer par quel art ensemble détala
Trop d'hymen souhaité de qui cherche le *la*:
Alors m'éveillerai-je à la ferveur première,
Droit et seul, sous un flot antique de lumière,
Lys! et l'un de vous tous pour l'ingénuité.

Autre que ce doux rien par leur lèvre ébruité,
Le baiser, qui tout bas des perfides assure,
Mon sein, vierge de preuve, atteste une morsure
Mystérieuse, due à quelque auguste dent;
Mais, bast! arcane tel élut pour confident
Le jonc vaste et jumeau dont sous l'azur on joue:
Qui, détournant à soi le trouble de la joue,
Rêve, dans un solo long, que nous amusions
La beauté d'alentour par des confusions
Fausses entre elle-même et notre chant crédule;
Et de faire aussi haut que l'amour se module
Évanouir du songe ordinaire de dos
Ou de flanc pur suivis avec mes regards clos,
Une sonore, vaine et monotone ligne.

Motionless, everything burns in the tawny hour without show-
ing by what art there ran off together too much Hymen desired by
him who seeks *A natural*: then shall I awaken to the first fervour,
upright and alone, beneath an ancient flood of light, lilies! and
one of you both for ingenuousness.

Other than this sweet nothing divulged by their lip, the kiss that
softly gives assurance of the treacherous, my breast, virgin of proof,
bears witness to a mysterious wound due to some august tooth; but
let it pass! A certain secret chose for confidant the great twin reed,
on which we play beneath the blue sky: which, diverting the cheek's
emotion to itself, dreams in a long solo that we entertained the
beauty of roundabout by false confusions between itself and our
credulous song; and, as high as love is sung, of making a resound-
ing, empty, monotonous line disappear from the habitual dream of
back or pure side followed by my half-shut glances.

Tâche donc, instrument des fuites, ô maligne
Syrinx, de refleurir aux lacs où tu m'attends!
Moi, de ma rumeur fier, je vais parler longtemps
Des déesses; et par d'idolâtres peintures,
A leur ombre enlever encore des ceintures:
Ainsi, quand des raisins j'ai sucé la clarté,
Pour bannir un regret par ma feinte écarté,
Rieur, j'élève au ciel d'été la grappe vide
Et, soufflant dans ses peaux lumineuses, avide
D'ivresse, jusqu'au soir je regarde au travers.

O nymphes, regonflons des SOUVENIRS divers.
«*Mon œil, trouant les joncs, dardait chaque encolure*
«*Immortelle, qui noie en l'onde sa brûlure*
«*Avec un cri de rage au ciel de la forêt;*
«*Et le splendide bain de cheveux disparaît*
«*Dans les clartés et les frissons, ô pierreries!*
«*J'accours; quand, à mes pieds, s'entrejoignent (meurtries*
«*De la langueur goûtée à ce mal d'être deux)*
«*Des dormeuses parmi leurs seuls bras hasardeux;*
«*Je les ravis, sans les désenlacer, et vole*
«*A ce massif, haï par l'ombrage frivole,*

Try then, instrument of flights, O malignant Syrinx, to flower once more upon the lakes where you await me! Proud of my murmuring, I shall speak of goddesses for many days; and by idolatrous paintings again remove girdles from their shadow: so, when I have sucked the brightness of grapes, to banish a regret removed by my pretence, laughing I raise the empty cluster to the summer sky and, blowing into its luminous skins, desiring drunkenness, I look through it till the evening.

O nymphs, let us swell various MEMORIES once again. '*My eye, piercing the reeds, touched with its dart each immortal neck that drowns its burning in the wave with a cry of rage to the forest sky; and the splendid bath of hair disappears in light and shuddering, O precious stones! I run up; when at my feet are joined (bruised by the languor tasted in this evil of being two) girls sleeping amid their perilous arms alone; I carry them off, without disentangling them, and fly to this bank, hated by the frivolous shade, of roses drying up every perfume in*

«De roses tarissant tout parfum au soleil,
«Où notre ébat au jour consumé soit pareil.»
Je t'adore, courroux des vierges, ô délice
Farouche du sacré fardeau nu qui se glisse
Pour fuir ma lèvre en feu buvant, comme un éclair
Tressaille! la frayeur secrète de la chair:
Des pieds de l'inhumaine au cœur de la timide
Que délaisse à la fois une innocence, humide
De larmes folles ou de moins tristes vapeurs.
«Mon crime, c'est d'avoir, gai de vaincre ces peurs
«Traîtresses, divisé la touffe échevelée
«De baisers que les dieux gardaient si bien mêlée:
«Car, à peine j'allais cacher un rire ardent
«Sous les replis heureux d'une seule (gardant
«Par un doigt simple, afin que sa candeur de plume
«Se teignît à l'émoi de sa sœur qui s'allume,
«La petite, naïve et ne rougissant pas:)
«Que de mes bras, défaits par de vagues trépas,
«Cette proie, à jamais ingrate se délivre
«Sans pitié du sanglot dont j'étais encore ivre.»

the sun, where our sport may be like to the day consumed.' I adore you,
virgin's wrath, O wild delight of the holy naked burden slipping
away to flee my lip aflame which, like quivering lightning, drinks
the secret terror of the flesh: from the feet of the heartless to the
heart of the timid one, abandoned at the same time by an innocence,
wet with wild tears or less sad vapours. '*Being gay at conquering*
these treacherous fears, my crime is to have divided the dishevelled tuft
of kisses that the gods kept so thoroughly mingled; for I scarcely went
to hide passionate laughter beneath the happy sinuosities of a single girl
(holding the little one, who was naïve and did not blush, by a mere finger
so that her feathery whiteness might be tinted at her sister's passion
taking fire) when from my arms, untwined by vague deaths, this ever
ungrateful prey frees herself, not pitying the tear with which I still was
drunk.'

Tant pis! vers le bonheur d'autres m'entraîneront
Par leur tresse nouée aux cornes de mon front:
Tu sais, ma passion, que, pourpre et déjà mûre,
Chaque grenade éclate et d'abeilles murmure;
Et notre sang, épris de qui le va saisir,
Coule pour tout l'essaim éternel du désir.
A l'heure où ce bois d'or et de cendres se teinte,
Une fête s'exalte en la feuillée éteinte:
Etna! c'est parmi toi visité de Vénus
Sur ta lave posant ses talons ingénus,
Quand tonne un somme triste où s'épuise la flamme.
Je tiens la reine!

       Ô sûr châtiment . . .

                         Non, mais l'âme
De paroles vacante et ce corps alourdi
Tard succombent au fier silence de midi:
Sans plus il faut dormir en l'oubli du blasphème,
Sur le sable altéré gisant et comme j'aime
Ouvrir ma bouche à l'astre efficace des vins!

Couple, adieu; je vais voir l'ombre que tu devins.

No matter! Others will lead me towards happiness by their braids knotted in the horns of my brow: you know, my passion, that, purple and ripe already, every pomegranate bursts and murmurs with bees; and our blood, enamoured of what shall seize upon it, flows for all the eternal swarm of desire. At the hour when the wood is coloured with gold and ashes a feast is exalted in the dead leaves: Etna! It is upon your slopes visited by Venus, who places her ingenuous heels upon your lava, when a melancholy slumber thunders in which the flame dies out. I hold the queen!

O certain punishment . . .

No, but the soul empty of words and this heavy body succumb slowly to the proud silence of noon: with no more ado we must sleep, forgetting blasphemy, lying on the thirsty sand and as I love to open my mouth to the effective star of wine!

Couple, farewell; I go to see the shadow you became.

Quand l'ombre menaça de la fatale loi . . .

QUAND l'ombre menaça de la fatale loi
Tel vieux Rêve, désir et mal de mes vertèbres,
Affligé de périr sous les plafonds funèbres
Il a ployé son aile indubitable en moi.

Luxe, ô salle d'ébène où, pour séduire un roi
Se tordent dans leur mort des guirlandes célèbres,
Vous n'êtes qu'un orgueil menti par les ténèbres
Aux yeux du solitaire ébloui de sa foi.

Oui, je sais qu'au lointain de cette nuit, la Terre
Jette d'un grand éclat l'insolite mystère
Sous les siècles hideux qui l'obscurcissent moins.

L'espace à soi pareil qu'il s'accroisse ou se nie
Roule dans cet ennui des feux vils pour témoins
Que s'est d'un astre en fête allumé le génie.

When the shadow threatened . . .

WHEN the shadow threatened with the fatal law a certain old dream, desire and sickness of my spine, afflicted at dying beneath funereal ceilings it folded its undoubted wing within me.

Pomp, O ebony hall where, to seduce a king, famous garlands writhe in death, you are only pride, a lie uttered by the shadows to the eyes of a hermit dazzled by his faith.

Yes, I know that in the distance of this night the Earth throws the unwonted mystery of a vast brilliance beneath the hideous centuries that darken it the less.

Space, like to itself whether it grows or is denied, revolves in this tedium base fires for witnesses that there has been kindled the genius of a festive star.

Le vierge, le vivace et le bel aujourd'hui ...

LE vierge, le vivace et le bel aujourd'hui
Va-t-il nous déchirer avec un coup d'aile ivre
Ce lac dur oublié que hante sous le givre
Le transparent glacier des vols qui n'ont pas fui!

Un cygne d'autrefois se souvient que c'est lui
Magnifique mais qui sans espoir se délivre
Pour n'avoir pas chanté la région où vivre
Quand du stérile hiver a resplendi l'ennui.

Tout son col secouera cette blanche agonie
Par l'espace infligée à l'oiseau qui le nie,
Mais non l'horreur du sol où le plumage est pris.

Fantôme qu'à ce lieu son pur éclat assigne,
Il s'immobilise au songe froid de mépris
Que vêt parmi l'exil inutile le Cygne.

The virginal, living, and beautiful day ...

THE virginal, living, and beautiful day, will it tear for us with a blow of its drunken wing this hard, forgotten lake haunted beneath the frost by the transparent glacier of flights that have not flown!

A swan of long ago remembers that it is he, magnificent but freeing himself without hope, for not having sung the country to live in, when the tedium of sterile winter shone.

His whole neck will shake off this white agony inflicted by space on the bird that denies it, but not the horror of the earth where his feathers are caught.

A phantom condemned to this place by his pure brilliance, he stays motionless in the cold dream of scorn worn in his useless exile by the Swan.

Prose

pour des Esseintes

HYPERBOLE! de ma mémoire
Triomphalement ne sais-tu
Te lever, aujourd'hui grimoire
Dans un livre de fer vêtu:

Car j'installe, par la science,
L'hymne des cœurs spirituels
En l'œuvre de ma patience,
Atlas, herbiers et rituels.

Nous promenions notre visage
(Nous fûmes deux, je le maintiens)
Sur maints charmes de paysage,
Ô sœur, y comparant les tiens.

L'ère d'autorité se trouble
Lorsque, sans nul motif, on dit
De ce midi que notre double
Inconscience approfondit

Prose

*for des Esseintes**

HYPERBOLE! From my memory can you not triumphantly arise, today like an occult language copied into a book bound in iron:

For by my science I install the hymn of spiritual hearts in the work of my patience, atlases, herbals, rituals.

We led our faces (I maintain that we were two) over many landscapes' charms, Sister, comparing yours to them.

The era of authority is disturbed when, without any motive, we say of this noon, which our double unconsciousness fathoms,

---

Des Esseintes: a character in Huysmans' novel, *A Rebours*, whose determination to live a life of pure art is there described. The sense of this poem is obscure, but it would seem to deal with an attempt to contemplate the eternal Ideas directly and with the poet's inevitable failure to do so (stanzas 9–12).

Que, sol des cent iris, son site,
Ils savent s'il a bien été,
Ne porte pas de nom que cite
L'or de la trompette d'Été.

Oui, dans une île que l'air charge
De vue et non de visions
Toute fleur s'étalait plus large
Sans que nous en devisions.

Telles, immenses, que chacune
Ordinairement se para
D'un lucide contour, lacune
Qui des jardins la sépara.

Gloire du long désir, Idées
Tout en moi s'exaltait de voir
La famille des iridées
Surgir à ce nouveau devoir,

Mais cette sœur sensée et tendre
Ne porta son regard plus loin
Que sourire et, comme à l'entendre
J'occupe mon antique soin.

That its site, the earth of a hundred irises – they know if it has really existed – bears no name quoted by the gold of summer's trumpet.

Yes, in an island that the air loads with sight and not with visions, every flower showed itself to be larger without our discussing it.

Such huge flowers that each one was usually adorned with a lucid contour, a hiatus that separated it from the gardens.

Glory of long desire, Ideas – everything in me was exalted to see the family of irises rise to this new duty,

But this sensible, tender sister carried her glance no further than to smile, and how to understand her is an old care of mine.

Oh! sache l'Esprit de litige,
A cette heure où nous nous taisons,
Que de lis multiples la tige
Grandissait trop pour nos raisons

Et non comme pleure la rive,
Quand son jeu monotone ment
A vouloir que l'ampleur arrive
Parmi mon jeune étonnement

D'ouïr tout le ciel et la carte
Sans fin attestés sur mes pas,
Par le flot même qui s'écarte,
Que ce pays n'exista pas.

L'enfant abdique son extase
Et docte déjà par chemins
Elle dit le mot: Anastase!
Né pour d'éternels parchemins,

Avant qu'un sépulcre ne rie
Sous aucun climat, son aïeul,
De porter ce nom: Pulchérie!
Caché par le trop grand glaïeul.

O let the litigious spirit know, at this hour when we are silent, that the stem of multiple lilies grew too much for our reasons

And not as weeps the shore, when its monotonous game plays false in wishing for abundance to arrive amid my young astonishment

To hear the whole sky and the map endlessly called upon to bear witness behind my steps, even by the withdrawing wave, that this land did not exist.

The child abdicates from its ecstasy and, already a scholar in the ways, she says the word: Anastasius!* born for eternal parchments,

Her ancestor, before a tomb laughs beneath any clime to bear this name: Pulcheria! hidden by the too large gladiolus.

Anastasius: this proper name means in Greek *arise. Pulcheria* means *beauty.*

STÉPHANE MALLARMÉ

Le Tombeau de Charles Baudelaire

Le temple enseveli divulgue par la bouche
Sépulcrale d'égout bavant boue et rubis
Abominablement quelque idole Anubis
Tout le museau flambé comme un aboi farouche

Ou que le gaz récent torde la mèche louche
Essuyeuse on le sait des opprobres subis
Il allume hagard un immortel pubis
Dont le vol selon le réverbère découche

Quel feuillage séché dans les cités sans soir
Votif pourra bénir comme elle se rasseoir
Contre le marbre vainement de Baudelaire

Au voile qui la ceint absente avec frissons
Celle son Ombre même un poison tutélaire
Toujours à respirer si nous en périssons.

The Tomb of Charles Baudelaire

THE buried temple gives forth by the sewer's sepulchral mouth, slobbering mud and rubies, abominably some idol of Anubis, the whole muzzle ablaze like a wild howl,

Or when the recent gas twists the foul wick which, we know, wipes away insults suffered, wildly it lights up an immortal pubis, whose flight moves according to the lamp.

What leaves, dried in cities without evening, votive, can bless as she, seating herself in vain against the marble of Baudelaire,

Shudderingly absent from the veil that girdles her, she, his very Shade, a guardian poison, always to be breathed although we die of it.

Toute l'âme résumée ...

TOUTE l'âme résumée
Quand lente nous l'expirons
Dans plusieurs ronds de fumée
Abolis en autres ronds

Atteste quelque cigare
Brûlant savamment pour peu
Que la cendre se sépare
De son clair baiser de feu

Ainsi le chœur des romances
A la lèvre vole-t-il
Exclus-en si tu commences
Le réel parce que vil

Le sens trop précis rature
Ta vague littérature.

All the soul summed up ...

ALL the soul summed up, when slowly we breathe it out in several rings of smoke vanishing in other rings,

Bears witness to some cigar burning skilfully as long as the ash is separated from its bright kiss of fire.

So the choir of romances flies to the lip; exclude from it, if you begin, the real because it is base.

Too precise a meaning erases your mysterious literature.

Tombeau

Anniversaire – Janvier 1897

LE noir roc courroucé que la bise le roule
Ne s'arrêtera ni sous de pieuses mains
Tâtant sa ressemblance avec les maux humains
Comme pour en bénir quelque funeste moule.

Ici presque toujours si le ramier roucoule
Cet immatériel deuil opprime de maints
Nubiles plis l'astre mûri des lendemains
Dont un scintillement argentera la foule.

Qui cherche, parcourant le solitaire bond
Tantôt extérieur de notre vagabond –
Verlaine? Il est caché parmi l'herbe, Verlaine

A ne surprendre que naïvement d'accord
La lèvre sans y boire ou tarir son haleine
Un peu profond ruisseau calomnié la mort.

Tomb

Anniversary . . . January 1897.

THE black rock, angered that the north wind should roll it, will not stop nor under pious hands feeling for its resemblance with human ills as if to bless some fatal mould of them.

Here almost always, if the dove coos, this immaterial mourning oppresses with many a nubile fold the ripe star of tomorrows, whose gleam is to colour the crowd silver.

Who seeks, following the solitary leap – exterior once – of our vagabond – Verlaine? He is hidden among the grass, Verlaine

Only to surprise, naïvely in agreement, the lip without drinking from it or drying up its breath, a shallow stream ill-spoken of, death.

PAUL VERLAINE

Nuit du Walpurgis classique

C'est plutôt le sabbat du second Faust que l'autre,
Un rhythmique sabbat, rhythmique, extrêmement
Rhythmique. – Imaginez un jardin de Lenôtre,
    Correct, ridicule et charmant.

Des ronds-points; au milieu, des jets d'eau; des allées
Toutes droites; sylvains de marbre; dieux marins
De bronze; çà et là, des Vénus étalées;
    Des quinconces, des boulingrins;

Des châtaigniers; des plants de fleurs formant la dune;
Ici, des rosiers nains qu'un goût docte affila;
Plus loin, des ifs taillés en triangles. La lune
    D'un soir d'été sur tout cela.

Minuit sonne, et réveille au fond du parc aulique
Un air mélancolique, un sourd, lent et doux air
De chasse: tel, doux, lent, sourd et mélancolique,
    L'air de chasse de *Tannhäuser*.

A Classical Walpurgisnacht

It is rather the sabbath of the second Faust than the other, a rhythmical sabbath, rhythmical, most rhythmical. – Imagine one of Lenôtre's gardens, correct, ridiculous, and charming.

Circuses; in the middle, fountains; straight alleys; marble sylvans; bronze sea-gods; here and there Venuses displayed; quincunxes and lawns;

Some chestnut trees; flowering shrubs forming a bank; here, dwarf rose-trees arranged by a skilful taste; further on, yews cut in triangles. A summer evening's moon over all that.

Midnight strikes and wakens in the depth of the aulic park a melancholy tune, a hollow, slow, sweet hunting tune: like the sweet, slow, hollow, melancholy hunting tune from *Tannhäuser*.

441

Des chants voilés de cors lointains, où la tendresse
Des sens étreint l'effroi de l'âme en des accords
Harmonieusement dissonants dans l'ivresse;
    Et voici qu'à l'appel des cors

S'entrelacent soudain des formes toutes blanches,
Diaphanes, et que le clair de lune fait
Opalines parmi l'ombre verte des branches,
    – Un Watteau rêvé par Raffet! –

S'entrelacent parmi l'ombre verte des arbres
D'un geste alangui, plein d'un désespoir profond;
Puis, autour des massifs, des bronzes et des marbres,
    Très lentement dansent en rond.

– Ces spectres agités, sont-ce donc la pensée
Du poète ivre, ou son regret ou son remords,
Ces spectres agités en tourbe cadencée,
    Ou bien tout simplement des morts?

Sont-ce donc ton remords, ô rêvasseur qu'invite
L'horreur, ou ton regret, ou ta pensée, – hein? – tous
Ces spectres qu'un vertige irrésistible agite,
    Ou bien des morts qui seraient fous? –

The muffled strains of distant horns, where the senses' tenderness clasps the soul's terror in notes melodiously discordant in their intoxication; and now at the call of the horns

Pure white, diaphanous forms, turned opaline by the moonlight in the green shadow of the branches, suddenly entwine – a Watteau dreamed by Raffet! –

Entwine in the green shadow of the trees with a languid gesture full of deep despair; then, around thickets, bronzes, and marbles, very slowly dance in a ring.

– These moving ghosts, are they then the thoughts of a drunken poet or his regret or his remorse, these ghosts moving in a rhythmic crowd, or else quite simply some of the dead?

Are they then your remorse, O dreamer, called up by horror or your regrets or your thoughts – say! – all these ghosts moved by an irresistible vertigo, or else some dead who may be mad? –

N'importe! ils vont toujours, les fébriles fantômes,
Menant leur ronde vaste et morne et tressautant
Comme dans un rayon de soleil des atomes,
     Et s'évaporant à l'instant

Humide et blême où l'aube éteint l'un après l'autre
Les cors, en sorte qu'il ne reste absolument
Plus rien – absolument – qu'un jardin de Lenôtre,
        Correct, ridicule et charmant.

Nevermore

SOUVENIR, souvenir, que me veux-tu? L'automne
Faisait voler la grive à travers l'air atone,
Et le soleil dardait un rayon monotone
Sur le bois jaunissant où la bise détone.

Nous étions seul à seule et marchions en rêvant,
Elle et moi, les cheveux et la pensée au vent.
Soudain, tournant vers moi son regard émouvant:
«Quel fut ton plus beau jour?» fit sa voix d'or vivant,

No matter! the feverish phantoms still continue leading their vast and dismal ring and leaping like motes in a sunbeam, and turning to mist

At the damp pale moment when dawn silences the horns one after another, so that there remains absolutely nothing more – absolutely nothing – than one of Lenôtre's gardens, correct, ridiculous, and charming.

Nevermore

MEMORY, memory, what do you want from me? Autumn made the thrush fly through the dull air, and the sun darted a monotonous ray over the yellowing wood where the north wind is loud.

We were by ourselves and walked dreaming, she and I, our hair and thoughts in the wind. Suddenly, turning her touching gaze upon me: 'What was your loveliest day?' said her voice of living gold,

Sa voix douce et sonore, au frais timbre angélique.
Un sourire discret lui donna la réplique,
Et je baisai sa main blanche, dévotement.

– Ah! les premières fleurs, qu'elles sont parfumées!
Et qu'il bruit avec un murmure charmant
Le premier *oui* qui sort de lèvres bien-aimées!

Clair de lune

VOTRE âme est un paysage choisi
Que vont charmant masques et bergamasques,
Jouant du luth, et dansant, et quasi
Tristes sous leurs déguisements fantasques.

Tout en chantant sur le mode mineur
L'amour vainqueur et la vie opportune,
Ils n'ont pas l'air de croire à leur bonheur
Et leur chanson se mêle au clair de lune,

Her gentle, resonant voice with the fresh angelic notes. A discreet
smile gave her her reply, and I kissed her white hand devoutly.
– Ah! how full of perfume the first flowers are! And with what a
charming murmur the first *yes* sounds, coming from beloved lips!

Moonlight

YOUR soul is a chosen landscape that masks and bergomasks go
charming, playing the lute and dancing and almost melancholy be-
neath their fantastic disguises.

While singing in the minor key of Love the conqueror and the
pleasant life, they have the air of not believing in their happiness,
and their song is mingled with the moonlight,

Au calme clair de lune triste et beau,
Qui fait rêver les oiseaux dans les arbres
Et sangloter d'extase les jets d'eau,
Les grands jets d'eau sveltes parmi les marbres.

Colloque sentimental

DANS le vieux parc solitaire et glacé
Deux formes ont tout à l'heure passé.

Leurs yeux sont morts et leurs lèvres sont molles,
Et l'on entend à peine leurs paroles.

Dans le vieux parc solitaire et glacé
Deux spectres ont évoqué le passé.

– Te souvient-il de notre extase ancienne?
– Pourquoi voulez-vous donc qu'il m'en souvienne?

– Ton cœur bat-il toujours à mon seul nom?
Toujours vois-tu mon âme en rêve? – Non.

– Ah! les beaux jours de bonheur indicible
Où nous joignions nos bouches! – C'est possible.

With the calm, beautiful, melancholy moonlight that makes the birds in the trees dream and the fountains sob with ecstasy, the tall, slender fountains among the statues.

Sentimental Dialogue

IN the old, solitary, frosty park two shapes passed by just now.

Their eyes are dead and their lips are slack, and their words can hardly be heard.

In the old, solitary, frosty park two ghosts recalled the past.

'Do you remember our old ecstasy?' 'Why will you have me remember it?'

'Does your heart still beat at my mere name? Do you still see my soul in dreams?' 'No.'

'Ah! The sweet days of unspeakable happiness when we joined our lips together!' 'It is possible.'

– Qu'il était bleu, le ciel, et grand, l'espoir!
– L'espoir a fui, vaincu, vers le ciel noir.

Tels ils marchaient dans les avoines folles,
Et la nuit seule entendit leurs paroles.

Il pleure dans mon cœur . . .

> *Il pleut doucement sur la ville.*
> ARTHUR RIMBAUD

IL pleure dans mon cœur
Comme il pleut sur la ville.
Quelle est cette langueur
Qui pénètre mon cœur?

Ô bruit doux de la pluie
Par terre et sur les toits!
Pour un cœur qui s'ennuie,
Ô le chant de la pluie!

'How blue the sky was and how great our hope!' 'Hope has fled defeated towards the dark sky.'

So they walked in the oat-grass, and night alone heard their words.

There is weeping in my heart . . .

> *It rains gently on the town.*
> ARTHUR RIMBAUD

THERE is weeping in my heart as it rains on the town. What languor is this that pierces my heart?

O gentle noise of the rain on the ground and the roofs! For a heart that is troubled, O the song of the rain!

Il pleure sans raison
Dans ce cœur qui s'écœure.
Quoi! nulle trahison?
Ce deuil est sans raison.

C'est bien la pire peine
De ne savoir pourquoi,
Sans amour et sans haine,
Mon cœur a tant de peine.

Sagesse d'un Louis Racine, je t'envie! ...

SAGESSE d'un Louis Racine, je t'envie!
Ô n'avoir pas suivi les leçons de Rollin,
N'être pas né dans le grand siècle à son déclin,
Quand le soleil couchant, si beau, dorait la vie,

Quand Maintenon jetait sur la France ravie
L'ombre douce et la paix de ses coiffes de lin,
Et, royale, abritait la veuve et l'orphelin,
Quand l'étude de la prière était suivie,

There is no cause for weeping in this sickened heart. What! No treason? This sorrow has no cause.

Indeed, it is the worst grief not to know why, without love or hate, my heart has so much grief.

Wisdom of a Louis Racine, I envy you! ...

WISDOM of a Louis Racine, I envy you! O not to have followed Rollin's lectures, not to have been born in the decline of the great century, when the setting sun gilded life so beautifully,

When Maintenon cast upon enraptured France the gentle shadow and peace of her linen coifs, and royally sheltered the widow and orphan, when the study of prayer was observed,

Quand poète et docteur, simplement, bonnement,
Communiaient avec des ferveurs de novices,
Humbles servaient la Messe et chantaient aux offices,

Et, le printemps venu, prenaient un soin charmant
D'aller dans les Auteuils cueillir lilas et roses
En louant Dieu, comme Garo* de toutes choses!

Non. Il fut gallican, ce siècle, et janséniste! ...

NON. Il fut gallican, ce siècle, et janséniste!
C'est vers le moyen âge, énorme et délicat,
Qu'il faudrait que mon cœur en panne naviguât,
Loin de nos jours d'esprit charnel et de chair triste.

Roi, politicien, moine, artisan, chimiste,
Architecte, soldat, médecin, avocat,
Quel temps! Oui, que mon cœur naufragé rembarquât
Pour toute cette force ardente, souple, artiste!

When poet and doctor simply and honestly took communion
with the zeal of novices, humbly serving the Mass and singing in the
church services,
   And, when Spring came, taking pleasant pains to go out Auteuil
way to gather lilac and roses, like Garo* praising God for all things!

No. That century was Gallican and Jansenist! ...

No. That century was Gallican and Jansenist! It is towards the
vast, delicate Middle Ages that my becalmed heart must steer, far
from our days of carnal spirit and melancholy flesh.
   King, politician, monk, craftsman, chemist, architect, soldier,
doctor, lawyer, what an age! Yes, would that my shipwrecked heart
might re-embark for all this passionately supple, artistic strength!

---

*The character of Garo is to be found in a fable of La Fontaine,
The Acorn and the Pumpkin.

Et là que j'eusse part – quelconque, chez les rois
Ou bien ailleurs, n'importe, – à la chose vitale,
Et que je fusse un saint, actes bons, pensers droits,

Haute théologie et solide morale
Guidé par la folie unique de la Croix,
Sur tes ailes de pierre, ô folle Cathédrale!

Parsifal

A Jules Tellier

PARSIFAL a vaincu les Filles, leur gentil
Babil et la luxure amusante – et sa pente
Vers la Chair de garçon vierge que cela tente
D'aimer les seins légers et ce gentil babil;

Il a vaincu la Femme belle, au cœur subtil,
Étalant ses bras frais et sa gorge excitante;
Il a vaincu l'Enfer et rentre sous sa tente
Avec un lourd trophée à son bras puéril,

And would I might have part there – some part or other, with
the kings or elsewhere, no matter – in the thing that is vital, and be
a saint with good actions, upright thoughts,
Lofty theology and firm morality, guided by the unique mad-
ness of the Cross, on your stone wings, O mad Cathedral!

Parsifal

To Jules Tellier

PARSIFAL has conquered the Girls, their pleasant chatter and
amusing lust – and his virgin boy's bent towards the Flesh which is
tempted to love the light breasts and this gentle chatter;
He has conquered the fair Woman with the subtle heart, display-
ing her cool arms and provoking bosom; he has conquered Hell and
comes back to his tent with a heavy trophy on his boyish arm,

449

Avec la lance qui perça le Flanc suprême!
Il a guéri le roi, le voici roi lui-même,
Et prêtre du très saint Trésor essentiel.

En robe d'or il adore, gloire et symbole,
Le vase pur où resplendit le Sang réel,
— Et, ô ces voix d'enfants chantant dans la coupole!

TRISTAN CORBIÈRE

Vénerie

Ô VENUS, dans ta Vénerie,
Limier et piqueur à la fois,
Valet-de-chiens et d'écurie,
J'ai vu l'Hallali, les Abois! ...

With the lance that pierced the supreme Side! He has cured the king; here he is king himself and priest of the holiest quintessential Treasure.

In a golden robe he worships, as glory and symbol, the pure vessel where shines the real Blood — and, O those children's voices singing in the dome!

Venery*

O VENUS, in your venery, staghound and huntsman at the same time, kennel-boy and stable-boy, I have seen the mort and seen the bay! ...

---

*This poem depends on a series of puns impossible to express in English, but playing for the most part on the idea of hunting a wild beast and hunting a woman. The third stanza is especially difficult: *pied-de-biche* can mean either *a hind's track* or *the handle of a bell-pull*. *Pied-de-grue* means *standing about and waiting*, and there is also a pun on *grue* in its slang sense of *prostitute*. In the fourth stanza there seems to be a play on the words *laie: a wild sow* and *Laïs: Laïs, courtezan*. The ambiguity existing in the word *vénerie* suggesting at the same time *hunting* and various derivatives of *Venus* is also present in English.

Que Diane aussi me sourie! ...
A cors, à cris, à pleine voix
Je fais le pied, je fais le bois;
Car on dit que: *bête varie* ...

– Un pied de biche: Le voici,
Cordon de sonnette sur rue,
– Bois de cerf: de la porte aussi;
– Et puis un pied: un pied-de-grue! ...

Ô Fauve après qui j'aboyais,
– Je suis fourbu, qu'on me relaie! –
Ô Bête, es-tu donc une laie?
....
Biens moins sauvage te croyais!

Paria

Qu'ils se payent des républiques,
Hommes libres! – carcan au cou –
Qu'ils peuplent leurs nids domestiques! ...
– Moi je suis le maigre coucou.

Let Diana too smile upon me! ... With horns, with shouts, at the top of my voice, I go on foot, I beat the wood; for they say that *beasts differ* ...

A hind's track: here it is, a bell-pull on the street, – a stag's antlers: the wooden door too; and then a foot: myself kicking my heels! ...

O wild beast after whom I bayed, – I am foundered, let them repla ce me! – O beast, are you a wild sow? – I thought you much less savage!

Pariah

Let them have their republics, free men! – with a yoke on their necks – let them people their homely nests! ... I am the lean cuckoo.

– Moi, – cœur eunuque, dératé
De ce qui mouille et ce qui vibre ...
Que me chante leur Liberté,
A moi? toujours seul. Toujours libre.

– Ma Patrie ... elle est par le monde;
Et, puisque la planète est ronde,
Je ne crains pas d'en voir le bout ...
Ma patrie est où je la plante:
Terre ou mer, elle est sous la plante
De mes pieds – quand je suis debout.

– Quand je suis couché: ma patrie
C'est la couche seule et meurtrie
Où je vais forcer dans mes bras
Ma moitié, comme moi sans âme;
Et ma moitié: c'est une femme ...
Une femme que je n'ai pas.

– L'idéal à moi: c'est un songe
Creux; mon horizon – l'imprévu –
Et le mal du pays me ronge ...
Du pays que je n'ai pas vu.

I – a eunuch heart deprived of all ecstasy and excitement ...
What does their freedom mean to me? Always alone. Always free.

My country ... is throughout the world; and, since the planet is
round, I am not afraid of seeing its end ... My country is where I
place it: on land or sea it is beneath the sole of my feet – when I am
standing up.

When I am lying down, my country is the lonely bruised bed
where I shall force into my arms my other half, soulless like myself;
and my other half is a woman ... A woman I do not possess.

My ideal is a hollow dream; my horizon – the unforeseen – and
homesickness consumes me ... For a home I have never seen.

Que les moutons suivent leur route,
De Carcassonne à Tombouctou ...
– Moi, ma route me suit. Sans doute
Elle me suivra n'importe où.

Mon pavillon sur moi frissonne,
Il a le ciel pour couronne:
C'est la brise dans mes cheveux ...
Et dans n'importe quelle langue;
Je puis subir une harangue;
Je puis me taire si je veux.

Ma pensée est un souffle aride:
C'est l'air. L'air est à moi partout.
Et ma parole est l'écho vide
Qui ne dit rien – et c'est tout.

Mon passé: c'est ce que j'oublie.
La seule chose qui me lie,
C'est ma main dans mon autre main.
Mon souvenir – Rien – C'est ma trace.
Mon présent, c'est tout ce qui passe.
Mon avenir – Demain ... demain.

Let the sheep follow their road from Carcassonne to Timbuctoo.
... My road follows me. Doubtless it will follow me anywhere.

Above me flutters my ensign with the sky for a crown: it is the
breeze in my hair ... And in any language I can put up with a
speech or be silent if I want.

My thought is an arid breath: it is the air. Everywhere the air be-
longs to me. And my speech is the empty echo which says nothing –
and that is all.

My past is what I forget. The only thing that binds me is my
hand in my other hand. My memory – nothing – it is my track. My
present is everything that passes by. My future – tomorrow ...
tomorrow.

Je ne connais pas mon semblable;
Moi, je suis ce que je me fais.
— *Le Moi humain est haïssable* . . .
— Je ne m'aime ni ne me hais.

— Allons! la vie est une fille
Qui m'a pris à son bon plaisir . . .
Le mien, c'est: la mettre en guenille,
La prostituer sans désir.

— Des dieux? . . . — Par hasard j'ai pu naître;
Peut-être en est-il — par hasard . . .
Ceux-là, s'ils veulent me connaître,
Me trouveront bien quelque part.

— Où que je meure: ma patrie
S'ouvrira bien, sans qu'on l'en prie,
Assez grande pour mon linceul . . .
Un linceul encor: pour que faire? . . .
Puisque ma patrie est en terre
Mon os ira bien là tout seul . . .

I know no fellow; I am what I make myself. — *The human Ego is hateful.* . . . I neither love nor hate myself.

Come! Life is a girl who took me for her pleasure . . . Mine is : to reduce her to rags and prostitute her without desire.

Gods? . . . By chance I was born; perhaps there are some — by chance . . . They, if they want to know me, will easily find me somewhere or other.

Wherever I die, without being asked my country will open wide enough for my shroud . . . Why even a shroud? . . . Since my country is the earth, my bones will easily go there by themselves . . .

ARTHUR RIMBAUD

Le Cœur volé

MON triste cœur bave à la poupe,
Mon cœur couvert de caporal:
Ils y lancent des jets de soupe,
Mon triste cœur bave à la poupe:
Sous les quolibets de la troupe
Qui pousse un rire général,
Mon triste cœur bave à la poupe,
Mon cœur couvert de caporal!

Ithyphalliques et pioupiesques
Leurs quolibets l'ont dépravé!
Au gouvernail on voit des fresques
Ithyphalliques et pioupiesques.
Ô flots abracadabrantesques,
Prenez mon cœur, qu'il soit lavé!
Ithyphalliques et pioupiesques,
Leurs quolibets l'ont dépravé!

The Stolen Heart

MY sad heart slobbers at the stern, my heart covered with shag tobacco: they spurt soup over it, my sad heart slobbers at the stern: under the jokes of the crew, who utter a general laugh, my sad heart slobbers at the stern, my heart covered with shag tobacco!

Their ithyphallic, barrack-room jokes have corrupted it! On the tiller one sees ithyphallic, barrack-room drawings. O magical waves take my heart that it may be washed! Their ithyphallic, barrack-room jokes have corrupted it!

Quand ils auront tari leurs chiques,
Comment agir, ô cœur volé?
Ce seront des hoquets bachiques
Quand ils auront tari leurs chiques:
J'aurai des sursauts stomachiques,
Moi, si mon cœur est ravalé:
Quand ils auront tari leurs chiques
Comment agir, ô cœur volé?

Les Premières Communions

I

VRAIMENT, c'est bête, ces églises des villages
Où quinze laids marmots encrassant les piliers
Écoutent, grasseyant les divins babillages,
Un noir grotesque dont fermentent les souliers:
Mais le soleil éveille, à travers des feuillages,
Les vieilles couleurs des vitraux irréguliers.

La pierre sent toujours la terre maternelle.
Vous verrez des monceaux de ces cailloux terreux

When they have chewed their quids dry, how shall I act, O
stolen heart? There will be Bacchanalian hiccoughs when they have
chewed their quids dry: I shall have tremors in my stomach myself,
if my heart is degraded again: when they have chewed their quids
dry, how shall I act, O stolen heart?

First Communions

I

REALLY, it is idiotic, these village churches where fifteen ugly
brats, dirtying the pillars and pronouncing the divine prattle with a
thick burr, listen to a black grotesque with sweaty shoes: but the
sun through the leaves awakens the old colours of the uneven
windows.

The stone still smells of the maternal earth. You will see piles of

Dans la campagne en rut qui frémit solennelle,
Portant près des blés lourds, dans les sentiers ocreux,
Ces arbrisseaux brûlés où bleuit la prunelle,
Des nœuds de mûriers noirs et de rosiers fuireux.

Tous les cent ans on rend ces granges respectables
Par un badigeon d'eau bleue et de lait caillé:
Si des mysticités grotesques sont notables
Près de la Notre-Dame ou du Saint empaillé,
Des mouches sentant bon l'auberge et les étables
Se gorgent de cire au plancher ensoleillé.

L'enfant se doit surtout à la maison, famille
Des soins naïfs, des bons travaux abrutissants;
Ils sortent, oubliant que la peau leur fourmille
Où la Prêtre de Christ plaqua ses doigts puissants.
On paie au Prêtre un toit ombré d'une charmille
Pour qu'il laisse au soleil tous ces fronts brunissants.

Le premier habit noir, le plus beau jour de tartes
Sous le Napoléon ou le Petit Tambour

these earthy stones in the rutting countryside, which quivers
solemnly and bears near the heavy corn, on the ochre paths, those
scorched shrubs on which the sloe is blue, clumps of blackberry
bushes and pale roses.

Every hundred years they make these barns respectable with a
wash of blue water and curdled milk: if grotesque mystifications are
to the fore near the statue of Our Lady or the stuffed Saint, flies
smelling pleasantly of the inn or the stables cram themselves with
wax on the sunny ceiling.

The child is bound to his home above all, the family of naïve
cares, of good exhausting work; they emerge, forgetting that their
skin crawls where Christ's priest laid his powerful fingers. The
Priest is paid a roof shaded by a hornbeam to leave all these bronzed
foreheads in the sun.

The first black coat, the nicest day of cakes, beneath the
Napoleon or the Little Drummer some coloured print where

Quelque enluminure où les Josephs et les Marthes
Tirent la langue avec un excessif amour
Et que joindront, au jour de science, deux cartes:
Ces seuls doux souvenirs lui restent du grand Jour.

Les filles vont toujours à l'église, contentes
De s'entendre appeler garces par les garçons
Qui font du genre après Messe ou vêpres chantantes.
Eux qui sont destinés au chic des garnisons,
Ils narguent au café les maisons importantes,
Blousés neuf, et gueulant d'effroyables chansons.

Cependant le Curé choisit pour les enfances
Des dessins; dans son clos, les vêpres dites, quand
L'air s'emplit du lointain nasillement des danses,
Il se sent, en dépit des célestes défenses,
Les doigts de pied ravis et le mollet marquant;
– La Nuit vient, noir pirate aux cieux d'or débarquant.

2

Le Prêtre a distingué parmi les catéchistes,
Congrégés des Faubourgs ou des Riches Quartiers,

Josephs and Marys put out their tongues with excessive love, to be joined by two cards on the day of the catechism: these sweet memories of the great day alone remain to him.

The girls still go to church, glad to be called lasses by the boys showing off after Mass or after singing vespers. They, destined for the fashionable life of garrison towns, snap their fingers in the café at important houses, with new blouses on and yelling frightful songs.

Meanwhile the *Curé* chooses drawings for the children; in his garden, vespers over, when the air is filled with the distant humming of dances, in spite of heavenly prohibitions, he feels his toes itching and calf beating time; – Night comes like a black pirate landing on the golden skies.

2

The Priest noticed among the catechists, who came from the suburbs or rich parts of the town, this unknown little girl with sad

Cette petite fille inconnue, aux yeux tristes,
Front jaune. Les parents semblent de doux portiers.
«Au grand Jour, le marquant parmi les Catéchistes,
Dieu fera sur ce front neiger ses bénitiers.»

3

La veille du grand Jour, l'enfant se fait malade.
Mieux qu'à l'Église haute aux funèbres rumeurs,
D'abord le frisson vient, – le lit n'étant pas fade –
Un frisson surhumain qui retourne: «Je meurs . . .»

Et, comme un vol d'amour fait à ses sœurs stupides,
Elle compte, abattue et les mains sur son cœur,
Les Anges, les Jésus et ses Vierges nitides
Et, calmement, son âme a bu tout son vainqueur.

Adonaï! . . . – Dans les terminaisons latines,
Des cieux moirés de vert baignent les Fronts vermeils,
Et, tachés du sang pur des célestes poitrines,
De grands linges neigeux tombent sur les soleils!

eyes and sallow brow. The parents seem to be peaceable door-keepers. 'On the great day, remarking it among the catechists, God will cause his fonts to drop snow upon this brow.'

3

On the eve of the great day the child becomes ill. Stronger than in the tall church with its dreary noises, first comes a fit of shivering – it is not that her bed is damp – a superhuman shivering that returns: 'I am dying . . .'

And, as if stealing love from her stupid sisters, dejectedly, her hands on her heart, she counts the Angels, the Jesuses, and her snowy Virgins and calmly her soul drank all its conqueror.

Adonai! . . . – In the Latin endings skies watered with green bathe crimson brows, and great snowy cloths spotted with the pure blood of heavenly bosoms fall on the suns!

— Pour ses virginités présentes et futures
Elle mord aux fraîcheurs de ta Rémission,
Mais plus que les lys d'eau, plus que les confitures,
Tes pardons sont glacés, ô Reine de Sion!

4

Puis la Vierge n'est plus que la vierge du livre.
Les mystiques élans se cassent quelquefois . . .
Et vient la pauvreté des images, que cuivre
L'ennui, l'enluminure atroce et les vieux bois;

Des curiosités vaguement impudiques
Épouvantent le rêve aux chastes bleuités
Qui s'est surpris autour des célestes tuniques,
Du linge dont Jésus voile ses nudités.

Elle veut, elle veut, pourtant, l'âme en détresse,
Le front dans l'oreiller creusé par les cris sourds,
Prolonger les éclairs suprêmes de tendresse,
Et bave . . . — L'ombre emplit les maisons et les cours.

For her present and future virginities she gnaws at the coolness of your forgiveness, but your pardons are icier, O Queen of Sion, than water-lilies or preserves!

4

Then the Virgin is no more than the virgin of the book. Mystical soarings are sometimes broken . . . And there comes the poverty of images coppered by boredom, the frightful coloured print and old wood-cuts;

Vaguely shameless curiosity frightens the chaste blue dream that surprised itself round heavenly tunics, the cloth with which Jesus veils his nakedness.

She wants, yet she wants, her soul in distress, her forehead in the pillow hollowed by muffled cries, to prolong the last flashes of tenderness, and dribbles . . . — The shadow fills houses and court-yards.

Et l'enfant ne peut plus. Elle s'agite, cambre
Les reins et d'une main ouvre le rideau bleu
Pour amener un peu la fraîcheur de la chambre
Sous le drap, vers son ventre et sa poitrine en feu ...

5

A son réveil, – minuit, – la fenêtre était blanche.
Devant le sommeil bleu des rideaux illunés,
La vision la prit des candeurs du dimanche;
Elle avait rêvé rouge. Elle saigna du nez,

Et, se sentant bien chaste et pleine de faiblesse,
Pour savourer en Dieu son amour revenant
Elle eut soif de la nuit où s'exalte et s'abaisse
Le cœur, sous l'œil des cieux doux, en les devinant;

De la nuit, Vierge-Mère impalpable, qui baigne
Tous les jeunes émois de ses silences gris;
Elle eut soif de la nuit forte où le cœur qui saigne
Écoule sans témoin sa révolte sans cris.

And the child can stand it no longer. She moves, arches her loins,
and with one hand opens the blue curtain to bring a little of the
room's coolness beneath the sheet, towards her burning stomach
and chest ...

5

At her awakening – midnight – the window was white. Before the
blue slumber of curtains lit by the moon, the vision of Sunday puri-
ties took her; she had dreamed red. She bled from the nose,

And feeling herself chaste indeed and full of weakness to savour
her love returning to God, she thirsted for the night where the
heart is exalted or cast down beneath the eye of the gentle heavens,
while guessing their secrets;

For the night, impalpable Virgin-Mother, bathing all young
emotions in her grey silences; she thirsted for the strong night
where the bleeding heart may utter its dumb revolt without a wit-
ness.

Et faisant la Victime et la petite épouse,
Son étoile la vit, une chandelle aux doigts,
Descendre dans la cour où séchait une blouse,
Spectre blanc, et lever les spectres noirs des toits.

6

Elle passa sa nuit sainte dans des latrines.
Vers la chandelle, aux trous du toit coulait l'air blanc,
Et quelque vigne folle aux noirceurs purpurines,
En deçà d'une cour voisine s'écroulant.

La lucarne faisait un cœur de lueur vive
Dans la cour où les cieux bas plaquaient d'ors vermeils
Les vitres; les pavés puant l'eau de lessive
Souffraient l'ombre des murs bondés de noirs sommeils.

7

Qui dira ces langueurs et ces pitiés immondes,
Et ce qu'il lui viendra de haine, ô sales fous

And playing the Victim and the little wife, her star saw her go down, a candle in her fingers, into the courtyard, where a blouse was drying like a white ghost, and raise the black ghosts of the roofs.

6

She passed her holy night in a privy. From the holes in the roof the white air flowed towards the candle, and some wild vine with its purple blackness collapsing this side of a neighbouring courtyard.

The skylight made a heart of bright light in the courtyard where the low skies touched the panes with ruby gold; the paving stones stinking of washing water sulphured the shadow of walls crammed with dark sleep.

7

Who shall tell of these languors and of this impure pity, and of the hatred that will come to her, when in the end leprosy shall devour

Dont le travail divin déforme encor les mondes,
Quand la lèpre à la fin mangera ce corps doux?

8

Et quand, ayant rentré tous ses nœuds d'hystéries,
Elle verra, sous les tristesses du bonheur,
L'amant rêver au blanc million des Maries,
Au matin de la nuit d'amour, avec douleur:

«Sais-tu que je t'ai fait mourir? J'ai pris ta bouche,
Ton cœur, tout ce qu'on a, tout ce que vous avez;
Et moi, je suis malade: Oh! je veux qu'on me couche
Parmi les Morts des eaux nocturnes abreuvés!

«J'étais bien jeune, et Christ a souillé mes haleines.
Il me bonda jusqu'à la gorge de dégoûts!
Tu baisais mes cheveux profonds comme les laines,
Et je me laissais faire . . . Ah! va, c'est bon pour vous,

that gentle body, O filthy fools, whose divine work still disfigures
the universe?

8

And when, having drawn all her coils of hysteria in, she will see
with grief, on the morning of the night of love, beneath the melan-
choly of happiness, her lover dreaming of the white million of
Marys:

'Do you know I made you die? I took your mouth, your heart,
all there is to be had, all you have; and I am sick: Oh! would I were
laid among the dead whose thirst is quenched with the waters of
night!

'I was very young, and Christ soiled my breath. He crammed me
full to the throat with disgust! You kissed my hair deep as a fleece,
and I let you do it . . . ah! go, it is all right for you,

«Hommes! qui songez peu que la plus amoureuse
Est, sous sa conscience aux ignobles terreurs,
La plus prostituée et la plus douloureuse,
Et que tous nos élans vers vous sont des erreurs!

«Car ma Communion première est bien passée.
Tes baisers, je ne puis jamais les avoir sus:
Et mon cœur et ma chair par ta chair embrassée
Fourmillent du baiser putride de Jésus!»

9

Alors l'âme pourrie et l'âme désolée
Sentiront ruisseler tes malédictions.
– Ils auront couché sur ta Haine inviolée,
Échappés, pour la mort, des justes passions,

Christ! ô Christ, éternel voleur des énergies,
Dieu qui pour deux mille ans vouas à ta paleur,
Cloués au sol, de honte et de céphalalgies,
Ou renversés, les fronts des femmes de douleur.

'Men! Who little think that beneath her consciousness, with its
vile terrors, the most amorous woman is the most prostituted and
sorrowful, and that all our movements towards you are mistakes!
  'For my first Communion is long past. I can never have known
your kisses: and my heart and flesh embraced by your flesh crawl
with the putrid kiss of Jesus!'

9

Then the corrupt soul and the desolate soul will feel your curses
flow. – They will have lain down on your inviolate Hatred, escaped
from their just passions for death,
  Christ! O Christ, perpetual thief of energy, God who for two
thousand years consecrated to your own pallor the brows of the
women of sorrow, nailed to the ground with shame and head-
aches or thrown back.

Les Chercheuses de poux

QUAND le front de l'enfant, plein de rouges tourmentes,
Implore l'essaim blanc des rêves indistincts,
Il vient près de son lit deux grandes sœurs charmantes
Avec de frêles doigts aux ongles argentins.

Elles assoient l'enfant devant une croisée
Grande ouverte où l'air bleu baigne un fouillis de fleurs,
Et dans ses lourds cheveux où tombe la rosée
Promènent leurs doigts fins, terribles et charmeurs.

Il écoute chanter leurs haleines craintives
Qui fleurent de longs miels végétaux et rosés,
Et qu'interrompt parfois un sifflement, salives
Reprises sur la lèvre ou désirs de baisers.

Il entend leurs cils noirs battant sous les silences
Parfumés; et leurs doigts électriques et doux
Font crépiter parmi ses grises indolences
Sous leurs ongles royaux la mort des petits poux.

Women Hunting Lice

WHEN the child's brow full of red torments begs for the white swarm of hazy dreams, two tall charming sisters with delicate fingers and silvery nails come near his bed.

They seat the child in front of a wide-open window, where the blue air bathes a mass of flowers, and through his heavy hair, on which the dew falls, they run their terrible, slender, magic fingers.

He hears their timid breath singing, smelling of slow vegetable honey made from roses, and interrupted sometimes by a hissing, saliva drawn back on the lip or the desire of kisses.

He listens to their dark lashes fluttering under the scented silence; and in his grey indolence their gentle, electric fingers make the death of the little lice crackle beneath their royal nails.

Voilà que monte en lui le vin de la Paresse,
Soupir d'harmonica qui pourrait délirer;
L'enfant se sent, selon la lenteur des caresses,
Sourdre et mourir sans cesse un désir de pleurer.

Qu'est-ce pour nous, mon cœur, que les nappes
de sang ...

QU'EST-CE pour nous, mon cœur, que les nappes de
sang
Et de braise et mille meurtres, et les longs cris
De rage, sanglots de tout enfer renversant
Tout ordre; et l'Aquilon encor sur les débris;

Et toute vengeance? Rien! ... – Mais si, toute encor,
Nous la voulons! Industriels, princes, senats:
Périssez! Puissance, justice, histoire: à bas!
Ça nous est dû. Le sang! le sang! la flamme d'or!

Now swells in him the wine of idleness, a harmonica's sighing that
might end in delirium; according to the slowness of the caresses
the child feels a desire to weep endlessly rising and dying within
him.

What does it mean to us, my heart, the sheets of blood ...?

WHAT does it mean to us, my heart, the sheets of blood and ash,
and a thousand killings, and the long shrieks of frenzy, the sobs of
every hell overturning all order, and the north wind still above the
ruins,

And each revenge? Nothing! – But yes, we still want it all! In-
dustrialists, princes, senates: perish! Down with power, justice, and
history! That is our due. Blood! blood! The golden flame!

Tout à la guerre, à la vengeance, à la terreur,
Mon esprit! Tournons dans la morsure: Ah! passez,
Républiques de ce monde! Des empereurs,
Des regiments, des colons, des peuples, assez!

Qui remuerait les tourbillons de feu furieux,
Que nous et ceux que nous nous imaginons frères?
A nous, romanesques amis: ça va nous plaire,
Jamais nous ne travaillerons, ô flots de feux!

Europe, Asie, Amérique, disparaissez.
Notre marche vengeresse a tout occupé,
Cités et campagnes! – Nous serons écrasés!
Les volcans sauteront! Et l'Océan frappé . . .

Oh! mes amis! – Mon cœur, c'est sûr, ils sont des frères:
Noirs inconnus, si nous allions! Allons! Allons!
Ô malheur! je me sens frémir, la vieille terre,
Sur moi de plus en plus à vous! la terre fond.

Ce n'est rien: j'y suis; j'y suis toujours.

Everything for war, revenge, terror, my soul! Let us take to biting: Ah! pass away, republics of this world! Enough of emperors, regiments, colonists, and peoples!

Who should move the fierce whirlwinds of fire but we and those we imagine to be our brothers? Help us, romantic friends: this will please us. Never shall we toil, O waves of fire!

Europe, Asia, America, disappear. Our avenging march has occupied everything, cities and country! – We shall be crushed! The volcanoes will explode! And the smitten ocean . . .

Oh! my friends! – My heart, it is certain, they are brothers: dark strangers, if we should march! March! March! O misfortune! I feel myself shivering, the ancient earth, the earth falls on me as I belong more and more to you!

It is nothing: I am there; I am still there.

Chanson de la plus haute tour

OISIVE jeunesse
A tout asservie,
Par délicatesse
J'ai perdu ma vie.
Ah! Que le temps vienne
Où les cœurs s'éprennent.

Je me suis dit: laisse,
Et qu'on ne te voie:
Et sans la promesse
De plus hautes joies.
Que rien ne t'arrête,
Auguste retraite.

J'ai tant fait patience
Qu'à jamais j'oublie;
Craintes et souffrances
Aux cieux sont parties.
Et la soif malsaine
Obscurcit mes veines.

Ainsi la Prairie
A l'oubli livrée
Grandie, et fleurie

Song of the Highest Tower

IDLE youth enslaved by everything; I have destroyed my life
through sensitivity. Ah! let the time come when hearts fall in love.

I said to myself: Let it go and be seen no more: without the pro-
mise of higher joys. Let nothing stop you, solemn withdrawal.

I have been so patient that I forget for evermore; fear and suffer-
ing have left for the skies. And unhealthy thirst darkens my veins.

Like the meadow given over to neglect, grown and flowering

D'encens et d'ivraies
Au bourdon farouche
De cent sales mouches.

Ah! Mille veuvages
De la si pauvre âme
Qui n'a que l'image
De la Notre-Dame!
Est-ce que l'on prie
La Vierge Marie?

Oisive jeunesse
A tout asservie,
Par délicatesse
J'ai perdu ma vie.
Ah! Que le temps vienne
Où les cœurs s'éprennent!

with incense and darnel to the savage buzzing of a hundred dirty
flies.

Ah, the thousand widowhoods of the poor soul who only has the
image of Our Lady! Does one pray to the Virgin Mary?

Idle youth enslaved by everything; I have destroyed my life
through sensitivity. Ah, let the time come when hearts fall in love!

Aube

J'ai embrassé l'aube d'été.

Rien ne bougeait encore au front des palais. L'eau était morte. Les camps d'ombres ne quittaient pas la route du bois. J'ai marché, réveillant les haleines vives et tièdes, et les pierreries regardèrent, et les ailes se levèrent sans bruit.

La première entreprise fut, dans le sentier déjà empli de frais et blêmes éclats, une fleur qui me dit son nom.

Je ris au wasserfall blond qui s'échevela à travers les sapins: à la cime argentée je reconnus la déesse.

Alors je levai un à un les voiles. Dans l'allée, en agitant les bras. Par la plaine, où je l'ai dénoncée au coq. A la grand'ville, elle fuyait parmi les clochers et les dômes, et, courant comme un mendiant sur les quais de marbre, je la chassais.

En haut de la route, près d'un bois de lauriers, je l'ai entourée avec ses voiles amassés, et j'ai senti un peu son immense corps. L'aube et l'enfant tombèrent au bas du bois.

Au réveil, il était midi.

Dawn

I have clasped the summer dawn.

Nothing moved as yet on the brow of the palaces. The water was dead. The camps of shadows did not leave the road in the wood. I walked, awakening warm and living breaths, and the precious stones watched, and the wings rose noiselessly.

The first venture, on the path already filled with cool, pale radiance, was a flower who told me her name.

I laughed at the blond *Wasserfall* dishevelling its hair through the pine trees: on the silver summit I recognized the goddess.

Then one by one I raised the veils. In the path shaking my arms. On the plain, where I denounced her to the cock. In the great city she fled among the belfries and the domes; and, running like a beggar on the marble quays, I pursued her.

At the top of the road, near a laurel wood, I enclosed her with her clustering veils, and I felt her vast body a little. The dawn and the child fell at the foot of the wood.

At the awakening it was noon.

Matin

N'eus-je pas *une fois* une jeunesse aimable, heroïque, fabuleuse, à écrire sur des feuilles d'or, – trop de chance! Par quel crime, par quelle erreur, ai-je mérité ma faiblesse actuelle? Vous qui prétendez que des bêtes poussent des sanglots de chagrin, que des malades désespèrent, que des morts rêvent mal, tâchez de raconter ma chute et mon sommeil. Moi, je ne puis pas plus m'expliquer que le mendiant avec ses continuels *Pater* et *Ave Maria*. *Je ne sais plus parler!*

Pourtant, aujourd'hui, je crois avoir fini la relation de mon enfer. C'était bien l'enfer; l'ancien, celui dont le fils de l'homme ouvrit les portes.

Du même désert, à la même nuit, toujours mes yeux las se réveillent à l'étoile d'argent, toujours, sans que s'émeuvent les Rois de la vie, les trois mages, le cœur, l'âme, l'esprit. Quand irons-nous, par delà les grèves et les monts, saluer la naissance du travail nouveau, la sagesse

Morning

Did I not *once* have a pleasant, heroic, legendary youth to be written on leaves of gold – I was too lucky! Through what crime, what mistake have I deserved my present weakness? You who claim that beasts utter sobs of anger, that sick men despair, that the dead dream bad dreams, try to narrate my fall and my sleep. I can no more make myself clear than the beggar with his continual *Paters* and *Ave Marias*. *I no longer know how to speak!*

Yet today I think I have finished the account of my hell. It was really hell; the old one whose gates were opened by the son of man.

From the same desert, on the same night, my tired eyes always awaken to the silver star, always without the Kings of life, the three Wise Men from the east, the heart, soul and mind, being stirred. When shall we go, beyond the shores and mountains, to hail the birth of new labour, new wisdom, the flight of tyrants and demons,

nouvelle, la fuite des tyrans et des démons, la fin de la
superstition, adorer – les premiers! – Noël sur la terre?

Le chant des cieux, la marche des peuples! Esclaves, ne
maudissons pas la vie.

ÉMILE VERHAEREN

Le Moulin

Le moulin tourne au fond du soir, très lentement,
Sur un ciel de tristesse et de mélancolie;
Il tourne et tourne, et sa voile, couleur de lie,
Est triste et faible et lourde et lasse, infiniment.

Depuis l'aube, ses bras, comme des bras de plainte,
Se sont tendus et sont tombés; et les voici
Qui retombent encor, là-bas, dans l'air noirci
Et le silence entier de la nature éteinte.

Un jour souffrant d'hiver sur les hameaux s'endort,
Les nuages sont las de leurs voyages sombres,

the end of superstition, to worship – for the first time! – Christmas
on earth?

The song of the heavens, the advance of the peoples! Slaves, let
us not blaspheme life.

The Mill

Very slowly the mill turns in the depth of the evening against a
sorrowful, melancholy sky; it turns and turns, and its purple sail
is infinitely sad and weak, heavy and tired.

Since dawn its arms, like arms of entreaty, have been held out
and have fallen; and here they are falling again down there in the
blackened air and the total silence of lifeless nature.

A sick winter's day sleeps above the hamlets, the clouds are tired

Et le long des taillis qui ramassent leurs ombres,
Les ornières s'en vont vers un horizon mort.

Autour d'un vieil étang, quelques huttes de hêtre
Très misérablement sont assises en rond;
Une lampe de cuivre éclaire leur plafond
Et glisse une lueur aux coins de leur fenêtre.

Et dans la plaine immense, au bord du flot dormeur,
Ces torpides maisons, sous le ciel bas, regardent,
Avec les yeux fendus de leurs vitres hagardes,
Le vieux moulin qui tourne et, las, qui tourne et meurt.

Vers le futur

Ô RACE humaine aux destins d'or vouée,
As-tu senti de quel travail formidable et battant,
Soudainement, depuis cent ans,
Ta force immense est secouée?

of their dark journeys, and along the copses that gather their shadows the dirt tracks go towards a dead horizon.

Around an old pond some beech-wood huts are wretchedly placed in a circle; a copper lamp lights up their ceilings and slips a gleam to the corners of their windows.

And in the vast plain, beside the sleeping wave, these torpid houses beneath the low sky gaze with the split eyes of their sunken window-panes at the old mill turning, turning, alas! and dying.

Towards the Future

O HUMAN race vowed to golden destinies, have you felt by what powerfully driving labour your vast strength has suddenly been shaken for the last hundred years?

L'acharnement à mieux chercher, à mieux savoir,
Fouille comme à nouveau l'ample forêt des êtres,
Et malgré la broussaille où tel pas s'enchevêtre
L'homme conquiert sa loi des droits et des devoirs.

Dans le ferment, dans l'atôme, dans la poussière,
La vie énorme est recherchée et apparaît.
Tout est capté dans une infinité de rets
Que serre ou que distend l'immortelle matière.

Héros, savant, artiste, apôtre, aventurier,
Chacun troue à son tour le mur noir des mystères
Et grâce à ces labeurs groupés ou solitaires,
L'être nouveau se sent l'univers tout entier.

Et c'est vous, vous les villes,
Debout
De loin en loin, là-bas, de l'un à l'autre bout
Des plaines et des domaines,
Qui concentrez en vous assez d'humanité,
Assez de force rouge et de neuve clarté,
Pour enflammer de fièvre et de rage fécondes

The fury to discover more, to know more, ransacks, as if anew,
the wide forest of being, and, in spite of the briars where certain
footsteps are entangled, man conquers his law of rights and duties.

In the leaven, in the atom, in the dust, vast life is sought and ap-
pears. Everything is snared in an infinity of nets that immortal mat-
ter compresses or distends.

Hero, scholar, artist, apostle, explorer, each one in his turn
pierces the dark wall of mystery and, thanks to this collective or
solitary toil, the new being feels itself the whole universe.

And it is you, you the towns, standing at intervals from one end
to the other of the plains and estates, who concentrate within your-
selves enough humanity, enough red strength and new light to en-
flame with fertile rage and fever the patient or violent brains of

Les cervelles patientes ou violentes
De ceux
Qui découvrent la règle et résument en eux
Le monde.

L'esprit de la campagne était l'esprit de Dieu;
Il eut la peur de la recherche et des révoltes,
Il chut; et le voici qui meurt, sous les essieux
Et sous les chars en feu des nouvelles récoltes.

La ruine s'installe et souffle aux quatre coins
D'où s'acharnent les vents, sur la plaine finie,
Tandis que la cité lui soutire de loin
Ce qui lui reste encor d'ardeur dans l'agonie.

L'usine rouge éclate où seuls brillaient les champs;
La fumée à flots noirs rase les toits d'église;
L'esprit de l'homme avance et le soleil couchant
N'est plus l'hostie en or divin qui fertilise.

Renaîtront-ils, les champs, un jour, exorcisés
De leurs erreurs, de leurs affres, de leur folie;
Jardins pour les efforts et les labeurs lassés,
Coupes de clarté vierge et de santé remplies?

those who discover the rule and resume the world in themselves.

The spirit of the countryside was the spirit of God; it was afraid of discovery and revolts, it fell; and now it is dying beneath the axle-trees and the fiery chariots of the new harvests.

Ruin sits down and blows to the four corners whence the winds rage, over the desolate plain, while from afar the city draws away from it what still remains of passion in its agony.

The red factory flares where the fields alone shone; the black waves of smoke shave the church roofs; man's spirit marches on, and the setting sun is no more the fertilizing Host in divine gold.

Will the fields one day be born again exorcized of their mistakes, their terrors, their stupidity; gardens for tired effort and labour, cups filled with virgin light and health?

Referont-ils, avec l'ancien et bon soleil,
Avec le vent, la pluie et les bêtes serviles,
En des heures de sursaut libre et de réveil,
Un monde enfin sauvé de l'emprise des villes?

Ou bien deviendront-ils les derniers paradis
Purgés des dieux et affranchis de leurs présages,
Où s'en viendront rêver, à l'aube et aux midis,
Avant de s'endormir dans les soirs clairs, les sages?

En attendant, la vie ample se satisfait
D'être une joie humaine, effrénée et féconde;
Les droits et les devoirs? Rêves divers que fait,
Devant chaque espoir neuf, la jeunesse du monde!

JULES LAFORGUE

Esthétique

La Femme mûre ou jeune fille,
J'en ai frôlé toutes les sortes,
Des faciles, des difficiles;
Voici l'avis que j'en rapporte:

Will they create again with the old kind sun, with the wind, the rain, and menial animals, at hours of free uprising and awakening, a world saved at last from the grip of the towns?

Or else will they become the last paradises, purged of the gods and freed from their omens, where sages will come to dream at dawn or noon before falling asleep in the clear evenings?

Meanwhile, abundant life is satisfied to be immoderate, fertile human joy; rights and duties? The various dreams that the world's youth creates before each new hope!

Aesthetic

Ripe woman or young girl, I have had a brush with every kind, easy ones, difficult ones. Here is the opinion I bring back:

C'est des fleurs diversement mises,
Aux airs fiers ou seuls selon l'heure;
Nul cri sur elles n'a de prise;
Nous jouissons, Elle demeure.

Rien ne les tient, rien ne les fâche,
Elles veulent qu'on les trouve belles,
Qu'on le leur râle et leur rabâche,
Et qu'on les use comme telles;

Sans souci de serments, de bagues,
Suçons le peu qu'elles nous donnent,
Notre respect peut être vague,
Leurs yeux sont hauts et monotones.

Cueillons sans espoirs et sans drames,
La chair vieillit après les roses;
Oh! parcourons le plus de gammes!
Car il n'y a pas autre chose.

They are flowers variously dressed, with proud or lonely airs according to the hour; no cry has any power over them; we enjoy, She remains.

Nothing holds them, nothing angers them, they want us to find them beautiful, to croak it at them and keep on saying it and use them as such;

Without worrying about oaths and rings, let us suck the little that they give us; our respect can be vague, their eyes are haughty and monotonous.

Without hope or scenes let us pluck; after roses the flesh grows old; Oh let us run through as many scales as possible! For there is nothing else.

La Mélancolie de Pierrot

LE premier jour, je bois leurs yeux ennuyés ...
　　Je baiserais leurs pieds,
　　A mort. Ah! qu'elles daignent
　　Prendre mon cœur qui saigne!
Puis on cause ... – et ça devient de la Pitié;
Et enfin je leur offre mon amitié.

C'est de pitié, que je m'offre en frère, en guide;
　　Elles me croient timide,
　　Et clignent d'un œil doux:
　　«Un mot, je suis à vous!»
(Je te crois) Alors, moi, d'étaler les rides
De ce cœur, et de sourire dans le vide ...

Et soudain j'abandonne la garnison,
　　Feignant de trahisons!
　　(Je l'ai échappé belle!)
　　Au moins, m'écrira-t-elle?
Point. Et je la pleure toute la saison ...
– Ah! J'en ai assez de ces combinaisons!

Pierrot's Melancholy

THE first day I drink their bored eyes ... I would kiss their feet to death. Ah, let them consent to take my bleeding heart! Then we chat ... and it becomes pity, and at last I offer them my friendship.

It is from pity that I offer myself as brother and guide; they think me timid and wink a gentle eye: 'A word and I am yours!' (I believe you.) Then I begin to show the wrinkles of this heart and to smile into the void ...

And suddenly I surrender the town, alleging treason! (I have had a narrow escape!) At least she will write to me? No, and I weep for her all that season ... Ah, I have enough of these arrangements!

Qui m'apprivoisera le cœur! belle cure...
Suis si vrai de nature
Aie la douceur des sœurs!
Oh viens! suis pas noceur,
Serait-ce donc une si grosse aventure
Sous le soleil? dans toute cette verdure...

Dimanches

BREF, j'allais me donner d'un «Je vous aime»
Quand je m'avisai non sans peine
Que d'abord je ne me possédais pas bien moi-même.

(Mon Moi, c'est Galathée aveuglant Pygmalion!
Impossible de modifier cette situation.)

Ainsi donc, pauvre, pâle et piètre individu
Qui ne croit à son Moi qu'à ses moments perdus,
Je vis s'effacer ma fiancée
Emportée par le cours des choses,
Telle l'épine voit s'effeuiller,
Sous prétexte de soir sa meilleure rose.

Who will tame my heart! A fine cure... I am so true by nature;
have the gentleness of sisters! Oh come! I am no rake, would it be
such a big adventure under the sun? In all this greenery...

Sundays

IN short, I was going to give myself with an 'I love you', when I
realized not without anguish that, in the first place, I did not really
possess myself.
(My self is Galathea blinding Pygmalion! It is impossible to
change this situation.)
So then, a poor, pale and wretched creature, only believing in his
self at forgotten moments, I saw my fiancée disappear, carried away
by the course of things, as the briar sees its loveliest rose shed its
petals under pretext of its being evening.

Or, cette nuit anniversaire, toutes les Walkyries du vent
Sont revenues beugler par les fentes de ma porte:
Væ soli!
Mais, ah! qu'importe?
Il fallait m'en étourdir avant!
Trop tard! ma petite folie est morte!
Qu'importe *Væ soli!*
Je ne retrouverai plus ma petite folie.

Le grand vent bâillonné,
S'endimanche enfin le ciel du matin.
Et alors, eh! allez donc, carillonnez,
Toutes cloches des bons dimanches!
Et passez layettes et collerettes et robes blanches
Dans un frou-frou de lavande et de thym
Vers l'encens et les brioches!
Tout pour la famille, quoi! *Væ soli!* C'est certain.

La jeune demoiselle à l'ivoirin paroissien
Modestement rentre au logis.
On le voit, son petit corps bien reblanchi
Sait qu'il appartient
A un tout autre passé que le mien!

Now, on this anniversary night, all the Valkyries of the wind
have returned to bellow through the cracks of my door: *Woe to the
lonely!* But, ah! What does it matter? They should have deafened
me with it before! Too late! My little folly is dead! What does *Woe
to the lonely* matter! I shall not find my little folly again.

With the vast wind gagged, the morning sky at last puts on its
Sunday clothes. And then, come, ring out, all you bells of fine
Sundays! And put on baby linen and collarettes and white frocks in
a rustling of lavender and thyme towards incense and rolls! Every-
thing for the family, eh! *Woe to the lonely!* Certainly.

The young lady with the ivory prayer-book modestly comes
back to her home. It is apparent that her little body, made all white
once again, knows that it belongs to quite another past than mine!

Mon corps, ô ma sœur, a bien mal à sa belle âme ...

Oh! voilà que ton piano
Me recommence, si natal maintenant!
Et ton cœur qui s'ignore s'y ânonne
En ritournelles de bastringues à tout venant,
Et ta pauvre chair s'y fait mal! ...
A moi, Walkyries!
Walkryies des hypocondries et des tueries!

Ah! que je te les tordrais avec plaisir,
Ce corps bijou, ce cœur à ténor,
Et te dirais leur fait, et puis encore
La manière de s'en servir,
De s'en servir à deux.
Si tu voulais seulement m'approfondir ensuite un peu!

Non, non! C'est sucer la chair d'un cœur élu,
Adorer d'incurables organes
S'entrevoir avant que les tissus se fanent
En monomanes, en reclus!

My body, O my sister, has quite a pain in its beautiful soul ...
O how your piano renews me – so like a birth now! And your heart,
ignorant of itself, stammers to every comer in the burdens of dance-
halls, and your poor flesh hurts itself! ... Help, Valkyries! Valkyries
of hypochondria and slaughter!

Ah! How gladly I would wring them for you, that darling body,
that tenor heart, and would tell you their business, and then again
the way to use them, to use them both of us together. If you would
only look into me a little afterwards!

No, no! That would be to suck the flesh of a dedicated heart, to
adore incurable organs, to get a glimpse of one another before the
tissues wither into monomaniacs, into hermits!

Et ce n'est pas sa chair qui me serait tout,
Et je ne serais pas qu'un grand cœur pour elle,
Mais quoi s'en aller faire les fous
Dans des histoires fraternelles!
L'âme et la chair, la chair et l'âme,
C'est l'Esprit édénique et fier
D'être un peu l'Homme avec la Femme.

En attendant, oh! garde-toi des coups de tête,
Oh! file ton rouet et prie et reste honnête.

– Allons, dernier des poètes,
Toujours enfermé tu te rendras malade!
Vois, il fait beau temps, tout le monde est dehors,
Va donc acheter deux sous d'ellébore,
Ça te fera une petite promenade.

And it is not her flesh that would be everything to me. And I
would be something more than a great heart for her, but how can
one go playing the fool with this talk of brotherly love! The soul
and the flesh, the flesh and the soul, it is the proud spirit of Eden to
play the Man a bit with a Woman.

Meanwhile, Oh keep yourself from rash actions, Oh spin your
wheel and pray and remain honest.

Come, meanest of poets, you will make yourself ill, if you are
always shut up! See, the weather is fine, everyone is out of doors;
then go and buy a pennyworth of hellebore. That will make a little
walk for you.

PART FOUR

THE TWENTIETH CENTURY

Introduced and edited by
Anthony Hartley

INTRODUCTION

The discussion of contemporary poetry faces a critic with special problems. Among most twentieth-century French verse time has had no chance to make its own selection. Only the very beginning of the period comes within the ken of literary history. Moreover, the attitudes and tensions expressed in this poetry are so specifically those of our own age that it is hard to judge them objectively or to perceive their significance in relation to the future. Many of them are connected with the mortal crisis which has affected Europe over the last sixty years. As Paul Valéry wrote after the First World War, 'tout ne s'est pas perdu, mais tout s'est senti périr'.* How can a sick man look dispassionately at the symptoms of his own disease? An English critic necessarily feels the European malady in his bones.

Still, there are compensations for someone concerned to explain French literature to an English audience. An all too similar experience may lead to easier understanding. Other factors also make twentieth-century French poetry more accessible to English contemporaries than was the case in the preceding century. Modern communications have led to closer contacts and to the mixed blessing of a cosmopolitan eclecticism, often fostered by the transatlantic melting-pot. It is doubtful if a work of such wide and indigestible cultural references as Pound's *Cantos* would have been possible before 1900. Since 1914 – and even before – there has been an invasion of the English-speaking domain by French poetry and prose. This was not coincidental: poets such as Eliot and Pound found in Baudelaire, Rimbaud, or Laforgue the modernity for which they were looking, but they would not have been looking for it had they not wanted answers to questions largely ignored by the English and American nineteenth centuries.

However, this very fact suggests one great difference between modern French and English poetry. Whereas the English writer

*All was not lost, but everything felt itself dying.

in search of modernity had to find his models abroad, his French *confrère* had before him great nineteenth-century ancestors. French poetry began to be 'modern' with Baudelaire. Innovators though they were, recent French poets have carried out no such sweeping revolution as that led by Pound and Eliot between 1914 and 1918. Their work had largely been done for them by Baudelaire, Rimbaud, and Mallarmé, and these remain their masters, even if they are not always acknowledged. The modern French poet's conception of his own work shows an unbroken line of continuity with the nineteenth century. Like their predecessors, twentieth-century poets have justified the pre-eminent importance they attach to poetry by a series of myths. They, too, have attributed to language all the magical power of a spell pronounced by the poet/mage intent upon the creation of his own universe. Up to 1914 that universe was usually to be a *re-creation*, a celebration, of the natural world around the poet, and for this return from the azure distances of Mallarmé or the mythomania of Rimbaud a wave of vitalistic optimism was responsible. After the War and the broken aspirations it left in its wake, there was a retreat from exterior reality. Poetry was once again felt to offer an alternative universe rather than a re-creation of the one immediately visible to the eye of the poet. This alternative might be found in the unconscious or in some fracturing of everyday phenomena, in the delirium of the machine or the horror of madness, but there was no doubt that the poem/spell could conjure up a new heaven and earth, and, with the Surrealists, poetry, from being a form of magic, was to become a religion, a self-sufficient way of life. All this has its roots deep in the nineteenth century, and it is significant that the best book on modern French poetry should be called *De Baudelaire au surréalisme*. The implicit unity is real enough.

Stylistically, there is also a considerable gap between modern English and French verse. French poets have continued to live off the Romantic inheritance at a time when, in this country, writers were turning to a dry, witty style frequently based on Corbière and Laforgue as well as on English seventeenth-century poets. Despite Apollinaire, Max Jacob, or even Raymond Queneau, this tradition has been played down in France. Also there are the old difficulties for the English reader: rhetoric and the more abstract quality of the French language. Although attempts have been made to arrive at a barer type of verse, poets such as Claudel or Saint-John Perse remain great rhetoricians, while even the purer lyricism of an Éluard or a Supervielle is more of an oration than would be the case in English.

To these difficulties must be added the use by modern French poets of an increasingly wide range of imagery. The English reader, who might find French classical poetry lacking in surprise, is likely to be dazzled and bewildered by a coruscating use of language. A good deal of the obscurity of modern French poetry lies in the ceaseless succession of images often only connected by an arbitrary act of the poet's will. Instead of a logical progression in the poem, which might be represented graphically by a straight line, we often – particularly since Apollinaire and Reverdy – get a sun-burst effect, with the subject of the poem giving off imagery in all directions, so that the reader is faced with a number of disparates connected only through the very themes they are meant to incarnate. A poem like Apollinaire's *Fête* shows the process at work – much affected by modern poster techniques:

> *Deux fusants*
> *Rose éclatement*
> *Comme deux seins que l'on dégrafe*
> *Tendent leurs bouts insolemment*
> IL SUT AIMER
> *quelle épitaphe*

Two shells, a pink burst, like two breasts undone, insolently hold out their tips. HE KNEW HOW TO LOVE – what an epitaph!

There is a logical thread, but it is tenuous. On the other hand, the sexual imagery arises directly out of the subject of the poem – the nostalgia of a soldier at the front. There is no denying, however, that this way of handling language makes many modern French poems hard for a foreigner to understand. Yet, with a little care, any English reader familiar with his own contemporary poetry should be able to get used to it. The difference is one of degree rather than kind.

Metrically, recent French poetry might seem to mark a considerable departure from previous tradition. The *vers libre* has become more popular, and the somewhat eccentric stylistic habits of many moderns – lack of punctuation, use of capitals, irregular spacing of lines, and so forth – emphasize the break. In fact, the actual rhythms of poetry have changed far less than the style. Beneath the prose poems of Saint-John Perse marches the sounding alexandrine of Hugo and even the quieter tones of Racine. Apollinaire or Desnos, for all their modernity, rely on traditional lyrical rhythms. I think it would be possible to argue that no great changes in metre are possible without some corresponding revolution in language. In the seventeenth century a revolution was carried out and did profoundly affect verse rhythms, but no such change is easily conceivable today. The rigid patterns of universal education, the wireless, the cinema, all militate against it. In some ways modern French poetry has made large gains: its vocabulary has been notably increased, its range widened, and its techniques made more flexible. Yet, what is surprising is the amount of continuity, considering the professedly revolutionary aims of its practitioners. Nobody writes more classically than André Breton, the acknowledged head of the Surrealist movement.*

*The best general guide to twentieth-century French poetry is still Marcel Raymond's *De Baudelaire au surréalisme*. All discussion must start from this excellent book. On individual poets, Donat O'Donnell's essays on Péguy and Claudel in *Maria Cross* are the best introduction to their work. There is also good criticism of these two poets to be found in Jacques Rivière's essay on Claudel (*Études*) and in Daniel Halévy's *Péguy et les Cahiers de la quinzaine*. For Saint-John Perse see Roger Caillois's *Le Poétique de Saint-John Perse*. On Dada Rivière's *Reconnaissance à Dada* (*Nouvelles Études*) is the best study. There is no satisfactory history of Surrealism. Maurice Nadeau's *Histoire du surréalisme* is quite uncritical, though the documents he prints, both in the book and in a supplementary volume, are very helpful. Anyone interested should read André Breton's *Les Manifestes du surréalisme*, while some pertinent remarks about the

*

By 1900 the spirit informing French intellectual and literary life was singularly unlike that of 1880. Out of the muddle of symbolists, decadents, and naturalists emerged a new generation, whose preoccupations gave a unity to its diverse talents. Something of all this can be seen in the voluminous correspondence exchanged between two young men, Henri Alain-Fournier and Jacques Rivière, from 1905 onwards. Their letters are full of their enthusiasms. They admire Barrès with some reservations. They are enchanted by Francis Jammes, swept off their feet by Claudel, and a little mystified by Gide. The clue to their preferences is to be found in the reason given by Alain-Fournier for his love of Jammes: 'J'ai aimé Francis Jammes parce qu'il n'a pas séparé la vie d'avec l'art.'* The reaction against what must have seemed the ivory tower of a Mallarmé or, on a lower level, of a Huysmans is evident. Their mood was one of conscious glorification of existence, of an acceptance of the universe, which might take the form of pantheism – 'Je sais me mêler à tout ce qui m'entoure, extasié, silencieux et accepter tout ce qui est – avec le mot: "voici que ..."'† – or else of a more philosophical vitalism bordering on a Nietzschean pursuit of energy for its own sake: 'C'est la croyance à la nécessité de chaque vie, et du bien et du mal ... Il faut que nous fassions le mal avec autant de terreur que l'ignorant; mais il faut que nous sachions que nous devions le faire.'‡

---

movement will be found in *La Poésie moderne et le sacré* by Jules Monnerot and *Qu'est-ce que la littérature?* by Jean-Paul Sartre (*Situations 2*). The third volume of Georges Poulet's *Études Sur le Temps* and the same critic's *Conscience critique* contain more essays on twentieth-century French poetry.

*I have loved Francis Jammes because he has not separated life from art.

†I can involve myself with everything surrounding me, ecstatic, silent, accepting everything that exists – with the word: 'behold' ...

‡It is the belief in the necessity of every life and of good and evil ... We must do wrong with as much terror as someone who is ignorant; but we must know that we have to do it.

This climate of feeling – it is difficult to call it anything else – was widespread in French intellectual circles before 1914. On one level, it might lead to the exaltation of the peasant virtues by a Péguy; on another, to the fascination with his own childhood of a Saint-John Perse; on yet another, to the pagan intoxication of a part of André Gide. The precise reasons for its appearance are not easy to discern. No doubt, there were a number of concordant intellectual and literary influences. Whitman, the increasing knowledge of the great Russians – the Marquis de Vogüé had begun to translate them from 1884 onwards – the philosophy of Bergson and Nietzsche – 'ce qu'on ne pardonne pas à Bergson, c'est qu'il a rompu nos fers',* said Péguy – the influence of biology with its evolutionary faith, the optimism of Comte and certain types of Socialism, the increasing effect of 'social' Catholicism – all these different currents flowed in the same direction, in the direction of a *Zeitgeist* which placed its values in mere existence, the constant dialectic of being and becoming. The onset of the new mood can be traced by the dates of some key works: Claudel's *Tête d'Or* (1890), Francis Jammes' *De l'angélus de l'aube à l'angélus du soir* (1888–97), Saint-Pol-Roux's *Les Reposoirs de la procession* (1893), Valéry's *Introduction à la méthode de Léonard de Vinci* (1895), Gide's *Les Nourritures terrestres* (1897), Péguy's *Jeanne d'Arc* (1898). The new century was to see many works follow these precursors.

There is some danger and some folly in proclaiming any general cultural movement of this kind to depend on 'influences'. What are called literary influences are usually only literary symptoms springing from the same cause as the works they are deemed to have affected.† In the case of this particular phenomenon we are faced with a spontaneous reaction on the part of a generation which had got over the disasters of the Franco–Prussian war and the Commune and was tired of the official

---

*What they do not forgive Bergson is that he has broken our chains.

†Valéry, for example, has specifically denied being influenced by Bergson, but there is an obvious similarity in many of their preoccupations.

rationalism of the Third Republic. The year 1900 lived up to its reputation as *la belle époque*. These were the years of the Dreyfus case and the sordid anti-clericalism of Combes, but they were also the years when Claudel would descend from Foochow or Tientsin leaving a trail of *crises de conscience* behind him, when there was a re-awakening of the religious spirit among intellectuals. In the world of art there was the aged Renoir and the young Picasso with his pink and blue pictures. Péguy was editing the *Cahiers de la quinzaine* and Proust ruminating his great novel. Maillol's first statue was produced at the same time as Bergson published *Le Rire*. It was a profoundly creative period, and the excitement of it vibrates in all the documents of the time.

Of course, there were some writers unaffected by the spirit of the age. Charles Maurras and the team of brilliantly corrosive young men he gathered round him at the *Action française* affirmed the power of human reason along with authoritarian political doctrines and an ill-defined cultural *latinità*. The literary side of the *Action française* was to have its influence later, playing its part in the formation of the idea of *la poésie pure* and the rediscovery of sixteenth- and early seventeenth-century French poetry.* To Maurras and his followers the Whitmanesque vitalism of the rising generation was abhorrent.

To most young men, however, life seemed good between 1900 and 1914, and they set off, cheerfully enough, to take possession of it. Their solution was to trust to instinct, to beware of the mere intellect, and, whether it led into the Catholic church, to a new paganism, or to the Abbaye de Créteil along with Jules Romains and the Unanimists, it expressed the same aspirations. In intellectual terms these might be conceived very differently; emotionally they were the same. The bad side of this widespread

---

*The concept of *poésie pure* is not, I believe, as important for the study of modern French poetry as has sometimes been thought. It can be used as a critical standard, but only after the initial creation of the poem. A poet can say that this or that is *poésie pure*. What he cannot do is to set out to write it, and, in fact, very few poets have tried to do so.

desire to possess the world was a priggish tone, a consciousness of the surpassing virtue of enjoying life, which occasionally makes a poem by Jammes or a letter by Alain-Fournier read like a boy-scout manual. Yet the main current was one of liberation. Gide put it well in *Les Nourritures terrestres*: 'Tu ne sauras jamais les efforts qu'il nous a fallu faire pour nous intéresser à la vie; mais maintenant qu'elle nous intéresse, ce sera comme toute chose – passionément.'* The duration of this feeling marks out one of the two great periods into which twentieth-century French poetry can be divided. The other runs from 1918 to 1939 and is mostly occupied by the Surrealist movement. The transition between them was the First World War.

*

Apart from their general continuity with the nineteenth century, many poets of the pre-war years were directly affected by one or other of their predecessors. It was no accident that the two greatest of them, Claudel and Valéry, had frequented Mallarmé's *salon* in the Rue de Rome; and, if Valéry was attracted by the asceticism of the older poet, Claudel was profoundly influenced by Rimbaud, to whom he ascribed his return to Catholicism. Other poets also renewed the tones of the nineteenth century. A Francis Jammes or a Charles van Lerberghe repeated the gentle lyricism of Lamartine or the *larmoyant* pathos of Verlaine. Jammes was not always fortunate in his assertion of the poetic value of common life. Jacques Rivière speaks of 'ces scènes touchantes faites pour émouvoir les bons cœurs',† and the implied accusation is just. Van Lerberghe's *Chanson d'Ève*, on the other hand, is a masterpiece of the tactful use of an intangibly feminine style. Unlike Jammes, he never falls into bathos. More of a future, however, was reserved for the flow of complex imagery to be found in Saint-Pol-Roux's poems, the

*You will never know the efforts we have had to make to become interested in life; but, now that it interests us, it will be like everything else – passionately.

†Those touching scenes created to move simple hearts.

significance of which was hardly grasped at the time even by Rémy de Gourmont, but which anticipated later styles. In his symphonic brilliance we can feel for the first time that total celebration of the universe to which the age aspired.

However, the major poets of this period are Valéry and Claudel, though the former stood aside from his contemporaries and was only to publish *La Jeune Parque* and *Charmes* in 1917 and 1922 respectively. He was one of the very few poets ever to have had the mind of a philosopher and, in this sense, continues the line of Mallarmé. Only, where Mallarmé postulated a language as his final value, Valéry postulates a consciousness, autonomous and ceaselessly self-regarding: 'Je suis étant, et me voyant; me voyant me voir, et ainsi de suite . . .'* In this introverted world of mirrors creation itself can hardly appear, or is felt as an impurity. In poems like *La Jeune Parque* or *La Pythie* recurs the theme of a violation. The consciousness of the poet is soiled by the work of which he is only the vehicle:

> *Qu'ai-je donc fait qui me condamne*
> *Pure, à ces rites odieux?*
> *Une sombre carcasse d'âne*
> *Eût bien servi de ruche aux dieux!*

What have I done then that condemns my purity to these hateful ceremonies? A dark ass's carcass would have served well enough as a hive for the gods!

For Mallarmé an aesthetic of absence had been the necessary consequence of the imperfections of language. Valéry – and it was his greatness – enlarged the debate to a point where the whole of human action is brought into question and opposed to the pure contemplation of the mind by itself which he alone valued:

> *Mais moi, Narcisse aimé, je ne suis curieux*
> *Que de ma seule essence:*
> *Tout autre n'a pour moi qu'un cœur mystérieux,*
> *Tout autre n'est qu'absence.*

But I, Narcissus beloved, am but curious of my own essence alone; any other has only a heart of mystery for me, any other is but absence.

*I exist, being and seeing myself; seeing myself see myself and so on . . .

At a moment when other poets were passionately seeking to possess themselves of the world, Valéry sought to put it from him. The question before him was, indeed, the same, but his answer was a refusal: '– Non, dit l'arbre. Il dit: *Non!* par l'étincellement de sa tête superbe . . .'*

Yet Valéry's philosophy itself illustrates the importance poetry had for him. Every time he wrote a poem he refuted his own mystery of contemplation. For him the poem became the act *par excellence*, and, in so using literature to symbolize life, he reversed the conclusions of Mallarmé without detracting from the eminent dignity which the latter had assigned to the poem within his universe. Where poetry had been for Mallarmé the opposite of chance, the nearest thing to pure being, for Valéry it became the flow of life, the disorderly return to the biological springs of existence.

Not that his poetry lacks order. In fact, its importance for him is shown by his insistence on the necessary difficulty of the craft: 'Les exigences d'une stricte prosodie sont l'artifice qui confère au langage naturel les qualités d'une matière résistante, étrangère à notre âme et comme sourde à nos désirs . . . A un dieu seulement est réservée l'ineffable indistinction de son acte et de sa pensée. Mais nous, il faut peiner; il faut connaître amèrement leur différence.'† Just as, in the realm of the mind, Valéry's nature pushed him to attempt the impossible, so his poetry had to exist at the intersection of complexity of thought and rigour of form. It, too, was a re-creation of the world, but one achieved in some sense against its author's will.

The lines of Valéry's poems are vibrant with these tensions, and the total effect is consonant with the poet's deepest pre-occupations. Nothing resembles more the Valéryan idea of a dynamic consciousness gyrating on itself than the Valéryan pic-

---

*– No, says the tree. It says: *No!* by the sparkling of its proud head . . .

†The requirements of a strict prosody are the artifice that endows natural language with the qualities of resistant matter, foreign to our soul and as though deaf to our desires . . . The ineffable coincidence of his act and thought is reserved for a god alone. But we must toil; bitterly must we know their difference.

ture of a plane-tree or palm, whose autonomy is subtly distinguished from the very first lines of the poem:

> *Tu penches, grand Platane, et te proposes nu,*
> *Blanc comme un jeune Scythe . . .*

You bend, vast plane-tree, and offer yourself naked, white as a young Scythian . . .

By the use of the verb *se proposer* the poet's own ideal of an entire self-consciousness is communicated to the object, and finds there the fulfilment which he himself could never accord it.

For, despite all Valéry's philosophical skill, the ideal of a self-regarding consciousness was deeply contradictory. The effect of the hall of mirrors within the brain could only be to validate a universal scepticism. 'C'est avec notre propre substance que nous imaginons et que nous formons une pierre, une plante, un mouvement, un *objet*: une image quelconque n'est peut-être qu'un commencement de nous-mêmes . . .'* To believe this is to indulge in a fundamental criticism of reality – a criticism which cannot be sustained in practice. As his creator came to see, Monsieur Teste will always be a monster, a distorted image formed by Valéry as a result of his experiments with consciousness: 'Je m'étais fait une île intérieure que je perdais mon temps à reconnaître et à fortifier . . .'† Where other poets make their work out of myth, it was typical of Valéry that his should be based on a hypothesis.

Life, after all, has to be lived. Poems have to be written. Valéry's scepticism casts a fine patina of illusion over his poetry, but it does not conceal the fact that the very existence of these poems depends on a necessary impurity in the immaculate consciousness of their parent. *Le Cimetière marin*, which is the greatest of Valéry's poems, is the account of such an invasion.

---

*It is with our own substance that we imagine and create a stone, a plant, a movement, an *object*: any image is perhaps only a beginning of ourselves . . .

†I had made myself an inner island, which I wasted my time exploring and fortifying . . .

The movement by which the sparkling, hypnotic mirror, in which mind finds its own reflection, is changed into the breaking waves of the fertile, life-giving sea, the Apollonian into the Dionysiac, represents the dialectic normally present within the poet. Although Valéry's philosophy of life carried him towards self-contemplation, there was no real conflict waiting to abort his poetry. He was able to seize the flow of life as easily as the contemplative ecstasy. No poet has written with more energy of the forces that move the world; in no poetry is the tension between the form and an inner dynamism so strongly felt. If Narcissus the philosopher was compelled to become Pygmalion the poet, at least his creation was one in which his own features were to remain carved for posterity.

*

Paul Claudel's relationship to the world around him was to be more direct. The keynote of his poetry is a passionate celebration of created things, a celebration justified by a carefully developed logic. The doctrine behind his poetry is mostly contained in the section *Traité de la co-naissance du monde* of his *Art poétique*. The pun – *co-naissance* meaning both 'knowledge' and 'simultaneous birth with . . .' – is significant. For Claudel the relationship existing between things is fundamentally one of passion: 'Vraiment le bleu connaît la couleur d'orange, vraiment la main son ombre sur le mur; vraiment et réellement l'angle d'un triangle connaît les deux autres au même sens qu'Isaac a connu Rebecca. Toute chose qui est, de toutes parts, désigne cela sans quoi elle n'aurait pu être.'* Any being, and man above all, is defined by its contacts with the phenomena around it. By knowing them, by a penetration of their essence, it also affirms itself, since without the limits assigned by them it could not exist. To 'know' things is therefore really to bring about their

---

*Really blue knows the colour orange, really the hand knows its shadow on the wall; really and truly the angle of a triangle knows the two others in the same sense as Isaac knew Rebecca. Everything that exists indicates on all sides that, without which it would not have been able to do so.

birth and our own. *Connaissance* and *co-naissance* are the same, and the sexual imagery is deliberate. It is precisely carnal knowledge that we have of the things of this world.

At this point language enters into the argument. For language is the sign by which we evoke objects. 'Nous les appelons, en effet, nous les évoquons en constituant en nous l'état de connaissance qui répond à leur présence sensible ... Je deviens maître, avec le mot, de l'objet qu'il représente, je puis le transporter où je veux avec moi, je puis faire comme s'il était là.'* Words then are a short cut to that establishment of the universe which is necessary to the affirmation of our own being, and here Claudel shares the belief in the magical power of language held by Baudelaire or Rimbaud. A poet can possess the universe through poetry. It is in this sense that Claudel could write: 'Mon désir est d'être le rassembleur de la terre de Dieu.'†

For the ultimate knowledge is the knowledge of God, and without it, so Claudel would claim, we are none of us complete. At the end of the possession of the world lies the possession of its first cause. As Marcel Raymond has pointed out, there is nothing Jansenist about this conception of Christianity. Claudel approaches God through the flesh of creatures made by Him. The carnal union he desires with the object in no way contradicts the aspiration towards union with God. Rather, it prefigures it.

Yet, Claudel's Christianity is very unlike the usual expression of religious feeling. Donat O'Donnell in the only significant study I know of the deepest level of Claudel's inspiration has shown the dichotomy running through his use of imagery. The opposition is between *gold* and *water* in the first place, and the meanings developed through these images are summed up by Mr O'Donnell as 'Ormuzd and Ahriman, Yin and Yang,

---

*We call them, indeed, we evoke them by creating within ourselves the state of knowledge which corresponds to their tangible presence ... With the word I become master of the object it represents, I can carry it with me where I will, I can behave as if it were there.

†My wish is to be the assembler of the land of God.

man-light and woman-dark'. What is going on inside Claudel's poetry is a continuous representation of the primal dynamic of life. Now, this dynamism might possibly be called God, but, if so, there is little resemblance to any Christian deity. No questions of right or wrong can arise in a world of perpetual orgasm. Claudel has fully realized Kierkegaard's divorce between religion and ethics. The theme of his poetry is a cosmological act which stands beyond good and evil.

Small wonder then that there are not many poets whose work is so highly charged with sensuality. Claudel is, in fact, one of the few poets to have achieved that tactile solidity which English readers often miss in French verse. Because his theme is one of constant drama, it is natural that the poetry should be dramatic in form. Even a poem like *Cantique du Rhône* is spoken – by a lay-figure, it is true. Yet, the exclamations and interrogations, succeeding one another, add to the urgency of the tone, while the loose, rather shambling metres express the human voice more closely than would be possible in stricter measures. Claudel's skill in the handling of rhythms should never be underestimated: large-scale constructions like the great Odes or the *Cantique de Mesa* are beautifully orchestrated. The danger comes when this style is applied to subjects unfitted for it. Then bathos is inevitable.

Taken as a whole, Claudel's poetry is of an epic solemnity. 'L'Art de Claudel est primitif et continu',* wrote Jacques Rivière: primitive by its erupting vitality and continuous by its creation of a whole world. The giant metaphors, the constant interplay of imagery are the outward signs of a conviction of the possibilities open to the shifting combinations of matter in its raw state. Claudel is a very great poet – even at his silliest (and he can be silly) he remains that. From his poetry as from no other we can get the swing of life's frenzied dialectic. It is hard to decide whether he should be classed as the last of the Romantics or as a baroque writer born out of his century, but both agnostic and Christian can unite to find in his work the gush of

* Claudel's art is primitive and continuous.

undifferentiated energy, the *mana* which may express itself as easily on the sexual as on the transcendental level. His possession of the world is certain. What remains obscure is in whose name it has been effected – Jehovah, the great Pan, or some more Chthonian deity.

> *Tu n'expliques rien, ô poète, mais toutes choses par toi nous deviennent explicables.*

> You explain nothing, O poet, but all things become explicable to us through you.

*

The comparison between Claudel and Péguy is almost inevitable. These two Catholic poets would, in fact, make very good material for some future Plutarch's diptych, where Claudel the intellectual and diplomat might contrast with Péguy the peasant and prophet, the universal Catholic with the French nationalist. The opposition is by no means absolute; in his own way Péguy, too, celebrates life. Only the quality is different. Instead of the fierce urges of Claudel there is something vegetable about the slow evolution of Péguy's poetry, where one line may be repeated dozens of times, while gradually changing and fulfilling itself. It is the earth – *la terre charnelle* – that he seeks to possess, and the slow laborious vitality of peasant life informs all his work. The simplicity of his poetry is the simplicity of growth. There is a calm of fulfilment in it, which is not to be found in Claudel, where the frantic tussle of procreation is always there to convulse the lines of verse. Péguy's creation of his own universe is no less total, but the resulting world is more of a real stretch of land with real trees and real human beings and less of a principle of pure energy.

> *Tel est mon paradis, dit Dieu. Mon paradis est tout ce qu'il y a de plus simple ...*
> *Ces simples enfants jouent avec leur palme et avec leurs couronnes de martyrs.*

> Such is my Paradise, says God. My Paradise is all the simplest things ... Those simple children *play* with their palms and their martyrs' crowns.

And the simple earth which Péguy celebrated was a specific earth. It was the land of France and, more particularly, that part of it lying between Orléans and Chartres – the Beauce with its rolling cornfields. Péguy's nationalism – it is a platitude to say so – takes exactly the tone of a French peasant speaking of his *pays*, a tone half pride, half exasperation. *Les Sept contre Paris* is one example of this fond enumeration of national furniture. Even God is made to testify to the greater glory of France:

> *C'est embêtant, dit Dieu. Quand il n'y aura plus ces Français,*
> *Il y a des choses que je fais, il n'y aura plus personne pour les*
> *comprendre.*

> It is tiresome, says God. When those French are no longer there, some things I do will have no one to understand them any more.

Gesta Dei per Francos . . . Péguy hardly envisaged any other demonstration of divine providence than what might be performed between the Rhine and the Pyrenees. No wonder that the cult of Jeanne d'Arc and the literary cult of Péguy – the two have gone hand in hand – have carried imperialist rather than Christian implications – notably in Indochina.

For a Catholic poet this restriction of his world was potentially serious. In fact, Péguy was usually on the generous political side. He only betrayed his own basic decency by calling for the death of Jaurès: 'la politique de la Convention Nationale c'est Jaurès dans une charette et un roulement de tambour pour couvrir cette grande voix'.* It is impossible to talk about the 'thought' of Péguy. Profoundly anti-rational, what Mr O'Donnell has called his 'darkly atavistic mind' continually returned to the grass-roots that lay somewhere at the back of childhood. In that image he made France, and in France's image he made God, thereby gravely over-simplifying all the terms in his mythical equation.

Moreover, the want of form in Péguy's poems, the *longueurs* which ruin some and the endless repetitions which disconcert in

---

*The policy of the National Convention is Jaurès in a tumbril and the roll of a drum to cover that great voice.

all, is due to this same failure to apply a critical intelligence, which he possessed, indeed, but from whose operations he exempted large areas of his basic compulsions. André Gide may have been unjust when he wrote that he did not feel any urge to select from Péguy's poetry, since the author had himself omitted to make any selection, but the magnificence of this verse, when the necessary compression is achieved, shows what was lost by sheer unwillingness to cut. The intellect also has its revenges.

At his best Péguy is capable of strength and simplicity unequalled save by Hugo. He had a firm grasp of one or two fundamental truths, and, if his peasant France seems to be a land of Cockayne, the emotion uniting men to the earth on which they were born remains real and permanent. Nationalism, after all, is a distortion of the noble emotion called patriotism, and some passages from Péguy such as the famous *Heureux ceux qui sont morts* . . . are among the most powerful expressions it has ever received. At the back of this longing to be joined to the earth lies, perhaps, a death-wish, as Mr O'Donnell has pointed out, but also the desire for a kind of consonance with the natural rhythms of growth and decay dimly felt by the dark, instinctive side of the human mind. For every mind has its dark side, and it is no criticism of Péguy as a poet that he should have drawn upon his own secret impulses. Where he might have destroyed himself as a man and a politician would have been in some attempt to compel the obedience of others to his own obsessions. But, for that, his time was too short.

*

Another poet who may be associated with the vitalist currents of the years before 1914 is Oscar Venceslas de Lubicz Milosz, who brought to the themes of Jammes a Slav intensity which lifted them out of sentimentality. Some of his stylistic devices can be criticized – his trick of repeating words or phrases is irritating – but his poems are among the most effective ever to deal with the themes of daily life from which he distilled a melancholy objectivity reminiscent of Leopardi. Valéry Larbaud found his own tone in the exaltation of travel. Anyone fascinated by frontiers will like his poems. Quite unlike most of his contemporaries was Paul-Jean Toulet, who poured an exquisite and fantastic poetry into his *Les Contrerimes* – quatrains of eight and six syllables rhymed a–b–b–a. A throwback to the minor poetry of the eighteenth century or even to earlier *gauloiserie*, his poems give something of the pleasure of the true epigram. Their eroticism is as carefully calculated as their form.

There is also a good case for connecting the work of a far greater poet with this pre-war period. Saint-John Perse had already published *Éloges* in 1909, and, in these first poems, we can see many of the elements of his poetry in their mature state. *Anabase* followed in 1922, and by that time he had assembled the whole recondite matter and manner of his verse. It is hard for a critic to penetrate its secret. Like Claudel, like Péguy, Saint-John Perse strives to create a universe, but this time it is a universe without metaphysics. The theme is the infinite wonder of the world for man, of the world as man, in some sense, creates it with his eye. Roger Caillois has emphasized the reality of all the bizarre and tumultuous imagery which this poet uses. A poem like *Vents* is encyclopaedic in its evocation of men and things, and the word gives some clue to the nature of Saint-John Perse's attempt. He would be a humanist – as Leonardo was a humanist. His poetry aspires to universality in something of the same way as a Renaissance artist or writer might have conceived it.

Unlike that of Claudel or Péguy, there is nothing primitive about Saint-John Perse's inspiration. His poetry is of an extreme sophistication, and, if he must take possession of the world, it will not be as the mystic possesses it, but as the conqueror or scientist subdues it. Only sophisticated writing enters into the spirit of childhood. Nostalgia is a civilized emotion – it is even the most destructive of civilized emotions – and it was from nostalgia for the primitive freshness of the object that Saint-John Perse made *Éloges*, the evocation of his early life in the West Indies. 'Sinon l'enfance, qu'y avait-il alors qu'il n'y a plus? . . .'*

*Except for childhood, what was there then that is there no longer? . . .

asks the poet. The whole sequence of poems expresses longing for a time when a child's contemplation served to bring people, beasts, and things into a stereoscopic focus lost with age.

Yet nostalgia brings disillusionment with it: 'Enfance, mon amour, n'était-ce que cela? . . .'* Indeed, this emotion about the past is itself the result of an acute sense of historic movement – no doubt sharpened by diplomatic duties carried out during a peculiarly insecure period. The themes of subsequent poems deal with man on the march, with exile and the mastering of the elements. To possess the earth like a conqueror, to found cities, to promulgate laws – these are the poet's preoccupations, and his poems are addressed to those who have felt the same sense of the movement of the tribes:

> *Ô vous que rafraîchit l'orage, la force vive et l'idée neuve rafraî-*
> *chiront votre couche de vivants . . .*

> O you whom the storm refreshes, the live strength and the new
> idea will refresh your human strata . . .

In these poems there is a perpetual struggle between the principles of order and disorder. On the one hand, there is the overthrow of old civilizations – 'Nous en avions assez de ces genoux trop calmes où s'enseignait le blé'† – on the other, the institution of law, rites, and ceremonies – 'ainsi la ville fut fondée et placée au matin sous les labiales d'un nom pur'.‡ The ceaseless dialectic of history which founds one civilization upon the dead carcass of another is the matter out of which a poem like *Anabase* is made.

All this is not without an inevitable pessimism and even nihilism. Man – 'les cavaleries de bronze vert sur de vastes chaussées'§ – is perpetually on the move, driven by his own consuming desires. The city is always destroyed, the tents never

---

*Childhood, my love, was it only that? . . .

†We had had enough of those too calm knees where the corn was taught.

‡So the town was founded and placed in the morning beneath the labials of a pure name.

§The cavalries of green bronze on immense highways.

pitched for long in the same spot. Saint-John Perse accepts the movement of history with all its violence and brutality:

> *Mais si un homme tient pour agréable sa tristesse, qu'on le produise dans le jour! et mon avis est qu'on le tue, sinon il y aura une sédition.*

> But if a man hold his melancholy to be pleasant, let him be brought forth into the daylight! And my opinion is that he should be killed, otherwise there will be a sedition.

In the last analysis these poems are desperately sad – tragedy is the normal form taken by humanism in art.

Saint-John Perse's style is best described by the word 'noble'. The tone is constantly aristocratic, and this is emphasized by the long, regular rhythms beneath the surface of the prose poems. The syntax is full of inversions and other departures from normal grammatical practice, and there are few poets who have as wide or as recondite a vocabulary. Saint-John Perse evidently learnt much from Rimbaud, Mallarmé, and Claudel, while there are aspects of his later poetry – the lack of transitions, the sense of a dream-like infinity – which show that the Surrealists have not been without influence on him. But his work is epic rather than lyrical, frequently showing a strong dramatic quality – which, of course, is epic too – and for this he had no model, apart from the first *Tête d'Or*, which, indeed, *Anabase* resembles.

When all allowances have been made for *Zeitgeist* and influences, Saint-John Perse remains a most original poet. His passionate *constatation* of the world and of history is the more moving in that he offers no remedy. His consolation is the assurance of immortality through creation, one that represents possibly the only valid answer for man desperate before the problem of his own transience:

> *Levez un peuple de miroirs sur l'ossuaire des fleuves, qu'ils interjettent appel dans la suite des siècles! Levez des pierres à ma gloire, levez des pierres au silence ...*

> Raise up a people of mirrors over the rivers' charnel-house, let them make appeal to the succession of centuries! Raise up stones to my fame, raise up stones to the silence ...

The appetite for the world, the desire for the brightness of things, only makes for more anguish as they ceaselessly and inevitably pass away. 'Enfance, mon amour . . .'* Is it an accident that the twentieth century has produced a literature of nostalgia for childhood in quantities never seen before? The poetry of Saint-John Perse was formed in its essentials before 1914, but it looks forward to the catastrophes of the coming years as well as back to the *élan vital* of 1900.

*

The year 1914 is the key date for the spiritual development of twentieth-century France. Despite the continuing productivity and ruthless longevity of the generation of 1900, nothing was the same afterwards. For some years before there had been signs that the serene horizon of the early century was breaking up. Already in 1909 Marinetti's First Futurist Manifesto had given vent to a dithyrambic adoration of the age of the machine: 'We shall sing of great crowds in the excitement of Labour, Pleasure or Rebellion; of the nocturnal vibration of arsenals and workshops beneath their electric moons; of greedy stations swallowing smoking snakes; of adventurous liners scenting the horizon; of broad-chested locomotives galloping on rails . . .' And the exaltation of the modern was accompanied by maxims of violence which were to have a familiar ring some years later: 'We are out to glorify War – the only health-giver of the world – Militarism, Patriotism, the Destructive arm of the Anarchist, Ideas that kill, Contempt for Women . . .' 'Poetry must be a violent onslaught. There is no masterpiece without aggressiveness.'† Associated with this rather psychopathic modernity was the advent of Cubist painting and the dark humours of Alfred Jarry, whose *Ubu Roi* had been staged as far back as 1896. In 1908 Jacques Rivière produced his *Introduction à la métaphysique du rêve*, where the exploration of the unconscious is set

*Childhood, my love . . .

† Quoted from *Modern French Painters*, by R. H. Wilenski, p. 223. The subsequent use made of these ideas certainly justifies us in regarding contemporary cults of 'toughness' with the deepest suspicion.

before the writer both as theme and ideal. M. Raymond has shown that these two currents, in appearance contradictory, were really complementary. Rivière and the Futurists had this in common: they both encouraged the artist to draw his material from outside the bounds of normal human experience. To an unlimited confidence in the natural world was to succeed a withdrawal from it. The new appeal was to be to a universe of anarchic powers, where the vitalism of Claudel or Péguy would issue from depths uncontrolled by the human will or be found in the autonomous action of a robot world rebelling against its masters. And, just as an earlier generation of poets had re-created natural life through language, so their successors would construct worlds, whose materials they found within themselves. Denying the everyday horrors of the post-Sarajevo world, they, like their nineteenth-century predecessors, endeavoured to find their own solutions through the operation of the word. After 1914 that word was most frequently to be *Merde!* – the expletive in which Jarry so accurately anticipated the cynicism of a generation to come.

*

There was, however, little in the way of cynicism about the first poet to incarnate the new spirit. In Guillaume Apollinaire many different types of poetry meet. The popular lyricism of the traditional French *chanson*, the sentimentality of Verlaine or Lamartine, a Slav passion, a central European pathos, an eye for the modern that made him the first 'Cubist' poet – all these varied elements went to compose a *persona* which was always the main theme of his poetry. The result was a Chaplinesque figure, *le pauvre Guillaume*, a little man always hoping for the miraculous, always a prey to nostalgia and melancholy in the world of the modern city. In one sense Apollinaire inherited the half-serious, half-mocking attitude of Laforgue, in another he developed the *poésie des villes* which Baudelaire had inaugurated.

His main talent was lyrical. Poems such as *Le Pont Mirabeau* or *La Blanche Neige* are in the most constant tradition of the songs which Alceste preferred to bad sonnets – 'Voilà ce que peut dire un cœur vraiment épris.'* The innocence of Apollinaire's eye is shown by the way in which he described the sordid trench warfare of 1914–18:

> *Ah Dieu! que la guerre est jolie*
> *Avec ses chants, ses longs loisirs ...*

Ah! God! how pretty war is with its songs, its long rests.

Few other poets would have chosen precisely that epithet for modern war, and the contrast produces that effect of some harsh reality emerging from make-believe which is part of Apollinaire's secret. His modernity can be illustrated from *Zone*, where the verbal skill, the play on words, the irregular metre might serve to hide the fundamentally lyrical character of the poem from anyone not acquainted with his technique. Apollinaire was a great technical innovator – though the poems shaped like objects in *Calligrammes* hardly seem his happiest invention – and he brought to the simplest traditional themes an artistry which lifted them into major poetry. The *Chanson du mal-aimé* is a great poem by any standard.

The most original gift to French poetry of Apollinaire, coming when he did, was to reproduce in verse the eclectic and disordered consciousness of modern man with its scraps of culture, its vague reminiscences of tradition, its hot sensuality, and its longing for innocence. More virile than Verlaine, less grim than Villon, like them he represented *l'homme moyen sensuel*. *L'homme moderne* too: Apollinaire's poems often seem to dissolve into images naturally suited to the cinema. How curious that it should have been left to this poet of Polish origin to re-introduce the heritage of an older France and link it with contemporary Paris, the bars, the tramways, and the posters by Toulouse-Lautrec. And how ironic that a poet concerned above all with fantasy should have had to cope with so horrible a reality as war. Finally, in one of his best poems, *La Jolie Rousse*, Apollinaire wears the dazed expression of a man crushed

---

*That is what a heart really in love might say.

by a fate he does not understand. The last line is full of pathos: 'Ayez pitié de moi.'* In this, too, he was modern.

Along with Apollinaire can be classed Max Jacob, who was his friend, and whose fate it was to be trapped in a second Armageddon, as Apollinaire had been in the first. Jacob's poetry is again that of an innocent – an innocent with deep religious intuitions. Unlike Apollinaire he is at his best when speaking through the mouth of some invented character – a Breton seaman or a girl waiting for her lover. Most of his poetry is basically dramatic, and its tone varies widely, passing from fantasy to satire to simple sentimentality. He is not a great poet, but he is an agreeable one. Léon-Paul Fargue also became known just before and after the First World War. His prose poems contain some of the best descriptions ever written of the seamier parts of Paris, the cheap hotels and the desolation of the *zone*. His dominant emotion is nostalgia and he adds to it a capacity for conveying blank unhappiness which is all his own. The poems of Jules Supervielle are in some ways more like those of the pre-war poets. They are re-creations of the world of men and beasts, but tinged with metaphysical disquiet. Behind his consciousness of life's goodness lies an uneasy sense of its brevity. His verse is impregnated with natural piety and humility before the surprising variety of the universe, and tragic grandeur is added to it by the poet's certainty of death's advent and his pity for those about to die. The subtly natural rhythms of his verse convey as well as that of any other twentieth-century poet the loneliness, the grandeur, and the feebleness of man. Balanced between optimism and pessimism, he is fully of this transitional period between 1914 and the Surrealists. Pierre-Jean Jouve also looks both ways in his sprawling, rather apocalyptic verse. Some of his compositions stem from the Unanimists, while others anticipate Surrealism in their use of the human unconscious, and their association of religious and sexual imagery.

The most considerable poet of this period is Pierre Reverdy, who throughout the War published in the reviews *Sic* and *Nord-*

*Take pity on me.

Sud, which were to play a part in preparing movements like Dada and Surrealism. His poems are metaphysical, and their characteristic feeling is that of anguish. He constantly comes back to the same moment: the moment when the mask drops, the curtain is pulled aside, the wall cracks, or the mirror is broken – the moment of disquiet:

> *Voici le point du jour*
> *Voici la tête grise*
> *Le masque de la nuit tombe dans les étangs*
> *Et la figure rit . . .*

Here is the dawn, here is the grey head, the mask of the night falls into the ponds, and the face laughs . . .

Amid a kaleidoscopic jumble of images and syntax, a curiously abstract tragedy makes itself felt – again a tragedy of the impermanence of things. Reverdy has realized almost completely the spiritual exercise involved in an interior dissolution of the world of appearances. He was the true precursor of Dada except for the fact that he does express the human side of the possible disaster. For him:

> *La vie entière est en jeu*
> *Constamment*
> *Nous passons à côté du vide élégamment*
> > *sans tomber*
> *Mais parfois quelque chose en nous fait tout trembler*
> *Et le monde n'existe plus.*

The whole of life is at stake constantly. We pass beside the void elegantly, without falling, but sometimes something in us makes everything tremble, and the world no longer exists.

To perceive this is the poet's *raison d'être*: 'Prisonnier dans les apparences, à l'étroit dans ce monde, d'ailleurs purement imaginaire, dont se contente le commun, il en franchit l'obstacle pour atteindre l'absolu et le réel; là, son esprit se meut avec aisance.'* The claim takes us back to the nineteenth century.

*A prisoner in appearances, cramped in this world – a purely imaginary one, moreover – with which the majority is content, he crosses the obstacle presented by it to reach the absolute and the real; there his spirit moves at ease.

Reverdy's disbelief in appearances, however, never becomes entirely nihilistic. He is capable of pity for the ills to which men are subject, superficial though they may be. Out of his contemplation of the cracks in the façade of physical reality he creates a classical lyricism which is highly original. This is a world of broken glass, of reflections on steel, of sombre landscapes, but it is one which, more than any other, provides a lyrical equivalent for the ravaged Europe of 1918 and 1945.

*

The reaction after the war years and, with it, the full force of the younger generation's protest against the world in which they found themselves was to be felt with Dada and the Surrealists.* The two movements can be taken together as different moments of the same rebellion, and there is little point in entering into the doctrinal clash between Tristan Tzara and André Breton. Dada was theoretically founded in Zürich on 8 February 1916, by Tzara, R. Hülsenbeck, and Hans Arp, but its extension to France dated from the arrival of Tzara in Paris in 1919, and the form it took there owed a great deal to native French influence – to Breton, who, under the guidance of Jacques Vaché, inventor of *humour noir*, had been thinking along the same lines, and even to Apollinaire, who had written in 1917: 'La surprise est le plus grand ressort nouveau. C'est par la surprise, par la place importante qu'il fait à la surprise, que l'esprit nouveau se distingue de tous les mouvements artistiques et littéraires qui l'ont

---

*A good account of the state of feeling among young French intellectuals in the immediate post-war period can be found in *Âge de l'homme*, by Michel Leiris, who was himself a Surrealist. Paul Nizan's *La Conspiration* is also a typical document, but deals with the more specifically political side of the general demoralization. The relationship of the French bourgeois intellectuals with the Communist Party during the twenties was distinguished by just as much mutual misunderstanding and just as pathetic attempts to find relief in action as was that of their English fellows during the thirties.

précédé . . .'* Between 1919 and 1924 the Dadaists published in the review *Littérature*.

The spirit of Dada was almost entirely negative. 'Qu'est-ce que c'est beau? qu'est-ce que c'est laid? Qu'est-ce que c'est grand, fort, faible? Qu'est-ce que c'est Carpentier, Renan, Foch? Connais pas. Qu'est-ce que c'est moi? Connais pas, connais pas, connais pas, connais pas.'† Jacques Rivière defined the ambitions of Dada as follows: 'Saisir l'être avant qu'il n'ait cédé à la compatibilité, l'atteindre dans son incohérence, ou mieux dans sa cohérence primitive . . . substituer à son unité logique, forcément acquise, son unité absurde, seule originelle: tel est le but que poursuivent tous les Dadas en écrivant . . .'‡ And the result is that 'les Dadas renoncent, très consciemment, à faire des *œuvres*'.§ 'Les Dadas ne considèrent plus les mots que comme des accidents: ils les laissent se produire.'‖ The connection of all this with Surrealism is obvious enough, as is that of the violent attempts to shock the bourgeoisie, with which the Dadaists diversified their literary activity. Only, from the point of view of someone interested in poetry rather than in the sociology of the twenties, Dada has the disadvantage of having left little behind it. As Rivière wrote: 'La plupart des poèmes Dada sont non pas seulement indéchiffrables, mais proprement illisibles . . .'¶

* Surprise is the greatest new main-spring. It is by surprise, by the important place it assigns to surprise, that the new spirit is differentiated from all the literary and artistic movements which have preceded it.

† What is beautiful? What is ugly? What is big, strong, weak? What is Carpentier, Renan, Foch? Don't know. What am I? Don't know, don't know, don't know, don't know.

‡ To seize upon being before it has yielded to compatibility, to reach it in its incoherence, or rather in its primitive coherence . . . to substitute for its logical unity, necessarily an acquired characteristic, its unity of absurdity, which is the only original one: such is the goal which all the Dadas try to reach when writing . . .

§ The Dadas quite consciously renounce the creation of *works*.

‖ The Dadas no longer consider words as anything other than accidents: they let them happen.

¶ Most of the Dada poems are not only indecipherable, but really unreadable.

Surrealism is a more positive affair and was to have a far deeper influence on French poetry. In relation to Dada it represents the moment when the latter's sterility became apparent. In defining its essentials we may neglect a great deal of the more public side of it – the rows, the mutual exchange of abuse, the excommunications, the narrowly sectarian atmosphere imposed by the powerful personality of Breton, who, if not the Pope, frequently behaved like the Lenin of the Parisian literary world. Neither do mere bad manners, which was the form all too often taken by the revolt of the young men of the twenties, need any notice here. Yet, as Jules Monnerot and Jean-Paul Sartre have pointed out, these things have a symptomatic significance. The indiscriminate violence of the Surrealists had unpleasant political overtones, while Breton's theological approach to controversy lies at the heart of the movement's history.

In an early Surrealist tract the thing is put clearly: 'Le surréalisme n'est pas un moyen d'expression nouveau ou plus facile, ni même une métaphysique de la poésie. Il est un moyen de libération totale de l'esprit et de tout ce qui lui ressemble.'* Surrealism then is a way of life: 'Nous sommes des spécialistes de la Révolte.'† Yet we are faced at once with a paradox. How does this connect with literature and art? How is it that Breton's first manifesto deals basically with the production of works of the imagination? The essential of the manifesto is aesthetic: 'Pour cette fois, mon intention était de faire justice de la *haine du merveilleux* qui sévit chez certains hommes, de ce ridicule sous lequel ils veulent le faire tomber. Tranchons-en: le merveilleux est toujours beau, n'importe quel merveilleux est beau, il n'y a même que le merveilleux qui soit beau.'‡ And Aragon

---

*Surrealism is not a new or easier means of expression or even a metaphysic of poetry. It is a means of total liberation of the spirit and of everything resembling it.

†We are specialists of Revolt.

‡This time my intention was to attack the *hatred of the marvellous*, which plagues certain men, that ridicule with which they wish to cover it. Let us cut the matter short: the marvellous is always beautiful, anything marvellous is beautiful, it is even only the marvellous which is beautiful.

was later to write: 'Le surréalisme est l'inspiration reconnue, acceptée et pratiquée. Non plus comme une visitation inexplicable, mais comme une faculté qui s'exerce.'* In other words, Surrealism envisages as its main activity a return to the sources of the imagination, which shall itself be a sufficient principle of renewal for the whole of life. 'L'homme propose et dispose. Il ne tient qu'à lui de s'appartenir tout entier, c'est-à-dire de maintenir à l'état anarchique la bande chaque jour plus redoutable de ses désirs. La poèsie le lui enseigne.'† The result of artistic activity, the poem or the painting, is seen as merely incidental to the inner regeneration of man brought about by the *ascesis* involved in its production. The means which the Surrealists, under the guidance of Freud, chose for the creation of the work of art – automatic writing or free association of words – were entirely subordinate to the main end of a strictly religious conversion: 'Le surréalisme n'est pas une forme poétique. Il est un cri de l'esprit qui retourne vers lui-même et est bien décidé à broyer désespérément ses entraves.'‡

Surrealism, in fact, may be regarded as a continuation of the effort to make of art a substitute religion which runs through the whole French nineteenth century. Under the influence of the powerfully logical mind of Breton, the Surrealists were prepared to be more consequent than Rimbaud or Mallarmé. For regeneration they looked to the powers of the human imagination rather than to a magical use of language. And the weakness of this approach, from a literary point of view, was that it shifted the emphasis from the work of art to the processes which produced it. Dada and then Surrealism were the logical development of the nineteenth century's attempt to attribute a

---

*Surrealism is inspiration recognized, accepted, and practised. No longer as an inexplicable visitation, but as a faculty which is used.

†Man proposes and disposes. It only depends on him to belong wholly to himself, that is, to keep in their anarchic state the company of his desires which grows more formidable every day. Poetry teaches him this.

‡Surrealism is not a poetic form. It is a cry of the spirit turning on itself and quite decided to crush its fetters in desperation.

transcendental value to the poet's work. All that was lost in the extrapolation was the primacy of the poem.

And what was gained? Surrealism is most often described as a 'liberation', and that it may well have been for a generation of young intellectuals sick of the rationalism of the *lycée* philosophy class, unable or unwilling to accept the solution of orthodox religion, disgusted with the world their elders had made, wishing desperately to believe – if only in literature. For, of course, the Surrealist movement was only literature. No more than the poet-mages of the nineteenth century could change the world by the spells they tried to cast through language could the Surrealists in any sense be 'saved' by the curious disciplines to which they submitted themselves. Claiming, as they did, a total liberation, once the inner world they sought had been revealed to them, their only possible action was in the field of expression– anything else would have been a constraint. To seek total liberty is a contradiction in any other terms than those of imaginative creation. This dilemma the Surrealists could not avoid.

So some of them entered the Communist Party to alter the world more effectively, if not necessarily for the better, and the others continued to write. Their style was naturally affected by the various techniques they had practised. Breton had written: 'Le poète à venir surmontera l'idée déprimante du divorce irréparable de l'action et du rêve.'* This meant still further suppression of logical transitions, still greater freedom of imagery, and the introduction into poetry of slices of the poet's consciousness or semi-consciousness, between dream and waking. Inevitably this poetry was almost wholly lyrical in character, and its favourite theme was to be the short moments of perception and disquiet, which Reverdy had already chosen as his poetic terrain. None of the Surrealists went farther towards the disintegration of image and poem than he had already done, unless we count as poems the automatic writing of the twenties or the enigmas of Dada.

* The poet to come will surmount the depressing idea of the irreparable divorce between action and dream.

*

The paradox of the Surrealist movement lies in the fact that, though numbers of poets belonged to it, there is nobody who can be singled out as the archetypal Surrealist. Much less is there an archetypal Surrealist poem. Of these poets the best seems to me to have been Robert Desnos, whose love lyrics – for example, the *Dernier Poème* he wrote from a concentration camp – are of great beauty. He harks back to a graver tradition of lyricism than Apollinaire – it is significant that he should have named Nerval and Góngora as his masters – while his popular poems have the genuine ring about them. France is one of the few countries where reputable poets write songs to be sung in cabarets and night-clubs, and Desnos in one of his moods, together with Jacques Prévert and Raymond Queneau, represents the half-mocking, half-sentimental production of the *chansonnier*. A purer type of poetry – in the technical sense of the word – was written by Paul Éluard, whose delicate rhythms and intangible use of words are more in the main line of French verse. Éluard writes with the minimum of rhetoric, and, even in a denunciatory piece like *La Tête contre les murs*, the general effect is smooth and graceful. He was the exception to the rule which says that *poésie pure* can be distinguished by critics, but not written by poets. His fault is a lack of concentration that sometimes allows his flow of mellifluous language to destroy the poem's shape. Colder and more cerebral is the poetry of André Breton himself. Among the second generation of the Surrealists Henri Michaux produced a more extroverted poetry, which, turning from consideration of wide horizons and exotic scenes, attained a terrible intensity during the Second World War and the German occupation. René Char, under similar stresses, went back to the fields and rivers of his native countryside, writing verse which is never simple in expression, but which deals with human aspirations towards happiness and good harvests.

The great crop of lyric poets produced by the Surrealist

movement – by no means all of them are mentioned here – is its main title to fame, and it remained until 1939 by far the most powerful influence affecting French poetry as well as being the only organized body of poetic theory in the field. Of course, there were those who remained outside it: Patrice de la Tour du Pin wrote strangely archaic poems in which haunted figures move in a landscape which might be that of some medieval Brittany of the mind. Francis Ponge brought the equipment of a materialist Pascal to his analysis of, and concentration on, the object – he is a humanist poet in the true sense of the word. With the War and the shock of occupation a more direct style came into vogue, allowing Louis Aragon, who had been a Surrealist, to produce, in *Le Crèvecœur*, his angry *tableaux vivants* of the defeat of 1940. André Frénaud's *Les Rois-Mages* (1943) is probably the best book of verse published at this time.

Since the War French poetry has split up into factions, and it is naturally difficult to observe any pronounced trend from so short a distance. Two outstanding volumes are *Hélène ou le règne végétal* (1952–3), by René Guy Cadou, and *Du Mouvement et de l'immobilité de Douve* (1954), by Yves Bonnefoy. Cadou, who died in 1951, was influenced by Apollinaire and Reverdy, but his poems sometimes read more like a reversion to the sentiment of Lamartine or Jammes. Bonnefoy's poetry is noble and hermetic, recalling Valéry or, farther back, Scève; and a somewhat similar note is struck by two poets who are his contemporaries: Philippe Jaccottet and Jacques Dupin. This group of poets, with their nobility of style and their preoccupation with the tragic elements in the human situation, provide a certain unity of tone on which to end this selection and a good augury for the future of French poetry.

*

In making a selection of contemporary verse, even in one's own language, there is more than the usual room for errors of judgement. I certainly should not claim that my choice is the result of anything other than backing my own taste or that time will not prove me wrong in a number of instances. In the original edition of this selection thirty-three poets were represented. This number has had to be reduced – not, I hope, inordinately – but this has meant that I have had to be fairly ruthless in excluding many very talented writers whose poems would certainly lay claim to a place in any extended anthology of recent French poetry. As before, in the selection of nineteenth-century verse, I have tried to make the translations as literal as possible.

Once again I have to thank Dr Joseph Chiari and Mr Donat O'Donnell for help with this selection.

ACKNOWLEDGEMENTS

THE following acknowledgements are due to poets, publishers, and copyright owners for permission to reprint poems used in this anthology. GUILLAUME APOLLINAIRE: to Éditions de la NRF for poems from *Œuvres poétiques* (Éditions de la Pléiade). LOUIS ARAGON: to Éditions de la NRF for poems from *Le Crève-cœur*. YVES BONNEFOY: to Éditions du Mercure de France for poems from *Du Mouvement et de l'immobilité de Douve* and *Pierre Écrite*. RENÉ CHAR: to Éditions de la NRF for poems from *Fureur et mystère*. PAUL CLAUDEL: to Éditions de la NRF for poems from *Œuvre poétique* (Éditions de la Pléiade) and to Éditions du Mercure de France for extracts from *Tête d'Or* and *Partage de midi*. ROBERT DESNOS: to Éditions de la NRF for poems from *Domaine public*. JACQUES DUPIN: to Éditions de la NRF for poems from *Gravir*. PAUL ÉLUARD: to Éditions de la NRF for poems from *Œuvres complètes* (Éditions de la Pléiade). LÉON-PAUL FARGUE: to Éditions de la NRF for poems from *Poèmes* and *Sous la Lampe*. ANDRÉ FRÉNAUD: to Éditions Pierre Seghers for a poem from *Les Rois-Mages* and to Éditions Ides et Calendes for a poem from *Soleil irréductible*. PHILIPPE JACCOTTET: to Éditions de la NRF for poems from *L'Ignorant*. MAX JACOB: to Éditions de la NRF for poems from *Derniers Poèmes*, and to Éditions Kra for a poem from *Les Pénitents en maillots roses*. FRANCIS JAMMES: to Éditions du Mercure de France for poems from *De l'Angélus de l'aube à l'angélus du soir*. VALÉRY LARBAUD: to Éditions de la NRF for a poem from *Les poésies de A. O. Barnabooth*. PATRICE DE LA TOUR DU PIN: to Éditions de la NRF for a poem from *Une Somme de poésie*. HENRI MICHAUX: to Éditions de la NRF for a poem from *Épreuves, Exorcismes*. OSCAR VENCESLAS DE LUBICZ MILOSZ: to the Librairie Des Lettres for a poem from *Poèmes*. CHARLES PÉGUY: to Éditions de la NRF for poems and extracts from *Œuvre poétiques complètes* (Éditions de la Pléiade). FRANCIS PONGE:

ACKNOWLEDGEMENTS

to Éditions de la NRF for poems from *Le Parti pris des choses* and *Proèmes*. CATHERINE POZZI: to Éditions de Mesures for a poem from *Poèmes*. JACQUES PRÉVERT: to Éditions de la NRF for a poem from *Paroles*. PIERRE REVERDY: to Éditions du Mercure de France for poems from *Main d'œuvre*. SAINT-JOHN PERSE: to Éditions de la NRF for poems from *Œuvre Poétique*. JULES SUPERVIELLE: to Éditions de la NRF for poems from *Choix de Poèmes*. PAUL-JEAN TOULET: to Éditions du Divan for poems from *Les Contrerimes*. PAUL VALÉRY: to Éditions de la NRF for poems from *Œuvres* (Éditions de la Pléiade).

PAUL-JEAN TOULET

Puisque tes jours ne t'ont laissé
Qu'un peu de cendre dans la bouche,
Avant qu'on ne tende la couche
Où ton cœur dorme, enfin glacé,

Retourne, comme au temps passé,
Cueillir, près de la dune instable,
Le lys qu'y courbe un souffle amer,
– Et grave ces mots sur le sable:
Le rêve de l'homme est semblable
Aux illusions de la mer.

Vous qui retournez du Cathai
Par les Messageries,
Quand vous berçaient à leurs féeries
L'opium ou le thé,

Dans un palais d'aventurine
Où se mourait le jour,
Avez-vous vu Boudroulboudour,
Princesse de la Chine,

Since your days have only left you a little ash in your mouth,
before the bed is spread where your heart may sleep, frozen at last,
return, as in time past, to gather, near the shifting dune, the lily that
a bitter breath bends there, – and mark these words upon the sand:
man's dream is like the illusions of the sea.

You who return from Cathay by the ocean-liners, when opium or
tea rocked you with their enchantments,
    In a sunstone palace where day was dying, did you see Badroul-
boudour, Princess of China,

Plus blanche en son pantalon noir
    Que nacre sous l'écaille?
Au clair de lune, Jean Chicaille,
    Vous est-il venu voir,

En pleurant comme l'asphodèle
    Aux îles d'Ouac-Wac,
Et jurer de coudre en un sac
    Son épouse infidèle,

Mais telle qu'à travers le vent
    Des mers sur le rivage
S'envole et brille un paon sauvage
    Dans le soleil levant?

FRANCIS JAMMES

J'AIME dans les temps Clara d'Ellébeuse,
l'écolière des anciens pensionnats,
qui allait, les soirs chauds, sous les tilleuls
lire les *magazines* d'autrefois.

Je n'aime qu'elle, et je sens sur mon cœur
la lumière bleue de sa gorge blanche.

  Whiter in her black trousers than mother-of-pearl beneath the
shell? Did Jean Chicaille come to see you by the light of the moon,
  Weeping like the asphodel in the Ouac-Wac islands, and swear
to sew up his faithless wife in a sack,
  – Faithless, but like a wild peacock that through the sea wind on
the shore flies away and shines in the rising sun?

I LOVE in the past Clara d'Ellébeuse, the pupil of old boarding
schools, who used to go beneath the may-trees on warm evenings
to read the magazines of other days
  I love her alone, and I feel the blue light of her white bosom on

Où est-elle? Où était donc ce bonheur?
Dans sa chambre claire il entrait des branches.

Elle n'est peut-être pas encore morte
– ou peut-être que nous l'étions tous deux.
La grande cour avait des feuilles mortes
dans le vent froid des fins d'Étés très vieux.

Te souviens-tu de ces plumes de paon,
dans un grand vase, auprès de coquillages? . . .
on apprenait qu'on avait fait naufrage,
on appelait Terre-Neuve: *le Banc.*

Viens, viens, ma chère Clara d'Ellébeuse:
aimons-nous encore si tu existes.
Le vieux jardin a de vieilles tulipes.
Viens toute nue, ô Clara d'Ellébeuse.

A Charles de Bordeu

LE soleil faisait luire l'eau du puits dans le verre.
Les pierres de la ferme étaient cassées et vieilles,

---

my heart. Where is she? Where was that happiness then? Into her
bright room branches came.

Perhaps she is not yet dead – or perhaps we were both dead. The
big courtyard had dead leaves in the cold wind of the end of sum-
mers long past.

Do you remember those peacock's feathers, in a big vase, beside
ornaments made of shells? . . . We heard there had been a ship-
wreck; we called Newfoundland: *the Bank.*

Come, come, my dear Clara d'Ellébeuse: let us still love one
another if you exist. The old garden has old tulips. Come quite
naked, O Clara d'Ellébeuse.

To Charles de Bordeu

THE sun made the well-water shine in the glass. The farm's stones
were broken and old, and the blue mountains had soft lines like the

et les montagnes bleues avaient des lignes douces
comme l'humidité qui luisait dans la mousse.
La rivière était noire et les racines d'arbres
étaient noires et tordues sur les bords qu'elle râpe.
On fauchait au soleil où les herbes bougeaient,
et le chien, timide et pauvre, par devoir aboyait.
La vie existait. Un paysan disait de gros mots
à une mendiante volant des haricots.
Les morceaux de forêt étaient des pierres noires.
Il sortait des jardins l'odeur tiède des poires.
La terre était pareille aux faucheuses de foin.
La cloche de l'église toussait au loin.
Et le ciel était bleu et blanc, et, dans la paille,
on entendait se taire le vol lourd des cailles.

PAUL CLAUDEL

Cébès. – Me voici,
Imbécile, ignorant,
Homme nouveau devant les choses inconnues,
Et je tourne ma face vers l'Année et l'arche pluvieuse,
j'ai plein mon cœur d'ennui!

dampness shining in the moss. The river was dark, and the tree
roots were dark and twisted on the banks worn away by it. They
were reaping in the sun where the grass was moving, and the poor
timid dog was barking out of duty. Life existed. A peasant was
swearing at a beggar woman stealing beans. The patches of forest
were black stones. From the gardens came the warm smell of pears.
The earth was like the women reaping hay. Far off the church bell
was coughing. And the sky was blue and white, and, in the straw,
we heard the heavy flight of the quails come to rest.

Cébès. – Here I am, imbecile, ignorant, a new man before un-
known things, and I turn my face towards the year and the rainy
arch, I have my heart full of weariness!

Je ne sais rien et je ne peux rien. Que dire? que faire?
A quoi emploierai-je ces mains qui pendent, ces pieds
Qui m'emmènent comme le songe nocturne?
La parole n'est qu'un bruit et les livres ne sont que du papier.
Il n'y a personne que moi ici. Et il me semble que tout
L'air brumeux, les labours gras,
Et les arbres et les basses nuées
Me parlent, avec un discours sans mots, douteusement.
Le laboureur
S'en revient avec la charrue, on entend le cri tardif.
C'est l'heure où les femmes vont au puits.
Voici la nuit. – Qu'est-ce que je suis?
Qu'est-ce que je fais? qu'est-ce que j'attends?
Et je réponds: je ne sais pas! et je désire en moi-même
Pleurer, ou crier
Ou rire, ou bondir et agiter les bras!
«Qui je suis»? Des plaques de neige restent encore, je
tiens une branche de minonnets à la main.
Car Mars est comme une femme qui souffle sur un feu de bois vert.

I know nothing and I can do nothing. What shall I say? What shall I do? How shall I use these dangling hands, these feet that lead me like a dream by night? The word is only a noise, and books are only paper. There is no one but myself here. And it seems to me that all the misty air, the rich ploughlands, and the trees and the low clouds speak to me doubtfully, in a speech without words. The ploughman returns with his plough, the belated shout is heard. It is the time when the women go to the well. Here is the night. – What am I? What am I doing? What am I waiting for?

And I answer: I do not know! And within myself I desire to weep or shout or laugh or leap and wave my arms! 'Who am I?' Some patches of snow still remain, I hold a branch of catkins in my hand. For March is like a woman blowing on a fire of green wood.

– Que l'Été

Et la journée épouvantable sous le soleil soient oubliés,
ô choses, ici,

Je m'offre à vous!

Je ne sais pas!

Voyez-moi! j'ai besoin,

Et je ne sais pas de quoi et je pourrais crier sans fin

Tout haut, tout bas, comme un enfant qu'on entend au
loin, comme les enfants qui sont restés tout seuls, près de
la braise rouge!

Ô ciel chagrin! arbres, terre! ombre, soirée pluvieuse!

Voyez-moi! que cette demande ne me soit pas refusée,
que je fais!

Cantique de Mesa

ME voici dans ma chapelle ardente!

Et de toutes parts, à droite, à gauche, je vois la forêt des
flambeaux qui m'entoure!

Non point de cires allumées, mais de puissants astres,
pareils à de grandes vierges flamboyantes

– May Summer and the terrible day beneath the sun be forgotten
here, O things; I offer myself to you! I do not know! Behold me!
I have need, and I know not of what and I could cry endlessly,
loudly, softly, like a child heard far away, like children who have
stayed all alone by the red embers! O sad sky! Trees, earth!
Shadow, rainy evening! Behold me! Let this request that I make
not be refused me!*

Mesa's Canticle

HERE I am lying in state in my burning chapel, and on every side,
to right and to left, I see the forest of torches surrounding me! Not
lighted candles, but puissant stars like great virgins blazing before

---

*This extract is taken from the beginning of the second version
of *Tête d'Or*.

Devant la face de Dieu, telles que dans les saintes pein-
tures on voit Marie qui se récuse.
Et moi, l'homme, l'Intelligent,
Me voici couché sur la Terre, prêt à mourir, comme sur
un catafalque solennel,
Au plus profond de l'univers et dans le milieu même de
cette bulle d'étoiles et de l'essaim et du culte.
Je vois l'immense clergé de la Nuit avec ses Évêques et ses
Patriarches.
Et j'ai au-dessus de moi le Pôle et à mes côtés la tranche,
et l'Équateur des animaux fourmillants de l'étendue,
Cela que l'on appelle Voie lactée, pareil à une forte
ceinture!
Salut, mes sœurs! aucune de vous, brillantes!
Ne supporte l'esprit, mais seule au centre de tout, la
Terre
A germé son homme, et vous, comme un million de
blanches brebis,
Vous tournez la tête vers elle qui est comme le Pasteur et
comme le Messie des mondes!
Salut, étoiles! Me voici seul! Aucun prêtre entouré de la
pieuse communauté
Ne viendra m'apporter le Viatique.

the face of God, as in the holy paintings we see Mary declare herself
unworthy. And I, man, intelligent man, here I am laid upon the
earth, ready to die, as upon a solemn bier at the deepest point of
the universe and in the very middle of this bubble of stars and of
the crowd and the worship. I see night's vast clergy with its bishops
and patriarchs. And above me I have the Pole and at my sides the
edge and the Equator of the swarming animals of space, that which
is called the Milky Way, like to a strong girdle! Hail, my sisters!
None of you, shining ones, supports the spirit, but, alone in the
centre of all, earth has brought forth her man, and, like a million
white sheep, you turn your heads towards her who is as the Shep-
herd and the Messiah of worlds! Hail, stars! Here I am alone! No
priest surrounded by the pious community will come to bring me

Mais déjà les portes du Ciel
Se rompent et l'armée de tous les Saints, portant des
    flambeaux dans leurs mains,
S'avancent à ma rencontre, entourant l'Agneau terrible!

Pourquoi?

Pourquoi cette femme? pourquoi la femme tout d'un
    coup sur ce bateau?
Qu'est-ce qu'elle s'en vient faire avec nous? est-ce que
    nous avions besoin d'elle? Vous seul!
Vous seul en moi tout d'un coup à la naissance de la Vie,
Vous avez été en moi la victoire et la visitation et le
    nombre et l'étonnement et la puissance et la merveille
    et le son!
Et cette autre, est-ce que nous croyions en elle? et que le
    bonheur est entre ses bras?
Et un jour j'avais inventé d'être à vous et de me donner,
Et cela était pauvre. Mais ce que je pouvais,
Je l'ai fait, je me suis donné,
Et vous ne m'avez point accepté, et c'est l'autre qui nous
    a pris.

the Viaticum. But already the gates of heaven are broken, and the
army of all the saints bearing torches in their hands advance to
meet me, surrounding the terrible Lamb.
    Why?
    Why this woman? Why this woman suddenly on that boat? What
does she come to do with us? Had we need of her? You alone! You
alone in me suddenly at the birth of life, within me You were victory
and visitation and number and astonishment and power and admira-
tion and sound! And that other – did we believe in her? And that
happiness is in her arms? And one day I had the idea of belonging
to you and of giving myself, and that was a poor thing. But what I
could, I did, I gave myself, and you did not accept me, and it was
the other who took us. And in a brief moment I am going to see

Et dans un petit moment je vais Vous voir et j'en ai effroi
Et peur dans l'Os des mes os!
Et vous m'interrogez. Et moi aussi je Vous interrogerai!
Est-ce que je ne suis pas un homme? Pourquoi est-ce que
　　vous faites le Dieu avec moi?

Non, non, mon Dieu! Allez, je ne vous demande rien!
Vous êtes là et c'est assez. Taisez-vous seulement,
Mon Dieu, afin que votre créature entende. Qui a goûté à
　　votre silence,
Il n'a pas besoin d'explication.

Parce que je Vous ai aimé
Comme on aime l'or beau à voir ou un fruit, mais alors il
　　faut se jeter dessus!
La gloire refuse les curieux, l'amour refuse les holocaustes
　　mouillés. Mon Dieu, j'ai exécration de mon orgueil!
Sans doute que je ne vous aimais pas comme il faut, mais
　　pour l'augmentation de ma science et de mon plaisir.
Et je me suis trouvé devant Vous comme quelqu'un qui
　　s'aperçoit qu'il est seul.
Eh bien! j'ai refait connaissance avec mon néant, j'ai
　　regoûté à la matière dont je suis fait.

You, and of that I have terror and fear in the bone of my bones!
And you question me. And I, too, will question You! Am I not a
man? Why do you play the God with me?

No, no, my God! Come, I ask nothing of you! You are there,
and that is enough. Only be silent, my God, that your creature may
listen. He who has tasted your silence has no need of explanations.

Because I loved You as gold fair to the eye or a fruit is loved, but
then we should throw ourselves upon it! Fame refuses the inquisi-
tive, love refuses damp burnt offerings. My God, I loathe my pride!
Doubtless I did not love You as I should, but for the increase of my
knowledge and pleasure. And I have found myself before You as
someone who sees that he is alone. Well, I have become acquainted
again with my nothingness. I have tasted again the stuff of which I

J'ai pêché fortement.

Et maintenant, sauvez-moi, mon Dieu, parce que c'est
  assez!

C'est vous de nouveau, c'est moi! Et vous êtes mon Dieu,
  et je sais que vous savez tout.

Et je baise votre main paternelle, et me voici entre vos
  mains comme une pauvre chose sanglante et broyée!

Comme la canne sous le cylindre, comme le marc sous le
  madrier.

Et parce que j'étais un égoïste, c'est ainsi que vous me
  punissez

Par l'amour épouvantable d'un autre!

Ah! je sais maintenant

Ce que c'est que l'amour! et je sais ce que vous avez
  enduré sur votre croix, dans ton Cœur,

Si vous avez aimé chacun de nous

Terriblement comme j'ai aimé cette femme, et le râle, et
  l'asphyxie, et l'étau!

Mais je l'aimais, ô mon Dieu, et elle m'a fait cela! Je
  l'aimais, et je n'ai point peur de vous,

am made. I sinned strongly. And now save me, my God, because it
is enough! Once more it is You, it is I! And You are my God, and
I know that You know everything. And I kiss your paternal hand,
and here I am in your hands like a poor thing bleeding and crushed!
Like the sugar-cane beneath the roller, like the marc beneath the
beam. And because I was an egoist it is in this way that You punish
me by the terrible love of another!

Ah! Now I know what love is! And I know what You suffered
on your cross, in your heart, if You loved each of us terribly as I
loved this woman, and the rattle in the throat and the suffocation
and the grip of the vice! But I loved her, O my God, and she did
that to me! I loved her, and I am not afraid of You, and above love

Et au-dessus de l'amour

Il n'y a rien, et pas vous-même et vous avez vu de quelle
    soif, ô Dieu, et grincement des dents,

Et sécheresse, et horreur et extraction,

Je m'étais saisi d'elle! Et elle m'a fait cela!

Ah, vous vous y connaissez, vous savez, vous,

Ce que c'est que l'amour trahi! Ah, je n'ai point peur de
    vous!

Mon crime est grand et mon amour est plus grand, et
    votre mort seule, ô mon Père,

La mort que vous m'accordez, la mort seule est à la
    mesure de tous deux!

Mourons donc et sortons de ce corps misérable!

Sortons, mon âme, et d'un seul coup éclatons cette
    détestable carcasse!

La voici déjà à demi-rompue, habillée comme une viande
    au croc, par terre ainsi qu'un fruit entamé.

Est-ce que c'est moi? Cela de cassé,

C'est l'œuvre de la femme, qu'elle le garde pour elle; et
    pour moi je m'en vais ailleurs.

Déjà elle m'avait détruit le monde et rien pour moi

N'existait qui ne fût pas elle et maintenant elle me détruit
    moi-même.

there is nothing and not Yourself, and You saw with what thirst, O
God, and grinding of teeth and dryness and horror and drawing
out I possessed myself of her! And she did that to me! Ah! You are
a good judge. You know indeed what love betrayed is! Ah! I am
not afraid of You! My crime is great and my love is greater, and
Your death alone, O my Father, the death You grant me, death
alone is to the scale of both of them!

    Let us die then and issue from this wretched body! Come forth,
my soul, and let us burst this loathesome carcass at a single blow!
Here it is already half-broken, dressed like meat on a hook, on the
ground like a spoiled fruit. Is it I? This broken thing, it is the
woman's work – let her keep it for herself; and on my side I depart
elsewhere. Already she had destroyed the world for me, and noth-
ing existed for me which was not her and now she is destroying me.

Et voici qu'elle me fait le chemin plus court.
Soyez témoin que je ne me plais pas à moi-même!
Vous voyez bien que ce n'est plus possible
Et que je ne puis me passer d'amour, et à l'instant, et non
    pas demain, mais toujours, et qu'il me faut la vie
    même, et la source même,
Et la différence même, et que je ne puis plus
Je ne puis plus supporter d'être sourd et mort!
Vous voyez bien qu'ici je ne suis bon à rien et que j'ennuie
    tout le monde
Et que pour tous je suis un scandale et une interrogation.
C'est pourquoi reprenez-moi et cachez-moi, ô père, en
    votre giron!

Strasbourg

A M. le Dr Bucher

La Cathédrale, toute rose entre les feuilles d'avril, comme un être que le sang anime, à demi humain.

And behold she has made the path shorter for me. Be witness that I am not pleasing to myself! You see clearly that it is no longer possible, and that I cannot do without love now, and not tomorrow, but forever, and that I must have life itself, and the spring itself and the difference itself, and that I can no longer, I can no longer bear to be dumb and dead! You see clearly that here I am good for nothing and that I weary everyone and that for all men I am a scandal and a question.

For that reason take me back and hide me, O Father, in your bosom.*

Strasbourg

To Dr Bucher

The cathedral, all pink among the April leaves, half-human, like a being quickened by blood, the great pink angel of Strasbourg

---

*This speech is taken from the last act of *Partage de Midi*.

Le grand Ange rose de Strasbourg qui est debout entre les Vosges et le Rhin,

Contient bien des mystères dans son livre et des choses qui ne sont pas racontées

Pour l'enfant qui vers ce frère géant lève les yeux avec bonne volonté.

Salut, Mères de la France là-bas, Paris et Chartres et Rouen,

Grandes Maries toutes usées et chenues, ô Mères toutes noires de temps!

Mais qu'il est jeune! qu'il est droit! comme il tient fièrement sa lance!

Qu'il fait de plaisir à voir dans le soleil, plein de menaces et d'élégance,

Tel que le bon écuyer qui soutient son maître face-à-face,

L'Ange de Strasbourg en fleur, rose comme une fille d'Alsace!

Dieu n'a point fermé les yeux de la mère pour qu'elle ignore

Ce Fils mystérieux au-dessus d'elle et ce grand laurier dans l'aurore!

C'est aussi présent que moi! c'est de la pierre! c'est aussi sain,

standing between the Vosges and the Rhine, contains many mysteries in his book and things that are not told to the child who raises his eyes with good will towards this giant brother.

Hail, mothers of France over there, Paris and Chartres and Rouen, great Marys all worn and white-haired, O mothers all black with time! But how young he is! How upright! How proudly he holds his lance! How pleasant it is to see him in the sun, full of threats and elegance, like the good squire supporting his master face to face, the angel of Strasbourg in bloom, pink as a girl of Alsace! God has not shut the mother's eyes for her not to know this mysterious Son above her and this great bay-tree in the dawn! It is as present as I am! It is stone! It is as healthy, as new, as living, as

Aussi neuf, aussi vivant, aussi dru que la rose de ce matin,

Ce qui de toutes parts à moi s'ouvre et m'accueille, et qui enfin

M'immerge, profond et divers, quand j'ai franchi le portail,

Asile comme le sein des mers, aussi vermeil que le corail!

De quel soleil au dehors ces feux sont-ils le reflet?

Comme la voix en dix mille syllabes qui devient un seul grand poëme diapré,

Le jour, en ce silence hors du monde pour y pénétrer,

Raconte à travers les vitraux tous les siècles, toute l'histoire profane et sacrée.

Les deux testaments sont ici, la double table de pierre.

Dieu est ici, et non seulement Dieu le Fils, mais Dieu le Père.

Quatre piliers, quatre colosses comme des arbres sont ses témoins

Dans la fosse fortifiée qui garde le Saint des Saints.

Quelqu'un est là, écoutant toute la vie et le cri que fait le sang d'Abel,

strong as this morning's rose, that which on all sides is opened to me and welcomes me, and which at last swallows me up, deep and various, when I have crossed the gateway, a refuge like the breast of the seas, as red as coral!

Of what sun outside are those fires the reflection? Like the voice in ten thousand syllables that becomes a single great, variegated poem, the daylight, in this silence out of the world, in order to penetrate there, tells through the stained-glass windows of all the centuries, of the whole of sacred and profane history. Both the testaments are here, the double tablet of stone. God is here, and not only God the Son, but God the Father. Four pillars, four giants like trees, are his witnesses in the fortified moat that guards the Holy of Holies. Someone is there listening to the whole of life and the cry made by Abel's blood, within silence and time, blind as

Dans le silence et le temps, aveugle comme Samuel!

Le Père et le Fils qu'Il engendre et l'Esprit qui En fait procession,

Résident là, c'est là! dans le mystère de la Circumin-session,

Cependant qu'un rayon suave et lent indique

L'heure fausse que contredit le grand Coq astrono-mique.

Dieu est présent, et avec lui toute l'Église dans l'église,

Tout le passé, mais autant que les histoires précises,

Autant que les Prophètes et les Vertus et le séducteur de la Parabole,

Qui avec un doux souris à reculons entraîne son troupeau de Vierges folles,

M'attirent ces débris, et ces têtes sans corps, et la notice

Sur une pierre déchue: ERWIN MAGISTER OPERIS,

Et ces Longs Hommes tout travaillés par le temps, qu'on a retirés du Ciel,

Comme un plongeur à grands coups de talons de la mer extrait un mort plein de sel.

Samuel! The Father and the Son He engenders and the Spirit that makes procession of Them dwell there – it is there! in the mystery of the reciprocal existence of the Trinity, while a gentle slow beam shows the false hour contradicted by the great astronomical Cock.

God is present and with him all the Church in the church, the whole past, but as much as precise stories, as the Prophets and Virtues and the Seducer of the Parable, leading backwards with a gentle smile his flock of foolish virgins, those ruins attract me, and those bodiless heads and the inscription of a fallen stone: ERWIN MASTER OF THE WORK, and those long men worked on by time and withdrawn from the sky, as a diver with strong kicks of his heels brings up a dead man full of salt from the sea.

Qui n'a senti quelquefois, dans les tristes après-midis
d'été,

Quelque chose vers nous languir comme une rose
desséchée?

Ah! de ceux ou de celles-là que nous étions faits pour
comprendre et pour aimer,

Ce n'est pas la distance seulement, c'est le temps qui
nous tient séparés,

L'irréparable temps, la distance qui efface le nom et le
visage:

Un regard seul pour nous seuls survit et traverse tous
les âges!

Dangereuse Nymphe d'autrefois! ah, qu'on lui bande
les yeux,

Qu'on l'attache fortement à la porte du Sainr-Lieu,

Comme cette figure sous le porche latéral qu'on
appelle la Synagogue!

Ah, qu'on lui rompe ce long dard pour notre perte,
analogue

A l'aiguillon même de la mort dont l'Apôtre nous a
parlé,

La grande femme folle et vague avec son visage de fée!

Plus vaine que l'eau qui fuit, plus que le Rhin flexueuse,

Who has not sometimes felt on a sad summer's afternoon some-
thing languish towards us like a withered rose? Ah! Of the men or
women we were made to understand and love, it is not distance
only, it is time that keeps us separated, irreparable time, distance
blotting out name and face: a single glance lives for us alone and
crosses all the ages!

Dangerous Nymph of former times! Ah! Let her eyes be bound,
let her be tightly chained to the gate of the sanctuary like that figure
under the lateral porch called the Synagogue! Ah! Let her long
dart for our destruction be broken, analogous to the very sting of
death of which the Apostle spoke to us, the tall, mad, wandering
woman with her fairy face! More empty than ebbing water, more
winding than the Rhine, she does not allow her tortuous weapon to

Elle ne laisse point tomber son arme tortueuse,

Et montre, les yeux bandés, sa charte où il n'y a rien écrit.

Mais de l'autre côté de la Porte est debout avec mépris,

Sans relâche la tenant sous ses yeux froids qui sont faits pour voir,

L'Église sans aucuns rêves qui ne pense qu'à son devoir,

L'Église qui est appuyée sur la croix et non ce jonc illusoire,

Héritière des jours passés, forte maîtresse d'aujourd'-hui:

Et antiquum documentum novo cedat ritui.

Nous, dédaignant le jour d'hier, réjouissons-nous dans le matin d'avril!

Laborieux présent, auteur des tâches difficiles,

Moins tu nous laisses d'avenir, plus le passé fut cruel,

Plus grande en nous la douceur amère des choses réelles!

Plus l'œuvre est dure et plus elle est honorable pour nous.

fall and, with her eyes blindfolded, displays her charter where there is nothing written. But on the other side of the gate stands with scorn, relentlessly holding her under her cold eyes that are made to see, the undreaming church, only thinking of her duty, the church which is supported on the cross and not this vain reed, heiress of past days, strong mistress of today: *and let the old law yield to the new rite.*

Scorning yesterday's day, let us rejoice in the April morning! Laborious present, author of difficult tasks, the less future you leave us, the more the past was cruel, the greater within us the bitter sweetness of real things! The harder the work the more honourable it is for us! How beautiful the Spring is this year! And how sweet

Que le printemps est beau, cette année! et qu'il est
doux

De voir peu à peu dans le brouillard se découvrir et se
dresser

L'Ange de Strasbourg éternel, rose comme une fiancée!

Ballade

LES négociateurs de Tyr et ceux-là qui vont à leurs
affaires aujourd'hui sur l'eau dans de grandes imagi-
nations mécaniques,

Ceux que le mouchoir par les ailes de cette mouette en-
core accompagne quand le bras qui l'agitait a disparu,

Ceux à qui leur vigne et leur champ ne suffisaient pas,
mais Monsieur avait son idée personelle sur l'Améri-
que,

Ceux qui sont partis pour toujours et qui n'arriveront pas
non plus,

Tous ces dévoreurs de la distance, c'est la mer elle-même
à présent qu'on leur sert, penses-tu qu'ils en auront
assez?

to see the eternal angel of Strasbourg, pink as a betrothed girl, little
by little revealed standing upright in the mist!

Ballad

THE merchants of Tyre and those who go to their business today
over the water in great mechanical imaginings, those whom the
handkerchief still accompanies through the wings of this seagull
when the arm that waved it has disappeared, those for whom their
vine and their field were not sufficient, but the gentleman had his
own ideas about America, those who have gone for ever and will
not arrive either, all those eaters-up of distance, it is the sea itself
that they are served now, do you think they will have enough of it?

Qui une fois y a mis les lèvres ne lâche point facilement la
    coupe:
Ce sera long d'en venir à bout, mais on peut tout de
    même essayer.

Il n'y a que la première gorgée qui coûte.

Équipages des bâtiments torpillés dont on voit les noms
    dans les statistiques,
Garnisons des cuirassés tout à coup qui s'en vont par le
    plus court à la terre,
Patrouilleurs de chalutiers poitrinaires, pensionnaires de
    sous-marins ataxiques,
Et tout ce que décharge un grand transport pêle-mêle
    quand il se met la quille en l'air,
Pour eux tous voici le devoir autour d'eux à la mesure de
    cet horizon circulaire.
C'est la mer qui se met en mouvement vers eux, plus
    besoin d'y chercher sa route.
Il n'y a qu'à ouvrir la bouche toute grande et à se laisser
    faire:

He who has once put his lips to it does not easily leave the cup:
it will take a long time to finish with it, but we can try all the same.

Only the first mouthful is hard to swallow.

Crews of torpedoed vessels whose names we see in the statistics,
garrisons of iron-clads who all at once go to ground by the shortest
route, consumptives patrolling in drifters, ataxic boarders in sub-
marines, and all that a big transport unloads pell-mell when it puts
its keel in the air, for them all here is duty around them to the scale
of this circular horizon. It is the sea beginning to move towards
them, no more need to seek one's path. You only have to open
your mouth wide and abandon yourself to it:

Ce n'est que la première gorgée qui coûte.

Qu'est-ce qu'ils disaient, la dernière nuit, les passagers des
    grands transatlantiques,
La nuit même avant le dernier jour où le sans-fil a dit:
    «Nous sombrons!»
Pendant que les émigrants de troisième classe là-bas
    faisaient timidement un peu de musique
Et que la mer inlassablement montait et redescendait à
    chaque coupée du salon?
«Les choses qu'on a une fois quittées, à quoi bon leur
    garder son cœur?
«Qui voudrait que la vie recommence quand il sait qu'elle
    est finie toute?
«Retrouver ceux qu'on aime serait bon, mais l'oubli est
    encore meilleur:

Il n'y a que la première gorgée qui coûte.»

ENVOI

Rien que la mer à chaque côté de nous, rien que cela qui
    monte et qui descend!

It is only the first mouthful that is hard to swallow.

What were they saying on the last night, the passengers of the
great transatlantic liners, the very night before the last day when the
wireless said: 'We are sinking!', while the emigrants down there in
the third class timidly played a little music, and the sea untiringly
rose and fell at each port of the saloon? 'What good is it to keep our
hearts on the things we have once left? Who would want life to
begin again when he knows it is quite ended? To find again those
we love would be good, but forgetfulness is still better:

Only the first mouthful is hard to swallow.'

ENVOI

Nothing but the sea on every side of us, nothing but that rising
and falling! Enough of this perpetual thorn in the heart, enough of

Assez de cette épine continuelle dans le cœur, assez de ces
    journées goutte à goutte!
Rien que la mer éternelle pour toujours, et tout à la fois
    d'un seul coup! la mer et nous sommes dedans!

Il n'y a que la première gorgée qui coûte.

PAUL VALÉRY

Narcisse parle

Narcissæ placandis manibus

Ô FRÈRES! tristes lys, je languis de beauté
Pour m'être désiré dans votre nudité,
Et vers vous, Nymphe, nymphe, ô nymphe des fontaines,
Je viens au pur silence offrir mes larmes vaines.

Un grand calme m'écoute, où j'écoute l'espoir.
La voix des sources change et me parle du soir;
J'entends l'herbe d'argent grandir dans l'ombre sainte,
Et la lune perfide élève son miroir
Jusque dans les secrets de la fontaine éteinte.

these days passed drop by drop! Nothing but the eternal sea for
evermore, and all at once at a single blow! The sea and we are in it!

Only the first mouthful is hard to swallow.

Narcissus Speaks

Narcissæ placandis manibus

O BROTHERS! Sad lilies, I languish with beauty for having desired
myself in your nakedness, and I come towards you, nymph, nymph,
O nymph of the fountains, to offer my vain tears to the pure silence.

    A great stillness listens to me, in which I listen to hope. The
springs' voice changes and speaks to me of evening; I hear the silver
grass growing in the holy shadow, and the treacherous moon raises
her mirror even in the secrets of the quenched fountain.

Et moi! de tout mon cœur dans ces roseaux jeté,
Je languis, ô saphir, par ma triste beauté!
Je ne sais plus aimer que l'eau magicienne
Où j'oubliai le rire et la rose ancienne.

Que je déplore ton éclat fatal et pur,
Si mollement de moi fontaine-environnée,
Où puisèrent mes yeux dans un mortel azur
Mon image de fleurs humides couronnée!

Hélas! L'image est vaine et les pleurs éternels!
A travers les bois bleus et les bras fraternels,
Une tendre lueur d'heure ambiguë existe,
Et d'un reste du jour me forme un fiancé
Nu, sur la place pâle où m'attire l'eau triste . . .
Délicieux démon, désirable et glacé!

Voici dans l'eau ma chair de lune et de rosée,
Ô forme obéissante à mes yeux opposée!
Voici mes bras d'argent dont les gestes sont purs! . . .
Mes lentes mains dans l'or adorable se lassent

And I! Thrown into these reeds with all my heart, I languish, O sapphire, on account of my sad beauty! I can no longer love anything except the magical water in which I forgot laughter and the antique rose.

How I deplore your pure and deadly lustre, fountain so indolently encompassed by myself, where from a fatal azure my eyes drew up my own image crowned with wet flowers!

Alas! The image is empty and the tears unending! Through the blue woods and arms of brothers exists a tender light of an uncertain hour, and, on the pale spot where the sad water lures me, from a remnant of day forms for me a naked fiancé . . . a delicious demon, icy and desirable!

Here in the water is my flesh of moonlight and dew, O obedient shape placed before my eyes! Here are my silver arms whose gestures are pure! . . . My sluggish hands weary themselves in the

D'appeler ce captif que les feuilles enlacent,
Et je crie aux échos les noms des dieux obscurs! . . .

Adieu, reflet perdu sur l'onde calme et close,
Narcisse . . . ce nom même est un tendre parfum
Au cœur suave. Effeuille aux mânes du défunt
Sur ce vide tombeau la funérale rose.

Sois, ma lèvre, la rose effeuillant le baiser
Qui fasse un spectre cher lentement s'apaiser,
Car la nuit parle à demi-voix, proche et lointaine,
Aux calices pleins d'ombre et de sommeils légers.
Mais la lune s'amuse aux myrtes allongés.

Je t'adore, sous ces myrtes, ô l'incertaine
Chair pour la solitude éclose tristement
Qui se mire dans le miroir au bois dormant.
Je me délie en vain de ta présence douce,
L'heure menteuse est molle aux membres sur la mousse
Et d'un sombre délice enfle le vent profond.

Adieu, Narcisse . . . meurs! Voici le crépuscule.
Au soupir de mon cœur mon apparence ondule,

lovely gold with calling this prisoner entwined with leaves, and I cry the names of the dark gods to the echoes! . . .

Farewell, reflection lost upon the still, closed wave, Narcissus . . . that very name is a tender perfume for the soft heart. Scatter the funereal rose on this empty tomb to the spirit of the dead.

My lip, be the rose scattering the kiss that may cause a beloved ghost slowly to be reconciled, for night speaks in a low voice, near and far, to calyxes full of shadow and light slumbers. But the moon plays with the long myrtles.

Beneath these myrtles I worship you, O wavering flesh sadly blooming for solitude and reflected in the mirror sleeping in the wood. I free myself in vain from your sweet presence, the false hour is soft for limbs upon the moss and swells the deep wind with a dark delight.

Farewell, Narcissus . . . die! Here is the twilight. My image ripples to the sighing of my heart, the flute through the buried

La flûte, par l'azur enseveli module
Des regrets de troupeaux sonores qui s'en vont.
Mais sur le froid mortel où l'étoile s'allume,
Avant qu'un lent tombeau ne se forme de brume,
Tiens ce baiser qui brise un calme d'eau fatal!
L'espoir seul peut suffire à rompre ce cristal.
La ride me ravisse au souffle qui m'exile
Et que mon souffle anime une flûte gracile
Dont le joueur léger me serait indulgent! . . .

Évanouissez-vous, divinité troublée!
Et toi, verse à la lune, humble flûte isolée,
Une diversité de nos larmes d'argent.

Au platane

A André Fontainas

Tu penches, grand Platane, et te proposes nu,
    Blanc comme un jeune Scythe,
Mais ta candeur est prise, et ton pied retenu
    Par la force du site.

azure modulates regrets of sonorous herds departing. But on the deadly chill where the star is lit, before a slow tomb is formed of mist, take this kiss that breaks the water's fatal stillness!

Hope alone can serve to shatter this crystal. Let the ripple snatch me from the breath by which I am exiled, and let my breath give life to a slender flute whose frivolous player may be indulgent to me! . . .

Vanish away, troubled divinity! And you, humble, lonely flute, pour out a variety of our silver tears to the moon.

To the Plane-tree

To André Fontainas

You bend, vast plane-tree, and offer yourself naked, white as a young Scythian, but your candour is caught and your foot held back by the strength of the site.

Ombre retentissante en qui le même azur
     Qui t'emporte, s'apaise,
La noire mère astreint ce pied natal et pur
     A qui la fange pèse.

De ton front voyageur les vents ne veulent pas;
     La terre tendre et sombre,
Ô Platane, jamais ne laissera d'un pas
     S'émerveiller ton ombre!

Ce front n'aura d'accès qu'aux degrés lumineux
     Où la sève l'exalte;
Tu peux grandir, candeur, mais non rompre les nœuds
     De l'éternelle halte!

Pressens autour de toi d'autres vivants liés
     Par l'hydre vénérable;
Tes pareils sont nombreux, des pins aux peupliers,
     De l'yeuse à l'érable,

Qui, par les morts saisis, les pieds échevelés
     Dans la confuse cendre,
Sentent les fuir les fleurs, et leurs spermes ailés
     Le cours léger descendre.

Resounding shadow in which the same blue sky that carries you off is appeased, the dark mother compels that pure, new-born foot on which the mud weighs heavily.

The winds do not want your journeying brow; the dark, tender earth, O plane-tree, will never let your shadow marvel at its stride!

This brow will only have access to the shining steps to which the sap raises it; you may grow, O candour, but not burst the knots of the eternal halt!

Figure around you other creatures bound by the venerable hydra; your fellows are numerous, from pines to poplars, from the holly-oak to the maple,

Who, gripped by the dead, their tousled hairy feet in the confused ashes, feel the flowers leave them and their winged sperms go down the light current.

Le tremble pur, le charme, et ce hêtre formé
    De quatre jeunes femmes,
Ne cessent point de battre un ciel toujours fermé,
    Vêtus en vain de rames.

Ils vivent séparés, ils pleurent confondus
    Dans une seule absence,
Et leurs membres d'argent sont vainement fendus
    A leur douce naissance.

Quand l'âme lentement qu'ils expirent le soir
    Vers l'Aphrodite monte,
La vierge doit dans l'ombre, en silence, s'asseoir,
    Toute chaude de honte.

Elle se sent surprendre, et pâle, appartenir
    A ce tendre présage
Qu'une présente chair tourne vers l'avenir
    Par un jeune visage . . .

Mais toi, de bras plus purs que les bras animaux,
    Toi qui dans l'or les plonges,
Toi qui formes au jour le fantôme des maux
    Que le sommeil fait songes,

The pure aspen, the hornbeam, and this beech formed of four young women continue beating a sky always closed, vainly dressed in boughs.*

They live separate, they weep mingled in a single absence, and their silver limbs are vainly split at their gentle birth.

When the soul they breathe forth in the evening slowly climbs towards Aphrodite, the virgin must sit down in silence in the shadow, all hot with shame.

She feels herself surprised and palely belong to that tender omen which a present flesh turns towards the future through a young face . . .

But you, with arms purer than animal arms, you who plunge them in gold, you who form by day the ghost of evils that slumber makes dreams,

---

Rame can mean *oar* or *bough.*

Haute profusion de feuilles, trouble fier
    Quand l'âpre tramontane
Sonne, au comble de l'or, l'azur du jeune hiver
    Sur tes harpes, Platane,

Ose gémir! . . . Il faut, ô souple chair du bois,
    Te tordre, te détordre,
Te plaindre sans te rompre, et rendre aux vents la voix
    Qu'ils cherchent en désordre!

Flagelle-toi! . . . Parais l'impatient martyr
    Qui soi-même s'écorche,
Et dispute à la flamme impuissante à partir
    Ses retours vers la torche!

Afin que l'hymne monte aux oiseaux qui naîtront,
    Et que le pur de l'âme
Fasse frémir d'espoir les feuillages d'un tronc
    Qui rêve de la flamme,

Je t'ai choisi, puissant personnage d'un parc,
    Ivre de ton tangage,
Puisque le ciel t'exerce, et te presse, ô grand arc,
    De lui rendre un langage!

Tall abundance of leaves, proud tumult when the harsh north wind sounds, at the height of the gold, the young winter's azure on your harps, O plane-tree,

Dare to groan! . . . O supple wooden flesh, you must twist and untwist yourself, complain without breaking and give the winds the voice they look for in disorder!

Whip yourself! . . . Appear the impatient martyr flaying himself and dispute to the flame, powerless to depart, its returns towards the torch!

So that the hymn may rise to the birds about to be born and the pure of soul may make the leaves of a trunk dreaming of flame shudder with hope,

I have chosen you, powerful dweller in a park, drunk with your pitching, since the sky exercises you and urges you, O great bow, to give it back a language!

Ô qu'amoureusement des Dryades rival,
　　　Le seul poète puisse
Flatter ton corps poli comme il fait du Cheval
　　　L'ambitieuse cuisse! ...

– Non, dit l'arbre. Il dit: *Non!* par l'étincellement
　　　De sa tête superbe,
Que la tempête traite universellement
　　　Comme elle fait une herbe!

Le Sylphe

Ni vu ni connu
Je suis le parfum
Vivant et défunt
Dans le vent venu!

Ni vu ni connu,
Hasard ou génie?
A peine venue
La tâche est finie!

Ni lu ni compris?
Aux meilleurs esprits
Que d'erreurs promises!

O, lovingly rivalling the Dryads, may the poet alone caress your polished body as he does the ambitious thigh of the horse! ...
– No, says the tree. It says: *No!* by the sparkling of its proud head, which the storm universally treats as it does a blade of grass.

The Sylph

Neither seen nor known, I am the perfume living and dead come on the wind!

　　Neither seen nor known, chance or genius? Hardly come, the task is ended!

　　Neither read nor understood? What mistakes destined for the best minds!

PAUL VALÉRY

Ni vu ni connu,
Le temps d'un sein nu
Entre deux chemises!

Le Cimetière marin

Μή, φίλα ψυχά, βίον ἀθάνατον
σπεῦδε, τὰν δ'ἔμπρακτον
ἄντλει μαχανάν

PINDARE. Pythiques III

CE toit tranquille, où marchent des colombes,
Entre les pins palpite, entre les tombes;
Midi le juste y compose de feux
La mer, la mer, toujours recommencée!
Ô récompense après une pensée
Qu'un long regard sur le calme des dieux!

Quel pur travail de fins éclairs consume
Maint diamant d'imperceptible écume,
Et quelle paix semble se concevoir!

Neither seen nor known, the time of a bare breast between two
smocks!

The Graveyard by the Sea

Seek not, my soul, the life of
the immortals; but enjoy to
the full the resources that are
within thy reach.
PINDAR. Pythics III

THIS quiet roof, where doves walk, shimmers among the pines,
among the tombs; Noon the just composes there out of fires the
sea, the sea, ever without end! O what a reward after thought is
a long glance at the gods' calm!
What pure labour of quick lightnings devours many a diamond
of invisible foam, and what peace seems to be conceived! When a

Quand sur l'abîme un soleil se repose,
Ouvrages purs d'une éternelle cause,
Le Temps scintille et le Songe est savoir.

Stable trésor, temple simple à Minerve,
Masse de calme, et visible réserve,
Eau sourcilleuse, Œil qui gardes en toi
Tant de sommeil sous un voile de flamme,
Ô mon silence! . . . Édifice dans l'âme,
Mais comble d'or aux mille tuiles, Toit!

Temple du Temps, qu'un seul soupir résume,
A ce point pur je monte et m'accoutume,
Tout entouré de mon regard marin;
Et comme aux dieux mon offrande suprême,
La scintillation sereine sème
Sur l'altitude un dédain souverain.

Comme le fruit se fond en jouissance,
Comme en délice il change son absence
Dans une bouche où sa forme se meurt,
Je hume ici ma future fumée,
Et le ciel chante à l'âme consumée
Le changement des rives en rumeur.

---

sun rests above the abyss – the pure creations of an eternal cause –
time sparkles and the dream is knowledge.

Firm treasure, simple temple to Minerva, mass of calm and apparent reticence, proud water, eye containing in yourself so much slumber beneath a veil of flame, O my silence! . . . Building in the soul, but golden eaves with a thousand tiles, O roof!

Time's temple summed up in a single sigh, to this pure spot I climb and become accustomed, quite surrounded by my sea gaze; and like my final offering to the gods the calm brilliance sows a sovereign scorn over the height.

As the fruit melts in enjoyment, as it changes its absence into delight in a mouth where its shape dies, here I sniff my future smoke, and the sky sings to the burnt-up soul the changing of the murmuring shores.

Beau ciel, vrai ciel, regarde-moi qui change!
Après tant d'orgueil, après tant d'étrange
Oisiveté, mais pleine de pouvoir,
Je m'abandonne à ce brillant espace,
Sur les maisons des morts mon ombre passe
Qui m'apprivoise à son frêle mouvoir.

L'âme exposée aux torches du solstice,
Je te soutiens, admirable justice
De la lumière aux armes sans pitié!
Je te rends pure à ta place première:
Regarde-toi! . . . Mais rendre la lumière
Suppose d'ombre une morne moitié.

Ô pour moi seul, à moi seul, en moi-même,
Auprès d'un cœur, aux sources du poème,
Entre le vide et l'événement pur,
J'attends l'écho de ma grandeur interne,
Amère, sombre et sonore citerne,
Sonnant dans l'âme un creux toujours futur!

Sais-tu, fausse captive des feuillages,
Golfe mangeur de ces maigres grillages,
Sur mes yeux clos, secrets éblouissants,

Fair sky, true sky, watch me changing! After so much pride,
after so much strange but powerful idleness, I give myself to this
shining space, my shadow passes over the houses of the dead,
accustoming me to its frail motion.

With my soul exposed to the solstice's torches, I bear you,
light's admirable justice pitilessly armed! Pure I give you back to
your first resting-place: look at yourself! . . . But to give back the
light supposes a dreary half of shadow.

O for myself alone, by myself, within myself, beside a heart, at
the poem's fountainhead, between the void and the pure event, I
await the echo of my inner greatness, the bitter, dark, and sonorous
well, sounding within the soul a hollowness that is always in the
future!

Do you know, false prisoner of the foliage, gulf that devours
these scanty lattices, dazzling secrets above my closed eyes, what

Quel corps me traîne à sa fin paresseuse,
Quel front l'attire à cette terre osseuse?
Une étincelle y pense à mes absents.

Fermé, sacré, plein d'un feu sans matière,
Fragment terrestre offert à la lumière,
Ce lieu me plaît, dominé de flambeaux,
Composé d'or, de pierre et d'arbres sombres,
Où tant de marbre est tremblant sur tant d'ombres;
La mer fidèle y dort sur mes tombeaux!

Chienne splendide, écarte l'idolâtre!
Quand solitaire au sourire de pâtre,
Je pais longtemps, moutons mystérieux,
Le blanc troupeau de mes tranquilles tombes,
Éloignes-en les prudentes colombes,
Les songes vains, les anges curieux!

Ici venu, l'avenir est paresse.
L'insecte net gratte la sécheresse;
Tout est brûlé, défait, reçu dans l'air
A je ne sais quelle sévère essence . . .
La vie est vaste, étant ivre d'absence,
Et l'amertume est douce, et l'esprit clair.

body drags me to its idle end, what brow draws it to this bony
ground? There a spark thinks of my departed ones.

Closed and consecrated, full of an immaterial fire, earthly frag-
ment offered to the light, this place pleases me, commanded by
torches, made up of gold, of stone, and of dark trees, where so much
marble trembles over so many shadows; the faithful sea sleeps there
upon my tombs!

Resplendent bitch, keep the idolator away! When alone and with
a shepherd's smile, long time I graze the mysterious sheep, the
white flock of my quiet tombs, keep far away from them the pru-
dent doves, vain dreams, and inquisitive angels!

Once come here, the future is idleness. The sharp insect scratches
the dryness; everything is burnt, dissolved, received in the air to I
know not what strict essence . . . Life is huge, being drunk with
absence, and bitterness is sweet, and the mind clear.

Les morts cachés sont bien dans cette terre
Qui les réchauffe et sèche leur mystère.
Midi là-haut, Midi sans mouvement
En soi se pense et convient à soi-même . . .
Tête complète et parfait diadème,
Je suis en toi le secret changement.

Tu n'as que moi pour contenir tes craintes!
Mes repentirs, mes doutes, mes contraintes
Sont le défaut de ton grand diamant . . .
Mais dans leur nuit toute lourde de marbres,
Un peuple vague aux racines des arbres
A pris déjà ton parti lentement.

Ils ont fondu dans une absence épaisse,
L'argile rouge a bu la blanche espèce,
Le don de vivre a passé dans les fleurs!
Où sont des morts les phrases familières,
L'art personnel, les âmes singulières?
La larve file où se formaient des pleurs.

Les cris aigus des filles chatouillées,
Les yeux, les dents, les paupières mouillées,
Le sein charmant qui joue avec le feu,

The hidden dead are at rest in this earth which warms them and
dries their mystery. Up there Noon, motionless Noon, conceives
itself and suffices to itself . . . Complete head and perfect diadem, I
am the secret change within you.

To hold your fears you have only me! My repentances, my
doubts, my compulsions are the flaw in your great diamond . . . But
in their night heavy with marbles a vague people at the roots of the
trees has already slowly made your choice.

They have melted into a thick absence, the red clay has drunk up
the white creature, the gift of life has passed into the flowers!
Where are the usual phrases of the dead, the personal art, the in-
dividual souls? The worm crawls where tears used to form.

The high shrieks of tickled girls, the eyes, the teeth, the damp
eyelids, the charming breast playing with fire, the blood shining in

Le sang qui brille aux lèvres qui se rendent,
Les derniers dons, les doigts qui les défendent,
Tout va sous terre et rentre dans le jeu!

Et vous, grande âme, espérez-vous un songe
Qui n'aura plus ces couleurs de mensonge
Qu'aux yeux de chair l'onde et l'or font ici?
Chanterez-vous quand serez vaporeuse?
Allez! Tout fuit! Ma présence est poreuse,
La sainte impatience meurt aussi!

Maigre immortalité noire et dorée,
Consolatrice affreusement laurée,
Qui de la mort fais un sein maternel,
Le beau mensonge et la pieuse ruse!
Qui ne connaît, et qui ne les refuse,
Ce crâne vide et ce rire éternel!

Pères profonds, têtes inhabitées,
Qui sous le poids de tant de pelletées,
Êtes la terre et confondez nos pas,
Le vrai rongeur, le ver irréfutable
N'est point pour vous qui dormez sous la table,
Il vit de vie, il ne me quitte pas!

lips surrendering, the final gifts, the fingers that defend them –
everything goes underground and returns back into play!

And you, vast soul, do you hope for a dream which shall no
longer have those lying colours which the wave and the gold make
here for the eyes of flesh? Will you sing when you are vapour?
Come! Everything passes away! My presence is porous; holy
impatience also dies!

Meagre immortality in black and gold, comforter terribly
adorned with laurels, that makes a mother's breast of death – what
a fine lie and pious trick! Who does not know, who does not reject,
that empty skull and that eternal laugh!

Deep fathers, uninhabited heads, who, beneath the weight of so
many spade-fulls of soil, are the earth and confuse our steps, the
true rodent, the irrefutable worm is not for you who sleep beneath
the slab – he lives on life, he does not leave me!

Amour, peut-être, ou de moi-même haine?
Sa dent secrète est de moi si prochaine
Que tous les noms lui peuvent convenir!
Qu'importe! Il voit, il veut, il songe, il touche!
Ma chair lui plaît, et jusque sur ma couche,
A ce vivant je vis d'appartenir!

Zénon! Cruel Zénon! Zénon d'Élée!
M'as-tu percé de cette flèche ailée
Qui vibre, vole, et qui ne vole pas!
Le son m'enfante et la flèche me tue!
Ah! le soleil ... Quelle ombre de tortue
Pour l'âme, Achille immobile à grands pas!

Non, non! ... Debout! Dans l'ère successive!
Brisez, mon corps, cette forme pensive!
Buvez, mon sein, la naissance du vent!
Une fraîcheur, de la mer exhalée,
Me rend mon âme ... Ô puissance salée!
Courons à l'onde en rejaillir vivant!

Oui! Grande mer de délires douée,
Peau de panthère et chlamyde trouée
De mille et mille idoles du soleil,

Love, perhaps, or hatred of myself? His secret tooth is so close to me that any name may suit him! What does it matter? He sees, he desires, he dreams, he touches! My flesh pleases him, and, even in my bed, I live to belong to this living creature!

Zeno! Cruel Zeno! Zeno of Elea! Have you pierced me with that winged arrow which quivers, flies, and does not fly! The noise brings me forth, and the arrow kills me! Ah! The sun ... What a tortoise's shadow for the soul, that Achilles motionless with his vast strides!

No, no! ... Up! Into the coming era! My body, shatter this pensive shape! My breast, drink the wind's birth! A coolness breathed forth by the sea gives me back my soul ... O salt power! Let us run to the waves and spring from them again alive!

Yes! Vast sea gifted with delirium, panther skin and mantle pierced with thousands and thousands of idols of the sun, absolute

Hydre absolue, ivre de ta chair bleue,
Qui te remords l'étincelante queue
Dans un tumulte au silence pareil,

Le vent se lève! . . . il faut tenter de vivre!
L'air immense ouvre et referme mon livre,
La vague en poudre ose jaillir des rocs!
Envolez-vous, pages tout éblouies!
Rompez, vagues! Rompez d'eaux réjouies
Ce toit tranquille où picoraient des focs!

CHARLES PÉGUY

Les Sept contre Thèbes

Tydée allait foncer sur la porte Prœtide.
Mais elle n'était pas laissée à l'abandon.
Car la Ville opposait au roi de Calydon
L'ardent Mélanippos, indomptable Astacide.

hydra, drunk with your own blue flesh, biting your sparkling tail
in a commotion like silence,

The wind is rising! . . . We must try to live! The huge air opens
and closes my book, the powdered wave dares to spout from the
rocks! Fly away, bedazzled pages! Break, waves! Break with joyous
waters this calm roof where sails pecked like doves!

The Seven against Thebes

Tydeus was going to attack the Prœtid gate. But it was not left
forsaken. For the town opposed to the king of Calydon the pas-
sionate Melanippus, the unconquerable son of Astacus.

Capanée en avait à la porte d'Électre.
Mais la Ville opposait au fils d'Hipponoos,
A l'énorme géant gendre du roi d'Argos,
L'effrayant Polyphonte impénétrable spectre.

Étéoclos visait la porte Néïtide.
Mais la Ville opposait à ce fier cavalier
Mégarée immuable et vivant bouclier,
Cousin-neveu d'Œdipe aveugle et parricide.

Vers la porte et la tour près de Minerve Oncée
Marchait Hippomédon, gigantesque figure.
Mais la Ville opposait à cet horrible augure
Hyperbios portier de la porte avancée.

Vers la cinquième, (et c'est la porte Boréïde
Ou la porte du Nord), marchait Parthénopée.
Mais la Ville opposait à cette jeune épée
L'inébranlable Actor, le deuxième Œnopide.

Et la sixième était la porte Homoloïde,
Pour qui venait d'Épire et du mont Homolos,
Mais la Ville y posait, contre Amphiaraos,
Lasthène non moins sage et sept fois plus rapide.

Capaneus had to do with the Electran gate. But the town opposed to Hipponous's son, to the huge giant who was son-in-law to the king of Argos, the terrifying Polyphontes, an unfathomable apparition.

Eteoclus aimed at the Neïstan gate. But the town opposed to this proud horseman Megareus, an immovable and living shield, cousin and nephew of the blind parricide Oedipus.

Towards the gate and the tower near Onca Minerva marched Hippomedon, a giant shape. But the town opposed to this horrible omen Hyperbius, porter of the forward gate.

Towards the fifth (and it is the Borean or Northern gate) marched Parthenopœus. But the town opposed to this youthful sword the unshakable Actor, the second child of Oenops.

And the sixth was the Homoloian gate for those who came from Epirus and Mount Homolos, but the town placed there, against Amphiaraüs, Lasthenes, not less wise and seven times more swift.

Or la septième porte apparaissait vacante.
Nul sort ne la donnait à nul homme vivant.
Nuls chefs ne s'affrontaient derrière ni devant,
Bondissant des buissons de lauriers et d'acanthe.

Le vieux Bacchus lui-même et la lourde bacchante,
Assis devers le temple au cœur de la cité,
Avaient vu se fermer pour la Nécessité
La septième et dernière et la seule éloquente.

Mais la septième porte on ne la nommait pas.
Qu'importait qu'elle fût la porte Dircéenne,
Dircé, source au flot d'or, la terreur cadméenne
Nulle part n'y voyait nulles traces de pas.

Qu'importait qu'elle fût la porte Crénéïde,
La porte de la source, une bien autre source,
Avant que le soleil eût achevé sa course,
Allait éclabousser la robe thébaïde.

Deux tonneaux plus crevés que ceux des Danaïdes
Allaient laisser couler un vin plus généreux.
Deux fleuves s'en iraient, se combattant entre eux,
Souiller jusques en mer les blanches Néréïdes.

Now the seventh gate appeared empty. No lot gave it to any living man. No chiefs faced each other behind or before, leaping from the clumps of laurels and acanthus.

Old Bacchus himself and the heavy Bacchanal, seated before the temple in the city's heart, had seen the seventh and the last and the only eloquent gate be closed for Necessity.

But the seventh gate was not named. What matter that it was the Dircean gate, *Dirce, the spring with waves of gold,* the Cadmean terror nowhere saw any footprints there.

What matter that it was the Creneidean gate, *the gate of the spring*; a very different spring was going to spatter the Theban dress before the sun had finished its course.

Two barrels more broken than those of the Danaides were going to allow a more generous wine to flow. Two rivers would go, fighting among themselves, to soil even in the sea the white Nereids.

Deux flots abreuveraient la terre maternelle,
Séparant, confondant, jaillis d'un double flanc,
Dans une même horreur un seul et même sang
Pour l'assouvissement d'une haine charnelle.

Or le peuple septuple et la septuple armée
Tous deux épouvantés de la même épouvante,
Comme on regarderait le Hadès mis en vente,
Considéraient la porte obstinément fermée.

Deux mondes contemplaient la porte solennelle.
Tout un peuple couché vers les genoux des dieux,
Tout un peuple courbé sous la fureur des cieux
Savait qu'elle serait la porte Fraternelle.

Qu'elle ne serait pas simplement homicide,
Qu'elle ne serait pas une fois criminelle,
Qu'elle rassasierait la rage originelle,
Porte à double versant doublement régicide.

Prosterné sur le seuil de la triple Euménide
Tout un peuple formait un chœur inaltérable.
Tout un peuple observait cette porte d'érable,
Sachant qu'elle serait la porte Fratricide.

Two waves would water mother earth, separating, mingling, sprung from a double flank, in the same horror one and the same blood for the satisfaction of a carnal hatred.

Now the sevenfold people and the sevenfold army, both frightened with the same fear, gazed at the obstinately closed gate as you might look at Hades put up for sale.

Two worlds contemplated the solemn gate. A whole people lying towards the knees of the gods, a whole people bent beneath the wrath of the heavens, knew that it would be the Brothers' gate.

That it would not simply be homicidal, that it would not be singly criminal, that it would satisfy the original rage, gate with double sides doubly regicidal.

Prostrated on the threshold of the threefold Eumenides a whole people formed an unfailing chorus. A whole people watched that gate of maple-wood, knowing it would be the Fratricidal gate.

Les corbeaux, connaissant la race Labdacide,
Attendaient en silence un auguste repas.
Les destins attendaient un mutuel trépas,
Deux fois inexpiable et presque déïcide.

Ce fut alors qu'il dit: Il faut qu'on en finisse,
Et marchant devant lui vers la porte propice,
Vers la pleine infortune et la pleine injustice,
Sans autre compagnon que la Parque complice,

Pour l'accomplissement du malheur paternel,
Pour le couronnement d'un opprobre éternel,
Pour le contentement de son sort temporel,
S'étant avancé seul d'un pas sacramentel,

Soldats du même orgueil et de la même guerre,
Nourris du même ciel et de la même terre,
Enfants du même père et de la même mère,

Étéocle attendait son frère Polynice.

The crows, knowing the race of Labdacus, silently awaited a
solemn meal. The fates awaited a mutual death, doubly inexpiable
and almost deicidal.

It was then that he said: We must finish with it, and marching
before him towards the propitious gate, towards the whole mis-
fortune and the whole injustice, without other companion than
Fate, his accomplice,

For the fulfilment of the father's misfortune, for the crowning of
an eternal reproach, for the contentment of his temporal lot, having
gone forward alone with a sacramental tread,

Soldiers of the same pride and the same war, fed by the same sky
and the same earth, *children of the same father and the same mother,*

Eteocles awaited his brother Polynices.

— HEUREUX ceux qui sont morts pour la terre charnelle,
Mais pourvu que ce fût dans une juste guerre.
Heureux ceux qui sont morts pour quatre coins de terre.
Heureux ceux qui sont morts d'une mort solennelle.

Heureux ceux qui sont morts dans les grandes batailles,
Couchés dessus le sol à la face de Dieu.
Heureux ceux qui sont morts sur un dernier haut lieu,
Parmi tout l'appareil des grandes funérailles.

Heureux ceux qui sont morts pour des cités charnelles.
Car elles sont le corps de la cité de Dieu.
Heureux ceux qui sont morts pour leur âtre et leur feu,
Et les pauvres honneurs des maisons paternelles.

Car elles sont l'image et le commencement
Et le corps et l'essai de la maison de Dieu.
Heureux ceux qui sont morts dans cet embrassement,
Dans l'étreinte d'honneur et le terrestre aveu.

Car cet aveu d'honneur est le commencement
Et le premier essai d'un éternel aveu.
Heureux ceux qui sont morts dans cet écrasement,
Dans l'accomplissement de ce terrestre vœu.

HAPPY those who have died for the carnal earth, but provided it
was in a just war. Happy those who have died for four corners of
land. Happy those who have died a death of solemnity.

Happy those who have died in the great battles, laid on the
ground in the face of God. Happy those who have died on a final
high place amid all the pomp of great funeral ceremonies.

Happy those who have died for carnal cities. For they are the
body of the city of God. Happy those who have died for their
hearth and their fire and the poor honours of their fathers' houses.

For they are the image and the beginning and the body and the
trial of God's house. Happy those who have died in this embrace,
in the grip of honour and the earthly confession.

For this confession of honour is the beginning and the first trial
of an eternal confession. Happy those who have died in this pros-
tration, in the fulfilment of this earthly vow.

Car ce vœu de la terre est le commencement
Et le premier essai d'une fidélité.
Heureux ceux qui sont mort dans ce couronnement
Et cette obéissance et cette humilité.

Heureux ceux qui sont morts, car ils sont retournés
Dans la première argile et la première terre.
Heureux ceux qui sont morts dans une juste guerre.
Heureux les épis mûrs et les blés moissonnés.

Heureux ceux qui sont morts, car ils sont retournés
Dans la première terre et l'argile plastique.
Heureux ceux qui sont morts dans une guerre antique.
Heureux les vases purs, et les rois couronnés.

Heureux ceux qui sont morts, car ils sont retournés
Dans la première terre et dans la discipline.
Ils sont redevenus la pauvre figuline.
Ils sont redevenus des vases façonnés.

Heureux ceux qui sont morts, car ils sont retournés
Dans leur première forme et fidèle figure.

For this vow of the earth is the beginning and the first trial of a
fidelity. Happy those who have died in this coronation and this
obedience and this humility.

Happy those who have died, for they have returned to the primal
clay and the primal earth. Happy those who have died in a just war.
Happy the ripe ears and the harvested corn.

Happy those who have died, for they have returned to the primal
earth and the malleable clay. Happy those who have died in an
ancient war. Happy the pure vessels, and the crowned kings.

Happy those who have died, for they have returned to the primal
earth and to discipline. They have again become poor earthen-
ware. They have again become moulded vessels.

Happy those who have died, for they have returned to their first

Ils sont redevenus ces objets de nature
Que le pouce d'un Dieu lui-même a façonnés.

Heureux ceux qui sont morts, car ils sont retournés
Dans la première terre et la première argile.
Ils se sont remoulés dans le moule fragile
D'où le pouce d'un Dieu les avait démoulés.

Heureux ceux qui sont morts, car ils sont retournés
Dans la première terre et le premier limon.
Ils sont redescendus dans le premier sillon
D'où le pouce de Dieu les avait défournés.

Heureux ceux qui sont morts, car ils sont retournés
Dans ce même limon d'où Dieu les réveilla.
Ils se sont rendormis dans cet alléluia
Qu'ils avaient désappris devant que d'être nés.

Heureux ceux qui sont morts, car ils sont revenus
Dans la demeure antique et la vieille maison.
Ils sont redescendus dans la jeune saison
D'où Dieu les suscita misérables et nus.

shape and faithful image. They have again become those natural
objects which were fashioned by the thumb of a God himself.
   Happy those who have died, for they have returned to the primal
earth and the primal clay. They have remoulded themselves in the
fragile mould whence the thumb of a God had lifted them.
   Happy those who have died, for they have returned to the primal
earth and the primal mud. They have gone back down into the
primal furrow whence the thumb of God had drawn them.
   Happy those who have died, for they have returned into that
same mud whence God awakened them. They have gone to sleep
again in that allelujah which they had unlearned before being born.
   Happy those who have died, for they have returned to the ancient
dwelling and the old home. They have gone back down into the
young season whence God raised them up miserable and naked.

Heureux ceux qui sont morts, car ils sont retournés
Dans cette grasse argile où Dieu les modela,
Et dans ce réservoir d'où Dieu les appela.
Heureux les grands vaincus, les rois découronnés.

Heureux ceux qui sont morts, car ils sont retournés
Dans ce premier terroir d'où Dieu les révoqua,
Et dans ce reposoir d'où Dieu les convoqua.
Heureux les grands vaincus, les rois dépossédés.

Heureux ceux qui sont morts, car ils sont retournés
Dans cette grasse terre où Dieu les façonna.
Ils se sont recouchés dedans ce hosanna
Qu'ils avaient désappris devant que d'être nés.

Heureux ceux qui sont morts, car ils sont retournés
Dans ce premier terreau nourri de leur dépouille,
Dans ce premier caveau, dans la tourbe et la houille.
Heureux les grands vaincus, les rois désabusés.

Happy those who have died, for they have returned to that oily
clay in which God modelled them, and to that reservoir whence
God called them. Happy the great defeated, the uncrowned kings.

Happy those who have died, for they have returned to that
primal soil whence God recalled them, and to that station of the
cross whence God called them together. Happy the great defeated,
the dispossessed kings.

Happy those who have died, for they have returned to that oily
earth whence God fashioned them. They have lain down again
within that hosannah which they had unlearned before being born.

Happy those who have died, for they have returned to that first
compost-heap fed with their bodies, to that first vault, to the peat
and the coal. Happy the great defeated, the disillusioned kings.*

---

*This extract was taken from *Ève*.

MAX JACOB

La Roue du moulin

Le chant de ma rivière où est le pont du gué
comme voix de chapelle et voix de sansonnet
pour y conter ma peine j'y vais après souper
au fil de l'eau courante ma peine et mon regret.

Au chant de l'eau courante je me suis endormi
alors j'ai vu ma belle et la belle a souri:
«Pour qui sont donc, lui dis-je, ces pierres de rubis?
et ces fleurs de jardin inconnues au pays?
– Meunier, répondit-elle, c'est ton cœur que je tiens.
qu'il aille à la rivière sous la roue du moulin.
Que la roue le boulange comme on fait du pétrin.»

A la roue donc, la belle, ces pierres et ces fleurs!
elle en fera des larmes, des larmes et des pleurs
quant au rubis, ma belle, il faudrait un fondeur
qu'ils sautent jusqu'au ciel: ce serait le meilleur.

The Mill Wheel

My river's song, where the bridge of the ford is, like the chapel's voice and the starling's voice – I go there after supper to tell my grief, to the flow of the running water my grief and my regret.

I went to sleep to the song of the running water. Then I saw my love, and my love smiled: 'For whom then,' said I to her, 'are those ruby stones? And those garden flowers unknown in this part of the country?' 'Miller,' answered she, 'it is your heart I hold. Let it go to the river beneath the mill wheel. Let the wheel knead it as you make dough.'

To the wheel then, my love, those stones and those flowers! It will make tears of them, salt water and tears – as to the rubies, my love, you would need a smelter – let them leap up to heaven: that would be the best.

«Connaissez-vous Maître Eckart?»

(*Paul Petit*)

CONNAISSEZ-VOUS le grand Albert?
Joachim? Amaury de Bène?
à Thöss, Margareta Ebner
de Christ enceinte en chair humaine?

Connaissez-vous Henri Suso?
Ruysbrock surnommé l'Admirable?
et Joseph de Cupertino
qui volait comme un dirigeable?

Et les sermons de Jean Tauler?
et le jeune homme des Sept Nonnes
qu'on soigna comme une amazone
débarquant des Ciels-univers?

Connaissez-vous Jacob Boehm
et la Signatura Rerum?
et Paracelse l'archidoxe,
le précurseur des rayons X?

'*Do You Know Master Eckart?*'*

(*Paul Petit*)

Do you know Albert the Great? Joachim? Amaury de Bène? At Thöss, Margareta Ebner made pregnant by Christ in human flesh?

Do you know Henry Suso? Ruysbroeck surnamed the Admirable? And Joseph of Copertino who used to fly like an airship?

And the sermons of John Tauler? And the young man of the Seven Nuns whom they looked after like an amazon disembarking from universes in the sky?

Do you know Jacob Boehm and the *Signatura Rerum*? And Paracelsus the archidoxis, the forerunner of X-rays?

---

*The names in this poem are mostly those of medieval philosophers or mystics.

On connaît bien peu ceux qu'on aime
mais je les comprends assez bien
étant tous ces gens-là moi-même
qui ne suis pourtant qu'un babouin.

OSCAR VENCESLAS DE LUBICZ MILOSZ

– Et surtout que Demain n'apprenne pas où je suis –
Les bois, les bois sont pleins de baies noires –
Ta voix est comme un son de lune dans le vieux puits
Où l'écho, l'écho de juin vient boire.

Et que nul ne prononce mon nom là-bas, en rêve,
Les temps, les temps sont bien accomplis –
Comme un tout petit arbre souffrant de prime sève
Est ta blancheur en robe sans pli.

Et que les ronces se referment derrière nous,
Car j'ai peur, car j'ai peur du retour.
Les grandes fleurs blanches caressent tes doux genoux
Et l'ombre, et l'ombre est pâle d'amour.

We little know those we love, but I understand them well enough, being all those folk myself, who yet am only a baboon.

* * *

And above all let not tomorrow learn where I am – the woods, the woods are full of dark berries – your voice is like a moon-sound in the old well, where the echo, the echo of June comes to drink.

And let no one speak my name down there in a dream. The times, the times are fulfilled indeed – your whiteness in an uncreased dress is like a small tree ill from its first sap.

And let the briars close again behind us, for I am afraid, I am afraid of the return. The great white flowers caress your soft knees, and the shade, and the shade is pale with love.

Et ne dis pas à l'eau de la forêt qui je suis;
Mon nom, mon nom est tellement mort.
Tes yeux ont la couleur heureuse des jeunes pluies,
Des jeunes pluies sur l'étang qui dort.

Et ne raconte rien au vent du vieux cimetière.
Il pourrait m'ordonner de le suivre.
Ta chevelure sent l'été, la lune et la terre.
Il faut vivre, vivre, rien que vivre . . .

LÉON-PAUL FARGUE

ILS entrèrent au crépuscule. – Une lampe étendit ses
ailes dans la chambre. Et quelqu'un posa la main sur mon
épaule. Elle est partie. Dit une voix déserte. – Par la porte
ouverte, on entendit des piétinements las de chaleur, des
voix sourdes, une voix caressante, et puis les bruits plus
frais du soir. Une fenêtre sans rideaux laissait voir la ville
où baissaient les mirages, et le profond des rues qui bouge
comme un fleuve . . .

And do not say to the forest water who I am; my name, my
name is so dead. Your eyes have the happy colour of young rains,
of young rains over the sleeping pond.

And tell nothing to the wind of the old graveyard. It might order
me to follow it. Your hair smells of summer, the moon and the
earth. We must live, live, do nothing but live . . .

THEY went in at twilight. – A lamp spread its wings in the room.
And someone placed a hand on my shoulder. She is gone. Said a
forsaken voice. – Through the open door could be heard steps
weary with heat, dull voices, a caressing voice, and then the cooler
sounds of evening. A window without curtains left the town visible
where the mirages were coming down low, and the depth of the
streets moving like a river . . .

Elle est partie. J'ouvris sans bruit la porte sur l'escalier sans lumière. On n'entendait sur le palier que la plainte obscure d'une fontaine. Mais je vis la main du Soir glisser sur la rampe, devant la mienne . . .

J'entrai dans la chambre. Je vis tout de suite quelques vêtements que je connaissais tant et qu'elle avait laissés sur une chaise. J'allai les toucher et les sentir. Elle tremblait vraiment partout dans la chambre crépusculaire. Et son regard y rayonnait comme un élément dans sa forme la plus belle.

Et je restais là sans oser bouger et sans pleurer, car je sentais éperdument sa présence par un frisson léger contre mes lèvres . . .

Postface

Un long bras timbré d'or glisse du haut des arbres
Et commence à descendre et tinte dans les branches.
Les fleurs et les feuilles se pressent et s'entendent.

She is gone. Noiselessly I opened the door on to the unlighted staircase. On the landing only the secret complaint of a cistern was to be heard. But I saw the evening's hand slip over the banisters before mine . . .

I went into the room. I saw at once some clothes which I knew so well and which she had left on a chair. I went to touch and feel them. Indeed, she trembled everywhere in the twilit room. And her glance shone there as a component in its loveliest form.

And I remained there without daring to move and without weeping, for I felt her presence desperately by a faint shudder against my lips . . .

Postface

A long arm crested with gold slips from the top of the trees and begins to come down and tinkles in the branches. The flowers and the leaves press against one another and make friends. I have seen

J'ai vu l'orvet glisser dans la douceur du soir.
Diane sur l'étang se penche et met son masque.
Un soulier de satin court dans la clairière
Comme un rappel du ciel qui rejoint l'horizon.
Les barques de la nuit sont prêtes à partir.
D'autres viendront s'asseoir sur la chaise de fer.
D'autres verront cela quand je ne serai plus.
La lumière oubliera ceux qui l'ont tant aimée.
Nul appel ne viendra rallumer nos visages.
Nul sanglot ne fera retentir notre amour.
Nos fenêtres seront éteintes.
Un couple d'étrangers longera la rue grise.
Les voix
D'autres voix chanteront, d'autres yeux pleureront
Dans une maison neuve.
Tout sera consommé, tout sera pardonné,
La peine sera fraîche et la forêt nouvelle,
Et peut-être qu'un jour, pour de nouveaux amis,
Dieu tiendra ce bonheur qu'il nous avait promis.

the slowworm sliding in the softness of evening. Diana leans down over the pool and puts on her mask. A satin shoe runs in the clearing like a reminder of the sky rejoining the horizon. The ships of the night are ready to leave. Others will come to sit on the iron chair. Others will see that when I shall be no more. The light will forget those who loved it so much. No call will come to light up our faces again. No sob will make our love resound. Our windows will be put out. A pair of strangers will go along the grey street. The voices of other voices will sing, other eyes will weep in a new house. All will be consummated, all will be forgiven, the sorrow will be fresh and the forest new, and perhaps one day, for new lovers, God will keep that happines swhich he had promised us.

GUILLAUME APOLLINAIRE

La Chanson du mal-aimé

A Paul Léautaud

*ET je chantais cette romance
En 1903 sans savoir
Que mon amour à la semblance
Du beau Phénix s'il meurt un soir
Le Matin voit sa renaissance*

*Un soir de demi-brume à Londres
Un voyou qui ressemblait à
Mon amour vint à ma rencontre
Et le regard qu'il me jeta
Me fit baisser les yeux de honte*

*Je suivis ce mauvais garçon
Qui sifflotait mains dans les poches
Nous semblions entre les maisons
Onde ouverte de la mer Rouge
Lui les Hébreux moi Pharaon*

The Song of the Ill-beloved

To Paul Léautaud

AND I sang this ballad in 1903 without knowing that my love like the beautiful Phoenix, if it dies one evening, the morning sees its rebirth.

One foggy evening in London a rascal who resembled my love came to meet me, and the glance he threw me made me lower my eyes for shame.

I followed that bad lad who whistled with his hands in his pockets. Between the houses, which were like the parted waves of the Red Sea, we seemed to be, he, the Hebrews, and I, Pharaoh.

Que tombent ces vagues de briques
Si tu ne fus pas bien aimée
Je suis le souverain d'Égypte
Sa sœur-épouse son armée
Si tu n'es pas l'amour unique

Au tournant d'une rue brûlant
De tous les feux de ses façades
Plaies du brouillard sanguinolent
Où se lamentaient les façades
Une femme lui ressemblant

C'était son regard d'inhumaine
La cicatrice à son cou nu
Sortit saoule d'une taverne
Au moment où je reconnus
La fausseté de l'amour même

Lorsqu'il fut de retour enfin
Dans sa patrie le sage Ulysse
Son vieux chien de lui se souvint
Près d'un tapis de haute lisse
Sa femme attendait qu'il revînt

Let these waves of brick fall, if you were not really loved! I am the sovereign of Egypt, his sister-wife, his army, if you are not the only love.

At the corner of a street burning with all the fires of its façades, wounds of the fog tinged with blood, where the façades bemoaned their lot, a woman resembling her

(It was her inhuman glance, the scar on her bare neck) came out drunk from a tavern at the instant when I recognized the falsity of love itself.

When the wise Ulysses returned at last to his native land, his old dog remembered him; his wife waited for him to come back near a cloth of high warp.

L'époux royal de Sacontale
Las de vaincre se réjouit
Quand il la retrouva plus pâle
D'attente et d'amour yeux pâlis
Caressant sa gazelle mâle

J'ai pensé à ces rois heureux
Lorsque le faux amour et celle
Dont je suis encore amoureux
Heurtant leurs ombres infidèles
Me rendirent si malheureux

Regrets sur quoi l'enfer se fonde
Qu'un ciel d'oubli s'ouvre à mes vœux
Pour son baiser les rois du monde
Seraient morts les pauvres fameux
Pour elle eussent vendu leur ombre

J'ai hiverné dans mon passé
Revienne le soleil de Pâques
Pour chauffer un cœur plus glacé
Que les quarante de Sébaste
Moins que ma vie martyrisée

The royal husband of Sakontala tired of conquering rejoiced when he found her paler, her eyes grown pale with expectancy and love, stroking her male gazelle.

I thought of those happy kings, when false love and she whom I still desire, jostling each other's faithless shadows, made me so unhappy.

Regrets on which hell is based! May a heaven of forgetfulness be opened to my desires! For her kiss the kings of the world would have died, poor famous wretches, for her they would have sold their shadow.

I have wintered in my past. Let the Easter sun return to heat a heart icier than the forty belonging to Sebasta who was tormented less than my life.

Mon beau navire ô ma mémoire
Avons-nous assez navigué
Dans une onde mauvaise à boire
Avons-nous assez divagué
De la belle aube au triste soir

Adieux faux amour confondu
Avec la femme qui s'éloigne
Avec celle que j'ai perdue
L'année dernière en Allemagne
Et que je ne reverrai plus

Voie lactée ô sœur lumineuse
Des blancs ruisseaux de Chanaan
Et des corps blancs des amoureuses
Nageurs morts suivrons-nous d'ahan
Ton cours vers d'autres nébuleuses

Je me souviens d'une autre année
C'était l'aube d'un jour d'avril
J'ai chanté ma joie bien-aimée
Chanté l'amour à voix virile
Au moment d'amour de l'année

My fine ship, O my memory, have we sailed enough in waves unfit to drink? Have we wandered enough from lovely dawn to sad evening?

Farewell, false love merged with the woman departing, with her whom I lost last year in Germany and whom I shall see no more.

Milky Way, O shining sister of the white streams of Canaan and the white bodies of women in love, shall we follow your track towards other nebulae, panting like dead swimmers?

I remember another year. It was the dawn of an April day. I sang my beloved joy, sang my love with a manly voice at the year's loving time.

AUBADE
CHANTÉE
A
LAETARE
UN AN
PASSÉ

C'est le printemps viens-t'en Pâquette
Te promener au bois joli
Les poules dans la cour caquètent
L'aube au ciel fait de roses plis
L'amour chemine à ta conquête

Mars et Vénus sont revenus
Ils s'embrassent à bouches folles
Devant des sites ingénus
Où sous les roses qui feuillolent
De beaux dieux roses dansent nus

Viens ma tendresse est la régente
De la floraison qui paraît
La nature est belle et touchante
Pan sifflote dans la forêt
Les grenouilles humides chantent

Beaucoup de ces dieux ont péri
C'est sur eux que pleurent les saules
Le grand Pan l'amour Jésus-Christ
Sont bien morts et les chats miaulent
Dans la cour je pleure à Paris

An aubade sung *a laetare* a year past

It is the Spring. Come, Pâquette, to walk in the pretty wood. The
hens in the yard are clucking. The dawn makes pink folds in the
sky. Love is marching to conquer you.

Mars and Venus have returned. With mouths grown wild they
kiss each other in front of artless beauty spots, where lovely pink
gods dance naked beneath leafy roses.

Come, my tenderness is the ruler of the apparent blossoming.
Nature is beautiful and moving. Pan is whistling in the forest. The
damp frogs are singing.

Many of these gods have died. It is over them the willows weep.
The great Pan, love, Jesus Christ are quite dead, and the cats are
miaowing in the courtyard I am weeping for in Paris.

Moi qui sais des lais pour les reines
Les complaintes de mes années
Des hymnes d'esclave aux murènes
La romance du mal-aimé
Et des chansons pour les sirènes

L'amour est mort j'en suis tremblant
J'adore de belles idoles
Les souvenirs lui ressemblant
Comme la femme de Mausole
Je reste fidèle et dolent

Je suis fidèle comme un dogue
Au maître le lierre au tronc
Et les Cosaques Zaporogues
Ivrognes pieux et larrons
Aux steppes et au décalogue

Portez comme un joug le Croissant
Qu'interrogent les astrologues
Je suis le Sultan tout-Puissant
Ô mes Cosaques Zaporogues
Votre Seigneur éblouissant

I who know lays for queens, my years' complaints, slaves' hymns to lampreys, the ballad of the ill-beloved and songs for sirens.

Love is dead. I tremble for it. I worship beautiful idols, the memories that resemble it. Like the wife of Mausolus I remain faithful and plaintive.

I am faithful as a mastiff to its master, as ivy to a tree-trunk and the Zaporogian Cossacks, pious drunkards and thieves, to the steppes and the decalogue.

Bear for a yoke the Crescent, which the astrologers question. O my Zaporogian Cossacks, I am the all-powerful Sultan, your dazzling Lord.

Devenez mes sujets fidèles
Leur avait écrit le Sultan
Ils rirent à cette nouvelle
Et répondirent à l'instant
A la lueur d'une chandelle

Plus criminel que Barrabas
Cornu comme les mauvais anges
Quel Belzébuth es-tu là-bas
Nourri d'immondice et de fange
Nous n'irons pas à tes sabbats

RÉPONSE
DES
COSAQUES
ZAPOROGUES
AU SULTAN
DE
CONSTANTINOPLE

Poisson pourri de Salonique
Long collier des sommeils affreux
D'yeux arrachés à coup de pique
Ta mère fit un pet foireux
Et tu naquis de sa colique

Bourreau de Podolie Amant
Des plaies des ulcères des croûtes
Groin de cochon cul de jument
Tes richesses garde-les toutes
Pour payer tes médicaments

Become my faithful subjects, the Sultan had written to them. They laughed at this news and answered immediately by the light of a candle.

Answer of the Zaporogian Cossacks to the
Sultan of Constantinople

More criminal than Barrabas, horned like the bad angels, what a Beelzebub you are there, fed on filth and dirt. We shall not go to your Sabbaths.

Rotten fish of Salonika, long necklace of frightful slumbers of eyes torn out by pike blows, your mother gave a loose fart, and you were born from her colic.

Podolia's hangman. Lover of sores, ulcers, scabs. Pig's snout, mare's arse, keep all your riches to pay for your medicines.

Voie lactée ô sœur lumineuse
Des blancs ruisseaux de Chanaan
Et des corps blancs des amoureuses
Nageurs morts suivrons-nous d'ahan
Ton cours vers d'autres nébuleuses

Regret des yeux de la putain
Et belle comme une panthère
Amour vos baisers florentins
Avaient une saveur amère
Qui a rebuté nos destins

Ses regards laissaient une traîne
D'étoiles dans les soirs tremblants
Dans ses yeux nageaient les sirènes
Et nos baisers mordus sanglants
Faisaient pleurer nos fées marraines

Mais en vérité je l'attends
Avec mon cœur avec mon âme
Et sur le pont des Reviens-t'en
Si jamais revient cette femme
Je lui dirai Je suis content

Milky Way, O shining sister of the white streams of Canaan and the white bodies of women in love, shall we follow your track towards other nebulae, panting like dead swimmers?

Regret for the eyes of the whore beautiful as a panther – love, your Florentine kisses had a bitter taste that discouraged our destinies.

Her glances left a trail of stars in the trembling evenings. In her eyes the sirens swarmed, and our bitten bleeding kisses made our fairy godmothers weep.

But in truth I wait for her with my heart and with my soul, and on the bridge of come-you-back, if ever that woman returns, I shall say to her, 'I am glad.'

Mon cœur et ma tête se vident
Tout le ciel s'écoule par eux
Ô mes tonneaux des Danaïdes
Comment faire pour être heureux
Comme un petit enfant candide

Je ne veux jamais l'oublier
Ma colombe ma blanche rade
Ô marguerite exfoliée
Mon île au loin ma Désirade
Ma rose mon giroflier

Les satyres et les pyraustes
Les égypans les feux follets
Et les destins damnés ou faustes
La corde au cou comme à Calais
Sur ma douleur quel holocauste

Douleur qui doubles les destins
La licorne et le capricorne
Mon âme et mon corps incertain
Te fuient ô bûcher divin qu'ornent
Des astres des fleurs du matin

My heart and head are emptied. The whole sky flows out through them. O my Danaides' casks! What should I do to be happy like a simple little child?

I wish never to forget her, my dove, my white roadstead, O open daisy! My far-off island, my Désirade, my rose, my clove-tree.

The Satyrs and the Pyraustas, the horned Pans, the St Elmo's fires, and the fatal or propitious destinies, cords round their necks as at Calais – what a holocaust on my grief!

Sorrow doubling the fates, the unicorn and capricorn, my soul and wavering body flee from you, O divine pyre adorned with stars, the morning flowers.

Malheur dieu pâle aux yeux d'ivoire
Tes prêtres fous t'ont-ils paré
Tes victimes en robe noire
Ont-elles vainement pleuré
Malheur dieu qu'il ne faut pas croire

Et toi qui me suis en rampant
Dieu de mes dieux morts en automne
Tu mesures combien d'empans
J'ai droit que la terre me donne
Ô mon ombre ô mon vieux serpent

Au soleil parce que tu l'aimes
Je t'ai menée souviens-t'en bien
Ténébreuse épouse que j'aime
Tu es à moi en n'étant rien
Ô mon ombre en deuil de moi-même

L'hiver est mort tout enneigé
On a brulé les ruches blanches
Dans les jardins et les vergers
Les oiseaux chantent sur les branches
Le printemps clair l'avril léger

Misfortune, pale god with ivory eyes, have your mad priests decked your victims for you in a black robe? Have they wept in vain, misfortune, god who must not be believed?

And you who follow me crawling, god of my gods that died in the autumn, you measure how many spans I have the right to be given by the earth, O my shadow, my old serpent!

Because you like it I have led you into the sun, remember, dark companion whom I love. You belong to me, while being nothing, O my shadow in mourning for myself!

Winter is dead full of snow. They have burned the white hives. In the gardens and the orchards the birds on the branches sing of clear Spring and light April.

Mort d'immortels argyraspides
La neige aux boucliers d'argent
Fuit les dendrophores livides
Du printemps cher aux pauvres gens
Qui resourient les yeux humides

Et moi j'ai le cœur aussi gros
Qu'un cul de dame damascène
Ô mon amour je t'aimais trop
Et maintenant j'ai trop de peine
Les sept épées hors du fourreau

Sept épées de mélancolie
Sans morfil ô claires douleurs
Sont dans mon cœur et la folie
Veut raisonner pour mon malheur
Comment voulez-vous que j'oublie

LES SEPT ÉPÉES   La première est toute d'argent
Et son nom tremblant c'est Pâline
Sa lame un ciel d'hiver neigeant
Son destin sanglant gibeline
Vulcain mourut en la forgeant

Death of silver-shielded immortals, the snow with silver bucklers flees from the pale caterpillars of Spring, dear to poor folk who smile again with moist eyes.

And I have a heart as big as a damascene lady's behind. O my love, I loved you too much, and now I have too much pain, the seven swords out of their sheath.

Seven swords of melancholy with no blunt edge, O shining griefs, are in my heart, and madness wants to reason to my cost: how do you think I can forget?

The Seven Swords

The first is all of silver, and its trembling name is Pâline, its blade a snowy winter sky, its fate bloody and Ghibelline. Vulcan died forging it.

La seconde nommée Noubosse
Est un bel arc-en-ciel joyeux
Les dieux s'en servent à leurs noces
Elle a tué trente Bé-Rieux
Et fut douée par Carabosse

La troisième bleu féminin
N'en est pas moins un chibriape
Appelé Lul de Faltenin
Et que porte sur une nappe
L'Hermès Ernest devenu nain

La quatrième Malourène
Est un fleuve vert et doré
C'est le soir quand les riveraines
Y baignent leurs corps adorés
Et des chants de rameurs s'y traînent

La cinquième Sainte-Fabeau
C'est la plus belle des quenouilles
C'est un cyprès sur un tombeau
Où les quatre vents s'agenouillent
Et chaque nuit c'est un flambeau

The second called Noubosse is a fine joyful rainbow. The gods make use of it at their weddings. It has killed thirty Bé-Rieux and was endowed by Carabosse.

The third, a feminine blue, is nonetheless a phallus called Lul de Faltenin and carried on a cloth by the messenger Ernest, become a dwarf.

The fourth Malourène is a green and golden river. It is the evening when the women dwelling on the banks bathe their lovely bodies there, and songs of rowers die away over it.

The fifth Sainte-Fabeau is the finest of distaffs. It is a cypress on a tomb where the four winds kneel down, and every night it is a torch.

La sixième métal de gloire
C'est l'ami aux si douces mains
Dont chaque matin nous sépare
Adieu voilà votre chemin
Les coqs s'épuisaient en fanfares

Et la septième s'exténue
Une femme une rose morte
Merci que le dernier venu
Sur mon amour ferme la porte
Je ne vous ai jamais connue

Voie lactée ô sœur lumineuse
Des blancs ruisseaux de Chanaan
Et des corps blancs des amoureuses
Nageurs morts suivrons-nous d'ahan
Ton cours vers d'autres nébuleuses

Les démons du hasard selon
Le chant du firmament nous mènent
A sons perdus leurs violons
Font danser notre race humaine
Sur la descente à reculons

The sixth metal of fame is the friend with such gentle hands from whom each morning severs us. Farewell, there is your road. The cocks wore themselves out in fanfares.

And the seventh wears itself away. A woman, a dead rose. Thanks be that the last arrival shuts the door on my love. I never knew you.

Milky Way, O shining sister of the white streams of Canaan and the white bodies of women in love, shall we follow your track towards other nebulæ, panting like dead swimmers?

The demons of chance lead us according to the song of the firmament. To lunatic sounds their violins make our human race dance backwards down the slope.

Destins destins impénétrables
Rois secoués par la folie
Et ces grelottantes étoiles
De fausses femmes dans vos lits
Aux déserts que l'histoire accable

Luitpold le vieux prince régent
Tuteur de deux royautés folles
Sanglote-t-il en y songeant
Quand vacillent les lucioles
Mouches dorées de la Saint-Jean

Près d'un château sans châtelaine
La barque aux barcarols chantants
Sur un lac blanc et sous l'haleine
Des vents qui tremblent au printemps
Voguait cygne mourant sirène

Un jour le roi dans l'eau d'argent
Se noya puis la bouche ouverte
Ils s'en revint en surnageant
Sur la rive dormir inerte
Face tournée au ciel changeant

Destinies, impenetrable destinies! Kings shaken by madness and those trembling stars of false women in your beds in deserts overwhelmed by history.

Does Luitpold, the old prince-regent, guardian of two mad royalties, weep for thinking of it, when the fireflies waver, the golden flies of St John's day.

Near a castle without a chatelaine, the barge full of the singing of sea songs, on a white lake beneath the breath of Spring's trembling winds, floated like a dying swan or a siren.

One day the king drowned himself in the silvery water; then with his mouth open returned floating to sleep motionless on the shore, his face turned to the changing sky.

Juin ton soleil ardente lyre
Brûle mes doigts endoloris
Triste et mélodieux délire
J'erre à travers mon beau Paris
Sans avoir le cœur d'y mourir

Les dimanches s'y éternisent
Et les orgues de Barbarie
Y sanglotent dans les cours grises
Les fleurs aux balcons de Paris
Penchent comme la tour de Pise

Soirs de Paris ivres de gin
Flambant de l'électricité
Les tramways feux verts sur l'échine
Musiquent au long des portées
De rails leur folie de machines

Les cafés gonflés de fumée
Crient tout l'amour de leurs tziganes
De tous leurs siphons enrhumés
De leurs garçons vêtus d'un pagne
Vers toi toi que j'ai tant aimée

June, your sun, a fiery lyre, burns my aching fingers. O sad melodious delirium! I wander through my beautiful Paris without having the heart to die there.

Sundays draw out interminably, and the barrel organs are sobbing in the grey courtyards. The flowers on the balconies of Paris lean like the tower of Pisa.

Parisian evenings drunk with gin, flaring with electricity, the tramways, green fires on their backs, set their mechanical madness to music as far as the rails reach.

The cafés swollen with smoke cry all the love of their gipsies, of all their snuffling syphons, and of their waiters dressed in aprons, towards you, you whom I loved so much.

Moi qui sais des lais pour les reines
Les complaintes de mes années
Des hymnes d'esclave aux murènes
La romance du mal-aimé
Et des chansons pour les sirènes

Fête

A André Rouveyre

Feu d'artifice en acier
Qu'il est charmant cet éclairage
   Artifice d'artificier
Mêler quelque grâce au courage

Deux fusants
Rose éclatement
Comme deux seins que l'on dégrafe
Tendent leurs bouts insolemment
IL SUT AIMER
      quelle épitaphe

I who know lays for queens, my years' complaints, slaves' hymns to lampreys, the ballad of the ill-beloved, and songs for sirens.

Festival

To André Rouveyre

Fireworks in steel. How charming this lighting is. Cunning of a firework-maker – to mix a little grace with bravery.

Two shells, a pink burst, like two breasts undone, insolently hold out their tips. HE KNEW HOW TO LOVE – what an epitaph! A poet

Un poète dans la forêt
Regarde avec indifférence
   Son revolver au cran d'arrêt
Des roses mourir d'espérance

Il songe aux roses de Saadi
Et soudain sa tête se penche
Car une rose lui redit
La molle courbe d'une hanche

L'air est plein d'un terrible alcool
Filtré des étoiles mi-closes
Les obus caressent le mol
Parfum nocturne où tu reposes
   Mortification des roses

Les Grenadines repentantes

En est-il donc deux dans Grenade
Qui pleurent sur ton seul péché
Ici l'on jette la grenade
Qui se change en un œuf coché

in the forest looks with indifference at his revolver with the safety catch on, at roses dying of hope. He dreams of the roses of Saadi, and suddenly his head droops, for a rose repeats the soft curve of a hip.

The air is full of a terrible alcohol filtered from the half-closed stars. The shells caress the soft perfume of night in which you lie, gangrene of the roses.

The Repentant Women of Granada*

ARE there then two of them in Granada weeping over your single sin? Here we throw the grenade that changes to a fertile egg.

*This poem depends on a pun. *Grenade* can mean 'hand-grenade', 'pomegranate', or the Spanish town of Granada.

Puisqu'il en naît des coqs Infante
Entends-les chanter leurs dédains
Et que la grenade est touchante
Dans nos effroyables jardins

Tourbillon de mouches

UN cavalier va dans la plaine
La jeune fille pense à lui
Et cette flotte à Mytilène
Le fil de fer est là qui luit

Comme ils cueillaient la rose ardente
Leurs yeux tout à coup ont fleuri
Mais quel soleil la bouche errante
A qui la bouche avait souri

VALÉRY LARBAUD

Ode

PRÊTE-MOI ton grand bruit, ta grande allure si douce,
Ton glissement nocturne à travers l'Europe illuminée,

Since cocks are born from it, Infanta, hear them singing their
scorn, and how touching the pomegranate is in our terrible gardens.

Swarm of Flies

A HORSEMAN passes in the plain. The young girl thinks of him
and that fleet at Mytilene. The iron blade is there shining.

As they gathered the burning rose all at once their eyes blos-
somed. But what a sun is the wandering mouth to which the mouth
had smiled.

Ode

LEND me your vast noise, your vast gentle speed, your nightly
slipping through a lighted Europe, O luxury train! And the

Ô train de luxe! et l'angoissante musique
Qui bruit le long de tes couloirs de cuir doré,
Tandis que derrière les portes laquées, aux loquets de
cuivre lourd,
Dorment les millionaires.

Je parcours en chantonnant tes couloirs
Et je suis ta course vers Vienne et Budapesth,
Mêlant ma voix à tes cent mille voix,
Ô Harmonika-Zug!

J'ai senti pour la première fois toute la douceur de vivre,
Dans une cabine du Nord-Express, entre Wirballen et
Pskow.
On glissait à travers des prairies où des bergers,
Au pied de groupes de grands arbres pareils à des
collines,
Étaient vêtus de peaux de moutons crues et sales . . .
(Huit heures du matin en automne, et la belle cantatrice
Aux yeux violets chantait dans la cabine à côté.)

agonizing music that sounds the length of your gilt leather corridors, while behind the japanned doors with heavy copper latches sleep the millionaires.

Singing, I pass through your corridors and follow your path towards Vienna and Budapest, mingling my voice to your hundred thousand voices, O harmonicat rain!

I felt all the sweetness of life for the first time in a compartment of the Nord express between Wirballen and Pskov. We were slipping through grasslands where shepherds, at the foot of clumps of big trees like hills, were dressed in dirty, raw sheepskins . . . (Eight o'clock on an autumn morning, and the beautiful singer with violet eyes was singing in the next compartment.)

Et vous, grandes glaces à travers lesquelles j'ai vu passer
     la Sibérie et les Monts du Samnium,
La Castille âpre et sans fleurs, et la mer de Marmara sous
     une pluie tiède!
Prêtez-moi, ô Orient-Express, Sud-Brenner-Bahn, prê-
     tez-moi
Vos miraculeux bruits sourds et
Vos vibrantes voix de chanterelle;
Prêtez-moi la respiration légère et facile
Des locomotives hautes et minces, aux mouvements
Si aisés, les locomotives des rapides,
Précédant sans effort quatre wagons jaunes à lettres d'or
Dans les solitudes montagnardes de la Serbie,
Et, plus loin, à travers la Bulgarie pleine de roses . . .

Ah! il faut que ces bruits et que ce mouvement
Entrent dans mes poèmes et disent
Pour moi ma vie indicible, ma vie
D'enfant qui ne veut rien savoir, sinon
Espérer éternellement des choses vagues.

    And you, huge plate-glass windows, through which I have seen
Siberia and the hills of Samnium go by, harsh flowerless Castille and
the sea of Marmara under a downpour of lukewarm rain! Lend me,
O Orient Express, South Brenner line, lend me your miraculous
muffled noises and your high quivering voices; lend me the light,
easy breathing of the tall, thin locomotives, whose movements are
so easy, the locomotives of the express trains, effortlessly guiding
four yellow coaches with gilt lettering into the mountainous soli-
tudes of Serbia and, farther on, across Bulgaria full of roses . . .
    Ah! these noises and this motion must enter into my poems and
tell my indescribable life for me, my child's life – a child who
wishes to know nothing except eternally to hope for uncertain
things.

CATHERINE POZZI

Ave

Très haut amour, s'il se peut que jė meure
Sans avoir su d'où je vous possédais,
En quel soleil était votre demeure,
En quel passé votre temps, en quelle heure
     Je vous aimais,

Très haut amour qui passez la mémoire,
Feu sans foyer dont j'ai fait tout mon jour,
En quel destin vous traciez mon histoire,
En quel sommeil se voyait votre gloire,
     Ô mon séjour . . .

Quand je serai pour moi-même perdue
Et divisée à l'abîme infini,
Infiniment, quand je serai rompue,
Quand le présent dont jė suis revêtue
     Aura trahi,

Par l'univers en mille corps brisée,
De mille instants non rassemblés encor,

Ave

Most lofty love, if it be that I die without having known whence I possessed you, in what sun your dwelling was, in what past your time, in what hour I loved you,

    Most lofty love, surpassing memory, fire without hearth from which I made all my day, in what destiny you marked my story, in what slumber your glory was seen, O my dwelling-place . . .

    When I am lost to myself and divided to the infinite abyss, when I am infinitely broken, when the present in which I am clad has betrayed me,

    Broken into a thousand pieces throughout the universe, you will

De cendre aux cieux jusqu'au néant vannée,
Vous referez pour une étrange année
Un seul trésor,

Vous referez mon nom et mon image
De mille corps emportés par le jour,
Vive unité sans nom et sans visage,
Cœur de l'esprit, ô centre du mirage
Très haut amour.

JULES SUPERVIELLE

Whisper in Agony

NE vous étonnez pas,
Abaissez les paupières
Jusqu'à ce qu'elles soient
De véritable pierre.

Laissez faire le cœur,
Et même s'il s'arrête.
Il bat pour lui tout seul
Sur sa pente secrète.

re-create a single treasure for a strange year from a thousand
moments not yet brought together, from ashes winnowed to the
skies till nothing remains,

You will re-create my name and my image from a thousand
pieces carried away by the day, a living unity nameless and faceless,
the spirit's heart, O centre of the mirage, most lofty love.

Whisper in Agony

Do not be surprised; close the eyelids until they become real
stone.

Let the heart alone and even if it stop. It beats for itself all
alone on its secret slope.

Les mains s'allongeront
Dans leur barque de glace,
Et le front sera nu
Comme une grande place
Vide, entre deux armées.

La Chambre voisine

TOURNEZ le dos à cet homme
Mais restez auprès de lui,
(Écartez votre regard,
Sa confuse barbarie),
Restez debout sans mot dire,
Voyez-vous pas qu'il sépare
Mal le jour d'avec la nuit,
Et les cieux les plus profonds
Du cœur sans fond qui l'agite?
Éteignez tous ces flambeaux
Regardez: ses veines luisent.
Quand il avance la main,
Un souffle de pierreries,
De la circulaire nuit
Jusqu'à ses longs doigts parvient.

The hands will be stretched out in their icy barge, and the
brow will be naked like a great empty square between two armies.

The Neighbouring Room

TURN your back on this man, but stay beside him (turn away your
gaze, its muddled barbarity); stay standing without saying a word;
do you not see that he hardly distinguishes day from night and the
deepest of the skies from the bottomless heart that torments him?
Put out all those torches. Watch: his veins are shining. When he
puts out his hand a breath of precious stones comes from the circu-
lar night right to his slender fingers. Leave him alone on his bed.

Laissez-le seul sur son lit,
Le temps le borde et le veille,
En vue de ces hauts rochers
Où gémit, toujours caché,
Le cœur des nuits sans sommeil.
Qu'on n'entre plus dans la chambre
D'où doit sortir un grand chien
Ayant perdu la mémoire
Et qui cherchera sur terre
Comme le long de la mer
L'homme qu'il laissa derrière
Immobile, entre ses mains
Raides et définitives.

CE bruit de la mer où nous sommes tous,
Il le connaît bien, l'arbre à chevelure,
Et le cheval noir y met l'encolure
Allongeant le cou comme pour l'eau douce,
Comme s'il voulait quitter cette dune,
Devenir au loin cheval fabuleux
Et se mélanger aux moutons d'écume,
A cette toison faite pour les yeux,
Être enfin le fils de cette eau marine,
Brouter l'algue au fond de la profondeur.

Time tucks him in and watches over him in sight of those tall rocks where, ever hidden, there groans the heart of sleepless nights. Let nobody enter the room whence will come forth a big dog, who has lost his memory and will search on earth and the length of the sea for the man he left behind, motionless, between his stiff final hands.

THIS sea noise where we all are, the tree with its hairy head knows it well, and the black horse goes into it up to the withers, stretching out his neck as if for the sweet water, as if he wanted to leave this sandbank, to become far off a legendary horse and to be mingled with the white sheep of the foam, with that fleece made for the eyes, in short to be the son of this sea-water, to crop the seaweed at the

Mais il faut savoir attendre au rivage,
Se promettre encore aux vagues du large,
Mettre son espoir dans la mort certaine,
Baisser de nouveau la tête dans l'herbe.

SAINT-JOHN PERSE

Éloges

I

LES viandes grillent en plein vent, les sauces se com-
posent
    et la fumée remonte les chemins à vif et rejoint qui
marchait.
    Alors le Songeur aux joues sales
    se tire
    d'un vieux songe tout rayé de violences, de ruses et
d'éclats,
    et orné de sueurs, vers l'odeur de la viande
    il descend
    comme une femme qui traîne: ses toiles, tout son linge
et ses cheveux défaits.

bottom of the deep. But he must know how to wait on the shore,
still promise himself to the waves of the open sea, put his hope in
certain death, lower once more his head in the grass.

Panegyrics

I

THE meats are grilling in the open wind, the sauces are made, and
the smoke goes sharp back up the paths and catches up with the
one who was walking. Then the Dreamer with the dirty cheeks
comes out of an old dream all striped with violence, tricks, and bril-
liants, and, ornamented with sweat, he goes down towards the
scent of the meat like a loitering woman; his duck clothes, all his
linen and his hair disarranged.

II

J'ai aimé un cheval – qui était-ce? – il m'a bien regardé de face, sous ses mèches.

Les trous vivants de ses narines étaient deux choses belles à voir – avec ce trou vivant qui gonfle au-dessus de chaque œil.

Quand il avait couru, il suait: c'est briller! – et j'ai pressé des lunes à ses flancs sous mes genoux d'enfant...

J'ai aimé un cheval – qui était-ce? – et parfois (car une bête sait mieux quelles forces nous vantent)

il levait à ses dieux une tête d'airain: soufflante, sillonnée d'un pétiole de veines.

III

Les rythmes de l'orgueil descendent les mornes rouges.

Les tortues roulent aux détroits comme des astres bruns.

Des rades font un songe plein de têtes d'enfants...

Sois un homme aux yeux calmes qui rit,

II

I loved a horse – which was it? – he certainly looked straight at me beneath his mane. The living holes of his nostrils were two things fair to see – with that living hole of each eye swelling above. When he had run he used to sweat: that is, to shine! – and I pressed moons to his sides beneath my child's knees ... I loved a horse – which was it? – and sometimes (for a beast knows better what strength brings us praise) he raised a brazen head to his gods: blowing, furrowed with a network of veins.

III

The rhythms of pride go down the red hills. The turtles wallow in the straits like dark stars. Roadsteads make a dream full of children's heads ...

Be a man with calm eyes laughing, a silent man laughing under

silencieux qui rit sous l'aile calme du sourcil, perfection
du vol (et du bord immobile du cil il fait retour aux
choses qu'il a vues, empruntant les chemins de la mer
frauduleuse . . . et du bord immobile du cil

il nous a fait plus d'une promesse d'îles,

comme celui qui dit à un plus jeune: «Tu verras!»

Et c'est lui qui s'entend avec le maître du navire.)

IV

AZUR! nos bêtes sont bondées d'un cri!

Je m'éveille, songeant au fruit noir de l'Anibe dans sa
cupule verruqueuse et tronquée . . . Ah bien! les crabes ont
dévoré tout un arbre à fruits mous. Un autre est plein de
cicatrices, ses fleurs poussaient, succulentes, au tronc. Et
un autre, on ne peut le toucher de la main, comme on
prend à témoin, sans qu'il pleuve aussitôt de ces mouches,
couleurs! . . . Les fourmis courent en deux sens. Des
femmes rient toutes seules dans les abutilons, ces fleurs
jaunes-tachées-de-noir-pourpre-à-la-base que l'on em-

the calm wing of his eyebrow, flight's perfection (and with the
motionless edge of his eyelash he returns to the things he has seen,
borrowing the paths of the fraudulent sea . . . and with the motion-
less edge of his eyelash he has made us more than one promise of
islands, as he who says to a younger man: 'You will see!' And it is
he who comes to an understanding with the ship's master).

IV

AZURE! Our beasts are crammed with a shriek!

I awaken, dreaming of the dark fruit of the Anibis in its warty,
truncated husk . . . Ah indeed! The crabs have eaten up a whole
soft-fruit tree. Another is full of scars, its flowers used to grow,
juicily, on its trunk. And another, you cannot touch it with your
hand, as you might touch wood, without it at once raining those
flies, colours! . . . The ants are running in both directions. Women
are laughing all by themselves in the flowering maples, those yellow

ploie dans la diarrhée des bêtes à cornes . . . Et le sexe sent
bon. La sueur s'ouvre un chemin frais. Un homme seul
mettrait le nez dans le pli de son bras. Ces rives gonflent,
s'écroulent sous des couches d'insectes aux noces sau-
grenues. La rame a bourgeonné dans la main du rameur.
Un chien vivant au bout d'un croc est le meilleur appât
pour le requin . . .

— Je m'éveille songeant au fruit noir de l'Anibe; à des
fleurs en paquets sous l'aisselle des feuilles.

V

. . . OR ces eaux calmes sont de lait
   et tout ce qui s'épanche aux solitudes molles du matin.
   Le pont lavé, avant le jour, d'une eau pareille en songe
au mélange de l'aube, fait une belle relation du ciel. Et
l'enfance adorable du jour, par la treille des tentes roulées,
descend à même ma chanson.

   Enfance, mon amour, n'était-ce que cela? . . .

flowers marked with black-purple at the base which are used for the
diarrhoea of horned beasts . . . And the sex smells good. The sweat
opens a cool path for itself. A solitary man would put his nose into
the fold of his arm. Those banks swell and collapse beneath layers
of insects with their mad nuptials. The oar has budded in the rower's
hand. A living dog at the end of a hook is the best bait for sharks . . .

— I awaken, dreaming of the dark fruit of the Anibis; of flowers
in bundles beneath the arm-pit of the leaves.

V

. . . NOW these calm waters are like milk and everything that is
poured out to the soft emptiness of the morning. The deck washed
before day with a water resembling in dreams the dawn's mixture,
makes a fine report of the sky. And the day's adorable childhood,
through the lattice of rolled up awnings, comes down to the level
of my song.

   Childhood, my love, was it only that? . . . Childhood, my love

Enfance, mon amour . . . ce double anneau de l'œil et
l'aisance d'aimer . . .
    Il fait si calme et puis si tiède,
    il fait si continuel aussi,
    qu'il est étrange d'être là, mêlé des mains à la
    facilité du jour . . .

    Enfance, mon amour! il n'est que de céder . . . Et l'ai-je
dit, alors? je ne veux plus même de ces linges
    à remuer, dans l'incurable, aux solitudes vertes du
matin . . . Et l'ai-je dit, alors? il ne faut que servir
    comme de vieille corde . . . Et ce cœur, et ce cœur, là!
qu'il traîne sur les ponts, plus humble et plus sauvage et
plus, qu'un vieux faubert,
    exténué . . .

VI

Et d'autres montent, à leur tour, sur le pont
    et moi je prie, encore, qu'on ne tende la toile . . . mais
pour cette lanterne, vous pouvez bien l'éteindre . . .
    Enfance, mon amour! c'est le matin, ce sont

. . . That double link of the eye and the ease of loving . . . It is so
calm and then so mild, so continual too, that it is strange to be there,
connected by the hands to the day's complaisance . . .
    Childhood, my love! There is nothing to do but yield . . . And did
I say it then? I no longer want to move even these clothes, in hope-
lessness, in the green emptiness of morning . . . And did I say it
then? We must only serve like old rope . . . And that heart, and that
heart, there! Let it loiter on the decks, humbler and wilder and more
worn out than an old swab . . .

VI

And others in their turn come up on the deck, and I still ask them
not to set the sail . . . but, as to that lantern, you may well put it
out . . . Childhood, my love! It is morning; there are things im-

des choses douces qui supplient, comme la haine de chanter,

douces comme la honte, qui tremble sur les lèvres, des choses dites de profil,

ô douces, et qui supplient, comme la voix la plus douce du mâle s'il consent à plier son âme rauque vers qui plie ...

Et à présent je vous le demande, n'est-ce pas le matin ... une aisance du souffle

et l'enfance agressive du jour, douce comme le chant qui étire les yeux?

XVIII

A présent laissez-moi, je vais seul.

Je sortirai, car j'ai affaire: un insecte m'attend pour traiter. Je me fais joie

du gros œil à facettes: anguleux, imprévu, comme le fruit du cyprès.

Ou bien j'ai une alliance avec les pierres veinées-bleu: et vous me laissez également,

assis, dans l'amitié de mes genoux.

1908

ploring and sweet as the hatred of song, sweet as shame trembling on the lips, things spoken in profile, O things sweet and imploring like the sweetest voice of the male, if he agree to incline his harsh soul towards the woman's inclining ... And now I ask you, is it not morning ... an ease of breath and the aggressive childhood of the day, sweet as the song which draws out the eyes?

XVIII

Now leave me, I am going alone. I shall go forth, for I have business: an insect awaits me to negotiate. I have joy of the great eye with facets: angular, unforeseen like the cypress fruit. Or else I have a union with the blue-veined stones: and you leave me likewise, seated, in the friendship of my knees.

Anabase

I

SUR trois grandes saisons m'établissant avec honneur,
j'augure bien du sol où j'ai fondé ma loi.

Les armes au matin sont belles et la mer. A nos chevaux
livrée la terre sans amandes

nous vaut ce ciel incorruptible. Et le soleil n'est point
nommé, mais sa puissance est parmi nous

et la mer au matin comme une présomption de l'esprit.

Puissance, tu chantais sur nos routes nocturnes! . . .
Aux ides pures du matin que savons-nous du songe, notre
aînesse?

Pour une année encore parmi vous! Maître du grain,
maître du sel, et la chose publique sur de justes balances!

Je ne hélerai point les gens d'une autre rive. Je ne
tracerai point de grands

quartiers de villes sur les pentes avec le sucre des
coraux. Mais j'ai dessein de vivre parmi vous.

Anabasis

I

ESTABLISHING myself with honour over three great seasons, I
prophesy well of the ground where I have founded my law. Wea-
pons are beautiful in the morning, and the sea. Given over to our
horses the earth without almonds brings us this incorruptible sky.
And the sun is not named, but its power is among us, and the sea in
the morning like a presumption of the spirit. Power, you used to
sing upon our night roads! . . . At the pure ides of morning what do
we know of the dream, our birthright? For a year more among
you! Master of the grain, master of the salt, and the affairs of state
on equal scales! I shall not call the people of another shore. I shall
not draw great districts of towns on the slopes with powdered
coral. But I purpose to live among you. Glory in the highest to the

Au seuil des tentes toute gloire! ma force parmi vous!
et l'idée pure comme un sel tient ses assises dans le jour.

*

... Or je hantais la ville de vos songes et j'arrêtais sur les
marchés déserts ce pur commerce de mon âme, parmi
vous

invisible et fréquente ainsi qu'un feu d'épines en plein
vent.

Puissance, tu chantais sur nos routes splendides! ...
«Au délice du sel sont toutes lances de l'esprit ... J'avi-
verai du sel les bouches mortes du désir!

Qui n'a, louant la soif, bu l'eau des sables dans un
casque,

je lui fais peu crédit au commerce de l'âme ...» (Et le
soleil n'est point nommé, mais sa puissance est parmi
nous.)

Hommes, gens de poussière et de toutes façons, gens
de négoce et de loisir, gens des confins et gens d'ailleurs,
ô gens de peu de poids dans la mémoire de ces lieux; gens

threshold of the tents! My strength in the midst of you! And the
idea pure as a salt holds its assizes in the day.

*

... Now I used to haunt the town of your dreams and on the de-
serted market places decide this pure commerce of my soul, in-
visible in your midst and rapid as a thorn fire in the open wind.
Power, you used to sing upon our shining roads! ... 'All lances of
the spirit belong to the salt's delight... With the salt I shall quicken
the dead mouths of desire! He who has not drunk the water of the
sands in a helmet, praising his thirst, I give him little credit in the
commerce of the soul...' (And the sun is not named, but its power
is among us.)

Men, people of dust and of all ways, people of business and
leisure, people of the borders, and people of elsewhere, O people of
little weight in the memory of these places; peoples of the valleys

des vallées et des plateaux et des plus hautes pentes de
ce monde à l'échéance de nos rives; flaireurs de signes, de
semences, et confesseurs de souffles en Ouest; suiveurs de
pistes, de saisons, leveurs de campements dans le petit
vent de l'aube; ô chercheurs de points d'eau sur l'écorce
du monde; ô chercheurs, ô trouveurs de raisons pour s'en
aller ailleurs,

vous ne trafiquez pas d'un sel plus fort quand, au
matin, dans un présage de royaumes et d'eaux mortes
hautement suspendues sur les fumées du monde, les
tambours de l'exil éveillent aux frontières

l'éternité qui bâille sur les sables.

*

. . . En robe pure parmi vous. Pour une année encore
parmi vous. «Ma gloire est sur les mers, ma force est
parmi vous!

A nos destins promis ce souffle d'autres rives et, por-
tant au delà les semences du temps, l'éclat d'un siècle sur
sa pointe au fléau des balances . . .»

Mathématiques suspendues aux banquises du sel! Au

and plateaux and of this world's highest slopes to the falling of our
shores; you who smell out omens and seeds, and you who confess
breaths of wind in the West; you who follow trails and seasons, you
who break camps in the faint wind of dawn; O you who seek
springs of water on the husk of the world; O seekers, O finders of
reasons to depart elsewhere, you traffic not with a stronger salt
when, in the morning, in a foreshadowing of kingdoms and dead
waters hung high above the smoke of the world, the drums of exile
awaken on the frontiers eternity yawning upon the sands.

*

. . . In pure raiment among you. For a year more among you. 'My
fame is on the seas, my strength is in your midst! Engaged to our
destinies this breath of wind from other shores and, bearing the
seeds of time beyond, the brightness of a century on its tip on the
beam of the scales . . .' Mathematics hung on ice-floes of salt! On

point sensible de mon front où le poème s'établit,
j'inscris ce chant de tout un peuple, le plus ivre,
 à nos chantiers tirant d'immortelles carènes!

VII

Nous n'habiterons pas toujours ces terres jaunes, notre
délice . . .

L'Été plus vaste que l'Empire suspend aux tables de
l'espace plusieurs étages de climats. La terre vaste sur son
aire roule à pleins bords sa braise pâle sous les cendres. –
Couleur de soufre, de miel, couleur de choses immortelles,
toute la terre aux herbes s'allumant aux pailles de l'autre
hiver – et de l'éponge verte d'un seul arbre le ciel tire son
suc violet.

Un lieu de pierres à mica! Pas une graine pure dans les
barbes du vent. Et la lumière comme une huile. – De la
fissure des paupières au fil des cimes m'unissant, je sais la
pierre tachée d'ouïes, les essaims du silence aux ruches de
lumière; et mon cœur prend souci d'une famille d'acri-
diens . . .

the sensitive point of my brow, where the poem is seated, I inscribe
this song of a whole people, the most exalted, dragging immortal
keels to our shipyards!

VII

We shall not always dwell in these yellow lands, our delight . . .
 Summer vaster than the Empire hangs several layers of climate
on the tables of space. The huge earth rolls over its surface brim-
ful its embers pale beneath the ashes. – The colour of sulphur, of
honey, the colour of immortal things, the whole earth with grass
lighting up at the straw of the other winter – and the sky draws its
violet juice from the green sponge of a single tree. A place of mica
stones! Not a pure seed in the whiskers of the wind. And the light
like an oil. – Joining myself to the edge of the peaks with the cleft
of my eyelids, I know the stone marked with ears, the swarms of
silence in the hives of light; and my heart is worried by a family of
acritans . . .

Chamelles douces sous la tonte, cousues de mauves cicatrices, que les collines s'acheminent sous les données du ciel agraire – qu'elles cheminent en silence sur les incandescences pâles de la plaine; et s'agenouillent à la fin, dans la fumée des songes, là où les peuples s'abolissent aux poudres mortes de la terre.

Ce sont de grandes lignes calmes qui s'en vont à des bleuissements de vignes improbables. La terre en plus d'un point mûrit les violettes de l'orage; et ces fumées de sable qui s'élèvent au lieu des fleuves morts, comme des pans de siècles en voyage . . .

A voix plus basse pour les morts, à voix plus basse dans le jour. Tant de douceur au cœur de l'homme, se peut-il qu'elle faille à trouver sa mesure? . . . «Je vous parle, mon âme! – mon âme tout enténébrée d'un parfum de cheval!» Et quelques grands oiseaux de terre, naviguant en Ouest, sont de bons mimes de nos oiseaux de mer.

A l'orient du ciel si pâle, comme un lieu saint scellé des linges de l'aveugle, des nuées calmes se disposent, où tournent les cancers du camphre et de la corne . . . Fumées

Like she-camels, gentle beneath the shears, sewn with mauve scars, let the hills proceed beneath the data of the agrarian sky – let them go in silence over the pale incandescence of the plain; and at the end kneel down in the smoke of dreams in the place where peoples vanish into the dead dust of the earth. There are great calm lines leading away to the blue of improbable vines. In more than one spot the earth matures the storm's violets; and those smoke clouds of sand that arise in the place of dead rivers like skirts of centuries on the march . . . With a lower voice for the dead, with a lower voice in the day. Can it be that so much sweetness in the heart of man fails to find its measure? . . . 'I am speaking to you, my soul! – My soul all shadowed by a horse's scent!' And some great land birds, steering to the West, are good mimics of our sea-birds. To the east of so pale a sky, like a holy place sealed with the linen of the blind, calm clouds are arranged, where the cancers of camphor and horn circle . . . Smoke clouds disputed to us by a

qu'un souffle nous dispute! la terre tout attente en ses barbes d'insectes, la terre enfante des merveilles! . . .

Et à midi, quand l'arbre jujubier fait éclater l'assise des tombeaux, l'homme clôt ses paupières et rafraîchit sa nuque dans les âges . . . Cavaleries du songe au lieu des poudres mortes, ô routes vaines qu'échevèle un souffle jusqu'à nous! où trouver, où trouver les guerriers qui garderont les fleuves dans leurs noces?

Au bruit des grandes eaux en marche sur la terre, tout le sel de la terre tressaille dans les songes. Et soudain, ah! soudain que nous veulent ces voix? Levez un peuple de miroirs sur l'ossuaire des fleuves, qu'ils interjettent appel dans la suite des siècles! Levez des pierres à ma gloire, levez des pierres au silence, et à la garde de ces lieux les cavaleries de bronze vert sur de vastes chaussées! . . .

(L'ombre d'un grand oiseau me passe sur la face.)

breath of wind! The earth all expectation in its insects' whiskers, the earth brings forth wonders! . . .

And at noon, when the jujube tree causes the foundation of tombs to burst asunder, man closes his eyelids and cools the nape of his neck in the ages . . . Dream's cavalries in the place of dead dust, O empty roads dishevelled by a breath of wind come to us! Where to find, where to find the warriors to guard the rivers in their nuptials? To the noise of great waters marching over the earth all the earth's salt starts up in dreams. And suddenly, ah! suddenly what do those voices want of us? Raise up a people of mirrors over the rivers' charnel-house, let them make appeal to the succession of centuries! Raise up stones to my fame, raise up stones to the silence, and to guard these places the cavalries of green bronze on immense highways! . . .

(The shadow of a great bird passes over my face.)

PIERRE REVERDY

Quai aux fleurs

PETITE poitrine
  Ô
nuages
      Dans l'étang où elle se noya
      L'hiver ne souffle plus
Et
loin de son bord
Il passe ayant remis son pardessus
Dans la vitrine tout le monde la regarde
Elle est morte et sourit à ces gens
                qui ne savent que douter
Sa petite poitrine a l'air de remuer
Avec vos lèvres vous soufflez dessus
Et ses yeux se ferment en vous regardant
Ces messieurs habillés de noir
Ont les yeux brillants de malice
Une petite femme que j'ai beaucoup connue
La misère passe avec le vent
et balaie le boulevard

The Flower-market Quay

LITTLE breast – O clouds – In the pond where she drowned herself the winter no longer blows. And far from its bank he passes by, having once again donned his overcoat. In the glass case everyone looks at her. She is dead and smiles at these people who do not know what to suspect. Her little breast appears to move – you are blowing on it with your lips – and her eyes are shut as they watch you. These gentlemen dressed in black have their eyes shining with malice. 'A little woman I've often had dealings with.' Wretchedness passes with the wind and sweeps the boulevard. She had very pretty

Elle avait de bien jolies jambes
Elle dansait elle riait
Et maintenant que va-t-elle devenir
Tournant la tête
elle demandait qu'on la laissât dormir

Spectacle des yeux

Les têtes qui dépassaient la ligne sont tombées
Tout le monde crie aux fenêtres
D'autres sont aussi dans la rue
Au milieu du bruit et des rires
Il y a des animaux qu'on n'avait jamais vus
Les passants familiers
Et les visages d'or
Les voix sur les sentiers
Et les accents plus forts
Puis vers midi le soleil les clairons
Les hommes plus joyeux qui se mettent à rire
Les maisons qui ouvrent leurs yeux
Les seuils s'accueillent d'un sourire
Quand le cortège flotte dans la poussière
L'enfant aux yeux brûlés d'étonnement

legs. She used to dance, she used to laugh. And now what is going to happen to her? Turning her head, she asked to be left to sleep.

Show for the Eyes

THE heads that topped the line have fallen, everyone shouts at the windows, others are in the street too. In the midst of the noise and the laughter there are animals you had never seen, the familiar passers-by and the golden faces, the voices on the paths and the louder tones; then, towards noon, the sun, the trumpets, more joyous men beginning to laugh, the houses opening their eyes. The thresholds greet one another with a smile, when the procession sets floating in dust the child with his eyes burned with wonder against

Contre la femme en tablier bleu
L'enfant blond et l'ange peureux
Devant ces gens venus d'ailleurs
qui ne ressemblent pas à ceux que l'on connaît
Avec qui l'on voudrait partir
Étrangers merveilleux qui passent sans mourir
Le soir rallume ses lumières
Le spectacle dresse ses feux
La danseuse enflammée sort du portemanteau
Les maillots gonflés se raniment
La fortune court sur le corps
La lune roule dans la piste
On saute à travers ce décor
Pendant que l'ombre basse équivoque du cirque
Tourne avec les clameurs
Et que l'enfant rêveur aux songes magnifiques
Pleure sur sa laideur

Chauffage central

UNE petite lumière
Tu vois une petite lumière descendre sur ton ventre pour
    t'éclairer

the woman in a blue apron, the fair-haired child and angel, afraid of
all these people come from elsewhere, not like those you know,
with whom you would like to leave, wonderful strangers who pass
by without dying.

The evening lights its lamps again, the show prepares its lights,
the blazing dancing girl comes out of her portmanteau, the swollen
tights take on life, the spotlight runs over the body, the moon re-
volves in its track, they leap through this scenery, while the low
equivocal shadow of the circus goes round with the uproar, and
the child, dreamer of wonderful dreams, weeps over his own ugli-
ness.

Central Heating

A LITTLE light, you see a little light come down on your stomach

609

– Une femme s'étire comme une fusée –
Au coin là-bas une ombre lit
Ses pieds libres sont trop jolis

Court-circuit au cœur
Une panne au moteur
Quel aimant me soutient
Mes yeux et mon amour se trompent de chemin

Un rien
Un feu que l'on rallume et qui s'éteint
J'ai assez du vent
J'ai assez du ciel
Au fond tout ce qu'on voit est artificiel
Même ta bouche
Pourtant j'ai chaud là où ta main me touche
La porte est ouverte et je n'entre pas
Je vois ton visage et je n'y crois pas
Tu es pâle
Un soir qu'on était triste on a pleuré sur une malle
Là-bas des hommes riaient
Des enfants presque nus parfois se promenaient
L'eau était claire

to light you up – a woman stretches herself like a rocket – over
there in the corner a shadow is reading. Her uncovered feet are too
pretty.

Short-circuit in the heart, a break-down in the motor, what
magnet keeps me going? My eyes and my love take the wrong road.

A nothing, a fire that is lighted again and goes out. I have
enough of the wind. I have enough of the sky. At bottom every-
thing we see is artificial, even your mouth. Yet I feel hot in the
place where your hand touches me. The door is open, and I do not
go in. I see your face, and I do not believe in it. You are pale. One
evening when we were sad we wept on a trunk. Down there men
were laughing, sometimes children walked by, almost naked. The

Un fil de cuivre rouge y conduit la lumière
Le soleil et ton cœur sont de même matière

FIGURE délayée dans l'eau
Dans le silence
Trop de poids sur la gorge
Trop d'eau dans le bocal
Trop d'ombre renversée
Trop de sang sur la rampe
Il n'est jamais fini
Ce rêve de cristal

Outre mesure

LE monde est ma prison
Si je suis loin de ce que j'aime
Vous n'êtes pas trop loin barreaux de l'horizon
L'amour la liberté dans le ciel trop vide
Sur la terre gercée de douleurs
Un visage éclaire et réchauffe les choses dures
Qui faisaient partie de la mort

water was clear. A red copper wire leads the light there. The sun and your heart are made of the same substance.

FACE dissolved in water, in silence. Too much weight on the bosom, too much water in the jar, too much shadow spilled, too much blood on the stairs. It is never finished this crystal dream.

Out of Proportion

THE world is my prison, if I am far from what I love. You are not too far, bars of the horizon, love, liberty in the too empty sky. On the earth blistered by suffering a face lights up and warms the harsh things which used to be part of death. Starting from that face, from

A partir de cette figure
De ces gestes de cette voix
Ce n'est que moi-même qui parle
Mon cœur qui résonne et qui bat
Un écran de feu abat-jour tendre
Entre les murs familiers de la nuit
Cercle enchanté des fausses solitudes
Faisceaux de reflets lumineux
Regrets
Tous ces débris du temps crépitent au foyer
Encore un plan qui se déchire
Un acte qui manque à l'appel
Il reste peu de chose à prendre
Dans un homme qui va mourir

PAUL ÉLUARD

Par une nuit nouvelle

FEMME avec laquelle j'ai vécu
Femme avec laquelle je vis
Femme avec laquelle je vivrai
Toujours la même

those gestures, from that voice, it is only I myself who am speaking, my heart resounding and beating. A screen of fire, a tender blind between the familiar walls of the night, enchanted circle of false solitudes, bundles of luminous reflections, regrets – all these ruins of time crackle on the hearth. One more plane torn apart, one more deed missing at the roll-call. There remain few things to be taken from a man who is going to die.

On a New Night

WOMAN with whom I have lived, woman with whom I live, woman with whom I shall live always the same. You must have a

Il te faut un manteau rouge
Des gants rouges un masque rouge
Et des bas noirs
Des raisons des preuves
De te voir toute nue
Nudité pure ô parure parée

Seins ô mon cœur.

ON ne peut me connaître
Mieux que tu me connais

Tes yeux dans lesquels nous dormons
Tous les deux
Ont fait à mes lumières d'homme
Un sort meilleur qu'aux nuits du monde

Tes yeux dans lesquels je voyage
Ont donné aux gestes des routes
Un sens détaché de la terre

Dans tes yeux ceux qui nous révèlent
Notre solitude infinie
Ne sont plus ce qu'ils croyaient être

red cloak, red gloves, a red mask, and black stockings: reasons,
proofs of seeing you quite naked, pure nakedness, O ornament
adorned!
  Breasts, O my heart!

I CANNOT be known better than you know me.
  Your eyes in which we both of us sleep have made a better lot
for my man's gleams than for the nights of the world.
  Your eyes in which I journey have given the gestures of the
roads a meaning detached from the earth.
  In your eyes those who reveal our infinite solitude to us are no
longer what they thought themselves to be.

On ne peut te connaître
Mieux que je te connais.

La Tête contre les murs

ILS n'étaient que quelques-uns
Sur toute la terre
Chacun se croyait seul
Ils chantaient ils avaient raison
De chanter
Mais ils chantaient comme on saccage
Comme on se tue

Nuit humide râpée
Allons-nous te supporter
Plus longtemps
N'allons-nous pas secouer
Ton évidence de cloaque
Nous n'attendrons pas un matin
Fait sur mesure
Nous voulions voir clair dans les yeux des autres
Leurs nuits d'amour épuisées
Ils ne rêvent que de mourir
Leurs belles chairs s'oublient

You cannot be known better than I know you.

Head against the Walls

THEY were only a few over the whole earth. Each thought himself
alone. They used to sing, they were right to sing, but they sang
as people pillage, as people kill each other.

Damp, shabby night, are we going to put up with you any
longer? Shall we not shake off your manifest filth? We shall not
wait for a morning made to measure. We wanted to see clearly in
others' eyes. Their nights of love exhausted, they only dream of
dying, their beautiful bodies are forgotten. Pavanes of spinning

Pavanes en tournecœur
Abeilles prises dans leur miel
Ils ignorent la vie
Et nous en avons mal partout

Toits rouges fondez sous la langue
Canicule dans les lits pleins
Viens vider tes sacs de sang frais
Il y a encore une ombre ici
Un morceau d'imbécile là
Au vent leurs masques leurs défroques
Dans du plomb leurs pièges leurs chaînes
Et leurs gestes prudents d'aveugles
Il y a du feu sous roche
Pour qui éteint le feu

Prenez-y garde nous avons
Malgré la nuit qu'il couve
Plus de force que le ventre
De vos sœurs et de vos femmes
Et nous nous reproduirons
Sans elles mais à coups de hache
Dans vos prisons

hearts, bees caught in their honey, they know not life, and we suffer for it everywhere.

Red roofs, melt beneath the tongue; dog-star, come and empty your bags of fresh blood into full beds. There is still a shadow here, a bit of a fool there. To the wind with their masks and cast-off clothes, into lead with their snares and chains and their prudent blind-man's gestures. There is fire beneath the rock for him who puts out the fire.

Pay heed. In spite of the night it hatches we have more strength than the stomach of your sisters and your wives, and we shall reproduce ourselves without them, but with axe blows in your prisons.

Torrents de pierre labours d'écume
Où flottent des yeux sans rancune
Des yeux justes sans espoir
Qui vous connaissent
Et que vous auriez dû crever
Plutôt que de les ignorer

D'un hameçon plus habile que vos potences
Nous prendrons notre bien où nous voulons qu'il soit.

Bonne Justice

C'EST la chaude loi des hommes
Du raisin ils font du vin
Du charbon ils font du feu
Des baisers ils font des hommes

C'est la dure loi des hommes
Se garder intact malgré
Les guerres et la misère
Malgré les dangers de mort

Torrents of stone, tillage of foam where float eyes without spite, just eyes without hope that know you and which you should have put out rather than be unaware of them.

With a cleverer hook than your gallows we shall take our wealth where we want it to be.

Honest Justice

IT is the hot law of men: from grapes they make wine, from coal they make fire, from kisses they make men.

It is the harsh law of men: to keep themselves untouched in spite of wars and wretchedness, in spite of death's dangers.

C'est la douce loi des hommes
De changer l'eau en lumière
Le rêve en réalité
Et les ennemis en frères

Une loi vieille et nouvelle
Qui va se perfectionnant
Du fond du cœur de l'enfant
Jusqu'à la raison suprême.

LOUIS ARAGON

Richard II quarante

M A patrie est comme une barque
Qu'abandonnèrent ses haleurs
Et je ressemble à ce monarque
Plus malheureux que le malheur
Qui restait roi de ses douleurs

Vivre n'est plus qu'un stratagème
Le vent sait mal sécher les pleurs

It is the gentle law of men: to change water into light, dream
into reality, and enemies into brothers.

An old and new law that continues to perfect itself from the bot-
tom of the child's heart up to the final reason.

Richard II Forty

M Y country is like a barge abandoned by its towers, and I resemble
that monarch, more unfortunate than misfortune, who remained
king of his griefs.

Living is no more than a trick. The wind does not know how to

Il faut haïr tout ce que j'aime
Ce que je n'ai plus donnez-leur
Je reste roi de mes douleurs

Le cœur peut s'arrêter de battre
Le sang peut couler sans chaleur
Deux et deux ne fassent plus quatre
Au Pigeon-Vole des voleurs
Je reste roi de mes douleurs

Que le soleil meure ou renaisse
Le ciel a perdu ses couleurs
Tendre Paris de ma jeunesse
Adieu printemps du Quai-aux-Fleurs
Je reste roi de mes douleurs

Fuyez les bois et les fontaines
Taisez-vous oiseaux querelleurs
Vos chants sont mis en quarantaine
C'est le règne de l'oiseleur
Je reste roi de mes douleurs

Il est un temps pour la souffrance
Quand Jeanne vint à Vaucouleurs

dry tears. I must hate everything I love. Give them what I no longer possess. I remain king of my griefs.

The heart can stop beating. The blood can flow without warmth. Let two and two no longer make four in the thieves' game of forfeits. I remain king of my griefs.

Whether the sun die or be reborn, the sky has lost its colours. Tender Paris of my youth – Farewell, Spring on the flower-market quay. I remain king of my griefs.

Flee the woods and the springs. Be silent wrangling birds. Your songs are sent to Coventry. It is the reign of the bird-catcher. I remain king of my griefs.

There is a time for suffering. When Joan came to Vaucouleurs –

Ah coupez en morceaux la France
Le jour avait cette pâleur
Je reste roi de mes douleurs

FRANCIS PONGE

Le Tronc d'arbre

PUISQUE bientôt l'hiver va nous mettre en valeur
Montrons-nous préparés aux offices du bois

Grelots par moins que rien émus à la folie
Effusions à nos dépens cessez ô feuilles
Dont un change d'humeur nous couvre ou nous dépouille
Avec peine par nous sans cesse imaginées
Vous n'êtes déjà plus qu'avec peine croyables

Détache-toi de moi ma trop sincère écorce
Va rejoindre à mes pieds celles des autres siècles
De visages passés masques passés public
Contre moi de ton sort demeurés pour témoins

ah! cut France in pieces – the day had this pallor. I remain king of
my griefs.

The Tree Trunk

SINCE winter is soon going to exploit us, let us show ourselves
prepared for the offices of the wood.

Bells moved to madness by less than nothing, effusions at our
expense, cease, O leaves, whose change of mood covers us or strips
us bare, ceaselessly hardly imagined by us, you are already hardly
credible to us any longer.

Fall away from me, my too sincere bark. Go and join at my feet
those of other centuries, the past masks of past faces, a public re-
maining for witnesses to your fate against me. Like you, all those

Tous ont eu comme toi la paume un instant vive
Que par terre et par eau nous voyons déconfits
Bien que de mes vertus je te croie la plus proche
Décède aux lieux communs tu es faite pour eux
Meurs exprès De ton fait déboute le malheur
Démasque volontiers ton volontaire auteur . . .

Ainsi s'efforce un arbre encore sous l'écorce
A montrer vif ce tronc que parfera la mort.

Notes pour un coquillage

UN coquillage est une petite chose, mais je peux la
démesurer en la replaçant où je la trouve, posée sur
l'étendue du sable. Car alors je prendrai une poignée de
sable et j'observerai le peu qui me reste dans la main
après que par les interstices de mes doigts presque toute
la poignée aura filé, j'observerai quelques grains, puis
chaque grain, et aucun de ces grains de sable à ce moment
ne m'apparaîtra plus une petite chose, et bientôt le coquil-

we see discomfited by land and water have had the palm of their
hand living for a moment. Although I believe you to be the nearest
of my virtues, die in the common places, you are made for them.
Die on purpose. By your deed dismiss misfortune. Voluntarily
unmask your voluntary author . . .

Thus a tree still beneath its bark endeavours to show quick this
trunk that death will perfect.

Notes for a Seashell

A SEASHELL is a small thing, but I can measure it by putting it
back where I found it, placed on the stretch of sand. For then I shall
take a handful of sand and observe the little that remains in my
hand after almost all the handful has slipped through the gaps in my
fingers. I shall observe a few grains, then each grain, and none of
those grains of sand at that time will appear any longer to me as a
little thing, and soon the formal seashell, this oyster shell or this

lage formel, cette coquille de huître ou cette tiare bâtarde, ou ce «couteau», m'impressionera comme un énorme monument, en même temps colossal, et précieux, quelque chose comme le temple d'Angkor, Saint-Maclou, ou les Pyramides, avec une signification beaucoup plus étrange que ces trop incontestables produits d'hommes.

Si alors il me vient à l'esprit que ce coquillage, qu'une lame de la mer peut sans doute recouvrir, est habité par une bête, si j'ajoute une bête à ce coquillage en l'imaginant replacé sous quelques centimètres d'eau, je vous laisse à penser de combien s'accroîtra, s'intensifiera de nouveau mon impression, et deviendra différente de celle que peut produire le plus remarquable des monuments que j'évoquais tout à l'heure!

*

Les monuments de l'homme ressemblent aux morceaux de son squelette ou de n'importe quel squelette, à de grands os décharnés: ils n'évoquent aucun habitant à leur taille. Les cathédrales les plus énormes ne laissent sortir qu'une foule informe de fourmis, et même la villa, le

bastard tiara or this razor-fish shell, will impress me like a huge monument, at the same time vast and precious, something like the temple of Angkor, Saint-Maclou, or the Pyramids, with a meaning much stranger than these too indisputably human creations.

If, then, it comes to my mind that this seashell, which a wave of the sea can doubtless cover again, is inhabited by an animal, if I add an animal to this seashell and imagine it put back under a few centimetres of water, I leave you to think to what extent my impression will grow, be freshly intensified, and become different from that which can be produced by the most remarkable of the monuments I conjured up just now.

*

Man's monuments resemble the pieces of his skeleton or of any skeleton, great fleshless bones: they invoke no inhabitant of their shape. The most huge cathedrals only let a formless crowd of ants go forth, and even the villa or the most sumptuous country-house

château le plus somptueux faits pour un seul homme sont encore plutôt comparables à une ruche ou à une fourmilière à compartiments nombreux, qu'à un coquillage. Quand le seigneur sort de sa demeure il fait certes moins d'impression que lorsque le bernard-l'hermite laisse apercevoir sa monstrueuse pince à l'embouchure du superbe cornet qui l'héberge.

Je puis me plaire à considérer Rome, ou Nîmes, comme le squelette épars, ici le tibia, là le crane d'une ancienne ville vivante, d'un ancien vivant, mais alors il me faut imaginer un énorme colosse en chair et en os, qui ne correspond vraiment à rien de ce qu'on peut raisonnablement inférer de ce qu'on nous a appris, même à la faveur d'expressions au singulier, comme le Peuple Romain, ou la Foule Provençale.

Que j'aimerais qu'un jour l'on me fasse entrevoir qu'un tel colosse a réellement existé, qu'on nourrisse en quelque sorte la vision très fantomatique et uniquement abstraite sans aucune conviction que je m'en forme! Qu'on me fasse toucher ses joues, la forme de son bras et comment il le posait le long de son corps.

---

made for a single man are still comparable rather to a hive or an antheap with numerous compartments than to a shell. When the master leaves his dwelling he certainly makes less impression than when the hermit-crab lets his monstrous claw be seen at the mouth of the magnificent horn that shelters him.

I can take pleasure in considering Rome or Nîmes as the scattered skeleton – here the tibia, there the skull – of an ancient living town, of an ancient human being, but then I must imagine a huge colossus of flesh and bone, which really corresponds to nothing that we can reasonably infer from what we have been taught, even by the grace of expressions put in the singular like the Roman People or the Provençal Crowd.

How I should love to be given an inkling one day that such a colossus really has existed, that the very ghostly, purely abstract, and quite unconvinced vision I have of it should be nourished in some way! To be made to touch its cheeks, the shape of its arm and how it placed it along its body!

Nous avons tout cela avec le coquillage: nous sommes avec lui en pleine chair, nous ne quittons pas la nature: le mollusque ou le crustacé sont là présents. D'où, une sorte d'inquiétude qui décuple notre plaisir.

*

Je ne sais pourquoi je souhaiterais que l'homme, au lieu de ces énormes monuments qui ne témoignent que de la disproportion grotesque de son imagination et de son corps (ou alors de ses ignobles mœurs sociales, compagniales), au lieu encore de ces statues à son échelle ou légèrement plus grandes (je pense au David de Michel-Ange) qui n'en sont que de simples représentations, sculpte des espèces de niches, de coquilles à sa taille, des choses très différentes de sa forme de mollusque mais cependant y proportionnées (les cahutes nègres me satisfont assez de ce point de vue), que l'homme mette son soin à se créer aux générations une demeure pas beaucoup plus grosse que son corps, que toutes ses imaginations, ses raisons soient là comprises, qu'il emploie son

We have all that with the seashell: we are with it right in the flesh, we do not leave nature: the shell-fish or crustacean are there present. Whence a kind of uneasiness that increases our pleasure tenfold.

*

I do not know why I should desire that man, instead of these vast monuments, which only bear witness to the grotesque disproportion between his imagination and his body (or then to his base habits in society or companionship), instead also of those statues to his own scale or slightly bigger (I am thinking of Michelangelo's David) which are only mere representations of him, should carve kinds of niches, shells of his own shape, things very different from his shell-fish form, but yet proportionate to it (the negro huts satisfy me well enough from this point of view), that man should take pains to create for his generations a dwelling not much larger than his body, that all his imaginings, all his reasonings should be included in it, that he should employ his genius for adjustment, not

génie à l'ajustement, non à la disproportion, – ou, tout au moins, que le génie se reconnaisse les bornes du corps qui le supporte.

Et je n'admire même pas ceux comme Pharaon qui font exécuter par une multitude des monuments pour un seul: j'aurais voulu qu'il employât cette multitude à une œuvre pas plus grosse ou pas beaucoup plus grosse que son propre corps, – ou – ce qui aurait été plus méritoire encore, qu'il témoignât de sa supériorité sur les autres hommes par le caractère de son œuvre propre.

De ce point de vue j'admire surtout certains écrivains ou musiciens mesurés, Bach, Rameau, Malherbe, Horace, Mallarmé –, les écrivains par-dessus tous les autres parce que leur monument est fait de la véritable sécrétion commune du mollusque homme, de la chose la plus proportionnée et conditionnée à son corps, et cependant la plus différente de sa forme que l'on puisse concevoir: je veux dire la PAROLE.

Ô Louvre de lecture, qui pourra être habité, après la fin de la race peut-être par d'autres hôtes, quelques singes

for disproportion, – or, at least, that genius should recognize the boundaries of the body supporting it.

And I do not even admire those, like Pharaoh, who cause a multitude to construct monuments for a single man: I should have wished him to employ this multitude for a work not bigger or not much bigger than his own body, – or – what would have been more praise-worthy still – to bear witness to his superiority over other men by the character of his own work.

From this point of view I admire above all certain restrained writers or musicians, Bach, Rameau, Malherbe, Horace, Mallarmé – the writers above all the others because their monument is made from the true common secretion of the shell-fish man, from the thing the most proportionate and conditioned to his body, and yet the most different from its form that can be imagined: I mean the WORD.

O Louvre of books, that may be inhabited after the end of our race perhaps by other guests, some monkeys, for instance, or some

par exemple, ou quelque oiseau, ou quelque être supérieur, comme le crustacé se substitue au mollusque dans la tiare bâtarde.

Et puis après la fin de tout le règne animal, l'air et le sable en petit grains lentement y pénètrent, cependant que sur le sol il luit encore et s'érode, et va brillament se désagréger, ô stérile, immatérielle poussière, ô brillant résidu, quoique sans fin brassé et trituré entre les laminoirs aériens et marins, ENFIN! *l'on* n'est plus là et ne peut rien reformer du sable, même pas du verre, et C'EST FINI!

HENRI MICHAUX

Voix

J'ENTENDIS une voix en ces jours de malheur et j'entendis: «Je les réduirai ces hommes, je les réduirai et «déjà ils sont réduits quoiqu'ils n'en sachent encore rien. «Je les réduirai à si peu de chose qu'il n'y aura pas moyen «de distinguer qui est homme de qui est femme et déjà ils

bird, or some superior being, as the crustacean takes the place of the shell-fish in the bastard tiara.

And then, after the end of the whole animal kingdom, the air and sand in little grains slowly enter it, while on the ground it still shines and wears away, and will disintegrate in brilliance, O sterile, immaterial dust, O shining remnant, though endlessly turned over and ground between the rollers of air and sea, AT LAST! *Someone* is no longer there and can form nothing again from the sand, not even glass, and IT IS FINISHED!

Voices

I HEARD a voice in those days of misfortune, and I heard: 'I shall reduce them, these men, I shall reduce them, and already they are reduced, though they know nothing of it yet. I shall reduce them to so little that there will be no means of telling man from woman, and

«ne sont plus ce qu'ils étaient autrefois, mais comme leurs
«organes savent encore s'interpénétrer, ils se croient
«toujours différents, l'un ceci, l'autre cela. Mais si fort je
«les ferai souffrir qu'il n'y aura plus organe qui compte.
«Je ne leur laisserai que le squelette, un simple trait de
«leur squelette pour y attacher leur malheur. Assez
«couru! Qu'ont-ils encore besoin de jambes? Petits, leurs
«déplacements, petits! Et ce sera tant mieux. Comme une
«statue dans un parc, quoiqu'il arrive, n'a plus qu'un
«geste, ainsi les pétrifierai-je; mais plus petits, plus petits.»

Cette voix, je l'entendis et j'avais le frisson, mais pas
tellement, car je l'admirais, pour sa sombre détermination
et son projet vaste quoiqu'apparemment insensé. Cette
voix n'était qu'une voix dans cent autres, remplissant le
haut et le bas de l'atmosphère et l'Est et l'Ouest, et toutes
étaient agressives, mauvaises, haineuses, et promettaient
à l'homme un funèbre avenir.

Mais l'homme, affolé ici, là du plus grand sang-froid,
avait des réflexes et des calculs au cas qu'il se présentât un

already they are no longer what they once were, but, as their organs
still know how to penetrate one another, they still think them-
selves different, the one this, the other that. But so much shall I
make them suffer that there will no longer be any organ which
counts. I shall only leave them the skeleton, their skeleton's mere
wire to attach their unhappiness to. They have run enough! Why
have they still need of legs? Small, their movements, small! And it
will be so much the better. As a statue in a park, whatever happens,
has only one gesture, so shall I turn them into stone; but smaller,
smaller.'

That voice, I heard it, and I shuddered, but not so much, for I
admired it because of its dark determination and its huge, though
apparently mad plan. That voice was only one voice among a hun-
dred others, filling the top and bottom of the atmosphere and the
East and the West, and all were aggressive, bad, hateful, and
promised man a sinister future.

But man, here distracted, there with the greatest calm, had re-
flexes and calculations in case a catastrophe should take place, and

coup dur, et il était prêt quoiqu'il eût paru en général plutôt vain et traqué.

Celui qu'un caillou fait trébucher marchait déjà depuis deux cent mille ans quand j'entendis les voix de haine et de menaces, qui prétendaient lui faire peur.

JACQUES PRÉVERT

Barbara

RAPPELLE-TOI Barbara
Il pleuvait sans cesse sur Brest ce jour-là
Et tu marchais souriante
Épanouie ravie ruisselante
Sous la pluie
Rappelle-toi Barbara
Il pleuvait sans cesse sur Brest
Et je t'ai croisée rue de Siam
Tu souriais
Et moi je souriais de même
Rappelle-toi Barbara

he was ready, though in general he might have appeared, on the contrary, empty and hunted.

He, whom a pebble causes to stumble, had already been walking for two hundred thousand years when I heard the voices of hatred and threats which aspired to frighten him.

Barbara

REMEMBER, Barbara, it was raining without stopping over Brest that day, and you were walking, smiling, blooming, happy and dripping beneath the rain. Remember, Barbara, it was raining without stopping over Brest, and I passed you in the Rue de Siam. You were smiling, and I smiled as well. Remember, Barbara. You whom

Toi que je ne connaissais pas
Toi qui ne me connaissais pas
Rappelle-toi
Rappelle-toi quand même ce jour-là
N'oublie pas
Un homme sous un porche s'abritait
Et il a crié ton nom
Barbara
Et tu as couru vers lui sous la pluie
Ruisselante ravie épanouie
Et tu t'es jetée dans ses bras
Rappelle-toi cela Barbara
Et ne m'en veux pas si je te tutoie
Je dis tu à tous ceux que j'aime
Même si je ne les ai vus qu'une seule fois
Je dis tu à tous ceux qui s'aiment
Même si je ne les connais pas
Rappelle-toi Barbara
N'oublie pas
Cette pluie sage et heureuse
Sur ton visage heureux
Sur cette ville heureuse
Cette pluie sur la mer
Sur l'arsenal
Sur le bateau d'Ouessant

I did not know, you who did not know me. Remember, remember that day all the same. Do not forget.

A man was sheltering beneath a porch, and he shouted your name: Barbara! And you ran towards him under the rain, dripping, happy and blooming, and you threw yourself into his arms. Remember that, Barbara, and don't be annoyed with me if I say *tu*. I say *tu* to all those I love, even if I have only seen them a single time. I say *tu* to all those who love one another, even if I do not know them. Remember, Barbara. Do not forget that wise and happy rain on your happy face, on that happy town, that rain on the sea, on the arsenal, on the Ushant boat. Oh, Barbara, what a sod

Oh Barbara
Quelle connerie la guerre
Qu'es-tu devenue maintenant
Sous cette pluie de fer
De feu d'acier de sang
Et celui qui te serrait dans ses bras
Amoureusement
Est-il mort disparu ou bien encore vivant
Oh Barbara
Il pleut sans cesse sur Brest
Comme il pleuvait avant
Mais ce n'est plus pareil et tout est abîmé
C'est une pluie de deuil terrible et désolée
Ce n'est même plus l'orage
De fer d'acier de sang
Tout simplement des nuages
Qui crèvent comme des chiens
Des chiens qui disparaissent
Au fil de l'eau sur Brest
Et vont pourrir au loin
Au loin très loin de Brest
Dont il ne reste rien.

war is! What has happened to you now beneath this rain of iron, of fire, steel and blood? And he who lovingly pressed you in his arms, is he dead, missing, or else still living?

Oh, Barbara! It is raining without stopping over Brest as it rained before. But it is not the same any more, and everything is ruined. It is a terrible, desolate rain of mourning. It is no longer even the storm of iron, steel, and blood. Quite simply clouds dying like dogs, dogs that disappear downstream over Brest and go to rot far away. Far away, very far from Brest, of which nothing remains.

ROBERT DESNOS

Non, l'amour n'est pas mort en ce cœur et ces yeux et cette bouche qui proclamait ses funérailles commencées.

Écoutez, j'en ai assez du pittoresque et des couleurs et du charme.

J'aime l'amour, sa tendresse et sa cruauté.

Mon amour n'a qu'un seul nom, qu'une seule forme.

Tout passe. Des bouches se collent à cette bouche.

Mon amour n'a qu'un nom, qu'une forme.

Et si quelque jour tu t'en souviens

Ô toi, forme et nom de mon amour,

Un jour sur la mer entre l'Amérique et l'Europe,

A l'heure où le rayon final du soleil se réverbère sur la surface ondulée des vagues, ou bien une nuit d'orage sous un arbre dans la campagne ou dans une rapide automobile,

Un matin de printemps boulevard Malesherbes,

Un jour de pluie,

A l'aube avant de te coucher,

Dis-toi, je l'ordonne à ton fantôme familier, que je fus seul à t'aimer davantage et qu'il est dommage que tu ne l'aies pas connu.

No, love is not dead in this heart and these eyes and this mouth which announced its funeral begun. Listen, I have had enough of the picturesque and of colours and charm. I love love, its tenderness and its cruelty. My love has only a single name, only a single form. Everything passes by. Mouths press themselves against this mouth. My love has only one name, only one form. And if some day you remember it, O you, form and name of my love, a day on the sea between America and Europe, at the time when the last beam of the sun is reflected on the undulating surface of the waves, or else on a stormy night beneath a tree in the country, or in a swift motor-car, on a spring morning in the boulevard Malesherbes, on a rainy day, at dawn before going to bed, say to yourself, I command it to your familiar spirit, that I was the only one to love you more and that it is a pity you did not know it. Say to yourself that we must not re-

Dis-toi qu'il ne faut pas regretter les choses: Ronsard avant moi et Baudelaire ont chanté le regret des vieilles et des mortes qui méprisèrent le plus pur amour.

Toi quand tu seras morte

Tu seras belle et toujours désirable.

Je serai mort déjà, enclos tout entier en ton corps immortel, en ton image étonnante présente à jamais parmi les merveilles perpétuelles de la vie et de l'éternité, mais si je vis

Ta voix et son accent, ton regard et ses rayons,

L'odeur de toi et celle de tes cheveux et beaucoup d'autres choses encore vivront en moi,

En moi qui ne suis ni Ronsard ni Baudelaire,

Moi qui suis Robert Desnos et qui pour t'avoir connue et aimée,

Les vaux bien.

Moi qui suis Robert Desnos, pour t'aimer

Et qui ne veux pas attacher d'autre réputation à ma mémoire sur la terre méprisable.

gret things: Ronsard before me and Baudelaire have sung the regrets of old and dead women who scorned the purest love.

You, when you are dead, will be beautiful and still desirable. I shall be dead already, enclosed completely in your immortal body, in your astonishing image ever present among the perpetual wonders of life and eternity, but, if I live, your voice and its tone, your glance and its beams, your smell and that of your hair, and many other things more will live in me, in me who am neither Ronsard nor Baudelaire; I who am Robert Desnos and, because I have known and loved you, am indeed their equal. I who am Robert Desnos in order to love you and wish to attach no other reputation to my memory on the despicable earth.

Le Paysage

J'AVAIS rêvé d'aimer. J'aime encor mais l'amour
Ce n'est plus ce bouquet de lilas et de roses
Chargeant de leur parfums la forêt où repose
Une flamme à l'issue de sentiers sans détours.

J'avais rêvé d'aimer. J'aime encor mais l'amour
Ce n'est plus cet orage où l'éclair superpose
Ses bûchers aux châteaux, déroute, décompose,
Illumine en fuyant l'adieu du carrefour.

C'est le silex en feu sous mon pas dans la nuit,
Le mot qu'aucun lexique au monde n'a traduit,
L'écume sur la mer, dans le ciel ce nuage.

A vieillir tout devient rigide et lumineux,
Des boulevards sans noms et des cordes sans nœuds.
Je me sens me roidir avec le paysage.

The Landscape

I HAD dreamed of loving. I still love, but love is no longer this bunch of lilac and roses burdening with their perfumes the forest where lies a flame at the end of paths without turnings.

I had dreamed of loving. I still love, but love is no longer this storm in which the lightning lays its pyres over the castles, confuses, distorts, and, vanishing, lights up the farewell in the square.

It is the flint fiery beneath my tread in the night, the word that no dictionary in the world has translated, the foam on the sea, this cloud in the sky.

In ageing everything becomes rigid and full of light, boulevards without names and cords without knots. I feel myself stiffen with the landscape.

Le Dernier Poème

J'AI rêvé tellement fort de toi,
J'ai tellement marché, tellement parlé,
Tellement aimé ton ombre,
Qu'il ne me reste plus rien de toi.

Il me reste d'être l'ombre parmi les ombres
D'être cent fois plus ombre que l'ombre
D'être l'ombre qui viendra et reviendra
dans ta vie ensoleillée.

RENÉ CHAR

Seuil

QUAND s'ébranla le barrage de l'homme, aspiré par la faille géante de l'abandon du divin, des mots dans le lointain, des mots qui ne voulaient pas se perdre, tentèrent de résister à l'exorbitante poussée. Là se décida la dynastie de leur sens.

The Last Poem

I HAVE dreamed so intensely of you, walked so much, spoken so much, loved your shadow so much that nothing more remains to me of you. It remains for me to be the shadow among shadows, to be a hundred times more shadow than the shadow, to be the shadow which will come and come again into your sunny life.

Threshold

WHEN man's dam began to move, breathed in by the giant flaw of the abandonment of the divine, words in the distance, words that did not want to be lost, tried to resist the exorbitant pressure. There the dynasty of their meaning was decided.

J'ai couru jusqu'à l'issue de cette nuit diluvienne.
Planté dans le flageolant petit jour, ma ceinture pleine de
saisons, je vous attends, ô mes amis qui allez venir. Déjà
je vous devine derrière la noirceur de l'horizon. Mon âtre
ne tarit pas de vœux pour vos maisons. Et mon bâton de
cyprès rit de tout son cœur pour vous.

REDONNEZ-LEUR ce qui n'est plus présent en eux,
Ils reverront le grain de la moisson s'enfermer dans l'épi
    et s'agiter sur l'herbe.
Apprenez-leur, de la chute à l'essor, les douze mois de
    leur visage,
Ils chériront le vide de leur cœur jusqu'au désir suivant;
Car rien ne fait naufrage ou ne se plaît aux cendres;
Et qui sait voir la terre aboutir à des fruits,
Point ne l'émeut l'échec quoiqu'il ait tout perdu.

I have run to the exit of this diluvian night. Standing in the quak-
ing dawn, with my belt full of seasons, I await you, O my friends
who are about to arrive. Already I feel you behind the darkness of
the horizon. My hearth's good wishes for your houses are not dried
up. And my staff of cypress laughs for you with all its heart.

GIVE them back what is no longer present in them; they will see
again the harvest's grain enclosed in the ear and waving on the
stalk. Teach them, from the fall to the arising, the twelve months
of their face; they will cherish the emptiness of their hearts until the
next desire; for nothing makes shipwreck or is pleased with ashes;
and he who knows how to see the earth end in fruit, no setback
moves him, though he has lost everything.

La Sorgue

Chanson pour Yvonne

RIVIÈRE trop tôt partie, d'une traite, sans compagnon,
Donne aux enfants de mon pays le visage de ta passion.

Rivière où l'éclair finit et où commence ma maison,
Qui roule aux marches d'oubli la rocaille de ma raison.

Rivière, en toi terre est frisson, soleil anxiété.
Que chaque pauvre dans sa nuit fasse son pain de ta
    moisson.
Rivière souvent punie, rivière à l'abandon.

Rivière des apprentis à la calleuse condition,
Il n'est vent qui ne fléchisse à la crête de tes sillons.

Rivière de l'âme vide, de la guenille et du soupçon,
Du vieux malheur qui se dévide, de l'ormeau, de la com-
    passion.

The Sorgue

Song for Yvonne

RIVER too soon parted, at a stretch, without a companion, give
the children of my native countryside the face of your passion.

River where the lightning ends, and my home begins, which
rolls the rubble of my reason to the steps of forgetfulness.

River, in you land is a shiver, sun, anxiety. Let every poor man
in his night make his bread of your harvest. River often punished,
river forsaken.

River of apprentices to the horny-handed condition, there is no
wind that does not yield at the crest of your furrows.

River of the empty soul, of the rag and of suspicion, of old mis-
fortune unravelling itself, of the young elm, of compassion.

Rivière des farfelus, des fiévreux, des équarisseurs,
Du soleil lâchant sa charrue pour s'acoquiner au menteur.

Rivière des meilleurs que soi, rivière des brouillards
éclos,
De la lampe qui désaltère l'angoisse autour de son
chapeau.

Rivière des égards au songe, rivière qui rouille le fer,
Où les étoiles ont cette ombre qu'elles refusent à la mer.

Rivière des pouvoirs transmis et du cri embouquant les
eaux,
De l'ouragan qui mord la vigne et annonce le vin
nouveau.

Rivière au cœur jamais détruit dans ce monde fou de
prison,
Garde-nous violent et ami des abeilles de l'horizon.

River of whipper-snappers, of the feverish, of stone-cutters, of
the sun leaving its plough to sink to the liar's level.

River of better than oneself, river of blossoming fogs, of the
lamp quenching the fear around its shade.

River of concern for dreams, river that rusts iron, where the stars
have that shadow which they refuse to the sea.

River of transmitted powers and of the shriek entering the
waters' mouth, of the hurricane that gnaws the vine and announces
the new wine.

River with heart never destroyed in this mad world of prison,
keep us violent and friendly to the horizon's bees.

ANDRÉ FRÉNAUD

Fraternité

UN plein filet de souvenirs
Pourquoi me l'ont-ils remonté
L'œil de mon chien l'écolier
les chansons que je leur chantais
le passionné de coquecigrues

Je ne me reconnais pas dans cet enfant
Je chasse cette brume douloureuse
Que le vent emporte cette petite fumée
et me laisse seul comme je suis seul

Pourtant je voudrais l'étreindre quand je le fuis
recomposer l'homme entier jusqu'à mon âge
celui qui acceptait sa place et leurs jeux
Ô chaleur qui me blesse aujourd'hui

Pitié pour vous et pour moi puisqu'il n'est pas permis
Frères

Brotherhood

A FULL net of memories – why have they drawn it up for me –:
my dog's eye, the schoolboy, the songs I used to sing them, the
lover of chimeras.

I do not recognize myself in this child. I drive away this painful
mist. Let the wind carry off this little bit of smoke and leave me
alone, as I am alone.

Yet I should like to clasp it when I flee it, to reconstruct the
whole man right up to my age, he who used to accept his place and
their games – O warmth that hurts me today.

Pity for you and for me, since it is not allowed, Brothers, to be

d'être un seul être fraternel
avant le sein froid de la nuit
dans l'unité de notre mère.

Je ne t'ai jamais oubliée

Sans nom maintenant sans visage
sans plus rien de tes yeux ni de ta pâleur

Dénoué de l'assaut de mon désir dans ton égarante image
dénué par les faux aveux du temps
par les fausses pièces de l'amour racheté
par tous ces gains perdu
libéré de toi maintenant
libre comme un mort
vivant de seule vie moite
enjoué avec les pierres et les feuillages

Quand je glisse entre les seins des douces mal aimées
je gis encore sur ton absence
sur la vivante morte que tu fais
par ton pouvoir ordonné à me perdre
jusqu'au bout de mon silence.

one single being in brotherhood before the cold breast of the night
in our mother's unity.

I Have Never Forgotten You

Now without name, without face, with nothing more of your eyes
or your pallor.
  Untangled from my desire's assault on your misleading image,
stripped by the false confessions of time, ransomed by the false
coins of love, destroyed by all those gains, freed from you now, free
as a dead man, living a flabby life alone, sprightly with stones and
leaves,
  When I slip between the breasts of gentle unloved women, I still
lie on your absence, on the living corpse you make through your
power ordained to destroy me right to the end of my silence.

PATRICE DE LA TOUR DU PIN

Les Laveuses

Il aurait fallu voir les arbres de plus haut,
A leurs crêtes, le vent qui joue parmi les branches,
Ce vent du Sud qui d'ordinaire est gonflé d'eau
Et qui rejoint si lentement l'autre lisière;
Tu l'entendras monter, Gemma, si tu te penches,
Car j'ai le nez d'un chien de chasse, pour prévoir
Les tempêtes qui font déborder ma rivière:
Nous n'avons plus le temps de battre avant ce soir
Les nippes d'un village qui va disparaître . . .

Nous n'avons plus le temps de nous enfuir: peut-être
As-tu déjà compris cette folle aventure,
Cette descente vers les pays de la mer,
A ce ruissellement où l'on voit des figures
Adorables, des voix d'enfants à la dérive
Et l'appel des hameaux que les eaux ont couverts.

Mais ce n'est pas le vent qui roule de la sorte,
Nous l'aurions reconnu d'une peur instinctive:

The Washerwomen

We should have seen the trees from higher up, on their crests, the wind playing among the branches, that South wind which is usually swollen with water and which rejoins the other forest border so slowly; you will hear it rising, Gemma, if you lean forward, for I have a hunting dog's nose to foresee the storms that make my river overflow: we have no longer time before this evening to pound the clothes of a village about to disappear . . .

We have no longer time to escape: perhaps you have already understood this wild adventure, this descent towards the countries of the sea, by this flood in which lovely faces can be seen, voices of children drifting and the call of villages covered by the waters!

But it is not the wind that rolls in this way; we should have

Les barrages ont dû se rompre, les eaux mortes,
Vont s'engouffrer à perdre haleine devant nous:
Gemma, ne pense pas de mal de ma rivière,
C'est toute la vallée en hiver, les remous
Qui tressaillent dans un frisson perpétuel:
Gemma, c'est beaucoup plus qu'un lavoir solitaire
Si doucement porté qu'on le croit immobile,
Mais devant nous des formes mouvantes défilent
– Et le vent qui déploie tes cheveux sur le ciel!

Tu perçois maintenant le bruit des eaux qui montent,
Nous sommes entraînés au milieu des courants:
Tu vas revivre la légende qu'on raconte
Le soir, dans les hameaux que la tempête isole:
Une maison de bois dérivant vers la mer,
Qui passe avec des chants et des rires de folles,
Et jamais retrouvée dans le vallon désert ...

Te souviens-tu, Gemma, d'une telle tempête?
Elle est gonflée de tant de rumeurs de là-bas,

recognized it with an instinctive fear: the dams must have broken, the dead waters will be breathlessly engulfed before us. Gemma, think no evil of my river: it is the whole winter valley, the eddies quivering in a perpetual shudder. Gemma, it is much more than a lonely washing-boat so gently carried that you think it motionless, but moving forms pass before us – and the wind unfurling your hair on the sky!

Now you notice the noise of the rising waters; we are carried away into the middle of the currents. You are going to live once again the legend they tell in the evening in villages cut off by the storm: a wooden house drifting towards the sea, passing by with songs and mad women's laughter, and never found again in the forsaken valley ...

Do you remember such a storm, Gemma? It is big with so many noises from over there, those of villages reached by the waters, of

Celles des villages que l'eau gagne, des bêtes
Bousculées d'une peur que tu ne comprends pas:
Elles se sont enfuies sur les hautes jachères
Avec les hommes, tout un monde immobile et traqué
Qui regarde d'en haut déborder ma rivière
Où deux êtres s'en vont sans vouloir débarquer!

Et nous sommes les seules des âmes vivantes
Que les eaux mêleront aux choses irréelles
Dans l'émerveillement de retrouver en elles
Des régions aimées que leur passage enchante,
Les herbes des prairies qu'on connaît une à une,
Et les hameaux tous feux éteints, au clair de lune
Où va rôder la grande peur, en pleine nuit!

Mais nous serons si loin parmi d'autres villages,
Nous passerons avant la vague qui détruit,
Pour voir les champs perdus dans une nuit d'hiver,
Et les aubes givrées au fond des paysages,

Et dans l'aurore les premiers oiseaux de mer . . .

animals jostled by a fear you do not understand: they have fled with the men to the high fallow lands, a whole hunted, motionless world watching from above my river overflowing on which two human beings voyage without wanting to disembark!

And we are the only living souls whom the waters will mingle with unreal things in the wonder of finding once again in them well-loved places bewitched by their passage, the grasses of the meadows we know one by one, and the villages, all lights out, in the moonlight, where the great fear will prowl at dead of night!

But we shall be so far among other villages, we shall pass before the destroying wave, to see the fields lost in a winter night, and the frosty dawns in the depth of the countryside,

And in the sunrise the first sea-birds . . .

YVES BONNEFOY

Hic est locus patriae

Le ciel trop bas pour toi se déchirait, les arbres
Envahissaient l'espace de ton sang.
Ainsi d'autres armées sont venues, ô Cassandre,
Et rien n'a pu survivre à leur embrassement.

Un vase décorait le seuil. Contre son marbre
Celui qui revenait sourit en s'appuyant.
Ainsi le jour baissait sur le lieudit *Aux Arbres*.
C'était jour de parole et ce fut nuit de vent.

Lieu du combat

I

Voici défait le chevalier de deuil.
Comme il gardait une source, voici
Que je m'éveille et c'est par la grâce des arbres
Et dans le bruit des eaux, songe qui se poursuit.

Here is the Place of the Fatherland

The sky too low for you was torn, the trees invaded the space of
your blood. So other armies have come, O Cassandra, and nothing
could survive their embrace.

A vase adorned the threshold. He who returned smiled leaning
against its marble. So day was sinking over the place called *Of The
Trees*. It used to be day of speech and it was night of wind.

Field of Battle

I

Here is the knight of mourning undone. As he kept a fountain,
behold I awaken, and it is through the grace of the trees and in the
noise of the waters, continuing dream.

642

Il se tait. Son visage est celui que je cherche
Sur toutes sources ou falaises, frère mort.
Visage d'une nuit vaincue, et qui se penche
Sur l'aube de l'épaule déchirée.

Il se tait. Que peut dire au terme du combat
Celui qui fut vaincu par probante parole?
Il tourne vers le sol sa face démunie,
Mourir est son seul cri, de vrai apaisement.

2

Mais pleure-t-il sur une source plus
Profonde et fleurit-il, dahlia des morts
Sur le parvis des eaux terreuses de novembre
Qui poussent jusqu'à nous le bruit du monde mort?

Il me semble, penché sur l'aube difficile
De ce jour qui m'est dû et que j'ai reconquis,
Que j'entends sangloter l'éternelle présence
De mon démon secret jamais enseveli.

He is silent. His face is that which I seek in all fountains or cliffs, dead brother. Face of a conquered night, leaning over the torn shoulder's dawn.

He is silent. At the end of the fight what can he say who was conquered by word of proof? He turns his face laid bare towards the earth, to die is his sole cry, of true appeasement.

2

But does he weep over a deeper fountain and does he flower, like a dahlia of the dead on the court of November's earthy waters that utter to us the noise of the dead world?

It seems to me, leaning over the difficult dawn of this day which is my due and which I have reconquered, that I hear sobbing the eternal presence of my secret demon which was never buried.

Ô tu reparaîtras, rivage de ma force!
Mais que ce soit malgré ce jour qui me conduit.
Ombres, vous n'êtes plus. Si l'ombre doit renaître
Ce sera dans la nuit et par la nuit.

Jean et Jeanne

Tu demandes le nom
De cette maison basse délabrée,
C'est Jean et Jeanne en un autre pays.

Quand les larges vents passent
Le seuil où rien ne chante ni paraît.

C'est Jean et Jeanne et de leurs faces grises
Le plâtre du jour tombe et je revois
La vitre des étés anciens. Te souviens-tu?
La plus brillante au loin, l'arche fille des ombres.

O you will reappear, shore of my strength! But let it be in spite of this day that guides me. Shadows, you are no more. If the shadow is to be reborn, it will be in the night and through the night.

Jean and Jeanne

You ask the name of this low ruined house, it is Jean and Jeanne in another country.

When the wide winds pass the threshold where nothing sings or appears.

It is Jean and Jeanne, and day's plaster falls from their grey faces, and I see again the window-pane of old summers. Do you remember? Far off the most shining one, the arch daughter of shadows.

Aujourd'hui, ce soir, nous ferons un feu
Dans la grande salle.
Nous nous éloignerons,
Nous le laisserons vivre pour les morts.

PHILIPPE JACCOTTET

Le livre des Morts

1956

I

CELUI qui est entré dans les propriétés de l'âge,
il n'en cherchera plus les pavillons ni les jardins,
ni les livres, ni les canaux, ni les feuillages,
ni la trace, aux miroirs, d'une plus brève et tendre main:

l'oeil de l'homme, en ce lieu de sa vie, est voilé,
son bras trop faible pour saisir, pour conquérir,
je le regarde qui regarde s'éloigner
tout ce qui fut un jour son seul travail, son doux désir . . .

Today in the evening we shall make a fire in the great hall. We shall withdraw, we shall let it live for the dead.

The Book of the Dead

I

HE who has entered into the estates of age will no longer seek their pavilions or gardens, or the books or the canals or the leaves or the mark on the mirrors of a briefer and more tender hand: man's eye is veiled in this place of his life, his arm too weak to seize or to conquer; I watch him watching everything grow more remote that one day was his sole task, his sweet desire . . .

Force cachée, s'il en est une, je te prie,
qu'il ne s'enfonce pas dans l'épouvante de ses fautes,
qu'il ne rabâche pas de paroles d'amour factices,
que sa puissance usée une dernière fois sursaute,
se ramasse, et qu'une autre ivresse l'envahisse!

Ses combats les plus durs furent légers éclairs d'oiseaux,
ses plus graves hasards à peine une invasion de pluie;
ses amours n'ont jamais fait se briser que des roseaux,
sa gloire inscrire au mur bientôt ruiné un nom de suie . . .

*

Qu'il entre maintenant vêtu de sa seule impatience
dans cet espace enfin à la mesure de son cœur;
qu'il entre, avec sa seule adoration pour toute science,
dans l'énigme qui fut la sombre source de ses pleurs.

Nulle promesse ne lui a été donnée;
nulle assurance ne lui sera plus laissée;
nulle réponse ne peut plus lui parvenir;
nulle lampe, à la main d'une femme jadis connue,
éclairer ni le lit ni l'interminable avenue:

Hidden strength, if there is one, I beg you, let him not sink into
the terror of his transgressions, let him not harp on meretricious
words of love, let his exhausted power start up for one last time,
gather itself and let another intoxication invade him!

His harshest battles were gentle lightnings of birds, his most
serious risks hardly an invasion of rain; his loves have only ever
broken reeds, his fame only inscribed a name in soot on a quickly
ruined wall . . .

*

Dressed in his sole impatience let him now enter into this space
measured at last to his heart; with his adoration alone as his only
knowledge let him enter the enigma that was his tears' dark source.

No promise has been given to him; no assurance will be left to
him any more; no reply can reach him any longer; no lamp in the
hand of a woman he once knew shall light either the bed or the
endless avenue:

qu'il veuille donc attendre et seulement se réjouir,
comme le bois n'apprend qu'en la défaite à éblouir.

VI

Au lieu où ce beau corps descend dans la terre inconnue,
combattant ceint de cuir ou amoureuse morte nue,
je ne peindrai qu'un arbre qui retient dans son feuillage
le murmure doré d'une lumière de passage . . .

Nul ne peut séparer feu et cendre, rire et poussière,
nul n'aurait reconnu la beauté sans son lit de râles,
la paix ne règne que sur l'ossuaire et sur les pierres,
le pauvre quoi qu'il fasse est toujours entre deux rafales.

VII

L'amandier en hiver: qui dira si ce bois
sera bientôt vêtu de feux dans les ténèbres
ou de fleurs dans le jour une nouvelle fois?
Ainsi l'homme nourri de la terre funèbre.

Let him therefore consent to wait and only rejoice as the wood
only learns to dazzle in defeat.

6

In the place where this handsome body goes down into the un-
known earth, a soldier girded in leather or a dead naked mistress, I
shall only paint a tree that retains in its leaves the golden murmur
of a passing light . . .

Nobody can separate fire and ashes, laughter and dust, nobody
would have recognized beauty without its bed of death-rattles;
peace only reigns over the charnel-house and the stones; whatever
he does, the poor man is always between two bursts of gunfire.

7

The almond-tree in winter: who shall say if this wood will soon
be arrayed in fire in the shadows or in flowers once again in the
day? Likewise man nourished by the funereal earth.

JACQUES DUPIN

L'Égyptienne

Où tu sombres, la profondeur n'est plus.
Il a suffi que j'emporte ton souffle dans un roseau
Pour qu'une graine au désert éclatât sous mon talon.

Tout est venu d'un coup dont il ne reste rien.
Rien que la marque sur ma porte
Des mains brûlées de l'embaumeur.

L'Urne

Sans fin regarder poindre une seconde nuit
A travers cet inerte bûcher lucide
Que ne tempère aucune production de cendres.

Mais la bouche à la fin, la bouche pleine de terre
Et de fureur,
Se souvient que c'est elle qui brûle
Et guide les berceaux sur le fleuve.

The Egyptian Woman

Where you sink depth no longer exists. It was sufficient for me to carry off your breath in a reed for a seed in the desert to burst beneath my heel.

Everything came at a single blow of which nothing remains. Nothing but the mark on my door of the embalmer's burned hands.

The Urn

Endlessly to watch a second night coming on through this sluggish lucid pyre mitigated by no production of ashes.

But the mouth at the end, the mouth full of earth and rage, remembers that it itself is burning and guides the cradles on the river.

INDEX OF FIRST LINES

INDEX OF FIRST LINES

INDEX OF POETS

INDEX OF
POETS AND ANONYMOUS WORKS

NOTE: Page numbers in italic refer to the beginnings of the actual poems

MORE ABOUT PENGUINS
AND PELICANS

Penguinews, which appears every month, contains details of all the new books issued by Penguins as they are published. From time to time it is supplemented by *Penguins in Print*, which is a complete list of all titles available. (There are some five thousand of these.)

A specimen copy of *Penguinews* will be sent to you free on request. For a year's issues (including the complete lists) please send 50p if you live in the British Isles, or 75p if you live elsewhere. Just write to Dept EP, Penguin Books Ltd, Harmondsworth, Middlesex, enclosing a cheque or postal order, and your name will be added to the mailing list.

In the U.S.A.: For a complete list of books available from Penguin in the United States write to Dept CS, Penguin Books Inc., 7110 Ambassador Road, Baltimore, Maryland 21207.

In Canada: For a complete list of books available from Penguin in Canada write to Penguin Books Canada Ltd, 41 Steelcase Road West, Markham, Ontario.

RIMBAUD: SELECTED VERSE

Paul Claudel called Rimbaud 'a mystic in the savage state'. All his poetry was written between the ages of sixteen and nineteen, after which he showed no interest in literature or in his literary reputation but became a trader in Abyssinia. A symbolist, much influenced by Baudelaire for his themes and by Verlaine for his harmonic effects, Rimbaud was yet a most individual poet. He was determined to 'reach the unknown' through his poetry and believed that the poet should undergo the 'complete dislocation of all the senses', in order to enlarge experience and to achieve self-knowledge.

This dislocation of the senses is shown most clearly in *Les Illuminations* and may have been obtained by taking hashish or opium. It is a mystery why this poet, who excelled in the creation of startling images, and wrote some of the most original and moving works of French literature, gave up writing so young. In his introduction to this Penguin selection Oliver Bernard suggests that this may have been because he had hoped through alchemy and poetry to become 'god-like' and turned away in disgust when he found he had failed.

This edition, which includes some 140 poems, contains an introduction and plain prose translations by Oliver Bernard, himself a poet and the author of *Country Matters and Other Poems*.